THE OXFORD BOOK OF
ENGLISH DETECTIVE STORIES

Patricia Craig is a freelance critic and reviewer, and the author of a number of books including *You're a Brick, Angela! A New Look at the Girls' Story 1839–1976* (1976), *Women and Children First: The Fiction of Two World Wars* (1978), and *The Lady Investigates: Women Detectives* and *Spies in Fiction* (1981), all with Mary Cadogan. She has also edited a number of anthologies, including *The Oxford Book of Travel Stories*, *The Oxford Book of Modern Women's Stories*, and *Twelve Irish Ghost Stories*.

THE OXFORD BOOK OF

ENGLISH DETECTIVE STORIES

EDITED BY
PATRICIA CRAIG

Oxford   New York
OXFORD UNIVERSITY PRESS

Oxford University Press, Great Clarendon Street, Oxford OX2 6DP

Oxford New York

*Athens Auckland Bangkok Bogota Buenos Aires Calcutta
Cape Town Chennai Dar es Salaam Delhi Florence Hong Kong Istanbul
Karachi Kuala Lumpur Madrid Melbourne Mexico City Mumbai
Nairobi Paris São Paolo Singapore Taipei Tokyo Toronto Warsaw*

*and associated companies in
Berlin Ibadan*

Oxford is a registered trade mark of Oxford University Press

Introduction, Bibliographical Notes and selection © Patricia Craig 1990

*First published 1990
First issued as an Oxford University Press paperback 1992
Reissued 1998*

British Library Cataloguing in Publication Data

Data available

Library of Congress Cataloging in Publication Data
*The Oxford book of English detective stories / edited by Patricia
Craig. p. cm.*
*1. Detective and mystery stories, English. I. Craig, Patricia
II. Title : English detective stories.*
823.087208–dc20[PQ1309.D4094 1992] 91-43383
ISBN 0-19-282968-8 (pbk.)

9 10

*Printed in Great Britain by
Cox & Wyman Ltd,
Reading, Berkshire*

CONTENTS

INTRODUCTION

While the short story proper in England was evolving in one direction, under the auspices of Chekhov and de Maupassant, one of its most pungent offshoots, the detective story, was acquiring a framework of its own. It is less than a hundred years since the process got under way: it has often been remarked that the story in general is a modern art form—'a child of this century', Elizabeth Bowen pronounced it;[1] and indeed an extra modernity is claimed for the tale of detection. 'Of its nature, [it] could not have been invented in the . . . age of fancy dress,' wrote Brigid Brophy.[2] 'The detective quintessentially wears trousers.' He could not, in other words, have gone about his work of regulating society before a recognizable system of law and order existed. It was Poe, with his *Murders in the Rue Morgue*, who inaugurated fictional detecting in the 1840s; but it was not until the advent of Sherlock Holmes that the genre, as we know it, came into being.

Between 1841 and the first appearance of Sherlock Holmes over forty years later, there was no shortage of detective writers in either England or America, but they tended not to differentiate between the 'sensation' mode then prevalent, and plain detection (without gothic or picturesque embellishments, that is). They were drawn to the theatrical assignation and the bated breath. The emotional effects of a crime were played up rather than being subdued. Conan Doyle changed all that by devising a pattern in which the puzzle was paramount, the detective memorable, and the investigative procedure riveting. He made a virtue of the artifice inherent in the formula, and also located his stories in a rich atmosphere (richer to present-day readers, of course, than to those of his own time). He showed in his own work how the basic structure allowed for variation, and opened the way for a host of detective writers to follow suit.

It is generally agreed that the longish story, and not the novel, is the most effective vehicle for the Holmes adventures; and indeed—as Julian Symons has pointed out[3]—this is true of most detective

---

[1] Elizabeth Bowen, introduction to *The Faber Book of Modern Short Stories* (1936).

[2] Brigid Brophy, 'Detective Fiction', *Hudson Review* (1965); reprinted in *Don't Never Forget* (1966).

[3] Julian Symons, *Bloody Murder* (Faber, 1972; revised edn. 1985).

fiction up until 1920 and Agatha Christie's *Mysterious Affair at
Styles*. That was really the first novel in which the system of interlock-
ing episodes was put before an appreciative readership. The age of
'jigsaw' detection was about to occur—a significant departure. Before
this time, the detective audience was attuned to the magazine story
(with many periodicals, such as *Strand*, *Pearson's*, and so on, to cater
for the taste), and a good many writers, in the wake of Conan Doyle,
opted for the eight- to ten-thousand-word length as a matter of
course. It took a few intrepid authors to show how the full-length
investigation might evade the makeshift construction and other
weaknesses which bedevilled the four Holmes novels. In the hands of
Christie, Sayers, and others, the detective plot was expanded and
elaborated, while still relying for its impact on the author's ability to
spring surprises. However, even during the heyday of the novel (the
so-called 'Golden Age') there were those writers who, having opted
for the discipline of a predetermined form, relished the still further
discipline imposed by the need to be brief as well as intriguing. Most
detective novelists tried their hand at the short story as well, often
with considerable *élan*.

The story needs to be both pithy and highly charged; it cuts down
the range of suspects, and more or less cuts out the red herring
(which, in a number of longer works, tended to turn into a bloater). In
its earliest and most sedate phase it followed closely the conventions
established by Conan Doyle, with the hero generally as adept as
Holmes at elucidating 'clues'. (Holmes, in the story included here,
is prompt to spot the 'immense significance' of a dish of curried mutton, and thereby gets at the truth of a death and a disappearance.)
R. Austin Freeman's Dr Thorndyke, for example, who goes about
amazing his colleagues by the sharpness of his deductions, is a sleuth
of this supralogical type, and very engaging too, with his scientific box
of tricks. The Thorndyke stories are models of deftness and economy,
and the old-fashioned formality of the tone adds greatly to their
charm. Charm, indeed, is a quality that attaches to most early
detective fiction, whether it is an effect the authors intended or not,
and it is especially apparent in the Clarence Rook story with which
this collection opens. What do we have? Regent Street on a sunny
afternoon around the turn of the century, complete with flower girls
and hansom cabs, and a heroine sufficiently intrepid to enter the Café
Royal unaccompanied: 'American, you bet. . . . They'll go anywhere
and do anything.'

The pleasure to be gained from a story like this has more to do with its powers of evocation than with any talent for subterfuge on the part of the author; it was not until later that readers were enabled to savour the tang of a complex situation, miraculously compressed. All detective writers trade on the general human 'passion . . . for concealment and revelation', as Julian Symons has put it;[4] but some, like John Dickson Carr, make more of a feature of this expedient than others. Carr's 'The House in Goblin Wood' (written under the name of Carter Dickson) gets in, for example, everything required of the longer narrative, but in a highly concentrated form: egregious investigator, 'impossible' occurrence, and compelling denouement. Even before we reach this level of technical expertise, though, a good many shifts in emphasis and interesting departures have taken place. Crime writers, as exponents of a popular literary form, need to guard against resorting to ingredients already considered old hat by derisive readers: for example, even while the Holmes formula was being consolidated, there were authors who—anticipating ridicule—reacted against elements of the myth, such as the detective's infallibility. Such authors stressed instead the 'ordinariness' of their own investigators, even if the claim was not always borne out by their performances (Arthur Morrison's Martin Hewitt is a case in point). And while Holmes cries up the faculty of imagination—'I imagined what happened, acted on the supposition, and find myself justified'—there are others, like H. C. Bailey's Reggie Fortune, who profess to stick strictly to the facts in front of them (there is something a little tongue-in-cheek about this assertion of Mr Fortune's, as we shall see).

Still in the Edwardian era, if only just, comes G. K. Chesterton who extended the range of the genre by toying with detection in the service of metaphysics; however, his Father Brown stories do not always cut out tedium and melodrama, and it is really only when they do, that they fit the specifications of detective fiction proper. I have selected a Father Brown episode from the 1920s, 'The Oracle of the Dog', in which the author's well-known addiction to paradox is kept within reasonable bounds (hardly amounting to more than the priest's insistence on the mundane character of religious belief: the title is sardonic), and the plot is attuned to the classic requirements, which keeps things pleasantly devious.

Of course paradox, on a rather more basic level than Chesterton conceived it, is inseparable from the genre as a whole with its

[4] Julian Symons, *Critical Observations* (Faber, 1981).

invigorating fusion of realism and improbability. Murder—real-life murder—is apt to be harrowing and unintriguing, as many authors have noted; indeed, the first task facing detective writers is to superimpose a decorative outline over the disagreeable business in which they have involved themselves. The ritual of detection quite obscures the wretchedness of the crime, and the narrative tone, whether it is dispassionate or downright playful, gets between the blood-letting and the blood. Even grisly speculations ('You think it was her head in his bag?') do not arouse any more consternation than one of those folk tales in which people's heads are constantly being chopped off, and the unwary eaten.

The practice of decorous detection persisted for some time, as we see in the work of authors like Freeman Wills Crofts and even G. D. H. and M. Cole; however, the rather whimsical urbanity presaged by E. C. Bentley in his celebrated novel of 1913, *Trent's Last Case*, was soon established as the dominant tone. By the mid-1920s the aim of a good many detective writers was to be as insouciant as possible—and Anthony Berkeley's 'poisoned-chocolates' story, 'The Avenging Chance', shows the tendency at its most striking. Berkeley's central character, Roger Sheringham, carries out his detecting in an atmosphere of blitheness and panache. Understatement and apparent offhandedness are part of the game. 'A tremendous amount of cases get solved by a stroke of sheer luck, don't they?' murmurs Roger Sheringham at one point; however, we know that it requires considerable alertness, on the part of the detective, to spot the crucial error or inconsistency in the criminal's elaborately staged tableau. Sheringham does it in this story, and so does Philip Trent in E. C. Bentley's 'The Genuine Tabard', in which a tiny item of misinformation gives the show away.

The trifling circumstance by which a scoundrel is scuppered is the central feature of Roy Vickers's *Department of Dead Ends* (from which I have selected 'The Henpecked Murderer'), a collection of wonderfully intricate elaborations of the avenging chance. And in 'Superintendent Wilson's Holiday', by G. D. H. and M. Cole, the astute policeman first sees through a set of props arranged by a murderer in the middle of the Norfolk countryside, and then has the luck to light on a bit of hard evidence to back up his case. (His expertise is highlighted by a Watson figure who keeps making the wrong deductions.) What else? Well, for one thing, Father Ronald Knox's 'Solved by Inspection' (his only Miles Bredon story), which

deserves inclusion in any anthology on the strength of its peculiarity
of method.

It was Ronald Knox (in his Introduction to *The Best Detective
Stories of the Year 1928*) who suggested a basis for the subsequent
Detection Club of 1929, founded largely for the purpose of outlawing
accoutrements of the genre which had fallen into disrepute. 'Divine
Revelation, Feminine Intuition, Mumbo-Jumbo, Jiggery-Pokery'
and the like were definitely off the agenda as far as this exacting
society was concerned. 'The puzzle pure and complex' was the thing.
The earliest members of the Detection Club were scrupulous in their
observance of the rules (well, most of the time), but otherwise given
to merriment, as we see in their habit of poking amiable fun at one
another's creations:

> Lord Peter Wimsey
> May look a little flimsy,
> But he's simply sublime
> When nosing out a crime,

wrote Edmund Clerihew Bentley. And we do not have to look too
hard at Nicholas Blake's 'The Assassins' Club' to discern that the
author has made the Detection Club itself the scene of a murder—a
bold and pleasing stroke. The club's members were, indeed, a
remarkable bunch of authors; as one of them, R. Austin Freeman,
observed in his essay on 'The Art of the Detective Story',[5] you need
highly developed imaginative and ratiocinative faculties—'qualities
. . . seldom met with united in a single individual'—plus a fair
amount of specialized knowledge, to turn out creditable work in the
field. And, on top of all that, a capacity to entertain.

While H. C. Bailey's Reggie Fortune stories (starting in 1920 with
Call Mr Fortune) in a sense exemplify the mannerisms of the
period—'Bafflin' case, yes. Well, well'—there is an undercurrent of
malaise running through them, pointing forward to the bleaker view
of death and detection which came to characterize this distinctive
branch of fiction (not that the sportive element was ever completely
in abeyance). Mr Fortune, a doctor, is attached in some advisory
capacity to the Criminal Investigation Department, and, in the
course of carrying out his duties, keeps having to deny a tendency to
complicate some perfectly straightforward case of murder by letting
his imagination run away with him—'I haven't any imagination at all.

---

[5] *Detection Medley* (Hutchinson, 1939).

That's my weakness,' he reiterates. However, when it comes to 'imagining' what actually happened, on the strength of the available information, this faculty of Fortune's seems every bit as highly developed as Sherlock Holmes's. A detective's individuality is quite often established by means of a catchphrase or some other peculiarity, but really this is just a gloss on the ability, common to all of them, to get at the truth of a deadly occurrence.

They go about it in different ways, of course, some making no bones about being omniscient, and others hiding their razor-sharp brains behind a deferential, mundane, or burbling manner (which disarms the suspects). Some are *bona fide* policemen and paid for their work, while others come under the heading of affluent amateur, or are involved in some profession unconnected with sleuthing. Priests, doctors, psychiatrists, dons, and commercial travellers—in this collection—all try their hand at a little extraneous investigating. Certain authors go in to the fullest degree for the colourful, debonair, or painstaking approach—for example (in that order), Margery Allingham, Anthony Berkeley, and Freeman Wills Crofts. And, as we have seen, each period produced a savour all its own.

With the Thirties and Forties came a certain sobriety—though never, in the hands of the experts, anything approaching dullness. Such developments as occurred were indigenous. The glamour of gangsterism, on the whole, stayed out of English detective fiction even while it was giving rise to a whole new idiom in America—hardboiled, hard-hitting, and utterly urban. The typical private eye has no more scruples as regards violence or corruption than the organized killers he stalks; not for him an English upper-class disdain for the tactics of the streets. (When brute force is not disdained in England it is undertaken in a spirit of high jinks: 'By the way, before we get chatty, let's tie this fellow up. Amanda, the clothes line.') It took some time for the effects of the 'hardboiled' school to percolate through to English crime fiction, and even when this happened (*c.*1954) it was apparent only in the type of police novel in which the details of urban atrocities are not shirked. The Marlowe–Sam Spade type of investigator was never successfully transplanted. What we find in England, however—in the immediate pre-war period—is an increasing amount of acrimony in the home (as with Ngaio Marsh's 'Death on the Air'), and more than one suburban householder discovering an urgent motive for wiping out his wife. The frivolity and affectation of the 1920s man-about-town detective (not unpleasing, especially in retrospect) gave way to a different kind of urbanity—

with a literary flavour, *pace* Blake and Innes. Julian Symons has recorded his amazement at finding an allusion to T. S. Eliot on the opening page of the first Blake novel, *A Question of Proof* (1935): 'I should be prepared to offer odds that there are less than a dozen crime stories written . . . between the wars in which the name of any modern poet appears.'[6] Poets themselves, as ever, were busy encapsulating the spirit of the time:

> With an easy existence, and a cosy country place,
> And with hardly a wrinkle, at sixty, in his face,
> Growing old with old books, with old wine, and with grace,
> Unaware that events move at a breakneck pace . . .,

wrote William Plomer[7] about an old buffer between the wars—exactly the type of person, incidentally, who might find himself at the centre of a full-blooded murder mystery. All the assets of the well-to-do—the manor houses, gazebos, libraries, clubs full of leather armchairs, bachelor apartments, full complement of servants, testamentary expectations—all these loom large in the crime writer's iconography.

Apart from the dramatic effect (however artificial) to be gained from the undermining of such well-established ease (however illusory), such egregious narrative assumptions as we find in the genre are of the greatest possible interest to the social historian. 'Evidence of what ideas had common currency at this or that moment in the past is among the hardest to adduce,' observed the detective novelist Colin Watson in his amusing survey of crime fiction[8]—especially as far as its more unpalatable aspects are concerned. 'What a pity it is . . . that there was no Ronald Knox in the monastery of the Venerable Bede; no Dorothy L. Sayers looking over Holinshed's shoulder while he whitewashed the Tudors . . .'. In their own day, Knox and Sayers and others like them, attached a good deal of importance to such imponderables as a decent British upbringing, and the consequent touches of snobbery and xenophobia in their books are apparent, and sometimes abhorrent, to present-day readers attuned to a different system of values. (A recent reissue of an early Gladys Mitchell novel, *The Saltmarsh Murders*, comes complete with a warning about a racial *gaffe* on the part of the author, which seems as heavy-handed a

---

[6] *Bloody Murder.*

[7] William Plomer, *The Dorking Thigh* (Faber, 1945).

[8] Colin Watson, *Snobbery with Violence* (Eyre & Spottiswoode, 1971).

way of upholding tolerance as the impeachment of Little Black Sambo.) In Ronald Knox's 'Solved by Inspection' a poor view is taken of dubious easterners (not even pukka Indians, we are told) and their rotten esoteric cults; while Dorothy Sayers's adulation of the upper classes is very well known. She treated Wimsey, Colin Watson says, 'even at his most inane, with an auntie-like indulgence that amounted almost to fawning'.[9] Still, none of this detracts from the detecting content of the stories, or their high spirits.

One of the striking things about detective fiction, in fact, is the ease with which it accommodates all kinds of topical ideologies, from C. Day Lewis's Thirties repudiation of the extreme Right (especially notable in the Nicholas Blake novel of 1940, *The Smiler with the Knife*), to the neo-feminism of the present. (As far as the latter is concerned, it did not take feminist authors long to latch on to the detective genre as a means of pinpointing crimes against women; as yet, however, this particular standpoint is most amply illustrated in novels rather than stories.) The detective story comes right up to date with Reginald Hill's diverting 'Bring Back the Cat!', in which a black investigator called Joe Sixsmith makes the most of some fortuitous revelations concerning a wandering cat and an adulterous au pair. With this story, incidentally, Reginald Hill shows himself a master of a notoriously difficult form: comic crime.

Present-day terrorism, along with counter-terrorism, is the theme of Michael Gilbert's compelling story, 'The Killing of Michael Finnegan', which is written with the greatest economy and detachment, and presents a view of the Security Service in which integrity and ruthlessness are well to the fore. And Julian Symons's 'The Murderer'—another strong piece of writing—shows the reprehensible side of sexual outrage, as well as giving a new twist to the story of the suburb dweller in whom a murderous impulse is secreted. Crime and detective writers of the last thirty-odd years have worked under fewer restrictions than their predecessors, as far as all the previously unmentionable aspects of sex and death are concerned, but change along these lines was indicated from about the late 1940s, when realism, or at least a set of conventions passing for realism, began to replace the out-and-out artifice of the past. Indeed, as far back as 1930 the way forward was adumbrated by Anthony Berkeley who, in a preface to his novel *The Second Shot*, expressed his conviction that staginess in the detective genre had had its day, and that the plot of

[9] *Snobbery with Violence.*

the future would hold its audience 'less by mathematical than by psychological ties'—a view borne out by subsequent developments.

However, it was necessary to establish the conventions, if only to enable them to be subverted, or at the very least to prove their flexibility. What is common to all successful detective stories is the note of exhilaration they can't help sounding, whether it has to do with the sheer pleasure of setting out on an adventure (Holmes and Watson making tracks for Dorset, to investigate the disappearance of a horse and its trainer), or involves applauding the statutory exercise of wits on the part of the hero. They all deal with urgent matters—death by violence or danger or the threat to the country of some illiberal force. Some authors—Edmund Crispin comes to mind, especially in the story chosen for this collection, 'Baker Dies' (written with Geoffrey Bush)—take considerable delight in hoodwinking the reader (one of the reasons we read detective fiction is for the joy of being led up the garden path), while others go in for extremes of irony in devising the solution to a puzzle. P. D. James, for example, in 'Great Aunt Allie's Flypapers', sets her detective hero Adam Dalgliesh to investigating a death at the turn of the century, and extracts the fullest piquancy from what is brought to light. Indeed, it is something of a device of the present to introduce some supremely ironic shift at the climax of the narrative, as recent stories by Simon Brett and Robert Barnard show. Sometimes, in the interests of irony or counterpoint, the murderer will get off scot-free without seriously deranging the scheme of things. In place of the old-fashioned, clear-cut morality of the past we find an amiable cynicism and admiration for expediency, which is thoroughly bracing in effect.

The title of Simon Brett's recent collection, *A Box of Tricks*, alerts us to the element of prestidigitation in the genre, and of course, when it comes to this particular ploy, the author who turned out one *tour de force* after another is Agatha Christie: an achievement to be weighed in the balance against her novels' shortcomings, such as blandness of tone and a rather facile moral view. I say novels rather than stories, because the shorter compass tends to point up Christie's defects (for example, her concern with prettifying a series of plain problems by giving them a flowery surround, as we find with the elucidations of a tiresome character called Harley Quinn). However, even with the stories, there are instances of breathtaking ingenuity, though you have to look quite hard to find them. The same may be said of Dorothy L. Sayers (the other half of the 'Golden Age's' top female duo) whose stories, on the whole—though not without exceptions

—are not as impressive as her full-length works. With Sayers, I have opted for Montague Egg rather than Lord Peter Wimsey for this collection, because 'Murder at Pentecost' (in which Egg appears) seems to me admirably resourceful and succinct.

Wimsey, with his blue blood, connoisseurship, nonchalance, and unshakeable *savoir vivre*, has been known to irritate even detective *aficionados*; while for those unsusceptible to the allure of the genre, he may be written off in an exasperated aside: 'a dreadful stock English nobleman of the casual and debonair kind', snorted Edmund Wilson,[10] no doubt in bad humour through having set out to fathom the appeal of this colourful branch of fiction, and remaining mystified. Even if a fairly striking means of ill-doing is postulated, he says (like a gun rigged up inside a piano to shoot the player), it will lose in impact by being embedded in the 'dialogue and doings of a lot of faked-up English county people'. Edmund Wilson is the testy kind of reader who will see only the banal side of Agatha Christie (say) and miss her virtuosity. For others, as W. H. Auden put it,[11] including himself in the category, 'the reading of detective stories is an addiction like tobacco or alcohol.' Also, it involves the engagement of one's faculties—not, certainly, all of one's faculties, but those, perhaps, unappeased by more exalted types of reading. Elizabeth Bowen[12] put her finger on an essential quality of the genre when she described detective stories as 'the only above-board grown-up children's stories'. It is true that the genre itself has grown up somewhat since the comment was made, with authors like Ruth Rendell and P. D. James (the present-day counterpart of the Christie–Sayers alliance) setting out to gauge the amount of reality the factitious framework would stand; but still—like children's fiction—it stays in line with the basic storytelling requirements of straightforward progression and a proper finale.

It is simply for this reason that detective fiction is, and is likely to remain, popular, and not because of any quasi-psychological factor like the gratifying by proxy of one's murderous instincts: as Auden rightly remarked,[13] detective-story readers on the contrary enjoy the illusion of being dissociated from the culprit. However, the tapping of

[10] Edmund Wilson, 'Who Cares Who Killed Roger Ackroyd?' in *Classics and Commercials: A Literary Chronicle of the Forties* (1950).
[11] W. H. Auden, 'The Guilty Vicarage', in *The Dyer's Hand and Other Essays* (1948).
[12] Elizabeth Bowen, 'Out of a Book', in *Collected Impressions* (1950).
[13] 'The Guilty Vicarage', op. cit.

various sources of guilt or unease may be used to contribute reson-
ance to the detective plot. Since the scope of the murder mystery has
widened so considerably, it is no longer necessary to exclude disquiet
from its precincts, as a good many of Ruth Rendell's stories show
—even the wonderful 'Thornapple', in which the crime is approached
obliquely and the overall effect is engaging rather than anything else.
We are brought up smack against delinquency in a chilling form.
Ruth Rendell's subject is the murky side of human relations, just as
earlier authors were predominantly concerned with the surface
interaction of characters in a social setting (a house party, say, or a
village fête), with a central dramatic event—a murder—to focus
their behaviour. The novel (or story) of manners is one of the major
literary forms available to the crime genre—though it has, at various
times, been cast in many different moulds such as comedy, social
satire, psychoanalytic study, political, or moral undertaking.

Gladys Mitchell, in certain of her more convoluted works, perhaps
took the detective story as close as it comes to the shaggy dog story;
however, this author is more justly noted for her moments of clarity,
exuberance, and inspiration. She is also, of course, famous for having
invented the most eldritch investigator of them all, Mrs Bradley (later
Dame Beatrice) of the pterodactyl looks and inflexible aplomb. In
'Daisy Bell'—the Mitchell story included here—an allusion to a
shaggy dog occurs at the start, but is not to be read as a warning:
things thereafter are kept lively and to the point. Certain Mitchell
characteristics are easily recognizable. For example, however dire
the situations this author depicts, black comedy keeps breaking in:
'The bag and the blood, for some reason, sounds perfectly horrible,
George,' declares Mrs Bradley. Quite often, what Gladys Mitchell's
detective fiction amounts to, willy-nilly, is a celebration of the
untoward.

Certain writers approach the business of crime writing from a
particular angle—for example, from the standpoint of a relevant
profession, like the law. This is the practice of Cyril Hare (author of
what has been called the finest detective novel with a legal bearing,
Tragedy at Law of 1940), whose cogent story, 'Miss Burnside's
Dilemma', turns on an issue of brilliantly simple chicanery over an
inheritance. Michael Underwood is another who makes full use of
courtroom protocol, though not in the story chosen for this collection,
'Murder at St Oswald's', which is set in a boys' prep school in 1928,
and concerns the dovetailing of some enthralling events. For the
rest, H. R. F. Keating ('A Dangerous Thing') juxtaposes a piece of

academic jiggery-pokery and an observant charlady, to spirited effect; Christianna Brand ('The Hornets' Nest') is down on cupidity; Michael Innes ('The Furies') treats a case of odd extravagance, followed by death, in a penny-pinching old lady; and John Rhode ('The Purple Line') gets to the bottom of a very dicey business: the upending of a woman in a water-butt. Margery Allingham ('Three is a Lucky Number') contributes an agreeable turning-of-the-tables piece.

Throughout this Introduction I have used the terms 'detective fiction' and 'crime fiction' more or less interchangeably, and this perhaps requires a word of explanation. There is a simple distinction between the crime novel and the detective novel, in that one charts the course of a piece of wrongdoing, while the other focuses on the discovery of the wrongdoer; however, with the short story, this distinction tends to be blurred to the point of becoming irrelevant. The story may either be cast in the form of a step-by-step investigation (highly compressed), or go in for a trickier presentation (sometimes dispensing with an investigator or quasi-investigator altogether), but the difference is one of emphasis, not of genre. The story, in other words, has branched out considerably from the original Holmes formula, but the formula is still implicit even in the most innovative offerings.

One of the aims of this anthology, indeed, is to show the continuity in detective writing: from Holmes on, there are certain persistent features which may be pinpointed, like the story's power to absorb the reader, and the edge of tension which is a key ingredient. All detective/crime fiction posits an essential soundness in human affairs, however individual a form it takes. Justice is seen to be carried out, or if it is not, it is in the interests of playfulness or invigorating anarchy, which comes down to the same thing in the end. Just occasionally, it is true, the author may have a bleaker purpose in dispensing with an even-handed outcome, but even in these instances we find something salutary in the story's uncompromising realism. Basically, we are dealing with an optimistic genre. Like the ghost story, the detective story has been pronounced dead on various occasions, but it always rises up to confound its critics, decked out in the trappings best suited to the period. At the present time, it has every appearance of flourishing. In this collection (I hope) most of the stalwarts of detective fiction are represented, along with some of its more idiosyncratic practitioners.

Elizabeth Bowen, in her Introduction to *The Faber Book of*

Modern Short Stories (1936), mentions the large amount of work which did not come up to scratch—scratch (or as she put it, the mark) being the point at which everything falls into place and the author's aim is seen to have been fulfilled. Many detective stories, too, I have found tedious, banal, long-winded, slack, unconvincing, or frankly preposterous—these are the ones I hope I have left out. There are certain guidelines which help. As Aristophanes said and Gladys Mitchell quoted—and this injunction applies as much to the authors as to the characters of detective fiction—'Be valiant, daring and subtle, and never mind taking a risk.'

PATRICIA CRAIG

ACKNOWLEDGEMENTS

Thanks are due to Jeffrey Morgan, Nigel May, and Nora T. Craig, to Barbara Harris for making some valuable suggestions, and especially to Julian Symons for unfailing kindness and sound advice.

CLARENCE ROOK · ?–1915

The Stir Outside the Café Royal

A Story of Miss Van Snoop, Detective

Colonel Mathurin was one of the aristocrats of crime; at least Mathurin was the name under which he had accomplished a daring bank robbery in Detroit which had involved the violent death of the manager, though it was generally believed by the police that the Rossiter who was at the bottom of some long-firm frauds in Melbourne was none other than Mathurin under another name, and that the designer and chief gainer in a sensational murder case in the Midlands was the same mysterious and ubiquitous personage.

But Mathurin had for some years successfully eluded pursuit; indeed, it was generally known that he was the most desperate among criminals, and was determined never to be taken alive. Moreover, as he invariably worked through subordinates who knew nothing of his whereabouts and were scarcely acquainted with his appearance, the police had but a slender clue to his identity.

As a matter of fact, only two people beyond his immediate associates in crime could have sworn to Mathurin if they had met him face to face. One of them was the Detroit bank manager whom he had shot with his own hand before the eyes of his fiancée. It was through the other that Mathurin was arrested, extradited to the States, and finally made to atone for his life of crime. It all happened in a distressingly commonplace way, so far as the average spectator was concerned. But the story, which I have pieced together from the details supplied—firstly, by a certain detective sergeant whom I met in a tavern hard by Westminster, and secondly, by a certain young woman named Miss Van Snoop—has an element of romance, if you look below the surface.

It was about half-past one o'clock, on a bright and pleasant day, that a young lady was driving down Regent Street in a hansom which she had picked up outside her boarding-house near Portland Road Station. She had told the cabman to drive slowly, as she was nervous behind a horse; and so she had leisure to scan, with the curiosity of a stranger, the strolling crowd that at nearly all hours of the day throngs Regent Street. It was a sunny morning, and everybody looked cheerful. Ladies were shopping, or looking in at the shop windows. Men about town were collecting an appetite for lunch; flower girls were selling 'nice vi'lets, sweet vi'lets, penny a bunch'; and the girl in the cab leaned one arm on the apron and regarded the scene with alert attention. She was not exactly pretty, for the symmetry of her features was discounted by a certain hardness in the set of the mouth. But her hair, so dark as to be almost black, and her eyes of greyish blue set her beyond comparison with the commonplace.

Just outside the Café Royal there was a slight stir, and a temporary block in the foot traffic. A brougham was setting down, behind it was a victoria, and behind that a hansom; and as the girl glanced round the heads of the pair in the brougham, she saw several men standing on the steps. Leaning back suddenly, she opened the trapdoor in the roof.

'Stop here,' she said, 'I've changed my mind.'

The driver drew up by the kerb, and the girl skipped out.

'You shan't lose by the change,' she said, handing him half-a-crown.

There was a tinge of American accent in the voice; and the cabman, pocketing the half-crown with thanks, smiled.

'They may talk about that McKinley tariff,' he soliloquized as he crawled along the kerb towards Piccadilly Circus, 'but it's better 'n free trade—lumps!'

Meanwhile the girl walked slowly back towards the Café Royal, and, with a quick glance at the men who were standing there, entered. One or two of the men raised their eyebrows; but the girl was quite unconscious, and went on her way to the luncheon room.

'American, you bet,' said one of the loungers. 'They'll go anywhere and do anything.'

Just in front of her as she entered was a tall, clean-shaven man, faultlessly dressed in glossy silk hat and frock-coat, with a flower in his buttonhole. He looked around for a moment in search of a convenient table. As he hesitated, the girl hesitated; but when the waiter waved him to a small table laid for two, the girl immediately sat down behind him at the next table.

'Excuse me, madam,' said the waiter, 'this table is set for four; would you mind—'

'I guess,' said the girl, 'I'll stay where I am.' And the look in her eyes, as well as a certain sensation in the waiter's palm, ensured her against further disturbance.

The restaurant was full of people lunching, singly or in twos, in threes, and even larger parties; and many curious glances were directed to the girl who sat at a table alone and pursued her way calmly through the menu. But the girl appeared to notice no one. When her eyes were off her plate they were fixed straight ahead—on the back of the man who had entered in front of her. The man, who had drunk a half-bottle of champagne with his lunch, ordered a liqueur to accompany his coffee. The girl, who had drunk an aerated water, leaned back in her chair and wrinkled her brows. They were very straight brows, that seemed to meet over her nose when she wrinkled them in perplexity. Then she called a waiter.

'Bring me a sheet of notepaper, please,' she said, 'and my bill.'

The waiter laid the sheet of paper before her, and the girl proceeded, after a few moments' thought, to write a few lines in pencil upon it. When this was done, she folded the sheet carefully and laid it in her purse. Then, having paid her bill, she returned her purse to her dress pocket, and waited patiently.

In a few minutes the clean-shaven man at the next table settled his bill and made preparations for departure. The girl at the same time drew on her gloves, keeping her eyes immovably upon her neighbour's back. As the man rose to depart and passed the table at which the girl had been sitting, the girl was looking into the mirror upon the wall and patting her hair. Then she turned and followed the man out of the restaurant, while a pair at an adjacent table remarked to one another that it was a rather curious coincidence for a man and woman to enter and leave at the same moment when they had no apparent connection.

But what happened outside was even more curious.

The man halted for a moment upon the steps at the entrance. The porter, who was in conversation with a policeman, turned, whistle in hand.

'Hansom, sir?' he asked.

'Yes,' said the clean-shaven man.

The porter was raising his whistle to his lips when he noticed the girl behind.

'Do you wish for a cab, madam?' he asked, and blew upon his whistle.

As he turned again for an answer, he plainly saw the girl, who was standing close behind the clean-shaven man, slip her hand under his coat, and snatch from his hip pocket something which she quickly transferred to her own.

'Well, I'm—' began the clean-shaven man, swinging round and feeling in his pocket.

'Have you missed anything, sir?' said the porter, standing full in front of the girl to bar her exit.

'My cigarette case is gone,' said the man, looking from one side to another.

'What's this?' said the policeman, stepping forward.

'I saw the woman's hand in the gentleman's pocket, plain as a pikestaff,' said the porter.

'Oh, that's it, is it?' said the policeman, coming close to the girl. 'I thought as much.'

'Come now,' said the clean-shaven man, 'I don't want to make a fuss. Just hand back that cigarette case, and we'll say no more about it.'

'I haven't got it,' said the girl. 'How dare you? I never touched your pocket.'

The man's face darkened.

'Oh, come now!' said the porter.

'Look here, that won't do,' said the policeman, 'you'll have to come along of me. Better take a four-wheeler, eh, sir?'

For a knot of loafers, seeing something interesting in the wind, had collected round the entrance.

A four-wheeler was called, and the girl entered, closely followed by the policeman and the clean-shaven man.

'I was never so insulted in my life,' said the girl.

Nevertheless, she sat back quite calmly in the cab, as though she was perfectly ready to face this or any other situation, while the policeman watched her closely to make sure that she did not dispose in any surreptitious way of the stolen article.

At the police station hard by, the usual formalities were gone through, and the clean-shaven man was constituted prosecutor. But the girl stoutly denied having been guilty of any offence.

The inspector in charge looked doubtful.

'Better search her,' he said.

And the girl was led off to a room for an interview with the female searcher.

The moment the door closed the girl put her hand into her pocket, pulled out the cigarette case, and laid it upon the table.

'There you are,' she said. 'That will fix matters so far.'

The woman looked rather surprised.

'Now,' said the girl, holding out her arms, 'feel in this other pocket, and find my purse.'

The woman picked out the purse.

'Open it and read the note on the bit of paper inside.'

On the sheet of paper which the waiter had given her, the girl had written these words, which the searcher read in a muttered undertone:

I am going to pick this man's pocket as the best way of getting him into a police station without violence. He is Colonel Mathurin, alias Rossiter, alias Connell, and he is wanted in Detroit, New York, Melbourne, Colombo, and London. Get four men to pin him unawares, for he is armed and desperate. I am a member of the New York detective force—Nora Van Snoop.

'It's all right,' said Miss Van Snoop, quickly, as the searcher looked up at her after reading the note. 'Show that to the boss—right away.'

The searcher opened the door. After whispered consultation the inspector appeared, holding the note in his hand.

'Now then, be spry,' said Miss Van Snoop. 'Oh, you needn't worry! I've got my credentials right here,' and she dived into another pocket.

'But do you know—can you be sure,' said the inspector, 'that this is the man who shot the Detroit bank manager?'

'Great heavens! Didn't I see him shoot Will Stevens with my own eyes! And didn't I take service with the police to hunt him out?'

The girl stamped her foot, and the inspector left. For two, three, four minutes, she stood listening intently. Then a muffled shout reached her ears. Two minutes later the inspector returned.

'I think you're right,' he said. 'We have found enough evidence on him to identify him. But why didn't you give him in charge before to the police?'

'I wanted to arrest him myself,' said Miss Van Snoop, 'and I have. Oh, Will! Will!'

Miss Van Snoop sank into a cane-bottomed chair, laid her head upon the table, and cried. She had earned the luxury of hysterics. In half an hour she left the station, and, proceeding to a post office, cabled her resignation to the head of the detective force in New York.

Silver Blaze

'I am afraid, Watson, that I shall have to go,' said Holmes, as we sat down together to our breakfast one morning.

'Go! Where to?'

'To Dartmoor—to King's Pyland.'

I was not surprised. Indeed, my only wonder was that he had not already been mixed up in this extraordinary case, which was the one topic of conversation through the length and breadth of England. For a whole day my companion had rambled about the room with his chin upon his chest and his brows knitted, charging and recharging his pipe with the strongest black tobacco, and absolutely deaf to any of my questions or remarks. Fresh editions of every paper had been sent up by our newsagent only to be glanced over and tossed down into a corner. Yet, silent as he was, I knew perfectly well what it was over which he was brooding. There was but one problem before the public which could challenge his powers of analysis, and that was the singular disappearance of the favourite for the Wessex Cup, and the tragic murder of its trainer. When, therefore, he suddenly announced his intention of setting out for the scene of the drama, it was only what I had both expected and hoped for.

'I should be most happy to go down with you if I should not be in the way,' said I.

'My dear Watson, you would confer a great favour upon me by coming. And I think that your time will not be misspent, for there are points about this case which promise to make it an absolutely unique one. We have, I think, just time to catch our train at Paddington, and I will go further into the matter upon our journey. You would oblige me by bringing with you your very excellent field-glass.'

And so it happened that an hour or so later I found myself in the corner of a first-class carriage, flying along, *en route* for Exeter, while Sherlock Holmes, with his sharp, eager face framed in his ear-flapped travelling-cap, dipped rapidly into the bundle of fresh papers which he had procured at Paddington. We had left Reading far behind us before he thrust the last of them under the seat, and offered me his cigar-case.

'We are going well,' said he, looking out of the window, and glancing at his watch. 'Our rate at present is fifty-three and a half miles an hour.'

'I have not observed the quarter-mile posts,' said I.

'Nor have I. But the telegraph posts upon this line are sixty yards apart, and the calculation is a simple one. I presume that you have already looked into this matter of the murder of John Straker and the disappearance of Silver Blaze?'

'I have seen what the *Telegraph* and the *Chronicle* have to say.'

'It is one of those cases where the art of the reasoner should be used rather for the sifting of details than for the acquiring of fresh evidence. The tragedy has been so uncommon, so complete, and of such personal importance to so many people that we are suffering from a plethora of surmise, conjecture, and hypothesis. The difficulty is to detach the framework of fact—of absolute, undeniable fact—from the embellishments of theorists and reporters. Then, having established ourselves upon this sound basis, it is our duty to see what inferences may be drawn, and which are the special points upon which the whole mystery turns. On Tuesday evening I received telegrams, both from Colonel Ross, the owner of the horse, and from Inspector Gregory, who is looking after the case, inviting my co-operation.'

'Tuesday evening!' I exclaimed. 'And this is Thursday morning. Why did you not go down yesterday?'

'Because I made a blunder, my dear Watson—which is, I am afraid, a more common occurrence than anyone would think who only knew me through your memoirs. The fact is that I could not believe it possible that the most remarkable horse in England could long remain concealed, especially in so sparsely inhabited a place 'as the north of Dartmoor. From hour to hour yesterday I expected to hear that he had been found, and that his abductor was the murderer of John Straker. When, however, another morning had come and I found that, beyond the arrest of young Fitzroy Simpson, nothing had been done, I felt that it was time for me to take action. Yet in some ways I feel that yesterday has not been wasted.'

'You have formed a theory then?'

'At least I have a grip of the essential facts of the case. I shall enumerate them to you, for nothing clears up a case so much as stating it to another person, and I can hardly expect your co-operation if I do not show you the position from which we start.'

I lay back against the cushions, puffing at my cigar, while Holmes, leaning forward, with his long thin forefinger checking off the points upon the palm of his left hand, gave me a sketch of the events which had led to our journey.

'Silver Blaze,' said he, 'is from the Isonomy stock, and holds as brilliant a record as his famous ancestor. He is now in his fifth year, and has brought in turn each of the prizes of the turf to Colonel Ross, his fortunate owner. Up to the time of the catastrophe he was first favourite for the Wessex Cup, the betting being three to one on. He has always, however, been a prime favourite with the racing public, and has never yet disappointed them, so that even at short odds enormous sums of money have been laid upon him. It is obvious, therefore, that there were many people who had the strongest interest in preventing Silver Blaze from being there at the fall of the flag next Tuesday.

'This fact was, of course, appreciated at King's Pyland, where the Colonel's training stable is situated. Every precaution was taken to guard the favourite. The trainer, John Straker, is a retired jockey, who rode in Colonel Ross's colours before he became too heavy for the weighing-chair. He has served the Colonel for five years as jockey, and for seven as trainer, and has always shown himself to be a zealous and honest servant. Under him were three lads, for the establishment was a small one, containing only four horses in all. One of these lads sat up each night in the stable, while the others slept in the loft. All three bore excellent characters. John Straker, who is a married man, lived in a small villa about two hundred yards from the stables. He has no children, keeps one maid-servant, and is comfortably off. The country round is very lonely, but about half a mile to the north there is a small cluster of villas which have been built by a Tavistock contractor for the use of invalids and others who may wish to enjoy the pure Dartmoor air. Tavistock itself lies two miles to the west, while across the moor, also about two miles distant, is the larger training establishment of Capleton, which belongs to Lord Backwater, and is managed by Silas Brown. In every other direction the moor is a complete wilderness, inhabited only by a few roaming gipsies. Such was the general situation last Monday night, when the catastrophe occurred.

'On that evening the horses had been exercised and watered as usual, and the stables were locked up at nine o'clock. Two of the lads walked up to the trainer's house, where they had supper in the kitchen, while the third, Ned Hunter, remained on guard. At a few minutes after nine the maid, Edith Baxter, carried down to the stables his supper, which consisted of a dish of curried mutton. She took no liquid, as there was a water-tap in the stables, and it was the rule that the lad on duty should drink nothing else. The maid carried a lantern with her, as it was very dark, and the path ran across the open moor.

'Edith Baxter was within thirty yards of the stables when a man appeared out of the darkness and called to her to stop. As he stepped into the circle of yellow light thrown by the lantern she saw that he was a person of gentlemanly bearing, dressed in a grey suit of tweed with a cloth cap. He wore gaiters, and carried a heavy stick with a knob to it. She was most impressed, however, by the extreme pallor of his face and by the nervousness of his manner. His age, she thought, would be rather over thirty than under it.

'"Can you tell me where I am?" he asked. "I had almost made up my mind to sleep on the moor when I saw the light of your lantern."

'"You are close to the King's Pyland training stables," she said.

'"Oh, indeed! What a stroke of luck!" he cried. "I understand that a stable boy sleeps there alone every night. Perhaps that is his supper which you are carrying to him. Now I am sure that you would not be too proud to earn the price of a new dress, would you?" He took a piece of white paper folded up out of his waistcoat pocket. "See that the boy has this tonight, and you shall have the prettiest frock that money can buy."

'She was frightened by the earnestness of his manner, and ran past him to the window through which she was accustomed to hand the meals. It was already open, and Hunter was seated at the small table inside. She had begun to tell him of what had happened, when the stranger came up again.

'"Good evening," said he, looking through the window, "I wanted to have a word with you." The girl has sworn that as he spoke she noticed the corner of the little paper packet protruding from his closed hand.

'"What business have you here?" asked the lad.

'"It's business that may put something into your pocket," said the other. "You've two horses in for the Wessex Cup—Silver Blaze and Bayard. Let me have the straight tip, and you won't be a loser. Is it a fact that at the weights Bayard could give the other a hundred yards in five furlongs, and that the stable have put their money on him?"

'"So you're one of those damned touts," cried the lad. "I'll show you how we serve them in King's Pyland." He sprang up and rushed across the stable to unloose the dog. The girl fled away to the house, but as she ran she looked back, and saw that the stranger was leaning through the window. A minute later, however, when Hunter rushed out with the hound he was gone, and though the lad ran all round the buildings he failed to find any trace of him.'

'One moment!' I asked. 'Did the stable boy, when he ran out with the dog, leave the door unlocked behind him?'

'Excellent, Watson; excellent!' murmured my companion. 'The importance of the point struck me so forcibly, that I sent a special wire to Dartmoor yesterday to clear the matter up. The boy locked the door before he left it. The window, I may add, was not large enough for a man to get through.

'Hunter waited until his fellow-grooms had returned, when he sent a message up to the trainer and told him what had occurred. Straker was excited at hearing the account, although he does not seem to have quite realized its true significance. It left him, however, vaguely uneasy, and Mrs Straker, waking at one in the morning, found that he was dressing. In reply to her inquiries, he said that he could not sleep on account of his anxiety about the horses, and that he intended to walk down to the stables to see that all was well. She begged him to remain at home, as she could hear the rain pattering against the windows, but in spite of her entreaties he pulled on his large mackintosh and left the house.

'Mrs Straker awoke at seven in the morning, to find that her husband had not yet returned. She dressed herself hastily, called the maid, and set off for the stables. The door was open; inside, huddled together upon a chair, Hunter was sunk in a state of absolute stupor, the favourite's stall was empty, and there were no signs of his trainer.

'The two lads who slept in the chaff-cutting loft above the harness-room were quickly roused. They had heard nothing during the night, for they are both sound sleepers. Hunter was obviously under the influence of some powerful drug; and, as no sense could be got out of him, he was left to sleep it off while the two lads and the two women ran out in search of the absentees. They still had hopes that the trainer had for some reason taken out the horse for early exercise, but on ascending the knoll near the house, from which all the neighbouring moors were visible, they not only could see no signs of the favourite, but they perceived something which warned them that they were in the presence of a tragedy.

'About a quarter of a mile from the stables, John Straker's overcoat was flapping from a furze bush. Immediately beyond there was a bowl-shaped depression in the moor, and at the bottom of this was found the dead body of the unfortunate trainer. His head had been shattered by a savage blow from some heavy weapon, and he was wounded in the thigh, where there was a long, clean cut, inflicted evidently by some very sharp instrument. It was clear, however, that Straker had defended himself vigorously against his assailants, for in his right hand he held a small knife, which was clotted with blood up to the handle, while in his left he grasped a red and black silk cravat, which was recognized by the maid as having been worn on the preceding evening by the stranger who had visited the stables.

'Hunter, on recovering from his stupor, was also quite positive as to the ownership of the cravat. He was equally certain that the same stranger had, while standing at the window, drugged his curried mutton, and so deprived the stables of their watchman.

'As to the missing horse, there were abundant proofs in the mud which lay at the bottom of the fatal hollow, that he had been there at the time of the struggle. But from that morning he has disappeared; and although a large reward has been offered, and all the gipsies of Dartmoor are on the alert, no news has come of him. Finally an analysis has shown that the remains of his supper, left by the stable lad, contain an appreciable quantity of powdered opium, while the people of the house partook of the same dish on the same night without any ill effect.

'Those are the main facts of the case stripped of all surmise and stated as baldly as possible. I shall now recapitulate what the police have done in the matter.

'Inspector Gregory, to whom the case has been committed, is an extremely competent officer. Were he but gifted with imagination he might rise to great heights in his profession. On his arrival he promptly found and arrested the man upon whom suspicion naturally rested. There was little difficulty in finding him, for he was thoroughly well known in the neighbourhood. His name, it appears, was Fitzroy Simpson. He was a man of excellent birth and education, who had squandered a fortune upon the turf, and who lived now by doing a little quiet and genteel bookmaking in the sporting clubs of London. An examination of his betting-book shows that bets to the amount of five thousand pounds had been registered by him against the favourite.

'On being arrested he volunteered the statement that he had come down to Dartmoor in the hope of getting some information about the King's Pyland horses, and also about Desborough, the second favourite, which was in charge of Silas Brown, at the Capleton stables. He did not attempt to deny that he had acted as described upon the evening before, but declared that he had no sinister designs, and had simply wished to obtain first-hand information. When confronted with the cravat he turned very pale, and was utterly unable to account for its presence in the hand of the murdered man. His wet clothing showed that he had been out in the storm of the night before, and his stick, which was a Penang lawyer, weighted with lead, was just such a weapon as might, by repeated blows, have inflicted the terrible injuries to which the trainer had succumbed.

'On the other hand, there was no wound upon his person, while the state of Straker's knife would show that one, at least, of his assailants must bear his mark upon him. There you have it all in a nutshell, Watson, and if you can give me any light I shall be infinitely obliged to you.'

I had listened with the greatest interest to the statement which Holmes, with characteristic clearness, had laid before me. Though most of the facts were familiar to me, I had not sufficiently appreciated their relative importance, nor their connection with each other.

'Is it not possible,' I suggested, 'that the incised wound upon Straker may have been caused by his own knife in the convulsive struggles which follow any brain injury?'

'It is more than possible; it is probable,' said Holmes. 'In that case, one of the main points in favour of the accused disappears.'

'And yet,' said I, 'even now I fail to understand what the theory of the police can be.'

'I am afraid that whatever theory we state has very grave objections to it,' returned my companion. 'The police imagine, I take it, that this Fitzroy Simpson, having drugged the lad, and having in some way obtained a duplicate key, opened the stable door, and took out the horse, with the intention, apparently, of kidnapping him altogether. His bridle is missing, so that Simpson must have put it on. Then, having left the door open behind him, he was leading the horse away over the moor, when he was either met or overtaken by the trainer. A row naturally ensued, Simpson beat out the trainer's brains with his heavy stick without receiving any injury from the small knife which Straker used in self-defence, and then the thief either led the horse on to some secret hiding-place, or else it may have bolted during the struggle, and be now wandering out on the moors. That is the case as it appears to the police, and improbable as it is, all other explanations are more improbable still. However, I shall very quickly test the matter when I am once upon the spot, and until then I really cannot see how we can get much further than our present position.'

It was evening before we reached the little town of Tavistock, which lies, like the boss of a shield, in the middle of the huge circle of Dartmoor. Two gentlemen were awaiting us at the station; the one a tall fair man with lion-like hair and beard, and curiously penetrating light blue eyes, the other a small alert person, very neat and dapper, in a frock-coat and gaiters, with trim little side-whiskers and an eyeglass. The latter was Colonel Ross, the well-known sportsman, the other Inspector Gregory, a man who was rapidly making his name in the English detective service.

'I am delighted that you have come down, Mr Holmes,' said the Colonel. 'The Inspector here has done all that could possibly be suggested; but I wish to leave no stone unturned in trying to avenge poor Straker, and in recovering my horse.'

'Have there been any fresh developments?' asked Holmes.

'I am sorry to say that we have made very little progress,' said the Inspector. 'We have an open carriage outside, and as you would no doubt like to see the place before the light fails, we might talk it over as we drive.'

A minute later we were all seated in a comfortable landau and were rattling through the quaint old Devonshire town. Inspector Gregory was full of his case, and poured out a stream of remarks, while Holmes threw in an occasional question or interjection. Colonel Ross leaned back with his arms folded and his hat tilted over his eyes, while I listened with interest to the dialogue of the two detectives. Gregory was formulating his theory, which was almost exactly what Holmes had foretold in the train.

'The net is drawn pretty close round Fitzroy Simpson,' he remarked, 'and I believe myself that he is our man. At the same time, I recognize that the evidence is purely circumstantial, and that some new development may upset it.'

'How about Straker's knife?'

'We have quite come to the conclusion that he wounded himself in his fall.'

'My friend Dr Watson made that suggestion to me as we came down. If so, it would tell against this man Simpson.'

'Undoubtedly. He has neither a knife nor any sign of a wound. The evidence against him is certainly very strong. He had a great interest in the disappearance of the favourite, he lies under the suspicion of having poisoned the stable boy, he was undoubtedly out in the storm, he was armed with a heavy stick, and his cravat was found in the dead man's hand. I really think we have enough to go before a jury.'

Holmes shook his head. 'A clever counsel would tear it all to rags,' said he. 'Why should he take the horse out of the stable? If he wished to injure it, why could he not do it there? Has a duplicate key been found in his possession? What chemist sold him the powdered opium? Above all, where could he, a stranger to the district, hide a horse, and such a horse as this? What is his own explanation as to the paper which he wished the maid to give to the stable boy?'

'He says that it was a ten-pound note. One was found in his purse. But your other difficulties are not so formidable as they seem. He is not a stranger to the district. He has twice lodged at Tavistock in the summer. The opium was probably brought from London. The key, having served its purpose, would be hurled away. The horse may lie at the bottom of one of the pits or old mines upon the moor.'

'What does he say about the cravat?'

'He acknowledges that it is his, and declares that he had lost it. But a new element has been introduced into the case which may account for his leading the horse from the stable.'

Holmes pricked up his ears.

'We have found traces which show that a party of gipsies encamped on Monday night within a mile of the spot where the murder took place. On Tuesday they were gone. Now, presuming that there was some understanding between Simpson and these gipsies, might he not have been leading the horse to them when he was overtaken, and may they not have him now?'

'It is certainly possible.'

'The moor is being scoured for these gipsies. I have also examined every stable and outhouse in Tavistock, and for a radius of ten miles.'

'There is another training stable quite close, I understand?'

'Yes, and that is a factor which we must certainly not neglect. As Desborough, their horse, was second in the betting, they had an interest in the disappearance of the favourite. Silas Brown, the trainer, is known to have had large bets upon the event, and he was no friend to poor Straker. We have, however, examined the stables, and there is nothing to connect him with the affair.'

'And nothing to connect this man Simpson with the interests of the Capleton stable?'

'Nothing at all.'

Holmes leaned back in the carriage and the conversation ceased. A few minutes later our driver pulled up at a neat little red-brick villa with overhanging eaves, which stood by the road. Some distance off, across a paddock, lay a long grey-tiled outbuilding. In every other direction the low curves of the moor, bronze-coloured from the fading ferns, stretched away to the skyline, broken only by the steeples of Tavistock, and by a cluster of houses away to the west-ward, which marked the Capleton stables. We all sprang out with the exception of Holmes, who continued to lean back with his eyes fixed upon the sky in front of him, entirely absorbed in his own thoughts. It was only when I touched his arm that he roused himself with a violent start and stepped out of the carriage.

'Excuse me,' said he, turning to Colonel Ross, who had looked at him in some surprise. 'I was day-dreaming.' There was a gleam in his eyes and a suppressed excitement in his manner which convinced me, used as I was to his ways, that his hand was upon a clue, though I could not imagine where he had found it.

'Perhaps you would prefer at once to go on to the scene of the crime, Mr Holmes?' said Gregory.

'I think that I should prefer to stay here a little and go into one or two questions of detail. Straker was brought back here, I presume?'

'Yes, he lies upstairs. The inquest is tomorrow.'

'He has been in your service some years, Colonel Ross?'

'I have always found him an excellent servant.'

'I presume that you made an inventory of what he had in his pockets at the time of his death, Inspector?'

'I have the things themselves in the sitting-room, if you would care to see them.'

'I should be very glad.'

We all filed into the front room, and sat round the central table, while the Inspector unlocked a square tin box and laid a small heap of things before us. There was a box of vestas, two inches of tallow candle, an ADP briar-root pipe, a pouch of sealskin with half an ounce of long-cut cavendish, a silver watch with a gold chain, five sovereigns in gold, an aluminium pencil-case, a few papers, and an ivory-handled knife with a very delicate inflexible blade marked Weiss & Co., London.

'This is a very singular knife,' said Holmes, lifting it up and examining it minutely. 'I presume, as I see blood-stains upon it, that it is the one which was found in the dead man's grasp. Watson, this knife is surely in your line.'

'It is what we call a cataract knife,' said I.

'I thought so. A very delicate blade devised for very delicate work. A strange thing for a man to carry with him upon a rough expedition, especially as it would not shut in his pocket.'

'The tip was guarded by a disc of cork which we found beside his body,' said the Inspector. 'His wife tells us that the knife had lain for some days upon the dressing-table, and that he had picked it up as he left the room. It was a poor weapon, but perhaps the best that he could lay his hand on at the moment.'

'Very possible. How about these papers?'

'Three of them are receipted hay-dealers' accounts. One of them is a letter of instructions from Colonel Ross. This other is a milliner's account for thirty-seven pounds fifteen, made out by Madame Lesurier, of Bond Street, to William Darbyshire. Mrs Straker tells us that Darbyshire was a friend of her husband's, and that occasionally his letters were addressed here.'

'Madame Darbyshire had somewhat expensive tastes,' remarked Holmes, glancing down the account. 'Twenty-two guineas is rather heavy for a single costume. However, there appears to be nothing more to learn, and we may now go down to the scene of the crime.'

As we emerged from the sitting-room a woman who had been waiting in the passage took a step forward and laid her hand upon the Inspector's sleeve. Her face was haggard, and thin, and eager; stamped with the print of a recent horror.

'Have you got them? Have you found them?' she panted.

'No, Mrs Straker; but Mr Holmes, here, has come from London to help us, and we shall do all that is possible.'

'Surely I met you in Plymouth, at a garden party, some little time ago, Mrs Straker,' said Holmes.

'No, sir; you are mistaken.'

'Dear me; why, I could have sworn to it. You wore a costume of dove-coloured silk with ostrich feather trimming.'

'I never had such a dress, sir,' answered the lady.

'Ah; that quite settles it,' said Holmes; and, with an apology, he followed the Inspector outside. A short walk across the moor took us to the hollow in which the body had been found. At the brink of it was the furze bush upon which the coat had been hung.

'There was no wind that night, I understand,' said Holmes.

'None; but very heavy rain.'

'In that case the overcoat was not blown against the furze bushes, but placed there.'

'Yes, it was laid across the bush.'

'You fill me with interest. I perceive that the ground has been trampled up a good deal. No doubt many feet have been there since Monday night.'

'A piece of matting has been laid here at the side, and we have all stood upon that.'

'Excellent.'

'In this bag I have one of the boots which Straker wore, one of Fitzroy Simpson's shoes, and a cast horseshoe of Silver Blaze.'

'My dear Inspector, you surpass yourself!'

Holmes took the bag, and descending into the hollow he pushed the matting into a more central position. Then stretching himself upon his face and leaning his chin upon his hands he made a careful study of the trampled mud in front of him.

'Halloa!' said he, suddenly, 'what's this?'

It was a wax vesta, half burned, which was so coated with mud that it looked at first like a little chip of wood.

'I cannot think how I came to overlook it,' said the Inspector, with an expression of annoyance.

'It was invisible, buried in the mud. I only saw it because I was looking for it.'

'What! You expected to find it?'

'I thought it not unlikely.' He took the boots from the bag and compared the impressions of each of them with marks upon the ground. Then he clambered up to the rim of the hollow and crawled about among the ferns and bushes.

'I am afraid that there are no more tracks,' said the Inspector. 'I have examined the ground very carefully for a hundred yards in each direction.'

'Indeed!' said Holmes, rising, 'I should not have the impertinence to do it again after what you say. But I should like to take a little walk over the moors before it grows dark, that I may know my ground tomorrow, and I think that I shall put this horseshoe into my pocket for luck.'

Colonel Ross, who had shown some signs of impatience at my companion's quiet and systematic method of work, glanced at his watch.

'I wish you would come back with me, Inspector,' said he. 'There are several points on which I should like your advice, and especially as to whether we do not owe it to the public to remove our horse's name from the entries for the Cup.'

'Certainly not,' cried Holmes, with decision; 'I should let the name stand.'

The Colonel bowed. 'I am very glad to have had your opinion, sir,' said he. 'You will find us at poor Straker's house when you have finished your walk, and we can drive together into Tavistock.'

He turned back with the Inspector, while Holmes and I walked slowly across the moor. The sun was beginning to sink behind the stables of Capleton, and the long sloping plain in front of us was tinged with gold, deepening into rich, ruddy brown where the faded ferns and brambles caught the evening light. But the glories of the landscape were all wasted upon my companion, who was sunk in the deepest thought.

'It's this way, Watson,' he said, at last. 'We may leave the question of who killed John Straker for the instant, and confine ourselves to finding out what has become of the horse. Now, supposing that he broke away during or after the tragedy, where could he have gone to? The horse is a very gregarious creature. If left to himself, his instincts would have been either to return to King's Pyland or go over to Capleton. Why should he run wild upon the moor? He would surely have been seen by now. And why should gipsies kidnap him? These people always clear out when they hear of trouble, for they do not wish to be pestered by the police. They could not hope to sell such a horse. They would run a great risk and gain nothing by taking him. Surely that is clear.'

'Where is he, then?'

'I have already said that he must have gone to King's Pyland or to Capleton. He is not at King's Pyland, therefore he is at Capleton. Let us take that as a working hypothesis, and see what it leads us to. This part of the moor, as the Inspector remarked, is very hard and dry. But it falls away towards Capleton, and you can see from here that there is a long hollow over yonder, which must have been very wet on Monday night. If our supposition is correct, then the horse must have crossed that, and there is the point where we should look for his tracks.'

We had been walking briskly during this conversation, and a few more minutes brought us to the hollow in question. At Holmes' request I walked down the bank to the right, and he to the left, but I had not taken fifty paces before I heard him give a shout, and saw him waving his hand to me. The track of a horse was plainly outlined in the soft earth in front of him, and the shoe which he took from his pocket exactly fitted the impression.

'See the value of imagination,' said Holmes. 'It is the one quality which Gregory lacks. We imagined what might have happened, acted upon the supposition, and find ourselves justified. Let us proceed.'

We crossed the marshy bottom and passed over a quarter of a mile of dry, hard turf. Again the ground sloped and again we came on the tracks. Then we lost them for half a mile, but only to pick them up once more quite close to Capleton. It was Holmes who saw them first, and he stood pointing with a look of triumph upon his face. A man's track was visible beside the horse's.

'The horse was alone before,' I cried.

'Quite so. It was alone before. Halloa! what is this?'

The double track turned sharp off and took the direction of King's Pyland. Holmes whistled, and we both followed along after it. His eyes were on the trail, but I happened to look a little to one side, and saw to my surprise the same tracks coming back again in the opposite direction.

'One for you, Watson,' said Holmes, when I pointed it out; 'you have saved us a long walk which would have brought us back on our own traces. Let us follow the return track.'

We had not to go far. It ended at the paving of asphalt which led up to the gates of the Capleton stables. As we approached a groom ran out from them.

'We don't want any loiterers about here,' said he.

'I only wished to ask a question,' said Holmes, with his finger and thumb in his waistcoat pocket. 'Should I be too early to see your master, Mr Silas Brown, if I were to call at five o'clock tomorrow morning?'

'Bless you, sir, if anyone is about he will be, for he is always the first stirring. But here he is, sir, to answer your questions for himself. No, sir, no; it's as much as my place is worth to let him see me touch your money. Afterwards, if you like.'

As Sherlock Holmes replaced the half-crown which he had drawn from his pocket, a fierce-looking elderly man strode out from the gate with a hunting-crop swinging in his hand.

'What's this, Dawson?' he cried. 'No gossiping! Go about your business! And you—what the devil do you want here?'

'Ten minutes' talk with you, my good sir,' said Holmes, in the sweetest of voices.

'I've no time to talk to every gadabout. We want no strangers here. Be off, or you may find a dog at your heels.'

Holmes leaned forward and whispered something in the trainer's ear. He started violently and flushed to the temples.

'It's a lie!' he shouted. 'An infernal lie!'

'Very good! Shall we argue about it here in public, or talk it over in your parlour?'

'Oh, come in if you wish to.'

Holmes smiled. 'I shall not keep you more than a few minutes, Watson,' he said. 'Now, Mr Brown, I am quite at your disposal.'

It was quite twenty minutes, and the reds had all faded into greys before Holmes and the trainer reappeared. Never have I seen such a change as had been brought about in Silas Brown in that short time. His face was ashy pale, beads of perspiration shone upon his brow, and his hands shook until the hunting-crop wagged like a branch in the wind. His bullying, overbearing manner was all gone too, and he cringed along at my companion's side like a dog with its master.

'Your instructions will be done. It shall be done,' said he.

'There must be no mistake,' said Holmes, looking round at him. The other winced as he read the menace in his eyes.

'Oh, no, there shall be no mistake. It shall be there. Should I change it first or not?'

Holmes thought a little and then burst out laughing.

'No, don't,' said he. 'I shall write to you about it. No tricks now or———'

'Oh, you can trust me, you can trust me!'

'You must see to it on the day as if it were your own.'

'You can rely upon me.'

'Yes, I think I can. Well, you shall hear from me tomorrow.' He turned upon his heel, disregarding the trembling hand which the other held out to him, and we set off for King's Pyland.

'A more perfect compound of the bully, coward, and sneak than Master Silas Brown I have seldom met with,' remarked Holmes, as we trudged along together.

'He has the horse, then?'

'He tried to bluster out of it, but I described to him so exactly what his actions had been upon that morning, that he is convinced that I was watching him. Of course, you observed the peculiarly square toes in the impressions, and that his own boots exactly corresponded to them. Again, of course, no subordinate would have dared to have done such a thing. I described to him how when, according to his custom, he was the first down, he perceived a strange horse wandering over the moor; how he went out to it, and his astonishment at recognizing from the white forehead which has given the favourite its name that chance had put in his power the only horse which could beat the one upon which he had put his money. Then I described how his first impulse had been to lead him back to King's Pyland, and how the devil had shown him how he could hide the horse until the race was over, and how he had led it back and concealed it at Capleton. When I told him every detail he gave it up, and thought only of saving his own skin.'

'But his stables had been searched.'

'Oh, an old horse-faker like him has many a dodge.'

'But are you not afraid to leave the horse in his power now, since he has every interest in injuring it?'

'My dear fellow, he will guard it as the apple of his eye. He knows that his only hope of mercy is to produce it safe.'

'Colonel Ross did not impress me as a man who would be likely to show much mercy in any case.'

'The matter does not rest with Colonel Ross. I follow my own methods, and tell as much or as little as I choose. That is the advantage of being unofficial. I don't know whether you observed it, Watson, but the Colonel's manner has been just a trifle cavalier to me. I am inclined now to have a little amusement at his expense. Say nothing to him about the horse.'

'Certainly not, without your permission.'

'And, of course, this is all quite a minor case compared with the question of who killed John Straker.'

'And you will devote yourself to that?'

'On the contrary, we both go back to London by the night train.'

I was thunderstruck by my friend's words. We had only been a few hours in Devonshire, and that he should give up an investigation which he had begun so brilliantly was quite incomprehensible to me. Not a word more could I draw from him until we were back at the trainer's house. The Colonel and the Inspector were awaiting us in the parlour.

'My friend and I return to town by the midnight express,' said Holmes. 'We have had a charming little breath of your beautiful Dartmoor air.'

The Inspector opened his eyes, and the Colonel's lips curled in a sneer.

'So you despair of arresting the murderer of poor Straker,' said he.

Holmes shrugged his shoulders. 'There are certainly grave difficulties in the way,' said he. 'I have every hope, however, that your horse will start upon Tuesday, and I beg that you will have your jockey in readiness. Might I ask for a photograph of Mr John Straker?'

The Inspector took one from an envelope in his pocket and handed it to him.

'My dear Gregory, you anticipate all my wants. If I might ask you to wait here for an instant, I have a question which I should like to put to the maid.'

'I must say that I am rather disappointed in our London consultant,' said Colonel Ross, bluntly, as my friend left the room. 'I do not see that we are any further than when he came.'

'At least, you have his assurance that your horse will run,' said I.

'Yes, I have his assurance,' said the Colonel, with a shrug of his shoulders. 'I should prefer to have the horse.'

I was about to make some reply in defence of my friend, when he entered the room again.

'Now, gentlemen,' said he, 'I am quite ready for Tavistock.'

As we stepped into the carriage one of the stable lads held the door open for us. A sudden idea seemed to occur to Holmes, for he leaned forward and touched the lad upon the sleeve.

'You have a few sheep in the paddock,' he said. 'Who attends to them?'

'I do, sir.'

'Have you noticed anything amiss with them of late?'

'Well, sir, not of much account; but three of them have gone lame, sir.'

I could see that Holmes was extremely pleased, for he chuckled and rubbed his hands together.

'A long shot, Watson; a very long shot!' said he, pinching my arm. 'Gregory, let me recommend to your attention this singular epidemic among the sheep. Drive on, coachman!'

Colonel Ross still wore an expression which showed the poor opinion which he had formed of my companion's ability, but I saw by the Inspector's face that his attention had been keenly aroused.

'You consider that to be important?' he asked.

'Exceedingly so.'

'Is there any other point to which you would wish to draw my attention?'

'To the curious incident of the dog in the night-time.'

'The dog did nothing in the night-time.'

'That was the curious incident,' remarked Sherlock Holmes.

Four days later Holmes and I were again in the train bound for Winchester, to see the race for the Wessex Cup. Colonel Ross met us, by appointment, outside the station, and we drove in his drag to the course beyond the town. His face was grave and his manner was cold in the extreme.

'I have seen nothing of my horse,' said he.

'I suppose that you would know him when you saw him?' asked Holmes.

The Colonel was very angry. 'I have been on the turf for twenty years, and never was asked such a question as that before,' said he. 'A child would know Silver Blaze with his white forehead and his mottled off foreleg.'

'How is the betting?'

'Well, that is the curious part of it. You could have got fifteen to one yesterday, but the price has become shorter and shorter, until you can hardly get three to one now.'

'Hum!' said Holmes. 'Somebody knows something, that is clear!'

As the drag drew up in the enclosure near the grandstand, I glanced at the card to see the entries. It ran:

Wessex Plate. 50 sovs. each, h ft, with 1,000 sovs. added, for four- and five-year olds. Second £300. Third £200. New course (one mile and five furlongs).

1. Mr Heath Newton's The Negro (red cap, cinnamon jacket).
2. Colonel Wardlaw's Pugilist (pink cap, blue and black jacket).
3. Lord Backwater's Desborough (yellow cap and sleeves).
4. Colonel Ross's Silver Blaze (black cap, red jacket).
5. Duke of Balmoral's Iris (yellow and black stripes).
6. Lord Singleford's Rasper (purple cap, black sleeves).

'We scratched our other one and put all hopes on your word,' said the Colonel. 'Why, what is that? Silver Blaze favourite?'

'Five to four against Silver Blaze!' roared the ring. 'Five to four against Silver Blaze! Fifteen to five against Desborough! Five to four on the field!'

'There are the numbers up,' I cried. 'They are all six there.'

'All six there! Then my horse is running,' cried the Colonel, in great agitation. 'But I don't see him. My colours have not passed.'

'Only five have passed. This must be he.'

As I spoke a powerful bay horse swept out from the weighing enclosure and cantered past us, bearing on its back the well-known black and red of the Colonel.

'That's not my horse,' cried the owner. 'That beast has not a white hair upon its body. What is this that you have done, Mr Holmes?'

'Well, well, let us see how he gets on,' said my friend, imperturbably. For a few minutes he gazed through my field-glass. 'Capital! An excellent start!' he cried suddenly. 'There they are, coming round the curve!'

From our drag we had a superb view as they came up the straight. The six horses were so close together that a carpet could have covered them, but half-way up the yellow of the Capleton stable showed to the front. Before they reached us, however, Desborough's bolt was shot, and the Colonel's horse, coming away with a rush, passed the post a good six lengths before its rival, the Duke of Balmoral's Iris making a bad third.

'It's my race anyhow,' gasped the Colonel, passing his hand over his eyes. 'I confess that I can make neither head nor tail of it. Don't you think that you have kept up your mystery long enough, Mr Holmes?'

'Certainly, Colonel. You shall know everything. Let us all go round and have a look at the horse together. Here he is,' he continued, as we made our way into the weighing enclosure where only owners and their friends find admittance. 'You have only to wash his face and his leg in spirits of wine and you will find that he is the same old Silver Blaze as ever.'

'You take my breath away!'

'I found him in the hands of a faker, and took the liberty of running him just as he was sent over.'

'My dear sir, you have done wonders. The horse looks very fit and well. It never went better in its life. I owe you a thousand apologies for having doubted your ability. You have done me a great service by recovering my horse. You would do me a greater still if you could lay your hands on the murderer of John Straker.'

'I have done so,' said Holmes, quietly.

The Colonel and I stared at him in amazement. 'You have got him! Where is he, then?'

'He is here.'

'Here! Where?'

'In my company at the present moment.'

The Colonel flushed angrily. 'I quite recognize that I am under obligations to you, Mr Holmes,' said he, 'but I must regard what you have just said as either a very bad joke or an insult.'

Sherlock Holmes laughed. 'I assure you that I have not associated you with the crime, Colonel,' said he; 'the real murderer is standing immediately behind you!'

He stepped past and laid his hand upon the glossy neck of the thoroughbred.

'The horse!' cried both the Colonel and myself.

'Yes, the horse. And it may lessen his guilt if I say that it was done in self-defence, and that John Straker was a man who was entirely unworthy of your confidence. But there goes the bell; and as I stand to win a little on this next race, I shall defer a more lengthy explanation until a more fitting time.'

We had the corner of a Pullman car to ourselves that evening as we whirled back to London, and I fancy that the journey was a short one to Colonel Ross as well as to myself, as we listened to our companion's narrative of the events which had occurred at the Dartmoor training stables upon that Monday night, and the means by which he had unravelled them.

'I confess,' said he, 'that any theories which I had formed from the newspaper reports were entirely erroneous. And yet there were indications there, had they not been overlaid by other details which concealed their true import. I went to Devonshire with the conviction that Fitzroy Simpson was the true culprit, although, of course, I saw that the evidence against him was by no means complete.

'It was while I was in the carriage, just as we reached the trainer's house, that the immense significance of the curried mutton occurred to me. You may remember that I was distrait, and remained sitting after you had all alighted. I was marvelling in my own mind how I could possibly have overlooked so obvious a clue.'

'I confess,' said the Colonel, 'that even now I cannot see how it helps us.'

'It was the first link in my chain of reasoning. Powdered opium is by no means tasteless. The flavour is not disagreeable, but it is perceptible. Were it mixed with any ordinary dish, the eater would undoubtedly detect it, and would probably eat no more. A curry was exactly the medium which would disguise this taste. By no possible supposition could this stranger, Fitzroy Simpson, have caused curry to be served in the trainer's family that night, and it is surely too monstrous a coincidence to suppose that he happened to come along with powdered opium upon the very night when a dish happened to be served which would disguise the flavour. That is unthinkable. Therefore Simpson becomes eliminated from the case, and our attention centres upon Straker and his wife, the only two people who could have chosen curried mutton for supper that night. The opium was added after the dish was set aside for the stable boy, for the others had the same for supper with no ill effects. Which of them, then, had access to that dish without the maid seeing them?

'Before deciding that question I had grasped the significance of the silence of the dog, for one true inference invariably suggests others. The Simpson incident had shown me that a dog was kept in the stables, and yet, though someone had been in and had fetched out a horse, he had not barked enough to arouse the two lads in the loft. Obviously the midnight visitor was someone whom the dog knew well.

'I was already convinced, or almost convinced, that John Straker went down to the stables in the dead of the night and took out Silver Blaze. For what purpose? For a dishonest one, obviously, or why should he drug his own stable boy? And yet I was at a loss to know why. There have been cases before now where trainers have made sure of great sums of money by laying against their own horses, through agents, and then prevented them from winning by fraud. Sometimes it is a pulling jockey. Sometimes it is some surer and subtler means. What was it here? I hoped that the contents of his pockets might help me to form a conclusion.

'And they did so. You cannot have forgotten the singular knife which was found in the dead man's hand, a knife which certainly no sane man would choose for a weapon. It was, as Dr Watson told us, a form of knife which is used for the most delicate operations known in surgery. And it was to be used for a delicate operation that night. You must know, with your wide experience of turf matters, Colonel Ross, that it is possible to make a slight nick upon the tendons of a horse's ham, and to do it subcutaneously so as to leave absolutely no trace. A horse so treated would develop a slight lameness which would be put down to a strain in exercise or a touch of rheumatism, but never to foul play.'

'Villain! Scoundrel!' cried the Colonel.

'We have here the explanation of why John Straker wished to take the horse out on to the moor. So spirited a creature would have certainly roused the soundest of sleepers when it felt the prick of the knife. It was absolutely necessary to do it in the open air.'

'I have been blind!' cried the Colonel. 'Of course, that was why he needed the candle, and struck the match.'

'Undoubtedly. But in examining his belongings, I was fortunate enough to discover, not only the method of the crime, but even its motives. As a man of the world, Colonel, you know that men do not carry other people's bills about in their pockets. We have most of us quite enough to do to settle our own. I at once concluded that Straker was leading a double life, and keeping a second establishment. The nature of the bill showed that there was a lady in the case, and one who had expensive tastes. Liberal as you are with your servants, one hardly expects that they can buy twenty-guinea walking dresses for their women. I questioned Mrs Straker as to the dress without her knowing it, and having satisfied myself that it had never reached her, I made a note of the milliner's address, and felt that by calling there with Straker's photograph, I could easily dispose of the mythical Darbyshire.

'From that time on all was plain. Straker had led out the horse to a hollow where his light would be invisible. Simpson, in his flight, had dropped his cravat, and Straker had picked it up with some idea, perhaps, that he might use it in securing the horse's leg. Once in the hollow he had got behind the horse, and had struck a light, but the creature, frightened at the sudden glare, and with the strange instinct of animals feeling that some mischief was intended, had lashed out, and the steel shoe had struck Straker full on the forehead. He had already, in spite of the rain, taken off his overcoat in order to do his delicate task, and so, as he fell, his knife gashed his thigh. Do I make it clear?'

'Wonderful!' cried the Colonel. 'Wonderful! You might have been there.'

'My final shot was, I confess, a very long one. It struck me that so astute a man as Straker would not undertake this delicate tendon-nicking without a little practice. What could he practise on? My eyes fell upon the sheep, and I asked a question which, rather to my surprise, showed that my surmise was correct.'

'You have made it perfectly clear, Mr Holmes.'

'When I returned to London I called upon the milliner, who at once recognized Straker as an excellent customer, of the name of Darbyshire, who had a very dashing wife with a strong partiality for expensive dresses. I have no doubt that this woman had plunged him over head and ears in debt, and so led him into this miserable plot.'

'You have explained all but one thing,' cried the Colonel. 'Where was the horse?'

'Ah, it bolted and was cared for by one of your neighbours. We must have an amnesty in that direction, I think. This is Clapham

Junction, if I am not mistaken, and we shall be in Victoria in less than ten minutes. If you care to smoke a cigar in our rooms, Colonel, I shall be happy to give you any other details which might interest you.'

R. AUSTIN FREEMAN · 1862–1943

The Mysterious Visitor

'So,' said Thorndyke, looking at me reflectively, 'you are a full-blown medical practitioner with a practice of your own. How the years slip by! It seems but the other day that you were a student, gaping at me from the front bench of the lecture theatre.'

'Did I gape?' I asked incredulously.

'I use the word metaphorically,' said he, 'to denote ostentatious attention. You always took my lectures very seriously. May I ask if you have ever found them of use in your practice?'

'I can't say that I have ever had any very thrilling medico-legal experiences since that extraordinary cremation case that you investigated—the case of Septimus Maddock, you know. But that reminds me that there is a little matter that I meant to speak to you about. It is of no interest, but I just wanted your advice, though it isn't even my business, strictly speaking. It concerns a patient of mine, a man named Crofton, who has disappeared rather unaccountably.'

'And do you call that a case of no medico-legal interest?' demanded Thorndyke.

'Oh, there's nothing in it. He just went away for a holiday and he hasn't communicated with his friends very recently. That is all. What makes me a little uneasy is that there is a departure from his usual habits—he is generally a fairly regular correspondent—that seems a little significant in view of his personality. He is markedly neurotic and his family history is by no means what one would wish.'

'That is an admirable thumb-nail sketch, Jardine,' said Thorndyke; 'but it lacks detail. Let us have a full-size picture.'

'Very well,' said I, 'but you mustn't let me bore you. To begin with Crofton: he is a nervous, anxious, worrying sort of fellow, everlastingly fussing about money affairs, and latterly this tendency has been getting worse. He fairly got the jumps about his financial position; felt that he was steadily drifting into bankruptcy and couldn't get the subject out of his mind. It was all bunkum. I am more or less a friend of the family, and I know that there was nothing to worry about. Mrs Crofton assured me that, although they were a trifle hard up, they could rub along quite safely.

'As he seemed to be getting the hump worse and worse, I advised him to go away for a change and stay in a boarding-house where he would see some fresh faces. Instead of that, he elected to go down to a bungalow that he has at Seasalter, near Whitstable, and lets out in the season. He proposed to stay by himself and spend his time in sea-bathing and country walks. I wasn't very keen on this, for solitude was the last thing that he wanted. There was a strong family history of melancholia and some unpleasant rumours of suicide. I didn't like his being alone at all. However, another friend of the family, Mrs Crofton's brother, in fact, a chap named Ambrose, offered to go down and spend a weekend with him to give him a start, and afterwards to run down for an afternoon whenever he was able. So off he went with Ambrose on Friday, the sixteenth of June, and for a time all went well. He seemed to be improving in health and spirits and wrote to his wife regularly two or three times a week. Ambrose went down as often as he could to cheer him up, and the last time brought back the news that Crofton thought of moving on to Margate for a further change. So, of course, he didn't go down to the bungalow again.

'Well, in due course, a letter came from Margate; it had been written at the bungalow, but the postmark was Margate and bore the same date—the sixteenth of July—as the letter itself. I have it with me. Mrs Crofton sent it for me to see and I haven't returned it yet. But there is nothing of interest in it beyond the statement that he was going on to Margate by the next train and would write again when he had found rooms there. That was the last that was heard of him. He never wrote and nothing is known of his movements excepting that he left Seasalter and arrived at Margate. This is the letter.'

I handed it to Thorndyke, who glanced at the postmark and then laid it on the table for examination later.

'Have any inquiries been made?' he asked.

'Yes. His photograph has been sent to the Margate police, but, of course—well, you know what Margate is like in July. Thousands of strangers coming and going every day. It is hopeless to look for him in that crowd; and it is quite possible that he isn't there now. But his disappearance is most inopportune, for a big legacy has just fallen in, and, naturally, Mrs Crofton is frantically anxious to let him know. It is a matter of about thirty thousand pounds.'

'Was this legacy expected?' asked Thorndyke.

'No. The Croftons knew nothing about it. They didn't know that the old lady—Miss Shuler—had made a will or that she had very much to leave; and they didn't know that she was likely to die, or even that she was ill. Which is rather odd; for she was ill for a month or two, and, as she suffered from a malignant abdominal tumour, it was known that she couldn't recover.'

'When did she die?'

'On the thirteenth of July.'

Thorndyke raised his eyebrows. 'Just three days before the date of this letter,' he remarked; 'so that, if he should never reappear, this letter will be the sole evidence that he survived her. It is an important document. It may come to represent a value of thirty thousand pounds.'

'It isn't really so important as it looks,' said I. 'Miss Shuler's will provides that if Crofton should die before the testatrix, the legacy should go to his wife. So whether he is alive or not, the legacy is quite safe. But we must hope that he is alive, though I must confess to some little anxiety on his account.'

Thorndyke reflected awhile on this statement. Presently he asked:

'Do you know if Crofton has made a will?'

'Yes, he has,' I replied; 'quite recently. I was one of the witnesses and I read it through at Crofton's request. It was full of the usual legal verbiage, but it might have been stated in a dozen words. He leaves practically everything to his wife, but instead of saying so it enumerates the property item by item.'

'It was drafted, I suppose, by the solicitor?'

'Yes; another friend of the family named Jobson, and he is the executor and residuary legatee.'

Thorndyke nodded and again became deeply reflective. Still meditating, he took up the letter, and as he inspected it, I watched him curiously and not without a certain secret amusement. First he looked over the envelope, back and front. Then he took from his pocket a powerful Coddington lens and with this examined the flap and the postmark. Next, he drew out the letter, held it up to the light, then read it through and finally examined various parts of the writing through his lens.

'Well,' I asked, with an irreverent grin, 'I should think you have extracted the last grain of meaning from it.'

He smiled as he put away his lens and handed the letter back to me.

'As this may have to be produced in proof of survival,' said he, 'it had better be put in a place of safety. I notice that he speaks of returning later to the bungalow. I take it that it has been ascertained that he did not return there?'

'I don't think so. You see, they have been waiting for him to write. You think that someone ought————'

I paused; for it began to be borne in on me that Thorndyke was taking a somewhat gloomy view of the case.

'My dear Jardine,' said he. 'I am merely following your own suggestion. Here is a man with an inherited tendency to melancholia and suicide who has suddenly disappeared. He went away from an empty house and announced his intention of returning to it later. As that house is the only known locality in which he could be sought, it is obvious that it ought to have been examined. And even if he never came back there, the house might contain some clues to his present whereabouts.'

This last sentence put an idea into my mind which I was a little shy of broaching. What was a clue to Thorndyke might be perfectly meaningless to an ordinary person. I recalled his amazing interpretations of the most commonplace facts in the mysterious Maddock case and the idea took fuller possession. At length I said tentatively:

'I would go down myself if I felt competent. Tomorrow is Saturday and I could get a colleague to look after my practice; there isn't much doing just now. But when you speak of clues, and when I remember what a duffer I was last time—I wish it were possible for you to have a look at the place.'

To my surprise, he assented almost with enthusiasm.

'Why not?' said he. 'It is a weekend. We could put up at the bungalow, I suppose, and have a little gipsy holiday. And there are undoubtedly points of interest in the case. Let us go down tomorrow. We can lunch in the train and have the afternoon before us. You had better get a key from Mrs Crofton, or, if she hasn't got one, an authority to visit the house. We may want that if we have to enter without a key. And we go alone, of course.'

I assented joyfully. Not that I had any expectations as to what we might learn from our inspection. But something in Thorndyke's manner gave me the impression that he had extracted from my account of the case some significance that was not apparent to me.

The bungalow stood on a space of rough ground a little way behind the sea-wall, along which we walked towards it from Whitstable, passing on our way a shipbuilder's yard and a slipway, on which a collier brigantine was hauled up for repairs. There were one or two other bungalows adjacent, but a considerable distance apart, and we looked at them as we approached to make out the names painted on the gates.

'That will probably be the one,' said Thorndyke, indicating a small building enclosed within a wooden fence and provided, like the others, with a bathing hut, just above high-water mark. Its solitary, deserted aspect and lowered blinds supported his opinion and when we reached the gate, the name 'Middlewick' painted on it settled the matter.

'The next question is,' said I, 'how the deuce we are going to get in? The gate is locked, and there is no bell. Is it worth while to hammer at the fence?'

'I wouldn't do that,' replied Thorndyke. 'The place is pretty certainly empty or the gate wouldn't be locked. We shall have to climb over unless there is a back gate unlocked, so the less noise we make the better.'

We walked round the enclosure, but there was no other gate, nor was there any tree or other cover to disguise our rather suspicious proceedings.

'There's no help for it, Jardine,' said Thorndyke, 'so here goes.'

He put his green canvas suitcase on the ground, grasped the top of the fence with both hands and went over like a harlequin. I picked up the case and handed it over to him, and, having taken a quick glance round, followed my leader.

'Well,' I said, 'here we are. And now, how are we going to get into the house?'

'We shall have to pick a lock if there is no door open, or else go in by a window. Let us take a look round.'

We walked round the house to the back door, but found it not only locked but bolted top and bottom, as Thorndyke ascertained with his knife-blade. The windows were all casements and all fastened with their catches.

'The front door will be the best,' said Thorndyke. 'It can't be bolted unless he got out by the chimney, and I think my "smoker's companion" will be able to cope with an ordinary door-lock. It looked like a common builder's fitting.'

As he spoke, we returned to the front of the house and he produced the 'smoker's companion' from his pocket (I don't know what kind of smoker it was designed to accompany). The lock was apparently a simple affair, for the second trial with the 'companion' shot back the bolt, and when I turned the handle, the door opened. As a precaution, I called out to inquire if there was anybody within, and then, as there was no answer, we entered, walking straight into the living-room, as there was no hall or lobby.

A couple of paces from the threshold we halted to look round the room, and on me the aspect of the place produced a vague sense of discomfort. Though it was early in a bright afternoon, the room was almost completely dark, for not only were the blinds lowered, but the curtains were drawn as well.

'It looks', said I, peering about the dim and gloomy apartment with sun-dazzled eyes, 'as if he had gone away at night. He wouldn't have drawn the curtains in the daytime.'

'One would think not,' Thorndyke agreed; 'but it doesn't follow.'

He stepped to the front window and drawing back the curtains pulled up the blind, revealing a half-curtain of green serge over the lower part of the window. As the bright daylight flooded the room, he stood with his back to the window looking about with deep attention, letting his eyes travel slowly over the walls, the furniture, and especially the floor. Presently he stooped to pick up a short match-end which lay just under the table opposite the door, and as he looked at it thoughtfully, he pointed to a couple of spots of candle grease on the linoleum near the table. Then he glanced at the mantelpiece and from that to an ash-bowl on the table.

'These are only trifling discrepancies,' said he, 'but they are worth noting. You see,' he continued in response to my look of inquiry, 'that this room is severely trim and orderly. Everything seems to be in its place. The matchbox, for instance, has its fixed receptacle above the mantelpiece, and there is a bowl for the burnt matches, regularly used, as its contents show. Yet here is a burnt match thrown on the floor, although the bowl is on the table quite handy. And the match, you notice, is not of the same kind as those in the box over the mantelpiece, which is a large Bryant and May, or as the burnt matches in the bowl which have evidently come from it. But if you look in the bowl,' he continued, picking it up, 'you will see two burnt matches of this same kind—apparently the small size Bryant and May—one burnt quite short and one only half burnt. The suggestion is fairly obvious, but, as I say, there is a slight discrepancy.'

'I don't know,' said I, 'that either the suggestion or the discrepancy is very obvious to me.'

He walked over to the mantelpiece and took the matchbox from its case.

'You see,' said he, opening it, 'that this box is nearly full. It has an appointed place and it was in that place. We find a small match, burnt right out, under the table opposite the door, and two more in the bowl under the hanging lamp. A reasonable inference is that some one came in in the dark and struck a match as he entered. That match must have come from a box that he brought with him in his pocket. It burned out and he struck another, which also burned out while he was raising the chimney of the lamp, and he struck a third to light the lamp. But if that person was Crofton, why did he need to strike a match to light the room when the matchbox was in its usual place; and why did he throw the match-end on the floor?'

'You mean that the suggestion is that the person was not Crofton; and I think you are right. Crofton doesn't carry matches in his pocket. He uses wax vestas and carries them in a silver case.'

'It might possibly have been Ambrose,' Thorndyke suggested.

'I don't think so,' said I. 'Ambrose uses a petrol lighter.'

Thorndyke nodded. 'There may be nothing in it,' said he, 'but it offers a suggestion. Shall we look over the rest of the premises?'

He paused for a moment to glance at a small key-board on the wall on which one or two keys were hanging, each distinguished by a little ivory label and by the name written underneath the peg; then he opened a door in the corner of the room. As this led into the kitchen, he closed it and opened an adjoining one which gave access to a bedroom.

'This is probably the extra bedroom,' he remarked as we entered. 'The blinds have not been drawn down and there is a general air of trimness that suggests a tidy up of an unoccupied room. And the bed looks as if it had been out of use.'

After an attentive look round, he returned to the living-room and crossed to the remaining door. As he opened it, we looked into a nearly dark room, both the windows being covered by thick serge curtains.

'Well,' he observed, when he had drawn back the curtains and raised the blinds, 'there is nothing painfully tidy here. That is a very roughly-made bed, and the blanket is outside the counterpane.'

He looked critically about the room and especially at the bedside table.

'Here are some more discrepancies,' said he. 'There are two candlesticks, in one of which the candle has burned itself right out, leaving a fragment of wick. There are five burnt matches in it, two large ones from the box by its side, and three small ones, of which two are mere stumps. The second candle is very much guttered, and I think'—he lifted it out of the socket—'yes, it has been used out of the candlestick. You see that the grease has run down right to the bottom and there is a distinct impression of a thumb—apparently a left thumb—made while the grease was warm. Then you notice the mark on the table of a tumbler which had contained some liquid that was not water, but there is no tumbler. However, it may be an old mark, though it looks fresh.'

'It is hardly like Crofton to leave an old mark on the table,' said I. 'He is a regular old maid. We had better see if the tumbler is in the kitchen.'

'Yes,' agreed Thorndyke. 'But I wonder what he was doing with that candle. Apparently he took it out of doors, as there is a spot on the floor of the living-room; and you see that there are one or two spots on the floor here.' He walked over to a chest of drawers near the door and was looking into a drawer which he had pulled out, and which I could see was full of clothes, when I observed a faint smile spreading over his face. 'Come round here, Jardine,' he said in a low voice, 'and take a peep through the crack of the door.'

I walked round, and, applying my eye to the crack, looked across the living-room at the end window. Above the half-curtain I could distinguish the unmistakable top of a constabulary helmet.

'Listen,' said Thorndyke. 'They are in force.'

As he spoke, there came from the neighbourhood of the kitchen a furtive scraping sound, suggestive of a pocket-knife persuading a window-catch. It was followed by the sound of an opening window and then of a stealthy entry. Finally, the kitchen door opened softly, someone tip-toed across the living-room and a burly police-sergeant appeared framed in the bedroom doorway.

'Good afternoon, Sergeant,' said Thorndyke, with a genial smile.

'Yes, that's all very well,' was the response, 'but the question is, who might you be, and what might you be doing in this house?'

Thorndyke briefly explained our business, and, when we had presented our cards and Mrs Crofton's written authority, the sergeant's professional stiffness vanished like magic.

'It's all right, Tomkins,' he sang out to an invisible myrmidon. 'You had better shut the window and go out by the front door. You must excuse me, gentlemen,' he added; 'but the tenant of the next bungalow cycled down and gave us the tip. He watched you through his glasses and saw you pick the front-door lock. It did look a bit queer, you must admit.'

Thorndyke admitted it freely with a faint chuckle, and we walked across the living-room to the kitchen. Here, the sergeant's presence seemed to inhibit comments, but I noticed that my colleague cast a significant glance at a frying-pan that rested on a Primus stove. The congealed fat in it presented another 'discrepancy'; for I could hardly imagine the fastidious Crofton going away and leaving it in that condition.

Noting that there was no unwashed tumbler in evidence, I followed my friend back to the living-room, where he paused with his eye on the key-board.

'Well,' remarked the sergeant, 'if he ever did come back here, it's pretty clear that he isn't here now. You've been all over the premises, I think?'

'All excepting the bathing-hut,' replied Thorndyke; and, as he spoke, he lifted the key so labelled from its hook.

The sergeant laughed softly. 'He's not very likely to have taken up his quarters there,' said he. 'Still, there's nothing like being thorough. But you notice that the key of the front door and that of the gate have both been taken away, so we can assume that he has taken himself away too.'

'That is a reasonable inference,' Thorndyke admitted; 'but we may as well make our survey complete.'

With this he led the way out into the garden and to the gate, where he unblushingly produced the 'smoker's companion' and insinuated its prongs into the keyhole.

'Well, I'm sure!' exclaimed the sergeant as the lock clicked and the gate opened. 'That's a funny sort of tool; and you seem quite handy with it, too. Might I have a look at it?'

He looked at it so very long and attentively, when Thorndyke handed it to him, that I suspected him of an intention to infringe the patent. By the time he had finished his inspection we were at the bottom of the bank below the sea-wall and Thorndyke had inserted the key into the lock of the bathing-hut. As the sergeant returned the 'companion' Thorndyke took it and pocketed it; then he turned the key and pushed the door open; and the officer started back with a shout of amazement.

It was certainly a grim spectacle that we looked in on. The hut was a small building about six feet square, devoid of any furniture or fittings excepting one or two pegs high up the wall. The single, unglazed window was closely shuttered and on the bare floor in the farther corner a man was sitting, leaning back into the corner, with his head dropped forward on his breast. The man was undoubtedly Arthur

Crofton. That much I could say with certainty, notwithstanding the horrible changes wrought by death and the lapse of time. 'But,' I added when I had identified the body, 'I should have said that he had been dead more than a fortnight. He must have come straight back from Margate and done this. And that will probably be the missing tumbler,' I concluded, pointing to one that stood on the floor close to the right hand of the corpse.

'No doubt,' replied Thorndyke, somewhat abstractedly. He had been looking critically about the interior of the hut, and now remarked: 'I wonder why he did not shoot the bolt instead of locking himself in; and what has become of the key? He must have taken it out of the lock and put it in his pocket.'

He looked interrogatively at the sergeant, who having no option but to take the hint, advanced with an expression of horrified disgust and proceeded very gingerly to explore the dead man's clothing.

'Ah!' he exclaimed at length,' here we are.' He drew from the waistcoat pocket a key with a small ivory label attached to it. 'Yes, this is the one. You see, it is marked "Bathing Hut".'

He handed it to Thorndyke, who looked at it attentively, and even with an appearance of surprise, and then, producing an indelible pencil from his pocket, wrote on the label, 'Found on body.'

'The first thing,' said he, 'is to ascertain if it fits the lock.'

'Why, it must,' said the sergeant, 'if he locked himself in with it.'

'Undoubtedly,' Thorndyke agreed, 'but that is the point. It doesn't look quite similar to the other one.'

He drew out the key which we had brought from the house and gave it to me to hold. Then he tried the key from the dead man's pocket; but it not only did not fit, it would not even enter the keyhole.

The sceptical indifference faded suddenly from the sergeant's face. He took the key from Thorndyke, and having tried it with the same result, stood up and stared, round-eyed, at my colleague.

'Well!' he exclaimed. 'This is a facer! It's the wrong key!'

'There may be another key on the body,' said Thorndyke. 'It isn't likely, but you had better make sure.'

The sergeant showed no reluctance this time. He searched the dead man's pockets thoroughly and produced a bunch of keys. But they were all quite small keys, none of them in the least resembling that of the hut door. Nor, I noticed, did they include those of the bungalow door or the garden gate. Once more the officer drew himself up and stared at Thorndyke.

'There's something rather fishy about this affair,' said he.

'There is,' Thorndyke agreed. 'The door was certainly locked; and as it was not locked from within, it must have been locked from without. Then that key—the wrong key—was presumably put in the dead man's pocket by some other person. And there are some other suspicious facts. A tumbler has disappeared from the bedside table, and there is a tumbler here. You notice one or two spots of candle-grease on the floor here, and it looks as if a candle had been stood in that corner near the door. There is no candle here now; but in the bedroom there is a candle which has been carried without a candle-stick and which, by the way, bears an excellent impression of a thumb. The first thing to do will be to take the deceased's finger-prints. Would you mind fetching my case from the bedroom, Jardine?'

I ran back to the house (not unobserved by the gentleman in the next bungalow) and, catching up the case, carried it down to the hut. When I arrived there I found Thorndyke holding the tumbler delicately in his gloved left hand while he examined it against the light with the aid of his lens. He handed the latter to me and observed:

'If you look at this carefully, Jardine, you will see a very interesting thing. There are the prints of two different thumbs—both left thumbs, and therefore of different persons. You will remember that the tumbler stood by the right hand of the body and that the table, which bore the mark of a tumbler, was at the left-hand side of the bed.'

When I had examined the thumb-prints he placed the tumbler carefully on the floor and opened his 'research-case', which was fitted as a sort of portable laboratory. From this he took a little brass box containing an ink tube, a tiny roller and some small cards, and, using the box-lid as an inking-plate, he proceeded methodically to take the dead man's fingerprints, writing the particulars on each card.

'I don't quite see what you want with Crofton's fingerprints,' said I. 'The other man's would be more to the point.'

'Undoubtedly,' Thorndyke replied. 'But we have to prove that they are another man's—that they are not Crofton's. And there is that print on the candle. That is a very important point to settle; and as we have finished here, we had better go and settle it at once.'

He closed his case, and, taking up the tumbler with his gloved hand, led the way back to the house, the sergeant following when he had locked the door. We proceeded direct to the bedroom, where Thorndyke took the candle from its socket and, with the aid of his lens, compared it carefully with the two thumb-prints on the card, and then with the tumbler.

'It is perfectly clear,' said he. 'This is a mark of a left thumb. It is totally unlike Crofton's and it appears to be identical with the strange thumb-print on the tumbler. From which it seems to follow that the stranger took the candle from this room to the hut and brought it back. But he probably blew it out before leaving the house and lit it again in the hut.'

The sergeant and I examined the cards, the candle, and the tumbler, and then the former asked:

'I suppose you have no idea whose thumb-print that might be? You don't know, for instance, of anyone who might have had any motive for making away with Mr Crofton?'

'That,' replied Thorndyke, 'is rather a question for the coroner's jury.'

'So it is,' the sergeant agreed. 'But there won't be much question about their verdict. It is a pretty clear case of wilful murder.'

To this Thorndyke made no reply excepting to give some directions as to the safekeeping of the candle and tumbler; and our proposed 'gipsy holiday' being now evidently impossible, we took our leave of the sergeant—who already had our cards—and wended back to the station.

'I suppose,' said I, 'we shall have to break the news to Mrs Crofton.'

'That is hardly our business,' he replied. 'We can leave that to the solicitor or to Ambrose. If you know the lawyer's address, you might send him a telegram, arranging a meeting at eight o'clock tonight. Give no particulars. Just say "Crofton found", but mark the telegram "urgent" so that he will keep the appointment.'

On reaching the station, I sent off the telegram, and very soon afterwards the London train was signalled. It turned out to be a slow train, which gave us ample time to discuss the case and me ample time for reflection. And, in fact, I reflected a good deal; for there was a rather uncomfortable question in my mind—the very question that the sergeant had raised and that Thorndyke had obviously evaded. Was there anyone who might have had a motive for making away with Crofton? It was an awkward question when one remembered the great legacy that had just fallen in and the terms of Miss Shuler's will; which expressly provided that, if Crofton died before his wife, the legacy should go to her. Now Ambrose was the wife's brother; and Ambrose had been in the bungalow alone with Crofton, and nobody else was known to have been there at all. I meditated on these facts uncomfortably and would have liked to put the case to Thorndyke; but his reticence, his evasion of the sergeant's question and his decision to communicate with the solicitor rather than with the family, showed pretty clearly what was in his mind and that he did not wish to discuss the matter.

Promptly at eight o'clock, having dined at a restaurant, we presented ourselves at the solicitor's house and were shown into the study, where we found Mr Jobson seated at a writing-table. He looked at Thorndyke with some surprise, and when the introductions had been made, said somewhat dryly:

'We may take it that Dr Thorndyke is in some way connected with our rather confidential business?'

'Certainly,' I replied. 'That is why he is here.'

Jobson nodded. 'And how is Crofton?' he asked, 'and where did you dig him up?'

'I am sorry to say,' I replied, 'that he is dead. It is a dreadful affair. We found his body locked in the bathing-hut. He was sitting in a corner with a tumbler on the floor by his side.'

'Horrible! horrible!' exclaimed the solicitor. 'He ought never to have gone there alone. I said so at the time. And it is most unfortunate on account of the insurance, though that is not a large amount. Still the suicide clause, you know————'

'I doubt whether the insurance will be affected,' said Thorndyke. 'The coroner's finding will amost certainly be wilful murder.'

Jobson was thunderstruck. In a moment his face grew livid and he gazed at Thorndyke with an expression of horrified amazement.

'Murder!' he repeated incredulously. 'But you said he was locked in the hut. Surely that is clear proof of suicide.'

'He hadn't locked himself in, you know. There was no key inside.'

'Ah!' The solicitor spoke almost in a tone of relief. 'But, perhaps—did you examine his pockets?'

'Yes; and we found a key labelled "Bathing Hut". But it was the wrong key. It wouldn't go into the lock. There is no doubt whatever that the door was locked from the outside.'

'Good God!' exclaimed Jobson, in a faint voice. 'It does look suspicious. But still, I can't believe—it seems quite incredible.'

'That may be,' said Thorndyke, 'but it is all perfectly clear. There is evidence that a stranger entered the bungalow at night and that the affair took place in the bedroom. From thence the stranger carried the body down to the hut and he also took a tumbler and a candle from the bedside table. By the light of the candle—which was stood on the floor of the hut in a corner—he arranged the body, having put into its pocket a key from the board in the living-room. Then he locked the hut, went back to the house, put the key on its peg and the candle in its candlestick. Then he locked up the house and the garden gate and took the keys away with him.'

The solicitor listened to this recital in speechless amazement. At length he asked:

'How long ago do you suppose this happened?'

'Apparently on the night of the fifteenth of this month,' was the reply.

'But,' objected Jobson, 'he wrote home on the sixteenth.'

'He wrote,' said Thorndyke, 'on the sixth. Somebody put a one in front of the six and posted the letter at Margate on the sixteenth. I shall give evidence to that effect at the inquest.'

I was becoming somewhat mystified. Thorndyke's dry, stern manner—so different from his usual suavity—and the solicitor's uncalled-for agitation, seemed to hint at something more than met the eye. I watched Jobson as he lit a cigarette—with a small Bryant and May match, which he threw on the floor—and listened expectantly for his next question. At length he asked:

'Was there any sort of—er—clue as to who this stranger might be?'

'The man who will be charged with the murder? Oh, yes. The police have the means of identifying him with absolute certainty.'

'That is, if they can find him,' said Jobson.

'Naturally. But when all the very remarkable facts have transpired at the inquest, that individual will probably come pretty clearly into view.'

Jobson continued to smoke furiously with his eyes fixed on the floor as if he were thinking hard. Presently he asked, without looking up:

'Supposing they do find this man. What then? What evidence is there that he murdered Crofton?'

'You mean direct evidence?' said Thorndyke. 'I can't say, as I did not examine the body; but the circumstantial evidence that I have given you would be enough to convict unless there were some convincing explanation other than murder. And I may say,' he added, 'that if the suspected person has a plausible explanation to offer, he would be well advised to produce it before he is charged. A voluntary statement has a good deal more weight than the same statement made by a prisoner in answer to a charge.'

There was an interval of silence, in which I looked in bewilderment from Thorndyke's stern visage to the pale face of the solicitor. At length the latter rose abruptly, and, after one or two quick strides up and down the room, halted by the fireplace, and, still avoiding Thorndyke's eye, said, somewhat brusquely, though in a low, husky voice:

'I will tell you how it happened. I went down to Seasalter, as you said, on the night of the fifteenth, on the chance of finding Crofton at the bungalow. I wanted to tell him of Miss Shuler's death and of the provisions of her will.'

'You had some private information on that subject, I presume?' said Thorndyke.

'Yes. My cousin was her solicitor and he kept me informed about the will.'

'And about the state of her health?'

'Yes. Well, when I arrived at the bungalow, it was in darkness. The gate and the front door were unlocked, so I entered, calling out Crofton's name. As no one answered, I struck a match and lit the lamp. Then I went into the bedroom and struck a match there; and by its light I could see Crofton lying on the bed, quite still. I spoke to him, but he did not answer or move. Then I lighted a candle on his table; and now I could see what I had already guessed, that he was dead, and that he had been dead some time—probably more than a week.

'It was an awful shock to find a dead man in this solitary house, and my first impulse was to rush out and give the alarm. But when I went into the living-room, I happened to see a letter lying on the writing-table and noticed that it was in his own handwriting and addressed to his wife. Unfortunately, I had the curiosity to take it out of the unsealed envelope and read it. It was dated the sixth and stated his intention of going to Margate for a time and then coming back to the bungalow.

'Now, the reading of that letter exposed me to an enormous temptation. By simply putting a one in front of the six and thus altering the date from the sixth to the sixteenth and posting the letter at Margate, I stood to gain thirty thousand pounds. I saw that at a glance. But I did not decide immediately to do it. I pulled down all the blinds, drew the curtains and locked up the house while I thought it over. There seemed to be practically no risk, unless someone should come to the bungalow and notice that the state of the body did not agree with the altered date on the letter. I went back and looked at the dead man. There was a burnt-out candle by his side and a tumbler containing the dried-up remains of some brown liquid. He had evidently poisoned himself. Then it occurred to me that, if I put the body and the tumbler in some place where they were not likely to be found for some time, the discrepancy between the condition of the body and the date of the letter would not be noticed.

'For some time I could think of no suitable place, but at last I remembered the bathing-hut. No one would look there for him. If they came to the bungalow and didn't find him there, they would merely conclude that he had not come back from Margate. I took the candle and the key from the key-board and went down to the hut; but there was a key in the door already, so I brought the other key back and put it in Crofton's pocket, never dreaming that it might not be the duplicate. Of course, I ought to have tried it in the door.

'Well, you know the rest. I took the body down, about two in the morning, locked up the hut, brought away the key and hung it on the board, took the counterpane off the bed, as it had some marks on it, and re-made the bed with the blanket outside. In the morning I took the train to Margate, posted the letter, after altering the date, and threw the gate-key and that of the front door into the sea.

'That is what really happened. You may not believe me; but I think you will as you have seen the body and will realize that I had no motive for killing Crofton before the fifteenth, whereas Crofton evidently died before that date.'

'I would not say "evidently",' said Thorndyke; 'but, as the date of his death is the vital point in your defence, you would be wise to notify the coroner of the importance of the issue.'

'I don't understand this case,' I said, as we walked homewards (I was spending the evening with Thorndyke). 'You seemed to smell a rat from the very first. And I don't see how you spotted Jobson. It is a mystery to me.'

'It wouldn't be if you were a lawyer,' he replied. 'The case against Jobson was contained in what you told me at our first interview. You yourself commented on the peculiarity of the will that he drafted for Crofton. The intention of the latter was to leave all his property to his wife. But instead of saying so, the will specified each item of property, and appointed a residuary legatee, which was Jobson himself. This might have appeared like mere legal verbiage; but when Miss Shuler's legacy was announced, the transaction took on a rather different aspect. For this legacy was not among the items specified in the will. Therefore it did not go to Mrs Crofton. It would be included in the residue of the estate and would go to the residuary legatee—Jobson.'

'The deuce it would!' I exclaimed.

'Certainly; until Crofton revoked his will or made a fresh one. This was rather suspicious. It suggested that Jobson had private information as to Miss Shuler's will and had drafted Crofton's will in accordance with it; and as she died of malignant disease, her doctor must have known for some time that she was dying and it looked as if Jobson had information on that point, too. Now the position of affairs that you described to me was this: Crofton, a possible suicide, had disappeared and had made no fresh will.

'Miss Shuler died on the thirteenth, leaving thirty thousand pounds to Crofton, if he survived her, or if he did not, then to Mrs Crofton. The important question then was whether Crofton was alive or dead; and if he was dead, whether he had died before or after the thirteenth. For if he died before the thirteenth the legacy went to Mrs Crofton, but if he died after that date the legacy went to Jobson.

'Then you showed me that extraordinarily opportune letter dated the sixteenth. Now, seeing that that date was worth thirty thousand pounds to Jobson, I naturally scrutinized it narrowly. The letter was written with ordinary blue-black ink. But this ink, even in the open, takes about a fortnight to blacken completely. In a closed envelope it takes considerably longer. On examining this date through a lens, the one was very perceptibly bluer than the six. It had therefore been added later. But for what reason? And by whom?

'The only possible reason was that Crofton was dead and had died before the thirteenth. The only person who had any motive for making the alteration was Jobson. Therefore, when we started for Seasalter I already felt sure that Crofton was dead and that the letter had been posted at Margate by Jobson. I had further no doubt that Crofton's body was concealed somewhere on the premises of the bungalow. All that I had to do was to verify those conclusions.'

'Then you believe that Jobson has told us the truth?'

'Yes. But I suspect that he went down there with the deliberate intention of making away with Crofton before he could make a fresh will. The finding of Crofton's body must have been a fearful disappointment, but I must admit that he showed considerable resource in dealing with the situation; and he failed only by the merest chance. I think his defence against the murder charge will be admitted; but, of course, it will involve a plea of guilty to the charge of fraud in connection with the legacy.'

Thorndyke's forecast turned out to be correct. Jobson was acquitted of the murder of Arthur Crofton, but is at present 'doing time' in respect of the forged letter and the rest of his too-ingenious scheme.

ARTHUR MORRISON · 1863–1945

The Case of Laker, Absconded

There were several of the larger London banks and insurance offices from which Hewitt held a sort of general retainer as detective adviser, in fulfilment of which he was regularly consulted as to the measures to be taken in different cases of fraud, forgery, theft, and so forth, which it might be the misfortune of the particular firms to encounter. The more important and intricate of these cases were placed in his hands entirely, with separate commissions, in the usual way. One of the most important companies of the sort was the General Guarantee Society, an insurance corporation which, among other risks, took those of the integrity of secretaries, clerks, and cashiers. In the case of a cash-box elopement on the part of any person guaranteed by the society, the directors were naturally anxious for a speedy capture of the culprit, and more especially of the booty, before too much of it was spent, in order to lighten the claim upon their funds, and in work of this sort Hewitt was at times engaged, either in general advice and direction, or in the actual pursuit of the plunder and the plunderer.

Arriving at his office a little later than usual one morning, Hewitt found an urgent message awaiting him from the General Guarantee Society, requesting his attention to a robbery which had taken place on the previous day. He had gleaned some hint of the case from the morning paper, wherein appeared a short paragraph, which ran thus:—

SERIOUS BANK ROBBERY.—In the course of yesterday a clerk employed by Messrs Liddle, Neal & Liddle, the well-known bankers, disappeared, having in his possession a large sum of money, the property of his employers —a sum reported to be rather over £15,000. It would seem that he had been entrusted to collect the money in his capacity of 'walk-clerk' from various other banks and trading concerns during the morning, but failed to return at the usual time. A large number of the notes which he received had been cashed at the Bank of England before suspicion was aroused. We understand that Detective-Inspector Plummer, of Scotland Yard, has the case in hand.

The clerk, whose name was Charles William Laker, had, it appeared from the message, been guaranteed in the usual way by the

General Guarantee Society, and Hewitt's presence at the office was at once desired, in order that steps might quickly be taken for the man's apprehension, and in the recovery, at any rate, of as much of the booty as possible.

A smart hansom brought Hewitt to Threadneedle Street in a bare quarter of an hour, and there a few minutes' talk with the manager, Mr Lyster, put him in possession of the main facts of the case, which appeared to be simple. Charles William Laker was twenty-five years of age, and had been in the employ of Messrs Liddle, Neal & Liddle for something more than seven years—since he left school, in fact—and until the previous day there had been nothing in his conduct to complain of. His duties as walk-clerk consisted in making a certain round, beginning at about half-past ten each morning. There were a certain number of the more important banks between which and Messrs Liddle, Neal & Liddle there were daily transactions, and a few smaller semi-private banks and merchant firms acting as financial agents, with whom there was business intercourse of less importance and regularity; and each of these, as necessary, he visited in turn, collecting cash due on bills and other instruments of a like nature. He carried a wallet, fastened securely to his person by a chain, and this wallet contained the bills and the cash. Usually at the end of his round, when all his bills had been converted into cash, the wallet held very large sums. His work and responsibilities, in fine, were those common to walk-clerks in all banks.

On the day of the robbery he had started out as usual—possibly a little earlier than was customary—and the bills and other securities in his possession represented considerably more than £15,000. It had been ascertained that he had called in the usual way at each establishment on the round, and had transacted his business at the last place by about a quarter-past one, being then, without doubt, in possession of cash to the full value of the bills negotiated. After that, Mr Lyster said, yesterday's report was that nothing more had been heard of him. But this morning there had been a message to the effect that he had been traced out of the country—to Calais, at least, it was thought. The directors of the society wished Hewitt to take the case in hand personally and at once, with a view of recovering what was possible from the plunder by way of salvage; also, of course, of finding Laker, for it is an important moral gain to guarantee societies, as an example, if a thief is caught and punished. Therefore Hewitt and Mr Lyster, as soon as might be, made for Messrs Liddle, Neal & Liddle's, that the investigation might be begun.

The bank premises were quite near—in Leadenhall Street. Having arrived there Hewitt and Mr Lyster made their way to the firm's private rooms. As they were passing an outer waiting-room, Hewitt noticed two women. One, the elder, in widow's weeds, was sitting with her head bowed in her hand over a small writing-table. Her face was not visible, but her whole attitude was that of a person overcome with unbearable grief; and she sobbed quietly. The other was a young woman of twenty-two or twenty-three. Her thick black veil revealed no more than that her features were small and regular, and that her face was pale and drawn. She stood with a hand on the elder woman's shoulder, and she quickly turned her head away as the two men entered.

Mr Neal, one of the partners, received them in his own room. 'Good morning, Mr Hewitt,' he said, when Mr Lyster had introduced the detective. 'This is a serious business—very. I think I am sorrier for Laker himself than for anybody else, ourselves included—or, at any rate, I am sorrier for his mother. She is waiting now to see Mr Liddle, as soon as he arrives—Mr Liddle has known the family for a long time. Miss Shaw is with her, too, poor girl. She is a governess, or something of that sort, and I believe she and Laker were engaged to be married. It's all very sad.'

'Inspector Plummer, I understand,' Hewitt remarked, 'has the affair in hand, on behalf of the police?'

'Yes,' Mr Neal replied; 'in fact, he's here now, going through the contents of Laker's desk, and so forth; he thinks it possible Laker may have had accomplices. Will you see him?'

'Presently. Inspector Plummer and I are old friends. We met last, I think, in the case of the Stanway cameo, some months ago. But, first, will you tell me how long Laker has been a walk-clerk?'

'Barely four months, although he has been with us altogether seven years. He was promoted to the walk soon after the beginning of the year.'

'Do you know anything of his habits—what he used to do in his spare time, and so forth?'

'Not a great deal. He went in for boating, I believe, though I have heard it whispered that he had one or two more expensive tastes—expensive, that is, for a young man in his position,' Mr Neal explained, with a dignified wave of the hand that he peculiarly affected. He was a stout old gentleman, and the gesture suited him.

'You have had no reason to suspect him of dishonesty before, I take it?'

'Oh, no. He made a wrong return once, I believe, that went for some time undetected, but it turned out, after all, to be a clerical error—a mere clerical error.'

'Do you know anything of his associates out of the office?'

'No, how should I? I believe Inspector Plummer has been making inquiries as to that, however, of the other clerks. Here he is, by the bye, I expect. Come in!'

It was Plummer who had knocked, and he came in at Mr Neal's call. He was a middle-sized, small-eyed, impenetrable-looking man, as yet of no great reputation in the force. Some of my readers may remember his connection with that case, so long a public mystery, that I have elsewhere fully set forth and explained under the title of 'The Stanway Cameo Mystery'. Plummer carried his billy-cock hat in one hand and a few papers in the other. He gave Hewitt good-morning, placed his hat on a chair, and spread the papers on the table.

'There's not a great deal here,' he said, 'but one thing's plain—Laker had been betting. See here, and here, and here'—he took a few letters from the bundle in his hand—'two letters from a book-maker about settling—wonder he trusted a clerk—several telegrams from tipsters, and a letter from some friend—only signed by initials—asking Laker to put a sovereign on a horse for the friend "with his own". I'll keep these, I think. It may be worth while to see that friend, if we can find him. Ah, we often find it's betting, don't we, Mr Hewitt? Meanwhile, there's no news from France yet.'

'You are sure that is where he is gone?' asked Hewitt.

'Well, I'll tell you what we've done as yet. First, of course, I went round to all the banks. There was nothing to be got from that. The cashiers all knew him by sight, and one was a personal friend of his. He had called as usual, said nothing in particular, cashed his bills in the ordinary way, and finished up at the Eastern Consolidated Bank at about a quarter-past one. So far there was nothing whatever. But I had started two or three men meanwhile making inquiries at the railway stations, and so on. I had scarcely left the Eastern Consolidated when one of them came after me with news. He had tried Palmer's Tourist Office, although that seemed an unlikely place, and there struck the track.'

'Had he been there?'

'Not only had he been there, but he had taken a tourist ticket for France. It was quite a smart move, in a way. You see it was the sort of ticket that lets you do pretty well what you like; you have the choice of two or three different routes to begin with, and you can break your journey where you please, and make all sorts of variations. So that a man with a ticket like that, and a few hours' start, could twist about on some remote branch route, and strike off in another direction altogether, with a new ticket, from some out-of-the-way place, while we were carefully sorting out and inquiring along the different routes he *might* have taken. Not half a bad move for a new hand; but he made one bad mistake, as new hands always do—as old hands do, in fact, very often. He was fool enough to give his own name, C. Laker! Although that didn't matter much, as the description was enough to fix him. There he was, wallet and all, just as he had come from the Eastern Consolidated Bank. He went straight from there to Palmer's, by the bye, and probably in a cab. We judge that by the time. He left the Eastern Consolidated at a quarter-past one, and was at Palmer's by twenty-five-past—ten minutes. The clerk at Palmer's remembered the time because he was anxious to get out to his lunch, and kept looking at the clock, expecting another clerk in to relieve him. Laker didn't take much in the way of luggage, I fancy. We inquired carefully at the stations, and got the porters to remember the passengers for whom they had been carrying luggage, but none appeared to have had any dealings with our man. That, of course, is as one would expect. He'd take as little as possible with him, and buy what he wanted on the way, or when he'd reached his hiding-place. Of course, I wired to Calais (it was a Dover to Calais route ticket) and sent a couple of smart men off by the 8.15 mail from Charing Cross. I expect we shall hear from them in the course of the day. I am being kept in London in view of something expected at headquarters, or I should have been off myself.'

'That is all, then, up to the present? Have you anything else in view?'

'That's all I've absolutely ascertained at present. As for what I'm going to do'—a slight smile curled Plummer's lip—'well, I shall see. I've a thing or two in my mind.'

Hewitt smiled slightly himself; he recognized Plummer's touch of professional jealousy. 'Very well,' he said, rising, 'I'll make an inquiry or two for myself at once. Perhaps, Mr Neal, you'll allow one of your clerks to show me the banks, in their regular order, at which Laker called yesterday. I think I'll begin at the beginning.'

Mr Neal offered to place at Hewitt's disposal anything or anybody the bank contained, and the conference broke up. As Hewitt, with the clerk, came through the rooms separating Mr Neal's sanctum from the outer office, he fancied he saw the two veiled women leaving by a side door.

The first bank was quite close to Liddle, Neal & Liddle's. There the cashier who had dealt with Laker the day before remembered nothing in particular about the interview. Many other walk-clerks had called during the morning, as they did every morning, and the only circumstances of the visit that he could say anything definite about were those recorded in figures in the books. He did not know Laker's name till Plummer had mentioned it in making inquiries on the previous afternoon. As far as he could remember, Laker behaved much as usual, though really he did not notice much; he looked chiefly at the bills. He described Laker in a way that corresponded with the photograph that Hewitt had borrowed from the bank; a young man with a brown moustache and ordinary-looking, fairly regular face, dressing much as other clerks dressed—tall hat, black cutaway coat, and so on. The numbers of the notes handed over had already been given to Inspector Plummer, and these Hewitt did not trouble about.

The next bank was in Cornhill, and here the cashier was a personal friend of Laker's—at any rate, an acquaintance—and he remembered a little more. Laker's manner had been quite as usual, he said; certainly he did not seem preoccupied or excited in his manner. He spoke for a moment or two—of being on the river on Sunday, and so on—and left in his usual way.

'Can you remember *everything* he said?' Hewitt asked. 'If you can tell me, I should like to know exactly what he did and said to the smallest particular.'

'Well, he saw me a little distance off—I was behind there, at one of the desks—and raised his hand to me, and said, "How d'ye do?" I came across and took his bills, and dealt with them in the usual way. He had a new umbrella lying on the counter—rather a handsome umbrella—and I made a remark about the handle. He took it up to show me, and told me it was a present he had just received from a friend. It was a gorse-root handle, with two silver bands, one with his monogram, C. W. L. I said it was a very nice handle, and asked him whether it was fine in his district on Sunday. He said he had been up the river, and it was very fine there. And I think that was all.'

'Thank you. Now about this umbrella. Did he carry it rolled? Can you describe it in detail?'

'Well, I've told you about the handle, and the rest was much as usual, I think; it wasn't rolled—just flapping loosely, you know. It was rather an odd-shaped handle, though. I'll try and sketch it, if you like, as well as I can remember.' He did so, and Hewitt saw in the result rough indications of a gnarled crook, with one silver band near the end, and another, with the monogram, a few inches down the handle. Hewitt put the sketch in his pocket, and bade the cashier good-day.

At the next bank the story was the same as at the first—there was nothing remembered but the usual routine. Hewitt and the clerk turned down a narrow paved court, and through into Lombard Street for the next visit. The bank—that of Buller, Clayton, Ladds & Co.—was just at the corner at the end of the court, and the imposing stone entrance-porch was being made larger and more imposing still, the way being almost blocked by ladders and scaffold-poles. Here there was only the usual tale, and so on through the whole walk. The cashiers knew Laker only by sight, and that not always very distinctly. The calls of walk-clerks were such matters of routine that little note was taken of the persons of the clerks themselves, who were called by the names of their firms, if they were called by any names at all. Laker had behaved much as usual, so far as the cashiers could remember, and when finally the Eastern Consolidated was left behind, nothing more had been learnt than the chat about Laker's new umbrella.

Hewitt had taken leave of Mr Neal's clerk, and was stepping into a hansom, when he noticed a veiled woman in widow's weeds hailing another hansom a little way behind. He recognized the figure again, and said to the driver, 'Drive fast to Palmer's Tourist Office, but keep your eye on that cab behind, and tell me presently if it is following us.'

The cabman drove off, and after passing one or two turnings, opened the lid above Hewitt's head, and said, 'That there other keb *is* a-follerin' us, sir, an' keepin' about even distance all along.'

'All right; that's what I wanted to know. Palmer's now.'

At Palmer's the clerk who had attended to Laker remembered him very well, and described him. He also remembered the wallet, and *thought* he remembered the umbrella—was practically sure of it, in fact, upon reflection. He had no record of the name given, but remembered it distinctly to be Laker. As a matter of fact, names were never asked in such a transaction, but in this case Laker appeared to be ignorant of the usual procedure, as well as in a great hurry, and asked for the ticket and gave his name all in one breath, probably assuming that the name would be required.

Hewitt got back to his cab, and started for Charing Cross. The cabman once more lifted the lid and informed him that the hansom with the veiled woman in it was again following, having waited while Hewitt had visited Palmer's. At Charing Cross Hewitt discharged his cab and walked straight to the lost property office. The man in charge knew him very well, for his business had carried him there frequently before.

'I fancy an umbrella was lost in the station yesterday,' Hewitt said. 'It was a new umbrella, silk, with a gnarled gorse-root handle and two silver bands, something like this sketch. There was a monogram on the lower band—"C. W. L." were the letters. Has it been brought here?'

'There was two or three yesterday,' the man said; 'let's see.' He took the sketch and retired to a corner of his room. 'Oh, yes—here it is, I think; isn't this it? Do you claim it?'

'Well, not exactly that, but I think I'll take a look at it, if you'll let me. By the way, I see it's rolled up. Was it found like that?'

'No; the chap rolled it up what found it—porter he was. It's a fad of his, rolling up umbrellas close and neat, and he's rather proud of it. He often looks as though he'd like to take a man's umbrella away and roll it up for him when it's a bit clumsy done. Rum fad, eh?'

'Yes; everybody has his little fad, though. Where was this found—close by here?'

'Yes, sir; just there, almost opposite this window, in the little corner.'

'About two o'clock?'

'Ah, about that time, more or less.'

Hewitt took the umbrella up, unfastened the band, and shook the silk out loose. Then he opened it, and as he did so a small scrap of paper fell from inside it. Hewitt pounced on it like lightning. Then, after examining the umbrella thoroughly, inside and out, he handed it back to the man, who had not observed the incident of the scrap of paper.

'That will do, thanks,' he said. 'I only wanted to take a peep at it—just a small matter connected with a little case of mine. Good-morning.'

He turned suddenly and saw, gazing at him with a terrified expression from a door behind, the face of the woman who had followed him in the cab. The veil was lifted, and he caught but a mere glance of the face ere it was suddenly withdrawn. He stood for a moment to allow the woman time to retreat, and then left the station and walked towards his office, close by.

Scarcely thirty yards along the Strand he met Plummer.

'I'm going to make some much closer inquiries all down the line as far as Dover,' Plummer said. 'They wire from Calais that they have no clue as yet, and I mean to make quite sure, if I can, that Laker hasn't quietly slipped off the line somewhere between here and Dover. There's one very peculiar thing,' Plummer added confidentially. 'Did you see the two women who were waiting to see a member of the firm at Liddle, Neal & Liddle's?'

'Yes. Laker's mother and his *fiancée*, I was told.'

'That's right. Well, do you know that girl—Shaw her name is—has been shadowing me ever since I left the Bank. Of course I spotted it from the beginning—these amateurs don't know how to follow anybody—and, as a matter of fact, she's just inside that jeweller's shop door behind me now, pretending to look at the things in the window. But it's odd, isn't it?'

'Well,' Hewitt replied, 'of course it's not a thing to be neglected. If you'll look very carefully at the corner of Villiers Street, without appearing to stare, I think you will possibly observe some signs of Laker's mother. She's shadowing *me*.'

Plummer looked casually in the direction indicated, and then immediately turned his eyes in another direction.

'I see her,' he said; 'she's just taking a look round the corner. That's a thing not to be ignored. Of course, the Lakers' house is being watched—we set a man on it at once, yesterday. But I'll put someone on now to watch Miss Shaw's place, too. I'll telephone through to Liddle's—probably they'll be able to say where it is. And the women themselves must be watched, too. As a matter of fact, I had a notion that Laker wasn't alone in it. And it's just possible, you know, that he has sent an accomplice off with his tourist ticket to lead us a dance while he looks after himself in another direction. Have you done anything?'

'Well,' Hewitt replied, with a faint reproduction of the secretive smile with which Plummer had met an inquiry of his earlier in the morning, 'I've been to the station here, and I've found Laker's umbrella in the lost property office.'

'Oh! Then probably he *has* gone. I'll bear that in mind, and perhaps have a word with the lost property man.'

Plummer made for the station and Hewitt for his office. He mounted the stairs and reached his door just as I myself, who had been disappointed in not finding him in, was leaving. I had called with the idea of taking Hewitt to lunch with me at my club, but he declined lunch. 'I have an important case in hand,' he said. 'Look here, Brett. See this scrap of paper. You know the types of the different newspapers—which is this?'

He handed me a small piece of paper. It was part of a cutting containing an advertisement, which had been torn in half.

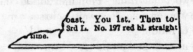

'I *think*,' I said, 'this is from the *Daily Chronicle*, judging by the paper. It is plainly from the "agony column", but all the papers use pretty much the same type for these advertisements, except the *Times*. If it were not torn I could tell you at once, because the *Chronicle* columns are rather narrow.'

'Never mind—I'll send for them all.' He rang, and sent Kerrett for a copy of each morning paper of the previous day. Then he took from a large wardrobe cupboard a decent but well-worn and rather roughened tall hat. Also a coat a little worn and shiny on the collar. He exchanged these for his own hat and coat, and then substituted an old necktie for his own clean white one, and encased his legs in mud-spotted leggings. This done, he produced a very large and thick pocket-book, fastened by a broad elastic band, and said, 'Well, what do you think of this? Will it do for Queen's taxes, or sanitary inspection, or the gas, or the water-supply?'

'Very well indeed, I should say,' I replied. 'What's the case?'

'Oh, I'll tell you all about that when it's over—no time now. Oh, here you are, Kerrett. By the bye, Kerrett, I'm going out presently by the back way. Wait for about ten minutes or a quarter of an hour after I am gone, and then just go across the road and speak to that lady in black, with the veil, who is waiting in that little foot-passage opposite. Say Mr Martin Hewitt sends his compliments, and he advises her not to wait, as he has already left his office by another door, and has been gone some little time. That's all; it would be a pity to keep the poor woman waiting all day for nothing. Now the papers. *Daily News*, *Standard*, *Telegraph*, *Chronicle*—yes, here it is, in the *Chronicle*.'

The whole advertisement read thus:—

Y OB.—H.R. Shop roast. You 1st. Then tonight. 02. 2nd top 3rd L. No. 197 red bl. straight
mon. One at a time.

'What's this,' I asked, 'a cryptogram?'

'I'll see,' Hewitt answered. 'But I won't tell you anything about it till afterwards, so you get your lunch. Kerrett, bring the directory.'

This was all I actually saw of this case myself, and I have written the rest in its proper order from Hewitt's information, as I have written some other cases entirely.

To resume at the point where, for the time, I lost sight of the matter. Hewitt left by the back way and stopped an empty cab as it passed. 'Abney Park Cemetery' was his direction to the driver. In little more than twenty minutes the cab was branching off down the Essex Road on its way to Stoke Newington, and in twenty minutes more Hewitt stopped it in Church Street, Stoke Newington. He walked through a street or two, and then down another, the houses of which he scanned carefully as he passed. Opposite one which stood by itself he stopped, and, making a pretence of consulting and arranging his large pocket-book, he took a good look at the house. It was rather larger, neater, and more pretentious than the others in the street, and it had a natty little coach-house just visible up the side entrance. There were red blinds hung with heavy lace in the front windows, and behind one of these blinds Hewitt was able to catch the glint of a heavy gas chandelier.

He stepped briskly up the front steps and knocked sharply at the door. 'Mr Merston?' he asked, pocket-book in hand, when a neat parlourmaid opened the door.

'Yes.'

'Ah!' Hewitt stepped into the hall and pulled off his hat; 'it's only the meter. There's been a deal of gas running away somewhere here, and I'm just looking to see if the meters are right. Where is it?'

The girl hesitated. 'I'll—I'll ask master,' she said.

'Very well. I don't want to take it away, you know—only to give it a tap or two, and so on.'

The girl retired to the back of the hall, and without taking her eyes off Martin Hewitt, gave his message to some invisible person in a back room, whence came a growling reply of 'All right.'

Hewitt followed the girl to the basement, apparently looking straight before him, but in reality taking in every detail of the place. The gas meter was in a very large lumber cupboard under the kitchen stairs. The girl opened the door and lit a candle. The meter stood on the floor, which was littered with hampers and boxes and odd sheets of brown paper. But a thing that at once arrested Hewitt's attention was a garment of some sort of bright blue cloth, with large brass buttons, which was lying in a tumbled heap in a corner, and appeared to be the only thing in the place that was not covered with dust. Nevertheless, Hewitt took no apparent notice of it, but stooped down and solemnly tapped the meter three times with his pencil, and listened with great gravity, placing his ear to the top. Then he shook his head and tapped again. At length he said:—

'It's a bit doubtful. I'll just get you to light the gas in the kitchen a moment. Keep your hand to the burner, and when I call out shut it off *at once*; see?'

The girl turned and entered the kitchen, and Hewitt immediately seized the blue coat—for a coat it was. It had a dull red piping in the seams, and was of the swallow-tail pattern—a livery coat, in fact. He held it for a moment before him, examining its pattern and colour, and then rolled it up and flung it again into the corner.

'Right!' he called to the servant. 'Shut off!'

The girl emerged from the kitchen as he left the cupboard.

'Well,' she asked, 'are you satisfied now?'

'Quite satisfied, thank you,' Hewitt replied.

'Is it all right?' she continued, jerking her hand towards the cupboard.

'Well, no, it isn't; there's something wrong there, and I'm glad I came. You can tell Mr Merston, if you like, that I expect his gas bill will be a good deal less next quarter.' And there was a suspicion of a chuckle in Hewitt's voice as he crossed the hall to leave. For a gas inspector is pleased when he finds at length what he has been searching for.

Things had fallen out better than Hewitt had dared to expect. He saw the key of the whole mystery in that blue coat; for it was the uniform coat of the hall porters at one of the banks that he had visited in the morning, though which one he could not for the moment remember. He entered the nearest post office and despatched a telegram to Plummer, giving certain directions and asking the inspector to meet him; then he hailed the first available cab and hurried towards the city.

At Lombard Street he alighted, and looked in at the door of each bank till he came to Buller, Clayton, Ladds & Co.'s. This was the bank he wanted. In the other banks the hall porters wore mulberry coats, brick-dust coats, brown coats, and what not, but here, behind the ladders and scaffold poles which obscured the entrance, he could see a man in a blue coat, with dull red piping and brass buttons. He sprang up the steps, pushed open the inner swing door, and finally satisfied himself by a closer view of the coat, to the wearer's astonishment. Then he regained the pavement and walked the whole length of the bank premises in front, afterwards turning up the paved passage at the side, deep in thought. The bank had no windows or doors on the side next the court, and the two adjoining houses were old and supported in places by wooden shores. Both were empty, and a great board announced that tenders would be received in a month's time for the purchase of the old materials of which they were constructed; also that some part of the site would be let on a long building lease.

Hewitt looked up at the grimy fronts of the old buildings. The windows were crusted thick with dirt—all except the bottom window of the house nearer the bank, which was fairly clean, and seemed to have been quite lately washed. The door, too, of this house was cleaner than that of the other, though the paint was worn. Hewitt reached and fingered a hook driven into the left-hand doorpost about six feet from the ground. It was new, and not at all rusted; also a tiny splinter had been displaced when the hook was driven in, and clean wood showed at the spot.

Having observed these things, Hewitt stepped back and read at the bottom of the big board the name, 'Winsor & Weekes, Surveyors and Auctioneers, Abchurch Lane.' Then he stepped into Lombard Street.

Two hansoms pulled up near the post office, and out of the first stepped Inspector Plummer and another man. This man and the two who alighted from the second hansom were unmistakably plain-clothes constables—their air, gait, and boots proclaimed it.

'What's all this?' demanded Plummer, as Hewitt approached.

'You'll soon see, I think. But, first, have you put the watch on No. 197, Hackworth Road?'

'Yes; nobody will get away from there alone.'

'Very good. I am going into Abchurch Lane for a few minutes. Leave your men out here, but just go round into the court by Buller, Clayton & Ladds's, and keep your eye on the first door on the left. I think we'll find something soon. Did you get rid of Miss Shaw?'

'No, she's behind now, and Mrs Laker's with her. They met in the Strand, and came after us in another cab. Rare fun, eh! They think we're pretty green! It's quite handy, too. So long as they keep behind me it saves all trouble of watching *them*.' And Inspector Plummer chuckled and winked.

'Very good. You don't mind keeping your eye on that door, do you?

I'll be back very soon,' and with that Hewitt turned off into Abchurch Lane.

At Winsor & Weekes's information was not difficult to obtain. The houses were destined to come down very shortly, but a week or so ago an office and a cellar in one of them was let temporarily to a Mr Westley. He brought no references; indeed, as he paid a fortnight's rent in advance, he was not asked for any, considering the circumstances of the case. He was opening a London branch for a large firm of cider merchants, he said, and just wanted a rough office and a cool cellar to store samples in for a few weeks till the permanent premises were ready. There was another key, and no doubt the premises might be entered if there were any special need for such a course. Martin Hewitt gave such excellent reasons that Winsor & Weekes's managing clerk immediately produced the key and accompanied Hewitt to the spot.

'I think you'd better have your men handy,' Hewitt remarked to Plummer when they reached the door, and a whistle quickly brought the men over.

The key was inserted in the lock and turned, but the door would not open; the bolt was fastened at the bottom. Hewitt stooped and looked under the door.

'It's a drop bolt,' he said. 'Probably the man who left last let it fall loose, and then banged the door, so that it fell into its place. I must try my best with a wire or a piece of string.'

A wire was brought, and with some manœuvring Hewitt contrived to pass it round the bolt, and lift it little by little, steadying it with the blade of a pocket-knife. When at length the bolt was raised out of the hole, the knife-blade was slipped under it, and the door swung open.

They entered. The door of the little office just inside stood open, but in the office there was nothing, except a board a couple of feet long in a corner. Hewitt stepped across and lifted this, turning its downward face towards Plummer. On it, in fresh white paint on a black ground, were painted the words—

'BULLER, CLAYTON, LADDS & CO.,
TEMPORARY ENTRANCE.'

Hewitt turned to Winsor & Weekes's clerk and asked, 'The man who took this room called himself Westley, didn't he?'

'Yes.'

'Youngish man, clean-shaven, and well-dressed?'

'Yes, he was.'

'I fancy,' Hewitt said, turning to Plummer, 'I *fancy* an old friend of yours is in this—Mr Sam Gunter.'

'What, the "Hoxton Yob"?'

'I think it's possible he's been Mr Westley for a bit, and somebody else for another bit. But let's come to the cellar.'

Winsor & Weekes's clerk led the way down a steep flight of steps into a dark underground corridor, wherein they lighted their way with many successive matches. Soon the corridor made a turn to the right, and as the party passed the turn, there came from the end of the passage before them a fearful yell.

'Help! help! Open the door! I'm going mad—mad! O my God!'

And there was a sound of desperate beating from the inside of the cellar door at the extreme end. The men stopped, startled.

'Come,' said Hewitt, 'more matches!' and he rushed to the door. It was fastened with a bar and padlock.

'Let me out, for God's sake!' came the voice, sick and hoarse, from the inside. 'Let me out!'

'All right!' Hewitt shouted. 'We have come for you. Wait a moment.'

The voice sank into a sort of sobbing croon, and Hewitt tried several keys from his own bunch on the padlock. None fitted. He drew from his pocket the wire he had used for the bolt of the front door, straightened it out, and made a sharp bend at the end.

'Hold a match close,' he ordered shortly, and one of the men obeyed. Three or four attempts were necessary, and several different bendings of the wire were effected, but in the end Hewitt picked the lock, and flung open the door.

From within a ghastly figure fell forward among them fainting, and knocked out the matches.

'Hullo!' cried Plummer. 'Hold up! Who are you?'

'Let's get him up into the open,' said Hewitt. 'He can't tell you who he is for a bit, but I believe he's Laker.'

'Laker! What, here?'

'I think so. Steady up the steps. Don't bump him. He's pretty sore already, I expect.'

Truly the man was a pitiable sight. His hair and face were caked in dust and blood, and his finger-nails were torn and bleeding. Water was sent for at once, and brandy.

'Well,' said Plummer hazily, looking first at the unconscious prisoner and then at Hewitt, 'but what about the swag?'

'You'll have to find that yourself,' Hewitt replied. 'I think my share of the case is about finished. I only act for the Guarantee Society, you know, and if Laker's proved innocent————'

'Innocent! How?'

'Well, this is what took place, as near as I can figure it. You'd better undo his collar, I think'—this to the men. 'What I believe has happened is this. There has been a very clever and carefully prepared conspiracy here, and Laker has not been the criminal, but the victim.'

'Been robbed himself, you mean? But how? Where?'

'Yesterday morning, before he had been to more than three banks—here, in fact.'

'But then how? You're all wrong. We *know* he made the whole round, and did all the collection. And then Palmer's office, and all, and the umbrella; why————'

The man lay still unconscious. 'Don't raise his head,' Hewitt said. 'And one of you had best fetch a doctor. He's had a terrible shock.' Then turning to Plummer he went on, 'As to *how* they managed the job, I'll tell you what I think. First it struck some very clever person that a deal of money might be got by robbing a walk-clerk from a bank. This clever person was one of a clever gang of thieves—perhaps the Hoxton Row gang, as I think I hinted. Now you know quite as well as I do that such a gang will spend any amount of time over a job that promises a big haul, and that for such a job they can always command the necessary capital. There are many most respectable persons living in good style in the suburbs whose chief business lies in financing such ventures, and taking the chief share of the proceeds. Well, this is their plan, carefully and intelligently carried out. They watch Laker, observe the round he takes, and his habits. They find that there is only one of the clerks with whom he does business that he is much acquainted with, and that this clerk is in a bank which is commonly second in Laker's round. The sharpest man among them —and I don't think there's a man in London could do this as well as young Sam Gunter—studies Laker's dress and habits just as an actor studies a character. They take this office and cellar, as we have seen, *because it is next door to a bank whose front entrance is being altered*—a fact which Laker must know from his daily visits. The smart man—Gunter, let us say, and I have other reasons for believing it to be he—makes up precisely like Laker, false moustache, dress, and everything, and waits here with the rest of the gang. One of the gang is dressed in a blue coat with brass buttons, like a hall-porter in Buller's bank. Do you see?'

'Yes, I think so. It's pretty clear now.'

'A confederate watches at the top of the court, and the moment Laker turns in from Cornhill,—having already been, mind, at the only bank where he was so well known that the disguised thief would not have passed muster—as soon as he turns in from Cornhill, I say, a signal is given, and that board'—pointing to that with the white letters—'is hung on the hook in the doorpost. The sham porter stands beside it, and as Laker approaches says, 'This way in, sir, this morning. The front way's shut for the alterations.' Laker, suspecting nothing, and supposing that the firm have made a temporary entrance through the empty house, enters. He is seized when well along the corridor, the board is taken down and the door shut. Probably he is stunned by a blow on the head—see the blood now. They take his wallet and all the cash he has already collected. Gunter takes the wallet and also the umbrella, since it has Laker's initials, and is therefore distinctive. He simply completes the walk in the character of Laker, beginning with Buller, Clayton & Ladds's just round the corner. It is nothing but routine work, which is quickly done, and nobody notices him particularly—it is the bills they examine. Meanwhile this unfortunate fellow is locked up in the cellar here, right at the end of the underground corridor, where he can never make himself heard in the street, and where next him are only the empty cellars of the deserted house next door. The thieves shut the front door and vanish. The rest is plain. Gunter, having completed the round, and bagged some £15,000 or more, spends a few pounds on a tourist ticket at Palmer's as a blind, being careful to give Laker's name. He leaves the umbrella at Charing Cross in a conspicuous place right opposite the lost property office, where it is sure to be seen, and so completes his false trail.'

'Then who are the people at 197, Hackworth Road?'

'The capitalist lives there—the financier, and probably the directing spirit of the whole thing. Merston's the name he goes by there, and I've no doubt he cuts a very imposing figure in chapel every Sunday. He'll be worth picking up—this isn't the first thing he's been in, I'll warrant.'

'But—but what about Laker's mother and Miss Shaw?'

'Well, what? The poor women are nearly out of their minds with terror and shame, that's all, but though they may think Laker a criminal, they'll never desert him. They've been following us about with a feeble, vague sort of hope of being able to baffle us in some way or help him if we caught him, or something, poor things. Did you ever hear of a real woman who'd desert a son or a lover merely because he was a criminal? But here's the doctor. When he's attended to him will you let your men take Laker home? I must hurry and report to the Guarantee Society, I think.'

'But,' said the perplexed Plummer, 'where did you get your clue? You must have had a tip from some one, you know—you can't have done it by clairvoyance. What gave you the tip?'

'The *Daily Chronicle*.'

'The *what*?'

'The *Daily Chronicle*. Just take a look at the "agony column" in yesterday morning's issue, and read the message to "Yob"—to Gunter, in fact. That's all.'

By this time a cab was waiting in Lombard Street, and two of Plummer's men, under the doctor's directions, carried Laker to it. No sooner, however, were they in the court than the two watching women threw themselves hysterically upon Laker, and it was long before they could be persuaded that he was not being taken to gaol. The mother shrieked aloud, 'My boy—my boy! Don't take him! Oh, don't take him! They've killed my boy! Look at his head—oh, his head!' and wrestled desperately with the men, while Hewitt attempted to soothe her, and promised to allow her to go in the cab with her son if she would only be quiet. The younger woman made no noise, but she held one of Laker's limp hands in both hers.

Hewitt and I dined together that evening, and he gave me a full account of the occurrences which I have here set down. Still, when he was finished I was not able to see clearly by what process of reasoning he had arrived at the conclusions that gave him the key to the mystery, nor did I understand the 'agony column' message, and I said so.

'In the beginning,' Hewitt explained, 'the thing that struck me as curious was the fact that Laker was said to have given his own name at Palmer's in buying his ticket. Now, the first thing the greenest and newest criminal thinks of is changing his name, so that the giving of his own name seemed unlikely to begin with. Still, he *might* have made such a mistake, as Plummer suggested when he said that criminals usually make a mistake somewhere—as they do, in fact. Still, it was the least likely mistake I could think of—especially as he actually didn't wait to be asked for his name, but blurted it out when it wasn't really wanted. And it was conjoined with another rather curious mistake, or what would have been a mistake, if the thief were Laker. Why should he conspicuously display his wallet—such a distinctive article—for the clerk to see and note? Why rather had he not got rid of it before showing himself? Suppose it should be somebody personating Laker? In any case I determined not to be prejudiced by what I had heard of Laker's betting. A man may bet without being a thief.

'But, again, supposing it *were* Laker? Might he not have given his name, and displayed his wallet, and so on, while buying a ticket for France, in order to draw pursuit after himself in that direction while he made off in another, in another name, and disguised? Each supposition was plausible. And, in either case, it might happen that whoever was laying this trail would probably lay it a little farther. Charing Cross was the next point, and there I went. I already had it from Plummer that Laker had not been recognized there. Perhaps the trail had been laid in some other manner. Something left behind with Laker's name on it, perhaps? I at once thought of the umbrella with his monogram, and, making a long shot, asked for it at the lost property office, as you know. The guess was lucky. In the umbrella, as you know, I found that scrap of paper. That, I judged, had fallen in from the hand of the man carrying the umbrella. He had torn the paper in half in order to fling it away, and one piece had fallen into the loosely flapping umbrella. It is a thing that will often happen with an omnibus ticket, as you may have noticed. Also, it was proved that the umbrella *was* unrolled when found, and rolled immediately after. So here was a piece of paper dropped by the person who had brought the umbrella to Charing Cross and left it. I got the whole advertisement, as you remember, and I studied it. "Yob" is back-slang for "boy", and it is often used in nicknames to denote a young smooth-faced thief. Gunter, the man I suspect, as a matter of fact, is known as the "Hoxton Yob". The message, then, was addressed to someone known by such a nickname. Next, "H. R. Shop roast." Now, in thieves' slang, to "roast" a thing or a person is to watch it or him. They call any place a shop—notably, a thieves' den. So that this meant that some resort —perhaps the "Hoxton Row shop"—was watched. "You 1st. Then tonight" would be clearer, perhaps, when the rest was understood. I thought a little over the rest, and it struck me that it must be a direction to some other house, since one was warned of as being watched. Besides, there was the number, 197, and "red bl.", which would be extremely likely to mean "red blinds", by way of clearly distinguishing the house. And then the plan of the thing was plain. You have noticed, probably, that the map of London which accompanies the Post Office Directory is divided, for convenience of reference, into numbered squares?'

'Yes. The squares are denoted by letters along the top margin and figures down the side. So that if you consult the directory, and find a place marked as being in D5, for instance, you find vertical division D, and run your finger down it till it intersects horizontal division 5, and there you are.'

'Precisely. I got my Post Office Directory, and looked for "O2". It was in North London, and took in parts of Abney Park Cemetery and Clissold Park; "2nd top" was the next sign. Very well, I counted the second street intersecting the top of the square—counting, in the usual way, from the left. That was Lordship Road. Then, "3rd L". From the point where Lordship Road crossed the top of the square, I ran my finger down the road till it came to "3rd L", or, in other words, the third turning on the left—Hackworth Road. So there we were, unless my guesses were altogether wrong. "Straight mon" probably meant "straight moniker"—that is to say, the proper name, a thief's *real* name, in contradistinction to that he may assume. I turned over the directory till I found Hackworth Road, and found that No. 197 was inhabited by a Mr Merston. From the whole thing I judged this. There was to have been a meeting at the "H. R. shop", but that was found, at the last moment, to be watched by the police for some purpose, so that another appointment was made for this house in the suburbs. "You 1st. Then tonight"—the person addressed was to come first, and the others in the evening. They were to ask for the householder's "straight moniker"—Mr Merston. And they were to come one at a time.

'Now, then, what was this? What theory would fit it? Suppose this were a robbery, directed from afar by the advertiser. Suppose, on the day before the robbery, it was found that the place fixed for division of spoils were watched. Suppose that the principal thereupon advertised (as had already been agreed in case of emergency) in these terms. The principal in the actual robbery—the "Yob" addressed —was to go first with the booty. The others were to come after, one at a time. Anyway, the thing was good enough to follow a little further, and I determined to try No. 197, Hackworth Road. I have told you what I found there, and how it opened my eyes. I went, of course, merely on chance, to see what I might chance to see. But luck favoured, and I happened on that coat—brought back rolled up, on the evening after the robbery, doubtless by the thief who had used it, and flung carelessly into the handiest cupboard. *That* was this gang's mistake.'

'Well, I congratulate you,' I said. 'I hope they'll catch the rascals.'

'I rather think they will, now they know where to look. They can scarcely miss Merston, anyway. There has been very little to go upon in this case, but I stuck to the thread, however slight, and it brought me through. The rest of the case, of course, is Plummer's. It was a peculiarity of my commission that I could equally well fulfil it by catching the man with all the plunder, or by proving him innocent. Having done the latter, my work was at an end, but I left it where Plummer will be able to finish the job handsomely.'

Plummer did. Sam Gunter, Merston, and one accomplice were taken—the first and last were well known to the police—and were identified by Laker. Merston, as Hewitt had suspected, had kept the lion's share for himself, so that altogether, with what was recovered from him and the other two, nearly £11,000 was saved for Messrs Liddle, Neal, & Liddle. Merston, when taken, was in the act of packing up to take a holiday abroad, and there cash his notes, which were found, neatly packed in separate thousands, in his portmanteau. As Hewitt had predicted, his gas bill *was* considerably less next quarter, for less than half-way through it he began a term in gaol.

As for Laker, he was reinstated, of course, with an increase of salary by way of compensation for his broken head. He had passed a terrible twenty-six hours in the cellar, unfed and unheard. Several times he had become insensible, and again and again he had thrown himself madly against the door, shouting and tearing at it, till he fell back exhausted, with broken nails and bleeding fingers. For some hours before the arrival of his rescuers he had been sitting in a sort of stupor, from which he was suddenly aroused by the sound of voices and footsteps. He was in bed for a week, and required a rest of a month in addition before he could resume his duties. Then he was quietly lectured by Mr Neal as to betting, and, I believe, dropped that practice in consequence. I am told that he is 'at the counter' now—a considerable promotion.

The Oracle of the Dog

'Yes,' said Father Brown, 'I always like a dog, so long as he isn't spelt backwards.'

Those who are quick in talking are not always quick in listening. Sometimes even their brilliancy produces a sort of stupidity. Father Brown's friend and companion was a young man with a stream of ideas and stories, an enthusiastic young man named Fiennes, with eager blue eyes and blond hair that seemed to be brushed back, not merely with a hairbrush but with the wind of the world as he rushed through it. But he stopped in the torrent of his talk in a momentary bewilderment before he saw the priest's very simple meaning.

'You mean that people make too much of them?' he said. 'Well, I don't know. They're marvellous creatures. Sometimes I think they know a lot more than we do.'

Father Brown said nothing; but continued to stroke the head of the big retriever in a half-abstracted but apparently soothing fashion.

'Why,' said Fiennes, warming again to his monologue, 'there was a dog in the case I've come to see you about; what they call the "Invisible Murder Case", you know. It's a strange story, but from my point of view the dog is about the strangest thing in it. Of course, there's the mystery of the crime itself, and how old Druce can have been killed by somebody else when he was all alone in the summer-house———'

The hand stroking the dog stopped for a moment in its rhythmic movement; and Father Brown said calmly, 'Oh, it was a summer-house, was it?'

'I thought you'd read all about it in the papers,' answered Fiennes. 'Stop a minute; I believe I've got a cutting that will give you all the particulars.' He produced a strip of newspaper from his pocket and handed it to the priest, who began to read it, holding it close to his blinking eyes with one hand while the other continued its half-conscious caresses of the dog. It looked like the parable of a man not letting his right hand know what his left hand did.

'Many mystery stories, about men murdered behind locked doors and windows, and murderers escaping without means of entrance and exit, have come true in the course of the extraordinary events at Cranston on the coast of Yorkshire, where Colonel Druce was found stabbed from behind by a dagger that has entirely disappeared from the scene, and apparently even from the neighbourhood.

'The summer-house in which he died was indeed accessible at one entrance, the ordinary doorway which looked down the central walk of the garden towards the house. But by a combination of events almost to be called a coincidence, it appears that both the path and the entrance were watched during the crucial time, and there is a chain of witnesses who confirm each other. The summer-house stands at the extreme end of the garden, where there is no exit or entrance of any kind. The central garden path is a lane between two ranks of tall delphiniums, planted so close that any stray step off the path would leave its traces; and both path and plants run right up to the very mouth of the summer-house, so that no straying from that straight path could fail to be observed, and no other mode of entrance can be imagined.

'Patrick Floyd, secretary of the murdered man, testified that he had been in a position to overlook the whole garden from the time when Colonel Druce last appeared alive in the doorway to the time when he was found dead; as he, Floyd, had been on the top of a step-ladder clipping the garden hedge. Janet Druce, the dead man's daughter, confirmed this, saying that she had sat on the terrace of the house throughout that time and had seen Floyd at his work. Touching some part of the time, this is again supported by Donald Druce, her brother, who overlooked the garden standing at his bedroom window in his dressing-gown, for he had risen late. Lastly the account is consistent with that given by Dr Valentine, a neighbour, who called for a time to talk with Miss Druce on the terrace, and by the Colonel's solicitor, Mr Aubrey Traill, who was apparently the last to see the murdered man alive—presumably with the exception of the murderer.

'All are agreed that the course of events was as follows: about half-past three in the afternoon, Miss Druce went down the path to ask her father when he would like tea; but he said he did not want any and was waiting to see Traill, his lawyer, who was to be sent to him in the summer-house. The girl then came away and met Traill coming down the path; she directed him to her father and he went in as directed. About half an hour afterwards he came out again, the Colonel coming with him to the door and showing himself to all appearance in health and even high spirits. He had been somewhat annoyed earlier in the day by his son's irregular hours, but seemed to recover his temper in a perfectly normal fashion, and had been rather markedly genial in receiving other visitors, including two of his nephews who came over for the day. But as these were out walking during the whole period of the tragedy, they had no evidence to give. It is said, indeed, that the Colonel was not on very good terms with Dr Valentine, but that gentleman only had a brief interview with the daughter of the house, to whom he is supposed to be paying serious attentions.

'Traill, the solicitor, says he left the Colonel entirely alone in the summer-house, and this is confirmed by Floyd's bird's-eye view of the garden, which showed nobody else passing the only entrance. Ten minutes later Miss Druce again went down the garden and had not reached the end of the path when she saw her father, who was conspicuous by his white linen coat, lying in a heap on the floor. She uttered a scream which brought others to the spot, and on entering the place they found the Colonel lying dead beside his basket-chair, which was also upset. Dr Valentine, who was still in the immediate neighbourhood, testified that the wound was made by some sort of stiletto, entering under the shoulder-blade and piercing the heart. The police have searched the neighbourhood for such a weapon, but no trace of it can be found.'

'So Colonel Druce wore a white coat, did he?' said Father Brown as he put down the paper.

'Trick he learnt in the tropics,' replied Fiennes with some wonder. 'He'd had some queer adventures there, by his own account; and I fancy his dislike of Valentine was connected with the doctor coming from the tropics, too. But it's all an infernal puzzle. The account there is pretty accurate; I didn't see the tragedy, in the sense of the discovery; I was out walking with the young nephews and the dog—the dog I wanted to tell you about. But I saw the stage set for it as described: the straight lane between the blue flowers right up to the dark entrance, and the lawyer going down it in his blacks and his silk hat, and the red head of the secretary showing high above the green hedge as he worked on it with his shears. Nobody could have mistaken that red head at any distance; and if people say they saw it there all the time, you may be sure they did. This red-haired secretary Floyd is quite a character; a breathless, bounding sort of fellow, always doing everybody's work as he was doing the gardener's. I think he is an American; he's certainly got the American view of life; what they call the viewpoint, bless 'em.'

'What about the lawyer?' asked Father Brown.

There was a silence and then Fiennes spoke quite slowly for him. 'Traill struck me as a singular man. In his fine black clothes he was almost foppish, yet you can hardly call him fashionable. For he wore a pair of long, luxuriant black whiskers such as haven't been seen since Victorian times. He had rather a fine grave face and a fine grave manner, but every now and then he seemed to remember to smile. And when he showed his white teeth he seemed to lose a little of his dignity and there was something faintly fawning about him. It may have been only embarrassment, for he would also fidget with his cravat and his tie-pin, which were at once handsome and unusual, like himself. If I could think of anybody—but what's the good, when the whole thing's impossible? Nobody knows who did it. Nobody knows how it could be done. At least there's only one exception I'd make, and that's why I really mentioned the whole thing. The dog knows.'

Father Brown sighed and then said absently: 'You were there as a friend of young Donald, weren't you? He didn't go on your walk with you?'

'No,' replied Fiennes smiling. 'The young scoundrel had gone to bed that morning and got up that afternoon. I went with his cousins, two young officers from India, and our conversation was trivial enough. I remember the elder, whose name I think is Herbert Druce and who is an authority on horse-breeding, talked about nothing but a mare he had bought and the moral character of the man who sold her; while his brother Harry seemed to be brooding on his bad luck at Monte Carlo. I only mention it to show you, in the light of what happened on our walk, that there was nothing psychic about us. The dog was the only mystic in our company.'

'What sort of a dog was he?' asked the priest.

'Same breed as that one,' answered Fiennes. 'That's what started me off on the story, your saying you didn't believe in believing in a dog. He's a big black retriever named Nox, and a suggestive name too; for I think what he did a darker mystery than the murder. You know Druce's house and garden are by the sea; we walked about a mile from it along the sands and then turned back, going the other way. We passed a rather curious rock called the Rock of Fortune, famous in the neighbourhood because it's one of those examples of one stone barely balanced on another, so that a touch would knock it over. It is not really very high, but the hanging outline of it makes it look a little wild and sinister; at least it made it look so to me, for I don't imagine my jolly young companions were afflicted with the picturesque. But it may be that I was beginning to feel an atmosphere; for just then the question arose of whether it was time to go back to tea, and even then I think I had a premonition that time counted for a good deal in the business. Neither Herbert Druce nor I had a watch, so we called out to his brother, who was some paces behind, having stopped to light his pipe under the hedge. Hence it happened that he shouted out the hour, which was twenty past four, in his big voice through the growing twilight; and somehow the loudness of it made it sound like the proclamation of something tremendous. His unconsciousness seemed to make it all the more so; but that was always the way with omens; and particular ticks of the clock were really very ominous things that afternoon. According to Dr Valentine's testimony, poor Druce had actually died just about half-past four.

'Well, they said we needn't go home for ten minutes, and we walked a little farther along the sands, doing nothing in particular —throwing stones for the dog and throwing sticks into the sea for him to swim after. But to me the twilight seemed to grow oddly oppressive and the very shadow of the top-heavy Rock of Fortune lay on me like a load. And then the curious thing happened. Nox had just brought back Herbert's walking-stick out of the sea and his brother had thrown his in also. The dog swam out again, but just about what must have been the stroke of the half-hour, he stopped swimming. He came back again on to the shore and stood in front of us. Then he suddenly threw up his head and sent up a howl or wail of woe, if ever I heard one in the world.

'"What the devil's the matter with the dog?" asked Herbert; but none of us could answer. There was a long silence after the brute's wailing and whining died away on the desolate shore; and then the silence was broken. As I live, it was broken by a faint and far-off shriek, like the shriek of a woman from beyond the hedges inland. We didn't know what it was then; but we knew afterwards. It was the cry the girl gave when she first saw the body of her father.'

'You went back, I suppose,' said Father Brown patiently. 'What happened then?'

'I'll tell you what happened then,' said Fiennes with a grim emphasis. 'When we got back into that garden the first thing we saw was Traill the lawyer; I can see him now with his black hat and black whiskers relieved against the perspective of the blue flowers stretching down to the summer-house, with the sunset and the strange outline of the Rock of Fortune in the distance. His face and figure were in shadow against the sunset; but I swear the white teeth were showing in his head and he was smiling.

'The moment Nox saw that man, the dog dashed forward and stood in the middle of the path barking at him madly, murderously, volleying out curses that were almost verbal in their dreadful distinctness of hatred. And the man doubled up and fled along the path between the flowers.'

Father Brown sprang to his feet with a startling impatience.

'So the dog denounced him, did he?' he cried. 'The oracle of the dog condemned him. Did you see what birds were flying, and are you sure whether they were on the right hand or the left? Did you consult the augurs about the sacrifices? Surely you didn't omit to cut open the dog and examine his entrails. That is the sort of scientific test you heathen humanitarians seem to trust when you are thinking of taking away the life and honour of a man.'

Fiennes sat gaping for an instant before he found breath to say, 'Why, what's the matter with you? What have I done now?'

A sort of anxiety came back into the priest's eyes—the anxiety of a man who has run against a post in the dark and wonders for a moment whether he has hurt it.

'I'm most awfully sorry,' he said with sincere distress. 'I beg your pardon for being so rude; pray forgive me.'

Fiennes looked at him curiously. 'I sometimes think you are more of a mystery than any of the mysteries,' he said. 'But anyhow, if you don't believe in the mystery of the dog, at least you can't get over the mystery of the man. You can't deny that at the very moment when the beast came back from the sea and bellowed, his master's soul was driven out of his body by the blow of some unseen power that no mortal man can trace or even imagine. And as for the lawyer, I don't go only by the dog; there are other curious details too. He struck me as a smooth, smiling, equivocal sort of person; and one of his tricks seemed like a sort of hint. You know the doctor and the police were on the spot very quickly; Valentine was brought back when walking away from the house, and he telephoned instantly. That, with the secluded house, small numbers, and enclosed space, made it pretty possible to search everybody who could have been near; and everybody was thoroughly searched—for a weapon. The whole house, garden, and shore were combed for a weapon. The disappearance of the dagger is almost as crazy as the disappearance of the man.'

'The disappearance of the dagger,' said Father Brown, nodding. He seemed to have become suddenly attentive.

'Well,' continued Fiennes, 'I told you that man Traill had a trick of fidgeting with his tie and tie-pin—especially his tie-pin. His pin, like himself, was at once showy and old-fashioned. It had one of those stones with concentric coloured rings that look like an eye; and his own concentration on it got on my nerves, as if he had been a Cyclops with one eye in the middle of his body. But the pin was not only large but long; and it occurred to me that his anxiety about its adjustment was because it was even longer than it looked; as long as a stiletto in fact.'

Father Brown nodded thoughtfully. 'Was any other instrument ever suggested?' he asked.

'There was another suggestion,' answered Fiennes, 'from one of the young Druces—the cousins, I mean. Neither Herbert nor Harry Druce would have struck one at first as likely to be of assistance in scientific detection; but while Herbert was really the traditional type of heavy Dragoon, caring for nothing but horses and being an ornament to the Horse Guards, his younger brother Harry had been in the Indian Police and knew something about such things. Indeed in his own way he was quite clever; and I rather fancy he had been too clever; I mean he had left the police through breaking some red-tape regulations and taking some sort of risk and responsibility of his own. Anyhow, he was in some sense a detective out of work, and threw himself into this business with more than the ardour of an amateur. And it was with him that I had an argument about the weapon—an argument that led to something new. It began by his countering my description of the dog barking at Traill; and he said that a dog at his worst didn't bark, but growled.'

'He was quite right there,' observed the priest.

'This young fellow went on to say that, if it came to that, he'd heard Nox growling at other people before then; and among others at Floyd the secretary. I retorted that his own argument answered itself; for the crime couldn't be brought home to two or three people, and least of all to Floyd, who was as innocent as a harum-scarum schoolboy, and had been seen by everybody all the time perched above the garden hedge with his fan of red hair as conspicuous as a scarlet cockatoo. 'I know there's difficulties anyhow,' said my colleague, 'but I wish you'd come with me down the garden a minute. I want to show you something I don't think anyone else has seen.' This was on the very day of the discovery, and the garden was just as it had been: the step-ladder was still standing by the hedge, and just under the hedge my guide stooped and disentangled something from the deep grass. It was the shears used for clipping the hedge, and on the point of one of them was a smear of blood.'

There was a short silence, and then Father Brown said suddenly, 'What was the lawyer there for?'

'He told us the Colonel sent for him to alter his will,' answered Fiennes. 'And, by the way, there was another thing about the business of the will that I ought to mention. You see, the will wasn't actually signed in the summer-house that afternoon.'

'I suppose not,' said Father Brown; 'there would have to be two witnesses.'

'The lawyer actually came down the day before and it was signed then; but he was sent for again next day because the old man had a doubt about one of the witnesses and had to be reassured.'

'Who were the witnesses?' asked Father Brown.

'That's just the point,' replied his informant eagerly, 'the witnesses were Floyd the secretary and this Dr Valentine, the foreign sort of surgeon or whatever he is; and the two have a quarrel. Now I'm bound to say that the secretary is something of a busybody. He's one of those hot and headlong people whose warmth of temperament has unfortunately turned mostly to pugnacity and bristling suspicion; to distrusting people instead of to trusting them. That sort of red-haired red-hot fellow is always either universally credulous or universally incredulous; and sometimes both. He was not only a Jack of all trades, but he knew better than all tradesmen. He not only knew everything, but he warned everybody against everybody. All that must be taken into account in his suspicions about Valentine; but in that particular case there seems to have been something behind it. He said the name of Valentine was not really Valentine. He said he had seen him elsewhere known by the name of De Villon. He said it would invalidate the will; of course he was kind enough to explain to the lawyer what the law was on that point. They were both in a frightful wax.'

Father Brown laughed. 'People often are when they are to witness a will,' he said, 'for one thing, it means that they can't have any legacy under it. But what did Dr Valentine say? No doubt the universal secretary knew more about the doctor's name than the doctor did. But even the doctor might have some information about his own name.'

Fiennes paused a moment before he replied.

'Dr Valentine took it in a curious way. Dr Valentine is a curious man. His appearance is rather striking but very foreign. He is young but wears a beard cut square; and his face is very pale, dreadfully pale and dreadfully serious. His eyes have a sort of ache in them, as if he ought to wear glasses or had given himself a headache with thinking; but he is quite handsome and always very formally dressed, with a top hat and a dark coat and a little red rosette. His manner is rather cold and haughty, and he has a way of staring at you which is very disconcerting. When thus charged with having changed his name, he merely stared like a sphinx and then said with a little laugh that he supposed Americans had no names to change. At that I think the Colonel also got into a fuss and said all sorts of angry things to the doctor; all the more angry because of the doctor's pretensions to a future place in his family. But I shouldn't have thought much of that but for a few words that I happened to hear later, early in the afternoon of the tragedy. I don't want to make a lot of them, for they weren't the sort of words on which one would like, in the ordinary way, to play the eavesdropper. As I was passing out towards the front gate with my two companions and the dog, I heard voices which told me that Dr Valentine and Miss Druce had withdrawn for a moment into the shadow of the house, in an angle behind a row of flowering plants, and were talking to each other in passionate whisperings—sometimes almost like hissings; for it was something of a lovers' quarrel as well as a lovers' tryst. Nobody repeats the sort of things they said for the most part; but in an unfortunate business like this I'm bound to say that there was repeated more than once a phrase about killing somebody. In fact, the girl seemed to be begging him not to kill somebody, or saying that no provocation could justify killing anybody; which seems an unusual sort of talk to address to a gentleman who has dropped in to tea.'

'Do you know,' asked the priest, 'whether Dr Valentine seemed to be very angry after the scene with the secretary and the Colonel—I mean about witnessing the will?'

'By all accounts,' replied the other, 'he wasn't half so angry as the secretary was. It was the secretary who went away raging after witnessing the will.'

'And now,' said Father Brown, 'what about the will itself?'

'The Colonel was a very wealthy man, and his will was important. Traill wouldn't tell us the alteration at that stage, but I have since heard, only this morning in fact, that most of the money was transferred from the son to the daughter. I told you that Druce was wild with my friend Donald over his dissipated hours.'

'The question of motive has been rather overshadowed by the question of method,' observed Father Brown thoughtfully. 'At that moment, apparently, Miss Druce was the immediate gainer by the death.'

'Good God! What a cold-blooded way of talking,' cried Fiennes, staring at him. 'You don't really mean to hint that she———'

'Is she going to marry that Dr Valentine?' asked the other.

'Some people are against it,' answered his friend. 'But he is liked and respected in the place and is a skilled and devoted surgeon.'

'So devoted a surgeon,' said Father Brown, 'that he had surgical instruments with him when he went to call on the young lady at tea-time. For he must have used a lancet or something, and he never seems to have gone home.'

Fiennes sprang to his feet and looked at him in a heat of inquiry. 'You suggest he might have used the very same lancet————'

Father Brown shook his head. 'All these suggestions are fancies just now,' he said. 'The problem is not who did it or what did it, but how it was done. We might find many men and even many tools—pins and shears and lancets. But how did a man get into the room? How did even a pin get into it?'

He was staring reflectively at the ceiling as he spoke, but as he said the last words his eye cocked in an alert fashion as if he had suddenly seen a curious fly on the ceiling.

'Well, what would you do about it?' asked the young man. 'You have a lot of experience, what would you advise now?'

'I'm afraid I'm not much use,' said Father Brown with a sigh. 'I can't suggest very much without having ever been near the place or the people. For the moment you can only go on with local inquiries. I gather that your friend from the Indian Police is more or less in charge of your inquiry down there. I should run down and see how he is getting on. See what he's been doing in the way of amateur detection. There may be news already.'

As his guests, the biped and the quadruped, disappeared, Father Brown took up his pen and went back to his interrupted occupation of planning a course of lectures on the Encyclical *Rerum Novarum*. The subject was a large one and he had to recast it more than once, so that he was somewhat similarly employed some two days later when the big black dog again came bounding into the room and sprawled all over him with enthusiasm and excitement. The master who followed the dog shared the excitement if not the enthusiasm. He had been excited in a less pleasant fashion, for his blue eyes seemed to start from his head and his eager face was even a little pale.

'You told me,' he said abruptly and without preface, 'to find out what Harry Druce was doing. Do you know what he's done?'

The priest did not reply, and the young man went on in jerky tones:

'I'll tell you what he's done. He's killed himself.'

Father Brown's lips moved only faintly, and there was nothing practical about what he was saying—nothing that has anything to do with this story or this world.

'You give me the creeps sometimes,' said Fiennes. 'Did you—did you expect this?'

'I thought it possible,' said Father Brown; 'that was why I asked you to go and see what he was doing. I hoped you might not be too late.'

'It was I who found him,' said Fiennes rather huskily. 'It was the ugliest and most uncanny thing I ever knew. I went down that old garden again and I knew there was something new and unnatural about it besides the murder. The flowers still tossed about in blue masses on each side of the black entrance into the old grey summerhouse; but to me the blue flowers looked like blue devils dancing before some dark cavern of the underworld. I looked all round; everything seemed to be in its ordinary place. But the queer notion grew on me that there was something wrong with the very shape of the sky. And then I saw what it was. The Rock of Fortune always rose in the background beyond the garden hedge and against the sea. And the Rock of Fortune was gone.'

Father Brown had lifted his head and was listening intently.

'It was as if a mountain had walked away out of a landscape or a moon fallen from the sky; though I knew, of course, that a touch at any time would have tipped the thing over. Something possessed me and I rushed down that garden path like the wind and went crashing through that hedge as if it were a spider's web. It was a thin hedge really, though its undisturbed trimness had made it serve all the purposes of a wall. On the shore I found the loose rock fallen from its pedestal; and poor Harry Druce lay like a wreck underneath it. One arm was thrown round it in a sort of embrace as if he had pulled it down on himself; and on the broad brown sands beside it, in large crazy lettering, he had scrawled the words, 'The Rock of Fortune falls on the Fool.'

'It was the Colonel's will that did that,' observed Father Brown. 'The young man had staked everything on profiting himself by Donald's disgrace, especially when his uncle sent for him on the same day as the lawyer, and welcomed him with so much warmth. Otherwise he was done; he'd lost his police job; he was beggared at Monte Carlo. And he killed himself when he found he'd killed his kinsman for nothing.'

'Here, stop a minute!' cried the staring Fiennes. 'You're going too fast for me.'

'Talking about the will, by the way,' continued Father Brown calmly, 'before I forget it, or we go on to bigger things, there was a simple explanation, I think, of all that business about the doctor's name. I rather fancy I have heard both names before somewhere. The doctor is really a French nobleman with the title of the Marquis de Villon. But he is also an ardent Republican and has abandoned his title and fallen back on the forgotten family surname. "With your Citizen Riquetti you have puzzled Europe for ten days."'

'What is that?' asked the young man blankly.

'Never mind,' said the priest. 'Nine times out of ten it is a rascally thing to change one's name; but this was a piece of fine fanaticism. That's the point of his sarcasm about Americans having no names —that is, no titles. Now in England the Marquis of Hartington is never called Mr Hartington; but in France the Marquis de Villon is called M. de Villon. So it might well look like a change of name. As for the talk about killing, I fancy that also was a point of French etiquette. The doctor was talking about challenging Floyd to a duel, and the girl was trying to dissuade him.'

'Oh, I *see*,' cried Fiennes slowly. 'Now I understand what she meant.'

'And what is that about?' asked his companion, smiling.

'Well,' said the young man, 'it was something that happened to me just before I found that poor fellow's body; only the catastrophe drove it out of my head. I suppose it's hard to remember a little romantic idyll when you've just come on top of a tragedy. But as I went down the lanes leading to the Colonel's old place, I met his daughter walking with Dr Valentine. She was in mourning of course, and he always wore black as if he were going to a funeral; but I can't say that their faces were very funereal. Never have I seen two people looking in their own way more respectably radiant and cheerful. They stopped and saluted me and then she told me they were married and living in a little house on the outskirts of the town, where the doctor was continuing his practice. This rather surprised me, because I knew that her old father's will had left her his property; and I hinted at it delicately by saying I was going along to her father's old place and had half expected to meet her there. But she only laughed and said, "Oh, we've given up all that. My husband doesn't like heiresses." And I discovered with some astonishment they really had insisted on restoring the property to poor Donald; so I hope he's had a healthy shock and will treat it sensibly. There was never much really the matter with him; he was very young and his father was not very wise. But it was in connection with that that she said something I didn't understand at the time; but now I'm sure it must be as you say. She said with a sort of sudden and splendid arrogance that was entirely altruistic:

"I hope it'll stop that red-haired fool from fussing any more about the will. Does he think my husband, who has given up a crest and a coronet as old as the Crusades for his principles, would kill an old man in a summer-house for a legacy like that?" Then she laughed again and said, "My husband isn't killing anybody except in the way of business. Why, he didn't even ask his friends to call on the secretary." Now, of course, I see what she meant.'

'I see part of what she meant, of course,' said Father Brown. 'What did she mean exactly by the secretary fussing about the will?'

Fiennes smiled as he answered. 'I wish you knew the secretary, Father Brown. It would be a joy to you to watch him make things hum, as he calls it. He made the house of mourning hum. He filled the funeral with all the snap and zip of the brightest sporting event. There was no holding him, after something had really happened. I've told you how he used to oversee the gardener as he did the garden, and how he instructed the lawyer in the law. Needless to say, he also instructed the surgeon in the practice of surgery; and as the surgeon was Dr Valentine, you may be sure it ended in accusing him of something worse than bad surgery. The secretary got it fixed in his red head that the doctor had committed the crime; and when the police arrived he was perfectly sublime. Need I say that he became on the spot the greatest of all amateur detectives: Sherlock Holmes never towered over Scotland Yard with more Titanic intellectual pride and scorn than Colonel Druce's private secretary over the police investigating Colonel Druce's death. I tell you it was a joy to see him. He strode about with an abstracted air, tossing his scarlet crest of hair and giving curt impatient replies. Of course it was his demeanour during these days that made Druce's daughter so wild with him. Of course he had a theory. It's just the sort of theory a man would have in a book; and Floyd is the sort of man who ought to be in a book. He'd be better fun and less bother in a book.'

'What was his theory?' asked the other.

'Oh, it was full of pep,' replied Fiennes gloomily. 'It would have been glorious copy if it could have held together for ten minutes longer. He said the Colonel was still alive when they found him in the summer-house and the doctor killed him with the surgical instrument on pretence of cutting the clothes.'

'I see,' said the priest. 'I suppose he was lying flat on his face on the mud floor as a form of siesta.'

'It's wonderful what hustle will do,' continued his informant. 'I believe Floyd would have got his great theory into the papers at any rate, and perhaps had the doctor arrested, when all these things were blown sky high as if by dynamite by the discovery of that dead body lying under the Rock of Fortune. And that's what we come back to after all. I suppose the suicide is almost a confession. But nobody will ever know the whole story.'

There was a silence, and then the priest said modestly, 'I rather think I know the whole story.'

Fiennes stared. 'But look here,' he cried, 'how do you come to know the whole story, or to be sure it's the true story? You've been sitting here a hundred miles away writing a sermon; do you mean to tell me you really know what happened already? If you've really come to the end, where in the world do you begin? What started you off with your own story?'

Father Brown jumped up with a very unusual excitement and his first exclamation was like an explosion.

'The dog!' he cried. 'The dog, of course! You had the whole story in your hands in the business of the dog on the beach, if you'd only noticed the dog properly.'

Fiennes stared still more. 'But you told me just now that my feelings about the dog were all nonsense, and the dog had nothing to do with it.'

'The dog had everything to do with it,' said Father Brown, 'as you'd have found out if you'd only treated the dog as a dog and not as God Almighty judging the souls of men.'

He paused in an embarrassed way for a moment, and then said, with a rather pathetic air of apology:

'The truth is, I happen to be awfully fond of dogs. And it seemed to me that in all this lurid halo of dog superstitions nobody was really thinking about the poor dog at all. To begin with a small point, about his barking at the lawyer or growling at the secretary. You asked how I could guess things a hundred miles away; but honestly it's mostly to your credit, for you described people so well that I know the types. A man like Traill who frowns usually and smiles suddenly, a man who fiddles with things, especially at his throat, is a nervous, easily embarrassed man. I shouldn't wonder if Floyd, the efficient secretary, is nervy and jumpy too; those Yankee hustlers often are. Otherwise he wouldn't have cut his fingers on the shears and dropped them when he heard Janet Druce scream.

'Now dogs hate nervous people. I don't know whether they make the dog nervous too; or whether, being after all a brute, he is a bit of a bully; or whether his canine vanity (which is colossal) is simply offended at not being liked. But anyhow there was nothing in poor Nox protesting against those people, except that he disliked them for being afraid of him. Now I know you're awfully clever, and nobody of sense sneers at cleverness. But I sometimes fancy, for instance, that you are too clever to understand animals. Sometimes you are too clever to understand men, especially when they act almost as simply as animals. Animals are very literal; they live in a world of truisms. Take this case; a dog barks at a man and a man runs away from a dog. Now you do not seem to be quite simple enough to see the fact; that the dog barked because he disliked the man and the man fled because he was frightened of the dog. They had no other motives and they needed none. But you must read psychological mysteries into it and suppose the dog had super-normal vision, and was a mysterious mouthpiece of doom. You must suppose the man was running away, not from the dog but from the hangman. And yet, if you come to think of it, all this deeper psychology is exceedingly improbable. If the dog really could completely and consciously realize the murderer of his master, he wouldn't stand yapping as he might at a curate at a tea-party; he's much more likely to fly at his throat. And on the other hand, do you really think a man who had hardened his heart to murder an old friend and then walk about smiling at the old friend's family, under the eyes of his old friend's daughter and post-mortem doctor—do you think a man like that would be doubled up by mere remorse because a dog barked? He might feel the tragic irony of it; it might shake his soul, like any other tragic trifle. But he wouldn't rush madly the length of a garden to escape from the only witness whom he knew to be unable to talk. People have a panic like that when they are frightened, not of tragic ironies, but of teeth. The whole thing is simpler than you can understand.

'But when we come to that business by the seashore, things are much more interesting. As you stated them, they were much more puzzling. I didn't understand that tale of the dog going in and out of the water; it didn't seem to me a doggy thing to do. If Nox had been very much upset about something else, he might possibly have refused to go after the stick at all. He'd probably go off nosing in whatever direction he suspected the mischief. But when once a dog is actually chasing a thing, a stone or a stick or a rabbit, my experience is that he won't stop for anything but the most peremptory command, and not always for that. That he should turn round because his mood changed seems to me unthinkable.'

'But he did turn round,' insisted Fiennes, 'and came back without the stick.'

'He came back without the stick for the best reason in the world,' replied the priest. 'He came back because he couldn't find it. He whined because he couldn't find it. That's the sort of thing a dog really does whine about. A dog is a devil of a ritualist. He is as particular about the precise routine of a game as a child about the precise repetition of a fairy-tale. In this case something had gone wrong with the game. He came back to complain seriously of the conduct of the stick. Never had such a thing happened before. Never had an eminent and distinguished dog been so treated by a rotten old walking-stick.'

'Why, what had the walking-stick done?' inquired the young man.

'It had sunk,' said Father Brown.

Fiennes said nothing, but continued to stare, and it was the priest who continued:

'It had sunk because it was not really a stick, but a rod of steel with a very thin shell of cane and a sharp point. In other words, it was a sword-stick. I suppose a murderer never got rid of a bloody weapon so oddly and yet so naturally as by throwing it into the sea for a retriever.'

'I begin to see what you mean,' admitted Fiennes; 'but even if a sword-stick was used, I have no guess of how it was used.'

'I had a sort of guess,' said Father Brown, 'right at the beginning when you said the word summer-house. And another when you said that Druce wore a white coat. As long as everybody was looking for a short dagger, nobody thought of it; but if we admit a rather long blade like a rapier, it's not so impossible.'

He was leaning back, looking at the ceiling, and began like one going back to his own first thoughts and fundamentals.

'All that discussion about detective stories like the Yellow Room, about a man found dead in sealed chambers which no one could enter, does not apply to the present case, because it is a summer-house. When we talk of a Yellow Room, or any room, we imply walls that are really homogeneous and impenetrable. But a summer-house is not made like that; it is often made, as it was in this case, of closely interlaced but still separate boughs and strips of wood, in which there are chinks here and there. There was one of them just behind Druce's back as he sat in his chair up against the wall. But just as the room was a summer-house, so the chair was a basket-chair. That also was a lattice of loopholes. Lastly, the summer-house was close up under the hedge; and you have just told me that it was really a thin hedge. A man standing outside it could easily see, amid a network of twigs and branches and canes, one white spot of the Colonel's coat as plain as the white of a target.

'Now, you left the geography a little vague; but it was possible to put two and two together. You said the Rock of Fortune was not really high; but you also said it could be seen dominating the garden like a mountain peak. In other words, it was very near the end of the garden, though your walk had taken you a long way round to it. Also, it isn't likely the young lady really howled so as to be heard half a mile. She gave an ordinary involuntary cry, and yet you heard it on the shore. And among other interesting things that you told me, may I remind you that you said Harry Druce had fallen behind to light his pipe under a hedge.'

Fiennes shuddered slightly. 'You mean he drew his blade there and sent it through the hedge at the white spot. But surely it was a very odd chance and a very sudden choice. Besides, he couldn't be certain the old man's money had passed to him, and as a fact it hadn't.'

Father Brown's face became animated.

'You misunderstand the man's character,' he said, as if he himself had known the man all his life. 'A curious but not unknown type of character. If he had really *known* the money would come to him, I seriously believe he wouldn't have done it. He would have seen it as the dirty thing it was.'

'Isn't that rather paradoxical?' asked the other.

'This man was a gambler,' said the priest, 'and a man in disgrace for having taken risks and anticipated orders. It was probably for something pretty unscrupulous, for every imperial police is more like a Russian secret police than we like to think. But he had gone beyond the line and failed. Now, the temptation of that type of man is to do a mad thing precisely because the risk will be wonderful in retrospect. He wants to say, "Nobody but I could have seized that chance or seen that it was then or never. What a wild and wonderful guess it was, when I put all those things together; Donald in disgrace; and the lawyer being sent for; and Herbert and I sent for at the same time— and then nothing more but the way the old man grinned at me and shook hands. Anybody would say I was mad to risk it; but that is how fortunes are made, by the man mad enough to have a little foresight."

In short, it is the vanity of guessing. It is the megalomania of the gambler. The more incongruous the coincidence, the more instantaneous the decision, the more likely he is to snatch the chance. The accident, the very triviality, of the white speck and the hole in the hedge intoxicated him like a vision of the world's desire. Nobody clever enough to see such a combination of accidents could be cowardly enough not to use them! That is how the devil talks to the gambler. But the devil himself would hardly have induced that unhappy man to go down in a dull, deliberate way and kill an old uncle from whom he'd always had expectations. It would be too respectable.'

He paused a moment; and then went on with a certain quiet emphasis.

'And now try to call up the scene, even as you saw it yourself. As he stood there, dizzy with his diabolical opportunity, he looked up and saw that strange outline that might have been the image of his own tottering soul; the one great crag poised perilously on the other like a pyramid on its point and remembered that it was called the Rock of Fortune. Can you guess how such a man at such a moment would read such a signal? I think it strung him up to action and even to vigilance. He who would be a tower must not fear to be a toppling tower. Anyhow, he acted; his next difficulty was to cover his tracks. To be found with a sword-stick, let alone a blood-stained sword-stick, would be fatal in the search that was certain to follow. If he left it anywhere, it would be found and probably traced. Even if he threw it into the sea the action might be noticed, and thought noticeable—unless indeed he could think of some more natural way of covering the action. As you know, he did think of one, and a very good one. Being the only one of you with a watch, he told you it was not yet time to return, strolled a little farther and started the game of throwing in sticks for the retriever. But how his eyes must have rolled darkly over all that desolate seashore before they alighted on the dog!'

Fiennes nodded, gazing thoughtfully into space. His mind seemed to have drifted back to a less practical part of the narrative.

'It's queer,' he said, 'that the dog really was in the story after all.'

'The dog could almost have told you the story, if he could talk,' said the priest. 'All I complain of is that because he couldn't talk, you made up his story for him, and made him talk with the tongues of men and angels. It's part of something I've noticed more and more in the modern world, appearing in all sorts of newspaper rumours and conversational catchwords; something that's arbitrary without being authoritative. People readily swallow the untested claims of this, that, or the other. It's drowning all your old rationalism and scepticism, it's coming in like a sea; and the name of it is superstition.' He stood up abruptly, his face heavy with a sort of frown, and went on talking almost as if he were alone. 'It's the first effect of not believing in God that you lose your common sense, and can't see things as they are. Anything that anybody talks about, and says there's a good deal in it, extends itself indefinitely like a vista in a nightmare. And a dog is an omen and a cat is a mystery and a pig is a mascot and a beetle is a scarab, calling up all the menagerie of polytheism from Egypt and old India; Dog Anubis and great green-eyed Pasht and all the holy howling Bulls of Bashan; reeling back to the bestial gods of the beginning, escaping into elephants and snakes and crocodiles; and all because you are frightened of four words: "He was made Man."'

The young man got up with a little embarrassment, almost as if he had overheard a soliloquy. He called to the dog and left the room with vague but breezy farewells. But he had to call the dog twice, for the dog had remained behind quite motionless for a moment, looking up steadily at Father Brown as the wolf looked at St Francis.

E. C. BENTLEY · 1875–1956

The Genuine Tabard

It was quite by chance, at a dinner party given by the American Naval Attaché, that Philip Trent met the Langleys, who were visiting Europe for the first time. During the cocktail time, before dinner was served, he had gravitated towards George D. Langley, because he was the finest looking man in the room—tall, strongly-built, carrying his years lightly, pink of face, with vigorous, massive features and thick grey hair.

They had talked about the Tower of London, the Cheshire Cheese, and the Zoo, all of which the Langleys had visited that day. Langley, so the Attaché had told Trent, was a distant relative of his own; he had made a large fortune manufacturing engineers' drawing-office equipment, was a prominent citizen of Cordova, Ohio, the headquarters of his business, and had married a Schuyler. Trent, though not sure what a Schuyler was, gathered that it was an excellent thing to marry, and this impression was confirmed when he found himself placed next to Mrs Langley at dinner.

Mrs Langley always went on the assumption that her own affairs were the most interesting subject of conversation; and as she was a vivacious and humorous talker and a very handsome and good-hearted woman, she usually turned out to be right. She informed Trent that she was crazy about old churches, of which she had seen and photographed she did not know how many in France, Germany, and England. Trent, who loved thirteenth-century stained glass, mentioned Chartres, which Mrs Langley said, truly enough, was too perfect for words. He asked if she had been to Fairford in Gloucester-shire. She had; and that was, she declared with emphasis, the greatest day of all their time in Europe; not because of the church, though that was certainly lovely, but because of the treasure they had found that afternoon.

Trent asked to be told about this; and Mrs Langley said that it was quite a story. Mr Gifford had driven them down to Fairford in his car. Did Trent know Mr Gifford—W. N. Gifford, who lived at the Suffolk Hotel? He was visiting Paris just now. Trent ought to meet him, because Mr Gifford knew everything there was to know about stained glass, and church ornaments, and brasses, and antiques in general. They had met him when he was sketching some traceries in Westminster Abbey, and they had become great friends. He had driven them about to quite a few places within reach of London. He knew all about Fairford, of course, and they had a lovely time there.

On the way back to London, after passing through Abingdon, Mr Gifford had said it was time for a cup of coffee, as he always did around five o'clock; he made his own coffee, which was excellent, and carried it in a thermos. They slowed down, looking for a good place to stop, and Mrs Langley's eye was caught by a strange name on a signpost at a turning off the road—something Episcopi. She knew that meant bishops, which was interesting; so she asked Mr Gifford to halt the car while she made out the weather-beaten lettering. The sign said 'Silcote Episcopi ½ mile.'

Had Trent heard of the place? Neither had Mr Gifford. But that lovely name, Mrs Langley said, was enough for her. There must be a church, and an old one; and anyway she would love to have Silcote Episcopi in her collection. As it was so near, she asked Mr Gifford if they could go there so she could take a few snaps while the light was good, and perhaps have coffee there.

They found the church, with the parsonage near by, and a village in sight some way beyond. The church stood back of the churchyard, and as they were going along the footpath they noticed a grave with tall railings round it; not a standing-up stone but a flat one, raised on a little foundation. They noticed it because, though it was an old stone, it had not been just left to fall into decay, but had been kept clean of moss and dirt, so you could make out the inscription, and the grass around it was trim and tidy. They read Sir Rowland Verey's epitaph; and Mrs Langley—so she assured Trent—screamed with joy.

There was a man trimming the churchyard boundary hedge with shears, who looked at them, she thought, suspiciously when she screamed. She thought he was probably the sexton; so she assumed a winning manner, and asked him if there was any objection to her taking a photograph of the inscription on the stone. The man said that he didn't know as there was; but maybe she ought to ask vicar, because it was his grave, in a manner of speaking. It was vicar's great-grandfather's grave, that was; and he always had it kep' in good order. He would be in the church now, very like, if they had a mind to see him.

Mr Gifford said that in any case they would have a look at the church, which he thought might be worth the trouble. He observed that it was not very old—about mid-seventeenth century, he would say—a poor little kid church, Mrs Langley commented with gay sarcasm. In a place so named, Mr Gifford said, there had probably been a church for centuries farther back: but it might have been burnt down, or fallen into ruin, and replaced by this building. So they went into the church; and at once Mr Gifford had been delighted with it. He pointed out how the pulpit, the screen, the pews, the glass, the organ-case in the west gallery, were all of the same period. Mrs Langley was busy with her camera when a pleasant-faced man of middle age, in clerical attire, emerged from the vestry with a large book under his arm.

Mr Gifford introduced himself and his friends as a party of chance visitors who had been struck by the beauty of the church and had ventured to explore its interior. Could the vicar tell them anything about the armorial glass in the nave windows? The vicar could and did; but Mrs Langley was not just then interested in any family history but the vicar's own, and soon she broached the subject of his great-grandfather's gravestone.

The vicar, smiling, said that he bore Sir Rowland's name, and had felt it a duty to look after the grave properly, as this was the only Verey to be buried in that place. He added that the living was in the gift of the head of the family, and that he was the third Verey to be vicar of Silcote Episcopi in the course of two hundred years. He said that Mrs Langley was most welcome to take a photograph of the stone, but he doubted if it could be done successfully with a hand-camera from over the railings—and of course, said Mrs Langley, he was perfectly right. Then the vicar asked if she would like to have a copy of the epitaph, which he could write for her if they would all come over to his house, and his wife would give them some tea; and at this, as Trent could imagine, they were just tickled to death.

'But what was it, Mrs Langley, that delighted you so much about the epitaph?' Trent asked. 'It seems to have been about a Sir Rowland Verey—that's all I have been told so far.'

'I was going to show it to you,' Mrs Langley said, opening her handbag. 'Maybe you will not think it so precious as we do. I have had a lot of copies made, to send to friends at home.' She unfolded a small typed sheet, on which Trent read what follows:

Within this Vault are interred
the Remains of
Lt.-Gen. Sir Rowland Edmund Verey,
Garter Principal King of Arms,
Gentleman Usher of the Black Rod
and
Clerk of the Hanaper,
who departed this Life
on the 2nd May 1795
in the 73rd Year of his Age
calmly relying
on the Merits of the Redeemer
for the Salvation of
his Soul.
Also of Lavinia Prudence,
Wife of the Above,
who entered into Rest
on the 12th March 1799
in the 68th Year of her Age.
She was a Woman of fine Sense
genteel Behaviour,
prudent Oeconomy
and
great Integrity.
'This is the Gate of the Lord:
The Righteous shall enter into it.'

'You have certainly got a fine specimen of that style,' Trent observed. 'Nowadays we don't run to much more, as a rule, than "in loving memory", followed by the essential facts. As for the titles, I don't wonder at your admiring them; they are like the sound of trumpets. There is also a faint jingle of money, I think. In Sir Rowland's time, Black Rod's was probably a job worth having; and though I don't know what a Hanaper is, I do remember that its Clerkship was one of the fat sinecures that made it well worth while being a courtier.'

Mrs Langley put away her treasure, patting the bag with affection. 'Mr Gifford said the Clerk had to collect some sort of legal fees for the Crown, and that he would draw maybe seven or eight thousand pounds a year for it, paying another man two or three hundred for doing the actual work. Well, we found the vicarage just perfect—an old house with everything beautifully mellow and personal about it. There was a long oar hanging on the wall in the hall, and when I asked about it the vicar said he had rowed for All Souls College when he was at Oxford. His wife was charming, too. And now listen! While she was giving us tea, and her husband was making a copy of the epitaph for me, he was talking about his ancestor, and he said the first duty that Sir Rowland had to perform after his appointment as King of Arms was to proclaim the Peace of Versailles from the steps of the Palace of St James's. Imagine that, Mr Trent!'

Trent looked at her uncertainly. 'So they had a Peace of Versailles all that time ago.'

'Yes, they did,' Mrs Langley said, a little tartly. 'And quite an important Peace, at that. We remember it in America, if you don't. It was the first treaty to be signed by the United States, and in that treaty the British Government took a licking, called off the war, and recognized our independence. Now when the vicar said that about his ancestor having proclaimed peace with the United States, I saw George Langley prick up his ears; and I knew why.

'You see, George is a collector of Revolution pieces, and he has some pretty nice things, if I do say it. He began asking questions; and the first thing anybody knew, the vicaress had brought down the old King of Arm's tabard and was showing it off. You know what a tabard is, Mr Trent, of course. Such a lovely garment! I fell for it on the spot, and as for George, his eyes stuck out like a crab's. That wonderful shade of red satin, and the Royal Arms embroidered in those stunning colours, red and gold and blue and silver, as you don't often see them.

'Presently George got talking to Mr Gifford in a corner, and I could see Mr Gifford screwing up his mouth and shaking his head; but George only stuck out his chin, and soon after, when the vicaress was showing off the garden, he got the vicar by himself and talked turkey.

'Mr Verey didn't like it at all, George told me; but George can be a very smooth worker when he likes, and at last the vicar had to allow that he was tempted, what with having his sons to start in the world, and the income tax being higher than a cat's back, and the death duties and all. And finally he said yes. I won't tell you or anybody what George offered him, Mr Trent, because George swore me to secrecy; but, as he says, it was no good acting like a piker in this kind of a deal, and he could sense that the vicar wouldn't stand for any bargaining back and forth. And anyway, it was worth every cent of it to George, to have something that no other curio-hunter possessed. He said he would come for the tabard next day and bring the money in notes, and the vicar said very well, then we must all three come to lunch, and he would have a paper ready giving the history of the tabard over his signature. So that was what we did; and the tabard is in our suite at the Greville, locked in a wardrobe, and George has it out and gloats over it first thing in the morning and last thing at night.'

Trent said with sincerity that no story of real life had ever interested him more. 'I wonder,' he said, 'if your husband would let me have a look at his prize. I'm not much of an antiquary, but I am interested in heraldry, and the only tabards I have ever seen were quite modern ones.'

'Why, of course,' Mrs Langley said. 'You make a date with him after dinner. He will be delighted. He has no idea of hiding it under a bushel, believe me!'

The following afternoon, in the Langleys' sitting-room at the Greville, the tabard was displayed on a coat-hanger before the thoughtful gaze of Trent, while its new owner looked on with a pride not untouched with anxiety.

'Well, Mr Trent,' he said. 'How do you like it? You don't doubt this is a genuine tabard, I suppose?'

Trent rubbed his chin. 'Oh yes, it's a tabard. I have seen a few before, and I have painted one, with a man inside it, when Richmond Herald wanted his portrait done in the complete get-up. Everything about it is right. Such things are hard to come by. Until recent times, I believe, a herald's tabard remained his property, and stayed in the family, and if they got hard up they might perhaps sell it privately, as this was sold to you. It's different now—so Richmond Herald told me. When a herald dies, his tabard goes back to the College of Arms, where he got it from.'

Langley drew a breath of relief. 'I'm glad to hear you say my tabard is genuine. When you asked me if you could see it, I got the impression you thought there might be something phoney about it.'

Mrs Langley, her keen eyes on Trent's face, shook her head. 'He thinks so still, George, I believe. Isn't that so, Mr Trent?'

'Yes, I am sorry to say it is. You see, this was sold to you as a particular tabard, with an interesting history of its own; and when Mrs Langley described it to me, I felt pretty sure that you had been swindled. You see, she had noticed nothing odd about the Royal Arms. I wanted to see it just to make sure. It certainly did not belong to the Garter King of Arms in the year 1783.'

A very ugly look wiped all the benevolence from Langley's face, and it grew several shades more pink. 'If what you say is true, Mr Trent, and if that old fraud was playing me for a sucker, I will get him jailed if it's my last act. But it certainly is hard to believe—a preacher—and belonging to one of your best families—settled in that lovely, peaceful old place, with his flock to look after and everything. Are you really sure of what you say?'

'What I know is that the Royal Arms on this tabard are all wrong.'

An exclamation came from the lady. 'Why, Mr Trent, how you talk! We have seen the Royal Arms quite a few times, and they are just the same as this—and you have told us it is a genuine tabard, anyway. I don't get this at all.'

'I must apologize,' Trent said unhappily, 'for the Royal Arms. You see, they have a past. In the fourteenth century Edward III laid claim to the Kingdom of France, and it took a hundred years of war to convince his descendants that that claim wasn't practical politics. All the same, they went on including the lilies of France in the Royal Arms, and they never dropped them until the beginning of the nineteenth century.'

'Mercy!' Mrs Langley's voice was faint.

'Besides that, the first four Georges and the fourth William were Kings of Hanover; so until Queen Victoria came along, and could not inherit Hanover because she was a female, the Arms of the House of Brunswick were jammed in along with our own. In fact, the tabard of the Garter King of Arms in the year when he proclaimed the peace with the United States of America was a horrible mess of the leopards of England, the lion of Scotland, the harp of Ireland, the lilies of France, together with a few more lions, and a white horse, and some hearts, as worn in Hanover. It was a fairly tight fit for one shield, but they managed it somehow—and you can see that the Arms on this tabard of yours are not nearly such a bad dream as that. It is a Victorian tabard—a nice, gentlemanly coat, such as no well-dressed herald should be without.'

Langley thumped the table. 'Well, I intend to be without it, anyway, if I can get my money back.'

'We can but try,' Trent said. 'It may be possible. But the reason why I asked to be allowed to see this thing, Mr Langley, was that I thought I might be able to save you some unpleasantness. You see, if you went home with your treasure, and showed it to people, and talked about its history, and it was mentioned in the newspapers, and then somebody got inquiring into its authenticity, and found out what I have been telling you, and made it public—well, it wouldn't be very nice for you.'

Langley flushed again, and a significant glance passed between him and his wife.

'You're damn right, it wouldn't,' he said. 'And I know the name of the buzzard who would do that to me, too, as soon as I had gone the limit in making a monkey of myself. Why, I would lose the money twenty times over, and then a bundle, rather than have that happen to me. I am grateful to you, Mr Trent—I am indeed. I'll say frankly that at home we aim to be looked up to socially, and we judged that we would certainly figure if we brought this doggoned thing back and had it talked about. Gosh! When I think—but never mind that now. The thing is to go right back to that old crook and make him squeal. I'll have my money out of him, if I have to use a can-opener.'

Trent shook his head. 'I don't feel very sanguine about that, Mr Langley. But how would you like to run down to his place tomorrow with me and a friend of mine, who takes an interest in affairs of this kind, and who would be able to help you if any one can?'

Langley said, with emphasis, that that suited him.

The car which called for Langley next morning did not look as if it belonged, but did belong, to Scotland Yard; and the same could be said of its dapper chauffeur. Inside was Trent, with a black-haired, round-faced man whom he introduced as Superintendent Owen. It was at his request that Langley, during the journey, told with as much detail as he could recall the story of his acquisition of the tabard, which he had hopefully brought with him in a suitcase.

A few miles short of Abingdon the chauffeur was told to go slow. 'You tell me it was not very far this side of Abingdon, Mr Langley, that you turned off the main road,' the superintendent said. 'If you will keep a look-out now, you might be able to point out the spot.'

Langley stared at him. 'Why, doesn't your man have a map?'

'Yes; but there isn't any place called Silcote Episcopi on his map.'

'Nor,' Trent added, 'on any other map. No, I am not suggesting that you dreamed it all; but the fact is so.'

Langley, remarking shortly that this beat him, glared out of the window eagerly; and soon he gave the word to stop. 'I am pretty sure this is the turning,' he said. 'I recognize it by these two haystacks in the meadow, and the pond with osiers over it. But there certainly was a signpost there, and now there isn't one. If I was not dreaming then, I guess I must be now.' And as the car ran swiftly down the side-road he went on, 'Yes; that certainly is the church on ahead—and the covered gate, and the graveyard—and there is the vicarage, with the yew trees and the garden and everything. Well, gentlemen, right now is when he gets what is coming to him, I don't care what the name of the darn place is.'

'The name of the darn place on the map,' Trent said, 'is Oakhanger.'

The three men got out and passed through the lych-gate.

'Where is the gravestone?' Trent asked.

Langley pointed. 'Right there.' They went across to the railed-in grave, and the American put a hand to his head. 'I must be nuts!' he groaned. 'I *know* this is the grave—but it says that here is laid to rest the body of James Roderick Stevens, of this parish.'

'Who seems to have died about thirty years after Sir Rowland Verey,' Trent remarked, studying the inscription; while the superintendent gently smote his thigh in an ecstasy of silent admiration. 'And now let us see if the vicar can throw any light on the subject.'

They went on to the parsonage; and a dark-haired, bright-faced girl, opening the door at Mr Owen's ring, smiled recognizingly at Langley. 'Well, you're genuine, anyway!' he exclaimed. 'Ellen is what they call you, isn't it? And you remember me, I see. Now I feel better. We would like to see the vicar. Is he at home?'

'The canon came home two days ago, sir,' the girl said, with a perceptible stress on the term of rank. 'He is down in the village now; but he may be back any minute. Would you like to wait for him?'

'We surely would,' Langley declared positively; and they were shown into the large room where the tabard had changed hands.

'So he has been away from home?' Trent asked. 'And he is a canon, you say?'

'Canon Maberley, sir; yes, sir, he was in Italy for a month. The lady and gentleman who were here till last week had taken the house furnished while he was away. Me and cook stayed on to do for them.'

'And did that gentleman—Mr Verey—do the canon's duty during his absence?' Trent inquired with a ghost of a smile.

'No, sir; the canon had an arrangement with Mr Giles, the vicar of Cotmore, about that. The canon never knew that Mr Verey was a clergyman. He never saw him. You see, it was Mrs Verey who came to see over the place and settled everything; and it seems she never mentioned it. When we told the canon, after they had gone, he was quite took aback. "I can't make it out at all," he says. "Why should he conceal it?" he says. "Well, sir," I says, "they was very nice people, anyhow, and the friends they had to see them here was very nice, and their chauffeur was a perfectly respectable man," I says.'

Trent nodded. 'Ah! They had friends to see them.'

The girl was thoroughly enjoying this gossip. 'Oh yes, sir. The gentleman as brought you down, sir'—she turned to Langley—'he brought down several others before that. They was Americans too, I think.'

'You mean they didn't have an English accent, I suppose,' Langley suggested dryly.

'Yes, sir; and they had such nice manners, like yourself,' the girl said, quite unconscious of Langley's confusion, and of the grins covertly exchanged between Trent and the superintendent, who now took up the running.

'This respectable chauffeur of theirs—was he a small, thin man with a long nose, partly bald, always smoking cigarettes?'

'Oh yes, sir; just like that. You must know him.'

'I do,' Superintendent Owen said grimly.

'So do I!' Langley exclaimed. 'He was the man we spoke to in the churchyard.'

'Did Mr and Mrs Verey have any—er—ornaments of their own with them?' the superintendent asked.

Ellen's eyes rounded with enthusiasm. 'Oh yes, sir—some lovely things they had. But they was only put out when they had friends coming. Other times they was kept somewhere in Mr Verey's bedroom, I think. Cook and me thought perhaps they was afraid of burglars.'

The superintendent pressed a hand over his stubby moustache. 'Yes, I expect that was it,' he said gravely. 'But what kind of lovely things do you mean? Silver—china—that sort of thing?'

'No, sir; nothing ordinary, as you might say. One day they had out a beautiful goblet, like, all gold, with little figures and patterns worked on it in colours, and precious stones, blue and green and white, stuck all round it—regular dazzled me to look at, it did.'

'The Debenham Chalice!' exclaimed the superintendent.

'Is it a well-known thing, then, sir?' the girl asked.

'No, not at all,' Mr Owen said. 'It is an heirloom—a private family possession. Only we happen to have heard of it.'

'Fancy taking such things about with them,' Ellen remarked. 'Then there was a big book they had out once, lying open on that table in the window. It was all done in funny gold letters on yellow paper, with lovely little pictures all round the edges, gold and silver and all colours.'

'The Murrane Psalter!' said Mr Owen. 'Come, we're getting on.'

'And,' the girl pursued, addressing herself to Langley, 'there was that beautiful red coat with the arms on it, like you see on a half-crown. You remember they got it out for you to look at, sir; and when I brought in the tea it was hanging up in front of the tallboy.'

Langley grimaced. 'I believe I do remember it,' he said, 'now you remind me.'

'There is the canon coming up the path now,' Ellen said, with a glance through the window. 'I will tell him you gentlemen are here.'

She hurried from the room, and soon there entered a tall, stooping old man with a gentle face and the indescribable air of a scholar.

The superintendent went to meet him.

'I am a police officer, Canon Maberley,' he said. 'I and my friends have called to see you in pursuit of an official inquiry in connection with the people to whom your house was let last month. I do not think I shall have to trouble you much, though, because your parlourmaid has given us already most of the information we are likely to get, I suspect.'

'Ah! That girl,' the canon said vaguely. 'She has been talking to you, has she? She will go on talking for ever, if you let her. Please sit down, gentlemen. About the Vereys—ah yes! But surely there was nothing wrong about the Vereys? Mrs Verey was quite a nice, well-bred person, and they left the place in perfectly good order. They paid me in advance, too, because they live in New Zealand, as she explained, and know nobody in London. They were on a visit to England, and they wanted a temporary home in the heart of the country, because that is the real England, as she said. That was so sensible of them, I thought—instead of flying to the grime and turmoil of London, as most of our friends from overseas do. In a way, I was quite touched by it, and I was glad to let them have the vicarage.'

The superintendent shook his head. 'People as clever as they are make things very difficult for us, sir. And the lady never mentioned that her husband was a clergyman, I understand.'

'No, and that puzzled me when I heard of it,' the canon said. 'But it didn't matter, and no doubt there was a reason.'

'The reason was, I think,' Mr Owen said, 'that if she had mentioned it, you might have been too much interested, and asked questions which would have been all right for a genuine parson's wife, but which she couldn't answer without putting her foot in it. Her husband could do a vicar well enough to pass with laymen, especially if they were not English laymen. I am sorry to say, canon, that your tenants were impostors. Their name was certainly not Verey, to begin with. I don't know who they are—I wish I did—they are new to us and they have invented a new method. But I can tell you what they are. They are thieves and swindlers.'

The canon fell back in his chair. 'Thieves and swindlers!' he gasped.

'And very talented performers too,' Trent assured him. 'Why, they have had in this house of yours part of the loot of several country-house burglaries which took place last year, and which puzzled the police because it seemed impossible that some of the things taken could ever be turned into cash. One of them was a herald's tabard, which Superintendent Owen tells me had been worn by the father of Sir Andrew Ritchie. He was Maltravers Herald in his day. It was taken when Sir Andrew's place in Lincolnshire was broken into, and a lot of very valuable jewellery was stolen. It was dangerous to try to sell the tabard in the open market, and it was worth little, anyhow, apart from any associations it might have. What they did was to fake up a story about the tabard which might appeal to an American purchaser, and, having found a victim, to induce him to buy it. I believe he parted with quite a large sum.'

'The poor simp!' growled Langley.

Canon Maberley held up a shaking hand. 'I fear I do not under-stand,' he said. 'What had their taking my house to do with all this?'

'It was a vital part of the plan. We know exactly how they went to work about the tabard; and no doubt the other things were got rid of in very much the same way. There were four of them in the gang. Besides your tenants, there was an agreeable and cultured person—I should think a man with real knowledge of antiquities and objects of art—whose job was to make the acquaintance of wealthy people visiting London, gain their confidence, take them about to places of interest, exchange hospitality with them, and finally get them down to this vicarage. In this case it was made to appear as if the proposal to look over your church came from the visitors themselves. They could not suspect anything. They were attracted by the romantic name of the place on a signpost up there at the corner of the main road.'

The canon shook his head helplessly. 'But there is no signpost at that corner.'

'No, but there was one at the time when they were due to be passing that corner in the confederate's car. It was a false signpost, you see, with a false name on it—so that if anything went wrong, the place where the swindle was worked would be difficult to trace. Then, when they entered the churchyard their attention was attracted by a certain gravestone with an inscription that interested them. I won't waste your time by giving the whole story—the point is that the gravestone, or rather the top layer which had been fitted on to it, was false too. The sham inscription on it was meant to lead up to the swindle, and so it did.'

The canon drew himself up in his chair. 'It was an abominable act of sacrilege!' he exclaimed. 'The man calling himself Verey————'

'I don't think,' Trent said, 'it was the man calling himself Verey who actually did the abominable act. We believe it was the fourth member of the gang, who masqueraded as the Vereys' chauffeur—a very interesting character. Superintendent Owen can tell you about him.'

Mr Owen twisted his moustache thoughtfully. 'Yes; he is the only one of them that we can place. Alfred Coveney, his name is; a man of some education and any amount of talent. He used to be a stage-carpenter and property-maker—a regular artist, he was. Give him a tub of papier-mâché, and there was nothing he couldn't model and colour to look exactly like the real thing. That was how the false top to the gravestone was made, I've no doubt. It may have been made to fit on like a lid, to be slipped on and off as required. The inscription was a bit above Alf, though—I expect it was Gifford who drafted that for him, and he copied the lettering from other old stones in the churchyard. Of course the fake signpost was Alf's work too—stuck up when required, and taken down when the show was over.

'Well, Alf got into bad company. They found how clever he was with his hands, and he became an expert burglar. He has served two terms of imprisonment. He is one of a few who have always been under suspicion for the job at Sir Andrew Ritchie's place, and the other two when the chalice was lifted from Eynsham Park and the Psalter from Lord Swanbourne's house. With what they collected in this house and the jewellery that was taken in all three burglaries, they must have done very well indeed for themselves; and by this time they are going to be hard to catch.'

Canon Maberley, who had now recovered himself somewhat, looked at the others with the beginnings of a smile. 'It is a new experience for me,' he said, 'to be made use of by a gang of criminals. But it is highly interesting. I suppose that when these confiding strangers had been got down here, my tenant appeared in the character of the parson, and invited them into the house, where you tell me they were induced to make a purchase of stolen property. I do not see, I must confess, how anything could have been better designed to prevent any possibility of suspicion arising. The vicar of a parish, at home in his own vicarage! Who could imagine anything being wrong? I only hope, for the credit of my cloth, that the deception was well carried out.'

'As far as I know,' Trent said, 'he made only one mistake. It was a small one; but the moment I heard of it I knew that he must have been a fraud. You see, he was asked about the oar you have hanging up in the hall. I didn't go to Oxford myself, but I believe when a man is given his oar it means that he rowed in an eight that did something unusually good.'

A light came into the canon's spectacled eyes. 'In the year I got my colours the Wadham boat went up five places on the river. It was the happiest week of my life.'

'Yet you had other triumphs,' Trent suggested. 'For instance, didn't you get a Fellowship at All Souls, after leaving Wadham?'

'Yes, and that did please me, naturally,' the canon said. 'But that is a different sort of happiness, my dear sir, and, believe me, nothing like so keen. And by the way, how did you know about that?'

'I thought it might be so, because of the little mistake your tenant made. When he was asked about the oar, he said he had rowed for All Souls.'

Canon Maberley burst out laughing, while Langley and the superintendent stared at him blankly.

'I think I see what happened,' he said. 'The rascal must have been browsing about in my library, in search of ideas for the part he was to play. I was a resident Fellow for five years, and a number of my books have a bookplate with my name and the name and arms of All Souls. His mistake was natural.' And again the old gentleman laughed delightedly.

Langley exploded. 'I like a joke myself,' he said, 'but I'll be skinned alive if I can see the point of this one.'

'Why, the point is,' Trent told him, 'that nobody ever rowed for All Souls. There never were more than four undergraduates there at one time, all the other members being Fellows.'

H. C. BAILEY · 1878–1961

The Dead Leaves

In his first dreamy meditations over the case, Mr Fortune remarked that it suggested one answer to the hard question why boys should be boys. He remains of that opinion.

The month was March. A day of sunshine had come after weeks of gloom. Gus Carter, a lusty twelve-year-old, felt the call to play truant, and took little Ernie Brooks with him that he might have a slave for teasing. They went to Richmond Park. It was, of course, Ernie whom the keeper caught when the deer were frightened. Dismissed in tears, Ernie found Gus exuberant with merry jests at a cry-baby. He could not bear it. He announced that he was going home. Gus snatched his cap, ran away, and threw it into one of the coverts which fences protect from small boys and other enemies of natural beauty.

Ernie scrambled over the palings to get it back, distracted by threats from Gus that the keeper was coming, and forced his woebegone way into the thicket. He found the cap, and he found something else—a woman. He saw what had been her face.

A scream frightened the joyous Gus. Ernie came back through the bushes, fighting at them with wild arms, stumbled to the fence, clutched at it, and was sick. That is the manner in which the death of the woman became known to the police. But for the diversions of Gus Carter it would not have been discovered till less was left of her—it might be still a secret. Even now it is classified as a case unsolved and insoluble. Mr Fortune admits the justice of this decision, and yet maintains that Gus had his uses in the scheme of the world.

Mr Fortune stood in his laboratory. A porcelain dish on the bench contained some little dry yellowish matter. His assistant watched while he let fall on it two drops of a colourless fluid. The pale yellow colour changed to a glaring purple-red, which soon became violet and then blue and changed no more.

'That's definite enough, sir,' said Jenks, the assistant, with satisfaction.

'My dear chap! Oh, my dear chap.' Mr Fortune sighed. He turned away. He contemplated some large glass jars which contained all the rest of the dead woman that could still be any use on earth. 'Send 'em on to Anneler. Let him estimate. It's no good. However!' He wandered out.

An hour afterwards Jenks came into the room behind the laboratory. Before the electric fire, Mr Fortune sat in an easy chair, on the small of his back. His feet were on another chair, and his knees as high as his head. On his thighs a woman's leather bag lay open. He was gazing at it with eyes half closed. 'Will there be anything else, sir?' said Jenks.

'What?' Mr Fortune's eyes opened to look at him as if he were a curiosity. Jenks repeated the question.

Mr Fortune held out to him the bag. 'Smell that,' he said. 'Centre.'

The bag had been of brown leather, but was much discoloured. It was of a common pattern, in several compartments, of which the inmost was a silk pocket for small intimate possessions.

Jenks smelt and smelt again. 'Just mouldy, isn't it?' he asked.

'You think so?'

Jenks applied his nose a third time. 'Something faintly aromatic,' he announced.

'Yes. The nose is not wholly effete.' Mr Fortune got out of his chair in one squirming movement. 'Put a name to the smell?'

'No, I can't, sir.' Jenks frowned.

Mr Fortune went to the table and took the stopper from a small, wide-mouthed glass bottle in which there was a twig of some dead leaves. 'And that?' He held it out.

Once more Jenks smelt. 'It's aromatic,' he decided. 'Very faint, though.'

'Not exact, Jenks,' Mr Fortune complained. 'The nose is not adequately scientific. Use the eye.'

Jenks took up a magnifying glass. 'Why, it's bog myrtle, isn't it?' he ventured.

'Yes. That is so. And the other exhibit?' Reggie presented a second bottle, containing a smaller sprig with smaller leaves.

Jenks sniffed. 'I get no smell at all. Oh, just faintly the same.'

'Yes. You would. Are they the same?'

Jenks applied the lens. 'No, they're not. This isn't bog myrtle. It might be willow.'

'Not so bad. Which willow?'

Jenks stared at him and puzzled over the twig. 'I don't know,' he said at last. 'It's so small and fragile. Is it willow?'

'Oh, my dear chap!' Mr Fortune reproached him. 'Don't hedge. Back your mind.'

'Well, I'll say it's a bit of a very young willow,' Jenks declared.

'Not young, no. Dwarf. *Salix herbacea*—the arctic willow. Smallest tree in the world.'

The sharp face of Jenks exhibited a certain stupor. 'I know.' He grumbled resentment. 'Never saw it before, though. Arctic willow—with bog myrtle!'

'Yes. That is so. One small sprig of each in bag of deceased female. Curious and interestin'. But the only useful things she left us. Poor woman.' He gazed at Jenks with round dreamy eyes. 'No, there isn't anything else, Jenks. Good night.'

Mr Fortune took up the house telephone and asked plaintively for China tea and muffins for two, applied himself to the other telephone, and was put through to the Chief of the Criminal Investigation Department. 'Fortune speaking. From laboratory. Work of science now concluded. Passed to you for requisite action. Act—act in the livin' present. Same like the poet says. Are you livin', Lomas? Come round.'

He rang off. He switched on a higher power of heat in the electric fire, and fell again to the depths of his easy chair.

The second muffin was being consumed when the Hon. Sidney Lomas came in swift and sprightly. 'Well, Reginald, what are you going to tell me?'

'Chair,' said Reggie, through mastication, and pointed with a foot. 'Tea?' His foot twisted to the tray on the hearth. Lomas poured himself a cup, without milk or sugar. 'Oh, my dear chap!' Reggie sighed. 'Muffin? They do butter 'em here.' Lomas made a grimace. 'Well, well. Sad life, your stomach's life. However. Let us then be up and doin'. The woman died not less than three, not more than six, months ago.'

'You have it as near as that!' Lomas was satirical. 'Marvellous. Any time between September and December. Thanks so much.'

'She was over thirty. Not a lot. About five foot nine, slim, rather wasted, in poor health. Fair woman, yellow-brown hair with red in it. Done some walking. Not a single woman. Had no children. Cause of death, probably morphia. There was morphia in her. Anneler's doing an estimate of the amount—which will be quite unreliable—owing to processes of putrefaction. I should say the dose which killed her wasn't the first she had. The hypodermic syringe found by the handbag had contained sulphate of morphia. That's the medical evidence.'

'Very clear, Reginald. Very useful.' Lomas smiled. 'The conclusion is: she was a drug addict who went into that covert and gave herself a final dose some time last autumn.'

'Yes, it could be,' Reggie said slowly. 'Your conclusion. Not mine.'

'What is yours, then?'

'I haven't one. No conclusion possible on the medical evidence. Other evidence curious and interesting.'

'How do you mean?'

'Oh, my Lomas!' Reggie complained. 'Think about it. Woman's clothes completely French. Hypodermic syringe also of French make. French money in handbag. But no name anywhere, no papers. Why not? Why should a Frenchwoman come to Richmond Park to kill herself carefully anonymous, but emphasizin' she was French? Bafflin' questions. Take in the medical evidence. Body suggests English rather than French. Probability, therefore, is she was made up French to confuse our intelligent police force. Involvin' probability she did not kill herself.'

Lomas lit a cigarette, inhaled the smoke, and gave him a condescending, tolerant, patient smile. 'Admirable, Reginald. One of your best efforts at seeing what isn't there.'

'Not me, no. I never do. Only insisting you should see all there is. That's what annoys the official mind.'

'I am only amused,' said Lomas gently. 'You do like to be brilliant, don't you? But what is your genius giving me now? A masterpiece. The woman was tall and slight and fair, so she was English. And, because she was English, her French clothes were put on to deceive. Therefore she was murdered.' He chuckled. 'I should like to hear you putting that rational argument to a jury. But I'm afraid I never shall, Reginald.'

'No. You won't. It isn't an argument. It's a provisional hypothesis. Probable hypothesis. Passed to you for proof. The police will have to do a little work. Sorry to trouble you.'

'Probable!' Lomas scoffed. 'My dear fellow, look at the foundation of it. A tall fair woman must be English!'

'Merely silly, yes. But you said that, not me. I said, body suggests she was English. General physical type rather English than French, and feet and legs show she was a walker. Women who walk hard more common in England than France. Take in other evidence not medical'—he stretched out from his chair and passed the two wide-mouthed bottles to Lomas.

'Dead leaves?' Lomas frowned at them.

'Correct. Dead leaves. Found in woman's bag; old and treasured souvenirs; sprigs of bog myrtle and arctic willow.'

'Arctic!' Lomas exclaimed. 'Good gad! Do you suggest the woman was an arctic explorer?'

'My poor Lomas! Education very defective. Arctic willow not confined to the polar regions. Dwarf tree found on British mountains above 2,000 feet or so. Bog myrtle is common in our mountain districts. A woman who goes mountain walking is much more likely to be English than French. So putting things together we have strong probability deceased was an Englishwoman fond of mountains and somebody wanted her to pass for French when she was dead. There you are. Action, action, and again action. You only have to get news of a woman as described sunk without trace since last September, and find the man who had a motive for murdering her.'

'Is that all?' said Lomas, and lit another cigarette and meditated. 'I agree you've worked out something, Reginald. But it's queer stuff. Somebody—it may have been herself, you know—somebody did take care that no sign of her name or origin should be found. Great care. Admitted. Then how can you make a clue out of dead leaves found in the handbag? If they had any value as evidence, they would have been removed. Everything else significant was. The bag itself needn't have been left—it wouldn't have been if it gave anything away.'

'Oh, yes. Bag was necessary. Didn't you notice that? It contained the syringe and case. That had to be with her to indicate suicide. The dead leaves weren't removed because they weren't noticed. Very small sprigs, you see, much same colour now as brown silk of pocket. I didn't notice 'em till I smelt the myrtle.'

'It's an answer,' Lomas admitted, and smoked his cigarette out. 'Well, accepting everything you say—what then? We put her down as an Englishwoman, fond of mountains, found dead, poisoned by morphia. We shall never be able to prove that she didn't kill herself. It wouldn't be the first time that a woman has hidden herself in a copse and taken poison. Common case. Your evidence is, this woman was in poor health and probably a morphia addict. Just the type for such a suicide. We may find that a woman as described is missing and get her history. We might—long odds against—but we might be able to prove somebody had a reason for wanting her dead. And then, Reginald? A million to one we can't get any further. We're months late. It's a hopeless case.'

'I wonder,' Reggie murmured. His eyes closed. His round face was pale and wistful. 'A hopeless case,' he drawled sleepily. 'Yes. Looks like that. Looks just like suicide—as you say—not the first time, just the type—and it wasn't. What about the other times? Useful little people, aren't we? The reasonably efficient murderer has us beat. Every time and all.'

'My dear fellow'—Lomas gave an impatient laugh—'that's fantastic. The moans of wounded pride. You're very able, but not quite omniscient. Your failure to prove a crime doesn't mean that the criminal escapes. It may be there wasn't one.'

'Pride!' Reggie's eyes opened. 'Oh, my hat! Pride!' He moaned. 'Not me, no. Thinkin' about that woman—and what she was thinkin' of when she picked her mountain plants—when she looked at 'em and smelt her myrtle the last time. I wonder.' He gazed solemnly at Lomas.

'God knows, poor wretch.' Lomas was uncomfortable.

'Yes. He does. Yes. What are we for?'

'For all you can ever tell, she may have been just driven to suicide.'

'It could be,' Reggie said slowly. 'One way of murder.'

'Very well, then. It's a useless enquiry,' said Lomas.

'Feeling pleased with yourself? I am not. I object to being useless. It annoys me. Let's annoy the murderer.'

'What the devil can we do?'

'Advertise her. Appeal for information about a woman as described. Any objection?'

'Oh, that—of course!' Lomas shrugged. 'That will be done; that's routine. Do you think it will bother your hypothetical murderer? You deceive yourself. If he exists, he's covered good and well, and he knows it.'

'You think so? Yes. It could be. I hate you. However. Do your stuff. He doesn't know everything. He doesn't know me.'

So every newspaper in the country announced that the woman found dead in Richmond Park was five foot nine and slim and of fair complexion, with bobbed hair of yellow red, and asked that anyone who knew of the disappearance of such a woman since September should give information to the police.

Several people did, and several women were sought for and found alive and indignant, but nothing was heard of a woman who could not be found.

As Lomas rose one morning, his telephone rang, and said: 'Fortune speaking. Are you up? Sorry. Meant to disturb your slumbers. Reference, woman of Richmond Park. Any results?'

With a bitter gusto Lomas told him what they were. 'There you are. Dead end. Absolutely. Hopeless case. I told you so.'

'You did. Yes. As answered the end of your bein' created. And acted accordin'. Seen the *Daily Life* this morning? You should.'

'What the deuce have you been up to?' said Lomas angrily.

'He only does it to annoy, because he knows it teases,' the telephone gurgled. 'You wouldn't. Good-bye.'

Lomas snatched at his papers. The *Daily Life* had a streamer headline: 'Woman of Richmond Park.' It gave a portrait of her, over the black caption: 'Do You Know Her?' The article printed round it picturesquely elaborated the official description of her, and explained that the portrait had been drawn by Our Special Artist from exclusive information. He had given her a background of melodramatic mountains. The *Daily Life* was able (exclusively) to announce that the police had in their hands evidence which proved that a murder had been committed and concealed with diabolical cunning. Startling revelations might be expected at any moment. The *Daily Life* appealed to its millions of readers for help. 'Have you seen her on the mountains?' a cross-head demanded. It was explained that the woman had been fond of mountain walking. Photographs of scenery in Wales, in Scotland, in the Lakes were printed with flamboyant description and a gush of sentiment about the devotion of mountain-lovers. Another question was then set out: 'Where could she get this?' Beneath it was a picture from a botany book of a plant of arctic willow, and information, not unnecessary, of what that rare and minute vegetable really looks like. In this passage only the *Daily Life* showed a cautious restraint. It did not say that the dead woman had got any arctic willow; it did not state the narrow limits within which the plant can be found, but concluded with a curt order that anyone who knew anything must speak out or be suspect of complicity in the murder.

Two days afterwards, Mr Fortune strolled into Lomas's room, after lunch, with a benign smile which was not returned. 'Like a ghost, aren't you?' he murmured, and deposited himself in the largest chair and took a cigar. 'Don't speak unless you're spoken to. Poor Reginald! Only waitin' for one kind word.'

'I didn't know you considered yourself responsible to me,' said Lomas.

'Oh, my Lomas! Absolutely. As to incarnate justice. With scales and sword complete. But blind! What's the matter? Wonderin' how do these things get into the papers, same like the late Mr Crummles? My dear chap! You approved usin' our invaluable Press to discover identity of woman. Well, it's been used. And, finally, used right. Object—to annoy the murderer. I should say he has been annoyed. Quite an effective bit of tump. Our murderer will be thinkin' rather hard. Has the interested public sent you anything about his thoughts?'

Lomas snorted. 'We're snowed under with nonsense, confound you. Deuced subtle, aren't you? You may be surprised to hear that the mountain districts swarm with thin ginger-haired women, and scores of people feel we'd like to know they've found your infernal vegetable all over Europe.'

'Yes. It would be like that. Who's dealing with the stuff?'

'The wretched Bell. I may tell you my note on his report this morning. "Fool answered according to his folly."'

'My dear old thing,' said Reggie affectionately. 'That must have made you feel better. Now let's have Bell in.'

'By all means. I expect he'll wring your neck. I hope so.'

Superintendent Bell came in, and gave Reggie a solemn, reproachful salutation. 'Tell him just what you think of him, Bell,' Lomas exhorted. 'He needs it.'

Bell shook his ample head. 'I've got to say, it's my experience we never do get anything to the purpose out of a newspaper stunt.' He sat down and opened a folder. 'More letters this morning, sir—same sort of chit-chat; nothing to work on; not worth putting before you —except one queer bit of goods.' He gave Lomas two quarto sheets of paper. 'And that's right off your line, Mr Fortune,' he admonished Reggie.

'Yet disturbin' to the expert mind, what?' Reggie came to look at the letter.

'It don't tell us anything about your arctic plant,' said Bell severely. 'Nor it don't help us to who the woman was. Another case altogether. You never know what you'll bring up if you start the Press going.'

'I didn't. No,' Reggie answered. He read the sheets, his hand on Lomas's shoulder. 'Well, well,' he murmured. 'I have brought something, haven't I?'

At the top of the first sheet was pasted a newspaper cutting of the first description of the woman's body in the copse. Then came the lines from the *Daily Life* which stated that she had been fond of mountain walking. There followed typing, headed with a reference to a paper of ten years ago: the report of an inquest on a woman found dead in a wood in the mountains of North Wales.

Her husband, Professor Loram of Cambridge, who was much

distressed, gave evidence that his wife had not been in good health. She suffered from insomnia, and her doctor had advised a holiday in mountain air. She had told him she was much better, and he had gone off for the day to climb on Tryfaen. At her suggestion. She was not allowed to walk far. She promised to rest. When he came back, in the evening, she was not to be found. No one at the farmhouse where they were staying had seen her go out. He organized a search at once, but it had not occurred to him to look in the wood in which she was found two days later. He was not surprised that she had a tube of medinal with her. She had been recommended to use it.

The medical evidence was that she had died from exhaustion and exposure (the month was September, the nights had been cold). From the condition of her shoes, it appeared she had walked some distance. Medinal was found in the body, but not a fatal quantity. Conclusion—she had taken a tablet, found herself unable to sleep, become restless, gone walking, and then been overcome by fatigue and the drug and slept till she died.

The coroner and the jury agreed, and recorded their deep sympathy with Professor Loram.

Lomas looked up from the typescript into Reggie's face, and gave him a complacent, contemptuous smile. 'I pointed out to you that the woman who hides herself with a narcotic and expires is a common type of hopeless case.'

'You did, yes. Recreations of the Hon. S. Lomas. Pointin' out to grandma that eggs have been sucked. Answer of grandma, not mine, thank you. I'm in this case. Perhaps you hadn't noticed that.'

'Indeed I have. Brilliant work. Amassing evidence; there is no case.'

'My only aunt!' Reggie's eyes opened wide. 'You did read this genial little contribution, didn't you? You have a brain, have you? Or not?'

'Thank you. It still functions. I know anonymous spite when I see it. We see a good deal here, Reginald. You may be surprised to hear that it's common, when we have a Press stunt about a mystery, for kindly souls to pitch in suspicions at large. Ask Bell.'

'Spite,' Reggie repeated. 'Yes, it could be.'

And Bell spoke: 'That's right. We've got to allow. But I want to say there is another thing to think of. Remember the brides in the bath case, Mr Lomas? That fellow went on doing his wives in quite comfortable, verdict letting him out every time, till somebody sent us the report of an inquest on a wife killed same way as his last. Then we got on to him. That's what I thought of when I read this.'

Reggie beamed upon him. 'Yes. You do think. The common case all too common.'

'Damme, there's no similarity at all!' Lomas exclaimed. 'In your brides in the bath case, who all the women were was known—and their connection with the man. There we had signed information. Here we haven't a scrap of evidence who the woman was connected with. And this effort to connect her with Loram—the one thing which sticks out of it is that the author daren't show.'

'Signs of returnin' consciousness,' Reggie murmured. 'Yes. Shyness of author is indicated. However. I shouldn't say that's the strikin' thing. What strikes me is the similarity of the two deaths. Faculty of imitation very strong in mankind. And monkeys.'

'Your usual form, Reginald. When you've made a beautiful theory you'll believe anything to maintain it. This Professor Loram murdered his wife, made a success of it, and imitated the method with a woman nobody's missed!'

'One of the possibilities. Attractive possibility,' Reggie murmured.

'And so probable—a professor whose profession is murdering women.' Lomas turned to Bell. 'What about this alleged inquest?'

'I've had it verified, sir. The report is genuine. We have no clue to the sender, except being somebody who knows a bit about Professor Loram and has a down on him. Postmark on the letter—London, E.C.; address typed.'

'And what do you know of Loram?' Reggie asked. 'Professor of some branch of useless knowledge, what?' He reached for a book of reference. 'Oh, yes. Mediæval economics. Well, well. Mediævally economic Loram was at his second wife at date of publication. One daughter. By first wife. I wonder.' He shut up the book; he gazed at Bell, and his eyes were pensive and dreamy. 'Beautiful life, university life! All members one of another. And lovin' accordin'. Everything against anybody joyously cultivated.'

'Quite,' said Lomas heartily. 'Hot-beds of scandal. And this is the result.' He pointed to the typescript.

'So nothing means anything, and all is gas and gaiters.' Reggie's eyelids drooped. 'I thank you, I am taking none. World not really irrational.' He rose slowly. 'Bad luck, Lomas. Good-bye.' He went out.

Then Lomas said to Bell that he was an offensive fellow when ineffective, and Bell coughed.

At dinner that night Mrs Fortune's amber eyes laughed when she tasted the claret. 'My dear, majestic!'

'Yes, right word, Joan. Mouton Rothschild 1900.'

'Libation for a triumph?'

'Oh, no. No. just fortifyin' the mind.'

He sat long, finishing the bottle; he was silent; he smoked a cigar with his eyes closed. Then he went in a sleep-walking manner to a bookcase, and took out a fat book, bound in grey morocco, and began to turn it over.

Mrs Fortune looked over his shoulder. 'Wordsworth! My child!' He had stopped at a page on which she read about Mr Wordsworth's perfect woman—'nobly planned, to warn, to comfort, and command.' 'Darling!' she gurgled, and kissed his nose.

'Thanks very much. Wasn't readin' that.' He recited from the poem below:

> I wandered lonely as a cloud
>   That floats on high o'er vales and hills———

'Lonely?' Mrs Fortune interrupted. 'Pig. Floating on high? No, dear, not Reginald. Not the figure. What a cloud!'

'Have you a soul, Joan?' he reproached her, and continued to murmur:

> When all at once I saw a crowd,
>   A host, of golden daffodils
> Beside the lake, beneath the trees,
>   Fluttering and dancing in the breeze.

He gazed at her. 'It's April. They'll be dancin' now. Beside the lake. I think we'll go to the Lakes, Joan. Sound man, the Wordsworth man. Fundamentally.'

'Yes?' Mrs Fortune smiled. 'Go to the Lakes and read Wordsworth. How like you, Reggie.'

'Daffodils along the margin of a bay. Pretty good, what? Let's go off tomorrow. Can do?'

'Bless you,' said Mrs Fortune maternally. And then sang to him something which Wordsworth did not write: '"The flowers which bloom in the spring—tra la—have nothing to do with the case!"' She showed him the tip of her tongue.

'Know everything, don't you, Joan?' Reggie sighed.

'Heaven forbid!' she said, as she went out.

'Yes, I hope so,' Reggie murmured, to the empty room. 'However.'

He took the telephone and rang up Lomas. 'Fortune here. Oh, hush. This is tonight's bedtime story. A fool, a fool—I met a fool in the club. A Cambridge fool, a solemn fool. You know. Cambridge man yourself. Fierce and earnest. I gather the mediævally economic Loram is not good enough for Cambridge. A sad dog—as they go there. A lion among ladies. Also, he's a marrier of money. Wife number one had a nice, warm fortune. Wife number two brought some more. And Loram does himself much better than professors ought to. A naughty, luxurious liver. But popular with youth, alas! So's his daughter by wife number one. A darling red-haired minx. Rather in father's line. Lots of affairs. The university was kindly hoping she'd thrown her cap over the windmill with one of father's research students, a bright lad called Elliot. But father put a flea in his ear and he dropped out. So they say. Well————'

'Damme, I don't want to listen to the gossip of the combination rooms!' Lomas exploded. 'Go to bed.'

'One moment. Our Professor Loram has cut a mediæval conference and buzzed off to the Lakes. Me too. That's all. Good-bye.'

'Hold on,' Lomas cried. 'What the devil do you think you're going to do?'

'I haven't the slightest idea,' said Reggie, and rang off.

Behold him, two days later, driving his car through the mists of the Kirkstone Pass down to the sunlight which shone on daffodils dancing, as Mr Wordsworth saw them, beside the sparkling waves of Ullswater. He stopped in the dappled shadows of trees from which the buds broke bright green and orange and crimson. 'There you are, Joan. A host of golden daffodils, beside the lake, beneath the trees. No deception.'

Mrs Fortune looked at them a long time. 'Happy,' she said, and turned to look at him. His round face had a sleepy solemnity. '"And then your heart with pleasure fills, And dances with the daffodils,"' she quoted. 'It does not!' She gave a little shudder. 'Go on, then.'

'Yes, I think so,' said Reggie. 'Difficult world. But there are daffodils, Joan.'

He drove on, away from the lake to bleak upland common, and Mrs Fortune endured one of his most *staccato* fantasias of speed, a wild surge over switchbacks and round corkscrew curves, suddenly checked to crawl through narrowing villages and as suddenly let go again. It was when they had threaded the needle's eye of Keswick, swirled over the flat beyond to stop dead before a blank wall and a lorry at an impossible turn and then shot forward up a long steep climb, that she spoke: '"Like the devil came through Athlone, in standing leaps."'

'What? Sorry. I was thinking,' Reggie said.

She laughed. 'Oh, I know that.'

But he has always maintained that no man drives more rationally than he. They swept down from the sombre fir-clad heights of the Whinlatter no faster than they had gone up. When they turned into a road which gave no room for anything else between its rough stone walls he was content with a maximum of forty, and slowed gently to its gates and the blind corners which came when it turned under cliff above Crummock Water. That lake lay black beneath the steep, red slopes on either side, and the high mountains ahead rose sharp and dark to wisps of fleeting cloud.

Crummock was lost and Buttermere came in sight, pale, lucid green in its frame of pasture and springtime woodland. On the peaks above the wood, sunlight and shadow played, making a crimson glow on the shoulder at one end, mysteries of grey and purple about the crags, and the streams which fell headlong down to the lake gleamed and flashed in the lacework of their foam between still, dull white and gloom.

Reggie stopped at the door of a hotel, and got out of the car and stood surveying all this. 'Good place.' He sighed. 'Well, well.' He glanced at the people sitting about, a rubicund and ample cleric with attentive females, and entered. The hotel was genially hospitable. Yes, their room was quite ready—a room with a view, yes. If he would register. . . . He did so, and saw that Professor Loram and family had registered four days earlier. He made small talk: supposed they had a good many clergy and school and university people; wondered if there was anybody he knew. Archdeacon Smith was suggested to him; Doctor Jones; Professor Loram. Was that a thin, scraggy man with a beard, rather shy? Oh, dear, no. A stout gentleman, clean shaven and full of his fun. No, Reggie did not know him. That room?—Oh, charming—a romantic view, what, Joan? . . .

The door was shut. 'So it is Professor Loram,' said Mrs Fortune.

'Sorry,' Reggie answered. 'I have to.'

She looked out at the lake and the heights. 'Romantic,' she repeated.

'Yes. "Comfortress of unsuccess, to bid the dead good night."'

She turned to him, her eyes dark, and put her hand in his.

'Dear.' He kissed it. 'Well, well. A pleasant pub.'

He confirmed that over a tea of hot scones and bilberry jam and pipes smoked outside with the ample archdeacon, who had been coming there for fifty years and was eager to tell the story of every one of them, a genial, soothing man, without a drop of gall in his flow of gossip. 'Regular meetin' place of old friends,' Reggie prompted him. 'Very jolly. Count on one another bein' here, what?' The archdeacon feared, with a professional intonation, some were missing as the years went by. Some had new claims, new calls. But then—he cheered up—there were pleasant surprises. A dear old friend would break in unexpected—like Professor Loram only the other day. Did Mr Fortune know Loram?—quite one of the old guard in the Lakes; a great climber in his day————

'Loram—professor,' Reggie said sleepily. 'No, I'm Oxford. Not there, I think'—and thus discovered that the archdeacon had never heard of Mr Fortune or failed to connect him with crime. It became clear, also, that the archdeacon's simple mind was unaware of any scandal about Loram. He babbled on of missing the man last summer —the first time in years—and being disappointed not to find him that spring till, unexpected, he came. The call of the mountains—no, one couldn't resist it. The archbishop said to him . . .

Reggie withdrew his attention and contemplated the universe.

In cars and afoot people came for tea, and lingered and strolled and departed. After a while he noticed that one man was recurring—a big fellow, seen along the road, now here now there, as though he waited for somebody or something which did not arrive; a fellow with a good deal of face between his scarf and his black hair—gloomy face. Reggie was classifying the expression as, 'She cometh not, he said,' when the archdeacon exclaimed, 'Dear me. Dear, dear!'

'Why is that?' Reggie enquired.

The archdeacon pointed, not to the man in the road, who, indeed, had passed out of sight, but to the mountain ridge beyond the lake. 'Do you see those two in Sour Milk Gill? They shouldn't, you know—really they shouldn't.'

'Sour Milk Gill? You mean the nearest waterfall. Well, well. Harsh name.' Reggie scanned the white water cascading in the darkness of the ravine, and made out two figures climbing down, a man and a woman. 'Bein' reckless, are they?'

The archdeacon explained anxiously. It was really dangerous. Of course it was a short cut to the summit of Red Pike and the ridge, and people did use it, but they ought not, and especially when there was so much water coming down. The proper path went round through the wood—perfectly safe, with a far better view. He did think it quite unpardonable to risk a serious accident for a trifle of time.

'Wouldn't fall far, would they?' Reggie asked, watching them. The woman was helping the man down a tall step in the cascade.

The archdeacon assured him, with gusto, that they could fall quite far enough. Only last year a poor fellow was found dead in one of the pools. He had slipped, and lay stunned under the water till he was drowned.

'Too bad,' Reggie murmured. 'However. This man's watchin' his step.' They came down and passed out of sight. 'I should say they're all right.'

The archdeacon could not understand how people could go that way after such a tragic warning . . .

Over the slope of the meadow between the hotel and the lake a woman rose into sight, a wild mop of red hair above a slim body in a faded leather jerkin, and stretches of lean pink leg revealed between shorts and fallen stockings. But the bedraggled legs bore her on fast, in a long springy stride. The man who followed her made heavier going. He was bulky; he bent under his rucksack, and his red face shone with sweat. She vaulted the meadow fence, looked up and down the road, and stood waiting for him with a smile which was not kindly.

The archdeacon gave a 'tut-tut' of surprised disapproval, and to Reggie's questioning eyebrows explained: 'It's Loram and his daughter. I shouldn't have thought it of them.'

Daughter and father came on to the hotel, and the archdeacon rose to reprove them. 'Molly, my dear! You brought my heart to my mouth. You mustn't take him by the gill.'

She tossed back her hair; her lip curled. 'Been watching the perilous climb? Thrills for you. The Prof. isn't what he was. Puff, puff.' She gave her father a jeering glance. 'But he would do it.' She vanished into the hotel.

'You're a terrible fellow, Loram,' the archdeacon said severely. 'It's not fair to lead the child into———'

Loram interrupted with a hoarse, breathless laugh. 'Don't be an old woman. I'm not her leader.' He unshipped his rucksack and dropped onto a bench in the porch and mopped his red face. Its fullness was sagging and deep-lined, and the eyes sunken.

'Dear, dear. You're quite exhausted,' said the archdeacon. 'It's been too much for you. The gill is a terrible place———'

Loram made an inarticulate exclamation of disgust. 'Gill's nothing.

Don't be silly.' He shook himself together. 'What's the matter with you?' He stared, frowning, from the archdeacon to Reggie.

'Had a good day, sir?' Reggie smiled.

'Just a training walk.' Loram's eyes dwelt on him. 'Up Floutern Tarn way, down over Red Pike. Are you staying here?'

'Yes, a little while. Quite new to me. Interestin' place.'

'Bit far from the big things. Are you a climber?'

'Oh, no. No. Passive person.'

Loram grunted an answer and went in, and Reggie saw him go to the visitors' book before he hung up his hat.

The archdeacon said anxiously that Loram was really a good fellow, one of the best fellows, but a little wild—eh, well, it was difficult to grow old wisely and happily. He became professional, and Reggie remarked that it was getting chilly and went for a walk. His walks are seldom long. This one took him to a knoll commanding a view of the road along the lake. The only wayfarers were sheep. Then, as the twilight darkened, came a small sports car, in which, as it slowed round the corkscrew curves of the little village, he made out the big fellow who had loitered by the hotel. 'Not stayin' here,' Reggie murmured. 'Well, well,' and strolled slowly back. The red head of Molly Loram came towards him through the gloom and was in the hotel before him.

The Loram family were incoherently late for dinner. Loram did not appear till the soup had gone round. A flaccid woman, who was beyond doubt his wife, came drifting in on the tail of the fish. His daughter arrived with the mutton. They did not unite in conversation. Loram paid attention to his wife, but she let him labour, and Molly had no interest in father or stepmother, preferring cross-talk with other tables, in which she was sharp and pert. Loram took his share of that eagerly.

'British family bein' very British,' Reggie murmured, and, having drunk his beer, reverted to sherry. 'One more glass, I think.' He finished it, and Mrs Fortune rose. 'Try the drawing-room, Joan,' he said, as they went into the hall, and himself turned into the lounge.

There was no one there. He dropped into an easy chair and lit his pipe.

The door opened behind him. He heard the high voice of one of the archdeacon's females say: 'It will be more amusing in the drawing-room.' The door was decisively closed.

'My poor Joan.' He sighed, and smoked on with his eyes shut.

He was opening them to fill the pipe again when Loram came in.

He mumbled a sleepy salutation, and Loram took a chair on the other side of the fire and said it was a comfortable place. Reggie thought so. Was he down for a rest? Reggie hoped so. Loram supposed his work was rather trying. Reggie always ran away from work. Loram laughed. Mr Fortune wasn't allowed to hide his light under a bushel, was he?

'What?' Reggie was shocked. 'Oh, my dear fellow. The shop is shut. And far away.'

Loram begged his pardon. Loram lit a cigar and talked mountains. Reggie displayed a mild, languid ignorance, and Loram let the cigar go out. 'That was an extraordinary story in the *Daily Life* last week, Mr Fortune.'

'Which was that?' Reggie mumbled.

'About the dead woman in Richmond Park, said to be a mountaineer.'

'Well, well!' Reggie's eyelids drooped. 'Wonder what they'll say next?'

'Did you read the stuff?'

'The papers!' Reggie was hurt. 'My dear fellow!'

'It was an astounding theory.'

'It would be,' Reggie mumbled. 'What astounded you?'

Loram lit his cigar a second time, and the door was flung open. 'Oh, that's where you've got to,' Molly snapped at him. 'What are you doing? Mother Bunch wants her bridge. Come on.' She waited for him to obey, and Loram heaved himself up and went out. The door slammed behind them.

Reggie sank deeper into his chair, and smoke emerged from him in slow, large clouds. Though he sat there till all the hotel was silent, Loram did not come back. . . .

Mrs Fortune lay in bed, but she had not put out her candle, and she turned to look at her tardy husband. With a sleep-walking manner he kissed her. 'My poor girl. How was it?'

'It wasn't anything. The most ordinary small talk and patience and bridge.'

'Oh. There was bridge?'

'Yes, quite vigorous. Mrs Loram became alive then.'

'Like that. Well, well. What did you think of the family relations?'

'She—she's just negative: not a person. He's a tired man, but he was very much the husband. And an anxious father. The daughter's fierce, but she's afraid of him all the time. And I think he's frightened of her. They're careful; they hold themselves in.'

'You didn't care for 'em?'

Mrs Fortune's smooth brow puckered. 'I don't know.' She hesitated. 'I haven't a reason. No, I didn't. I thought they were all selfish. But I was sorry for them.'

'My dear girl.' Reggie smiled and kissed her again.

'You're not?'

'Not me, no. Not my job. But I like you, Joan. Rather a lot. That's all.'

He has sometimes speculated how the case would have worked out if Molly Loram had not snatched her father away from him that night. His usual comfortable conclusion is that the desperate fears which determined events were at that stage beyond his control. If Loram had dared to talk, no knowing what he would have said, or what could have been made of it. The end might have been worse.

When he came down in the morning, Loram was packing a rucksack in the hall with Molly's assistance. 'Takin' daughter off for another climb?' he asked.

'Not much,' said Molly. 'I had enough of him yesterday. There you are, Prof. Be good.'

'She's a lazy chit,' Loram told Reggie. 'You're staying on? See you tonight.' He strode heavily away.

'Where's he off to, Miss Loram?'

'Search me.' She lit a cigarette and sauntered off to the garage.

As Reggie sat at breakfast he saw her drive off alone. A few minutes afterwards another car stopped at the door, and he heard a voice, which he knew, asking for him. 'Well, well,' he sighed, to his wife's troubled eyes. 'The sleepers awake. They won't like that.'

He went out to see Superintendent Bell's square face pale and puffy about the eyes. 'My dear chap! What a glad surprise! Night in the train? You do go it, don't you?'

'More than one, sir,' Bell grunted. 'Never mind me.'

'Oh, my Bell! Breakfast?'

'I've had it. You finish yours. Then we might have a stroll.'

'Now,' said Reggie, and took his arm and walked him out. 'The hunt is up, what?'

'I wouldn't like to say that, Mr Fortune. But you were right about the newspaper stunt. It did fish up something worth looking into, after all.'

'No, don't say that. So bad for me. So sad for you.'

'Well, sir, a letter came in from a solicitor in Manchester, saying he'd acted for a woman answering to the description, and he thought it right to give information—he felt uneasy about her. She was a school teacher, name of Grace Tyson, living alone; no relations except an old uncle, retired publican, who died leaving her a bit of house property. That's how the solicitor came in—he was the uncle's executor. Well, he wanted her to take over the houses or invest. She wouldn't. She told him she was going to get married and live abroad, and she turned the estate into cash—matter of £4,000 or so—and resigned her school and quit. Now that was about a year ago. So we have a gap between her leaving Manchester and the earliest time the woman in Richmond Park could have died—say the whole summer.'

'Her honeymoon,' Reggie murmured.

'Ah. That's what I had in mind,' Bell growled. 'Man takes her and gets all she's got, and then wipes her out. It happens, don't it? And her doings about the money look like she's fallen for just that kind o' man.'

'Yes, I think so. Always did think so. Faculty of imitation very strong in the human race. I pointed that out to you.'

'You mean, Loram's first wife died convenient for him to have her money?' Bell frowned. 'And then this woman—and somebody puts us on to Loram. All very well—but there's pretty big differences. Loram lived with that first wife for years, and everybody knew all about 'em. Then he was living with his second wife all the time this woman was cashing her legacy and vanishing and dying. I grant you, men do live double lives————'

'I had noticed it.' Reggie smiled awry. 'Found evidence Loram was doubling?'

'Not to say evidence,' Bell grunted. 'That's where we get stopped, when we try for firm evidence. The case just conks out with a vague nasty smell about. Loram—they say he is a woman's man; he's thought to live above his means; he did have a spell in Paris last summer, and, beyond that, there's nothing to fix him. We've done work on the woman, and she's a teaser—one of the lonely ones. Of course they're the sort that give us these cases.'

'I know. Yes. The lonely woman.' Reggie drew a long breath. 'Make the world safe, don't we?'

'The friendless haven't got friends,' said Bell profoundly. 'There it is. This Grace Tyson don't seem to have let anybody really know her. The teachers at her school, and the people where she lodged—I've put 'em through it, I give you my word, and what have I got? Not one of 'em has a guess who the man was, where she found him, or anything. The other teachers say she had a down on any talk about men, kind of shy and disgusted.'

'Oh, yes. Yes. It would be like that.' Reggie's round face hardened. 'Just the woman to give herself to a brute.'

'Maybe. That don't help us, does it? Well, anyway, nobody ever heard a hint there was a man except this solicitor. When she gave notice to leave, she just said she was going abroad, and they knew she'd come into money and thought no more about it. When I told the head mistress Miss Tyson had married, she wouldn't hardly believe me, and one of the young ones told me it was the shock of their lives. Funny, isn't it? Looks to me like there wasn't going to be a marriage. She went off with a man who couldn't marry her.' Bell paused and looked keenly at Reggie. 'How does that fit in with your ideas, Mr Fortune?'

'Fits the facts,' Reggie murmured. 'Always did. Obvious probable possibility.'

'Ah. You had that in mind when you were talking to Mr Lomas over that Professor Loram story. I give it to you, you've been wonderful in this case.'

Reggie checked; his eyes grew round. 'Me?' he gave a short, bitter laugh. 'Not me, no. Somebody's been wonderful clever. Devilish clever. But not on our side, Bell. I'm the futile, gapin' spectator. And still do gape.'

'I wouldn't like to have you gaping on my track.' Bell met the pensive innocent stare with a grim face. 'What exactly did you come down here for? Just to have a look at Loram?'

'Yes, speakin' broadly. Loram and family. And the place. Recallin' connection of the corpse with mountains and sudden unexpected action of Loram in coming here.'

'Have you had any results?'

'Slight comfort to wounded self-respect. Feel sure I was right to look into Loram. Loram has the wind up. Loram's daughter has the wind up. And they're not lovin' each other. Confirmation of Cambridge scandal. She has a young man not approved by father. She is fierce. But that's all. Nothing definite. Same like you said. Facts fade out into a fishy fume.'

'Ah.' Bell gave him a queer look, searching, suspicious, but respectful. 'What about the dead woman's being a mountaineer and Loram nipping off to these mountains? You haven't made anything of that line?'

'Nothing effective. Loram's bothered about me being here. Loram's active on the mountains. That's all.'

'Is it? Would you be surprised to hear Grace Tyson was a mountain fan?'

'No. Some further comfort to humiliated mind. However.' He gazed at Bell, who was showing a sort of gloomy satisfaction. 'My dear chap! You don't mean to say you have a real, reliable fact? Come on.'

'I have.' Bell nodded. 'Seems to be the one thing anybody did know about her private life. Every holiday she was off to these mountains. Always alone, as far as they can say, and moving about, they believe. Hiking. She sent her landlady a card now and then—about sending on clothes, or when she was coming back and so forth—nothing to help. But the old girl remembers pictures of Buttermere and having to address parcels here.'

'Well, well.' Reggie sighed. 'A real fact, yes. Small fact. The mind is not wholly impotent.'

Bell glowered at him. 'Small! My oath, it gave me a jump when I got it. The way you see through things beats me. You————'

'My dear chap! Oh, my dear chap! I don't. Don't see my way now. Just accept the evidence and act on it. Havin' faith in the human reason.'

'It isn't reason,' said Bell gloomily, 'it's a gift. I said to myself you were just chancing your luck, giving evidence away to the papers, taking up that Loram scandal, following the fellow out to this off-the-map place—and then I get proof it's here we've got to work.'

'Gratifyin', yes. Not wonderful. Only showin' evidence is evidence and reason is reasonable. And we haven't got anywhere now.' He contemplated Bell. 'Oh. Something still up the official sleeve. Tell me all.'

'Well, sir, I think I may have a bit of a line,' Bell grinned. 'The landlady says she sent parcels here to an address—Old Scar. Stuck in her mind, being funny.'

'Miss Grace Tyson—at Old Scar,' Reggie said plaintively. 'Doesn't sound real. However. Try everything.' They turned back and proceeded briskly to the post office. The lady who presided there had never heard of any place called Old Scar. She suggested, in the best post official manner, that Bell should try Ulscar, which was a cottage on the track to Floutern Tarn. Reggie, who had remained behind Bell's broad shoulders, went out backwards. Bell caught him up, and demanded, 'What do you know about that?'

'Old man Ulph left his mark in the Lakes,' Reggie complained. 'Place called Ulpha. Lake called Ullswater. And a cottage called Ulscar.'

Bell made an impatient noise. 'I suppose you've been there already!'

'Never heard of it,' Reggie protested. He stopped, and pointed up to the right of the cascade of Sour Milk Gill and the red peak above. 'But she said it was on the Floutern Tarn track—which is that way—and last night, when Loram and daughter came down that waterfall, doing acrobatics, he said they'd been round by Floutern Tarn.'

'My oath!' Bell grunted. 'Looks like we are getting somewhere, don't it?'

'I wonder,' Reggie murmured. 'Well, well. Seek duty's iron crown. Come on.' He trudged away in earnest gloom between the lakes, along the marshy shore of Crummock, and up by the base of another roaring waterfall over a dull, sodden slope. 'Oh, my aunt!' he complained. 'The next time you have a walker murdered, don't tell me.'

'I didn't,' Bell chuckled. 'You made this case.'

'Grrh, I hate you. You shall finish it,' Reggie groaned. But in that he was wrong.

Though he walks nowhere unless he must, he came first to the whitewashed cottage of Ulscar. It stood lonely on the drab fell, but it displayed a printed card: 'Teas. Bed and Breakfast.' A young, trim woman opened the door to them. No, she could not give them lunch, but she had eggs and bread and butter and tea. She produced these in a kitchen with a stone floor which smelt of soap and mint. Bell talked to her like a father. Very nice and homely—she ought to get a lot of people. Eh, holiday times; a flock at Easter surely, but quiet enough mostly. Nobody much about just now? No, not to count on. Just a few dropping in for tea. There was some yesterday, but then, maybe, wouldn't be none for weeks. Nobody staying? Eh, you wouldn't look for it, only the holidays. Bell wondered if she remembered a Miss Grace Tyson used to come there.

She shook her head. Ah, no, she wouldn't know; her man only took the place last summer, when old John Ritson gave up—his wife dying. She bustled away.

'Like that.' Reggie looked at Bell under drooping eyelids.

'It would be,' Bell growled. 'Hopeless case.'

'Yes. The murderer has the luck. All the luck. However. People came to tea yesterday. And Loram and daughter were this way.' He glanced about the kitchen, he took a greasy quarto from the window-sill. It was the usual visitors' book of such a place.

People had testified to their eatings and drinkings, been facetious about one another with bad sketches and worse rhymes. Snapshots of the cottage, of scenery, of persons single and very much connected were pasted in. Reggie stopped turning the leaves. 'Oh!' He looked up at Bell. 'Page gone. Page of summer before last. Recently removed. Well, well.'

Bell examined the book. 'My oath! That's right,' he grunted. 'And the Lorams were this way yesterday. I'll have a talk with your Professor Loram.'

'Yes. That is indicated,' Reggie agreed, and lifted up his voice and asked if they could have some honey.

The woman hurried from her wash-house, apologetic; too bad she hadn't any—she was going to start bees presently. She thrust upon them various confections—apple cake, Eccles cakes, ginger-bread—and still apologized. Reggie consoled her—it was a noble spread—they would have to put their bit in her visitors' book—jolly book—he fluttered the leaves and read out jocose praise, and she beamed upon him. 'Hullo! Page been cut out.'

'Eh, you don't say.' She came to look. She was angry. 'Well, now did you ever? There's a pretty thing!'

'Too bad.' Reggie sympathized. 'Why should anybody?'

She took the book out of his hands. 'I lay it was for to steal a picture,' she muttered. 'There's fine pictures.' She turned the pages. 'Eh, eh, I don't miss no drawing as I remember. It'll be a photo, likely. Ay, that's it. There was a rare funny photo of two folks straddling the fall up along Sour Milk Gill, and that ain't here no more. What was the words to it now?—funny words, they was. Some'at like "grace and graceless". That's gone. That's been stole.'

'Well, well,' Reggie sighed. 'Who'd steal it?'

'How would I tell?' she exclaimed. 'Anybody as comes in might have the book same as you did. Nor I can't be watching 'em.'

'No. It would have to be like that,' Reggie murmured. 'Two folks in the stolen photo, you said. What sort of folks?'

'I dunno.' She stared. 'Just a man and woman.'

'You couldn't recognize 'em?'

'How could I? They was before my time.'

'You haven't had people like 'em here lately?'

'Eh, I see what you mean,' she cried, and pondered. 'No, I couldn't say at all. They was just like any visitors. Only it was a funny picture. I reckon that's what 'twas stole for. Folks ha'n't no conscience.'

'No. I'm afraid not. No,' Reggie said, and they departed.

'Maddening, ain't it?' Bell growled. 'We keep on getting a bit and then we're beat. Everything dies on us.'

'Yes, you may be right,' Reggie murmured. 'Are we down-hearted? Yes. Being a feeble folk. However. Not quite dead, this line. Strong reason to believe lady of the photograph was the vanished Grace. And there was a graceless man with her. And Loram and daughter came this way yesterday, returnin' by the fall where Grace and the graceless one straddled. And the photograph has been removed, same like Grace. Curious and interestin'. You do want to talk to our Lorams.'

'You bet I do,' said Bell, and they trudged down to the hotel.

But they were again frustrated. Loram had not come back. Molly Loram had come back but gone out again, taking her mother with her.

'Elusive, aren't they?' Reggie condoled with Bell's gloom. 'Yes. My dear old thing. A drop of sleep would do you no harm. You're nearly all in.' And Bell, having been compelled to a bedroom, Reggie wandered away to the post office, where he used the telephone to Cambridge. . . .

Behold him, then, recumbent in a deck-chair, at its lowest pitch, contemplating the admirable profile of his wife and a background of golden sunset sky. Molly Loram drove up with her mother, but without her father. The archdeacon was heard remarking on that, and being snubbed. . . .

Bell came out, looking ashamed of himself. 'I have had a nap,' he apologized. 'Getting old, I suppose.' He gave Reggie a solemn questioning glance.

'Oh, no. No. Only wise. Same like Napoleon. When nothing to do—sleep till there is.'

'I don't know about Napoleon,' Bell lamented. 'Helpless, I'd say.'

'You're so proud,' said Mrs Fortune. 'Proud, earnest men. Too much conscience, Reggie.'

'Yes. I know. That hampers me.' They made fun of each other, and Bell did his best to play that game till it was time to change. . . .

Dinner was begun without any Lorams. Most people had nearly finished before mother and daughter came to their table. The archdeacon made a fuss of asking where the professor was, and Molly answered furiously, 'I should worry. One of his long hikes'; and her mother said he was so thoughtless.

The archdeacon tried to carry on the conversation. Loram said in the morning he was going to revisit the scene of his old exploits. He wondered if that meant climbing.

'Oh, don't bother,' Molly laughed. 'Leave him alone and he'll come home, bringing his tail behind him.' She turned the coldest of slim shoulders on the archdeacon, and ate fast. . . .

Bell and Reggie stood in the darkness in front of the hotel. The archdeacon had gathered a little congregation in the porch, and was preaching on the dangers of the mountains. Reggie glanced back into the light of the hall and gave Bell a nod. Molly and her mother were going upstairs.

Bell followed them. 'Excuse me, Miss Loram.' He touched her arm as they reached the first floor. 'I want to speak to you.' She took her mother into a bedroom and shut the door. He tapped at it.

After a minute she came out again. 'What is it? Who are you?'

'This way, please.' He pointed her across the corridor to a sitting-room, where Reggie stood waiting. She flashed a glance from one to the other, and obeyed him. 'I'm Superintendent Bell of the Metropolitan Police, Miss Loram. This is Mr Fortune. I may tell you that I came here to investigate a case of death.'

She stood between them, straining to her full height, slim shoulders up, hands clenched. Her pretty face was drawn and sharp and flushed crimson. She tossed back her mop of red hair. 'What death?' she cried.

'I want to know why your father went off this morning,' Bell answered.

'Don't be silly. He does a hike every day.'

'You went with him yesterday. Why not today?'

'He said he'd be going too hard for me.'

'Ah. Where was he going?'

'I don't know,' she said fiercely. 'That's all he told me.'

Bell frowned at her. 'Funny he hasn't come back by now, eh?'

'Just like him,' she declared.

'It don't worry you?' Bell grunted. 'Where have you been?'

'Out in the car. I haven't seen him.'

'I said where?'

'Oh, over the fell road, Eskdale way, in the morning. After lunch, I took Fram—I took my stepmother to Keswick.' There was a glow in her hazel eyes as she stared back at Bell's stolid, intent face. 'Anything else?'

'Yes, I think so,' Reggie murmured, and she swung round to confront him, 'About yesterday, Miss Loram. You went up to Ulscar with your father. Why?'

She seemed to be startled and puzzled. She bit her lip. 'I don't know where you mean. We went up by Floutern Tarn, and came down over Red Pike by the gill.'

'I know. I wondered about that. Taking a chance, what?'

She laughed contempt. 'Oh, if you listen to that old woman of a parson! It's nothing of a place. The Prof. wanted a scramble—don't blame him—the rest is the dullest drag.'

'Then why go that way? Why go to Ulscar?'

'You keep saying Ulscar! What is it? I never heard of it.'

'Really? Name of the tea cottage.'

'That hole! What about it?'

'The visitors' book,' Reggie murmured. 'What was on the leaf that's been cut out?'

'I don't know anything about the blinking book,' she cried.

'Oh. But you went there. You looked at it. Well?'

'I didn't. The Prof. would stop and have a go of milk. Something about old time's sake, he said. I don't know what he looked at. I was playing with the dog.'

'Well, well.' Reggie sighed. 'Nothing else you'd like to tell me?'

'There is not!' She was vehement. 'What is all this for? You said you were investigating a death. What death?'

'Woman's death. Woman who died last autumn.'

'What woman?'

'Did you ever hear of Grace Tyson?'

'No. Nobody I know. Nobody I ever knew.'

'I didn't ask that,' Reggie murmured.

'Well, I never heard of her,' she said defiantly.

'Oh. Did you go to see someone when you drove Eskdale way?'

She frowned at him; she compressed her lips. 'Yes, of course I did. A friend of mine's been in Wasdale for a bit and just going back. I wanted to look him up before he went.'

'Oh, yes. Friend who looked you up yesterday? Friend of the family?'

'You are being clever,' she jeered. 'Quite right. One of the Prof.'s old students—Jock Elliot.'

'Not clever, no, only careful.' Reggie sighed. 'Thanks very much.

That's all, Miss Loram.' He opened the door for her, and she swept out with a toss of her red head.

'She knows something,' Bell growled.

'Quite a lot, yes.' Reggie dropped into a chair and lit his pipe.

'Hard—my oath, girls can be hard!'

'You think so?' Reggie let a long stream of smoke out of the corner of his mouth. '"It is fear, O little hunter, it is fear."'

All night there were lights burning in the hotel, for Professor Loram did not come back. . . .

Soon after dawn Reggie and Bell and a long-legged inspector of the county police tramped away up the valley. The inspector set a brisk pace, but was lugubrious. 'I ought to warn you, gentlemen, I have no great hopes of this myself. The one bit of information you've got where he meant to go is the parson telling us he said he was going to look at the scene of his old exploits and remembering he used to climb on the Pillar Rock. That's all very well. But you can bet it wasn't the only place he'd climbed. There's the Gable just as handy, to go no further. And besides, by what you say, seems likely he meant to do a bunk.'

'Yes, it could be,' Reggie murmured. 'However. Try everything.'

'I grant you, we've got to make a search,' the inspector grumbled. 'I only say trying the Pillar is just blind guesswork.'

'Oh, no. Rational choice. The archdeacon thought he meant Pillar. And Pillar's the nearest high mountain to Ulscar. Only mountain near where dwarf willow would be likely to grow.'

'What's that?' The inspector laboured in thought. 'I don't rightly get it. Dwarf willow—the plant you found in the dead woman's bag—very rare, I'm told.'

'That is so. Only grows above 2,500 feet. Even then rare. But it might grow on Pillar.'

'This is beyond me. Maybe it does. But why the deuce should Loram have gone after it?'

'Take it he was bothered about the dead woman—bothered about a woman who'd been at Ulscar—and wanted to verify—well?'

'All right. If you think you understand, I don't. But we have to search—so we may as well begin this way.' The inspector looked with grim humour at Reggie's shape, which is not lithe. 'I warn you, you're in for a doing.' He strode out.

'The offensive expert.' Reggie moaned to Bell's ear. 'Despising the natural man.'

The inspector vanished into a farmhouse at the head of the lake, and came out again to report that a lad there thought he'd seen a gentleman going up Scarf Gap yesterday morning, alone. 'You'll note that don't mean much.'

'Nothing does, does it?' Reggie said bitterly.

'I believe you.' The inspector went on up the steep stony zigzags of a pass.

When Reggie reached the summit and sank down, panting, he was already far down the other side. 'Expert showin' off his futile expertise,' he complained, and surveyed the landscape. A deep valley lay below them, and on its far side a mountain, the top of which loomed through fleeting mist like a dome, on whose side stood isolated a tall crag. 'Oh, yes, Pillar and Pillar Rock. As in the book of the words. To resume'—he went on down into the valley.

The inspector was seen going into a small cottage. Bell made haste after him. Thankfully Reggie sat down again. They returned. 'That place is a Youth Hostel, sir,' Bell told him. 'There's a couple of lads, hiking, spent the night there. They saw some man round the Pillar Rock as they came up the valley in the evening. That's all they know.'

'N.B.G.,' the inspector growled. 'Well, come on. Best take it from the bottom.'

Having trudged some way along the welcome level of the valley, Reggie was led across the stream and up again through a young plantation of firs by a path which steepened sharply. The black crag of the Rock loomed close above, its ledges and gullies scraped pale and red by the scars of boot-nails. He heard through the throb of pulse and lung a hoarse shout, and forced himself on faster.

'My oath, you were right, sir,' Bell called to him.

At the base of the Rock, Loram lay, and his head was dabbled with blood, and flies buzzed about it where it was crushed out of shape.

Reggie stood still, mopped the sweat out of his eyes, got his breath back, gazed down at the body, gazed up at the Rock. 'Right?' he muttered. 'You said right. Well, well!' He knelt by the body. . . .

He sat back on his heels and looked up at them, and his face was without expression. 'Cause of death, injury to brain from extensive fractures of skull. Also various bones broken. Time of death, round about twelve hours ago. Say yesterday evening.'

'That's when the lads saw him at the Rock.' The inspector nodded. 'There we are. He tried a climb alone, and he fell, eh?'

'Yes, it could be,' Reggie murmured. 'On the medical evidence.' He laughed. 'Useful stuff, medical evidence. Just the right kind of death for a fall from that thing. Why are we, Bell?'

'Eh, not much need for a doctor,' the inspector agreed cheerfully. 'Plain enough. And he's not the first we've had here. Well, I'll go get some people.' Off he went.

'Not the first,' Reggie laughed. 'Woman at Richmond Park wasn't the first.'

'You're not satisfied, sir?' Bell frowned.

'Satisfied!' Reggie's voice rose shrill. 'God help us!' An invocation he is not wont to use. He bent over the body again and searched the pockets. A wallet came out, with some notes in it; a letter or two, insignificant; a small diary—from that fell a scrap of a twig: tiny buds of bright green leaves, round, serrated. Reggie held it out on the palm of his hand. 'Dwarf willow,' he murmured.

'Like you said,' Bell frowned. 'But what then?'

'He didn't get it on that Rock. It wouldn't grow there. He'd been higher. On the mountain.'

Bell watched him gaze up at it with a queer wistful look. His round face had the expression of a child wanting the cruel, difficult world to be kind. He wandered away; he vanished, scrambling among boulders round the mountainside.

Some two hours afterwards Bell reached the flat mossy summit, and peered about through swirls of mist which let him see glimpses of combe and crag only to hide them again. He strode to and fro; he shouted often. At last a faint shout answered, and he strode towards the sound and saw Reggie sitting in a hollow. 'My oath! You shouldn't have gone off like this,' he complained. 'You've given me a nasty half hour. Been wondering if you had taken a toss too.'

'My Bell! Sorry,' Reggie said affectionately. 'Not me. No. I am careful. It's the only use I can be.' He gave a queer short laugh. 'Just doin' a little botany. Fine natural rock garden, this combe. Sedums, saxifrages, all sorts. Look at that.' He pointed to a place where the earth between the rocks had been disturbed and a tiny shrub appeared with a broken twig. 'I didn't do that. And it's dwarf willow. The scrap Loram took fits the break.'

'Good God!' Bell muttered.

'Yes. As you say. See that too.' He pointed to dark flecks on a sedum. 'I didn't do that either. And I should say it's blood. Well, well. We will now collect the exhibits.' He dug up the little shrub; he cut off the blood-stained leaves.

Bell watched him a moment and turned away to peer down the precipitous combe. Pillar Rock stood close beside. 'What can you make of it?' he grunted. 'You've got good evidence he was here and had a fall here, but then, where we found him is pretty close below. How are you going to prove he didn't just stumble down here and then fall over?'

'I haven't the slightest idea,' Reggie mumbled, preparing his exhibits for transport. 'I should say we never shall. And yet he didn't stumble. He didn't fall. Not by accident. Isn't that nice? Well, well. On with the dance.' He shocked Bell by a performance of some waltz steps. He gave a little shrill laugh. 'Just doing our stuff. We've got to.'

'What's in your mind, sir?'

As they tramped away Reggie told him, and has always maintained that he told all there was. Bell was then convinced, Bell agreed, but has since had doubts.

The mist darkened and drove at them in cold rain.

When they came back to the hotel, the inspector met them with a condescending sarcastic smile for Reggie's sodden weariness. 'You have made a day of it, Mr Fortune. I've been here a couple of hours. Well, I told these poor ladies. They took it very hard, as you'd look for. There's nothing more for me to do here. I'll be————'

'Yes, there is,' Bell interrupted. 'You come along with me,' and walked him away.

Reggie went upstairs. As he reached the landing, Molly Loram came out of her mother's room. 'Well?' she demanded.

'I'm sorry,' Reggie said gravely, and pointed her into the sitting-room where she had been questioned the night before.

'He fell from Pillar Rock, didn't he?' She was breathless.

'He was found dead at the bottom.'

'Well, then!'

'No. It isn't well.'

'What do you mean?'

'Have you heard from Elliot?'

She gasped; she stammered. 'How—how could I? He went away yesterday. He's motoring. He wouldn't know.'

'You needn't tell him. That's all, Miss Loram.'

Reggie left her. . . .

In the morning Bell tapped at Reggie's door and brought him out of bed to hear that Elliot had been found: 'They picked him up in his rooms in London last night. Told him the police here wanted him for the inquest on Loram. He said he didn't know Loram was dead; he couldn't give any evidence about it. But he didn't refuse to come. He's on his way now. We'll have him in Cockermouth this afternoon.'

'And you waked me up to tell me that,' Reggie mourned. 'Oh, my Bell! Carry on. On with the dance.' . . .

Mr Jock Elliot sat down in a bare room at the police station, and was told portentously by the inspector that the gentleman was Super-intendent Bell from Scotland Yard.

'At your service.' Elliot nodded, and arranged his heavy frame more comfortably. 'But I'd better say at once, I don't see how I can be of any use to you.'

'Well, I hope you're wrong,' Bell grunted, studying a paper.

Elliot's long face watched him, carelessly, contemptuously. 'Go ahead.'

Bell looked up. 'It must have been a great shock to you, Professor Loram's sudden death.'

'Rather. Good man. No better in his own line, and years of work in him. Damnable bad luck. Rotten for his wife.'

'He was a great friend of yours?'

'I worked under him. He was very decent to me.'

'When did you see him last?'

'Oh, Lord, a long while ago. I haven't seen him for ages. Not since the last time I was in Cambridge. That would be twelve months back.'

'Had you got on bad terms with him?'

'Nothing of the sort!' Elliot gave an angry laugh. 'What the devil put that in your head?'

'The facts,' said Bell stolidly. 'My information is, you used to be his favourite student. But you say you haven't seen him for ages. You've just been on holiday here a few miles away from where he was, and yet you didn't care to meet one another. Why not?'

'I don't know about him. I dare say he didn't know I was in Wasdale.'

'Why were you?' Bell asked.

'Just snatching a few days on the mountains.'

'Ah! Know this country well, don't you?'

'Fair. I like it for a short spell.'

'Loram didn't know you were down here, you suggest. But you knew he was. Why didn't you look him up?'

'No dam' time.'

'You had time to meet his daughter,' said Bell.

Elliot laughed again, but his eyes were watchful. 'A fellow makes time to meet a girl.'

'That way, was it? You and her have an attachment?'

'What do you take me for? I shan't answer that without Miss Loram's permission.'

'Very proper.' Bell nodded. 'Anyhow, you two did meet. On the morning of the day Loram died she came over to Wasdale to you. The day before he died you went over to Buttermere to her. Now, Mr Elliot, did anything pass between you to explain Loram's actions down here?'

Elliot's black brows went up in surprise. 'I don't understand the question.'

'Oh, I'm sorry. Well, what did she say about her father?'

'Nothing much.' Elliot sniggered. 'Naturally, we didn't talk about him. I gathered he was being rather queer and trying. They never hit it off. Loram could be quite unaccountable. A kink somewhere in him. Always hard going for his women.'

'I see. That kind of man.' Bell nodded. 'Any idea what he was up to on these last walks of his?'

'How do you mean? I don't know where he was walking. Why shouldn't he walk? He always did.'

'I take it you want to help us to the truth about Loram, Mr Elliot?' Bell gave him a solemn, searching stare.

'Of course I do.'

'Very good.' Bell studied his paper, folded it up and put it away. 'I have to tell you we're not satisfied with Miss Loram's account of his doings—the round she had with him the day before he died, or why he went off without her the next day. Now you knew him—no one better. You'd been with him in these parts. I want you to come out with me to Buttermere and go over some of the ground she says they went and give me your ideas. See?'

'I don't see any use in it,' Elliot said slowly.

'That's for me to judge.'

'All right.' Elliot shrugged. 'I've no earthly objection. Don't blame me if it's a flop.' . . .

In the hall of the hotel at Buttermere a man sat with a camera on his knees. The telephone rang, and he was called to it and took a message for Mr Fortune.

Reggie knocked at Molly Loram's door. 'This is about the time, isn't it?' he said. She came out, thrust past him, hurried out of the hotel, and away towards the lake. He followed her, and the man with the camera followed him. As they did not catch her up she stood still and waited. 'Thanks very much,' he murmured. 'No hurry.'

'Oh, you're maddening. For God's sake, let's get it over.'

'I meant this was about the time you come down the gill with your father the other day,' he drawled. 'You quite understand, what? You're going to show me just where he stopped and looked at the waterfall and the rocks. You can't forget. Light's the same now. Then we'll take a photograph of the place. You won't make any mistake, will you? It wouldn't do.'

'Do you think you're frightening me?' she cried.

'Not me, no,' said Reggie. She made haste on. 'We won't go up the waterfall,' he told her. 'The safe path, please'; and he followed at his own pace. . . .

Bell and the inspector drove out with Elliot, left their car in the village, and walked away up the path to the cottage of Ulscar. 'Do you mean to say Loram spent a day on this sort of thing?' Elliot made a gesture at the featureless, drab slope.

'Didn't Miss Loram tell you?' Bell answered.

Elliot shook his head. 'It looks like the dullest trudge in the Lakes. I suppose Loram wasn't in condition and wanted an easy day—training walk, you know—and then felt he'd got himself fit enough to have a go at Pillar. Just the sort of way fellows' minds do work. Everybody wants to go big as soon as they can—and sooner. Poor old chap!'

'Ah! Accidents do come like that,' Bell agreed. 'You've never been round this way yourself?'

'Not me.' Elliot laughed. 'I like to get high and stay there.'

'Yes, I see what you mean,' Bell said. 'But Miss Loram says this is the way they did go. I suppose she's telling the truth.'

Elliot looked at him. 'Why the devil shouldn't she?'

Bell left that without an answer. They tramped on in silence till they were near Ulscar. 'She says he went in there and had a drink o' milk,' Bell remarked. 'Know anything about the place?'

'Never saw it before,' Elliot laughed. 'Never heard of it.'

'Takes visitors, I'm told,' Bell grunted. 'But you wouldn't know whether Loram had ever stayed there.'

Elliot shook his head. 'Not for certain. To hear him talk, you'd think he stayed at every shanty in the Lakes.'

'H'm.' Bell grunted. 'There's a visitors' book, but it's been cut about. Pity.'

'Why, they generally are. What's it matter?'

'You never know,' said Bell. While they were talking, the inspector had fallen behind. 'Well, somewhere here Loram and the girl turned up towards that red mountain—so she says. Not a usual round, I'm told.'

'Oh, anything does for a training walk,' Elliot answered.

The inspector, now out of their sight, went into the cottage.

'I can't see what good it is to go over the ground,' Elliot complained.

'Just want to get your ideas about why they picked it,' Bell told him. 'Might be very helpful.' . . .

Reggie came along the mountainside to the top of the waterfall of Sour Milk Gill. Molly stood there, her small, thin face flushed, her bosom beating fast, her hands clenched. 'How feeble you are!' she cried.

'You think so?' Reggie looked at his wrist-watch, turned and surveyed the ravine of the fall. Swollen by the night's rain the stream roared down in gleaming masses of water between clouds of white foam and still, black pools. Rocks broke bare from it, and were hidden again. It vanished to a sheer descent, flashed out again, and again vanished to appear far below, spreading wide and white. 'And you went down there,' he murmured. 'You were in a hurry.'

'There's more water coming down today,' she snapped.

'Is there? Yes, you may be right. Well, well.' He swung round, gazed at her and beyond her. Two men were coming round the shoulder of the mountain—Bell and Elliot, and Elliot was looking back. 'Where was it your father stopped?' Reggie asked sharply. She pointed to a place where the stream was held in a narrow, deep channel between rock walls before a long leap down. 'Do what he did, please.'

She moved slowly along the rock till she came to the sheer edge. There she stopped and glared at Reggie. 'He did that first one side and then the other. Then he stood here, one foot each side.'

'Straddled across,' Reggie drawled. 'Yes. Could you do that?'

'Of course I could.' She put out a slim leg.

'Stand fast,' he called.

Elliot came plunging down with a cry, 'Molly! What the devil are you doing?'

'Mr Jock Elliot, I presume?' Reggie smiled. 'Good. Photographer all ready for you. Stand where Miss Loram is. Straddlin' the stream.'

'Give your orders.' Elliot scowled at him, scowled at Molly. 'I'd like to know what sort of trick you think you're playing.'

'You do,' Reggie said.

Bell and the inspector came hurrying down with the woman of Ulscar. 'Do you recognize this place, ma'am?' Bell was saying.

'Eh, sure enough,' she panted. 'Here's where the picture was took.

'Ay, ay, and that fellow'—she pointed at Elliot—'that fellow was up to my place t'other night, in the gloaming, for a tea. I lay it's him as stole the picture from me.'

'Do you recognize him for the man in the picture?' Bell asked.

She stood silent, puckering her eyes at Elliot's red rage. 'The clothes is different,' she said slowly.

'The hell they are!' Elliot roared. 'I was never in any dam' picture of yours.'

'Don't you think to bully me.' She came a step nearer. 'Eh, it's the same make o' man, and the long face of him—the long, cruel face. But yon's not the lass.'

'No. That was Grace,' said Reggie. 'Grace who was murdered. Now you know, Miss Loram.'

She gave a cry; she shrank back from Elliot with a look of misery and loathing. 'Don't be a fool, Molly.' He laughed. 'It's a muddle-headed bluff. Grace was your father's woman.'

'Try again,' said Reggie.

'Oho!' Elliot turned, sneering. 'She wasn't the first of his women who had bad luck. Don't you know that?'

'You—you beast,' Molly gasped, and struck at him. He beat her off with such a blow that she reeled and fell.

'That'll do, thank you,' said Reggie, grappling with him. Elliot broke free and plunged away. Reggie dived for his feet. He went headlong down the fall.

'Look after the girl,' Reggie spluttered as he rose; he made for the edge of the rocks and lowered himself down. They heard crash and splash, then a shout.

'Can't see him. Got away. No sign of him down here. Cut across to the path. Quick!' The police photographer obeyed.

'Ay, that's the way,' the inspector told Bell. 'He could never do the Gill with this head o' water.' They left Molly to the woman of Ulscar, and lumbered away slanting down the mountainside. . . .

Through the mists of a chill night Bell came back to the hotel. Mr Fortune was then spread before the fire in the lounge, an inch of ash on his cigar, his round face sleepily benign. Bell stood before him, dank and muddy to the hair. Mr Fortune's eyes opened. 'My dear chap!' he sympathized.

'We haven't found the fellow,' Bell growled. 'God knows where he's got to. Nobody seems to have seen him come down. Can't do any more tonight.'

'Oh, no. No. All clear.'

'What?' Bell glowered. 'You mean we're bound to catch him? Of course we are. He hasn't a chance. But what then? Do you see your way? I don't.'

'Yes. I think so.' Reggie smiled. 'Thought so some time. Opinion kindly confirmed today by our Mr Elliot. Course of events now quite plain. Loram did well out of the death of his first wife. I should say that was quite natural. But Loram was left with one fortune and free to marry another. Which impressed Mr Elliot's nice mind. I don't suppose he ever thought it was a natural death. And, as I was saying, man is an imitative animal. Mr Elliot found a lonely woman with money. Grace Tyson. Loram had seen 'em together up here at Ulscar. When some thoughtful humorist photographed 'em, Elliot married Grace—or didn't—and took her and her money to Paris. I told you Cambridge can confirm he was there last summer, supposed to be doing research; we know Loram was there too. I should say Loram saw Grace with the graceless one. Confirmin' his lack of love for Elliot as a son-in-law. Elliot made an end of poor Grace neat and skilful, and was ready to take on Molly. Then I bothered him with my little proof Grace was a mountain walker. He put in that bold counter—Loram murdered the first Mrs Loram. Rather too bold. Loram also sat up and took notice when he read about my arctic willow. He wanted to connect Grace with that and with Elliot. But he was frightened too. He knew there was scandal about his first wife's death: not anxious to appear in a case of another woman found dead. Well, he hurried off here to make sure of the evidence, found the snapshot at Ulscar, went up to the Gill where it was taken, and then went off to Pillar to see if Grace could have got arctic willow there—I take it he knew she used to go up that side. All right. But Elliot had his eye very sharp on Loram—heard he'd come here, and followed good and quick. He looked up Molly. She told him about going to Ulscar and Sour Milk Gill. So he nipped up to Ulscar and eliminated the snapshot. Next morning she was meeting her Elliot again. Where was father? Off by himself, most likely Pillar way. That was enough for our Mr Elliot. He took action. Loram was flung down Pillar, and Elliot went off in his sports car. Rather misjudging my humble abilities. There you are.'

Bell stood steaming in front of the fire. 'Ah. All very well. I don't doubt everything did happen just like you say. How are we going to prove it?'

'Oh, my Bell!' Reggie laughed gently. 'Find our Mr Elliot. He's all the proof you want.'

'I don't see it,' Bell growled. 'I grant you, he cracked today————'

'Yes, quite nicely, yes,' Reggie murmured.

'But that's not evidence to convict him. It's a hopeless case.'

'You think so? Well, well. Go away. Go and change. Go and dine. Go and sleep. And tomorrow is another day.' Bell went heavily out. . . .

In the morning Reggie was sitting with Mrs Fortune in the hotel garden where daffodils danced to the music of thrush and willow wren. With a faint smile he gazed across the grey-green lake to the white water in the rocks of Sour Milk Gill. High up there, men were moving. . . .

Bell came slowly back to the hotel, saw Mr and Mrs Fortune, and stood still and stared and coughed. Reggie beckoned to him, but he shook his head and waited. 'Oh, my hat!' Reggie sighed. 'The mysterious expert,' and went to him.

'You were wrong, sir.' Bell spoke in a low voice, studying him with solemn eyes.

'Oh. When?'

'When you said Elliot had got out of that waterfall. He hadn't. We've found him in the pool just below.'

'Well, well. So that is that,' Reggie murmured.

'Ah.' Bell's eyes were sombrely intent on him. 'He was lying there in the water, with some rocks on top of him. I should say he lay there stunned till he was drowned.'

'Yes, it could be,' said Reggie cheerfully. 'Simple medical question. Want me to do the post-mortem?'

'Do you want to?' Bell put grim emphasis on the question.

'As you please. Don't matter who does it. Can't tell you anything. I may as well finish off the case.'

'My oath!' Bell muttered. 'I'll say you have.'

Reggie laughed and went back to Mrs Fortune. 'These experts, Joan!' he murmured. 'All over. "And then my heart with pleasure fills, and dances with the daffodils."' She gave him a queer look of awe. 'My dear girl! Not like that, no.' He smiled at her. 'Just the natural man.'

FREEMAN WILLS CROFTS · 1879–1957

The Mystery of the Sleeping-Car Express

No one who was in England in the autumn of 1909 can fail to
remember the terrible tragedy which took place in a North-Western
express between Preston and Carlisle. The affair attracted enormous
attention at the time, not only because of the arresting nature of the
events themselves, but even more for the absolute mystery in which
they were shrouded.

Quite lately a singular chance has revealed to me the true explanation of the terrible drama, and it is at the express desire of its chief
actor that I now take upon myself to make the facts known. As it is a
long time since 1909, I may, perhaps, be pardoned if I first recall the
events which came to light at the time.

One Thursday, then, early in November of the year in question,
the 10.30 p.m. sleeping-car train left Euston as usual for Edinburgh,
Glasgow, and the North. It was generally a heavy train, being popular
with business men who liked to complete their day's work in London,
sleep while travelling, and arrive at their northern destination with
time for a leisurely bath and breakfast before office hours. The night
in question was no exception to the rule, and two engines hauled
behind them eight large sleeping-cars, two firsts, two thirds, and two
vans, half of which went to Glasgow, and the remainder to
Edinburgh.

It is essential to the understanding of what follows that the
composition of the rear portion of the train should be remembered.
At the extreme end came the Glasgow van, a long eight-wheeled,
bogie vehicle, with Guard Jones in charge. Next to the van was one of
the third-class coaches, and immediately in front of it came a first-
class, both labelled for the same city. These coaches were fairly well
filled, particularly the third-class. In front of the first-class came the
last of the four Glasgow sleepers. The train was corridor throughout,
and the officials could, and did, pass through it several times during
the journey.

It is with the first-class coach that we are principally concerned,
and it will be understood from the above that it was placed in between

the sleeping-car in front and the third-class behind, the van following immediately behind the third. It had a lavatory at each end and six compartments, the last two, next the third-class, being smokers, the next three non-smoking, and the first, immediately beside the sleeping car, a 'Ladies only'. The corridors in both it and the third-class coach were on the left-hand side in the direction of travel—that is, the compartments were on the side of the double line.

The night was dark as the train drew out of Euston, for there was no moon and the sky was overcast. As was remembered and commented on afterwards, there had been an unusually long spell of dry weather, and, though it looked like rain earlier in the evening, none fell till the next day, when, about six in the morning, there was a torrential downpour.

As the detectives pointed out later, no weather could have been more unfortunate from their point of view, as, had footmarks been made during the night, the ground would have been too hard to take good impressions, while even such traces as remained would more than likely have been blurred by the rain.

The train ran to time, stopping at Rugby, Crewe, and Preston. After leaving the latter station Guard Jones found he had occasion to go forward to speak to a ticket-collector in the Edinburgh portion. He accordingly left his van in the rear and passed along the corridor of the third-class carriage adjoining.

At the end of this corridor, beside the vestibule joining it to the first-class, were a lady and gentleman, evidently husband and wife, the lady endeavouring to soothe the cries of a baby she was carrying. Guard Jones addressed some civil remark to the man, who explained that their child had been taken ill, and they had brought it out of their compartment as it was disturbing the other passengers.

With an expression of sympathy, Jones unlocked the two doors across the corridor at the vestibule between the carriages, and, passing on into the first-class coach, re-closed them behind him. They were fitted with spring locks, which became fast on the door shutting.

The corridor of the first-class coach was empty, and as Jones walked down it he observed that the blinds of all the compartments were lowered, with one exception—that of the 'Ladies Only'. In this compartment, which contained three ladies, the light was fully on, and the guard noticed that two out of the three were reading.

Continuing his journey, Jones found that the two doors at the vestibule between the first-class coach and the sleeper were also locked, and he opened them and passed through, shutting them behind him. At the sleeping-car attendant's box, just inside the last of these doors, two car attendants were talking together. One was actually inside the box, the other standing in the corridor. The latter moved aside to let the guard pass, taking up his former position as, after exchanging a few words, Jones moved on.

His business with the ticket-collector finished, Guard Jones returned to his van. On this journey he found the same conditions obtaining as on the previous—the two attendants were at the rear end of the sleeping-car, the lady and gentleman with the baby in the front end of the third-class coach, the first-class corridor deserted, and both doors at each end of the latter coach locked. These details, casually remarked at the time, became afterwards of the utmost importance, adding as they did to the mystery in which the tragedy was enveloped.

About an hour before the train was due at Carlisle, while it was passing through the wild moorland country of the Westmorland highlands, the brakes were applied—at first gently, and then with considerable power. Guard Jones, who was examining parcel way-bills in the rear end of his van, supposed it to be a signal check, but as such was unusual at this place, he left his work and, walking down the van, lowered the window at the left-hand side and looked out along the train.

The line happened to be in a cutting, and the railway bank for some distance ahead was dimly illuminated by the light from the corridors of the first- and third-class coaches immediately in front of his van. As I have said, the night was dark, and, except for this bit of bank, Jones could see nothing ahead. The railway curved away to the right, so, thinking he might see better from the other side, he crossed the van and looked out of the opposite window, next the up line.

There were no signal lights in view, nor anything to suggest the cause of the slack, but as he ran his eye along the train he saw that something was amiss in the first-class coach. From the window at its rear end figures were leaning, gesticulating wildly, as if to attract attention to some grave and pressing danger. The guard at once ran through the third-class to this coach, and there he found a strange and puzzling state of affairs.

The corridor was still empty, but the centre blind of the rear compartment—that is, the first reached by the guard—had been raised. Through the glass Jones could see that the compartment contained four men. Two were leaning out of the window on the opposite side, and two were fumbling at the latch of the corridor door, as if trying to open it. Jones caught hold of the outside handle to assist, but they pointed in the direction of the adjoining compartment, and the guard, obeying their signs, moved on to the second door.

The centre blind of this compartment had also been pulled up, though here, again, the door had not been opened. As the guard peered in through the glass he saw that he was in the presence of a tragedy.

Tugging desperately at the handle of the corridor door stood a lady, her face blanched, her eyes starting from her head, and her features frozen into an expression of deadly fear and horror. As she pulled she kept glancing over her shoulder, as if some dreadful apparition lurked in the shadows behind. As Jones sprang forward to open the door his eyes followed the direction of her gaze, and he drew in his breath sharply.

At the far side of the compartment, facing the engine and huddled down in the corner, was the body of a woman. She lay limp and inert, with head tilted back at an unnatural angle into the cushions and a hand hanging helplessly down over the edge of the seat. She might have been thirty years of age, and was dressed in a reddish-brown fur coat with toque to match. But these details the guard hardly glanced at, his attention being riveted to her forehead. There, above the left eyebrow, was a sinister little hole, from which the blood had oozed down the coat and formed a tiny pool on the seat. That she was dead was obvious.

But this was not all. On the seat opposite her lay a man, and, as far as Guard Jones could see, he also was dead.

He apparently had been sitting in the corner seat, and had fallen forward so that his chest lay across the knees of the woman and his head hung down towards the floor. He was all bunched and twisted up—just a shapeless mass in a grey frieze overcoat, with dark hair at the back of what could be seen of his head. But under that head the guard caught the glint of falling drops, while a dark, ominous stain grew on the floor beneath.

Jones flung himself on the door, but it would not move. It stood fixed, an inch open, jammed in some mysterious way, imprisoning the lady with her terrible companions.

As she and the guard strove to force it open, the train came to a standstill. At once it occurred to Jones that he could now enter the compartment from the opposite side.

Shouting to reassure the now almost frantic lady, he turned back to the end compartment, intending to pass through it on to the line and so back to that containing the bodies. But here he was again baffled, for the two men had not succeeded in sliding back their door. He seized the handle to help them, and then he noticed their companions had opened the opposite door and were climbing out on to the permanent way.

It flashed through his mind that an up-train passed about this time, and, fearing an accident, he ran down the corridor to the sleeping-car, where he felt sure he would find a door that would open. That at the near end was free, and he leaped out on to the track. As he passed he shouted to one of the attendants to follow him, and to the other to remain where he was and let no one pass. Then he joined the men who had already alighted, warned them about the up-train, and the four opened the outside door of the compartment in which the tragedy had taken place.

Their first concern was to get the uninjured lady out, and here a difficult and ghastly task awaited them. The door was blocked by the bodies, and its narrowness prevented more than one man from working. Sending the car attendant to search the train for a doctor, Jones clambered up, and, after warning the lady not to look at what he was doing, he raised the man's body and propped it back in the corner seat.

The face was a strong one with clean-shaven but rather coarse features, a large nose, and a heavy jaw. In the neck, just below the right ear, was a bullet hole which, owing to the position of the head, had bled freely. As far as the guard could see, the man was dead. Not without a certain shrinking, Jones raised the feet, first of the man, and then of the woman, and placed them on the seats, thus leaving the floor clear except for its dark, creeping pool. Then, placing his handkerchief over the dead woman's face, he rolled back the end of the carpet to hide its sinister stain.

'Now, ma'am, if you please,' he said; and keeping the lady with her back to the more gruesome object on the opposite seat, he helped her to the open door, from where willing hands assisted her to the ground.

By this time the attendant had found a doctor in the third-class coach, and a brief examination enabled him to pronounce both victims dead. The blinds in the compartment having been drawn down and the outside door locked, the guard called to those passengers who had alighted to resume their seats, with a view to continuing their journey.

The fireman had meantime come back along the train to ascertain what was wrong, and to say the driver was unable completely to release the brake. An examination was therefore made, and the tell-tale disc at the end of the first-class coach was found to be turned, showing that someone in that carriage had pulled the communication chain. This, as is perhaps not generally known, allows air to pass between the train pipe and the atmosphere, thereby gently applying the brake and preventing its complete release. Further investigation showed that the slack of the chain was hanging in the end smoking-compartment, indicating that the alarm must have been operated by one of the four men who travelled there. The disc was then turned back to normal, the passengers reseated, and the train started, after a delay of about fifteen minutes.

Before reaching Carlisle, Guard Jones took the name and address of everyone travelling in the first- and third-class coaches, together with the numbers of their tickets. These coaches, as well as the van, were thoroughly searched, and it was established beyond any doubt that no one was concealed under the seats, in the lavatories, behind luggage, or, in fact, anywhere about them.

One of the sleeping-car attendants having been in the corridor in the rear of the last sleeper from the Preston stop till the completion of this search, and being positive no one except the guard had passed during that time, it was not considered necessary to take the names of the passengers in the sleeping-cars, but the numbers of their tickets were noted.

On arrival at Carlisle the matter was put into the hands of the police. The first-class carriage was shunted off, the doors being locked and sealed, and the passengers who had travelled in it were detained to make their statements. Then began a most careful and searching investigation, as a result of which several additional facts became known.

The first step taken by the authorities was to make an examination of the country surrounding the point at which the train had stopped, in the hope of finding traces of some stranger on the line. The tentative theory was that a murder had been committed and that the murderer had escaped from the train when it stopped, struck across the country, and, gaining some road, had made good his escape.

Accordingly, as soon as it was light, a special train brought a force of detectives to the place, and the railway, as well as a tract of ground on each side of it, were subjected to a prolonged and exhaustive search. But no traces were found. Nothing that a stranger might have dropped was picked up, no footsteps were seen, no marks discovered. As has already been stated, the weather was against the searchers. The drought of the previous days had left the ground hard and unyielding, so that clear impressions were scarcely to be expected, while even such as might have been made were not likely to remain after the downpour of the early morning.

Baffled at this point, the detectives turned their attention to the stations in the vicinity. There were only two within walking distance of the point of the tragedy, and at neither had any stranger been seen. Further, no trains had stopped at either of these stations; indeed, not a single train, either passenger or goods, had stopped anywhere in the neighbourhood since the sleeping-car express went through. If the murderer had left the express, it was, therefore, out of the question that he could have escaped by rail.

The investigators then turned their attention to the country roads and adjoining towns, trying to find the trail—if there was a trail —while it was hot. But here, again, no luck attended their efforts. If there were a murderer, and if he had left the train when it stopped, he had vanished into thin air. No traces of him could anywhere be discovered.

Nor were their researches in other directions much more fruitful.

The dead couple were identified as a Mr and Mrs Horatio Llewelyn, of Gordon Villa, Broad Road, Halifax. Mr Llewelyn was the junior partner of a large firm of Yorkshire ironfounders. A man of five-and-thirty, he moved in good society and had some claim to wealth. He was of kindly though somewhat passionate disposition, and, so far as could be learnt, had not an enemy in the world. His firm was able to show that he had had business appointments in London on the Thursday and in Carlisle on the Friday, so that his travelling by the train in question was quite in accordance with his known plans.

His wife was the daughter of a neighbouring merchant, a pretty girl of some seven-and-twenty. They had been married only a little over a month, and had, in fact, only a week earlier returned from their honeymoon. Whether Mrs Llewelyn had any definite reason for accompanying her husband on the fatal journey could not be ascertained. She also, so far as was known, had no enemy, nor could any motive for the tragedy be suggested.

The extraction of the bullets proved that the same weapon had been used in each case—a revolver of small bore and modern design. But as many thousands of similar revolvers existed, this discovery led to nothing.

Miss Blair-Booth, the lady who had travelled with the Llewelyns, stated she had joined the train at Euston, and occupied one of the seats next the corridor. A couple of minutes before starting the deceased had arrived, and they sat in the two opposite corners. No other passengers had entered the compartment during the journey, nor had any of the three left it; in fact, except for the single visit of the ticket-collector shortly after leaving Euston, the door into the corridor had not been even opened.

Mr Llewelyn was very attentive to his young wife, and they had conversed for some time after starting, then, after consulting Miss Blair-Booth, he had pulled down the blinds and shaded the light, and they had settled down for the night. Miss Blair-Booth had slept at intervals, but each time she wakened she had looked round the compartment, and everything was as before. Then she was suddenly aroused from a doze by a loud explosion close by.

She sprang up, and as she did so a flash came from somewhere near her knee, and a second explosion sounded. Startled and trembling, she pulled the shade off the lamp, and then she noticed a little cloud of smoke just inside the corridor door, which had been opened about an inch, and smelled the characteristic odour of burnt powder. Swinging round, she was in time to see Mr Llewelyn dropping heavily forward across his wife's knees, and then she observed the mark on the latter's forehead and realized they had both been shot.

Terrified, she raised the blind of the corridor door which covered the handle and tried to get out to call assistance. But she could not move the door, and her horror was not diminished when she found herself locked in with what she rightly believed were two dead bodies. In despair she pulled the communication chain, but the train did not appear to stop, and she continued struggling with the door till, after what seemed to her hours, the guard appeared, and she was eventually released.

In answer to a question, she further stated that when her blind went up the corridor was empty, and she saw no one till the guard came.

The four men in the end compartment were members of one party travelling from London to Glasgow. For some time after leaving they had played cards, but, about midnight, they too had pulled down their blinds, shaded their lamp, and composed themselves to sleep. In this case also, no person other than the ticket-collector had entered the compartment during the journey. But after leaving Preston the door had been opened. Aroused by the stop, one of the men had eaten some fruit, and having thereby soiled his fingers, had washed them in the lavatory. The door then opened as usual. This man saw no one in the corridor, nor did he notice anything out of the common.

Some time after this all four were startled by the sound of two shots. At first they thought of fog signals, then, realizing they were too far from the engine to hear such, they, like Miss Blair-Booth, unshaded their lamp, raised the blind over their corridor door, and endeavoured to leave the compartment. Like her they found themselves unable to open their door, and, like her also, they saw that there was no one in the corridor. Believing something serious had happened, they pulled the communication chain, at the same time lowering the outside window and waving from it in the hope of attracting attention. The chain came down easily as if slack, and this explained the apparent contradiction between Miss Blair-Booth's statement that she had pulled it, and the fact that the slack was found hanging in the end compartment. Evidently the lady had pulled it first, applying the brake, and the second pull had simply transferred the slack from one compartment to the next.

The two compartments in front of that of the tragedy were found to be empty when the train stopped, but in the last of the non-smoking compartments were two gentlemen, and in the 'Ladies Only', three ladies. All these had heard the shots, but so faintly above the noise of the train that the attention of none of them was specially arrested, nor had they attempted any investigation. The gentlemen had not left their compartment or pulled up their blinds between the time the train left Preston and the emergency stop, and could throw no light whatever on the matter.

The three ladies in the end compartment were a mother and two daughters, and had got in at Preston. As they were alighting at Carlisle they had not wished to sleep, so they had left their blinds up and their light unshaded. Two of them were reading, but the third was seated at the corridor side, and this lady stated positively that no one except the guard had passed while they were in the train.

She described his movements—first, towards the engine, secondly, back towards the van, and a third time, running, towards the engine after the train had stopped—so accurately in accord with the other evidence that considerable reliance was placed on her testimony. The stoppage and the guard's haste had aroused her interest, and all three ladies had immediately come out into the corridor, and had remained there till the train proceeded, and all three were satisfied that no one else had passed during that time.

An examination of the doors which had jammed so mysteriously revealed the fact that a small wooden wedge, evidently designed for the purpose, had been driven in between the floor and the bottom of the framing of the door, holding the latter rigid. It was evident therefore that the crime was premeditated, and the details had been carefully worked out beforehand. The most careful search of the carriage failed to reveal any other suspicious object or mark.

On comparing the tickets issued with those held by the passengers, a discrepancy was discovered. All were accounted for except one. A first single for Glasgow had been issued at Euston for the train in question, which had not been collected. The purchaser had therefore either not travelled at all, or had got out at some intermediate station. In either case no demand for a refund had been made.

The collector who had checked the tickets after the train left London believed, though he could not speak positively, that two men had then occupied the non-smoking compartment next to that in which the tragedy had occurred, one of whom held a Glasgow ticket, and the other a ticket for an intermediate station. He could not recollect which station nor could he describe either of the men, if indeed they were there at all.

But the ticket collector's recollection was not at fault, for the police succeeded in tracing one of these passengers, a Dr Hill, who had got out at Crewe. He was able, partially at all events, to account for the missing Glasgow ticket. It appeared that when he joined the train at Euston, a man of about five and thirty was already in the compartment. This man had fair hair, blue eyes, and a full moustache, and was dressed in dark well-cut clothes. He had no luggage, but only a waterproof and a paper-covered novel. The two travellers had got into conversation, and on the stranger learning that the doctor lived at Crewe, said he was alighting there also, and asked to be recommended to a hotel. He then explained that he had intended to go on to Glasgow and had taken a ticket to that city, but had since decided to break his journey to visit a friend in Chester next day. He asked the doctor if he thought his ticket would be available to complete the journey the following night, and if not, whether he could get a refund.

When they reached Crewe, both these travellers had alighted, and the doctor offered to show his acquaintance the entrance to the Crewe Arms, but the stranger, thanking him, declined, saying he wished to see to his luggage. Dr Hill saw him walking towards the van as he left the platform.

Upon interrogating the staff on duty at Crewe at the time, no one could recall seeing such a man at the van, nor had any inquiries about luggage been made. But as these facts did not come to light until several days after the tragedy, confirmation was hardly to be expected.

A visit to all the hotels in Crewe and Chester revealed the fact that no one in any way resembling the stranger had stayed there, nor could any trace whatever be found of him.

Such were the principal facts made known at the adjourned inquest on the bodies of Mr and Mrs Llewelyn. It was confidently believed that a solution to the mystery would speedily be found, but as day after day passed away without bringing to light any fresh information, public interest began to wane, and became directed into other channels.

But for a time controversy over the affair waxed keen. At first it was argued that it was a case of suicide, some holding that Mr Llewelyn had shot first his wife and then himself; others that both had died by the wife's hand. But this theory had only to be stated to be disproved.

Several persons hastened to point out that not only had the revolver disappeared, but on neither body was there powder blackening, and it was admitted that such a wound could not be self-inflicted without leaving marks from this source. That murder had been committed was therefore clear.

Rebutted on this point, the theorists then argued that Miss Blair-Booth was the assassin. But here again the suggestion was quickly negatived. The absence of motive, her known character and the truth of such of her statements as could be checked were against the idea. The disappearance of the revolver was also in her favour. As it was not in the compartment nor concealed about her person, she could only have rid herself of it out of the window. But the position of the bodies prevented access to the window, and, as her clothes were free from any stain of blood, it was impossible to believe she had moved these grim relics, even had she been physically able.

But the point that finally demonstrated her innocence was the wedging of the corridor door. It was obvious she could not have wedged the door on the outside and then passed through it. The belief was universal that whoever wedged the door fired the shots, and the fact that the former was wedged an inch open strengthened that view, as the motive was clearly to leave a slot through which to shoot.

Lastly, the medical evidence showed that if the Llewelyns were sitting where Miss Blair-Booth stated, and the shots were fired from where she said, the bullets would have entered the bodies from the direction they were actually found to have done.

But Miss Blair-Booth's detractors were loath to recede from the position they had taken up. They stated that of the objections to their theory only one—the wedging of the doors—was overwhelming. And they advanced an ingenious theory to meet it. They suggested that before reaching Preston Miss Blair-Booth had left the compartment, closing the door after her, that she had then wedged it, and that, on stopping at the station, she had passed out through some other compartment, re-entering her own through the outside door.

In answer to this it was pointed out that the gentleman who had eaten the fruit had opened his door *after* the Preston stop, and if Miss Blair-Booth was then shut into her compartment she could not have wedged the other door. That two people should be concerned in the wedging was unthinkable. It was therefore clear that Miss Blair-Booth was innocent, and that some other person had wedged both doors, in order to prevent his operations in the corridor being interfered with by those who would hear the shots.

It was recognized that similar arguments applied to the four men in the end compartment—the wedging of the doors cleared them also.

Defeated on these points the theorists retired from the field. No further suggestions were put forward by the public or the daily Press. Even to those behind the scenes the case seemed to become more and more difficult the longer it was pondered.

Each person known to have been present came in turn under the microscopic eye of New Scotland Yard, but each in turn had to be eliminated from suspicion, till it almost seemed proved that no murder could have been committed at all. The prevailing mystification was well summed up by the chief at the Yard in conversation with the inspector in charge of the case.

'A troublesome business, certainly,' said the great man, 'and I admit that your conclusions seem sound. But let us go over it again. There *must* be a flaw somewhere.'

'There must, sir. But I've gone over it and over it till I'm stupid, and every time I get the same result.'

'We'll try once more. We begin, then, with a murder in a railway carriage. We're sure it was a murder, of course?'

'Certain, sir. The absence of the revolver and of powder blackening and the wedging of the doors prove it.'

'Quite. The murder must therefore have been committed by some person who was either in the carriage when it was searched, or had left before that. Let us take these two possibilities in turn. And first, with regard to the searching. Was that efficiently done?'

'Absolutely, sir. I have gone into it with the guard and attendants. No one could have been overlooked.'

'Very good. Taking first, then, those who were in the carriage. There were six compartments. In the first were the four men, and in the second Miss Blair-Booth. Are you satisfied these were innocent?'

'Perfectly, sir. The wedging of the doors eliminated them.'

'So I think. The third and fourth compartments were empty, but in the fifth there were two gentlemen. What about them?'

'Well, sir, you know who they were. Sir Gordon M'Clean, the great engineer, and Mr Silas Hemphill, the professor of Aberdeen University. Both utterly beyond suspicion.'

'But, as you know, inspector, *no one* is beyond suspicion in a case of this kind.'

'I admit it, sir, and therefore I made careful inquiries about them. But I only confirmed my opinion.'

'From inquiries I also have made I feel sure you are right. That brings us to the last compartment, the "Ladies Only". What about those three ladies?'

'The same remarks apply. Their characters are also beyond suspicion, and, as well as that, the mother is elderly and timid, and couldn't brazen out a lie. I question if the daughters could either. I made inquiries all the same, and found not the slightest ground for suspicion.'

'The corridors and lavatories were empty?'

'Yes, sir.'

'Then everyone found in the coach when the train stopped may be definitely eliminated?'

'Yes. It is quite impossible it could have been any that we have mentioned.'

'Then the murderer must have left the coach?'

'He must; and that's where the difficulty comes in.'

'I know, but let us proceed. Our problem then really becomes —*how* did he leave the coach?'

'That's so, sir, and I have never been against anything stiffer.'

The chief paused in thought, as he absently selected and lit another cigar. At last he continued:

'Well, at any rate, it is clear he did not go through the roof or the floor, or any part of the fixed framing or sides. Therefore he must have gone in the usual way—through a door. Of these, there is one at each end and six at each side. He therefore went through one of these fourteen doors. Are you agreed, inspector?'

'Certainly, sir.'

'Very good. Take the ends first. The vestibule doors were locked?'

'Yes, sir, at both ends of the coach. But I don't count that much. An ordinary carriage key opened them and the murderer would have had one.'

'Quite. Now, just go over again our reason for thinking he did not escape to the sleeper.'

'Before the train stopped, sir, Miss Bintley, one of the three in the "Ladies Only", was looking out into the corridor, and the two sleeper attendants were at the near end of their coach. After the train stopped, all three ladies were in the corridor, and one attendant was at the sleeper vestibule. All these persons swear most positively that no one but the guard passed between Preston and the searching of the carriage.'

'What about these attendants? Are they reliable?'

'Wilcox has seventeen years' service, and Jeffries six, and both bear excellent characters. Both, naturally, came under suspicion of the murder, and I made the usual investigation. But there is not a scrap of evidence against them, and I am satisfied they are all right.'

'It certainly looks as if the murderer did not escape towards the sleeper.'

'I am positive of it. You see, sir, we have the testimony of two separate lots of witnesses, the ladies and the attendants. It is out of the question that these parties would agree to deceive the police. Conceivably one or other might, but not both.'

'Yes, that seems sound. What, then, about the other end—the third-class end?'

'At that end,' replied the inspector, 'were Mr and Mrs Smith with their sick child. They were in the corridor close by the vestibule door, and no one could have passed without their knowledge. I had the child examined, and its illness was genuine. The parents are quiet persons, of exemplary character, and again quite beyond suspicion. When they said no one but the guard had passed I believed them. However, I was not satisfied with that, and I examined every person that travelled in the third-class coach, and established two things: first, that no one was in it at the time it was searched who had not travelled in it from Preston; and secondly, that no one except the Smiths had left any of the compartments during the run between

Preston and the emergency stop. That proves beyond question that no one left the first-class coach for the third after the tragedy.'

'What about the guard himself?'

'The guard is also a man of good character, but he is out of it, because he was seen by several passengers as well as the Smiths running through the third-class after the brakes were applied.'

'It is clear, then, the murderer must have got out through one of the twelve side doors. Take those on the compartment side first. The first, second, fifth, and sixth compartments were occupied, therefore he could not have passed through them. That leaves the third and fourth doors. Could he have left by either of these?'

The inspector shook his head.

'No, sir,' he answered, 'that is equally out of the question. You will recollect that two of the four men in the end compartment were looking out along the train from a few seconds after the murder until the stop. It would not have been possible to open a door and climb out on to the footboard without being seen by them. Guard Jones also looked out at that side of the van and saw no one. After the stop these same two men, as well as others, were on the ground, and all agree that none of these doors were opened at any time.'

'H'm,' mused the chief, 'that also seems conclusive, and it brings us definitely to the doors on the corridor side. As the guard arrived on the scene comparatively early, the murderer must have got out while the train was running at a fair speed. He must therefore have been clinging on to the outside of the coach while the guard was in the corridor working at the sliding doors. When the train stopped all attention was concentrated on the opposite, or compartment, side, and he could easily have dropped down and made off. What do you think of that theory, inspector?'

'We went into that pretty thoroughly, sir. It was first objected that the blinds of the first and second compartments were raised too soon to give him time to get out without being seen. But I found this was not valid. At least fifteen seconds must have elapsed before Miss Blair-Booth and the men in the end compartment raised their blinds, and that would easily have allowed him to lower the window, open the door, pass out, raise the window, shut the door, and crouch down on the footboard out of sight. I estimate also that nearly thirty seconds passed before Guard Jones looked out of the van at that side. As far as time goes he could have done what you suggest. But another thing shows he didn't. It appears that when Jones ran through the third-class coach, while the train was stopping, Mr Smith, the man with the sick child, wondering what was wrong, attempted to follow him into the first-class. But the door slammed after the guard before the other could reach it, and, of course, the spring lock held it fast. Mr Smith therefore lowered the end corridor window and looked out ahead, and he states positively no one was on the footboard of the first-class. To see how far Mr Smith could be sure of this, on a dark night we ran the same carriage, lighted in the same way, over the same part of the line, and we found a figure crouching on the footboard was clearly visible from the window. It showed a dark mass against the lighted side of the cutting. When we remember that Mr Smith was specially looking out for something abnormal, I think we may accept his evidence.'

'You are right. It is convincing. And, of course, it is supported by the guard's own testimony. He also saw no one when he looked out of his van.'

'That is so, sir. And we found a crouching figure was visible from the van also, owing to the same cause—the lighted bank.'

'And the murderer could not have got out while the guard was passing through the third-class?'

'No, because the corridor blinds were raised before the guard looked out.'

The chief frowned.

'It is certainly puzzling,' he mused. There was silence for some moments, and then he spoke again.

'Could the murderer, immediately after firing the shots, have concealed himself in a lavatory and then, during the excitement of the stop, have slipped out unperceived through one of these corridor doors and, dropping on the line, moved quietly away?'

'No, sir, we went into that also. If he had hidden in a lavatory he could not have got out again. If he had gone towards the third-class the Smiths would have seen him, and the first-class corridor was under observation during the entire time from the arrival of the guard till the search. We have proved the ladies entered the corridor *immediately* the guard passed their compartment, and two of the four men in the end smoker were watching through their door till considerably after the ladies had come out.'

Again silence reigned while the chief smoked thoughtfully.

'The coroner had some theory, you say?' he said at last.

'Yes, sir. He suggested the murderer might have, immediately after firing, got out by one of the doors on the corridor side— probably the end one—and from there climbed on the outside of the coach to some place from which he could not be seen from a window, dropping to the ground when the train stopped. He suggested the roof, the buffers, or the lower step. This seemed likely at first sight, and I tried therefore the experiment. But it was no good. The roof was out of the question. It was one of those high curved roofs—not a flat clerestory—and there was no hand-hold at the edge above the doors. The buffers were equally inaccessible. From the handle and guard of the end door to that above the buffer on the corner of the coach was seven feet two inches. That is to say, a man could not reach from one to the other, and there was nothing he could hold on to while passing along the step. The lower step was not possible either. In the first place it was divided—there was only a short step beneath each door—not a continuous board like the upper one—so that no one could pass along the lower while holding on to the upper, and secondly, I couldn't imagine anyone climbing down there, and knowing that the first platform they came to would sweep him off.'

'That is to say, inspector, you have proved the murderer was in the coach at the time of the crime, that he was not in it when it was searched, and that he did not leave it in the interval. I don't know that that is a very creditable conclusion.'

'I know, sir. I regret it extremely, but that's the difficulty I have been up against from the start.'

The chief laid his hand on his subordinate's shoulder.

'It won't do,' he said kindly. 'It really won't do. You try again. Smoke over it, and I'll do the same, and come in and see me again tomorrow.'

But the conversation had really summed up the case justly. My Lady Nicotine brought no inspiration, and, as time passed without bringing to light any further facts, interest gradually waned till at last the affair took its place among the long list of unexplained crimes in the annals of New Scotland Yard.

And now I come to the singular coincidence referred to earlier whereby I, an obscure medical practitioner, came to learn the solution of this extraordinary mystery. With the case itself I had no connection, the details just given being taken from the official reports made at the time, to which I was allowed access in return for the information I brought. The affair happened in this way.

One evening just four weeks ago, as I lit my pipe after a long and tiring day, I received an urgent summons to the principal inn of the little village near which I practised. A motor-cyclist had collided with a car at a crossroads and had been picked up terribly injured. I saw almost at a glance that nothing could be done for him; in fact, his life was a matter of a few hours. He asked coolly how it was with him, and, in accordance with my custom in such cases, I told him, inquiring was there anyone he would like sent for. He looked me straight in the eyes and replied:

'Doctor, I want to make a statement. If I tell it to you will you keep it to yourself while I live and then inform the proper authorities and the public?'

'Why, yes,' I answered; 'but shall I not send for some of your friends or a clergyman?'

'No,' he said, 'I have no friends, and I have no use for parsons. You look a white man; I would rather tell you.'

I bowed and fixed him up as comfortably as possible, and he began, speaking slowly in a voice hardly above a whisper.

'I shall be brief for I feel my time is short. You remember some few years ago a Mr Horatio Llewelyn and his wife were murdered in a train on the North-Western some fifty miles south of Carlisle?'

I dimly remembered the case.

'"The sleeping-car express mystery," the papers called it?' I asked.

'That's it,' he replied. 'They never solved the mystery and they never got the murderer. But he's going to pay now. I am he.'

I was horrified at the cool, deliberate way he spoke. Then I remembered that he was fighting death to make his confession and that, whatever my feelings, it was my business to hear and record it while yet there was time. I therefore sat down and said as gently as I could:

'Whatever you tell me I shall note carefully, and at the proper time shall inform the police.'

His eyes, which had watched me anxiously, showed relief.

'Thank you. I shall hurry. My name is Hubert Black, and I live at 24, Westbury Gardens, Hove. Until ten years and two months ago I lived at Bradford, and there I made the acquaintance of what I thought was the best and most wonderful girl on God's earth—Miss Gladys Wentworth. I was poor, but she was well off. I was diffident about approaching her, but she encouraged me till at last I took my courage in both hands and proposed. She agreed to marry me, but made it a condition our engagement was to be kept secret for a few days. I was so mad about her I would have agreed to anything she wanted, so I said nothing, though I could hardly behave like a sane man from joy.

'Some time before this I had come across Llewelyn, and he had been very friendly, and had seemed to like my company. One day we met Gladys, and I introduced him. I did not know till later that he had followed up the acquaintanceship.

'A week after my acceptance there was a big dance at Halifax. I was to have met Gladys there, but at the last moment I had a wire that my mother was seriously ill, and I had to go. On my return I got a cool little note from Gladys saying she was sorry, but our engagement had been a mistake, and I must consider it at an end. I made a few inquiries, and then I learnt what had been done. Give me some stuff, doctor; I'm going down.'

I poured out some brandy and held it to his lips.

'That's better,' he said, continuing with gasps and many pauses: 'Llewelyn, I found out, had been struck by Gladys for some time. He knew I was friends with her, and so he made up to me. He wanted the introduction I was fool enough to give him, as well as the chances of meeting her he would get with me. Then he met her when he knew I was at my work, and made hay while the sun shone. Gladys spotted what he was after, but she didn't know if he was serious. Then I proposed, and she thought she would hold me for fear the bigger fish would get off. Llewelyn was wealthy, you understand. She waited till the ball, then she hooked him, and I went overboard. Nice, wasn't it?'

I did not reply, and the man went on:

'Well, after that I just went mad. I lost my head and went to Llewelyn, but he laughed in my face. I felt I wanted to knock his head off, but the butler happened by, so I couldn't go on and finish him then. I needn't try to describe the hell I went through—I couldn't, anyway. But I was blind mad, and lived only for revenge. And then I got it. I followed them till I got a chance, and then I killed them. I shot them in that train. I shot her first and then, as he woke and sprang up, I got him too.'

The man paused.

'Tell me the details', I asked; and after a time he went on in a weaker voice:

'I had worked out a plan to get them in a train, and had followed them all through their honeymoon, but I never got a chance till then. This time the circumstances fell out to suit. I was behind him at Euston and heard him book to Carlisle, so I booked to Glasgow. I got into the next compartment. There was a talkative man there, and I tried to make a sort of alibi for myself by letting him think I would get out at Crewe. I did get out, but I got in again, and travelled on in the same compartment with the blinds down. No one knew I was there. I waited till we got to the top of Shap, for I thought I could get away easier in a thinly populated country. Then, when the time came, I fixed the compartment doors with wedges, and shot them both. I left the train and got clear of the railway, crossing the country till I came on a road. I hid during the day and walked at night till after dark on the second evening I came to Carlisle. From there I went by rail quite openly. I was never suspected.'

He paused, exhausted, while the Dread Visitor hovered closer.

'Tell me,' I said, 'just a word. How did you get out of the train?'

He smiled faintly.

'Some more of your stuff,' he whispered; and when I had given him a second dose of brandy he went on feebly and with long pauses which I am not attempting to reproduce:

'I had worked the thing out beforehand. I thought if I could get out on the buffers while the train was running and before the alarm was raised, I should be safe. No one looking out of the windows could see me, and when the train stopped, as I knew it soon would, I could drop down and make off. The difficulty was to get from the corridor to the buffers. I did it like this:

'I had brought about sixteen feet of fine, brown silk cord, and the same length of thin silk rope. When I got out at Crewe I moved to the corner of the coach and stood close to it by way of getting shelter to light a cigarette. Without anyone seeing what I was up to I slipped the end of the cord through the bracket handle above the buffers. Then I strolled to the nearest door, paying out the cord, but holding on to its two ends. I pretended to fumble at the door as if it was stiff to open, but all the time I was passing the cord through the handle-guard, and knotting the ends together. If you've followed me you'll understand this gave me a loop of fine silk connecting the handles at the corner and the door. It was the colour of the carriage, and was nearly invisible. Then I took my seat again.

'When the time came to do the job, I first wedged the corridor doors. Then I opened the outside window and drew in the end of the cord loop and tied the end of the rope to it. I pulled one side of the cord loop and so got the rope pulled through the corner bracket handle and back again to the window. Its being silk made it run easily, and without marking the bracket. Then I put an end of the rope through the handle-guard, and after pulling it tight, knotted the ends together. This gave me a loop of rope tightly stretched from the door to the corner.

'I opened the door and then pulled up the window. I let the door close up against a bit of wood I had brought. The wind kept it to, and the wood prevented it from shutting.

'Then I fired. As soon as I saw that both were hit I got outside. I kicked away the wood and shut the door. Then with the rope for handrail I stepped along the footboard to the buffers. I cut both the cord and the rope and drew them after me, and shoved them in my pocket. This removed all traces.

'When the train stopped I slipped down on the ground. The people were getting out at the other side so I had only to creep along close to the coaches till I got out of their light, then I climbed up the bank and escaped.'

The man had evidently made a desperate effort to finish, for as he ceased speaking his eyes closed, and in a few minutes he fell into a state of coma which shortly preceded his death.

After communicating with the police I set myself to carry out his second injunction, and this statement is the result.

JOHN RHODE · 1884–1964

The Purple Line

Inspector Purley picked up the telephone. But the torrent of words which poured into his ears was so turbid that he could make little of it. Something about a wife and a water-butt. The fellow was obviously in such a state that questioning him would elicit no coherent answer. 'I'll come along at once,' said Purley. 'Holly Bungalow, you say? On the Cadford road? Right!'

He took the police car, in which he drove out of the fair-sized market town of Faythorpe. The villas on the outskirts extended for a short distance, with a scarlet telephone kiosk near the further end. Beyond this the road, bordered with trees on either side, ran through agricultural country.

Purley kept a sharp look-out as he went, for he was by no means sure of the exact location of Holly Bungalow. It wasn't any too easy, for it was growing dark on a February afternoon, and it was pouring with rain, as it had been all day. Then, about half a mile beyond the kiosk, he saw, on the left, a white-painted gate between the trees and, standing beside it, a man with a bicycle. The Inspector slowed up as he saw 'Holly Bungalow' painted on the gate.

As he got out of the car the man at the gate began gabbling and gesticulating. He was short and stocky, round-faced and goggle-eyed, and was evidently labouring under some violent emotion. He wore a mackintosh, sodden with wet, and was hatless, with the rain pouring from his hair over his face. 'Rode at once to the kiosk,' he was rambling incoherently. 'That's where I rang you up from. We're not on the telephone, you know. I didn't know what else to do. It's a dreadful thing. Come, I'll show you.'

He turned and almost ran up the path leading from the gate. Purley followed him towards the bungalow, a few yards away. The man turned off round the side of the building to the back and stopped abruptly. 'There, look!'

At the back of the bungalow was a verandah, looking out over a lawn and garden surrounded by trees. At the further end of the verandah was a round galvanized water-butt, overflowing with the water pouring into it from a spout in the eaves. Projecting from the top of the butt, and resting against the edge, was a pair of inverted high-heeled shoes. 'It's my wife!' the little man exclaimed.

The butt was about five feet high and two feet six inches in diameter, standing on a brick foundation. Beside it was a folding wooden garden chair. Purley climbed on to this and leaned over the edge of the butt. Within it, completely submerged but for the feet, was a woman, head down and fully clothed.

The first problem was how to get her out. It might be possible to push the butt over on its side. He managed to tilt the butt, the water surging over the edge.

'Here, come and bear a hand!' he exclaimed. Between them they tilted the butt still further, the water pouring out and streaming across the lawn. Then it fell on its side.

The little man made no attempt to help Purley as he drew the woman out by the legs. She was fairly tall and slim, apparently in the thirties, wearing a dark frock, silk stockings, and high-heeled shoes, with no hat. Purley glanced into the butt. The water had drained out of it, and all it now contained was a layer of slime and a broken ridge-tile, which had at some time presumably fallen into it from the roof.

Purley carried the body into the shelter of the verandah. The little man was quivering like a jelly. 'You'd better come with me,' said Purley.

In a dazed fashion the other followed him back to the car. Purley drove to the kiosk, where he telephoned to the police station. Then the two drove back to the bungalow. 'We'll go inside, out of the rain,' said Purley. 'There you can tell me what you know about this.'

They entered by the front door. The bungalow was not large—lounge, dining-room, a couple of bedrooms, and the usual domestic offices. The furnishings, if not luxurious, were well-to-do. In the dining-room a french window leading on to the verandah was open. On the table were still some remains of a meal, apparently lunch, with one place only laid. Beside this, a tumbler, a siphon, and a bottle of whisky, half full.

As they sat down Purley took out his notebook and headed a page 'Monday, Feb. 13'. He said, 'You told me the name was Briston, I think?'

The other nodded. 'That's right. I am Henry Briston. My wife's name was Shirley. She had seemed rather depressed for the last few days. I wouldn't have left her alone if it had ever entered my head that she would do a thing like that.'

'When did you last see her alive?'

'About eight o'clock this morning,' Briston replied. 'She was in bed then. I got up early, for I was going to Mawnchester to see my brother, and I took her a cup of tea. She seemed quite cheerful then. I got my own breakfast, and while the egg was frying I put a new chart in the barograph yonder.'

He pointed to the instrument on a bracket fixed to the dining-room wall. Purley was familiar with barographs—there was one in the window of the optician's next door to the police station. The one on the wall was of the conventional type, with a revolving drum driven by clockwork, and a pen at the end of a long needle. The chart stuck round the drum bore out Briston's words. It ran from Monday to Sunday, ruled in two-hour divisions, the lines an eighth of an inch apart.

The pen had been set at eight o'clock that morning, and filled rather clumsily, for the deep purple oily ink had overflowed and run vertically down the chart. The time was now seven o'clock, and the pen pointed correctly between the six and eight o'clock lines. The graph it had drawn ran horizontally for an eighth of an inch, from eight to ten. After that time it sloped steeply downwards, indicating rapidly falling pressure.

'And after breakfast?' Purley asked. 'You saw Mrs Briston again?'

'I didn't see her,' Briston replied. 'I called through the door and told her I was going, and she answered me. Then I jumped on my bicycle and rode to the station to catch the 8.50 to Mawnchester.'

'Was Mrs Briston expecting anyone to call here during your absence?'

Briston shook his head. 'Not that I know of. The postman must have called, for I met him on the road as I was riding to the station. I called out to ask him if he had anything for me, and he said only a parcel for my wife.'

'Was that garden chair standing by the water-butt when you left home?'

'I don't think so. If it was, I didn't put it there. At this time of year it's kept folded up in the verandah. I sometimes use it to stand on and look into the butt to see how much water there is. But this morning the butt was empty. During the dry spell we had last week we used all the water for the plants in the greenhouse. It would have taken three or four hours to fill even with the heavy rain today.'

'Did you put this bottle of whisky on the table here?'

'No, I found it there when I came home. Latterly my wife had taken to drinking rather more than I liked to see. I didn't clear away my breakfast things before I left this morning. My wife must have done that, and got her own lunch later on.'

'You went to Mawnchester by the 8.50. What time did you come back?'

'By the train that gets to Faythorpe at 4.45. The ticket collector will remember that—we had some conversation. I had taken a cheap day ticket, but it wasn't available for return as early as the 4.45, and I had to pay the full fare. I lunched with my brother in Mawnchester, and saw several other people there.'

There came a loud knock. Purley opened the door, to find the divisional surgeon. 'This way, Doctor,' he said, leading him round the bungalow to the verandah. 'What can you tell me?' he asked.

'Not very much more than you can see for yourself,' said the doctor. 'She's been dead some hours. Death was due to drowning. There's a pretty severe contusion on the top of the head. It wouldn't have been fatal, for the skull isn't fractured. But you'll want to account for it, I expect.'

'Have a look inside the butt,' said Purley. 'You see that broken ridge-tile?'

The doctor nodded. 'Yes, I see it. You found her head downwards in the butt, you say? If, when she dived in, her head had struck the tile, the contusion would be accounted for.'

Another loud knock brought Purley once more to the front door. This time it was a couple of ambulance men with a stretcher. The body was carried to the ambulance, which set off for the mortuary, the doctor following in his car. Purley returned to the dining-room, to find Briston looking utterly dejected and exhausted. Purley feared he might have a second suicide on his hands. 'I don't think you ought to stop here all alone, Mr Briston,' he suggested.

'Oh, I shall be all right,' Briston replied drearily. 'I'll go along to the kiosk by-and-by and ring up my brother. If he can't come here he'll let me go to him, I daresay.'

Purley went back to Faythorpe. Accident, murder, or suicide? The only way she could have fallen headlong into the butt by accident was if she had been clambering about on the roof; such behaviour might surely be ruled out. Murder? By whom? Her husband's alibi seemed perfectly good, though of course it would have to be checked. And there was this finally convincing point. Nobody, certainly not her puny little husband, could, with the help only of the garden chair, have lifted a struggling victim above his shoulders and plunged her head downwards into the butt.

Suicide, then. Everything pointed to that. The depression from which Shirley Briston had been suffering. And possibly the whisky to supply Dutch courage. It had started to rain about half-past nine that morning, and had never ceased all day. Three or four hours, Briston had said. The butt would have been full by the time she might be expected to have had her lunch. She had taken out the garden chair, climbed on to it, and dived into the butt.

Verification of Briston's alibi followed naturally. The ticket collector remembered him perfectly well. 'I couldn't say what train he went by in the morning, for I wasn't on duty then,' he told Purley. 'But he came off the 4.45 and gave up the return half of a cheap day to Mawnchester. I told him that was no good, as cheap tickets are only available by trains leaving Mawnchester after six. So he paid me the difference, and I gave him a receipt for it.'

Purley ran the postman to earth in the bar of the Red Admiral. 'This morning's delivery?' he replied to Purley's question. 'Yes, I do recollect seeing Mr Briston while I was on my way to Cadford. He was riding his bike towards the town here, and as he passed he called out and asked me if I had anything for him. I told him that all there was for Holly Bungalow was a parcel for Mrs Briston.'

'You delivered the parcel, I suppose?' Purley remarked. 'Did you see anyone at the bungalow?'

'Why, yes,' the postman replied. 'The parcel was too big to go through the letter-box, so I knocked on the door. After a bit Mrs Briston opened it and took in the parcel. She wasn't what you might call properly dressed, but had a sort of wrap round her.'

'Can you tell me what time this was?'

'It must have been round about half-past eight when I spoke to Mr Briston. And maybe five minutes later when I got to the bungalow.'

All that remained was a final word with the doctor. There was just one possibility. Briston had arrived at Faythorpe station at 4.45. He should have reached home by 5.15. It had been after six when Purley had first seen the body in the butt. Only the faintest possibility, of course.

The doctor was at home when Purley called, and frowned irritably at his question. 'How the dickens can I tell to a split second? I'm ready to testify on oath that death was due to drowning. But I'm not prepared to say exactly when it took place. When a body has been in water for any length of time, that's impossible. My opinion is that the woman died not later than midday or thereabouts.'

So that settled it. Mrs Briston had been seen alive after her husband left the house that morning. The medical evidence showed that she must have been dead before his return that evening. Clearly, then, a case of suicide.

Next morning, Purley went to Holly Bungalow fairly early. The door was opened by a man who bore some resemblance to Henry Briston, though he was taller and not so plump. 'Do you want to see my brother?' he asked. 'I am Edward Briston, from Mawnchester. Henry rang me up last night and told me what had happened, and I came over at once. He's had a very bad night, and I told him he'd better stay in bed for a bit.'

'I won't disturb him,' Purley replied. 'I only looked in to see he was all right. You saw your brother in Mawnchester yesterday, didn't you, Mr Briston?'

'Yes, he lunched with me, and we spent the afternoon together in my office, till he left to catch his train.'

Purley nodded. 'Have you any personal knowledge of your sister-in-law's state of mind recently?'

Edward Briston glanced over his shoulder, led the way into the dining-room and shut the door. 'It was to talk about Shirley that Henry came to see me yesterday,' he said in a hushed voice. 'He told me she was terribly depressed. Just as if she had something on her mind that she wouldn't tell him about.

'I'm going to tell you something, Inspector, that I didn't tell Henry, and never shall, now. One day last week I saw Shirley in Mawnchester. She was with a man I didn't know, and they seemed to be getting on remarkably well together. I know she saw me, but the couple hurried away together in the opposite direction. It's my belief the poor woman had got herself into a situation from which she could see only one way of escape.'

That might be the case, Purley thought. Glancing round the room, he caught sight of the barograph. After that flat step, an eighth of an inch wide, the purple line traced by the pen had fallen steadily till about midnight. Then it had become horizontal, and was now beginning to rise. Fine weather might be expected. The prosperous appearance of the room prompted Purley's next question. 'Your brother is in comfortable circumstances?'

'Well, yes,' Edward Briston replied. 'Henry hasn't much of his own, but Shirley had considerable means. She was a widow when he married her, and her first husband had left her quite well off.'

Henry Briston's alibi was complete. There could be no doubt now that his wife had committed suicide, and Edward Briston's guess might explain why. Purley went back to the police station, and caught sight of the barograph in the window next door.

He looked at the instrument more closely. It was very similar to the one at Holly Bungalow; the only difference that Purley could see was the chart on the drum, which ran from Sunday to Saturday. A new chart had been fitted at ten o'clock the previous Sunday, for that was where the purple graph began. For the greater part of Sunday it ran almost horizontally. Then, late that evening, it began to decline. By the early hours of Monday morning, this decline had become a steep slope. As with the instrument at Holly Bungalow, this fall had continued till about midnight.

The queer thing about this graph was that it showed no horizontal step between eight and ten on Monday morning. Briston's barograph must be out of order. But it couldn't be, for in every other respect the two purple lines were exactly similar.

Purley went into the police station. A discrepancy only an eighth of an inch long in the graphs could be of no importance. And then the only possible explanation revealed itself to him.

His thoughts began to race. There was no confirmation of Henry Briston having left Faythorpe by the 8.50. He had certainly been seen by the postman riding in the direction of the station about 8.30. But he might have turned back when the postman had passed the bungalow on his way to Cadford. A later train would have given him plenty of time to meet his brother for lunch in Mawnchester.

Back to the bungalow, to find his wife dressed and having breakfast. Perhaps he had contrived to meet the postman. He could easily have ordered something to be sent her by post. That contusion the doctor had found. The kitchen poker! A blow, not enough to kill her, but to knock her out.

But it would manifestly have been beyond Briston's power to lift even an inert body over the edge of the butt. No, it wouldn't do. By jove, yes, it would! It hadn't begun to rain till 9.30, and before then the butt had been empty. Briston had tipped the butt over on its side. Easy enough, for it was of thin sheet metal, and comparatively light when empty.

First the broken tile, to explain the contusion that must be found. Then the unconscious woman, dragged through the french window of the dining-room and thrust head first into the butt. An effort, and the butt with its contents was upended in place. Perhaps the rainwater was already beginning to trickle into it from the spout. Then to set the scene, so as to suggest that the victim had been alive at a much later hour. To clear away the breakfast, and to lay the appearance of lunch, with that significant whisky bottle.

In his preoccupation with the crime, he had forgotten to change the barograph chart. It was by then ten o'clock. He put on a new chart, and set the pen on the eight o'clock line, to suggest the time of his action. Then he turned the drum till the pen rested on the ten o'clock line. He was bound to do that, otherwise it might be noticed later that the instrument was two hours slow. That was the only possible explanation of the purple line being horizontal for that vital eighth of an inch.

The motive might be deduced from Edward Briston's revelation. The only evidence for Shirley Briston's depressed state was her husband's. She hadn't been depressed, but determined. She had told him she was going to leave him. And if she did that her money would go with her.

It was beyond any doubt that the barograph had been set not at eight, but at ten. If it could be proved that Henry Briston had set it, his alibi was destroyed. He must have been in a state of great agitation. He had clumsily overfilled the pen, so that the ink had run down the chart. Might he not in his agitation have got some of it on his fingers? That oily purple fluid was not a true ink, but a dye, defying soap and water.

Purley drove again to Holly Bungalow. This time Henry Briston himself opened the door. 'Hold out your hands, Mr Briston,' said the Inspector sternly.

'My hands?' Briston replied. He held them out tremblingly, palms downwards. Purley seized the right hand and turned it over. There on the inner side of forefinger and thumb were two faint purple stains. 'You will come with me in my car,' said Purley sternly. 'And I must caution you————'

Solved by Inspection

Miles Bredon, the eminently indefatigable inquiry agent, was accustomed to describe himself as a perfect fool at his job. Here he was in agreement with his wife Angela; where he differed from her was in really regarding himself as a fool at his job. There she knew better; and so, fortunately for both of them, did the Indescribable—that vast insurance company which employed him to investigate the more questionable transactions of its clients, and saved itself about five thousand a year by doing so. On one occasion, however, Bredon did claim to have really solved a problem by inspection, without any previous knowledge to put him on the right track. Indeed, since he seldom read the cheaper kind of newspaper, it is probable that he had never heard of the eccentric millionaire, Herbert Jervison, until Herbert Jervison was found dead in his bed. He was only supplied with the facts of the situation as he travelled down in the train to Wiltshire with Dr Simmonds, the expensive medical man whom the Indescribable valued almost as much as Bredon himself. It was a bright summer's morning, and the dewy fields, horizoned by lazy stretches of canal, would have been food enough for meditation if Simmonds had not been so confoundedly anxious to impart information.

'You must have heard of him,' he was saying. 'He was a newspaper boom long before he was a casualty. The Million and a Half Mystic —that was the sort of thing they called him. Why is it that the grossly rich never have the least idea of how to spend money? This Jervison had pottered about in the East, and had got caught with all that esoteric bilge—talked about Mahatmas and Yogis and things till even the most sanguine of his poor relations wouldn't ask him to stay. So he settled down at Yewbury here with some Indian frauds he had picked up, and said he was the Brotherhood of Light. Had it printed on his notepaper, which was dark green. Ate nuts and did automatic writing and made all sorts of psychic experiments, till the papers were all over him; that sort of stuff gets them where they live. And then, you see, he went and died.'

'That's a kind of publicity we all achieve sooner or later. If they all did it later, our job with the Indescribable would be a soft one. Anyhow, why did they send for me? He probably choked on a Brazil nut or something. No question of murder or suicide or anything, is there?'

'That's just the odd part about it. He died suddenly, of starvation.'

'I suppose you want me to say that's impossible. No medical man myself, I am astute enough to see that my leg is being pulled. Let's hear more about it. Did you ever see the fellow?'

'Not till he came in to be vetted for his insurance. I've been kicking myself over that; because, you see, I thought he was about the soundest life I'd ever struck. He was only fifty-three, and of course these people who go in for Oriental food-fads do sometimes pull off a longevity record. In fact, he had the cheek to ask for a specially low premium, because he said he was in a fair way to discovering the secret of immortality—which, as he pointed out, would make his premium a permanent asset to the company. And then he goes and kills himself by refusing his mash. Mark you, I'm not sure I wouldn't sooner starve than eat the sort of muck he ate; but then, he seemed to flourish on it.'

'And there was really nothing wrong with him? What about his top storey?'

'Well, he admitted to nerves, and I must say he showed up badly over some of the nerve tests. You know we take the nervy people up to the top of the Indescribable building nowadays, to see whether it gives them the jim-jams. Well, this fellow was at the end of his tether; you couldn't get him to look over the edge for love or money. But if his relations had wanted him certified—and they'd every reason to—I couldn't have done it. Colney Hatch wasn't on the map; I'd swear to that, even at a directors' meeting.'

'So he went off and died suddenly of starvation. Could you amplify that statement a bit?'

'Well, what really happened was that he shut himself up for ten days or so in the room he calls his laboratory. I haven't seen it, but it's an old gymnasium or racket-court, they tell me. There was nothing queer in that, because he was always shutting himself up to do his fool experiments; locked himself in and wasn't to be disturbed on any account. Probably thought his astral body was wandering about in Tibet. But—this is the odd thing—he was fully victualled, so I hear, for a fortnight. And at the end of ten days he was found dead in his bed. The local doctor, who had been out in the East and served a famine area, says it's the clearest case of starvation he's ever met.'

'And the food?'

'The food was untouched. I say, this is Westbury, where the car's going to meet us. I didn't tell Dr Mayhew I was bringing a friend; how exactly am I going to explain you?'

'Tell him I'm the representative of the company. That always fetches them. Hallo, there's a black man on the platform.'

'That'll be the chauffeur. . . . No, thanks, no luggage. . . . Good morning, are you from Yewbury? Dr Simmonds, my name is; I think Dr Mayhew expects me. Outside, is he? Good. Come along, Bredon.'

Dr Mayhew was a little round-faced man who seemed incapable of suspicion and radiated hospitality. You saw at once that he was the kind of country doctor who suffers from having too little company, and can scarcely be got to examine your symptoms because he is so anxious to exchange all the news first. He outdid Simmonds himself in his offhand way of referring to the tragedy.

'Awfully good of you fellows to come,' he said. 'Not that I'm anxious for a second opinion here. Nine cases out of ten, *you* know that well enough, one signs the death certificate on an off-chance; but there ain't any doubt about this poor devil. I've been in a famine area, you know, and seen the symptoms often enough to make you dream of it; not pleasant, are they? I expect Mr—oh, yes, Bredon, to be sure; Mr Bredon won't want to see the corpus. They've got it parked up at the Brotherhood House, ready to be disposed of when it's finished with; the—er—symptoms come on rather suddenly, you know, Mr Bredon, in these cases. What about coming round to my house and having a spot of something on the way? Sure you won't? Oh, very well. Yes, they've got to bury him in some special way of their own, tuck him up with his feet towards Jericho, I expect, or something of that sort. Hope these niggers'll clear out after this,' he added, lowering his voice for fear the driver should overhear him. 'The neighbours don't like 'em, and that's a fact. They're not pukka Indians, you know; he picked them up in San Francisco or somewhere; lascars, I should call 'em.'

'I don't know that you're likely to be rid of them, doctor,' explained Bredon. 'I suppose you realize that they benefit heavily under Jervison's will? At least, his insurance policy is made out in favour of the Brotherhood, and I suppose there'll be a tidy piece of his own money coming to them as well.'

'And your company pays up, does it, Mr Bredon?' said the little doctor. 'Gad, I wonder if they'd let me into the Brotherhood? There are only four of them in it, and I could do with a few extra thousands.'

'Well,' explained Bredon, 'that's what we're here about. If it's suicide, you see, they can't touch the money. Our policies don't cover suicide; it would be too much of a temptation.'

'That so? Well, then, you're on velvet. The thing can only be suicide, and unsound mind at that. There's Yewbury, up on the hill. Queer place; very rich man had it, name of Rosenbach, and fitted it all up like a palace, with a real racket-court; that's the roof of it you see there. Then he crashed, and the place was sold for next to nothing; taken on as a preparatory school, it was, by a young fellow called Enstone; I liked him, but he never could make the place pay properly, one way and another, so he sold out and went to the South Coast, and then Jervison took it on. Well, here we are. Would you like to wander about the grounds, Mr Bredon, while we go in and look at the remains, or what?'

'I think I'd like to go into the room where he was found. Perhaps one of these natives would take me in; I'd like to have a chance of talking to one of them.'

The arrangement was made without difficulty, though Bredon found his guide a source of embarrassment, almost of nervousness. The driver of the car had worn an ordinary dark suit, but this other representative of the community was dressed in flowing white robes, with a turban to match, and seemed covered all over with cabalistic emblems. He was tall and strongly built; his manner was at once impassive and continually alert; nothing seemed to disturb him, yet you felt that nothing escaped him. And when he spoke, he belied his whole appearance by talking English with a violently American intonation.

The racket-court stood at a considerable distance from the main block of buildings; perhaps five hundred yards away. The gallery which had once existed close to the door had been cleared away to make space when it had been turned into a gymnasium, and you entered directly into a huge oblong room, with something of a cathedral vastness in its effects of distance and of silence. The floor had been fitted with shiny red oilcloth, so that your footsteps were deadened, and the echoes of the place awoke only at the sound of your voice. The light came chiefly, and the ventilation entirely, from a well in the centre of the roof; the top of this was of fixed glass, and only the iron slats at the side were capable of letting in air. There were still memories of the gymnasium period; at four points in the ceiling were iron rings, which looked as if ropes had hung down from them by hooks, and there were lockers at one side which still seemed to demand the presence of juvenile boots. Little had been done since in the way of furnishing; the eccentric had evidently used the place when he wanted to be separated from his kind, with the thick walls shutting out the sounds of the countryside, the heavy locked doors preventing intrusion. Bredon could not help wondering if the owner had felt safer sleeping in here than under the same roof with his questionable protégés.

But two pieces of furniture there were, which attracted attention almost equally as symptoms of the recent tragedy. One was a bed, standing out in the very middle of the floor; a temporary arrangement, apparently, since it was a wheeled bed with iron railings, of the type common in hospitals, and the wheels had dragged lines across the linoleum, which still shone from their passage. The bed itself was absolutely bare; even the under-blanket had been torn out from its position, and lay, with the other blankets and the sheets, on and around the bed in grotesque confusion. It had the air, Bredon felt, of a bed from which the occupant has been pulled out, rather than of one which the occupant has left, in whatever hurry or excitement, of his own free will. Beyond the bed, against the wall furthest from the entrance, stood a sideboard, plentifully laden with vegetarian food. There was a loaf of bread, made of some very coarse grain, a honeycomb in a glass dish, a box of dates, some biscuits which looked brittle as glue, even, in witness of Simmonds's accuracy, some nuts. It was not a room in which the ordinary man would have sat down cheerfully to a meal; but, what was more important, it was a room in which you could not possibly starve.

Bredon went to the sideboard first of all, and gave the exhibits a careful scrutiny. He felt the outside of the bread, and satisfied himself, from the hardness of the 'fly-walk,' that it had remained for several days untasted. He tried some milk from a jug which stood there, and found it, as he had expected, thoroughly sour. 'Did Mr Jervison always have sour milk?' he asked of his guide, who was watching all his movements with grave interest. 'No, sir,' was the answer. 'I took that milk in myself, the evening when we last saw the prophet alive. It was sweet milk, fresh from the dairy. It has not been drunk, not one drop of it, till you tasted it, sir, just now.' The box of dates, though it was opened, contained its full complement of fruit. The honey was thick, and furred over with dust. The place on which the biscuits lay was not covered with crumbs, as it should have been if any of them had been broken. Altogether, it seemed a safe conclusion that the dead man had starved in sight of plenty.

'I want to ask some questions, if I may,' said Bredon, turning to the native. 'My company wishes to satisfy itself whether Mr Jervison died by misadventure, or took his own life. You will not mind helping me?'

'I will tell you whatever you wish to know. I am sure you are a very just man.'

'Look here, then—did Jervison often sleep here? And why did he want to sleep here that night—the night when you last saw him?'

'Never before; but that night he was trying a very special experiment; you do not understand these things here in the West. He was meaning to take a narcotic drug, one which he had prepared himself, which would set his soul free from his body. But because it is very dangerous to be disturbed from outside, while the soul is away from the body, he wanted to sleep here, where nobody could disturb him, and we wheeled that bed in from the house. All this you will find written in his diary; he was very careful to do that, because, he said, if any harm came to him from the experiment, he wished it to be known that it was no fault of ours. I will show you the diary myself.'

'Oh, he was drugged, was he, that first night? You don't think he may have taken an overdose of the drug, and died from that?'

The Indian smiled ever so slightly, and shrugged his shoulders. 'But the doctor has told us that he starved to death. Your friend is a doctor also; he will tell you the same. No, I will tell you what I think. The prophet fasted very often, especially when he wished his soul to be free. And I think that when he woke up from his sleep he had had some revelation which made him want to go deeper into these mysteries; and therefore he fasted; only this time he fasted too long. He fasted perhaps till he fainted, and was too weak to reach his food, or to come out and find help. And we waited in the house, doing our own studies, while the prophet was dying in here. It was fated that it should be so.'

Bredon was less interested in the theological bearings of the question than in its legal aspect. Is a man who starves himself without meaning to kill himself a suicide? Anyhow, that was for the lawyers. 'Thank you,' he said, 'I will wait for my friend here; don't let me keep you.' The Indian bowed, and left him—with some reluctance, Bredon thought. But he was determined to search this room thoroughly; he did not like the look of things. The lock on the door—no, that did not seem to have been tampered with, unless there were a second key. The walls? You do not make secret doors in a racket-court. The windows? None, except those slats underneath the skylight, at the sides of the well; only just room for a man to put his hand in there, and that would be about forty feet up. Hang it all, the man had been alone for ten days; he had left the food untasted, and he had made no effort to get out. There was even a writing-tablet with a pencil tied to it, not far from the bed; he had meant, Bredon supposed, to write down his revelations on it as he woke from sleep; yet the dust stood on the top sheet, and the dead man had left no message. Could it really be madness? Or was the Indian right in his guess? Or was it even possible . . . one heard of strange tricks these Eastern jugglers played; was it possible that these four adepts had managed to tamper with the inside of the room without entering it?

And then Bredon noticed something on the floor which interested him; and when Simmonds came back with the little doctor they found him on all fours beside the bed, and the face he turned towards them as they came in was a very grave one, yet with a light in the eyes that suggested the anticipation of a victory.

'What a time you've been!' he said reproachfully.

'There's been a good deal in the way of alarms and excursions,' exclaimed Simmonds. 'Your friends the police have been round, and they've just taken off the whole Brotherhood in a suitably coloured Maria. Apparently they are known in Chicago. But I'm dashed if I see how they are going to fix anything on them over this business. The man starved to death. Don't talk to me about drugs, Bredon; there simply isn't any question of that.'

'It's murder, though,' said Bredon cheerfully. 'Look here!' And he pointed to the shiny tracks drawn across the oil-cloth by the movement of the bed's wheels. 'You see those tracks? They don't lead right up to the place where the bed stands; they stop about two inches short of it. And that means murder, and a dashed ingenious kind of murder too. By rights, the police oughtn't to be able to fix it on them, as you say. But that's the bother about a murder which takes four men to do it; one of them is certain to break down under examination, and give the others away. I was wondering, Dr Mayhew—when your friend Enstone left, did he take the fixtures away with him? The fixtures of this gymnasium, for example?'

'Sold the whole place, lock, stock and barrel. He needed all the money he could get, and the Brotherhood weren't particular. There's a sort of shed at the back, you know, where Enstone used to keep odds and ends, and I shouldn't be a bit surprised if you find the parallel bars and what not tidied away in there. Were you thinking of giving us a gymnastic display? Because I should suggest some lunch first.'

'I just thought I'd like to look at them, that's all. And then, as you say, lunch.' Dr Mayhew's prophecy proved accurate. The shed at the back was plentifully littered with the appropriate debris. A vaulting-horse stood there, mutely reproachful at having been so long turned out to grass; the parallel bars were still shiny from youthful hands; the horizontal ladder, folded in three, was propped at an uneasy angle, and the floor was a network of ropes and rings. Bredon took up a rope at random and brought it out into the daylight. 'You see,' he said, passing his hands down it; 'it's frayed all along. Boys don't fray ropes when they climb up them; they wear gym-shoes. Besides, the fraying is quite fresh; looks only a day or two old. Yes, that's what they did; and I suppose we had better tell the police about it. The company stands to lose, of course; but I don't see what is to be done with the policy now, unless they erect a mausoleum over the Brotherhood with it. There won't be any more Brotherhood now, Dr Mayhew.'

'You must excuse him,' apologized Simmonds; 'he is like this sometimes. I hate to say it, Bredon, but I haven't completely followed your train of thought. How did these fellows get at Jervison, when he was locked up in his gymnasium? You can't kill a man by starvation, unless you shut him up without any food, or hold him down so that he can't get at it.'

'You're wrong there,' objected Bredon. 'There are all sorts of ways. You can poison the food, and tell him it is poisoned. Not that that happened here, because I've tasted some of the milk myself, and here I am. Besides, I think a starving man would always risk it when it came to the point. You can hypnotize the man, in theory, and persuade him that the food isn't there, or that it isn't food at all. But that's only in theory; you never hear of a crime like that being pulled off in real life. No, the Indians had their alibi all right, when poor Jervison died.'

'You mean they starved him somewhere else, and brought his body in here afterwards?'

'Hardly that. You see, it would be very much simpler to starve your man in here, and bring the food in afterwards to look as if he'd starved himself deliberately. But to do either of those things you must have access to the building. Do you happen to know, Dr Mayhew, who it was that first found the body? And what sort of difficulty they had in making their way into the gymnasium?'

'The door was locked, and the key fixed on the inside. We had to take the lock off. I was one of the party myself. The police, of course, had charge of things; but the Indians had called me in as well, the moment they got the idea that something was wrong.'

'Really? Now, that's very instructive. It shows how criminals always overdo these things. You or I, if a friend locked himself up and didn't appear for ten days, would shout through the keyhole and then send for a locksmith. Whereas these gentlemen sent off at once for a doctor and the police, as if they knew that both would be wanted. That's the worst of thinking that you've covered your tracks.'

'My dear Bredon, we're still taking your word for it that it *is* murder. If it is, I should say the murderers covered their tracks quite remarkably well. It looks to me the clearest possible case of lunacy and suicide.'

'You're wrong there. Did you notice that there was a writing-tablet and a pencil by the side of the bed? Now, what madman ever resisted the temptation to scrawl something on any odd piece of paper he came across? Especially if he thought he was being starved, or poisoned. That applies, too, if he were really making some fasting experiment; he would have left us a last message. And what did you make of the way the bedclothes were piled on and round the bed? Nobody, mad or sane, wants to get out of bed that way.'

'Well, tell us all about it if you must. You may be mad or I may be mad, but I see no reason why either of us should starve, and we are keeping Dr Mayhew from his lunch.'

'Well, the outlines of the thing are simple. Jervison had picked up these rogues somewhere in America, and they were no more mystics than you or I are; they could talk the patter, that's all. They knew he was rich, and they stuck to him because they saw there was money to be made out of him. When they found he had made the Brotherhood his heirs, there remained nothing except to eliminate him; they went over the plan of the ground, and determined to make the fullest use of the weapons that lay ready to hand. Always a mistake to bring in weapons from outside; study your man's habits, and kill him along his own lines, so to speak. All they had to do was to encourage him in making these fool experiments, and to supply him with some ordinary kind of sleeping-draught which pretended to have a magical effect; probably it was they who suggested his retiring to the gymnasium, where he could be quiet, and they who insisted on wheeling his bed out into the middle of the room, telling him that he ought to catch the noonday sun, or some nonsense of that kind. Who ever heard of a man wanting to have his bed out in the middle of the room? It's human nature to want it next to the wall, though why, I've no idea.'

'And then?'

'They waited, that night, till the sleeping-draught had taken its full effect; waited till it was early dawn, and they could see what was happening without being noticed by inquisitive neighbours. They tied ladders together, or more probably used that horizontal ladder, stretched out into a straight line, and climbed up on to the roof. All they took with them was ropes—the four ropes that used to hang from those hooks in the ceiling. They still had iron hooks on them; I dare say they tied handkerchiefs round the hooks to prevent any noise. Through the skylight, they could look down on the sleeping man; between the iron slats they could let down the four ropes. The hooks acted as grapnels, and it did not take much fishing before they hooked the iron rails at the head and foot of the bed. Very quietly, very evenly, they pulled up the ropes; it was like a profane and ghastly parody of a scene you may remember in the Gospels. And still poor Jervison slept on, under the influence of his drug; dreaming, perhaps, that he was being levitated, and had at last got rid of the burden of the flesh. He nearly had.

'He slept on, and when he woke, he was hung up forty feet in the air, still in his bed. The bed-clothes had been removed; it would not do to let him have a chance of climbing down. He hung there for over a week; and if his cries reached the outside world at all, they only reached the ears of four pitiless men, his murderers. Perhaps a braver man would have jumped for it, and preferred to end his life that way. But Jervison, you told me yourself, Simmonds, was a coward about heights; he couldn't jump.'

'And if he had?'

'He would have been found dead, either from his fall or from its effects. And the Indians would have told us, gravely enough, that the prophet must have been making an experiment in levitation, or something of that kind. As it was, all they had to do was to come back when all was safely over, to let down the ropes again, to throw his bed-clothes in through the slats, falling where they would, and to take their ropes and ladder down again the way they had come. Only, as was natural, they did not bother to pay out the ropes quite evenly this time, and the bed came down in the wrong place, about two inches from where it had stood originally. So that it didn't fit in with the tracks across the oil-cloth, and it was that, somehow, which gave me a notion of what had happened. The bed, evidently, had been lifted; and you do not lift a wheeled bed unless you have a special purpose to be served, as these devils had. Jervison was a fool, but I hate to think of the way he died, and I am going to do my best to see these four fellows hanged. If I had my way with them, I would spare them the drop.'

ROY VICKERS · 1899–1965

The Henpecked Murderer

1

The case of Crippen has been retold so often and in so many languages
that the facts are known even to those students of criminal psychology
who were not born in 1910, when it all happened. That he was the
first murderer to be caught by wireless telegraphy, as it was then
called, is today of less interest than the fact that police, counsel, and
finally warders of the condemned cell all agreed that he was a 'decent
little man', a 'gentleman', in the moral rather than the social sense of
the word. Yet he buried portions of his wife under the floor-boards of
the kitchen.

Alfred Cummarten had much of the mentality of Crippen. The
Cummarten murder, in 1934, was a sort of tangent to the Crippen
murder. As he had not read the case, Cummarten made most of
Crippen's minor mistakes, avoiding the major mistake of flight. He
was not as anxious as the decent little Crippen that no one else should
suffer for his sins—a moral defect which brought its own penalty.

There was even a physical resemblance to the original, for
Cummarten was a shortish man, with brown, protuberant eyes, a
moustache, and a waxen complexion.

Moreover, there was, to start with, exactly the same set-up.
Gertrude Cummarten, like Cora Crippen, was regarded by her
husband with esteem and affection, although she was shrewish,
greedy, and wholly selfish. She drilled and bullied him—for Gertrude, too, was physically larger than her husband, and would
sometimes strike him in anger. That her attractions were fading at
thirty-seven had, really, nothing to do with the case, because the girl,
Isabel Redding, appealed primarily to Cummarten's thwarted
paternal instinct.

Isabel, as is now known, was of unidentifiable origin. Someone
contrived her admission to a convent school, where she acquired a
certain ladylike address, if nothing else. She was twenty-two when
she applied to Cummarten for employment as a stenographer.
Cummarten was a shipping agent with a small but steady clientele.

Isabel was decorative, docile, but remarkably inefficient. Cummarten saw in her an innocent child-woman who could be moulded into the kind of woman he would like his daughter to be—if he had a daughter. So he engaged another girl to be his secretary, and kept Isabel on to run the errands and stamp the envelopes.

Being a silly little man (though Scotland Yard would not agree) he asked her for the weekend to The Laurels, his modest house on the outskirts of Thadham, an old market town some twenty miles from London. He was guileless enough to suggest that his wife should elect herself an honorary aunt.

Gertrude's marked coldness did not deter Isabel from spending three more weekends at The Laurels during 1933, the last occasion being in July, when Cummarten took her to a flower-show and introduced her to most of his acquaintances.

He was deeply shocked when Gertrude said she did not believe a word of his angel-child nonsense, and that, if he could afford a mistress, which surprised her, he might have the decency not to humiliate his wife by flaunting the girl before the neighbours. The truth was that he himself did believe the angel-child nonsense.

Gertrude's allegation that he was spending money on the girl was true. There was her salary, the bulk of which was a dead weight on the business. There were other expenses—not indeed for dress or for any kind of entertainment, but for a special diet, to build up her nervous system; for massage to cure her insomnia, and even for books to nourish her mind.

Gertrude's accusation lost its horror through repetition. By the autumn of 1933, it no longer seemed outrageous to notice the physical charms of the young woman he had hitherto thought of as his spiritual daughter. In short, under some high-falutin phrase, she became his mistress in fact. In this period she betrayed a certain sophistication which compelled him to revise the angel-child theory, and to wonder what she had been doing between leaving the convent school and applying to him for employment.

By the turn of the year, his expenditure began to alarm him. This, he believed, was largely his own fault. He would discover little needs of Isabel's, and urge her to do the buying. It was he who suggested that she needed a new bag, not expecting that she would order one in crocodile, costing nine pounds. It was he who said she must have new hairbrushes. She ordered a dressing-table set in tortoiseshell. He had admired it before she revealed that it would cost one hundred guineas.

'You've been swindled, darling!' he gasped. 'I've noticed things exactly like this at Harridges—the whole layout for about a couple of pounds.'

'But this is real tortoiseshell, darling!' she explained. 'It comes from Perriere's, and they said they would always lend us sixty pounds on it if we should ever need the money. But, of course, I'll take it back if you think I've been extravagant.'

By ill luck he had knocked one of the scent bottles to the floor, slightly chipping the glass and slightly denting the tortoiseshell. She had been so nice about it—so anxious to cover up the damage so that the set could be returned—that he eventually sent the cheque to Perriere's, feeling that he had robbed Gertrude.

He was now leading a double life, which he hated. To rob it of some of its duplicity, the silly little man confided in his wife. She treated him with scorn and intensified bullying—which made him feel better, because he despised himself and felt that he ought to be punished.

In July, 1934, Isabel gave him the usual reason, true or false, for hurrying a divorce, to be followed by immediate marriage. He said he would put it to Gertrude, but did not, because he was afraid. For an utterly miserable fortnight he stalled Isabel with palpable lies.

On Monday, August 7th, a Bank Holiday, Isabel took the matter out of his hands by turning up uninvited at The Laurels—at half past two in the afternoon—for a showdown with Gertrude.

2

Gertrude had been visiting a cousin at Brighton and did not return until about nine o'clock. A light rain was falling and it was getting dark—but not too dark for the neighbours to observe her return from behind their curtains. They had been, in a sense, waiting for her. They had seen Isabel arrive: they had discussed the details of her dress: in particular, a magenta scarf which was unfashionable and strident but, in her case, effective: a crocodile bag, which they opined must have cost Mr Cummarten a matter of pounds. They knew that Gertrude had been to Brighton for the day. Whatever happened now, there was certain to be a scandal or at least a rumpus.

'As soon as I heard her footsteps I went into the hall and turned on the light,' wrote Cummarten. *'I meant to tell her about Isabel at once, but, of course, I had to lead up to it a bit. So in the hall I just said something ordinary, like I hoped she had enjoyed her day.'*

'Well, I did think you'd have the light on in the hall to welcome me home, even if it'd be a false welcome,' said Gertrude. 'But I expect we have to be careful with the housekeeping bills, now that you're spending so much money on that girl. And since you ask, I didn't go to Brighton for pleasure. I went to Mabel for advice and I'm going to take her advice. Come in here and sit down, Alfred.'

She took him into the little room which they called the morning-room because they had breakfast there. He obediently sat down at the table, knowing that he could not secure her attention until she had talked herself to a standstill.

'Mabel says I'm a soft-hearted fool to put up with it and she's right. And it's got to be one of two things, Alfred. Either you sack that girl from the office and break off with her altogether or I'm going to divorce you.'

'I was so surprised when she said this after all I'd been through that I said nothing but stared at her like a ninny.'

'You needn't pretend it would break your heart, Alfred. I've no doubt that you'd be glad enough to have done with our marriage altogether, after the mockery you've made of it. But Mabel says the judge would make an order for you to pay me at least a third of your income, and perhaps a half, and so you may want to think twice. *Alfred*, whose bag is that over there by the coal scuttle?'

'As soon as she saw the bag I knew she would tell herself everything and I needn't try to break it gently but just answer her questions.'

'It's Isabel's bag,' said Cummarten.

'So she has been here! I suspected it from your sly behaviour. What time did she go?'

'She didn't go. She's in the drawing-room.'

'Then she's going now. I'm going to turn her out.'

'You aren't,' said Cummarten. 'You can't get into the drawing-room. I've locked the door and I've got the key.'

The pitch of his voice made her spine tingle. She reached across the breakfast table, upsetting a vase of flowers, and grabbed him by the lapel of his coat.

'What're you trying to tell me, Alfred? Go on! Say it!'

'She's dead,' answered Cummarten. 'I killed her.'

'Oh-h!' It was a long-drawn, whispered moan. 'To think that this should happen to *me*! Oh, dear God, what have I done to deserve this!'

Characteristically, she was concerned solely with the impact of the murder on her own circumstances. She sprawled forward on the table, her face on her forearm, and burst into tears. So violent was her emotion that the silly little man went round to her side of the table to comfort her.

'There, there, my dear!' He patted her shoulder. 'Don't take on so, Gert! It won't bring the poor girl back to life. Something goes wrong sometimes, and this sort of thing happens. Stop, Gert—you'll make yourself ill!'

Presently she was able to speak, in a voice shaken with convulsive sobs.

'I was twenty-four when you married me and I'm thirty-seven now. You've had the best years of my life. I could put up with your wanting a younger woman, though it hurt my feelings more than you know. But I did believe you'd always look after me in my old age.'

'Thirty-seven isn't old age, dear. Now, do calm yourself, because we've got to settle practical matters before I'm arrested.'

That caught her attention.

'You haven't got any money outside the business, have you?'

'No. And I'm afraid you won't get much for that. It's largely a personal connection.'

'I can't even go back to nursing. No one would employ me after this!' Her imagination still struggled against accepting the fact of disaster to herself. 'Are you sure you've killed her, Alfred? Are you sure she isn't fooling you? How did you kill her? I don't believe you could kill anybody without a revolver, which you haven't got.'

'I killed her, all right! She made out we had to have a divorce and me marry her. Even if she was telling the truth about that, I've good reason to believe she could have picked on others besides me. There's one she called Len—I've seen him hanging about—big Spanish-looking feller. Never mind!'

'But you didn't have to kill her for that, Alfred!'

'Let me finish! She came down here on her own for a show-down with you. When she offered to say nothing to you and cut out all the divorce stuff if I'd hand over a thousand pounds, I got pretty angry. After a while, she tried to coax me into a good temper by love-making. Real love-making! I suppose I softened up a bit, and then I felt what a worm I was for letting a woman like that wheedle me. I'd got my arm round her neck in some way—can't remember quite how—and she was pretending to struggle. And I thought if I pushed her chin back it'd break her neck—sort of leverage. And I suddenly wanted to do that more than I'd ever wanted to do anything. And I did it. That's all!'

'I don't believe you killed her!' Gertrude was lashing herself into wishful disbelief. 'Give me that key!'

She went alone to the drawing-room. Her past training as a hospital nurse saved her from the normal revulsion. When she returned she was carrying the magenta scarf.

'You were right,' she said. 'I didn't think you could've done it, but you have.' She went on: 'I've brought this scarf, because it's the sort of thing you would leave lying about, same as you left that bag. You'd better put them both together. The neighbours will have noticed both. And we'll have a look round to see if there's anything else, before I go.'

'What's the use, Gert! As soon as you've gone, I'm going to ring the police.'

'I *thought* that was in your mind!' Her self-pity was lost in fury. 'Going to give up without lifting a finger to save yourself? And you call yourself a man!'

'I can take what's coming to me without squealing, anyhow!'

'You mean you can take what's coming to *me!*' she shrilled. 'You're ready to kick me into the gutter where I shall be branded for life as the wife of a murderer, and all you think about is how brave you are!'

'But what can I do? It's no good running away!'

'You can get rid of her if you keep your head. You can use a spade, can't you! And who's to know she didn't leave the house and run off with a man who's got more money than you—not that anyone will bother their heads about what happens to that sort!'

Cummarten had planned to give himself up, because he had not been able to imagine doing anything else. But already Gertrude had planted in his brain the idea of escape. For thirteen years he had lived under her domination. Always, after his domestic blunders, she had first bullied him and then cleared up the mess. The same process was now at work on a larger scale.

'Suppose something goes wrong?' he objected, in order to receive her reassurance, which promptly came.

'Nothing will go wrong if you do as you're told. I shall have to leave everything in your hands, because I know you wouldn't wish me to take any risk of being dragged into it. I shan't worry about myself. No one need know I've helped you. I wasn't seen coming home tonight. It so happened that I took the bus from the junction instead of waiting for the local train, and no one else got out at the corner and there was no one about, because it was raining. I'll get along to Ealing and spend the night with mother. You can say I went straight there from

Mabel's. You can give out that mother is ill and I'm looking after her. As soon as it's all clear, I'll come back.'

'You mean we can take up our life again as if nothing had happened!' There was awe in his voice as the idea took shape.

'I'm quite ready to try all over again to make you happy, Alfred, now that you've learnt your lesson.'

But she must, of course, take care not to burn her fingers. In a few minutes she had evolved a plan by which all risk was concentrated upon Cummarten. She made him repeat his orders and then:

'I'll slip out to the garage now and get into the car. The neighbours will hear the engine. And if anyone asks you afterwards, which they won't, remember to say that you were driving the girl back to her flat in London. If anyone wants to speak to me they can ring me up at mother's.'

3

With a course of action laid down for him, Cummarten's nerve steadied. He made good time to London. In Holborn he dropped Gertrude at the tube station, where she was to take a train to Ealing. He himself drove on to the flatlet, which was in one of the dingier blocks in Bloomsbury. The block had no resident porter—a fact which most of the residents regarded as an advantage. He chose his moment for leaving the car, his sole concern being that no one should observe that he was alone.

The flatlet consisted of a fair-sized room with two curtained recesses. It was clean but untidy. Three large fans nailed on the walls gave it a would-be artistic atmosphere, helped by an expensively elaborate cover on the ottoman bed. For the rest, there was the usual bed-sitting-room furniture.

Acting on Gertrude's instructions with all possible speed, Cummarten found Isabel's suitcase. Into it he crammed her night-dress and other small oddments. Next, 'any small articles you've given her that are expensive.' The tortoiseshell dressing-table set was certainly expensive though it was not small, as it consisted of eight pieces including the scent bottles. It occupied two-thirds of the suitcase and left no room for any additions.

The magenta scarf he placed 'carelessly' on the folding-table. The crocodile bag, emptied at The Laurels, he put on the floor near the stove, as if the girl had flung it down after emptying its contents into another bag.

By midnight, he was back at The Laurels.

He had brought his tools from the garage and a spade and pick from the adjoining tool shed. He moved the table and chairs from the morning-room into the hall. Then he untacked the carpet in the morning-room and removed some of the floor-boards.

This gave him no serious difficulty—he had finished before one. Below the beams holding the floor-boards he had expected to find soft earth. Instead, he found rubble, evenly spread to a depth of some eighteen inches. Clearing this was extremely laborious: he had to work very slowly because the rubble made a dangerous amount of noise. His courage fluctuated: while he was wielding the spade he was steady: but when he rested, which was often, he would fancy he heard footsteps on the garden path and would climb up and listen, to reassure himself.

It was half past three before he had cleared a sufficient area. Temporarily exhausted, he went into the kitchen and revived his strength with tea. When he re-started work, with the pick, he realized that his own stamina would be a major factor. Though the house had been built before cement was commonly used for the purpose, the foundations had been well laid and the earth was dry and very hard.

In an hour his strokes with the pick became feeble. By six o'clock his physical condition resembled that of a boxer who has just managed to keep on his feet for a twenty-round contest. His wrists were numb and his knees were undependable. It was all he could do to hoist himself back onto the floor of the morning-room. As he lay panting he knew that, in his present condition, he could not possibly carry the body and complete his task before eight o'clock, when Bessie, the daily help, would arrive. If he were to make the attempt and fail he would be worse off than if he were to leave it in the drawing-room.

He was moving so slowly that when he had replaced everything in the morning-room and re-tacked the carpet with his hammer-head muffled, half past seven was striking.

Having washed, he went upstairs, got into bed for a minute in order to tumble the bedclothes, then did his best to shave as usual. When he heard Bessie arrive he came down in his dressing-gown.

The drawing-room door was locked: the blinds were down, as he had left them the previous evening: the french windows giving on to the garden were bolted on the inside. He had only to keep his head and, as Gertrude had promised, everything would be all right.

'Mrs Cummarten,' he told Bessie, 'has had to go to her mother who has been taken ill. If you'll get me some breakfast, that'll be all. You can have another day off.'

'All right, sir!' Bessie was not overjoyed. After Sunday and the holiday on Monday there would be arrears of cleaning which would have to be made up later. 'But I'd better do the drawing-room before I go.'

'You can't,' said Cummarten. 'It is locked and Mrs Cummarten has evidently taken the key with her.'

'That doesn't matter,' returned Bessie. 'The key of the morning-room fits.'

To keep his head was the first essential. But what was the use if you couldn't think of things quickly, not being that sort of man.

'I'd rather you didn't, Bessie.' With sudden misinspiration, he added: 'Before Mrs Cummarten left yesterday morning she started to clean the china. She had to break off to catch her train—and she left the pieces all over the floor. She asked me to keep the room locked.'

Bessie stumped off to the kitchen. She heard him remove the keys from the morning-room and the dining-room. Knowing that something was being kept from her, she went into the garden and tried to look through the edges of the blind, but without seeing anything except part of a cushion from the settee lying on the floor.

Instead of leaving for the office at nine-fifteen, Cummarten stayed on in the morning-room, so that she could not clean it. Bessie left at ten. But before going home, she stepped across the road to The Cedars to tell her friend, who was help to Mrs Evershed, all about the locked drawing-room and the nonsense about the china being on the floor.

Cummarten was dozing in his chair at eleven when Mrs Evershed knocked at the front door.

'I didn't mean to disturb you, Mr Cummarten—I thought you'd be at the office. Can I have a word with Gertrude if she isn't busy?'

'Sorry, but she's in Ealing looking after her mother. I don't suppose it's anything much, but the doctor says the old lady had better stay in bed for a bit. Don't know when Gertrude will be back.'

Mrs Evershed delivered the usual polite platitudes, and then:

'Did she leave a message for me about Thursday? She said she'd know for certain by Monday night.'

'I haven't seen her since yesterday morning,' said Cummarten.

'Oh!' said Mrs Evershed, who was amongst those who had seen Gertrude return, 'I thought she was coming home last night.'

'She was, but she didn't. On her way back from Brighton she stopped off at Ealing, then phoned me that she would stay there.'

Bessie's friend had already repeated to Mrs Evershed the tale of the locked drawing-room. Mrs Evershed carried the tale to others. Before noon, there were two more callers for Gertrude, who received from Cummarten the same explanation.

During the afternoon he was left in peace and slept in his chair until nine. By midnight he was at work again on the grave. He was more careful of his strength this time and completed his task by four. The remains of Isabel and the contents of her crocodile bag and of the suitcase he had brought from the flatlet were buried four feet in the earth, with another eighteen inches of rubble on top. The floor-boards and the furniture were replaced.

In the drawing-room, the dozen odd pieces of china had been moved from the cabinet and placed on the floor, to give substance to the tale told to Bessie. Cummarten bathed, went to bed and slept until Bessie called him.

At breakfast he was surprised at his own freshness. 'I must be as strong as a horse, when I'm put to it,' he reflected with pride. That he had killed Isabel Redding ranked in his mind as a tragic misfortune, over which he must not allow himself to brood. He had a moral duty to Gertrude and, so far, had made a pretty good job of it, as Gertrude herself would have to admit.

When he arrived at the office he decided to ring Gertrude and let her know that the coast was clear—was about to do so when his secretary came in.

'Good morning, Miss Kyle; has Miss Redding been in to collect her belongings?'

'I have not seen Miss Redding since Friday last,' replied Miss Kyle with some hauteur, 'and her belongings are still here.'

'She came to my house on Monday and made it clear she would not be working for us any more. I fear,' he added, 'that Miss Redding has not been a success in this office.'

Miss Kyle, who was well aware of their intimacy, said nothing.

Having dealt with his mail, he rang his mother-in-law's flat in Ealing, but could get no answer. He tried again before going out to lunch and again when he returned. Then he rang the porter of the flats—to learn that Mrs Massell, his mother-in-law, had gone away for the weekend, had not yet come back and that the flat was therefore empty.

'Has Mrs Cummarten—my wife—been to you to make enquiries?'

'No, sir, there've been no enquiries for Mrs Massell since she went away last Friday.'

Cummarten replaced the receiver and found himself badly at a loss.

'Then where on earth is Gertrude?'

4

Others were already asking that question—including Mrs Massell herself. On her way back from a long weekend at Salisbury she had stopped off at Thadham to have a chat with her daughter. Arriving after Bessie had left, she was unable to obtain admission to the house. Mrs Evershed popped out of The Cedars. Explanations were being exchanged in the front garden of The Laurels when Cummarten himself appeared . . .

'That's what Gertrude told me on the telephone,' said Cummarten doggedly.

'But she knew I had gone to Salisbury!'

'I'm not saying what she knew. I'm saying what she told me.'

His mother-in-law walked him, by the sidepath, to the garden at the back of the house.

'You said all that because that Evershed woman was listening. Where is Gertrude?'

'I don't know! That's the maddening part of it!' cried Cummarten in genuine exasperation.

'When did you last see her?'

'Monday morning when she was going off to Mabel's.' He added a flourish: 'At least, that's where she said she was going.'

Mrs Massell gave him a hostile stare.

'Look here, Alfred, it's no use your trying to hint that she has run off with a lover. She's not that kind and wouldn't need to run when she could easily divorce you, as I happen to know, though you may have thought I didn't. If she has disappeared, something has happened. She may have lost her memory, like those people you hear about on the radio every night. Or she may have met with an accident—she might even have been murdered, for all you know or seem to care.'

A long, bitter laugh broke from him, which angered her further.

'You may not care much about her, but I warn you that you will find yourself in a very awkward position if anything has happened to her and you doing nothing about it.'

'But what *can* I do?'

'Come straight to the police with me and start inquiries.'

'That's no good!' he said sulkily. 'The police will take no notice.'

'Then I am going myself,' said Mrs Massell and promptly went.

5

In the Crippen case, the very similar lies were exposed within a few days of the murder. Nevertheless, six months passed before the police were able to take even the preliminary steps. But Crippen had no mother-in-law, nor did he employ domestic help.

Mrs Evershed's maid, in whom Bessie had confided, was being courted by a young constable, to whom she passed Bessie's tale and Mrs Evershed's comments. This she did to entertain the young man, not with any idea of informing the police as such—for even at this stage there was no suspicion that a crime had been committed, in spite of the locked drawing-room.

But everyone's sense of proportion was shattered by the arrival of Mrs Massell. When she was seen to enter the local police head-quarters there was hardly anyone in the neighbourhood who was not ready to believe that Cummarten had murdered his wife. In drawing-rooms, in gardens, at the local tennis club, the case of Crippen was recalled, the younger generation tactfully pretending they had not heard it all before.

If the police did not jump to that conclusion, they would seem to have toyed with it. By half past nine, when he went to The Laurels, Superintendent Hoylock had tapped all sources and primed himself with every available fact, even to the details of Isabel Redding's magenta scarf and crocodile bag. He wanted, he told Cummarten, confirmation of Mrs Massell's statement, before he could ask the BBC to broadcast an inquiry.

Cummarten took him into the dining-room, which was rarely used. He heard his mother-in-law's statement read and nodded confirmation of each item, inwardly fearing that Gertrude would be very angry at having her name called on the radio.

'When did you last see Mrs Cummarten?'

'About the middle of Monday morning—before she went to Brighton.'

Superintendent Hoylock folded the statement and returned it to his pocket.

'Mr Cummarten, your wife was seen to enter this house within a few minutes of nine o'clock on Monday night.'

It had not yet dawned on Cummarten that he was in immediate danger of anything but Gertrude's wrath. He looked positively angry.

'It's all Gertrude's fault for not telling me where she's gone!' he blurted out spontaneously. In spite of what Gertrude had said, he would now have to admit that she had returned on the Monday night. His anger stimulated him to a certain ingenuity in adapting the story which Gertrude had concocted.

'I'd better begin at the beginning, Superintendent. A young lady I employ at my office—a Miss Isabel Redding—came to see us in the afternoon. She has been here often—spent several weekends. She looked on us almost as relations. Lately, my wife became jealous, and everything was—well, not so pleasant as it used to be. Isabel came down to talk it all over. She waited until my wife came home. Words passed, and you may say there was a bit of a row. Soon we all calmed down and I drove the girl back to her flatlet. When I got back here—must have been about midnight—my wife had gone. Next morning the neighbours asked where she was. I wasn't going to tell 'em what I've been telling you, so I told 'em the first thing that came into my head. My wife may have walked out on me for all I know.'

The story held up under Hoylock's questions, because it covered all the facts known to him—with one exception.

'With one thing and another, Mr Cummarten, you've set people talking their heads off. There's a tale about something funny in your drawing-room—'

'That must be Bessie, our maid,' said Cummarten. 'You see, after breakfast on Monday, before my wife left for Brighton, she thought she'd clean the china—'

'So I heard,' interrupted Hoylock. 'It wouldn't do any harm to let me see that room.'

Cummarten produced a number of keys from his pocket, unlocked the drawing-room door. The Superintendent saw drawn blinds, and a litter of china on the floor—also on the floor, near the window, a cushion.

'Shows what people will say!' remarked the Superintendent. 'Now I'll tell you what we'll do. If nothing develops by tomorrow morning, we'll put it up to the BBC. People really do get lapses of memory sometimes when they're upset. Good night, Mr Cummarten. Don't you worry! We'll stop people talking!'

Talking! What were they saying?

Why, of course! Why hadn't he seen it before! They were saying that he had murdered *Gertrude*!

And what did they think he had done with her body?
Buried it under the floor-boards?

6

On Thursday, as Cummarten was about to leave the office for lunch, Superintendent Hoylock turned up, in plain clothes.

'Miss Redding might be able to help us find your wife,' he said. 'Can I have a word with her?'

Cummarten explained. He was pleased when Hoylock asked for her address, because he wanted the police to 'discover' the magenta scarf and the crocodile bag.

'It's a bit difficult to find. It'll save your time if I take you there.'

Outside the flatlet, Hoylock pointed to three milk bottles with the seals unbroken.

'Tuesday, Wednesday, and this morning!' he remarked and rapped on the door. 'Looks as if we shan't get an answer.'

Cummarten indicated that he was not surprised, and added: 'I have a key—she used to like me to have one.'

Inside the flatlet, the Superintendent behaved as Cummarten hoped he would, by immediately noticing the magenta scarf on the folding table.

'Is that the one she was wearing on Monday afternoon?'

'Let's have a look! Yes, that's the one all right.'

Hoylock's eye travelled to the crocodile bag lying on the floor near the stove.

'Wonder why she hasn't taken her bag with her!'

'She had more than one.' Cummarten picked up the bag and displayed the empty interior. 'She evidently shifted her money and whatnots to another bag.'

'So *she's* disappeared too!' exclaimed Hoylock. 'That's what I call a most peculiar coincidence!'

'Not much coincidence in it, really!' said Cummarten quickly. 'When I was up here with her on Monday night she said she was going straight off to a feller.'

'There and then? Without telling the man she was coming?'

'I didn't believe it any more than you,' said Cummarten. 'She started packing things before I left, but I thought she was putting on an act.'

'What's the man's name?'

'Don't know. She used to refer to him as "Len". I saw him hanging about outside once. Tall, dark chap, thick eyebrows and side-whiskers. Like a Spaniard. Sort o' chap who appeals to women. Probably a dancing partner by profession.'

Hoylock made a note of the description. Next, he opened the wardrobe, then the drawers of the dressing-table. Cummarten wished he would ask if there were anything missing from the dressing-table. But Hoylock said the wrong thing.

'She didn't take much with her, did she!'

'There was very little room in her one suitcase,' said Cummarten, 'because she had to take her dressing-table set—brushes, combs, scent bottles—eight pieces in all. I saw her packing them.'

'What! All that junk when she'd only got one suitcase! You'd think she'd leave that sort of thing till she came back for her clothes and furniture.'

'It was a very valuable set,' explained Cummarten. 'A present from myself—with my wife's approval, of course! It was real tortoiseshell. I paid Perriere's a hundred guineas for it.'

'A hundred guineas!' Hoylock was impressed and elaborated his notes.

Everything, thought Cummarten, was going just right, though he wondered why Hoylock was showing such detailed interest in Isabel's movements.

'Miss Redding,' he said, 'is certain to turn up in a few days to collect her things. Is it your idea, Superintendent, that she and my wife have gone off together?'

'I don't say they have. But I do say that if Mrs Cummarten doesn't turn up after the radio appeal we shall have to find this girl.'

Superintendent Hoylock returned to Thadham to file a detailed report—Cummarten to his office to spend the afternoon wondering what had happened to Gertrude.

After the nine o'clock news that night, Gertrude's name was called amongst those missing from their home and believed to be suffering from a loss of memory.

Cummarten sat up until after midnight in the hope that she might turn up. It didn't occur to him that her absence might have a wholly selfish explanation. For his peace of mind he forced himself to accept the loss of memory theory. Someone had told him that the broadcasts always found such persons, if they were alive. He saw clearly what his fate would be if the broadcast failed to produce results in a very few days.

7

When Cummarten entered his office the next morning he found a young man chatting to Miss Kyle.

'Mr Cummarten,' said Miss Kyle, 'this gentleman is from Scotland Yard.'

Cummarten managed to say 'good morning'. But it was a minute or more before he could understand what the young man was saying.

'In a boarding house in West Kensington, Mr Cummarten. We can get there in twenty minutes in a taxi. If the lady is Mrs Cummarten I can then notify the BBC.'

The lady was indeed Mrs Cummarten. She was being virtually held prisoner by the proprietress of the boarding-house, who had been suspicious from the first of this visitor who had paid a deposit in lieu of luggage.

Gertrude had the presence of mind to tell the plain-clothes youngster that her memory was a blank from the moment she left Brighton on the previous Monday. While the report for the BBC was being filled in, Cummarten telephoned a telegram to Superintendent Hoylock.

In the taxi that was taking them to the station, their first moment alone, Gertrude asked:

'Is everything all right, Alfred?'

'Absolutely! Only it would have been everything all wrong if you hadn't been found. I say—did you really have a lapse of memory?'

'Of course not! In the train I suddenly remembered mother was at Salisbury. I daren't ring you up—in case. It wouldn't have been safe to do anything but just keep out of the way. I was getting short of money. I tried yesterday to catch you on the Tube without anybody seeing me.'

He failed to perceive her callous indifference to his own fate, contented himself with a modest grumble.

'This time yesterday everybody thought I'd murdered you. In another day or two—'

'Well, then, that's the best thing that could have happened, when you come to think of it!'

In the train, in an unoccupied compartment, he gave her his account. To his surprise, she was extremely annoyed when he told her about the locked drawing-room door and the china ornaments.

'As if anybody would believe I'd be so silly! What would be the sense of putting the china on the floor?'

'I couldn't think of anything else to say on the spur of the moment.'

'The less you think about the whole thing now, the better. I shall pretend I've forgotten everything, and they can't get over that.'

The neighbours did not even try to get over it. The prestige of the BBC had the illogical effect of making everyone believe that the lapse of memory must have been genuine. Police interest vanished with the return of Mrs Cummarten. In a week or so, the neighbourhood, in effect, forgot its disappointment that a major scandal had failed to materialize.

A month later, Isabel Redding's landlord distrained on the flatlet for non-payment of rent. A dressmaker complained that Isabel had obtained a credit of forty pounds by false pretences. The Bloomsbury police, after a perfunctory attempt to find her, reported her as missing. As missing she appeared in the official police publication. Superintendent Hoylock, remembering the name, sent a copy of his report to Scotland Yard.

'Same old story!' grunted the inspector in charge. 'You can never trace these girls. You may pick 'em up by chance some day. Or you may not!'

With which remark he dropped the report into the basket which would eventually be emptied in the Department of Dead Ends.

The Cummartens resumed the even tenor of their life together. Though neither was strong in logic nor in law, they knew, in general terms, that before the police can start digging up a man's garden or lifting his floor-boards, they must establish before a magistrate a *prima facie* case that somewhere therein he has feloniously concealed a corpse.

They knew also that it was now impossible to establish such a case.

8

In May, 1935, the Cummartens went to Brighton to stay for a fortnight with Gertrude's cousin Mabel. While they were away, one Leonard Haenlin, a tall, dark, handsome scoundrel, remarkable for his sidewhiskers, was charged by a wealthy spinster with stealing her automobile and defrauding her in other ways.

The defence was that the car and the other articles and sums of money were gifts, and it looked as if the defence would succeed. The police had recognized that this man was a professional despoiler of women and were working up the case. His rooms were equipped with a number of expensive articles—including a handsome and obviously expensive dressing-table set of eight pieces, in real tortoiseshell.

When asked to account for the latter, he grinned in the face of Detective-Inspector Karslake.

'You think they are not mine. For once, you happen to be right. They belong to a girl friend, who lent them to me. Her name is Isabel Redding.' He added the address of the flatlet.

One of Karslake's men went to the flatlet to check up—to be humiliated by the information that Scotland Yard had posted the girl as missing the previous September.

A chit was duly sent to Detective-Inspector Rason asking for any available light on the ownership of the tortoiseshell set. Having found the reference in Superintendent Hoylock's report, Rason called on Haenlin, who was on bail, to see the set for himself.

'When did you borrow it, Len?'

'She lent it to me to pawn on July 20th, last year. If you look it up, you'll find that on that day I was fined forty quid for a little misunderstanding in Piccadilly. Perriere's, where it came from, said they'd always lend her sixty quid on it. But one of the bottles had a dent and a chip—the mutt who gave it her knocked it off her table—look for yourself—and they would only spring forty-five.'

'A good tale, old man—but you're switching this set with another,' chirped Rason. 'D'you know where Isabel got her set?'

'Yes. From a funny little bloke with a pasty face called Cummarten. You been a detective-inspector long, Mr Rason?'

'July 20th, you said,' returned Rason. 'Stand by for a shock! On the night of Monday, August 7th, Mr Cummarten saw Isabel packing her tortoiseshell set into her suitcase.'

'He didn't—he only thought he did,' grinned Haenlin. 'Listen! I knew I couldn't redeem the stuff for a bit, and Pasty Face might miss it from Isabel's table. So we went to Harridges and paid thirty-seven-and-six for an imitation set, like enough to that one for old Pasty Face not to know the difference. I redeemed the other set last month; you can check up if you want to.'

'That's big of you, Len. Where shall I find her to check up?'

'Wish I knew! She's a good kid, that!'

'Very good not to bother you about her tortoiseshell.'

'Can't make out why she hasn't been round!' Haenlin scowled. 'I'm not sure she isn't holding out on me. She went down to make a row between Pasty Face and his wife, saying she must have a divorce. It's not a sound line as a rule, but sometimes it works. She reckoned to touch for a thousand. Maybe she got it and is spending the dough on her own. Can't think of any other reason why she has kept out of my way.'

At Perriere's, Rason learnt that Haenlin's tale of the purchase and the subsequent pawning was true. Therefore the tale about the imitation set, which had successfully deceived Cummarten, must also be true. But it didn't make sense.

'If the girl was off in a hurry with one suitcase, she wouldn't stuff it with the whole eight pieces of doodah which she knew to be practically valueless. Even if she had pretended to Cummarten that she was taking them, she'd have unpacked 'em as soon as he left the flatlet. Hm! Probably Hoylock has muddled his facts.'

At Thadham, it soon became clear to Rason that Superintendent Hoylock had not muddled his facts. He heard Hoylock's full story, which included the story of the locked drawing-room and the china.

'So all Tuesday that door was locked—and most of Wednesday? And the blinds were down?'

When Hoylock assented, Rason asked for Bessie's address. By indirect means he contrived that the girl should show him the china, of which he noted that there were only a dozen small pieces.

On the way back he surveyed progress, if any.

'The next check-up is whether it's true the girl was blackmailing Cummarten for a thousand. Hm! Simplest way to do that would be to ask Cummarten.'

9

Two days later, when the Cummartens stepped out of the Brighton train at Victoria Station they were surprised to find that Bessie had come to meet them. And Bessie was not alone.

Rason stepped forward and announced himself, positively grovelling with apology.

'I'm very sorry indeed to pounce on you like this, Mr Cummarten, and I hope Mrs Cummarten will forgive me. It's about the Haenlin case—I daresay you read about it in the papers.'

Cummarten felt the pain in his breathing apparatus vanish.

'We have a strong suspicion that Haenlin is the man you told Superintendent Hoylock last year that you had seen outside the flatlet of Miss Redding. By the way, we haven't traced that girl yet.'

Cummarten, with something approaching graciousness, agreed to accompany Rason to the Yard to identify Haenlin. Now that the whole thing had blown over, he wished he had never mentioned 'Len' to the superintendent. Still, it had been a wise precaution at the time. He told Gertrude that he would come on by the one-fifteen to Thadham and his lunch could be kept hot.

'Haenlin,' said Rason in the taxi, 'is charged with swindling women. But we strongly suspect that he knows something about the disappearance of Miss Redding.'

'He struck me as a pretty rough type,' put in Cummarten, 'though I suppose one shouldn't judge on appearance.'

'You don't have to,' said Rason. 'He was working with that girl to trim you, Mr Cummarten. He knew all about her coming down to try and sting you for a thousand quid—he admitted it when we started work on him. But he wouldn't say whether you had paid her the thousand. Would you have any objection to telling us?'

'I have no objection to telling you,' said Cummarten gaining time to reflect that such a payment could be traced, 'that I did not. I couldn't afford such a sum.'

So it was true that the girl had tried. That altered the perspective of all Cummarten's statements and all his actions. But perspective isn't evidence. There was still a long way to go.

'To show you how he knew all about your affairs,' continued Rason, 'he even mentioned that you'd given her that tortoiseshell dressing-table set and that you yourself had chipped and dented a scent bottle, thereby reducing its value.'

Cummarten was shocked at this revelation of Isabel's treachery.

'I'm not the first man to make that sort of fool of himself,' he muttered. 'But I didn't know she was playing as low down as that.'

Rason's room, normally a disgrace to the orderliness of Scotland Yard, today looked more like a store room than an office. His desk had been pushed out of place to make room for a trestle table, the contents of which were covered with a white sheet which might almost have been a shroud.

'We shall have to keep you waiting a few minutes for the identification, Mr Cummarten,' apologized Rason. 'Take a seat.'

Cummarten sat down, uncomfortably close to the trestle table.

'In the train coming up from Thadham, your maid Bessie made me laugh,' chattered Rason. 'Told me how she thought once you had murdered Mrs Cummarten, because the drawing-room door was kept locked. And it all turned out to be something to do with the china being on the floor.'

Cummarten, being a silly little man, took the words at their face value.

'Yes. My wife was cleaning it when she had to run for her train, and—'

'Why did Mrs Cummarten clean the china in the dark?'

Cummarten blinked as if he had not heard aright. Rason added:

'Bessie says the blinds were down.'

Cummarten opened his mouth and shut it. Rason stood up, towering over him.

'D'you know, Mr Cummarten, if a girl tried to sting me for a thousand pounds I wouldn't see her home.' He drew at his cigarette. 'I'd be more likely to murder her.'

'And if I had murdered her I might sneak into her flat and plant her scarf and her bag—then carry off her expensive toilet set, to suggest that she had bolted.'

Again Cummarten had felt that pain in his breathing apparatus. It passed, as cold fear forced him to self-control.

'I don't begin to understand you, Mr Rason. You asked me here to identify that man—'

'Still trying to plant the murder on him, Cummarten? You packed that tortoiseshell stuff in the suitcase yourself and took it back to your house. And you know where you put it.'

'I deny it!' The words came in a whispered shout.

'You're wasting your breath, Cummarten. Look at that white sheet in front of you, Cummarten. Any idea what's underneath it, Cummarten? Well, lift up the sheet and see. Go on, man! It isn't Isabel—we couldn't bring her along.'

Cummarten sat as if paralysed. Rason tweaked the sheet, slowly raising one corner. Cummarten stared, uncertain whether he was experiencing hallucination. For he saw on the trestle table a scent bottle, with a chip in the glass and a dent in the tortoiseshell cap.

He sprang up, tore the sheet from Rason's hand and flung it back. Spread out on the table was a complete tortoiseshell set of eight pieces.

'*You know where you put it!*' repeated Rason.

With a cough-like sound in his throat, Cummarten collapsed into his chair, covering his eyes with his hands. When he removed his hands he looked like an old man, but he was wholly calm.

'I suppose it had to come some time,' he said. 'In a way, it's a relief to get it over. I can see now what a fool I've been, from the first. That tortoiseshell brings it all back.' He smiled wanly. 'Paid a hundred guineas for that set!'

It was indeed the set for which Cummarten had paid a hundred guineas—the set which Len Haenlin had pawned and redeemed. Rason had borrowed it when he had become morally certain that Cummarten had buried Isabel—and the imitation set.

But he still had no proof—still did not know precisely where Isabel was buried—could doubtfully have obtained an order to dig at random.

'You made a good fight of it!' remarked Rason. 'Weakest spot was that yarn about cleaning the china——'

'First thing that came into my head when Bessie wanted to do the drawing-room on the Tuesday morning! You see, I couldn't finish the job in the morning-room on the Monday night—all that rubble!'

Rason dug under the morning-room. With the remains of Isabel Redding, there was found an imitation tortoiseshell toilet set costing thirty-seven and sixpence.

Superintendent Wilson's Holiday

It is always a difficult job to persuade Wilson to take a holiday; for, as he is fond of saying, his work is his recreation, and he is apt to feel lost without it. On the occasion of which I am writing, however, I was adamant; for he was really badly run down after a succession of gruelling cases, and I was afraid that, unless he gave himself a rest, even his physique would give way. In my double capacity therefore, of friend and medical adviser, I brought strong pressure to bear. I not only ordered him positively to take an absolute rest, but proposed a joint walking tour, during which I made up my mind to ensure that neither cases nor adventures should come his way. Finally, as old Plato used to say, 'with great difficulty he agreed'; and that was how it was that a bright June afternoon found us walking together along the low sand-hills which border, but do not protect, the coast of Norfolk a few miles north of Yarmouth.

It was the third day of our tour. On the first we had been content with running to Norwich in my Morris-Oxford, and refreshing our memories of the old city. The next day we had poked about among the Broads, and ended up at Yarmouth, where we decided to leave the car behind and walk in a leisurely fashion right round the coast to King's Lynn, zigzagging inland to look at an old church or village as we felt inclined.

This afternoon we were walking through a region sparsely populated enough. It was a part where the sea was still steadily eating away the land, and in the memory of man whole villages had vanished. Already we had inspected the ruins of an old church, still lying strewn about the beach, where, we were told, the parson still preached one sermon yearly in order to maintain his right to the stipend. That left behind, we were walking along a very low range of sand-cliffs. One solitary house was in sight, perched on the very edge, and some miles ahead we could see the big black and white bulk of a lighthouse, and behind it a tall church tower.

'Upon my word, Michael,' said Wilson, 'I've got a thirst. A drink, or even a cup of tea, would come in mighty handy.' He took out the map.

200 G . D . H . Cole and M . Cole

'There doesn't appear to be a village nearer than that lighthouse, and that's a good three miles. There's a small place called Happisburgh just behind it, where that church tower is.'

I, too, looked at the map. 'There seem to be a few houses half a mile or so inland,' I said. 'We might get something at one of them.'

'Better push on,' said Wilson. 'There's sure to be a pub in the village. And the only house in our immediate neighbourhood doesn't look at all hospitable.' He pointed to the lonely building on the edge of the cliff ahead.

Most certainly it did not. We had come a good deal nearer while we were talking and could now see that it was no longer a house at all, but only its skeleton. More than half of it had slid right down off the edge on to the beach below; and the remainder stood desolate—roof and windows gone, with heaps of broken brickwork lying as they had fallen. The door was boarded up; but an intruder could have readily walked in through broken wall or window.

'That looks a little more promising,' I said, pointing to a bell-tent which had just come into view round the corner of the deserted house. 'If there are campers there, they will at any rate tell us the lie of the land.'

'There's quite a village of them beyond,' said Wilson. 'It looks to me like a boy scouts' camp, or something of the sort. Now's our chance, Michael, of giving one of them an opportunity for his daily good deed. The Good Samaritan up to date, you know.'

'I don't see a soul about,' I answered.

By this time, we had come abreast of the ruined cottage, and within twenty yards or so of the solitary tent. The scouts' camp, if it was so, still lay a good half mile ahead on the opposite side of a track which ran down to the beach through a gap in the cliffs. It looked very white and trim, with the sun upon it, whereas the tent nearer to us, even in the bright sunshine, still looked dirty and somehow forlorn. We passed the ruin and went towards it. Not a soul appeared. The tent flap was waving idly about in the light wind; and, as we came up to it, we saw the remains of a fire before it, scattered broadcast by the wind, and a number of cooking utensils and other miscellaneous objects lying about.

'Slovenly people, these campers,' said Wilson. 'Apparently there's no one here; but we may as well make sure.' So saying, he strode up to the tent opening and looked in. A minute later he withdrew his head. 'You have a look too,' he said.

The inside of the tent was in wild disorder. In two places the canvas had come away from the ground, and the wind had been blowing freely through the interior. Bedclothes and a few garments were flung about here and there in confusion. Moreover, it looked as if the rain had got in; for many of the things were wet and sodden, though the tent itself appeared quite dry. There was, however, on the farther side a long tear in the canvas, and through this a shaft of sunlight was streaming in.

'Well, Michael, any deductions?' my companion asked, as I turned away.

'Only that any sensible camper would have sewn up that hole, pegged the tent down, and put out his bedclothes in the sun to dry.'

'True, O sage. And, from the fact that these campers didn't, what do you conclude?'

'It looks as if they weren't here last night.'

'Because it hasn't rained since yesterday, you mean?'

'Yes,' I answered. 'Those things must have got wet at least eighteen hours ago. No one could have slept in them in that state.'

'True,' said Wilson, 'and equally, nobody would have left them in that state if he had been here since the weather turned fine. Ergo, these campers left here before last night, and presumably in a hurry, since they didn't even stop to straighten things up, or close the tent-flap. Queer campers, Michael. Now, why were they in such a devil of a hurry? It's not natural.' He stood pondering.

'Hanged if I know. Perhaps they were catching a train.'

Wilson strode round the little encampment. Suddenly, he stopped. 'Hullo!' he said. 'You see that bucket.'

'Yes; what about it?'

'Only that there isn't any water in it.'

'Why should there be?'

'My dear Michael, it rained heavily last night. A regular downpour. If that bucket had been standing there then, it wouldn't have been dry now.'

'You mean it shows they were here after it turned fine. Perhaps they went away in a hurry just after the rain stopped.'

'At midnight? To catch a train? Hardly.'

'Somebody else may have been here and put the bucket there since.'

'Perhaps,' said Wilson. He seemed to be hardly listening. Instead, he was poking about among the scattered remains of the fire. 'Eh? What's this?'

'Come off it,' I said. 'I've not brought you here to practise detecting why a pair of campers didn't wash up the dinner things. It's none of our business, thank heaven!'

'No,' said Wilson, hesitatingly, and with a faint note of interrogation in his voice. 'But this is interesting, all the same.' He held out for my inspection what looked like the charred fragment of a penny notebook.

I took it from him. 'Why,' I exclaimed, 'it's a bit of the butt-end of somebody's cheque-book.'

'It is; and somebody has been kind enough to leave the number of the cheques all ready for identification.'

'I suppose a man may burn the butt-end of his cheque-book if he likes.'

'But he doesn't usually burn the butt-ends of several different cheque-books over a camp-fire during his holidays.' Raking among the ashes, he had disinterred what were clearly the ends of two other cheque-books. In both, the numbering of the cheques was intact.

'You know, Michael,' Wilson went on, 'this is really extraordinarily odd.'

'Damn it, man, come away before you find any more mare's nests.'

Wilson chuckled. 'Mare's nests? Is this a mare's nest? That's exactly what I'm wondering, my dear fellow. It might be a singularly appropriate name. Let's have another look in here.' This time he dived right into the tent. Peering in, I saw him carefully turning over the various objects which lay strewn about it. Presently he gave a long whistle. 'Look here,' he said.

I looked. He was holding up a sheet on which, unmistakably, there was a long stain of blood. That it was blood I had no doubt. But it looked, not as if someone had bled upon the sheet, but as if some sharp, bloodstained implement had been wiped clean upon it. There were little tears in the midst of the stain, as if the sharp edge had cut into the fabric. 'What do you make of that?' Wilson asked. I told him. 'Right first time,' he observed. 'Is my medical adviser still of opinion that these campers' affairs are none of our business?'

I could no longer deny it. 'If they are,' I said, 'let me report it to the local police, while you clear out before you get involved. You've got to rest.'

'My dear Michael, I ask you. You bring me to this desolate spot, and walk me straight into the middle of a mystery. To begin with, I'm human; and secondly, this is evidently the hand of fate. Never flout Providence, Michael; she knows better even than my doctor what is good for me.'

I shrugged my shoulders helplessly. 'May it be a mare's nest,' I said, 'and may you quickly find the eggs.'

'I've just found something; but it's not an egg.' He held up his hand, and in it was a long, sharp steel blade, still unrusted.

'The weapon,' I gasped.

Wilson laughed. 'So doubting Thomas believes at last,' he said. 'Precisely—the weapon. All we require now is the corpse.'

'It doesn't follow there is a corpse,' I objected. 'Even if you strike a man with a knife, you don't always kill him.'

'A profoundly surgical observation, doctor. But we may as well see if there is a corpse all the same. At any rate, there seems to be—or to have been—a fair amount of blood about.' He went to the back of the tent and showed me on a patch of sand a large dark stain which had soaked deeply into the ground. 'The man who lost all that blood, Michael, didn't dash off at top speed to catch a train. Let's have another look round.'

He dived into the tent, and reappeared, carrying a Norfolk coat, a pair of grey flannel trousers, and an exceedingly dirty shirt. These he proceeded carefully to examine.

'Well,' I said at last, 'what are the conclusions?'

'They are fairly obvious. The shirt is marked "H.P." Inside the pocket of the coat is a tailor's label, which announces it as the property of Alec Courage, Esq., St Mary's Mansions, SW1. It is a large coat, obviously made for a fat, but fairly short man. The trousers, on the other hand, were made for a thin man, and bear no mark. Either they belong to "H.P.", the owner of the shirt, who, by the way, may also be identifiable by his laundry mark, or they are the property of some third person unknown. We will give "H.P.", for the present, the benefit of the doubt. We have thus the traces of two men, one fat and one thin, and we have good reason for believing that we know the name of one and the initials of the other. Beyond that, there are a few obvious indications. The large man is a heavy smoker, and in the habit of carrying tobacco loose in the pocket. The small man keeps a car or motorcycle—for there are numerous petrol and grease stains on his trousers, and they are of very varying age. He has the habit of keeping his hands in his trousers pockets, and he has something wrong with his left leg. There are other inferences; but for the present they seem unimportant. It is to be observed that there are no papers of any sort in either the coat or the trousers.'

'I think I follow you so far,' I said. 'What next?'

'We will now,' said Wilson, 'look a little farther afield. And the first thing we observe strikes me as distinctly interesting. May I call your attention to the footprints, Michael?'

I looked closely at the trodden sand before the tent and tried to follow what I knew of Wilson's methods. 'I can see signs,' I said, 'of four distinct pairs of feet—or at least I think so.'

'Good,' said Wilson.

'First, there is a large blank impression—with no nails or stud-marks or anything. Secondly, there is a rather smaller impression, in which the sole is blank, but the heel is round with a star-shaped figure in the middle. Thirdly, there is a very small pair of marks that might almost have been made by a woman. They are noticeable because of the barred impressions of the soles. And lastly, there is a pair with very large hobnails, or something of the sort. Am I right?'

'Quite right,' Wilson answered. 'And it can hardly have escaped you that pairs one and two are regularly on top of the others—or that, in fact, the large blank impression is your own crepe-rubber, while the star and the circle belong to me.' He held up his foot for my inspection.

'Oh,' I said rather ruefully. 'Then that leaves only the other two. And as we have signed our presence so plainly, and there are no other marks, it seems pretty plain that nobody except these two men has been here till we came.'

Wilson nodded. 'Yes,' he said; 'that is, since the rain, which would have washed away any previous impressions. But it also follows that these two men have been here since the rain.'

'But what about the wet camping clothes?'

'My dear Michael, that was the bucket, not the rain. Someone upset the bucket over them, and then set it upright again. And that was done since the rain, or the bucket would not have been empty. No, what we have proved is that these two men *were* here after the rain, and that they left in a hurry.'

Drawing out a piece of paper and a pencil, Wilson made a sketch. 'Let us call the small prints "A",' he said, 'and the big hobnails "B". Now, here we have "B" prints first coming towards the tent up from the road that leads inland from the beach. Then we have again "B's" prints going in the direction of that ruined cottage, and then return-ing. You see, he has trodden on one of his own steps just here, and that proves which way he went first. Lastly, on the opposite side, we have again "B's" prints going away inland, towards that road that comes up from the beach.' He cast about for a minute or two. 'No,' he said, 'I can find no other prints at all. "A" has left none except just in front of the tent, and "B" only some more just by the tent and these other two lines. It looks, then, as if they were both here at the same time. We have, however, tracks of "B" going away, but not of "A". Puzzle: where is "A"?'

'He's not here, at all events.'

'True. Now, suppose we try following "B's" tracks. Towards the cottage first, I think. Study the footprints carefully, and don't walk in them. They are, to say the least, suggestive.'

They suggested nothing to me, but I followed obediently. The steps led to a gap in the broken wall. Wilson, who was leading, looked in, and immediately uttered an exclamation.

In the half-room to which the gap in the wall led stood the remains of a deal table. The two walls nearest the sea had collapsed, and one leg of the table was actually standing upon air, protruding over the edge of the cliff. And on the table lay a cap, a walking-stick and a mackintosh. The stick lay a little apart, and under it, as under a paperweight, was a letter. Wilson silently picked it up. It was stuck down, stamped and addressed to George Chalmers, Esq., St Mary's Mansions, SW1.

Wilson held it irresolutely in his hand for a moment. Then he produced a pocket-knife and slowly and carefully worked the blade under the flap. In a few seconds he had the letter open, leaving the envelope to all appearance intact. 'I think, in the circumstances, we will take the liberty,' he said. A minute later, he handed me the letter.

'Dear George,' it ran, 'Very sorry to leave you in the lurch, and all that. But you'll find out soon enough why I'd better not live any longer. Forgive me, if you can. Yours, Hugh.'

'Suicide!' I said. 'But how . . . ?'

Wilson, meanwhile, was leaning over the edge of the cliff, gazing down at something below. 'Well?' I asked. 'The exhibits are complete,' he answered; 'item, one body.'

I climbed beside him and gazed down. Below us a clump of jejune bushes was growing precariously on the face of the cliff. And among them lay the body of a man, huddled up awkwardly, as it had fallen from the room in which we stood. 'I must get down to him,' I said.

It was an unpleasant scramble; but I managed it. In a minute or so, I stood beside the body. There was no doubt about the cause of death. The man's throat was slit from ear to ear. 'His throat's been cut,' I shouted up to Wilson. A minute later he stood beside me, and we gazed down together at the dead man. He was small and fair-haired, not more than thirty years old, with a face almost childishly pretty, but now frozen in a strange look of horror. And he had been dead many hours. There was no doubt of that.

Wilson spoke my thought. 'Does a suicide look like that, Michael?' he asked, gravely.

I bent down again, and studied the wound. 'This is no suicide,' I said. 'The man's been murdered.'

'Precisely,' said Wilson. 'Men do not commit suicide by first cutting their throats, and then jumping off a fifty foot cliff into a bush. Do you mean more than that?'

'Yes, I do. That wound is not self-inflicted. The man was seized from behind, and held roughly by someone who then slit his throat . . . But . . . what does that letter mean? He said he was committing suicide.'

'Or his murderer said it for him,' Wilson answered. 'But look! What's that?'

In the bush, close by the dead man, lay an open razor, stained with blood. 'The weapon,' I said.

Wilson smiled grimly. 'You said that before,' he said. 'Two blood-stained weapons are surely an undue allowance for one throat.'

'I'm out of my depth,' said I.

Wilson by now was bending down and making a search of the body. The murdered man was dressed in a silver grey lounge suit; and from this he quickly extracted a bundle of papers and letters. Among them were two envelopes addressed to 'Hugh Parsons, Esq.,' at an address in Hampstead. The letters and papers seemed to be purely personal, and, after a cursory examination, Wilson thrust them back into the dead man's pocket. '*Prima facie*,' he said, 'this appears to be the body of Hugh Parsons, whom we can identify with the "H.P." of the shirt we found in the tent and the "Hugh" of the letter.'

'But I don't understand,' I said. 'This man has been murdered; but he has left a letter announcing his suicide. What's the explanation?'

'On the face of it, there is one obvious answer. Parsons has been murdered, and his murderer has tried to make it look like suicide.'

'But the letter?'

'If we are right, then the letter is a forgery. We can't tell for certain, at present; but I think we may safely accept the hypothesis of murder. To begin with—we found sufficient reason to suspect a murderous attempt *before* we had even encountered the body or the suggestion of suicide.'

'As a suggested suicide,' I observed, 'it doesn't seem very success-ful. It didn't deceive you at all.'

'Nor could it have deceived anyone for five minutes,' Wilson said. 'Let's go over the points. First, we have a plain set of footprints leading to and from the cliff. They are not the dead man's. Secondly, there are no footprints of the dead man leading here, though he clearly came, or was brought, here after the rain; for his body is quite dry, though the ground under him is still damp. Thirdly, we have the traces up at the tent simply shouting "Murder." And, fourthly, we have two bloodstained weapons instead of one. No murderer could possibly have thought this arrangement made a plausible suicide. Yet he left it like that. Why?'

'Perhaps he staged the suicide, and then was surprised before he had time to remove either his own footprints or the traces up at the tent.'

'That is possible; but I don't think it is correct. For we know he wasn't actually surprised. There are no other footprints. Of course, he might have got panic and done a bunk. But he didn't. The steps leading inland from the tent are those of a man walking slowly.'

'Then what is the explanation?'

'Part of it, I think, is clear. The murder was done just by the tent. Then the murderer carried the body here and staged this absurd suicide. If you remember the tracks, "B's" stride was shorter, and the impressions of his feet were much deeper when he was coming this way than on his return. That suggests that he was carrying a heavy burden—to wit, the body. What I don't understand is why he didn't clear the traces away. As he left things, he was bound to be seen through. And then, again, you say the wound was obviously not self-inflicted.'

'He may not have had medical knowledge enough to know that,' I said.

'He must have had enough to know that two weapons were not likely,' Wilson said. 'And that just deepens the mystery. The thing's so well done in some respects, and so badly in others. Now, why?'

'I'm damned if I know,' said I. 'Do you?'

'I can think of at any rate one possible explanation,' Wilson said, puckering his brow. 'But I'm not at all sure that it will work. Anyway, our immediate job, I suppose, is to tell the local police what we've found.'

It was not, however, quite our next job. For at this moment a voice—a fresh, young voice—hailed us from above. 'Hullo!' it said. 'Something wrong here. Bill!' Looking up, we saw two boy scouts staring down at us as we stood beside the body.

'Something very much wrong,' said Wilson. 'Do either of you boys know this man?'

With extraordinary agility, the two boys clambered down beside us. 'It's one of the blokes from that tent up there,' he said.

'There were two of them, weren't there?' Wilson inquired.

'Three. Leastways, two of them was campin' out 'ere, and there was a friend of theirs stayin' at the Bear and Cross.'

'Where's that?'

''Bout a mile inland, up the track. 'E 'ad a car wiv 'im, and used to drive it down 'ere.'

'When did you last see any of them?'

'Mr Chalmers—'e's the chap with the car—ain't seen him for two or three days. But I seen the other two night before last. Quarrellin', they was. Oo! D'yer think t'other chap done this one in?'

'Somebody's done him in,' said Wilson. 'Now, mind, nothing up here or at the tent must be touched till the police come. But I've a job for you chaps. I want you to hunt all down this bit of cliff and see if you can find anything that might throw more light on this affair. And, Michael, I've a job for you too. I'm going to stay here till help comes. But I want you to buzz off and find the nearest telephone, and get straight on to the police station at Norwich. Tell them I'm here, and they're to send an inspector and some men out in a car at once. See? And then go to the Bear and Cross, and see if this Mr Chalmers is still about, or what's become of him. And find out anything you can about those two fellows down at the tent. When that's done, come back here, and, if you value your life, don't forget to bring a couple of bottles of beer and some sandwiches.'

By the time we had clambered up to the ruined cottage, several more boy scouts had appeared on the scene. Wilson at once took command, and set them to hunt the entire neighbourhood for clues. One was assigned to me as guide to the Bear and Cross, where, it appeared, the nearest telephone was to be found. As I left the scene of the crime, I saw Wilson neatly covering the tell-tale footsteps with a blanket taken from the tent.

At the Bear and Cross, I found no difficulty in carrying out Wilson's suggestions. In the presence of a gaping landlord, to whom I had given the barest minimum of information, I rang up the police station at Norwich, and was lucky enough to get through at once. A recital of the main facts sufficed to secure a promise that an inspector should be despatched at once to the scene of the crime, and, as soon as I mentioned Wilson's name, there was no mistaking the alacrity with which the local police took up the case. But I did not want to waste time; and as soon as I could, I rang off, and turned my attention to the landlord.

He seemed a typical country innkeeper enough—an ex-soldier by the look of him, and indeed I soon found he had been a sergeant in a regular regiment before the war and had seen plenty of service in France. His great desire was to question me; but I speedily made it plain that I meant to get more information than I gave, and before long I had him talking.

The two campers in the tent—Hugh Parsons and Alec Courage —had been there for about ten days, and had had their letters sent to the inn. The previous weekend, a friend of theirs, named George Chalmers, had come down with his car, and had put up at the inn. He had stayed only a few days, and had returned to town on Tuesday, leaving the other two behind. The two campers had been before his coming regular visitors at the inn; and during the weekend they had been there more than ever, and Chalmers had several times taken them out in his car—a Morris-Oxford. Three days ago, on Tuesday afternoon, Chalmers had received a telegram, and on receipt of it had announced that he must go back to town at once. The other two had been with him when it came, and they had stayed to take a farewell drink together and to see him off. The last the landlord had seen of them was their going off arm in arm, and a little unsteadily (for it had been a wet leave-taking) along the track towards the sea. He had been rather surprised to see nothing of them for the past three days; for previously they had been frequent and thirsty visitors at the inn. But it was quite possible that, now their friend was no longer there, they had transferred their attention to the Swan at Happisburgh. It was only a couple of miles or so from their camp.

At my suggestion the landlord rang up the Swan, and found that his surmise was correct. The two men had spent the greater part of Wednesday there, drinking and playing billiards and strumming on the piano—for the day had been wet. They had also walked over together on Thursday afternoon, and stayed for a drink and a game. The Swan, however, had seen nothing of them since then, and it was now late on Friday afternoon. There were, I ascertained, no other licensed premises within several miles. This seemed to bear out the conclusion already formed that the murder had taken place some time on Thursday night.

'What sort of man was Courage?' I asked. The landlord's view was that he was a bit of a sport—an athlete, too, by his talk; shortish, but very strongly and sturdily built, with curly dark hair and a small moustache—about thirty years of age.

'We found a queer-looking long knife down at the tent,' I said; 'a very thin, sharp blade about eight inches long, with a white bone handle. Do you know it?'

'Why,' said the landlord, staring. 'I shouldn't wonder if it was my ham and beef knife. I lost it on Tuesday after those chaps were here. You don't mean it was————'

'It may have been the weapon,' I said. 'Anyway, it's at the tent now. One of them must have picked it up. Could they have got at it easily?'

'It was kept in a drawer in the parlour, where they were all sitting. And, now you mention it, I remember Mr Courage went back in there after Mr Chalmers had driven off. He may have taken it then.'

'When did you see it last?'

'When I put it back in the drawer after lunch on Tuesday. When I wanted it on Wednesday morning it wasn't there.'

'Any of them could have taken it?'

'It must 'a' been Mr Courage, when he went back into the parlour.'

That was the sum of the information I gleaned; but, as I made my way back to the scene of the tragedy, accompanied by the boy scout bearing a plentiful supply of Bass and sandwiches, I felt well enough pleased with it. It all seemed to fit in; and especially the theft of the knife from the inn seemed to prove that the crime had been premeditated for at least two days before its actual execution. Parsons was dead, and Courage was presumably his murderer. Else why had the man vanished off the face of the earth? Courage, too, was proved to have had ample opportunity for stealing the knife. Things certainly looked black for Mr Alec Courage.

I found Wilson the centre of an excited group of boy scouts, among whom was a man, dressed as a scoutmaster, whom I had not seen before. Wilson hailed me cheerily, and, seizing a bottle of Bass from my companion, took a long pull. 'That's better,' he said.

I told my news, which seemed to please him, while he hungrily ate a sandwich. 'We've some news too,' he said, 'and it's rather curious. To begin with, Mr Evanson here knows a bit about our two friends.'

The scoutmaster proceeded to explain. He and Courage had been at school together; but they had not met for years until their accidental encounter a few days before. Indeed, Mr Evanson gave it clearly to be understood that, in his view, Courage was a good deal of a bad hat. Meeting, however, by chance on the beach, they had renewed their old acquaintance and exchanged experiences.

Courage had introduced Parsons to him, and explained that they were partners in a firm of outside brokers in the City. Evanson had gathered that their business was highly speculative; indeed, they had spoken of it in the spirit of gamblers who enjoyed playing for high stakes. He had met Chalmers once at the Bear and Cross, and gathered that he was the senior partner in the concern.

On the tragedy itself Evanson could throw no direct light. He said he had last spoken with the two friends on Thursday afternoon, when they were going down to the sea for a bathe. They had told him of Chalmers's return to town, and had announced that they were staying on at least for another week. They had seemed in the best of spirits and on excellent terms with each other.

That was the end of Evanson's direct evidence. But he produced one of his boys, who had been in the neighbourhood of the tent later on Thursday evening. The boy said that he had heard high voices, as of two men quarrelling, proceeding from the tent, and had caught some words about 'a tight place' and 'letting a pal down'. The boy had not thought much of it at the time, and had, in fact, forgotten all about it till the discovery of the tragedy brought the incident back to his mind.

Evanson's story seemed to me quite straightforward. He gave of Courage a most unflattering portrait, which showed that he thought him quite the sort of man who might be guilty of a serious crime. Of Parsons he seemed to know little, but to regard him as in all probability a harmless 'pigeon' who had fallen into Courage's skilful hands. But I, at any rate, was disposed to discount a good deal of Mr Evanson's testimony; for it was obvious that he was more than a bit of a prig.

'Come over here, Michael,' said Wilson; 'there's something I want to look at again.'

'Anything fresh since I went away?' I asked, as soon as we were alone.

'Yes and no,' was the answer. 'You know those footprints of "B" leading inland from the tent?' I nodded. 'Well, there's an odd thing about them. You remember I said that Mr "B's" stride was shorter and his footmarks deeper on the way to the ruined cottage than back?' Again I nodded acquiescence. 'Well, those steps leading inland from the tent are the same as those leading to the cottage—short and deep.'

'I don't quite see what you mean,' I said.

'I concluded from the first lot of footsteps that "B" had been carrying a heavy burden going to the cottage, but not on his return.

That squared with our finding the body on the cliffs below the cottage. But how does it square with our finding the same sort of footsteps—deep, and close together—leading from the tent in the opposite direction?'

'It doesn't seem to square at all,' I said. 'Where do the other footsteps lead, by the way?'

'They go to the road leading to the inn; and there they stop. The road surface is too hard to leave an impression.'

'Then you simply don't know where "B" went after he reached the road?'

'That's where those boy scouts come in. I set them to search, and one of them says he's found some of "B's" footsteps again a bit farther up the road, leading off into a disused path that apparently runs along parallel to the cliffs. I've had no chance to follow it yet; but the boy says the tracks are quite plain. Hullo, that must be the police!'

A car was running swiftly down the road that led from the Bear and Cross to the sea. In it were two policemen and a man in plain clothes. Wilson went to meet the car, and it came to a stop about a hundred yards from the tent. I hung in the background while the plain clothes man deferentially saluted Wilson. They remained a minute or two in conversation, and then came over towards me. 'This is Inspector Davey,' said Wilson. 'My friend, Dr Prendergast.'

In a few minutes Wilson had given the local inspector a full account of what we had so far discovered. 'We'll leave you to look round here,' he said then, 'while we follow up these footsteps.' But we were not destined to follow them just yet; for, as we turned to leave the inspector, a second car appeared, coming at full speed along the road from the Bear and Cross. 'Hullo, who's this?' said the inspector.

The second car—a new Morris-Oxford—came to a stop beside the police car, and its sole occupant, a tall, broad man of forty or so, came hastily towards us. 'What the devil's all this?' he said. 'My name's Chalmers. They told me up at the pub there was something wrong.'

The inspector glanced at Wilson. 'You are Mr George Chalmers,' said the latter.

'Yes. Is it true that Parsons is dead?' The big man seemed greatly agitated.

'He was a friend of yours?' Wilson asked.

'My partner—he and Mr Courage, who was staying here with him. I've just run down from town to see them, and they told me at the inn . . .'

'What did they tell you?'

'That Parsons was dead, and Courage had disappeared. Is that true? What has happened?'

'Mr Parsons left this letter for you, Mr Chalmers,' said Wilson, handing over the note which we had found at the ruined cottage. 'We took the liberty of opening it.'

Chalmers took the note, and read it with puckered brows. 'I don't understand,' he said. 'The landlord said Parsons had been murdered. But this means suicide. Though why————'

'You do not know of any reason why Mr Parsons should have taken his life?'

'The thing's preposterous. Now, if it had been Courage, I might have understood. This is the devil of a business. I say, I suppose anything I tell you won't go any further—I mean, unless it has to, you know.'

'I think,' said Wilson, 'you had better tell us frankly all you know, Mr Chalmers.'

'It's a beastly business,' said Chalmers, 'and I don't understand it at all. You realize, Parsons and Courage were my partners—we're stockbrokers, you know. Ten days ago, the two of them came away here on a holiday together, leaving me to run the show in town while they were away. Last Friday, my bank manager asked me to come round and see him. I went, and he produced a cheque, drawn to bearer for a very large sum on the firm's account, and asked me if it was all right. It was signed with Courage's name and mine. I told him at once the damned thing was a forgery and I'd never signed any such cheque. It was a damned good forgery, mind you; and I could hardly tell the signature from my own. Well, to cut a long story short, we went into the accounts, and we found that during the past week several other bearer cheques had been paid out, all purporting to be signed by Courage and me—and all forgeries, so far as my signature was concerned at any rate. Of course, I was in the devil of a stew—I may tell you the cheques were big enough to cause our firm serious embarrassment. We rang up the police at once and put the matter in their hands, and then I went back to the office, collected the cheque-books in which the counterfoils were, and buzzed off down here with them to see Courage. Of course, I assumed his signature had been forged as well as mine.

'Well, over the weekend, we had a tremendous confab about it. Courage said he'd never signed the cheques, and couldn't give any explanation. But we knew the cheque-books had been locked up in a safe to which only we three had the keys. Finally, Courage and

Parsons fell out about it, and accused each other of forging the cheques. I trusted them both, and told them it was all nonsense, and at length they made it up and shook hands. I stayed down here till Tuesday, keeping in telephonic communication with London all the time. Then, on Tuesday, I got a wire from the office, asking me to go up to town at once over some important business. And now comes the beastly part of the affair. I had to go to Courage's desk for some papers this morning, and there I found, in his blotting book, some unmistakable transfers of a series of attempts at my signature. Of course, that put the lid on it. I simply buzzed down here at once; and I don't mind telling you I meant to cut my losses and advise Courage to make himself scarce. We've been close friends, and I'd sooner lose all I have than have to put him in the dock over it. You can say that's compounding a felony if you like. Anyway, it's what I meant to do. I got to the Bear and Cross a few minutes ago, and there the landlord told me Parsons was dead and Courage vanished. Of course, I was dumbfounded. Forgery's one thing; but murder's another. I came right on here to tell you all I know. But, of course, if it's suicide . . . though why on earth . . .' His voice tailed away.

'It was not suicide, Mr Chalmers,' said Wilson. 'It was murder. The suicide was merely a clumsy pretence. The murderer burned, or endeavoured to burn, the butt-ends of the cheque-books, and then made off.' And in a few words he told Chalmers the state of the affair.

Chalmers seemed more and more downcast. 'I'd never have believed it,' he said at the close.

'Well, what's your conclusion now?' Wilson asked.

'I've no wish to draw conclusions. Unfortunately, they seem too obvious.'

'You mean that Courage killed Parsons and fled. But why should he kill Parsons?'

'I suppose Parsons must have found out that he had forged the cheques. He killed him in order to shut his mouth, and then got panic and ran away.'

'Parsons, you think, was entirely innocent?'

'Lord bless you, yes. Hugh Parsons had nothing to do with this. No, it was Courage who forged the cheques, sorry as I am to say it.'

'Well, Mr Chalmers, will you kindly go with the inspector here and identify Parsons, and give him any help you can?' Wilson drew the inspector aside and communed with him a moment. 'Now, Michael,' he said. '*A nos moutons.*' We waited until Inspector Davey and Chalmers had disappeared into the ruined cottage, and then set off up the road. 'About here is where the boy found the footprints,' said Wilson. 'Yes, here they are. He's a sharp lad.'

The footprints were rather faint; but there was no doubt that they had been made by the same boots as the 'B' prints by the tent. There were only two or three of them visible, for the track was loose sand, and so overgrown that the rain had only penetrated at one or two points. But it was quite clear that they were leading away from the tent along a sunken lane which ran parallel to the shore and about a hundred yards from it, and was screened from view by a thick covering of bushes on either side. We walked along the track for a little distance. I could see no further marks; but Wilson's more experienced eyes seemed to be satisfied that he was still on the trail. Eventually, after about five minutes' walking, the lane came out on a wider track leading on one side up to the main road inland, and on the other still keeping roughly parallel to the shore.

'Hullo!' said Wilson. 'There's been a car here. You notice the tracks. And just here it stood for some time. You can see the oil ran down and made a little pool. Dunlop tyres, with a noticeable patch on the left back wheel. That may come in useful. The tracks run both ways—up to the road, and in the other direction—a double track each way. Left turn, I think.' He led the way along the track, away from the main road.

For some distance we followed the track, which, though wider here, was still sunken. Marks were few and far between; but Wilson seemed sure that we were still following the trail of the car. After about a mile the track bent round in the direction of the shore, and within five minutes brought us out, through another gap in the low cliffs, right on the beach, and within a few yards of the ruined church we had already visited earlier in the day. No tyre marks were visible on the beach; either the wind had obliterated them all from the loose sand, or, if the car had descended below high-water mark, the tide had been up and washed them away. But Wilson strode unhesitatingly towards the ruin, which stood well above high-water mark, temporarily protected by a range of low artificial sand-hills planted with juniper. There he paused and stared meditatively at the bushes.

'What on earth do you expect to find here?' I asked.

'Who knows,' he returned. 'One can but look.'

'But for what?'

'For what one may find. Look here, for instance.' I looked, but could see nothing but the sandy soil between the ruins. 'Trampled ground,' Wilson interpreted. 'And recently trampled. But someone's obliterated all clear marks. Anyway, we might as well experiment there as anywhere. Prod with your stick.' So saying, he began prodding with his own, thrusting it in as deep as it would go into the sand at one place after another. I followed his example. In some places the stick, with a little coaxing, went right down. In others, it was speedily stopped by something hard below the surface. 'Never mind the hard stuff,' said Wilson. 'That's masonry from the church. Try for something soft but resistant.' A minute or so later he gave an exclamation. 'This feels like something, Michael,' he said. 'Come and help me clear away the sand.'

With sticks and hands we cleared away the loose sand as best we could. Less than a foot down, my hand caught hold of something hard but yielding. Together we scraped for a moment and brought to light a human boot. Another followed, and within a few minutes we had exposed to view the entire body of a man, buried a foot deep below the drifting sand. He was a young man, short but stout and strongly built, with a crisp black moustache, and to all appearances not long dead. And the manner of death was evident. Round his neck a cord had been tightly knotted, and the stained and swollen flesh plainly showed the marks.

I had been too occupied first in scraping away the sand and then in making a brief inspection of the body to give vent to my curiosity till now. But when I had assured myself how the man had died, I turned to Wilson. 'What in God's name does this mean?' I cried. 'Was this what you were looking for?'

'Permit me to introduce you to the suspected murderer, Mr Courage,' he said.

'Courage!' I exclaimed. 'Then who . . .' But a sharp exclamation from Wilson cut short my sentence. He had turned the body over, and now from beneath it he drew—a big gold cigar case, which gleamed brightly in the evening sun. He pressed the catch and the case flew open. Within were two fat cigars, and with them a scrap of paper—a tearing from a newspaper. Wilson read it and passed it to me. It was an extract from the city page of the *Financial Times*, describing the dramatic slump in the shares of the Anglo-Asiatic Corporation.

'From yesterday's paper,' said Wilson. '*Yesterday's*, mark you.'

'Why not?' I asked.

'The *Financial Times* is hardly likely to be on sale at Happisburgh,' he answered. 'This grave was made last night, or at all events the man died then. How did a bit of yesterday's *Financial Times* get into his grave?'

'It may have come by post,' I hazarded.

'We can probably find out whether he received any newspapers by post. The question is whether this is his cigar case or someone else's. If it's someone else's, we're in luck.'

'But how did it get into the grave?'

'Do you ever dig, Michael? If you do, and don't take precautions to secure your loose property, as likely as not you'll drop some of it, and cover it over before you find out your loss. If the murderer has been kind enough to drop his cigar case for us, I say we're in luck. And I'm inclined to think he has. Judging from Mr Courage's coat which we inspected at the tent, he was a pipe, and not a cigar smoker.'

'But how do you know this is Courage?'

For answer, Wilson bent down and felt in the dead man's pockets. They were entirely empty. 'I don't,' he said at last. 'But I'll bet you anything you like it is. You see, I've been looking for him.'

'You suspected—this?' I asked.

'Certainly. It was plain from the first that we were meant to see through the pretence of suicide—plain that the murderer had meant us to see through it. But, once we did see through it, all the surface indications pointed to Courage as the murderer. Clearly that would not do. If Courage had been the murderer, either he would not have wanted us to see through the suicide, or he would have arranged that, when we did see through it, the clues should not point to him. Ergo, Courage was not the murderer. Then where was Courage, and why had he disappeared? One possible explanation was that he had taken fright and run away, even though he was innocent of the murder. But a far more plausible theory was that he had been murdered too.

'That theory was confirmed by a study of the footprints. We concluded, on good evidence, that the murderer had been carrying a heavy burden on his way from the tent to the ruined cottage. We found we were right. He had been carrying Parsons. But we had equally good evidence that he was carrying a burden in the second set of footprints leading to the car; for they too were deep, and showed a shortened stride. The inference was clear. The murderer had also been carrying a body towards the car. But that body could not be Parsons. Who was it? Obviously Courage himself.'

I listened to this convincing deduction with increasing amazement. At this point I broke in. 'But his boots, man! Look at his boots!' For the boots on the feet of the body before us were identical with the 'B' tracks we had found at the tent.

'I have looked at his boots,' said Wilson. 'That is the final link in the

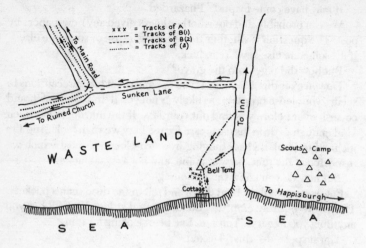

argument. We found three sets of "B" footprints, did we not? One set led up from the shore to the tent, a second from the tent to the ruined cottage and back again, and the third from the tent to the path we have just followed.' I nodded. 'Very well,' said Wilson. 'Now observe that the left boot on the body has two nails missing. If you go back to the tent, you'll find that of our "B" footprints, set number one has those two nails missing; sets number two and three have not. This man's boots have two nails missing. Otherwise, the tracks are the same. Now, do you see?'

'You never told me that,' I said reproachfully.

'You looked at them just as much as I did,' said the provoking fellow. 'Can you now tell me what they mean?'

'Mr "B" was two men,' I said, rather sulkily. 'And only one of them is Courage.'

'Precisely. Two men with almost identical boots—but fortunately not quite identical. Does that suggest anything to you?'

'Only a very odd coincidence, I'm afraid. And, of course, the fact that we have to look for a new murderer.'

'Yes,' said Wilson. 'Perhaps we'd better start.'

Wilson left me to watch by the body while he went back to the tent to inform the police and summon assistance. But hardly had he left me when the scoutmaster, Evanson, appeared, scrambling down the cliff by a narrow path. I did not quite know what to do; for Wilson had said that he was particularly anxious, for the present, to keep the finding of the second body a secret. But I did not see how I could keep the newcomer away. I went towards him in the hope of heading him off.

'What were you two doing here?' he asked. 'I happened to notice you from the path above and I thought I'd come down and see if you had found anything fresh. Have you?'

'I'm afraid,' I said, 'I'm hardly at liberty . . .'

Evanson shook his head. 'No, I'm going a bit farther along the pry. But, while I am here, I want to have a look at these ruins. Any objection?'

'Well,' I said, 'if you don't mind . . .'

At this moment his hat, lifted by a gust of wind, went flying along the beach. He followed it, and, with some dismay, I watched the chase end within a few feet of the shallow hole in which the body lay. I ran after him.

'My God! What's this?' I heard him say. 'Courage!'

I came up, panting, 'Well, Mr Evanson, since you have seen this, I must ask you not to say a word about it to anybody. It is most important that no one should————'

'But Courage! I thought Courage was the murderer.'

'If he was, Nemesis has soon overtaken him.'

'How did you find him? Who————?'

I was scarcely able to answer; for suddenly, on the firm sand, I had noticed the print of the scoutmaster's feet. They were, to say the least, extraordinarily like the 'B' footprints we had seen at the tent, and tracked to the lonely grave in the sand. And they were a perfect impression, without a nail missing. 'We tracked him here,' I said.

Evanson clearly noticed something odd in my manner, for he looked at me strangely. I did my best not to show my excitement; and I flattered myself that, after my first start of astonishment, I managed pretty well. Evanson went on plying me with questions, direct and indirect; and I did my best to make answers that sounded innocent, and at the same time gave nothing away. The man was not to know I suspected him if I could help it. But it was wearing work; and I was mightily relieved when the police car came running down the track and the local inspector leapt out beside us.

'Thank you, doctor, for keeping watch for us. I see Mr Evanson is here. Does he recognize the body?'

'It is Courage,' said Evanson. 'But I thought . . .'

'Lord bless you, sir, we all thought. In a case like this, one's apt to think a lot of the wrong things before thinking of the right one. And now, you won't mind leaving me to manage this little affair myself. The superintendent says he would like to see you at the inn, doctor.'

I had been hesitating whether or not to tell the inspector of my discovery. But it seemed best to keep it for Wilson's ear. 'Are you coming back towards the tent?' I asked the scoutmaster.

Evanson shook his head. 'No, I'm going a bit farther along the shore,' he answered. I wondered if Wilson would blame me for letting him go; but on the whole that seemed preferable to giving my knowledge away. I left him, and set off at a smart pace towards the inn.

There, the sound of voices attracted me to the sitting-room. I found Wilson there with George Chalmers. Eagerly I asked Wilson to let me speak to him for a moment alone. He came out at once, and I told him what I had found, and expressed my fear that Evanson might even now be making his escape. To my chagrin, I found that my news was no news to him. 'Yes,' he said, 'I noticed Evanson's boots when we were talking to him by the ruined cottage. But I don't think he'll run away, all the same.' He smiled.

'Not now he knows the other body has been found?'

'I think we'll chance it,' said Wilson, leaving me to wonder whether he had really something up his sleeve, or whether in this case he was not quite up to the mark. Sadly disappointed, and more than a little perplexed, I followed him back into the room where Chalmers was still sitting.

'I've just been getting Mr Chalmers to give me all the particulars about this man Courage', he said. 'For purposes of offering a reward for his apprehension, you know.' I took the hint. Chalmers was to know nothing yet of the discovery of Courage's body.

'Now, Mr Chalmers,' Wilson went on. 'You say Courage and Parsons quarrelled badly over the weekend, but had made it up before you left.'

'Yes.'

'Since you went away, have you either heard from, or communicated with, either of them?'

'No.'

'Is there any way you can think of in which either could have got to know what you have since discovered about Courage?'

'Impossible. I only found it out myself this morning.'

'But it is possible Mr Parsons may have found out somehow for himself?'

'Yes, that's possible. But I don't see how.'

'Then how do you explain what happened?'

'I don't like having to explain it at all. But I fear the facts speak for themselves.'

At this point Wilson's tone suddenly changed. 'Was your firm in Anglo-Asiatics, Mr Chalmers?' he said sharply.

Chalmers gave a violent start, and seemed unable to make up his mind what to answer. 'I don't see what bearing——' he began.

'I only asked,' said Wilson sweetly, 'because I noticed you cut out that bit about it from Wednesday's *Financial Times*.'

'What the devil d'you mean?'

'Well, you did, didn't you?'

'Certainly not,' Chalmers snapped.

'You see,' said Wilson, 'I thought you had, because we found the cutting in your cigar case. This is yours, isn't it?' He passed the heavy gold case across the table.

Chalmers stared down at it as if the opulent little object were a snake. 'Yes,' he said, 'that's mine. I must have left it behind here on Tuesday.'

'Oh, no, I think not, Mr Chalmers. The landlord here saw you take it out, and light a cigar just as you started the car. And he is sure you put it back in your pocket.'

'He's mistaken. I must have left it behind at the tent, or it couldn't have been found there.'

'It wasn't found at the tent, Mr Chalmers. It was found on the sands beside the old ruined church at Eccles. Does that refresh your memory?'

This time there was no mistaking Chalmers's consternation. His hand shook so violently that he knocked the cigar case to the floor with a clatter.

'What! Oh, I—I walked that way on Tuesday. I must have dropped it then.'

'With a cutting from Wednesday's *Financial Times* inside?'

'Somebody must have found the case, and put the cutting in, and dropped it later.'

'It was not dropped. It was buried.'

'I—can only say I have not had it since last Tuesday.'

Wilson changed the subject. 'On Tuesday, you drove back to London in your car?'

'Yes.'

'Where has the car been since then?'

'In my garage, except when I was using it in town.'

'It has not been out of your possession?'

'N—no.'

'Then, if your car was down here yesterday, we can take it that you were here too. Is that so?'

'It was not here yesterday. I was in London all day.'

'Supposing I tell you that you and your car were seen to turn off the main road and stop at a point where two tracks join on the way between here and Eccles, and that subsequently your car was driven down to a point near the church at Eccles, and near where the cigar case was found?'

Chalmers's alarm seemed to increase with every word that Wilson spoke. 'It's not true,' he said wildly. 'I tell you I've been here since Tuesday.'

'Are you aware that your car has a highly distinctive patch on the left back tyre, Mr Chalmers?'

Chalmers had apparently made up his mind by now what to say. 'Look here,' he said, 'this is a ridiculous misunderstanding. You're quite right. I did drive that way. But it was on Tuesday.'

'Come, come, Mr Chalmers. The marks could not possibly have survived the rain. Will you tell me where you were on Thursday, if you were not here?'

Chalmers sprang up. 'That's enough,' he said furiously. 'I thought third-degree methods were confined to the American police. I tell you I have not been near the place since Tuesday last, when I left Parsons and Courage alive and well!'

'And what makes you think Mr Courage is not alive now?' Wilson asked sharply. Chalmers saw his slip and made a sudden movement for the door. Opening it, he stepped straight into the arms of a large Norfolk policeman.

'George Chalmers,' said Wilson, signing to the policeman, 'I arrest you for the murder of Hugh Parsons and Alec Courage. And I warn you that anything you say may be used in evidence against you.'

A minute later, when the policeman, assisted by another, had led Chalmers away, I turned to Wilson.

'But what about Evanson's boots?' I cried.

'My dear Michael, what about them? They had the same arrangement of nails—it's a common one—but they were at least a size and a half too small.'

'Then it was I after all who discovered the mare's nest.'

'I'm afraid it was, Michael,' said Wilson gently. 'We all do at times.'

'I'll get my own back on you when you have that nervous break-down,' said I. But Wilson only laughed.

Of course, Wilson's work did not end with the arrest of Chalmers. We might be as morally certain as we liked that he had murdered both his partners, but proof was another matter. Wilson himself admitted that it was Chalmers's own suspicious manner at the interview just described which had decided him to risk an immediate arrest, rather than give the man the chance of destroying incriminating evidence. And it was as well that he did so; for in Chalmers's rooms at the flat which he shared with Courage in St Mary's Mansions were found not only the copy of the *Financial Times* from which the incriminating cutting had been torn, but also a pair of boots, the twin of those on the dead man's feet, except that they had all their nails intact. They were half a size smaller than Chalmers's own footgear, and were still partly covered with Norfolk sand. Thirdly, in the desk, at the back, there turned up a scrap of paper covered with attempts at Courage's signature.

Armed with this last piece of evidence, Wilson interviewed the bank, with the result that the forged bearer cheques were submitted to further expert examination; and it was discovered that, of the two signatures which they bore—those of Courage and Chalmers—the former was really the forgery, though it had been executed so cleverly that no suspicion of it had been entertained by the bank. Chalmers had deliberately so written his own signature that it would be easily recognized as a forgery, whereas he had been at pains to make the imitation of his partner's signature as plausible as possible. This conclusion was borne out by a piece of paper found where it had blown behind the desk in his study. On this he had actually tried out both signatures. This discovery led to a close investigation of Chalmers's affairs, from which it eventually transpired that, having got the firm into serious difficulties through unwarrantable speculation, Chalmers had converted the sums represented by these cheques into bearer securities, which he had retained in preparation for the inevitable collapse.

At this point Courage's solicitor, who had also been his personal friend, disclosed a statement made by the dead man just before leaving for his holiday. In this Courage explained that he had detected a certain amount of irregularity and had eventually connected it with Chalmers. Receiving no satisfactory explanation from the latter, he had taken with him to Norfolk certain of the papers and cheque-books of the firm, with the object of discussing the position fully with Parsons, and deciding on a line of action. (These were the cheque-books whose butt-ends we found at the tent, Chalmers having burnt just enough of them to create additional suspicion and bolster up his own story.)

Even with this evidence the Crown had a hard struggle to get its conviction. Chalmers and his lawyers fought to the very last gasp, blackened Courage's character—which, indeed, was none of the best—and poured scorn on the story reconstructed by Wilson; namely, that Chalmers, having failed to secure his partners' complicity in his frauds, had decided to murder them both, and then, knowing that suspicion would almost certainly be directed to himself, had staged the clumsy pretence of suicide, which was, of course, intended to lead straight to Courage as the murderer. Even supposing the police did not see through the pretence, Courage's disappearance, together with Chalmers's statements about the forged cheques, would have amply sufficed to throw suspicion on him, and prevent any search for another criminal. What finally clinched the case against Chalmers was, curiously enough, his own alibi for the fatal night, which he had prepared with care and which very nearly saved him. Eventually, however, the police proved it to be a palpable fraud; the defence collapsed, and Chalmers was hanged.

'The Happisburgh murderer,' Wilson said to me one day when the case was over, 'illustrates one important point in the science of crime. Chalmers had brains. No one could have planned murder much better than he planned it; but he was a clumsy executant. At every point, he lacked technique. Thus, he failed to make the suicide plausible enough. It was so barefaced a fake that it was obviously meant to be seen through. But, if that was so, one naturally distrusted the obvious explanation of the murder to which it pointed when one saw through it. Then again, he dropped his cigar case, and he failed to obliterate the traces of his car. If he had merely carried Courage's body a short distance and buried it in the sand, and then really carefully obliterated the traces, I very much doubt if we should ever have found it, and then the odds are he would have got off scot-free. No, Michael, a really good criminal needs two things —brains and technique. Chalmers had plenty of brains; but, as an executant, the fellow was a bungler. The combination of brains and technique is fortunately rare—or we policemen should never catch our hares. Which would be a great pity.'

I agreed. It was wonderful how well Wilson was looking. Our little holiday in Norfolk had quite set him up.

AGATHA CHRISTIE · 1890–1976

The Witness for the Prosecution

Mr Mayherne adjusted his pince-nez and cleared his throat with a little dry as dust cough that was wholly typical of him. Then he looked again at the man opposite him, the man charged with wilful murder.

Mr Mayherne was a small man, precise in manner, neatly, not to say foppishly dressed, with a pair of very shrewd and piercing grey eyes. By no means a fool. Indeed, as a solicitor, Mr Mayherne's reputation stood very high. His voice, when he spoke to his client, was dry but not unsympathetic.

'I must impress upon you again that you are in very grave danger, and that the utmost frankness is necessary.'

Leonard Vole, who had been staring in a dazed fashion at the blank wall in front of him, transferred his glance to the solicitor.

'I know,' he said hopelessly. 'You keep telling me so. But I can't seem to realize yet that I'm charged with murder—*murder*. And such a dastardly crime too.'

Mr Mayherne was practical, not emotional. He coughed again, took off his pince-nez, polished them carefully, and replaced them on his nose. Then he said:

'Yes, yes, yes. Now, my dear Mr Vole, we're going to make a determined effort to get you off—and we shall succeed—we shall succeed. But I must have all the facts. I must know just how damaging the case against you is likely to be. Then we can fix upon the best line of defence.'

Still the young man looked at him in the same dazed, hopeless fashion. To Mr Mayherne the case had seemed black enough, and the guilt of the prisoner assured. Now, for the first time, he felt a doubt.

'You think I'm guilty,' said Leonard Vole, in a low voice. 'But, by God, I swear I'm not! It looks pretty black against me, I know that. I'm like a man caught in a net—the meshes of it all round me, entangling me whichever way I turn. But I didn't do it, Mr Mayherne, I didn't do it!'

In such a position a man was bound to protest his innocence. Mr Mayherne knew that. Yet, in spite of himself, he was impressed. It might be, after all, that Leonard Vole was innocent.

'You are right, Mr Vole,' he said gravely. 'The case does look very black against you. Nevertheless, I accept your assurance. Now, let us get to facts. I want you to tell me in your own words exactly how you came to make the acquaintance of Miss Emily French.'

'It was one day in Oxford Street. I saw an elderly lady crossing the road. She was carrying a lot of parcels. In the middle of the street she dropped them, tried to recover them, found a 'bus was almost on top of her and just managed to reach the curb safely, dazed and bewildered by people having shouted at her. I recovered her parcels, wiped the mud off them as best I could, retied the string of one, and returned them to her.'

'There was no question of your having saved her life?'

'Oh! dear me, no. All I did was to perform a common act of courtesy. She was extremely grateful, thanked me warmly, and said something about my manners not being those of most of the younger generation—I can't remember the exact words. Then I lifted my hat and went on. I never expected to see her again. But life is full of coincidences. That very evening I came across her at a party at a friend's house. She recognized me at once and asked that I should be introduced to her. I then found out that she was a Miss Emily French and that she lived at Cricklewood. I talked to her for some time. She was, I imagined, an old lady who took sudden and violent fancies to people. She took one to me on the strength of a perfectly simple action which anyone might have performed. On leaving, she shook me warmly by the hand, and asked me to come and see her. I replied, of course, that I should be very pleased to do so, and she then urged me to name a day. I did not want particularly to go, but it would have seemed churlish to refuse, so I fixed on the following Saturday. After she had gone, I learned something about her from my friends. That she was rich, eccentric, lived alone with one maid and owned no less than eight cats.'

'I see,' said Mr Mayherne. 'The question of her being well off came up as early as that?'

'If you mean that I inquired——' began Leonard Vole hotly, but Mr Mayherne stilled him with a gesture.

'I have to look at the case as it will be presented by the other side. An ordinary observer would not have supposed Miss French to be a lady of means. She lived poorly, almost humbly. Unless you had been told the contrary, you would in all probability have considered her to be in poor circumstances—at any rate to begin with. Who was it exactly who told you that she was well off?'

'My friend, George Harvey, at whose house the party took place.'

'Is he likely to remember having done so?'

'I really don't know. Of course it is some time ago now.'

'Quite so, Mr Vole. You see, the first aim of the prosecution will be to establish that you were in low water financially—that is true, is it not?'

Leonard Vole flushed.

'Yes,' he said, in a low voice. 'I'd been having a run of infernal bad luck just then.'

'Quite so,' said Mr Mayherne again. 'That being, as I say, in low water financially, you met this rich old lady and cultivated her acquaintance assiduously. Now if we are in a position to say that you had no idea she was well off, and that you visited her out of pure kindness of heart——'

'Which is the case.'

'I dare say. I am not disputing the point. I am looking at it from the outside point of view. A great deal depends on the memory of Mr Harvey. Is he likely to remember that conversation or is he not? Could he be confused by counsel into believing that it took place later?'

Leonard Vole reflected for some minutes. Then he said steadily enough, but with a rather paler face:

'I do not think that that line would be successful, Mr Mayherne. Several of those present heard his remark, and one or two of them chaffed me about my conquest of a rich old lady.'

The solicitor endeavoured to hide his disappointment with a wave of the hand.

'Unfortunate,' he said. 'But I congratulate you upon your plain speaking, Mr Vole. It is to you I look to guide me. Your judgement is quite right. To persist in the line I spoke of would have been disastrous. We must leave that point. You made the acquaintance of Miss French, you called upon her, the acquaintanceship progressed. We want a clear reason for all this. Why did you, a young man of thirty-three, good-looking, fond of sport, popular with your friends, devote so much of your time to an elderly woman with whom you could hardly have anything in common?'

Leonard Vole flung out his hands in a nervous gesture.

'I can't tell you—I really can't tell you. After the first visit, she pressed me to come again, spoke of being lonely and unhappy. She made it difficult for me to refuse. She showed so plainly her fondness and affection for me that I was placed in an awkward position. You see, Mr Mayherne, I've got a weak nature—I drift—I'm one of those people who can't say "No". And believe me or not, as you like, after the third or fourth visit I paid her I found myself getting genuinely fond of the old thing. My mother died when I was young, an aunt brought me up, and she too died before I was fifteen. If I told you that I genuinely enjoyed being mothered and pampered, I dare say you'd only laugh.'

Mr Mayherne did not laugh. Instead he took off his pince-nez again and polished them, always a sign with him that he was thinking deeply.

'I accept your explanation, Mr Vole,' he said at last. 'I believe it to be psychologically probable. Whether a jury would take that view of it is another matter. Please continue your narrative. When was it that Miss French first asked you to look into her business affairs?'

'After my third or fourth visit to her. She understood very little of money matters, and was worried about some investments.'

Mr Mayherne looked up sharply.

'Be careful, Mr Vole. The maid, Janet Mackenzie, declares that her mistress was a good woman of business and transacted all her own affairs, and this is borne out by the testimony of her bankers.'

'I can't help that,' said Vole earnestly. 'That's what she said to me.'

Mr Mayherne looked at him for a moment or two in silence. Though he had no intention of saying so, his belief in Leonard Vole's innocence was at that moment strengthened. He knew something of the mentality of elderly ladies. He saw Miss French, infatuated with the good-looking young man, hunting about for pretexts that should bring him to the house. What more likely than that she should plead ignorance of business, and beg him to help her with her money affairs? She was enough of a woman of the world to realize that any man is slightly flattered by such an admission of his superiority. Leonard Vole had been flattered. Perhaps, too, she had not been averse to letting this young man know that she was wealthy. Emily French had been a strong-willed old woman, willing to pay her price for what she wanted. All this passed rapidly through Mr Mayherne's mind, but he gave no indication of it, and asked instead a further question.

'And you did handle her affairs for her at her request?'

'I did.'

'Mr Vole,' said the solicitor. 'I am going to ask you a very serious question, and one to which it is vital I should have a truthful answer. You were in low water financially. You had the handling of an old lady's affairs—an old lady who, according to her own statement, knew little or nothing of business. Did you at any time, or in any manner, convert to your own use the securities which you handled? Did you engage in any transaction for your own pecuniary advantage which will not bear the light of day?' He quelled the other's response. 'Wait a minute before you answer. There are two courses open to us. Either we can make a feature of your probity and honesty in conducting her affairs whilst pointing out how unlikely it is that you would commit murder to obtain money which you might have obtained by such infinitely easier means. If, on the other hand, there is anything in your dealings which the prosecution will get hold of—if, to put it baldly, it can be proved that you swindled the old lady in any way, we must take the line that you had no motive for the murder, since she was already a profitable source of income to you. You perceive the distinction. Now, I beg of you, take your time before you reply.'

But Leonard Vole took no time at all.

'My dealings with Miss French's affairs are all perfectly fair and above board. I acted for her interests to the very best of my ability, as anyone will find who looks into the matter.'

'Thank you,' said Mr Mayherne. 'You relieve my mind very much. I pay you the compliment of believing that you are far too clever to lie to me over such an important matter.'

'Surely,' said Vole eagerly, 'the strongest point in my favour is the lack of motive. Granted that I cultivated the acquaintanceship of a rich old lady in the hopes of getting money out of her—that, I gather, is the substance of what you have been saying—surely her death frustrates all my hopes?'

The solicitor looked at him steadily. Then, very deliberately, he repeated his unconscious trick with his pince-nez. It was not until they were firmly replaced on his nose that he spoke.

'Are you not aware, Mr Vole, that Miss French left a will under which you are the principal beneficiary?'

'What?' The prisoner sprang to his feet. His dismay was obvious and unforced. 'My God! What are you saying? She left her money to me?'

Mr Mayherne nodded slowly. Vole sank down again, his head in his hands.

'You pretend to know nothing of this will?'

'Pretend? There's no pretence about it. I knew nothing about it.'

'What would you say if I told you that the maid, Janet Mackenzie, swears that you *did* know? That her mistress told her distinctly that she had consulted you in the matter, and told you of her intentions?'

'Say? That she's lying! No, I go too fast. Janet is an elderly woman. She was a faithful watchdog to her mistress, and she didn't like me.

She was jealous and suspicious. I should say that Miss French confided her intentions to Janet, and that Janet either mistook something she said, or else was convinced in her own mind that I had persuaded the old lady into doing it. I dare say that she believes herself now that Miss French actually told her so.'

'You don't think she dislikes you enough to lie deliberately about the matter?'

Leonard Vole looked shocked and startled.

'No, indeed! Why should she?'

'I don't know,' said Mr Mayherne thoughtfully. 'But she's very bitter against you.'

The wretched young man groaned again.

'I'm beginning to see,' he muttered. 'It's frightful. I made up to her, that's what they'll say, I got her to make a will leaving her money to me, and then I go there that night, and there's nobody in the house—they find her the next day—oh! my God, it's awful!'

'You are wrong about there being nobody in the house,' said Mr Mayherne. 'Janet, as you remember, was to go out for the evening. She went, but about half-past nine she returned to fetch the pattern of a blouse sleeve which she had promised to a friend. She let herself in by the back door, went upstairs and fetched it, and went out again. She heard voices in the sitting-room, though she could not distinguish what they said, but she will swear that one of them was Miss French's and one was a man's.'

'At half-past nine,' said Leonard Vole. 'At half-past nine . . .' He sprang to his feet. 'But then I'm saved—saved——'

'What do you mean, saved?' cried Mr Mayherne, astonished.

'*By half-past nine I was at home again!* My wife can prove that. I left Miss French about five minutes to nine. I arrived home about twenty past nine. My wife was there waiting for me. Oh! Thank God—thank God! And bless Janet Mackenzie's sleeve pattern.'

In his exuberance, he hardly noticed that the grave expression of the solicitor's face had not altered. But the latter's words brought him down to earth with a bump.

'Who, then, in your opinion, murdered Miss French?'

'Why, a burglar, of course, as was thought at first. The window was forced, you remember. She was killed with a heavy blow from a crowbar, and the crowbar was found lying on the floor beside the body. And several articles were missing. But for Janet's absurd suspicions and dislike of me, the police would never have swerved from the right track.'

'That will hardly do, Mr Vole,' said the solicitor. 'The things that were missing were mere trifles of no value, taken as a blind. And the marks on the window were not at all conclusive. Besides, think for yourself. You say you were no longer in the house by half-past nine. Who, then, was the man Janet heard talking to Miss French in the sitting-room? She would hardly be having an amicable conversation with a burglar?'

'No,' said Vole. 'No——' He looked puzzled and discouraged. 'But anyway,' he added with reviving spirit, 'it lets me out. I've got an alibi. You must see Romaine—my wife—at once.'

'Certainly,' acquiesced the lawyer. 'I should already have seen Mrs Vole but for her being absent when you were arrested. I wired to Scotland at once, and I understand that she arrives back tonight. I am going to call upon her immediately I leave here.'

Vole nodded, a great expression of satisfaction settling down over his face.

'Yes, Romaine will tell you. My God! it's a lucky chance that.'

'Excuse me, Mr Vole, but you are very fond of your wife?'

'Of course.'

'And she of you?'

'Romaine is devoted to me. She'd do anything in the world for me.'

He spoke enthusiastically, but the solicitor's heart sank a little lower. The testimony of a devoted wife—would it gain credence?

'Was there anyone else who saw you return at nine-twenty? A maid, for instance?'

'We have no maid.'

'Did you meet anyone in the street on the way back?'

'Nobody I knew. I rode part of the way in a 'bus. The conductor might remember.'

Mr Mayherne shook his head doubtfully.

'There is no one, then, who can confirm your wife's testimony?'

'No. But it isn't necessary, surely?'

'I dare say not. I dare say not,' said Mr Mayherne hastily. 'Now there's just one thing more. Did Miss French know that you were a married man?'

'Oh, yes.'

'Yet you never took your wife to see her. Why was that?'

For the first time, Leonard Vole's answer came halting and uncertain. 'Well—I don't know.'

'Are you aware that Janet Mackenzie says her mistress believed you to be single, and contemplated marrying you in the future?'

Vole laughed.

'Absurd! There was forty years difference in age between us.'

'It has been done,' said the solicitor drily. 'The fact remains. Your wife never met Miss French?'

'No——' Again the constraint.

'You will permit me to say,' said the lawyer, 'that I hardly understand your attitude in the matter.'

Vole flushed, hesitated, and then spoke.

'I'll make a clean breast of it. I was hard up, as you know. I hoped that Miss French might lend me some money. She was fond of me, but she wasn't at all interested in the struggles of a young couple. Early on, I found that she had taken it for granted that my wife and I didn't get on—were living apart. Mr Mayherne—I wanted the money—for Romaine's sake. I said nothing, and allowed the old lady to think what she chose. She spoke of my being an adopted son to her. There was never any question of marriage—that must be just Janet's imagination.'

'And that is all?'

'Yes—that is all.'

Was there just a shade of hesitation in the words? The lawyer fancied so. He rose and held out his hand.

'Goodbye, Mr Vole.' He looked into the haggard young face and spoke with an unusual impulse. 'I believe in your innocence in spite of the multitude of facts arrayed against you. I hope to prove it and vindicate you completely.'

Vole smiled back at him.

'You'll find the alibi is all right,' he said cheerfully.

Again he hardly noticed that the other did not respond.

'The whole thing hinges a good deal on the testimony of Janet Mackenzie,' said Mr Mayherne. 'She hates you. That much is clear.'

'She can hardly hate me,' protested the young man.

The solicitor shook his head as he went out.

'Now for Mrs Vole,' he said to himself.

He was seriously disturbed by the way the thing was shaping.

The Voles lived in a small shabby house near Paddington Green. It was to this house that Mr Mayherne went.

In answer to his ring, a big slatternly woman, obviously a charwoman, answered the door.

'Mrs Vole? Has she returned yet?'

'Got back an hour ago. But I dunno if you can see her.'

'If you will take my card to her,' said Mr Mayherne quietly, 'I am quite sure that she will do so.'

The woman looked at him doubtfully, wiped her hand on her apron and took the card. Then she closed the door in his face and left him on the step outside.

In a few minutes, however, she returned with a slightly altered manner.

'Come inside, please.'

She ushered him into a tiny drawing-room. Mr Mayherne, examining a drawing on the wall, started up suddenly to face a tall pale woman who had entered so quietly that he had not heard her.

'Mr Mayherne? You are my husband's solicitor, are you not? You have come from him? Will you please sit down?'

Until she spoke he had not realized that she was not English. Now, observing her more closely, he noticed the high cheekbones, the dense blue-black of the hair, and an occasional very slight movement of the hands that was distinctly foreign. A strange woman, very quiet. So quiet as to make one uneasy. From the very first Mr Mayherne was conscious that he was up against something that he did not understand.

'Now, my dear Mrs Vole,' he began, 'you must not give way——'

He stopped. It was so very obvious that Romaine Vole had not the slightest intention of giving way. She was perfectly calm and composed.

'Will you please tell me all about it?' she said. 'I must know everything. Do not think to spare me. I want to know the worst.' She hesitated, then repeated in a lower tone, with a curious emphasis which the lawyer did not understand: 'I want to know the worst.'

Mr Mayherne went over his interview with Leonard Vole. She listened attentively, nodding her head now and then.

'I see,' she said, when he had finished. 'He wants me to say that he came in at twenty minutes past nine that night?'

'He did come in at that time?' said Mr Mayherne sharply.

'That is not the point,' she said coldly. 'Will my saying so acquit him? Will they believe me?'

Mr Mayherne was taken aback. She had gone so quickly to the core of the matter.

'That is what I want to know,' she said. 'Will it be enough? Is there anyone else who can support my evidence?'

There was a suppressed eagerness in her manner that made him vaguely uneasy.

'So far there is no one else,' he said reluctantly.

'I see,' said Romaine Vole.

She sat for a minute or two perfectly still. A little smile played over her lips.

The lawyer's feeling of alarm grew stronger and stronger.

'Mrs Vole——' he began. 'I know what you must feel——'

'Do you?' she said. 'I wonder.'

'In the circumstances——'

'In the circumstances—I intend to play a lone hand.'

He looked at her in dismay.

'But, my dear Mrs Vole—you are overwrought. Being so devoted to your husband——'

'I beg your pardon?'

The sharpness of her voice made him start. He repeated in a hesitating manner:

'Being so devoted to your husband——'

Romaine Vole nodded slowly, the same strange smile on her lips.

'Did he tell you that I was devoted to him?' she asked softly. 'Ah! yes, I can see he did. How stupid men are! Stupid—stupid—stupid——'

She rose suddenly to her feet. All the intense emotion that the lawyer had been conscious of in the atmosphere was now concentrated in her tone.

'I hate him, I tell you! I hate him. I hate him. I hate him! I would like to see him hanged by the neck till he is dead.'

The lawyer recoiled before her and the smouldering passion in her eyes.

She advanced a step nearer, and continued vehemently:

'Perhaps I *shall* see it. Supposing I tell you that he did not come in that night at twenty past nine, but at twenty past *ten*? You say that he tells you he knew nothing about the money coming to him. Supposing I tell you he knew all about it, and counted on it, and committed murder to get it? Supposing I tell you that he admitted to me that night when he came in what he had done? That there was blood on his coat? What then? Supposing that I stand up in court and say all these things?'

Her eyes seemed to challenge him. With an effort, he concealed his growing dismay, and endeavoured to speak in a rational tone.

'You cannot be asked to give evidence against your husband——'

'He is not my husband!'

The words came out so quickly that he fancied he had misunderstood her.

'I beg your pardon? I——'

'He is not my husband.'

The silence was so intense that you could have heard a pin drop.

'I was an actress in Vienna. My husband is alive but in a madhouse. So we could not marry. I am glad now.'

She nodded defiantly.

'I should like you to tell me one thing,' said Mr Mayherne. He contrived to appear as cool and unemotional as ever. 'Why are you so bitter against Leonard Vole?'

She shook her head, smiling a little.

'Yes, you would like to know. But I shall not tell you. I will keep my secret . . .'

Mr Mayherne gave his dry little cough and rose.

'There seems no point in prolonging this interview,' he remarked. 'You will hear from me again after I have communicated with my client.'

She came closer to him, looking into his eyes with her own wonderful dark ones.

'Tell me,' she said, 'did you believe—honestly—that he was innocent when you came here today?'

'I did,' said Mr Mayherne.

'You poor little man,' she laughed.

'And I believe so still,' finished the lawyer. 'Good evening, madam.'

He went out of the room, taking with him the memory of her startled face.

'This is going to be the devil of a business,' said Mr Mayherne to himself as he strode along the street.

Extraordinary, the whole thing. An extraordinary woman. A very dangerous woman. Women were the devil when they got their knife into you.

What was to be done? That wretched young man hadn't a leg to stand upon. Of course, possibly he did commit the crime . . .

'No,' said Mr Mayherne to himself. 'No—there's almost too much evidence against him. I don't believe this woman. She was trumping up the whole story. But she'll never bring it into court.'

He wished he felt more conviction on the point.

The police court proceedings were brief and dramatic. The principal witnesses for the prosecution were Janet Mackenzie, maid to the dead woman, and Romaine Heilger, Austrian subject, the mistress of the prisoner.

Mr Mayherne sat in court and listened to the damning story that the latter told. It was on the lines she had indicated to him in their interview.

The prisoner reserved his defence and was committed for trial.

Mr Mayherne was at his wits' end. The case against Leonard Vole was black beyond words. Even the famous KC who was engaged for the defence held out little hope.

'If we can shake the Austrian woman's testimony, we might do something,' he said dubiously. 'But it's a bad business.'

Mr Mayherne had concentrated his energies on one single point. Assuming Leonard Vole to be speaking the truth, and to have left the murdered woman's house at nine o'clock, who was the man whom Janet heard talking to Miss French at half-past nine?

The only ray of light was in the shape of a scapegrace nephew who had in bygone days cajoled and threatened his aunt out of various sums of money. Janet Mackenzie, the solicitor learned, had always been attached to this young man, and had never ceased urging his claims upon her mistress. It certainly seemed possible that it was this nephew who had been with Miss French after Leonard Vole left, especially as he was not to be found in any of his old haunts.

In all other directions, the lawyer's researches had been negative in their result. No one had seen Leonard Vole entering his own house, or leaving that of Miss French. No one had seen any other man enter or leave the house in Cricklewood. All inquiries drew blank.

It was the eve of the trial when Mr Mayherne received the letter which was to lead his thoughts in an entirely new direction.

It came by the six o'clock post. An illiterate scrawl, written on common paper and enclosed in a dirty envelope with the stamp stuck on crooked.

Mr Mayherne read it through once or twice before he grasped its meaning.

DEAR MISTER:
Youre the lawyer chap wot acks for the young feller. If you want that painted foreign hussy showd up for wot she is an her pack of lies you come to 16 Shaw's Rents Stepney tonight It ull cawst you 2 hundred quid Arsk for Missis Mogson.

The solicitor read and re-read this strange epistle. It might, of course, be a hoax, but when he thought it over, he became increasingly convinced that it was genuine, and also convinced that it was the one hope for the prisoner. The evidence of Romaine Heilger damned him completely, and the line the defence meant to pursue, the line that the evidence of a woman who had admittedly lived an immoral life was not to be trusted, was at best a weak one.

Mr Mayherne's mind was made up. It was his duty to save his client at all costs. He must go to Shaw's Rents.

He had some difficulty in finding the place, a ramshackle building in an evil-smelling slum, but at last he did so, and on inquiry for Mrs Mogson was sent up to a room on the third floor. On this door he knocked, and getting no answer, knocked again.

At this second knock, he heard a shuffling sound inside, and presently the door was opened cautiously half an inch and a bent figure peered out.

Suddenly the woman, for it was a woman, gave a chuckle and opened the door wider.

'So it's you, dearie,' she said, in a wheezy voice. 'Nobody with you, is there? No playing tricks? That's right. You can come in—you can come in.'

With some reluctance the lawyer stepped across the threshold into the small dirty room, with its flickering gas jet. There was an untidy unmade bed in a corner, a plain deal table and two rickety chairs. For the first time Mr Mayherne had a full view of the tenant of this unsavoury apartment. She was a woman of middle age, bent in figure, with a mass of untidy grey hair and a scarf wound tightly round her face. She saw him looking at this and laughed again, the same curious toneless chuckle.

'Wondering why I hide my beauty, dear? He, he, he. Afraid it may tempt you, eh? But you shall see—you shall see.'

She drew aside the scarf and the lawyer recoiled involuntarily before the almost formless blur of scarlet. She replaced the scarf again.

'So you're not wanting to kiss me, dearie? He, he, I don't wonder. And yet I was a pretty girl once—not so long ago as you'd think, either. Vitriol, dearie, vitriol—that's what did that. Ah! but I'll be even with 'em——'

She burst into a hideous torrent of profanity which Mr Mayherne tried vainly to quell. She fell silent at last, her hands clenching and unclenching themselves nervously.

'Enough of that,' said the lawyer sternly. 'I've come here because I have reason to believe you can give me information which will clear my client, Leonard Vole. Is that the case?'

Her eyes leered at him cunningly.

'What about the money, dearie?' she wheezed. 'Two hundred quid, you remember.'

'It is your duty to give evidence, and you can be called upon to do so.'

'That won't do, dearie. I'm an old woman, and I know nothing. But you give me two hundred quid, and perhaps I can give you a hint or two. See?'

'What kind of hint?'

'What should you say to a letter? A letter from *her*. Never mind how I got hold of it. That's my business. It'll do the trick. But I want my two hundred quid.'

Mr Mayherne looked at her coldly, and made up his mind.

'I'll give you ten pounds, nothing more. And only that if this letter is what you say it is.'

'Ten pounds?' She screamed and raved at him.

'Twenty,' said Mr Mayherne, 'and that's my last word.'

He rose as if to go. Then, watching her closely, he drew out a pocket-book, and counted out twenty one-pound notes.

'You see,' he said. 'That is all I have with me. You can take it or leave it.'

But already he knew that the sight of the money was too much for her. She cursed and raved impotently, but at last she gave in. Going over to the bed, she drew something out from beneath the tattered mattress.

'Here you are, damn you!' she snarled. 'It's the top one you want.'

It was a bundle of letters that she threw to him, and Mr Mayherne untied them and scanned them in his usual cool, methodical manner. The woman, watching him eagerly, could gain no clue from his impassive face.

He read each letter through, then returned again to the top one and read it a second time. Then he tied the whole bundle up again carefully.

They were love letters, written by Romaine Heilger, and the man they were written to was not Leonard Vole. The top letter was dated the day of the latter's arrest.

'I spoke true, dearie, didn't I?' whined the woman. 'It'll do for her, that letter?'

Mr Mayherne put the letters in his pocket, then he asked a question.

'How did you get hold of this correspondence?'

'That's telling,' she said with a leer. 'But I know something more. I heard in court what that hussy said. Find out where *she* was at twenty past ten, the time she says she was at home. Ask at the Lion Road Cinema. They'll remember—a fine upstanding girl like that—curse her!'

'Who is the man?' asked Mr Mayherne. 'There's only a Christian name here.'

The other's voice grew thick and hoarse, her hands clenched and unclenched. Finally she lifted one to her face.

'He's the man that did this to me. Many years ago now. She took him away from me—a chit of a girl she was then. And when I went after him—and went for him too—he threw the cursed stuff at me! And she laughed—damn her! I've had it in for her for years. Followed her, I have, spied upon her. And now I've got her! She'll suffer for this, won't she, Mr Lawyer? She'll suffer?'

'She will probably be sentenced to a term of imprisonment for perjury,' said Mr Mayherne quietly.

'Shut away—that's what I want. You're going, are you? Where's my money? Where's that good money?'

Without a word, Mr Mayherne put down the notes on the table. Then, drawing a deep breath, he turned and left the squalid room. Looking back, he saw the old woman crooning over the money.

He wasted no time. He found the cinema in Lion Road easily enough, and, shown a photograph of Romaine Heilger, the commissionaire recognized her at once. She had arrived at the cinema with a man some time after ten o'clock on the evening in question. He had not noticed her escort particularly, but he remembered the lady who had spoken to him about the picture that was showing. They stayed until the end, about an hour later.

Mr Mayherne was satisfied. Romaine Heilger's evidence was a tissue of lies from beginning to end. She had evolved it out of her passionate hatred. The lawyer wondered whether he would ever know what lay behind that hatred. What had Leonard Vole done to her? He had seemed dumbfounded when the solicitor had reported her attitude to him. He had declared earnestly that such a thing was incredible—yet it had seemed to Mr Mayherne that after the first astonishment his protests had lacked sincerity.

He *did* know. Mr Mayherne was convinced of it. He knew, but he had no intention of revealing the fact. The secret between those two remained a secret. Mr Mayherne wondered if some day he should come to learn what it was.

The solicitor glanced at his watch. It was late, but time was everything. He hailed a taxi and gave an address.

'Sir Charles must know of this at once,' he murmured to himself as he got in.

The trial of Leonard Vole for the murder of Emily French aroused widespread interest. In the first place the prisoner was young and good-looking, then he was accused of a particularly dastardly crime, and there was the further interest of Romaine Heilger, the principal witness for the prosecution. There had been pictures of her in many papers, and several fictitious stories as to her origin and history.

The proceedings opened quietly enough. Various technical evidence came first. Then Janet Mackenzie was called. She told substantially the same story as before. In cross-examination counsel for the defence succeeded in getting her to contradict herself once or twice over her account of Vole's association with Miss French, he emphasized the fact that though she had heard a man's voice in the sitting-room that night, there was nothing to show that it was Vole who was there, and he managed to drive home a feeling that jealousy and dislike of the prisoner were at the bottom of a good deal of her evidence.

Then the next witness was called.

'Your name is Romaine Heilger?'

'Yes.'

'You are an Austrian subject?'

'Yes.'

'For the last three years you have lived with the prisoner and passed yourself off as his wife?'

Just for a moment Romaine Heilger's eyes met those of the man in the dock. Her expression held something curious and unfathomable.

'Yes.'

The questions went on. Word by word the damning facts came out. On the night in question the prisoner had taken out a crowbar with him. He had returned at twenty minutes past ten, and had confessed to having killed the old lady. His cuffs had been stained with blood, and he had burned them in the kitchen stove. He had terrorized her into silence by means of threats.

As the story proceeded, the feeling of the court which had, to begin with, been slightly favourable to the prisoner, now set dead against him. He himself sat with downcast head and moody air, as though he knew he were doomed.

Yet it might have been noted that her own counsel sought to restrain Romaine's animosity. He would have preferred her to be a more unbiased witness.

Formidable and ponderous, counsel for the defence arose.

He put it to her that her story was a malicious fabrication from start to finish, that she had not even been in her own house at the time in question, that she was in love with another man and was deliberately seeking to send Vole to his death for a crime he did not commit.

Romaine denied these allegations with superb insolence.

Then came the surprising denouement, the production of the letter. It was read aloud in court in the midst of a breathless stillness.

Max, beloved, the Fates have delivered him into our hands! He has been arrested for murder—but, yes, the murder of an old lady! Leonard who would not hurt a fly! At last I shall have my revenge. The poor chicken! I shall say that he came in that night with blood upon him—that he confessed to me. I shall hang him, Max—and when he hangs he will know and realize that it was Romaine who sent him to his death. And then—happiness, Beloved! Happiness at last!

There were experts present ready to swear that the handwriting was that of Romaine Heilger, but they were not needed. Confronted with the letter, Romaine broke down utterly and confessed everything. Leonard Vole had returned to the house at the time he said, twenty past nine. She had invented the whole story to ruin him.

With the collapse of Romaine Heilger, the case for the Crown collapsed also. Sir Charles called his few witnesses, the prisoner himself went into the box and told his story in a manly straightforward manner, unshaken by cross-examination.

The prosecution endeavoured to rally, but without great success. The judge's summing up was not wholly favourable to the prisoner, but a reaction had set in and the jury needed little time to consider their verdict.

'We find the prisoner not guilty.'

Leonard Vole was free!

Little Mr Mayherne hurried from his seat. He must congratulate his client.

He found himself polishing his pince-nez vigorously, and checked himself. His wife had told him only the night before that he was getting a habit of it. Curious things, habits. People themselves never knew they had them.

An interesting case—a very interesting case. That woman, now, Romaine Heilger.

The case was dominated for him still by the exotic figure of Romaine Heilger. She had seemed a pale quiet woman in the house at Paddington, but in court she had flamed out against the sober background. She had flaunted herself like a tropical flower.

If he closed his eyes he could see her now, tall and vehement, her exquisite body bent forward a little, her right hand clenching and unclenching itself unconsciously all the time.

Curious things, habits. That gesture of hers with the hand was her habit, he supposed. Yet he had seen someone else do it quite lately. Who was it now? Quite lately——

He drew in his breath with a gasp as it came back to him. *The woman in Shaw's Rents* . . .

He stood still, his head whirling. It was impossible—impossible —— Yet, Romaine Heilger was an actress.

The KC came up behind him and clapped him on the shoulder.

'Congratulated our man yet? He's had a narrow shave, you know. Come along and see him.'

But the little lawyer shook off the other's hand.

He wanted one thing only—to see Romaine Heilger face to face.

He did not see her until some time later, and the place of their meeting is not relevant.

'So you guessed,' she said, when he had told her all that was in his mind. 'The face? Oh! that was easy enough, and the light of that gas jet was too bad for you to see the make-up.'

'But why—why——'

'Why did I play a lone hand?' She smiled a little, remembering the last time she had used the words.

'Such an elaborate comedy!'

'My friend— I had to save him. The evidence of a woman devoted to him would not have been enough—you hinted as much yourself. But I know something of the psychology of crowds. Let my evidence be wrung from me, as an admission, damning me in the eyes of the law, and a reaction in favour of the prisoner would immediately set in.'

'And the bundle of letters?'

'One alone, the vital one, might have seemed like a—what do you call it?—put-up job.'

'Then the man called Max?'

'Never existed, my friend.'

'I still think,' said little Mr Mayherne, in an aggrieved manner, 'that we could have got him off by the—er—normal procedure.'

'I dared not risk it. You see, you *thought* he was innocent——'

'And you *knew* it? I see,' said little Mr Mayherne.

'My dear Mr Mayherne,' said Romaine, 'you do not see at all. I knew—he was guilty!'

ANTHONY BERKELEY · 1893–1971

The Avenging Chance

Roger Sheringham was inclined to think afterwards that the Poisoned Chocolates Case, as the papers called it, was perhaps the most perfectly planned murder he had ever encountered. The motive was so obvious, when you knew where to look for it—but you didn't know; the method was so significant when you had grasped its real essentials—but you didn't grasp them; the traces were so thinly covered, when you had realized what was covering them—but you didn't realize. But for a piece of the merest bad luck, which the murderer could not possibly have foreseen, the crime must have been added to the classical list of great mysteries.

This is the gist of the case, as Chief Inspector Moresby told it one evening to Roger in the latter's rooms in the Albany a week or so after it happened:

On Friday morning, the fifteenth of November, at half-past ten in the morning, in accordance with his invariable custom, Sir William Anstruther walked into his club in Piccadilly, the very exclusive Rainbow Club, and asked for his letters. The porter handed him three and a small parcel. Sir William walked over to the fireplace in the big lounge hall to open them.

A few minutes later another member entered the club, a Mr Graham Beresford. There were a letter and a couple of circulars for him, and he also strolled over to the fireplace, nodding to Sir William, but not speaking to him. The two men only knew each other very slightly, and had probably never exchanged more than a dozen words in all.

Having glanced through his letters, Sir William opened the parcel and, after a moment, snorted with disgust. Beresford looked at him, and with a grunt Sir William thrust out a letter which had been enclosed in the parcel. Concealing a smile (Sir William's ways were a matter of some amusement to his fellow-members), Beresford read the letter. It was from a big firm of chocolate manufacturers, Mason & Sons, and set forth that they were putting on the market a new brand of liqueur-chocolates designed especially to appeal to men; would Sir William do them the honour of accepting the enclosed two-pound box and letting the firm have his candid opinion on them?

'Do they think I'm a blank chorus-girl?' fumed Sir William. 'Write 'em testimonials about their blank chocolates, indeed! Blank 'em! I'll complain to the blank committee. That sort of blank thing can't blank well be allowed here.'

'Well, it's an ill wind so far as I'm concerned,' Beresford soothed him. 'It's reminded me of something. My wife and I had a box at the Imperial last night. I bet her a box of chocolates to a hundred cigarettes that she wouldn't spot the villain by the end of the second act. She won. I must remember to get them. Have you seen it—*The Creaking Skull*? Not a bad show.'

Sir William had not seen it, and said so with force.

'Want a box of chocolates, did you say?' he added, more mildly. 'Well, take this blank one. I don't want it.'

For a moment Beresford demurred politely and then, most unfortunately for himself, accepted. The money so saved meant nothing to him for he was a wealthy man; but trouble was always worth saving.

By an extraordinarily lucky chance neither the outer wrapper of the box nor its covering letter were thrown into the fire, and this was the more fortunate in that both men had tossed the envelopes of their letters into the flames. Sir William did, indeed, make a bundle of the wrapper, letter and string, but he handed it over to Beresford, and the latter simply dropped it inside the fender. This bundle the porter subsequently extracted and, being a man of orderly habits, put it tidily away in the waste-paper basket, whence it was retrieved later by the police.

Of the three unconscious protagonists in the impending tragedy, Sir William was without doubt the most remarkable. Still a year or two under fifty, he looked, with his flaming red face and thick-set figure, a typical country squire of the old school, and both his manners and his language were in accordance with tradition. His habits, especially as regards women, were also in accordance with tradition—the tradition of the bold, bad baronet which he undoubtedly was.

In comparison with him, Beresford was rather an ordinary man, a tall, dark, not unhandsome fellow of two-and-thirty, quiet and reserved. His father had left him a rich man, but idleness did not appeal to him, and he had a finger in a good many business pies.

Money attracts money, Graham Beresford had inherited it, he made it, and, inevitably, he had married it, too. The daughter of a late shipowner in Liverpool, with not far off half a million in her own right. But the money was incidental, for he needed her and would have married her just as inevitably (said his friends) if she had not had a farthing. A tall, rather serious-minded, highly cultured girl, not so young that her character had not had time to form (she was twenty-five when Beresford married her, three years ago), she was the ideal wife for him. A bit of a Puritan perhaps in some ways, but Beresford, whose wild oats, though duly sown, had been a sparse crop, was ready enough to be a Puritan himself by that time if she was. To make no bones about it, the Beresfords succeeded in achieving that eighth wonder of the modern world, a happy marriage.

And into the middle of it there dropped with irretrievable tragedy, the box of chocolates.

Beresford gave them to her after lunch as they sat over their coffee, with some jesting remark about paying his honourable debts, and she opened the box at once. The top layer, she noticed, seemed to consist only of kirsch and maraschino. Beresford, who did not believe in spoiling good coffee, refused when she offered him the box, and his wife ate the first one alone. As she did so she exclaimed in surprise that the filling seemed exceedingly strong and positively burnt her mouth.

Beresford explained that they were samples of a new brand and then, made curious by what his wife had said, took one too. A burning taste, not intolerable but much too strong to be pleasant, followed the release of the liquid, and the almond flavouring seemed quite excessive.

'By Jove,' he said, 'they are strong. They must be filled with neat alcohol.'

'Oh, they wouldn't do that, surely,' said his wife, taking another. 'But they are very strong. I think I rather like them, though.'

Beresford ate another, and disliked it still more. 'I don't,' he said with decision. 'They make my tongue feel quite numb. I shouldn't eat any more of them if I were you, I think there's something wrong with them.'

'Well, they're only an experiment, I suppose,' she said. 'But they do burn. I'm not sure whether I like them or not.'

A few minutes later Beresford went out to keep a business appointment in the City. He left her still trying to make up her mind whether she liked them, and still eating them to decide. Beresford remembered that scrap of conversation afterwards very vividly, because it was the last time he saw his wife alive.

That was roughly half-past two. At a quarter to four Beresford arrived at his club from the City in a taxi, in a state of collapse. He was helped into the building by the driver and the porter, and both described him subsequently as pale to the point of ghastliness, with staring eyes and livid lips, and his skin damp and clammy. His mind seemed unaffected, however, and when they had got him up the steps he was able to walk, with the porter's help, into the lounge.

The porter, thoroughly alarmed, wanted to send for a doctor at once, but Beresford, who was the last man in the world to make a fuss, refused to let him, saying that it must be indigestion and he would be all right in a few minutes. To Sir William Anstruther, however, who was in the lounge at the time, he added after the porter had gone:

'Yes, and I believe it was those infernal chocolates you gave me, now I come to think of it. I thought there was something funny about them at the time. I'd better go and find out if my wife————' He broke off abruptly. His body, which had been leaning back limply in his chair, suddenly heaved rigidly upright; his jaws locked together, the livid lips drawn back in a horrible grin, and his hands clenched on the arms of his chair. At the same time Sir William became aware of an unmistakable smell of bitter almonds.

Thoroughly alarmed, believing indeed that the man was dying under his eyes, Sir William raised a shout for the porter and a doctor. The other occupants of the lounge hurried up, and between them they got the convulsed body of the unconscious man into a more comfortable position. Before the doctor could arrive a telephone message was received at the club from an agitated butler asking if Mr Beresford was there, and if so would he come home at once as Mrs Beresford had been taken seriously ill. As a matter of fact she was already dead.

Beresford did not die. He had taken less of the poison than his wife, who after his departure must have eaten at least three more of the chocolates, so that its action was less rapid and the doctor had time to save him. As a matter of fact it turned out afterwards that he had not had a fatal dose. By about eight o'clock that night he was conscious; the next day he was practically convalescent.

As for the unfortunate Mrs Beresford, the doctor had arrived too late to save her, and she passed away very rapidly in a deep coma.

The police had taken the matter in hand as soon as Mrs Beresford's death was reported to them and the fact of poison established, and it was only a very short time before things had become narrowed down to the chocolates as the active agent.

Sir William was interrogated, the letter and wrapper were recovered from the waste-paper basket, and, even before the sick man was out of danger, a detective inspector was asking for an interview with the managing-director of Mason & Sons. Scotland Yard moves quickly.

It was the police theory at this stage, based on what Sir William and the two doctors had been able to tell them, that by an act of criminal carelessness on the part of one of Mason's employees, an excessive amount of oil of bitter almonds had been included in the filling mixture of the chocolates, for that was what the doctors had decided must be the poisoning ingredient. However, the managing-director quashed this idea at once: oil of bitter almonds, he asserted, was never used by Mason's.

He had more interesting news still. Having read with undisguised astonishment the covering letter, he at once declared that it was a forgery. No such letter, no such samples had been sent out by the firm at all; a new variety of liqueur-chocolates had never been mooted. The fatal chocolates were their ordinary brand.

Unwrapping and examining one more closely, he called the inspector's attention to a mark on the underside, which he suggested was the remains of a small hole drilled in the case, through which the liquid could have been extracted and the fatal filling inserted, the hole afterwards being stopped up with softened chocolate, a perfectly simple operation.

He examined it under a magnifying-glass and the inspector agreed. It was now clear to him that somebody had been trying deliberately to murder Sir William Anstruther.

Scotland Yard doubled its activities. The chocolates were sent for analysis, Sir William was interviewed again, and so was the now conscious Beresford. From the latter the doctor insisted that the news of his wife's death must be kept till the next day, as in his weakened condition the shock might be fatal, so that nothing very helpful was obtained from him.

Nor could Sir William throw any light on the mystery or produce a single person who might have any grounds for trying to kill him. He was living apart from his wife, who was the principal beneficiary in his will, but she was in the South of France, as the French police subsequently confirmed. His estate in Worcestershire, heavily mortgaged, was entailed and went to a nephew; but as the rent he got for it barely covered the interest on the mortgage, and the nephew was considerably better off than Sir William himself, there was no motive there. The police were at a dead end.

The analysis brought one or two interesting facts to light. Not oil of bitter almonds but nitrobenzine, a kindred substance, chiefly used in the manufacture of aniline dyes, was the somewhat surprising poison employed. Each chocolate in the upper layer contained exactly six minims of it, in a mixture of kirsch and maraschino. The chocolates in the other layers were harmless.

As to the other clues, they seemed equally useless. The sheet of Mason's notepaper was identified by Merton's, the printers, as of their work, but there was nothing to show how it had got into the murderer's possession. All that could be said was that, the edges being distinctly yellowed, it must be an old piece. The machine on which the letter had been typed, of course, could not be traced. From the wrapper, a piece of ordinary brown paper with Sir William's address hand-printed on it in large capitals, there was nothing to be learnt at all beyond that the parcel had been posted at the office in Southampton Street between the hours of 8.30 and 9.30 on the previous evening.

Only one thing was quite clear. Whoever had coveted Sir William's life had no intention of paying for it with his or her own.

'And now you know as much as we do, Mr Sheringham,' concluded Chief Inspector Moresby, 'and if you can say who sent those chocolates to Sir William, you'll know a good deal more.'

Roger nodded thoughtfully.

'It's a brute of a case. I met a man only yesterday who was at school with Beresford. He didn't know him very well because Beresford was on the modern side and my friend was a classical bird, but they were in the same house. He says Beresford's absolutely knocked over by his wife's death. I wish you could find out who sent those chocolates, Moresby.'

'So do I, Mr Sheringham,' said Moresby gloomily.

'It might have been anyone in the whole world,' Roger mused. 'What about feminine jealousy, for instance? Sir William's private life doesn't seem to be immaculate. I dare say there's a good deal of off with the old light-o'-love and on with the new.'

'Why, that's just what I've been looking into, Mr Sheringham, sir,' retorted Chief Inspector Moresby reproachfully. 'That was the first thing that came to me. Because if anything does stand out about this business it is that it's a woman's crime. Nobody but a woman would send poisoned chocolates to a man. Another man would send a poisoned sample of whisky, or something like that.'

'That's a very sound point, Moresby,' Roger meditated. 'Very sound indeed. And Sir William couldn't help you?'

'Couldn't,' said Moresby, not without a trace of resentment, 'or wouldn't. I was inclined to believe at first that he might have his suspicions and was shielding some woman. But I don't think so now.'

'Humph!' Roger did not seem quite so sure. 'It's reminiscent, this case, isn't it? Didn't some lunatic once send poisoned chocolates to the Commissioner of Police himself? A good crime always gets imitated, as you know.'

Moresby brightened.

'It's funny you should say that, Mr Sheringham, because that's the very conclusion I've come to. I've tested every other theory, and so far as I know there's not a soul with an interest in Sir William's death, whether from motives of gain, revenge, or what you like, whom I haven't had to rule quite out of it. In fact, I've pretty well made up my mind that the person who sent those chocolates was some irresponsible lunatic of a woman, a social or religious fanatic who's probably never even seen him. And if that's the case,' Moresby sighed, 'a fat chance I have of ever laying hands on her.'

'Unless Chance steps in, as it so often does,' said Roger brightly, 'and helps you. A tremendous lot of cases get solved by a stroke of sheer luck, don't they? *Chance the Avenger*. It would make an excellent film-title. But there's a lot of truth in it. If I were superstitious, which I'm not, I should say it wasn't chance at all, but Providence avenging the victim.'

'Well, Mr Sheringham,' said Moresby, who was not superstitious either, 'to tell the truth, I don't mind what it is, so long as it lets me get my hands on the right person.'

If Moresby had paid his visit to Roger Sheringham with any hope of tapping that gentleman's brains, he went away disappointed.

To tell the truth, Roger was inclined to agree with the chief inspector's conclusion, that the attempt on the life of Sir William Anstruther and the actual murder of the unfortunate Mrs Beresford must be the work of some unknown criminal lunatic. For this reason, although he thought about it a good deal during the next few days, he made no attempt to take the case in hand. It was the sort of affair, necessitating endless inquiries that a private person would have neither the time nor the authority to carry out, which can be handled only by the official police. Roger's interest in it was purely academic.

It was hazard, a chance encounter nearly a week later, which translated this interest from the academic into the personal.

Roger was in Bond Street, about to go through the distressing ordeal of buying a new hat. Along the pavement he suddenly saw bearing down on him Mrs Verreker-le-Flemming. Mrs Verreker-le-Flemming was small, exquisite, rich, and a widow, and she sat at Roger's feet whenever he gave her the opportunity. But she talked. She talked, in fact, and talked and talked. And Roger, who rather liked talking himself, could not bear it. He tried to dart across the road, but there was no opening in the traffic stream. He was cornered.

Mrs Verreker-le-Flemming fastened on him gladly.

'Oh, Mr Sheringham! *Just* the person I wanted to see. Mr Sheringham, *do* tell me. In confidence. *Are* you taking up this dreadful business of poor Joan Beresford's death?'

Roger, the frozen and imbecile grin of civilized intercourse on his face, tried to get a word in; without result.

'I was horrified when I heard of it—simply horrified. You see, Joan and I were such *very* close friends. Quite intimate. And the awful thing, the truly *terrible* thing is that Joan brought the whole business on herself. Isn't that *appalling*?'

Roger no longer wanted to escape.

'What did you say?' he managed to insert incredulously.

'I suppose it's what they call tragic irony,' Mrs Verreker-le-Flemming chattered on. 'Certainly it was tragic enough, and I've never heard anything so terribly ironical. You know about that bet she made with her husband, of course, so that he had to get her a box of chocolates, and if he hadn't Sir William would never have given him the poisoned ones and he'd have eaten them and died himself and good riddance? Well, Mr Sheringham———' Mrs Verreker-le-Flemming lowered her voice to a conspirator's whisper and glanced about her in the approved manner. 'I've never told anybody else this, but I'm telling you because I know you'll appreciate it. *Joan wasn't playing fair!*'

'How do you mean?' Roger asked, bewildered.

Mrs Verreker-le-Flemming was artlessly pleased with her sensation.

'Why, she'd seen the play before. We went together, the very first week it was on. She *knew* who the villain was all the time.'

'By Jove!' Roger was as impressed as Mrs Verreker-le-Flemming could have wished. 'Chance the Avenger! We're none of us immune from it.'

'Poetic justice, you mean?' twittered Mrs Verreker-le-Flemming, to whom these remarks had been somewhat obscure. 'Yes, but Joan Beresford of all people! That's the extraordinary thing. I should never have thought Joan *would* do a thing like that. She was such a *nice* girl. A little close with money, of course, considering how well-off they are, but that isn't anything. Of course it was only fun, and pulling her husband's leg, but I always used to think Joan was such a *serious* girl, Mr Sheringham. I mean, ordinary people don't talk about honour and truth, and playing the game, and all those things one takes for granted. But Joan did. She was always saying that this wasn't honourable, or that wouldn't be playing the game. Well, she paid herself for not playing the game, poor girl, didn't she? Still, it all goes to show the truth of the old saying, doesn't it?'

'What old saying?' said Roger, hypnotized by this flow.

'Why, that still waters run deep. Joan must have been deep, I'm afraid.' Mrs Verreker-le-Flemming sighed. It was evidently a social error to be deep. 'I mean, she certainly took me in. She can't have been quite so honourable and truthful as she was always pretending, can she? And I can't help wondering whether a girl who'd deceived her husband in a little thing like that might not—oh, well, I don't want to say anything against poor Joan now she's dead, poor darling, but she can't have been *quite* such a plaster saint after all, can she? I mean,' said Mrs Verreker-le-Flemming, in hasty extenuation of these suggestions, 'I do think psychology is so very interesting, don't you, Mr Sheringham?'

'Sometimes, very,' Roger agreed gravely. 'But you mentioned Sir William Anstruther just now. Do you know him, too?'

'I used to,' Mrs Verreker-le-Flemming replied, without particular interest. 'Horrible man! Always running after some woman or other. And when he's tired of her, just drops her—biff!—like that. At least,' added Mrs Verreker-le-Flemming somewhat hastily, 'so I've heard.'

'And what happens if she refuses to be dropped?'

'Oh dear, I'm sure I don't know. I suppose you've heard the latest?' Mrs Verreker-le-Flemming hurried on, perhaps a trifle more pink than the delicate aids to nature on her cheeks would have warranted.

'He's taken up with that Bryce woman now. You know, the wife of the oil man, or petrol, or whatever he made his money in. It began about three weeks ago. You'd have thought that dreadful business of being responsible, in a way, for poor Joan Beresford's death would have sobered him up a little, wouldn't you? But not a bit of it; he———'

Roger was following another line of thought.

'What a pity you weren't at the Imperial with the Beresfords that evening. She'd never have made that bet if you had been.' Roger looked extremely innocent. 'You weren't, I suppose?'

'I?' queried Mrs Verreker-le-Flemming in surprise, 'Good gracious, no. I was at the new revue at the Pavilion. Lady Gavelstroke had a box and asked me to join her party.'

'Oh, yes. Good show, isn't it? I thought that sketch *The Sempiternal Triangle* very clever. Didn't you?'

'*The Sempiternal Triangle?*' wavered Mrs Verreker-le-Flemming.

'Yes, in the first half.'

'Oh! Then I didn't see it. I got there disgracefully late, I'm afraid. But then,' said Mrs Verreker-le-Flemming with pathos, 'I always do seem to be late for simply everything.'

Roger kept the rest of the conversation resolutely upon theatres. But before he left her he had ascertained that she had photographs of both Mrs Beresford and Sir William Anstruther and had obtained permission to borrow them some time. As soon as she was out of view he hailed a taxi and gave Mrs Verreker-le-Flemming's address. He thought it better to take advantage of her permission at a time when he would not have to pay for it a second time over.

The parlour maid seemed to think there was nothing odd in his mission, and took him up to the drawing-room at once. A corner of the room was devoted to the silver-framed photographs of Mrs Verreker-le-Flemming's friends, and there were many of them. Roger examined them with interest, and finally took away with him not two photographs but six, those of Sir William, Mrs Beresford, Beresford, two strange males who appeared to belong to the Sir William period, and, lastly a likeness of Mrs Verreker-le-Flemming herself. Roger liked confusing his trail.

For the rest of the day he was very busy.

His activities would have no doubt seemed to Mrs Verreker-le-Flemming not merely baffling but pointless. He paid a visit to a public library, for instance, and consulted a work of reference, after which he took a taxi and drove to the offices of the Anglo-Eastern Perfumery Company, where he inquired for a certain Mr Joseph Lea Hardwick and seemed much put out on hearing that no such gentleman was known to the firm and was certainly not employed in any of their branches. Many questions had to be put about the firm and its branches before he consented to abandon the quest.

After that he drove to Messrs Weall and Wilson, the well-known institution which protects the trade interests of individuals and advises its subscribers regarding investments. Here he entered his name as a subscriber, and explaining that he had a large sum of money to invest, filled in one of the special inquiry-forms which are headed Strictly Confidential.

Then he went to the Rainbow Club, in Piccadilly.

Introducing himself to the porter without a blush as connected with Scotland Yard, he asked the man a number of questions, more or less trivial, concerning the tragedy.

'Sir William, I understand,' he said finally, as if by the way, 'did not dine here the evening before?'

There it appeared that Roger was wrong. Sir William had dined in the club, as he did about three times a week.

'But I quite understood he wasn't here that evening?' Roger said plaintively.

The porter was emphatic. He remembered quite well. So did a waiter, whom the porter summoned to corroborate him. Sir William had dined, rather late, and had not left the dining-room till about nine o'clock. He spent the evening there, too, the waiter knew, or at least some of it, for he himself had taken him a whisky-and-soda in the lounge not less than half an hour later.

Roger retired.

He retired to Merton's, in a taxi.

It seemed that he wanted some new notepaper printed, of a very special kind, and to the young woman behind the counter he specified at great length and in wearisome detail exactly what he did want. The young woman handed him the books of specimen pieces and asked him to see if there was any style there which would suit him. Roger glanced through them, remarking garrulously to the young woman that he had been recommended to Merton's by a very dear friend, whose photograph he happened to have on him at that moment. Wasn't that a curious coincidence? The young woman agreed that it was.

'About a fortnight ago, I think, my friend was in here last,' said Roger, producing the photograph. 'Recognize this?'

The young woman took the photograph, without apparent interest.

'Oh, yes. I remember. About some notepaper, too, wasn't it? So that's your friend. Well, it's a small world. Now this is a line we're selling a good deal of just now.'

Roger went back to his rooms to dine. Afterwards, feeling restless, he wandered out of the Albany and turned up Piccadilly. He wandered round the Circus, thinking hard, and paused for a moment out of habit to inspect the photographs of the new revue hung outside the Pavilion. The next thing he realized was that he had got as far as Jermyn Street and was standing outside the Imperial Theatre. Glancing at the advertisements of *The Creaking Skull*, he saw that it began at half-past eight. Glancing at his watch, he saw that the time was twenty-nine minutes past that hour. He had an evening to get through somehow. He went inside.

The next morning, very early for Roger, he called on Moresby at Scotland Yard.

'Moresby,' he said without preamble, 'I want you to do something for me. Can you find me a taximan who took a fare from Piccadilly Circus or its neighbourhood at about ten past nine on the evening before the Beresford crime, to the Strand somewhere near the bottom of Southampton Street, and another who took a fare back between those points. I'm not sure about the first. Or one taxi might have been used for the double journey, but I doubt that. Anyhow, try to find out for me, will you?'

'What are you up to now, Mr Sheringham?' Moresby asked suspiciously.

'Breaking down an interesting alibi,' replied Roger serenely. 'By the way, I know who sent those chocolates to Sir William. I'm just building up a nice structure of evidence for you. Ring up my rooms when you've got those taximen.'

He strolled out, leaving Moresby positively gaping after him.

The rest of the day he spent apparently trying to buy a second-hand typewriter. He was very particular that it should be a Hamilton No. 4. When the shop-people tried to induce him to consider other makes he refused to look at them, saying that he had had the Hamilton No. 4 so strongly recommended to him by a friend, who had bought one about three weeks ago. Perhaps it was at this very shop? No? They hadn't sold a Hamilton No. 4 for the last three months? How odd.

But at one shop they had sold a Hamilton No. 4 within the last month, and that was odder still.

At half-past four Roger got back to his rooms to await the telephone message from Moresby. At half-past five it came.

'There are fourteen taxi-drivers here, littering up my office,' said Moresby offensively. 'What do you want me to do with 'em?'

'Keep them till I come, Chief Inspector,' returned Roger with dignity.

The interview with the fourteen was brief enough, however. To each man in turn Roger showed a photograph, holding it so that Moresby could not see it, and asked if he could recognize his fare. The ninth man did so, without hesitation.

At a nod from Roger, Moresby dismissed them, then sat at his table and tried to look official. Roger seated himself on the table, looking most unofficial, and swung his legs. As he did so, a photograph fell unnoticed out of his pocket and fluttered, face downwards, under the table. Moresby eyed it but did not pick it up.

'And now, Mr Sheringham, sir,' he said, 'perhaps you'll tell me what you've been doing?'

'Certainly, Moresby,' said Roger blandly. 'Your work for you. I really have solved the thing, you know. Here's your evidence.' He took from his note-case an old letter and handed it to the Chief Inspector. 'Was that typed on the same machine as the forged letter from Mason's, or was it not?'

Moresby studied it for a moment, then drew the forged letter from a drawer of his table and compared the two minutely.

'Mr Sheringham,' he said soberly, 'where did you get hold of this?'

'In a second-hand typewriter shop in St Martin's Lane. The machine was sold to an unknown customer about a month ago. They identified the customer from that same photograph. As it happened, this machine had been used for a time in the office after it was repaired, to see that it was OK, and I easily got hold of that specimen of its work.'

'And where is the machine now?'

'Oh, at the bottom of the Thames, I expect,' Roger smiled. 'I tell you, this criminal takes no unnecessary chances. But that doesn't matter. There's your evidence.'

'Humph! It's all right so far as it goes,' conceded Moresby. 'But what about Mason's paper?'

'That,' said Roger calmly, 'was extracted from Merton's book of sample notepapers, as I'd guessed from the very yellowed edges might be the case. I can prove contact of the criminal with the book, and there is a page which will certainly turn out to have been filled by that piece of paper.'

'That's fine,' Moresby said more heartily.

'As for that taximan, the criminal had an alibi. You've heard it broken down. Between ten past nine and twenty-five past, in fact during the time when the parcel must have been posted, the murderer took a hurried journey to that neighbourhood, going probably by 'bus or Underground, but returning as I expected, by taxi, because time would be getting short.'

'And the murderer, Mr Sheringham?'

'The person whose photograph is in my pocket,' Roger said unkindly. 'By the way, do you remember what I was saying the other day about Chance the Avenger, my excellent film-title? Well, it's worked again. By a chance meeting in Bond Street with a silly woman I was put, by the merest accident, in possession of a piece of information which showed me then and there who had sent those chocolates addressed to Sir William. There were other possibilities, of course, and I tested them, but then and there on the pavement I saw the whole thing, from first to last.'

'Who was the murderer, then, Mr Sheringham?' repeated Moresby.

'It was so beautifully planned,' Roger went on dreamily. 'We never grasped for one moment that we were making the fundamental mistake that the murderer all along intended us to make.'

'And what was that?' asked Moresby.

'Why, that the plan had miscarried. That the wrong person had been killed. That was just the beauty of it. The plan had *not* miscarried. It had been brilliantly successful. The wrong person was *not* killed. Very much the right person was.'

Moresby gaped.

'Why, how on earth do you make that out, sir?'

'Mrs Beresford was the objective all the time. That's why the plot was so ingenious. Everything was anticipated. It was perfectly natural that Sir William should hand the chocolates over to Beresford. It was foreseen that we should look for the criminal among Sir William's associates and not the dead woman's. It was probably even foreseen that the crime would be considered the work of a woman!'

Moresby, unable to wait any longer, snatched up the photograph.

'Good heavens! But Mr Sheringham, you don't mean to tell me that . . . Sir William himself!'

'He wanted to get rid of Mrs Beresford,' Roger continued. 'He had liked her well enough at the beginning, no doubt, though it was her money he was after all the time.

'But the real trouble was that she was too close with her money. He wanted it, or some of it, pretty badly; and she wouldn't part. There's no doubt about the motive. I made a list of the firms he's interested in and got a report on them. They're all rocky, every one. He'd got through all his own money, and he had to get more.

'As for the nitrobenzine which puzzled us so much, that was simple enough. I looked it up and found that beside the uses you told me, it's used largely in perfumery. And he's got a perfumery business. The Anglo-Eastern Perfumery Company. That's how he'd know about it being poisonous, of course. But I shouldn't think he got his supply from there. He'd be cleverer than that. He probably made the stuff himself. And schoolboys know how to treat benzol with nitric acid to get nitrobenzine.'

'But,' stammered Moresby, 'but Sir William . . . He was at Eton.'

'Sir William?' said Roger sharply. 'Who's talking about Sir William? I told you the photograph of the murderer was in my pocket.' He whipped out the photograph in question and confronted the astounded Chief Inspector with it. 'Beresford, man! Beresford's the murderer of his own wife.

'Beresford, who still had hankerings after a gay life,' he went on more mildly, 'didn't want his wife but did want her money. He contrived this plot, providing as he thought against every contingency that could possibly arise. He established a mild alibi, if suspicion ever should arise, by taking his wife to the Imperial, and slipped out of the theatre at the first interval. (I sat through the first act of the dreadful thing myself last night to see when the interval came.) Then he hurried down to the Strand, posted his parcel, and took a taxi back. He had ten minutes, but nobody would notice if he got back to the box a minute late.

'And the rest simply followed. He knew Sir William came to the club every morning at ten-thirty, as regularly as clockwork; he knew that for a psychological certainty he could get the chocolates handed over to him if he hinted for them; he knew that the police would go chasing after all sorts of false trails starting from Sir William. And as for the wrapper and the forged letter he carefully didn't destroy them because they were calculated not only to divert suspicion but actually to point away from him to some anonymous lunatic.'

'Well, it's very smart of you, Mr Sheringham,' Moresby said, with a little sigh, but quite ungrudgingly. 'Very smart indeed. What was it the lady told you that showed you the whole thing in a flash?'

'Why, it wasn't so much what she actually told me as what I heard between her words, so to speak. What she told me was that Mrs

Beresford knew the answer to that bet; what I deduced was that, being the sort of person she was, it was quite incredible that she should have made a bet to which she knew the answer. *Ergo*, she didn't. *Ergo*, there never was such a bet. *Ergo*, Beresford was lying. *Ergo*, Beresford wanted to get hold of those chocolates for some reason other than he stated. After all, we only had Beresford's word for the bet, hadn't we?

'Of course he wouldn't have left her that afternoon till he'd seen her take, or somehow made her take, at least six of the chocolates, more than a lethal dose. That's why the stuff was in those meticulous six-minim doses. And so that he could take a couple himself, of course. A clever stroke, that.'

Moresby rose to his feet.

'Well, Mr Sheringham, I'm much obliged to you, sir. And now I shall have to get busy myself.' He scratched his head. 'Chance the Avenger, eh? Well, I can tell you one pretty big thing Beresford left to Chance the Avenger, Mr Sheringham. Suppose Sir William hadn't handed over the chocolates after all? Supposing he'd kept 'em, to give to one of his own ladies?'

Roger positively snorted. He felt a personal pride in Beresford by this time.

'Really, Moresby! It wouldn't have had any serious results if Sir William had. Do give my man credit for being what he is. You don't imagine he sent the poisoned ones to Sir William, do you? Of course not! He'd send harmless ones, and exchange them for the others on his way home. Dash it all, he wouldn't go right out of his way to present opportunities to Chance.

'If,' added Roger, 'Chance really is the right word.'

DOROTHY L. SAYERS · 1893–1957

Murder at Pentecost

'Buzz off, Flathers,' said the young man in flannels. 'We're thrilled by your news, but we don't want your religious opinions. And, for the Lord's sake, stop talking about "undergrads", like a ruddy commercial traveller. Hop it!'

The person addressed, a pimply youth in a commoner's gown, bleated a little, but withdrew from the table, intimidated.

'Appalling little tick,' commented the young man in flannels to his companion. 'He's on my staircase, too. Thank Heaven, I move out next term. I suppose it's true about the Master? Poor old blighter —I'm quite sorry I cut his lecture. Have some more coffee?'

'No, thanks, Radcott. I must be pushing off in a minute. It's getting too near lunch-time.'

Mr Montague Egg, seated at the next small table, had pricked up his ears. He now turned, with an apologetic cough, to the young man called Radcott.

'Excuse me, sir,' he said, with some diffidence. 'I didn't intend to overhear what you gentlemen were saying, but might I ask a question?' Emboldened by Radcott's expression, which, though surprised, was frank and friendly, he went on: 'I happen to be a commercial traveller—Egg is my name, Montague Egg, representing Plummet & Rose, wines and spirits, Piccadilly. Might I ask what is wrong with saying "undergrads"? Is the expression offensive in any way?'

Mr Radcott blushed a fiery red to the roots of his flaxen hair:

'I'm frightfully sorry,' he said ingenuously, and suddenly looking extremely young. 'Damn stupid thing of me to say. Beastly brick.'

'Don't mention it, I'm sure,' said Monty.

'Didn't mean anything personal. Only, that chap Flathers gets my goat. He ought to know that nobody says "undergrads" except townees and journalists and people outside the university.'

'What ought we to say? "Undergraduates"?'

'"Undergraduates" is correct.'

'I'm very much obliged,' said Monty. 'Always willing to learn. It's easy to make a mistake in a thing like that, and, of course, it prejudices the customer against one. The *Salesman's Handbook* doesn't give any guidance about it; I shall have to make a memo for myself. Let me see. How would this do? "To call an Oxford gent an————"'

'I think I should say "Oxford man"—it's the more technical form of expression.'

'Oh, yes. "To call an Oxford man an undergrad proclaims you an outsider and a cad." That's very easy to remember.'

'You seem to have a turn for this kind of thing,' said Radcott, amused.

'Well, I think perhaps I have,' admitted Monty, with a touch of pride. 'Would the same thing apply at Cambridge?'

'Certainly,' replied Radcott's companion. 'And you might add that "To call the university the 'varsity is out of date, if not precisely narsity." I apologize for the rhyme. 'Varsity has somehow a flavour of the 'nineties.'

'So has the port I'm recommending,' said Mr Egg brightly. 'Still, one's sales-talk must be up to date, naturally; and smart, though not vulgar. In the wine and spirit trade we make refinement our aim. I am really much obliged to you, gentlemen, for your help. This is my first visit to Oxford. Could you tell me where to find Pentecost College? I have a letter of introduction to a gentleman there.'

'Pentecost?' said Radcott. 'I don't think I'd start there, if I were you.'

'No?' said Mr Egg, suspecting some obscure point of university etiquette. 'Why not?'

'Because,' replied Radcott surprisingly, 'I understand from the regrettable Flathers that some public benefactor has just murdered the Master, and in the circumstances I doubt whether the Bursar will be able to give proper attention to the merits of rival vintages.'

'Murdered the Master?' echoed Mr Egg.

'Socked him one—literally, I am told, with a brickbat enclosed in a Woolworth sock—as he was returning to his house from delivering his too-well-known lecture on Plato's use of the Enclitics. The whole school of *Literæ Humaniores* will naturally be under suspicion, but, personally, I believe Flathers did it himself. You may have heard him informing us that judgement overtakes the evil-doer, and inviting us to a meeting for prayer and repentance in the South Lecture-Room. Such men are dangerous.'

'Was the Master of Pentecost an evil-doer?'

'He has written several learned works disproving the existence of Providence, and I must say that I, in common with the whole Pentecostal community, have always looked on him as one of Nature's worst mistakes. Still, to slay him more or less on his own doorstep seems to me to be in poor taste. It will upset the examination candidates, who face their ordeal next week. And it will mean cancelling the Commem. Ball. Besides, the police have been called in, and are certain to annoy the Senior Common Room by walking on the grass in the quad. However, what's done cannot be undone. Let us pass to a pleasanter subject. I understand that you have some port to dispose of. I, on the other hand, have recently suffered bereavement at the hands of a bunch of rowing hearties, who invaded my rooms the other night and poured my last dozen of Cockburn '04 down their leathery and undiscriminating throttles. If you care to stroll round with me to Pentecost, Mr Egg, bringing your literature with you, we might be able to do business.'

Mr Egg expressed himself as delighted to accept Radcott's invitation, and was soon trotting along the Cornmarket at his conductor's athletic heels. At the corner of Broad Street the second undergraduate left them, while they turned on, past Balliol and Trinity, asleep in the June sunshine, and presently reached the main entrance of Pentecost.

Just as they did so, a small, elderly man, wearing a light overcoat and carrying an MA gown over his arm, came ambling short-sightedly across the street from the direction of the Bodleian Library. A passing car just missed whirling him into eternity, as Radcott stretched out a long arm and raked him into safety on the pavement.

'Look out, Mr Temple,' said Radcott. 'We shall be having *you* murdered next.'

'Murdered?' queried Mr Temple, blinking. 'Oh, you refer to the motor-car. But I saw it coming. I saw it quite distinctly. Yes, yes. But why "next"? Has anybody else been murdered?'

'Only the Master of Pentecost,' said Radcott, pinching Mr Egg's arm.

'The Master? Dr Greeby? You don't say so! Murdered? Dear me! Poor Greeby! This will upset my whole day's work.' His pale-blue eyes shifted, and a curious, wavering look came into them. 'Justice is slow but sure. Yes, yes. The sword of the Lord and of Gideon. But the blood—that is always so disconcerting, is it not? And yet, I washed my hands, you know.' He stretched out both hands and looked at them in a puzzled way. 'Ah, yes—poor Greeby has paid the price of his sins. Excuse my running away from you—I have urgent business at the police-station.'

'If,' said Mr Radcott, again pinching Monty's arm, 'you want to give yourself up for the murder, Mr Temple, you had better come along with us. The police are bound to be about the place somewhere.'

'Oh, yes, of course, so they are. Yes. Very thoughtful of you. That will save me a great deal of time, and I have an important chapter to finish. A beautiful day, is it not, Mr—I fear I do not know your name. Or do I? I am growing sadly forgetful.'

Radcott mentioned his name, and the oddly assorted trio turned together towards the main entrance to the college. The great gate was shut; at the postern stood the porter, and at his side a massive figure in blue, who demanded their names.

Radcott, having been duly identified by the porter, produced Monty and his credentials.

'And this,' he went on, 'is, of course, Mr Temple. You know him. He is looking for your Superintendent.'

'Right you are, sir,' replied the policeman. 'You'll find him in the cloisters . . . At his old game, I suppose?' he added, as the small figure of Mr Temple shuffled away across the sun-baked expanse of the quad.

'Oh, yes,' said Radcott. 'He was on to it like a shot. Must be quite exciting for the old bird to have a murder so near home. Where was his last?'

'Lincoln, sir; last Tuesday. Young fellow shot his young woman in the Cathedral. Mr Temple was down at the station the next day, just before lunch, explaining that he'd done it because the poor girl was the Scarlet Woman.'

'Mr Temple,' said Radcott, 'has a mission in life. He is the sword of the Lord and of Gideon. Every time a murder is committed in this country, Mr Temple lays claim to it. It is true that his body can always be shown to have been quietly in bed or at the Bodleian while the dirty work was afoot, but to an idealistic philosopher that need present no difficulty. But what *is* all this about the Master, actually?'

'Well, sir, you know that little entry between the cloisters and the Master's residence? At twenty minutes past ten this morning, Dr Greeby was found lying dead there, with his lecture-notes scattered all round him and a brickbat in a woollen sock lying beside his head. He'd been lecturing in a room in the Main Quadrangle at nine o'clock, and was, as far as we can tell, the last to leave the lecture-room. A party of American ladies and gentlemen passed through the cloisters a little after 10 o'clock, and they have been found, and say there was nobody about there then, so far as they could see—but, of course, sir, the murderer might have been hanging about the entry, because, naturally, they wouldn't go that way but through Boniface Passage to the Inner Quad and the chapel. One of the young gentlemen says he saw the Master cross the Main Quad on his way to the cloisters at 10.5, so he'd reach the entry in about two minutes after that. The Regius Professor of Morphology came along at 10.20, and found the body, and when the doctor arrived, five minutes later, he said Dr Greeby must have been dead about a quarter of an hour. So that puts it somewhere round about 10.10, you see, sir.'

'When did these Americans leave the chapel?'

'Ah, there you are, sir!' replied the constable. He seemed very ready to talk, thought Mr Egg, and deduced, rightly, that Mr Radcott was well and favourably known to the Oxford branch of the Force. 'If that there party had come back through the cloisters, they might have been able to tell us something. But they didn't. They went on through the Inner Quad into the garden, and the verger didn't leave the chapel, on account of a lady who had just arrived and wanted to look at the carving on the reredos.'

'And did the lady also come through the cloisters?'

'She did, sir, and she's the person we want to find, because it seems as though she must have passed through the cloisters very close to the time of the murder. She came into the chapel just on 10.15, because the verger recollected of the clock chiming a few minutes after she came in and her mentioning how sweet the notes was. You see the lady come in, didn't you, Mr Dabbs?'

'I saw *a* lady,' replied the porter, 'but then I see a lot of ladies one way and another. This one came across from the Bodleian round about 10 o'clock. Elderly lady, she was, dressed kind of old-fashioned, with her skirts round her heels and one of them hats like a rook's nest and a bit of elastic round the back. Looked like she might be a female don—leastways, the way female dons used to look. And she had the twitches—you know—jerked her head a bit. You get hundreds like 'em. They goes to sit in the cloisters and listen to the fountain and the little birds. But as to noticing a corpse or a murderer, it's my belief they wouldn't know such a thing if they saw it. I didn't see the lady again, so she must have gone out through the garden.'

'Very likely,' said Radcott. 'May Mr Egg and I go in through the cloisters, officer? Because it's the only way to my rooms, unless we go round by St Scholastica's Gate.'

'All the other gates are locked, sir. You go on and speak to the Super; he'll let you through. You'll find him in the cloisters with Professor Staines and Dr Moyle.'

'Bodley's Librarian? What's he got to do with it?'

'They think he may know the lady, sir, if she's a Bodley reader.'

'Oh, I see. Come along, Mr Egg.'

Radcott led the way across the Main Quadrangle and through a dark little passage at one corner, into the cool shade of the cloisters. Framed by the arcades of ancient stone, the green lawn drowsed tranquilly in the noonday heat. There was no sound but the echo of their own footsteps, the plash and tinkle of the little fountain and the subdued chirping of chaffinches, as they paced the alternate sunshine and shadow of the pavement. About midway along the north side of the cloisters they came upon another dim little covered passageway, at the entrance to which a police-sergeant was kneeling, examining the ground with the aid of an electric torch.

'Hullo, sergeant!' said Radcott. 'Doing the Sherlock Holmes stunt? Show us the blood-stained footprints.'

'No blood, sir, unfortunately. Might make our job easier if there were. And no footprints neither. The poor gentleman was sand-bagged, and we think the murderer must have climbed up here to do it, for the deceased was a tall gentleman and he was hit right on the top of the head, sir.' The sergeant indicated a little niche, like a blocked-up window, about four feet from the ground. 'Looks as if he'd waited up here, sir, for Dr Greeby to go by.'

'He must have been well acquainted with his victim's habits,' suggested Mr Egg.

'Not a bit of it,' retorted Radcott. 'He'd only to look at the lecture-list to know the time and place. This passage leads to the Master's House and the Fellows' Garden and nowhere else, and it's the way Dr Greeby would naturally go after his lecture, unless he was lecturing elsewhere, which he wasn't. Fairly able-bodied, your murderer, sergeant, to get up here. At least—I don't know.'

Before the policeman could stop him, he had placed one hand on the side of the niche and a foot on a projecting band of masonry below it, and swung himself up.

'Hi, sir! Come down, please. The Super won't like that.'

'Why? Oh, gosh! Fingerprints, I suppose. I forgot. Never mind; you can take mine if you want them, for comparison. Give you practice. Anyhow, a baby in arms could get up here. Come on, Mr Egg; we'd better beat it before I'm arrested for obstruction.'

But at this moment Radcott was hailed by a worried-looking don, who came through the passage from the far side, accompanied by three or four other people.

'Oh, Mr Radcott! One moment, Superintendent; this gentleman will be able to tell you what you want to know; he was at Dr Greeby's lecture. That is so, is it not, Mr Radcott?'

'Well, no, not exactly, sir,' replied Radcott, with some embarrassment. 'I should have been, but, by a regrettable accident, I cut—that is to say, I was on the river, sir, and didn't get back in time.'

'Very vexatious,' said Professor Staines, while the Superintendent merely observed:

'Any witness to your being on the river, sir?'

'None,' replied Radcott. 'I was alone in a canoe, up a backwater —earnestly studying Aristotle. But I really didn't murder the Master. His lectures were—if I may say so—dull, but not to that point exasperating.'

'That is a very impudent observation, Mr Radcott,' said the Professor severely, 'and in execrable taste.'

The Superintendent, murmuring something about routine, took down in a notebook the alleged times of Mr Radcott's departure and return, and then said:

'I don't think I need detain any of you gentlemen further. If we want to see you again, Mr Temple, we will let you know.'

'Certainly, certainly. I shall just have a sandwich at the café and return to the Bodleian. As for the lady, I can only repeat that she sat at my table from about half-past nine till just before ten, and returned again at ten-thirty. Very restless and disturbing. I do wish, Dr Moyle, that some arrangement could be made to give me that table to myself, or that I could be given a place apart in the library. Ladies are always restless and disturbing. She was still there when I left, but I very much hope she has now gone for good. You are sure you don't want to lock me up now? I am quite at your service.'

'Not just yet, sir. You will hear from us presently.'

'Thank you, thank you. I should like to finish my chapter. For the present, then, I will wish you good-day.'

The little bent figure wandered away, and the Superintendent touched his head significantly.

'Poor gentleman! Quite harmless, of course. I needn't ask you, Dr Moyle, where *he* was at the time?'

'Oh, he was in his usual corner of Duke Humfrey's Library. He admits it, you see, when he is asked. In any case, I know definitely that he was there this morning, because he took out a Phi book, and of course had to apply personally to me for it. He asked for it at 9.30 and returned it at 12.15. As regards the lady, I think I have seen her before. One of the older school of learned ladies, I fancy. If she is an outside reader, I must have her name and address somewhere, but she may, of course, be a member of the University. I fear I could not undertake to know them all by sight. But I will inquire. It is, in fact, quite possible that she is still in the library, and, if not, Franklin may know when she went and who she is. I will look into the matter immediately. I need not say, professor, how deeply I deplore this lamentable affair. Poor dear Greeby! Such a loss to classical scholarship!'

At this point, Radcott gently drew Mr Egg away. A few yards farther down the cloisters, they turned into another and rather wider passage, which brought them out into the Inner Quadrangle, one side of which was occupied by the chapel. Mounting three dark flights of stone steps on the opposite side, they reached Radcott's rooms, where the undergraduate thrust his new acquaintance into an armchair, and, producing some bottles of beer from beneath the window-seat, besought him to make himself at home.

'Well,' he observed presently, 'you've had a fairly lively introduction to Oxford life—one murder and one madman. Poor old Temple. Quite one of our prize exhibits. Used to be a Fellow here, donkey's years ago. There was some fuss, and he disappeared for a time. Then he turned up again, ten years since, perfectly potty; took lodgings in Holywell, and has haunted the Bodder and the police-station alternately ever since. Fine Greek scholar he is, too. Quite reasonable, except on the one point. I hope old Moyle finds his mysterious lady, though it's nonsense to pretend that they keep tabs on all the people who use the library. You've only got to walk in firmly, as if the place belonged to you, and, if you're challenged, say in a loud, injured tone that you've been a reader for years. If you borrow a gown, they won't even challenge you.'

'Is that so, really?' said Mr Egg.

'Prove it, if you like. Take my gown, toddle across to the Bodder, march straight in past the showcases and through the little wicket marked "Readers Only", into Duke Humfrey's Library; do what you like, short of stealing the books or setting fire to the place—and if anybody says anything to you, I'll order six dozen of anything you like. That's fair, isn't it?'

Mr Egg accepted this offer with alacrity, and in a few moments, arrayed in a scholar's gown, was climbing the stair that leads to England's most famous library. With a slight tremor, he pushed open the swinging glass door and plunged into the hallowed atmosphere of mouldering leather that distinguishes such temples of learning.

Just inside, he came upon Dr Moyle in conversation with the doorkeeper. Mr Egg, bending nonchalantly to examine an illegible manuscript in a showcase, had little difficulty in hearing what they said, since, like all official attendants upon reading-rooms, they took no trouble to lower their voices.

'I know the lady, Dr Moyle. That is to say, she has been here several times lately. She usually wears an MA gown. I saw her here this morning, but I didn't notice when she left. I don't think I ever heard her name, but seeing that she was a senior member of the University———'

Mr Egg waited to hear no more. An idea was burgeoning in his mind. He walked away, courageously pushed open the Readers' Wicket, and stalked down the solemn mediæval length of Duke Humfrey's Library. In the remotest and darkest bay, he observed Mr Temple, who, having apparently had his sandwich and forgotten about the murder, sat alone, writing busily, amid a pile of repellent volumes, with a large attaché-case full of papers open before him.

Leaning over the table, Mr Egg addressed him in an urgent whisper:

'Excuse me, sir. The police Superintendent asked me to say that they think they have found the lady, and would be glad if you would kindly step down at once and identify her.'

'The lady?' Mr Temple looked up vaguely. 'Oh, yes—the lady. To be sure. Immediately? That is not very convenient. Is it so very urgent?'

'They said particularly to lose no time, sir,' said Mr Egg.

Mr Temple muttered something, rose, seemed to hesitate whether to clear up his papers or not, and finally shovelled them all into the bulging attaché-case, which he locked upon them.

'Let me carry this for you, sir,' said Monty, seizing it promptly and shepherding Mr Temple briskly out. 'They're still in the cloisters, I think, but the Super said, would you kindly wait a few moments for him in the porter's lodge. Here we are.'

He handed Mr Temple and his attaché-case over to the care of the porter, who looked a little surprised at seeing Mr Egg in academic dress, but, on hearing the Superintendent's name, said nothing. Mr

Egg hastened through quad and cloisters and mounted Mr Radcott's staircase at a run.

'Excuse me, sir,' he demanded breathlessly of that young gentleman, 'but what is a Phi book?'

'A Phi book,' replied Radcott, in some surprise, 'is a book deemed by Bodley's Librarian to be of an indelicate nature, and catalogued accordingly, by some dead-and-gone humorist, under the Greek letter *phi*. Why the question?'

'Well,' said Mr Egg, 'it just occurred to me how simple it would be for anybody to walk into the Bodleian, disguise himself in a retired corner—say in Duke Humfrey's Library—walk out, commit a murder, return, change back to his own clothes and walk out. Nobody would stop a person from coming in again, if he—or she—had previously been seen to go out—especially if the disguise had been used in the library before. Just a change of clothes and an MA gown would be enough.'

'What in the world are you getting at?'

'This lady, who was in the cloisters at the time of the murder. Mr Temple says she was sitting at his table. But isn't it funny that Mr Temple should have drawn special attention to himself by asking for a Phi book, today of all days? If he was once a Fellow of this college, he'd know which way Dr Greeby would go after his lecture; and he may have had a grudge against him on account of that old trouble, whatever it was. He'd know about the niche in the wall, too. And he's got an attaché-case with him that might easily hold a lady's hat and a skirt long enough to hide his trousers. And why is he wearing a top-coat on such a hot day, if not to conceal the upper portion of his garments? Not that it's any business of mine—but—well, I just took the liberty of asking myself. And I've got him out there, with his case, and the porter keeping an eye on him.'

Thus Mr Egg, rather breathlessly. Radcott gaped at him.

'Temple? My dear man, you're as potty as he is. Why, he's always confessing—he confessed to this—you can't possibly suppose————?'

'I daresay I'm wrong,' said Mr Egg. 'But isn't there a fable about the man who cried "Wolf!" so often that nobody would believe him when the wolf really came? There's a motto in the *Salesman's Handbook* that I always admire very much. It says: "Discretion plays a major part in making up the salesman's art, for truths that no one can believe are calculated to deceive." I think that's rather subtle, don't you?'

Death on the Air

On the 25th of December at 7.30 a.m. Mr Septimus Tonks was found dead beside his wireless set.

It was Emily Parks, an under-housemaid, who discovered him. She butted open the door and entered, carrying mop, duster, and carpet-sweeper. At that precise moment she was greatly startled by a voice that spoke out of the darkness.

'Good morning, everybody,' said the voice in superbly inflected syllables, 'and a Merry Christmas!'

Emily yelped, but not loudly, as she immediately realized what had happened. Mr Tonks had omitted to turn off his wireless before going to bed. She drew back the curtains, revealing a kind of pale murk which was a London Christmas dawn, switched on the light, and saw Septimus.

He was seated in front of the radio. It was a small but expensive set, specially built for him. Septimus sat in an armchair, his back to Emily, his body tilted towards the radio.

His hands, the fingers curiously bunched, were on the ledge of the cabinet under the tuning and volume knobs. His chest rested against the shelf below and his head leaned on the front panel.

He looked rather as though he was listening intently to the interior secrets of the wireless. His head was bent so that Emily could see his bald top with its trail of oiled hairs. He did not move.

'Beg pardon, sir,' gasped Emily. She was again greatly startled. Mr Tonks's enthusiasm for radio had never before induced him to tune in at seven-thirty in the morning.

'Special Christmas service,' the cultured voice was saying. Mr Tonks sat very still. Emily, in common with the other servants, was terrified of her master. She did not know whether to go or to stay. She gazed wildly at Septimus and realized that he wore a dinner-jacket. The room was now filled with the clamour of pealing bells.

Emily opened her mouth as wide as it would go and screamed and screamed and screamed. . . .

Chase, the butler, was the first to arrive. He was a pale, flabby man but authoritative. He said: 'What's the meaning of this outrage?' and then saw Septimus. He went to the armchair, bent down, and looked into his master's face.

He did not lose his head, but said in a loud voice: 'My Gawd!' And then to Emily: 'Shut your face.' By this vulgarism he betrayed his agitation. He seized Emily by the shoulders and thrust her towards the door, where they were met by Mr Hislop, the secretary, in his dressing-gown. Mr Hislop said: 'Good heavens, Chase, what is the meaning————' and then his voice too was drowned in the clamour of bells and renewed screams.

Chase put his fat white hand over Emily's mouth.

'In the study if you please, sir. An accident. Go to your room, will you, and stop that noise or I'll give you something to make you.' This to Emily, who bolted down the hall, where she was received by the rest of the staff who had congregated there.

Chase returned to the study with Mr Hislop and locked the door. They both looked down at the body of Septimus Tonks. The secretary was the first to speak.

'But—but—he's dead,' said little Mr Hislop.

'I suppose there can't be any doubt,' whispered Chase.

'Look at the face. Any doubt! My God!'

Mr Hislop put out a delicate hand towards the bent head and then drew it back. Chase, less fastidious, touched one of the hard wrists, gripped, and then lifted it. The body at once tipped backwards as if it was made of wood. One of the hands knocked against the butler's face. He sprang back with an oath.

There lay Septimus, his knees and his hands in the air, his terrible face turned up to the light. Chase pointed to the right hand. Two fingers and the thumb were slightly blackened.

Ding, dong, dang, ding.

'For God's sake stop those bells,' cried Mr Hislop. Chase turned off the wall switch: Into the sudden silence came the sound of the door-handle being rattled and Guy Tonks's voice on the other side.

'Hislop! Mr Hislop! Chase! What's the matter?'

'Just a moment, Mr Guy.' Chase looked at the secretary. 'You go, sir.'

So it was left to Mr Hislop to break the news to the family. They listened to his stammering revelation in stupefied silence. It was not until Guy, the eldest of the three children, stood in the study that any practical suggestion was made.

'What has killed him?' asked Guy.

'It's extraordinary,' burbled Hislop. 'Extraordinary. He looks as if he'd been——'

'Galvanized,' said Guy.

'We ought to send for a doctor,' suggested Hislop timidly.

'Of course. Will you, Mr Hislop? Dr Meadows.'

Hislop went to the telephone and Guy returned to his family. Dr Meadows lived on the other side of the square and arrived in five minutes. He examined the body without moving it. He questioned Chase and Hislop. Chase was very voluble about the burns on the hand. He uttered the word 'electrocution' over and over again.

'I had a cousin, sir, that was struck by lightning. As soon as I saw the hand——'

'Yes, yes,' said Dr Meadows. 'So you said. I can see the burns for myself.'

'Electrocution,' repeated Chase. 'There'll have to be an inquest.'

Dr Meadows snapped at him, summoned Emily, and then saw the rest of the family—Guy, Arthur, Phillipa, and their mother. They were clustered round a cold grate in the drawing-room. Phillipa was on her knees, trying to light the fire.

'What was it?' asked Arthur as soon as the doctor came in.

'Looks like electric shock. Guy, I'll have a word with you if you please. Phillipa, look after your mother, there's a good child. Coffee with a dash of brandy. Where are those damn maids? Come on, Guy.'

Alone with Guy, he said they'd have to send for the police.

'The police!' Guy's dark face turned very pale. 'Why? What's it got to do with them?'

'Nothing, as like as not, but they'll have to be notified. I can't give a certificate as things are. If it's electrocution, how did it happen?'

'But the police!' said Guy. 'That's simply ghastly. Dr Meadows, for God's sake couldn't you——?'

'No,' said Dr Meadows, 'I couldn't. Sorry, Guy, but there it is.'

'But can't we wait a moment? Look at him again. You haven't examined him properly.'

'I don't want to move him, that's why. Pull yourself together, boy. Look here. I've got a pal in the CID—Alleyn. He's a gentleman and all that. He'll curse me like a fury, but he'll come if he's in London, and he'll make things easier for you. Go back to your mother. I'll ring Alleyn up.'

That was how it came about that Chief Detective-Inspector Roderick Alleyn spent his Christmas Day in harness. As a matter of fact he was on duty, and as he pointed out to Dr Meadows, would have had to turn out and visit his miserable Tonkses in any case. When he did arrive it was with his usual air of remote courtesy. He was accompanied by a tall, thick-set officer—Inspector Fox—and by the divisional police-surgeon. Dr Meadows took them into the study. Alleyn, in his turn, looked at the horror that had been Septimus.

'Was he like this when he was found?'

'No. I understand he was leaning forward with his hands on the ledge of the cabinet. He must have slumped forward and been propped up by the chair arms and the cabinet.'

'Who moved him?'

'Chase, the butler. He said he only meant to raise the arm. *Rigor* is well established.'

Alleyn put his hand behind the rigid neck and pushed. The body fell forward into its original position.

'There you are, Curtis,' said Alleyn to the divisional surgeon. He turned to Fox. 'Get the camera man, will you, Fox?'

The photographer took four shots and departed. Alleyn marked the position of the hands and feet with chalk, made a careful plan of the room and turned to the doctors.

'Is it electrocution, do you think?'

'Looks like it,' said Curtis. 'Have to be a p.m. of course.'

'Of course. Still, look at the hands. Burns. Thumb and two fingers bunched together and exactly the distance between the two knobs apart. He'd been tuning his hurdy-gurdy.'

'By gum,' said Inspector Fox, speaking for the first time.

'D'you mean he got a lethal shock from his radio?' asked Dr Meadows.

'I don't know. I merely conclude he had his hands on the knobs when he died.'

'It was still going when the housemaid found him. Chase turned it off and got no shock.'

'Yours, partner,' said Alleyn, turning to Fox. Fox stooped down to the wall switch.

'Careful,' said Alleyn.

'I've got rubber soles,' said Fox, and switched it on. The radio hummed, gathered volume, and found itself.

'No-oel, No-o-el,' it roared. Fox cut it off and pulled out the wall plug.

'I'd like to have a look inside this set,' he said.

'So you shall, old boy, so you shall,' rejoined Alleyn. 'Before you begin, I think we'd better move the body. Will you see to that, Meadows? Fox, get Bailey, will you? He's out in the car.'

Curtis, Hislop, and Meadows carried SeptimusTonks into a spare downstairs room. It was a difficult and horrible business with that contorted body. Dr Meadows came back alone, mopping his brow, to find Detective-Sergeant Bailey, a fingerprint expert, at work on the wireless cabinet.

'What's all this?' asked Dr Meadows. 'Do you want to find out if he'd been fooling round with the innards?'

'He,' said Alleyn, 'or—somebody else.'

'Umph!' Dr Meadows looked at the Inspector. 'You agree with me, it seems. Do you suspect——?'

'Suspect? I'm the least suspicious man alive. I'm merely being tidy. Well, Bailey?'

'I've got a good one off the chair arm. That'll be the deceased's, won't it, sir?'

'No doubt. We'll check up later. What about the wireless?'

Fox, wearing a glove, pulled off the knob of the volume control.

'Seems to be OK,' said Bailey. 'It's a sweet bit of work. Not too bad at all, sir.' He turned his torch into the back of the radio, undid a couple of screws underneath the set, lifted out the works.

'What's the little hole for?' asked Alleyn.

'What's that, sir?' said Fox.

'There's a hole bored through the panel above the knob. About an eighth of an inch in diameter. The rim of the knob hides it. One might easily miss it. Move your torch, Bailey. Yes. There, do you see?'

Fox bent down and uttered a bass growl. A fine needle of light came through the front of the radio.

'That's peculiar, sir,' said Bailey from the other side. 'I don't get the idea at all.'

Alleyn pulled out the tuning knob.

'There's another one there,' he murmured. 'Yes. Nice clean little holes. Newly bored. Unusual, I take it?'

'Unusual's the word, sir,' said Fox.

'Run away, Meadows,' said Alleyn.

'Why the devil?' asked Dr Meadows indignantly. 'What are you driving at? Why shouldn't I be here?'

'You ought to be with the sorrowing relatives. Where's your corpseside manner?'

'I've settled them. What are you up to?'

'Who's being suspicious now?' asked Alleyn mildly. 'You may stay for a moment. Tell me about the Tonkses. Who are they? What are they? What sort of a man was Septimus?'

'If you must know, he was a damned unpleasant sort of a man.'

'Tell me about him.'

Dr Meadows sat down and lit a cigarette.

'He was a self-made bloke,' he said, 'as hard as nails and—well, coarse rather than vulgar.'

'Like Dr Johnson perhaps?'

'Not in the least. Don't interrupt. I've known him for twenty-five years. His wife was a neighbour of ours in Dorset. Isabel Foreston. I brought the children into this vale of tears and, by jove, in many ways it's been one for them. It's an extraordinary household. For the last ten years Isabel's condition has been the sort that sends these psycho-jokers dizzy with rapture. I'm only an out-of-date GP, and I'd just say she is in an advanced stage of hysterical neurosis. Frightened into fits of her husband.'

'I can't understand these holes,' grumbled Fox to Bailey.

'Go on, Meadows,' said Alleyn.

'I tackled Sep about her eighteen months ago. Told him the trouble was in her mind. He eyed me with a sort of grin on his face and said: "I'm surprised to learn that my wife has enough mentality to————" But look here, Alleyn, I can't talk about my patients like this. What the devil am I thinking about.'

'You know perfectly well it'll go no further unless————'

'Unless what?'

'Unless it has to. Do go on.'

But Dr Meadows hurriedly withdrew behind his professional rectitude. All he would say was that Mr Tonks had suffered from high blood pressure and a weak heart, that Guy was in his father's city office, that Arthur had wanted to study art and had been told to read for law, and that Phillipa wanted to go on to the stage and had been told to do nothing of the sort.

'Bullied his children,' commented Alleyn.

'Find out for yourself. I'm off.' Dr Meadows got as far as the door and came back.

'Look here,' he said, 'I'll tell you one thing. There was a row here last night. I'd asked Hislop, who's a sensible little beggar, to let me know if anything happened to upset Mrs Sep. Upset her badly, you know. To be indiscreet again, I said he'd better let me know if Sep cut up rough because Isabel and the young had had about as much of that as they could stand. He was drinking pretty heavily. Hislop rang me up at ten-twenty last night to say there'd been a hell of a row; Sep bullying Phips—Phillipa, you know; always call her Phips—in her room. He said Isabel—Mrs Sep—had gone to bed. I'd had a big day and I didn't want to turn out. I told him to ring again in half an hour if things hadn't quieted down. I told him to keep out of Sep's way and stay in his own room, which is next to Phips's and see if she was all right when Sep cleared out. Hislop was involved. I won't tell you how. The servants were all out. I said that if I didn't hear from him in half an hour I'd ring again and if there was no answer I'd know they were all in bed and quiet. I did ring, got no answer, and went to bed myself. That's all. I'm off. Curtis knows where to find me. You'll want me for the inquest, I suppose. Goodbye.'

When he had gone Alleyn embarked on a systematic prowl round the room. Fox and Bailey were still deeply engrossed with the wireless.

'I don't see how the gentleman could have got a bump-off from the instrument,' grumbled Fox. 'These control knobs are quite in order. Everything's as it should be. Look here, sir.'

He turned on the wall switch and tuned in. There was a prolonged humming.

'. . . concludes the programme of Christmas carols,' said the radio.

'A very nice tone,' said Fox approvingly.

'Here's something, sir,' announced Bailey suddenly.

'Found the sawdust, have you?' said Alleyn.

'Got it in one,' said the startled Bailey.

Alleyn peered into the instrument, using the torch. He scooped up two tiny traces of sawdust from under the holes.

''Vantage number one,' said Alleyn. He bent down to the wall plug. 'Hullo! A two-way adapter. Serves the radio and the radiator. Thought they were illegal. This is a rum business. Let's have another look at those knobs.'

He had his look. They were the usual wireless fitments, bakelite knobs fitting snugly to the steel shafts that projected from the front panel.

'As you say,' he murmured, 'quite in order. Wait a bit.' He produced a pocket lens and squinted at one of the shafts. 'Ye-es. Do they ever wrap blotting-paper round these objects, Fox?'

'Blotting-paper!' ejaculated Fox. 'They do not.'

Alleyn scraped at both the shafts with his penknife, holding an envelope underneath. He rose, groaning, and crossed to the desk. 'A corner torn off the bottom bit of blotch,' he said presently. 'No prints on the wireless, I think you said, Bailey?'

'That's right,' agreed Bailey morosely.

'There'll be none, or too many, on the blotter, but try, Bailey, try,' said Alleyn. He wandered about the room, his eyes on the floor; got as far as the window and stopped.

'Fox!' he said. 'A clue. A very palpable clue.'

'What is it?' asked Fox.

'The odd wisp of blotting-paper, no less.' Alleyn's gaze travelled up the side of the window curtain. 'Can I believe my eyes?'

He got a chair, stood on the seat, and with his gloved hand pulled the buttons from the ends of the curtain-rod.

'Look at this.' He turned to the radio, detached the control knobs, and laid them beside the ones he had removed from the curtain-rod.

Ten minutes later Inspector Fox knocked on the drawing-room door and was admitted by Guy Tonks. Phillipa had got the fire going and the family was gathered round it. They looked as though they had not moved or spoken to one another for a long time.

It was Phillipa who spoke first to Fox. 'Do you want one of us?'

'If you please, miss,' said Fox. 'Inspector Alleyn would like to see Mr Guy Tonks for a moment, if convenient.'

'I'll come,' said Guy, and led the way to the study. At the door he paused. 'Is he—my father—still—?'

'No, no, sir,' said Fox comfortably. 'It's all ship-shape in there again.'

With a lift of his chin Guy opened the door and went in, followed by Fox. Alleyn was alone, seated at the desk. He rose to his feet.

'You want to speak to me?' asked Guy.

'Yes, if I may. This has all been a great shock to you, of course. Won't you sit down?'

Guy sat in the chair farthest away from the radio.

'What killed my father? Was it a stroke?'

'The doctors are not quite certain. There will have to be a *post-mortem*.'

'Good God! And an inquest?'

'I'm afraid so.'

'Horrible!' said Guy violently. 'What do you think was the matter? Why the devil do these quacks have to be so mysterious? What killed him?'

'They think an electric shock.'

'How did it happen?'

'We don't know. It looks as if he got it from the wireless.'

'Surely that's impossible. I thought they were fool-proof.'

'I believe they are, if left to themselves.'

For a second undoubtedly Guy was startled. Then a look of relief came into his eyes. He seemed to relax all over.

'Of course,' he said, 'he was always monkeying about with it. What had he done?'

'Nothing.'

'But you said—if it killed him he must have done something to it.'

'If anyone interfered with the set it was put right afterwards.'

Guy's lips parted but he did not speak. He had gone very white.

'So you see,' said Alleyn, 'your father could not have done anything.'

'Then it was not the radio that killed him.'

'That we hope will be determined by the *post-mortem*.'

'I don't know anything about wireless,' said Guy suddenly. 'I don't understand. This doesn't seem to make sense. Nobody ever touched the thing except my father. He was most particular about it. Nobody went near the wireless.'

'I see. He was an enthusiast?'

'Yes, it was his only enthusiasm except—except his business.'

'One of my men is a bit of an expert,' Alleyn said. 'He says this is a remarkably good set. You are not an expert you say. Is there anyone in the house who is?'

'My young brother was interested at one time. He's given it up. My father wouldn't allow another radio in the house.'

'Perhaps he may be able to suggest something.'

'But if the thing's all right now———'

'We've got to explore every possibility.'

'You speak as if—as—if—'

'I speak as I am bound to speak before there has been an inquest,' said Alleyn. 'Had anyone a grudge against your father, Mr Tonks?'

Up went Guy's chin again. He looked Alleyn squarely in the eyes.

'Almost everyone who knew him,' said Guy.

'Is that an exaggeration?'

'No. You think he was murdered, don't you?'

Alleyn suddenly pointed to the desk beside him.

'Have you ever seen those before?' he asked abruptly. Guy stared at two black knobs that lay side by side on an ashtray.

'Those?' he said. 'No. What are they?'

'I believe they are the agents of your father's death.'

The study door opened and Arthur Tonks came in.

'Guy,' he said, 'what's happening? We can't stay cooped up together all day. I can't stand it. For God's sake what happened to him?'

'They think those things killed him,' said Guy.

'Those?' For a split second Arthur's glance slewed to the curtain-rods. Then, with a characteristic flicker of his eyelids, he looked away again.

'What do you mean?' he asked Alleyn.

'Will you try one of those knobs on the shaft of the volume control?'

'But,' said Arthur, 'they're metal.'

'It's disconnected,' said Alleyn.

Arthur picked one of the knobs from the tray, turned to the radio, and fitted the knob over one of the exposed shafts.

'It's too loose,' he said quickly, 'it would fall off.'

'Not if it was packed—with blotting-paper, for instance.'

'Where did you find these things?' demanded Arthur.

'I think you recognized them, didn't you? I saw you glance at the curtain-rod.'

'Of course I recognized them. I did a portrait of Phillipa against those curtains when—he—was away last year. I've painted the damn things.'

'Look here,' interrupted Guy, 'exactly what are you driving at, Mr Alleyn? If you mean to suggest that my brother————'

'I!' cried Arthur. 'What's it got to do with me? Why should you suppose————'

'I found traces of blotting-paper on the shafts and inside the metal knobs,' said Alleyn. 'It suggested a substitution of the metal knobs for the bakelite ones. It is remarkable, don't you think, that they should so closely resemble one another? If you examine them, of course, you find they are not identical. Still, the difference is scarcely perceptible.'

Arthur did not answer this. He was still looking at the wireless.

'I've always wanted to have a look at this set,' he said surprisingly.

'You are free to do so now,' said Alleyn politely. 'We have finished with it for the time being.'

'Look here,' said Arthur suddenly, 'suppose metal knobs were substituted for bakelite ones, it couldn't kill him. He wouldn't get a shock at all. Both the controls are grounded.'

'Have you noticed those very small holes drilled through the panel?' asked Alleyn. 'Should they be there, do you think?'

Arthur peered at the little steel shafts. 'By God, he's right, Guy,' he said. 'That's how it was done.'

'Inspector Fox,' said Alleyn, 'tells me those holes could be used for conducting wires and that a lead could be taken from the—the transformer, is it?—to one of the knobs.'

'And the other connected to earth,' said Fox. 'It's a job for an expert. He could get three hundred volts or so that way.'

'That's not good enough,' said Arthur quickly; 'there wouldn't be enough current to do any damage—only a few hundredths of an amp.'

'I'm not an expert,' said Alleyn, 'but I'm sure you're right. Why were the holes drilled then? Do you imagine someone wanted to play a practical joke on your father?'

'A practical joke? On *him*?' Arthur gave an unpleasant screech of laughter. 'Do you hear that, Guy?'

'Shut up,' said Guy. 'After all, he is dead.'

'It seems almost too good to be true, doesn't it?'

'Don't be a bloody fool, Arthur. Pull yourself together. Can't you see what this means? They think he's been murdered.'

'Murdered! They're wrong. None of us had the nerve for that, Mr Inspector. Look at me. My hands are so shaky they told me I'd never be able to paint. That dates from when I was a kid and he shut me up in the cellars for a night. Look at me. Look at Guy. He's not so vulnerable, but he caved in like the rest of us. We were conditioned to surrender. Do you know———'

'Wait a moment,' said Alleyn quietly. 'Your brother is quite right, you know. You'd better think before you speak. This may be a case of homicide.'

'Thank you, sir,' said Guy quickly. 'That's extraordinarily decent of you. Arthur's a bit above himself. It's a shock.'

'The relief, you mean,' said Arthur. 'Don't be such an ass. I didn't kill him and they'll find it out soon enough. Nobody killed him. There must be some explanation.'

'I suggest that you listen to me,' said Alleyn. 'I'm going to put several questions to both of you. You need not answer them, but it will be more sensible to do so. I understand no one but your father touched this radio. Did any of you ever come into this room while it was in use?'

'Not unless he wanted to vary the programme with a little bully-ing,' said Arthur.

Alleyn turned to Guy, who was glaring at his brother.

'I want to know exactly what happened in this house last night. As far as the doctors can tell us, your father died not less than three and not more than eight hours before he was found. We must try to fix the time as accurately as possible.'

'I saw him at about a quarter to nine,' began Guy slowly. 'I was going out to a supper-party at the Savoy and had come downstairs. He was crossing the hall from the drawing-room to his room.'

'Did you see him after a quarter to nine, Mr Arthur?'

'No. I heard him, though. He was working in here with Hislop. Hislop had asked to go away for Christmas. Quite enough. My father discovered some urgent correspondence. Really, Guy, you know, he was pathological. I'm sure Dr Meadows thinks so.'

'When did you hear him?' asked Alleyn.

'Some time after Guy had gone. I was working on a drawing in my room upstairs. It's above his. I heard him bawling at little Hislop. It must have been before ten o'clock, because I went out to a studio party at ten. I heard him bawling as I crossed the hall.'

'And when,' said Alleyn, 'did you both return?'

'I came home at about twenty past twelve,' said Guy immediately. 'I can fix the time because we had gone on to Chez Carlo, and they had a midnight stunt there. We left immediately afterwards. I came home in a taxi. The radio was on full blast.'

'You heard no voices?'

'None. Just the wireless.'

'And you, Mr Arthur?'

'Lord knows when I got in. After one. The house was in darkness. Not a sound.'

'You had your own key?'

'Yes,' said Guy. 'Each of us has one. They're always left on a hook in the lobby. When I came in I noticed Arthur's was gone.'

'What about the others? How did you know it was his?'

'Mother hasn't got one and Phips lost hers weeks ago. Anyway, I knew they were staying in and that it must be Arthur who was out.'

'Thank you,' said Arthur ironically.

'You didn't look in the study when you came in,' Alleyn asked him.

'Good Lord, no,' said Arthur as if the suggestion was fantastic. 'I say,' he said suddenly, 'I suppose he was sitting here—dead. That's a queer thought.' He laughed nervously. 'Just sitting here, behind the door in the dark.'

'How do you know it was in the dark?'

'What d'you mean? Of course it was. There was no light under the door.'

'I see. Now do you two mind joining your mother again? Perhaps your sister will be kind enough to come in here for a moment. Fox, ask her, will you?'

Fox returned to the drawing-room with Guy and Arthur and remained there, blandly unconscious of any embarrassment his presence might cause the Tonkses. Bailey was already there, ostensibly examining the electric points.

Phillipa went to the study at once. Her first remark was characteristic. 'Can I be of any help?' asked Phillipa.

'It's extremely nice of you to put it like that,' said Alleyn. 'I don't want to worry you for long. I'm sure this discovery has been a shock to you.'

'Probably,' said Phillipa. Alleyn glanced quickly at her. 'I mean,' she explained, 'that I suppose I must be shocked but I can't feel anything much. I just want to get it all over as soon as possible. And then think. Please tell me what has happened.'

Alleyn told her they believed her father had been electrocuted and that the circumstances were unusual and puzzling. He said nothing to suggest that the police suspected murder.

'I don't think I'll be much help,' said Phillipa, 'but go ahead.'

'I want to try to discover who was the last person to see your father or speak to him.'

'I should think very likely I was,' said Phillipa composedly. 'I had a row with him before I went to bed.'

'What about?'

'I don't see that it matters.'

Alleyn considered this. When he spoke again it was with deliberation.

'Look here,' he said, 'I think there is very little doubt that your father was killed by an electric shock from his wireless set. As far as I know the circumstances are unique. Radios are normally incapable of giving a lethal shock to anyone. We have examined the cabinet and are inclined to think that its internal arrangements were disturbed last night. Very radically disturbed. Your father may have experimented with it. If anything happened to interrupt or upset him, it is possible that in the excitement of the moment he made some dangerous readjustment.'

'You don't believe that, do you?' asked Phillipa calmly.

'Since you ask me,' said Alleyn, 'no.'

'I see,' said Phillipa; 'you think he was murdered, but you're not sure.' She had gone very white, but she spoke crisply. 'Naturally you want to find out about my row.'

'About everything that happened last evening,' amended Alleyn.

'What happened was this,' said Phillipa; 'I came into the hall some time after ten. I'd heard Arthur go out and had looked at the clock at five past. I ran into my father's secretary, Richard Hislop. He turned aside, but not before I saw . . . not quickly enough. I blurted out: "You're crying." We looked at each other. I asked him why he stood it. None of the other secretaries could. He said he had to. He's a widower with two children. There have been doctor's bills and things. I needn't tell you about his . . . about his damnable servitude to my father nor about the refinements of cruelty he'd had to put up with. I think my father was mad, really mad, I mean. Richard gabbled it all out to me higgledy-piggledy in a sort of horrified whisper. He's been here two years, but I'd never realized until that moment that we . . . that . . .' A faint flush came into her cheeks. 'He's such a funny little man. Not at all the sort I've always thought . . . not good-looking or exciting or anything.'

She stopped, looking bewildered.

'Yes?' said Alleyn.

'Well, you see—I suddenly realized I was in love with him. He realized it too. He said: "Of course, it's quite hopeless, you know. Us, I mean. Laughable, almost." Then I put my arms round his neck and kissed him. It was very odd, but it seemed quite natural. The point is my father came out of his room into the hall and saw us.'

'That was bad luck,' said Alleyn.

'Yes, it was. My father really seemed delighted. He almost licked his lips. Richard's efficiency had irritated my father for a long time. It was difficult to find excuses for being beastly to him. Now, of course . . . He ordered Richard to the study and me to my room. He followed me upstairs. Richard tried to come too, but I asked him not to. My father . . . I needn't tell you what he said. He put the worst possible construction on what he'd seen. He was absolutely foul, screaming at me like a madman. He was insane. Perhaps it was d.t.'s. He drank terribly, you know. I dare say it's silly of me to tell you all this.'

'No,' said Alleyn.

'I can't feel anything at all. Not even relief. The boys are frankly relieved. I can't feel afraid either.' She stared meditatively at Alleyn. 'Innocent people needn't feel afraid, need they?'

'It's an axiom of police investigation,' said Alleyn and wondered if indeed she was innocent.

'It just *can't* be murder,' said Phillipa. 'We were all too much afraid to kill him. I believe he'd win even if you murdered him. He'd hit back somehow.' She put her hands to her eyes. 'I'm all muddled.'

'I think you are more upset than you realize. I'll be as quick as I can. Your father made this scene in your room. You say he screamed. Did anyone hear him?'

'Yes. Mummy did. She came in.'

'What happened?'

'I said: "Go away, darling, it's all right." I didn't want her to be involved. He nearly killed her with the things he did. Sometimes he'd . . . we never knew what happened between them. It was all secret, like a door shutting quietly as you walk along a passage.'

'Did she go away?'

'Not at once. He told her he'd found out that Richard and I were lovers. He said . . . it doesn't matter. I don't want to tell you. She was terrified. He was stabbing at her in some way I couldn't understand. Then, quite suddenly, he told her to go to her own room. She went at once and he followed her. He locked me in. That's the last I saw of him, but I heard him go downstairs later.'

'Were you locked in all night?'

'No. Richard Hislop's room is next to mine. He came up and spoke through the wall to me. He wanted to unlock the door, but I said better not in case—he—came back. Then, much later, Guy came home. As he passed my door I tapped on it. The key was in the lock and he turned it.'

'Did you tell him what had happened?'

'Just that there'd been a row. He only stayed a moment.'

'Can you hear the radio from your room?'

She seemed surprised.

'The wireless? Why, yes. Faintly.'

'Did you hear it after your father returned to the study?'

'I don't remember.'

'Think. While you lay awake all that long time until your brother came home?'

'I'll try. When he came out and found Richard and me, it was not going. They had been working, you see. No, I can't remember hearing it at all unless—wait a moment. Yes. After he had gone back to the study from mother's room I remember there was a loud crash of static. Very loud. Then I think it was quiet for some time. I fancy I heard it again later. Oh, I've remembered something else. After the static my bedside radiator went out. I suppose there was something wrong with the electric supply. That would account for both, wouldn't it? The heater went on again about ten minutes later.'

'And did the radio begin again then, do you think?'

'I don't know. I'm very vague about that. It started again sometime before I went to sleep.'

'Thank you very much indeed. I won't bother you any longer now.'

'All right,' said Phillipa calmly, and went away.

Alleyn sent for Chase and questioned him about the rest of the staff and about the discovery of the body. Emily was summoned and dealt with. When she departed, awestruck but complacent, Alleyn turned to the butler.

'Chase,' he said, 'had your master any peculiar habits?'

'Yes, sir.'

'In regard to the wireless?'

'I beg pardon, sir. I thought you meant generally speaking.'

'Well, then, generally speaking.'

'If I may say so, sir, he was a mass of them.'

'How long have you been with him?'

'Two months, sir, and due to leave at the end of this week.'

'Oh. Why are you leaving?'

Chase produced the classic remark of his kind.

'There are some things,' he said, 'that flesh and blood will not stand, sir. One of them's being spoke to like Mr Tonks spoke to his staff.'

'Ah. His peculiar habits, in fact?'

'It's my opinion, sir, he was mad. Stark, staring.'

'With regard to the radio. Did he tinker with it?'

'I can't say I've ever noticed, sir. I believe he knew quite a lot about wireless.'

'When he tuned the thing, had he any particular method? Any characteristic attitude or gesture?'

'I don't think so, sir. I never noticed, and yet I've often come into the room when he was at it. I can seem to see him now, sir.'

'Yes, yes,' said Alleyn swiftly. 'That's what we want. A clear mental picture. How was it now? Like this?'

In a moment he was across the room and seated in Septimus's chair. He swung round to the cabinet and raised his right hand to the tuning control.

'Like this?'

'No, sir,' said Chase promptly, 'that's not him at all. Both hands it should be.'

'Ah.' Up went Alleyn's left hand to the volume control. 'More like this?'

'Yes, sir,' said Chase slowly. 'But there's something else and I can't recollect what it was. Something he was always doing. It's in the back of my head. You know, sir. Just on the edge of my memory, as you might say.'

'I know.'

'It's a kind—something—to do with irritation,' said Chase slowly.

'Irritation? His?'

'No. It's no good, sir. I can't get it.'

'Perhaps later. Now look here, Chase, what happened to all of you last night? All the servants, I mean.'

'We were all out, sir. It being Christmas Eve. The mistress sent for me yesterday morning. She said we could take the evening off as soon as I had taken in Mr Tonks's grog-tray at nine o'clock. So we went,' ended Chase simply.

'When?'

'The rest of the staff got away about nine. I left at ten past, sir, and returned about eleven-twenty. The others were back then, and all in bed. I went straight to bed myself, sir.'

'You came in by a back door, I suppose?'

'Yes, sir. We've been talking it over. None of us noticed anything unusual.'

'Can you hear the wireless in your part of the house?'

'No, sir.'

'Well,' said Alleyn, looking up from his notes, 'that'll do, thank you.'

Before Chase reached the door Fox came in.

'Beg pardon, sir,' said Fox, 'I just want to take a look at the *Radio Times* on the desk.'

He bent over the paper, wetted a gigantic thumb, and turned a page.

'That's it, sir,' shouted Chase suddenly. 'That's what I tried to think of. That's what he was always doing.'

'But what?'

'Licking his fingers, sir. It was a habit,' said Chase. 'That's what he always did when he sat down to the radio. I heard Mr Hislop tell the doctor it nearly drove him demented, the way the master couldn't touch a thing without first licking his fingers.'

'Quite so,' said Alleyn. 'In about ten minutes, ask Mr Hislop if he will be good enough to come in for a moment. That will be all, thank you, Chase.'

'Well, sir,' remarked Fox when Chase had gone, 'if that's the case and what I think's right, it'd certainly make matters worse.'

'Good heavens, Fox, what an elaborate remark. What does it mean?'

'If metal knobs were substituted for bakelite ones and fine wires brought through those holes to make contact, then he'd get a bigger bump if he tuned in with *damp* fingers.'

'Yes. And he always used both hands. Fox!'

'Sir.'

'Approach the Tonkses again. You haven't left them alone, of course?'

'Bailey's in there making out he's interested in the light switches. He's found the main switchboard under the stairs. There's signs of a blown fuse having been fixed recently. In a cupboard underneath there are odd lengths of flex and so on. Same brand as this on the wireless and the heater.'

'Ah, yes. Could the cord from the adapter to the radiator be brought into play?'

'By gum,' said Fox, 'you're right! That's how it was done, Chief. The heavier flex was cut away from the radiator and shoved through. There was a fire, so he wouldn't want the radiator and wouldn't notice.'

'It might have been done that way, certainly, but there's little to prove it. Return to the bereaved Tonkses, my Fox, and ask prettily if any of them remember Septimus's peculiarities when tuning his wireless.'

Fox met little Mr Hislop at the door and left him alone with Alleyn. Phillipa had been right, reflected the Inspector, when she said Richard Hislop was not a noticeable man. He was nondescript. Grey eyes, drab hair; rather pale, rather short, rather insignificant; and yet last night there had flashed up between those two the realization of love. Romantic but rum, thought Alleyn.

'Do sit down,' he said. 'I want you, if you will, to tell me what happened between you and Mr Tonks last evening.'

'What happened?'

'Yes. You all dined at eight, I understand. Then you and Mr Tonks came in here?'

'Yes.'

'What did you do?'

'He dictated several letters.'

'Anything unusual take place?'

'Oh, no.'

'Why did you quarrel?'

'Quarrel!' The quiet voice jumped a tone. 'We did not quarrel, Mr Alleyn.'

'Perhaps that was the wrong word. What upset you?'

'Phillipa has told you?'

'Yes. She was wise to do so. What was the matter, Mr Hislop?'

'Apart from the . . . what she told you . . . Mr Tonks was a difficult man to please. I often irritated him. I did so last night.'

'In what way?'

'In almost every way. He shouted at me. I was startled and nervous, clumsy with papers, and making mistakes. I wasn't well. I blundered and then . . . I . . . I broke down. I have always irritated him. My very mannerisms——'

'Had he no irritating mannerisms, himself?'

'He! My God!'

'What were they?'

'I can't think of anything in particular. It doesn't matter does it?'

'Anything to do with the wireless, for instance?'

There was a short silence.

'No,' said Hislop.

'Was the radio on in here last night, after dinner?'

'For a little while. Not after—after the incident in the hall. At least, I don't think so. I don't remember.'

'What did you do after Miss Phillipa and her father had gone upstairs?'

'I followed and listened outside the door for a moment.' He had gone very white and had backed away from the desk.

'And then?'

'I heard someone coming. I remembered Dr Meadows had told me to ring him up if there was one of the scenes. I returned here and rang him up. He told me to go to my room and listen. If things got any worse I was to telephone again. Otherwise I was to stay in my room. It is next to hers.'

'And you did this?' He nodded. 'Could you hear what Mr Tonks said to her?'

'A—a good deal of it.'

'What did you hear?'

'He insulted her. Mrs Tonks was there. I was just thinking of ringing Dr Meadows up again when she and Mr Tonks came out and went along the passage. I stayed in my room.'

'You did not try to speak to Miss Phillipa?'

'We spoke through the wall. She asked me not to ring Dr Meadows, but to stay in my room. In a little while, perhaps it was as much as twenty minutes—I really don't know—I heard him come back and go downstairs. I again spoke to Phillipa. She implored me not to do anything and said that she herself would speak to Dr Meadows in the morning. So I waited a little longer and then went to bed.'

'And to sleep?'

'My God, no!'

'Did you hear the wireless again?'

'Yes. At least I heard static.'

'Are you an expert on wireless?'

'No. I know the ordinary things. Nothing much.'

'How did you come to take this job, Mr Hislop?'

'I answered an advertisement.'

'You are sure you don't remember any particular mannerism of Mr Tonks's in connection with the radio?'

'No.'

'And you can tell me no more about your interview in the study that led to the scene in the hall?'

'No.'

'Will you please ask Mrs Tonks if she will be kind enough to speak to me for a moment?'

'Certainly,' said Hislop, and went away.

Septimus's wife came in looking like death. Alleyn got her to sit down and asked her about her movements on the preceding evening. She said she was feeling unwell and dined in her room. She went to bed immediately afterwards. She heard Septimus yelling at Phillipa and went to Phillipa's room. Septimus accused Mr Hislop and her daughter of 'terrible things'. She got as far as this and then broke down quietly. Alleyn was very gentle with her. After a little while he learned that Septimus had gone to her room with her and had continued to speak of 'terrible things'.

'What sort of things?' asked Alleyn.

'He was not responsible,' said Isabel. 'He did not know what he was saying. I think he had been drinking.'

She thought he had remained with her for perhaps a quarter of an hour. Possibly longer. He left her abruptly and she heard him go along the passage, past Phillipa's door, and presumably downstairs. She had stayed awake for a long time. The wireless could not be heard from her room. Alleyn showed her the curtain knobs, but she seemed quite unable to take in their significance. He let her go, summoned Fox, and went over the whole case.

'What's your idea on the show?' he asked when he had finished.

'Well, sir,' said Fox, in his stolid way, 'on the face of it the young gentlemen have got alibis. We'll have to check them up, of course, and I don't see we can go much further until we have done so.'

'For the moment,' said Alleyn, 'let us suppose Masters Guy and Arthur to be safely established behind cast-iron alibis. What then?'

'Then we've got the young lady, the old lady, the secretary, and the servants.'

'Let us parade them. But first let us go over the wireless game. You'll have to watch me here. I gather that the only way in which the radio could be fixed to give Mr Tonks his quietus is like this: Control knobs removed. Holes bored in front panel with fine drill. Metal knobs substituted and packed with blotting paper to insulate them from metal shafts and make them stay put. Heavier flex from adapter to radiator cut and the ends of the wires pushed through the drilled holes to make contact with the new knobs. Thus we have a positive and negative pole. Mr Tonks bridges the gap, gets a mighty wallop as the current passes through him to the earth. The switchboard fuse is blown almost immediately. All this is rigged by murderer while Sep was upstairs bullying wife and daughter. Sep revisited study some time after ten-twenty. Whole thing was made ready between ten, when Arthur went out, and the time Sep returned—say, about ten-forty-five. The murderer reappeared, connected radiator with flex, removed wires, changed back knobs, and left the thing tuned in. Now I take it that the burst of static described by Phillipa and Hislop would be caused by the short-circuit that killed our Septimus?'

'That's right.'

'It also affected all the heaters in the house. *Vide* Miss Tonks's radiator.'

'Yes. He put all that right again. It would be a simple enough matter for anyone who knew how. He'd just have to fix the fuse on the main switchboard. How long do you say it would take to—what's the horrible word?—to recondition the whole show?'

'M'm,' said Fox deeply. 'At a guess, sir, fifteen minutes. He'd have to be nippy.'

'Yes,' agreed Alleyn. 'He or she.'

'I don't see a female making a success of it,' grunted Fox. 'Look here, Chief, you know what I'm thinking. Why did Mr Hislop lie about deceased's habit of licking his thumbs? You say Hislop told you he remembered nothing and Chase says he overheard him saying the trick nearly drove him dippy.'

'Exactly,' said Alleyn. He was silent for so long that Fox felt moved to utter a discreet cough.

'Eh?' said Alleyn. 'Yes, Fox, yes. It'll have to be done.' He consulted the telephone directory and dialled a number.

'May I speak to Dr Meadows? Oh, it's you, is it? Do you remember Mr Hislop telling you that Septimus Tonks's trick of wetting his fingers nearly drove Hislop demented. Are you there? You don't? Sure? All right. All right. Hislop rang up at ten-twenty, you said? And you telephoned him? At eleven. Sure of the times? I see. I'd be glad if you'd come round. Can you? Well, do if you can.'

He hung up the receiver.

'Get Chase again, will you, Fox?'

Chase, recalled, was most insistent that Mr Hislop had spoken about it to Dr Meadows.

'It was when Mr Hislop had flu, sir. I went up with the doctor. Mr Hislop had a high temperature and was talking very excited. He kept on and on, saying the master had guessed his ways had driven him crazy and that the master kept on purposely to aggravate. He said if it went on much longer he'd . . . he didn't know what he was talking about, sir, really.'

'What did he say he'd do?'

'Well, sir, he said he'd—he'd do something desperate to the master. But it was only his rambling, sir. I daresay he wouldn't remember anything about it.'

'No,' said Alleyn, 'I daresay he wouldn't.' When Chase had gone he said to Fox: 'Go and find out about those boys and their alibis. See if they can put you on to a quick means of checking up. Get Master Guy to corroborate Miss Phillipa's statement that she was locked in her room.'

Fox had been gone for some time and Alleyn was still busy with his notes when the study door burst open and in came Dr Meadows.

'Look here, my giddy sleuth-hound,' he shouted, 'what's all this about Hislop? Who says he disliked Sep's abominable habits?'

'Chase does. And don't bawl at me like that. I'm worried.'

'So am I, blast you. What are you driving at? You can't imagine that

. . . that poor little broken-down hack is capable of electrocuting anybody, let alone Sep?'

'I have no imagination,' said Alleyn wearily.

'I wish to God I hadn't called you in. If the wireless killed Sep, it was because he'd monkeyed with it.'

'And put it right after it had killed him?'

Dr Meadows stared at Alleyn in silence.

'Now,' said Alleyn, 'you've got to give me a straight answer, Meadows. Did Hislop, while he was semi-delirious, say that this habit of Tonks's made him feel like murdering him?'

'I'd forgotten Chase was there,' said Dr Meadows.

'Yes, you'd forgotten that.'

'But even if he did talk wildly, Alleyn, what of it? Damn it, you can't arrest a man on the strength of a remark made in delirium.'

'I don't propose to do so. Another motive has come to light.'

'You mean—Phips—last night?'

'Did he tell you about that?'

'She whispered something to me this morning. I'm very fond of Phips. My God, are you sure of your grounds?'

'Yes,' said Alleyn. 'I'm sorry. I think you'd better go, Meadows.'

'Are you going to arrest him?'

'I have to do my job.'

There was a long silence.

'Yes,' said Dr Meadows at last. 'You have to do your job. Goodbye, Alleyn.'

Fox returned to say that Guy and Arthur had never left their parties. He had got hold of two of their friends. Guy and Mrs Tonks confirmed the story of the locked door.

'It's a process of elimination,' said Fox. 'It must be the secretary. He fixed the radio while deceased was upstairs. He must have dodged back to whisper through the door to Miss Tonks. I suppose he waited somewhere down here until he heard deceased blow himself to blazes and then put everything straight again, leaving the radio turned on.'

Alleyn was silent.

'What do we do now, sir?' asked Fox.

'I want to see the hook inside the front-door where they hang their keys.'

Fox, looking dazed, followed his superior to the little entrance hall.

'Yes, there they are,' said Alleyn. He pointed to a hook with two latch-keys hanging from it. 'You could scarcely miss them. Come on, Fox.'

Back in the study they found Hislop with Bailey in attendance.

Hislop looked from one Yard man to another.

'I want to know if it's murder.'

'We think so,' said Alleyn.

'I want you to realize that Phillipa—Miss Tonks—was locked in her room all last night.'

'Until her brother came home and unlocked the door,' said Alleyn.

'That was too late. He was dead by then.'

'How do you know when he died?'

'It must have been when there was that crash of static.'

'Mr Hislop,' said Alleyn, 'why would you not tell me how much that trick of licking his fingers exasperated you?'

'But—how do you know! I never told anyone.'

'You told Dr Meadows when you were ill.'

'I don't remember.' He stopped short. His lips trembled. Then, suddenly he began to speak.

'Very well. It's true. For two years he's tortured me. You see, he knew something about me. Two years ago when my wife was dying, I took money from the cash-box in that desk. I paid it back and thought he hadn't noticed. He knew all the time. From then on he had me where he wanted me. He used to sit there like a spider. I'd hand him a paper. He'd wet his thumbs with a clicking noise and a sort of complacent grimace. Click, click. Then he'd thumb the papers. He knew it drove me crazy. He'd look at me and then . . . click, click. And then he'd say something about the cash. He'd never quite accused me, just hinted. And I was impotent. You think I'm insane. I'm not. I could have murdered him. Often and often I've thought how I'd do it. Now you think I've done it. I haven't. There's the joke of it. I hadn't the pluck. And last night when Phillipa showed me she cared, it was like Heaven—unbelievable. For the first time since I've been here I *didn't* feel like killing him. And last night someone else *did*!'

He stood there trembling and vehement. Fox and Bailey, who had watched him with bewildered concern, turned to Alleyn. He was about to speak when Chase came in. 'A note for you, sir,' he said to Alleyn. 'It came by hand.'

Alleyn opened it and glanced at the first few words. He looked up.

'You may go, Mr Hislop. Now I've got what I expected—what I fished for.'

When Hislop had gone they read the letter.

Dear Alleyn,

Don't arrest Hislop. I did it. Let him go at once if you've arrested him and don't tell Phips you ever suspected him. I was in love with Isabel before she met Sep. I've tried to get her to divorce him, but she wouldn't because of the kids. Damned nonsense, but there's no time to discuss it now. I've got to be quick. He suspected us. He reduced her to a nervous wreck. I was afraid she'd go under altogether. I thought it all out. Some weeks ago I took Phips's key from the hook inside the front door. I had the tools and the flex and wire all ready. I knew where the main switchboard was and the cupboard. I meant to wait until they all went away at the New Year, but last night when Hislop rang me I made up my mind at once. He said the boys and servants were out and Phips locked in her room. I told him to stay in his room and to ring me up in half an hour if things hadn't quieted down. He didn't ring up. I did. No answer, so I knew Sep wasn't in his study.

I came round, let myself in, and listened. All quiet upstairs but the lamp still on in the study, so I knew he would come down again. He'd said he wanted to get the midnight broadcast from somewhere.

I locked myself in and got to work. When Sep was away last year, Arthur did one of his modern monstrosities of painting in the study. He talked about the knobs making good pattern. I noticed then that they were very like the ones on the radio and later on I tried one and saw that it would fit if I packed it up a bit. Well, I did the job just as you worked it out, and it only took twelve minutes. Then I went into the drawing-room and waited.

He came down from Isabel's room and evidently went straight to the radio. I hadn't thought it would make such a row, and half expected someone would come down. No one came. I went back, switched off the wireless, mended the fuse in the main switchboard, using my torch. Then I put everything right in the study.

There was no particular hurry. No one would come in while he was there and I got the radio going as soon as possible to suggest he was at it. I knew I'd be called in when they found him. My idea was to tell them he had died of a stroke. I'd been warning Isabel it might happen at any time. As soon as I saw the burned hand I knew that cat wouldn't jump. I'd have tried to get away with it if Chase hadn't gone round bleating about electrocution and burned fingers. Hislop saw the hand. I daren't do anything but report the case to the police, but I thought you'd never twig the knobs. One up to you.

I might have bluffed through if you hadn't suspected Hislop. Can't let you hang the blighter. I'm enclosing a note to Isabel, who won't forgive me, and an official one for you to use. You'll find me in my bedroom upstairs. I'm using cyanide. It's quick.

I'm sorry, Alleyn. I think you knew, didn't you? I've bungled the whole game, but if you will be a supersleuth . . . Goodbye.

Henry Meadows

CYRIL HARE · 1900–1958

Miss Burnside's Dilemma

It's the fact that it's the vicar that makes the whole business so *difficult*. I simply don't know what to do about it. Those were his very words to me when I taxed him with it after matins last Sunday. 'Well, Miss Burnside,' he said, 'and what do you propose to do about it?' He smiled at me as he said it, I remember—just a friendly, amused sort of smile over his shoulder as he locked the vestry door, and then he took off his hat in that courteous way of his and walked back to the vicarage, leaving me standing there without an answer. That was nearly a week ago. And I don't know what the answer is. And he knows quite well that I don't know. I can see it in his eye whenever we meet. And in a small place like this it does make for a really impossible situation.

My first thought was to go to the police about it. In fact, if it had not been for the chance that my nephew John was staying with me at the time I think I should have done so. I call it chance, but looking back on it now I feel that it was rather the hand of Providence. Because if I had obeyed that first impulse I can see now what a terrible scandal there would have been. And much worse than a mere scandal, indeed! It so happened that on that Sunday evening John—he is studying for the Bar and is a very clever boy indeed—was talking to me about a big law case there had been recently in which a poor woman was made to pay enormous damages for—what did he call it?—Malicious Prosecution. That made me think a great deal of the danger of acting rashly in the matter, and in the end I told him all about it and asked his advice. After all, he is very nearly a lawyer, and as he is not one of the village it didn't seem to matter. John was tremendously interested—more interested than shocked, I'm afraid, but I suppose that is only natural—and he spent nearly the whole evening considering the matter when he ought to have been studying the Law of Real Property, which is his next examination, and in the end he told me that he could not find that any crime had been committed. Well, that may be the law, and of course I believe what my nephew tells me, but it does seem to me very wrong that the law should permit such things to be done—especially by a minister of the Church of England.

Of course, I could write to the bishop about it. Indeed, I have considered very seriously whether it is not my *duty* to write to the bishop. But it is a step that one shrinks from. In some ways it seems almost more serious than informing the police. I mean, it does seem almost equal to invoking the help of a Higher Power—I trust I am not being irreverent in putting it in that way. But I do not think the seriousness of it would deter me if I were only sure that the bishop would be able to do anything about it, and of that I cannot be sure. I asked John, but he could not help me. It appears that Church Law is not one of the subjects they examine him in, which seems a pity. However, he was very kind and helpful in explaining all kinds of points about the Law of Wills and so on, so that I do at least understand the whole of the dreadful story now quite clearly. Not that that is very much comfort to me, indeed! Rather the reverse. And situated as I am, there is literally *nobody* to whom I can turn for guidance. It is just the sort of problem that I could have set before the vicar himself until this terrible thing happened. But now————!

I want to be perfectly just to the vicar. In all the time that he has been in the village nobody, I am sure, has had a word to say against him, except indeed old Judd, and he, I fear, is irreclaimably ill disposed to every influence for good in the village. Of course, one might say that he—the vicar, I mean—has merely been a hypocrite all these years and that we have all been woefully deceived in him. But I prefer to think of him as a man suddenly exposed to a great Temptation and being carried away, as might happen to any of us. True, I cannot forget the way in which he brazened it out with me on Sunday, but neither can I believe that I have been utterly mistaken in the man, after knowing him so well for nearly ten years. That is the time that he has been in the village, and I remember quite well how good an impression he made when Mrs Wheeler presented him to the living. It was quite soon after Mrs Wheeler settled down among us, and bought the Hall and with it the patronage. I do not myself altogether approve of such a thing as a cure of souls being in the gift of a private person and I am very glad that Parliament has done something about it, though I can never understand quite *what*, but it seemed impossible to quarrel with Mrs Wheeler's choice, and the fact that he was her godson as well as her nephew made it so peculiarly appropriate. Certainly, we all agreed that it was a mercy that the old vicar had survived until after Sir John sold the place, for

Sir John's intellect was beginning to fail, and what with that and his dangerously Low Church tendencies one shudders to think what his choice might have been.

Altogether, there is no denying that the double change, at the Hall and the vicarage, was all to the good of the neighbourhood. Everybody liked Mrs Wheeler. Even Judd had hardly a word to say against her. True, she lived very quietly, as was after all only proper for a widow who was no longer young; but until last year, when her health began to fail, she took her full part in all the village activities, and whenever help was needed she was unfailingly generous. As indeed she could well afford to be— not that I consider that that detracts in any way from her kindness of heart, but it was common knowledge that Mr Wheeler, whoever he may have been, had left her very well provided for. The all-important thing was that she used her wealth for the good of others.

But if it is true to say that we respected the new vicar and admired Mrs Wheeler—and I think it is—there is no doubt that we loved Miss Dalrymple. She, I should explain, was Mrs Wheeler's companion. There is a lot of nonsense talked about the companions of rich old ladies who have no daughters of their own to look after them. They are always represented as poor abject creatures, perpetually bullied and down-trodden by their employers. Miss Dalrymple was not at all like that. She was a very cheerful, active young woman—not really young, of course, only in comparison with Mrs Wheeler she seemed so—and there was nothing in the least abject about her. Of course, she kept herself well in the background when Mrs Wheeler was present, but that is no more than one would expect. And there was no doubt that they were very fond of each other. They were indeed just like mother and daughter—or, rather, like what mother and daughter should be but so often, alas, are *not*.

The only person in the place who did not seem absolutely devoted to Miss Dalrymple, strangely enough, was the vicar himself. It was strange, because in many ways they had so much in common. At one time, indeed, I had hopes that the pair of them would make a match of it. It seemed so extremely suitable, and I know that I did my little best to bring it to pass. Certainly, I have always felt that a bachelor vicar, however excellent, is out of place in a parish like ours—though I know that Saint Paul thought otherwise. But it was not to be, and as the years went on it was impossible not to notice a certain coolness—I wouldn't go so far as to call it hostility—between him and Miss Dalrymple; although, of course, they always remained scrupulously polite and acted together quite harmoniously on committees and bazaars and at other parish functions.

That was how matters stood when Mrs Wheeler came to the village, and that was how they remained for a very long time. Nothing changes very much with the years in a quiet place like this, except that we all grow a little older, and I think it was quite a shock to most of us to realize last year how very much older and more infirm dear Mrs Wheeler had become. She went out less and less, and Miss Dalrymple, too, withdrew almost entirely from our little activities owing to the necessity of having to look after her. Mrs Wheeler had some objection to a nurse, so that all the burden fell upon poor Miss Dalrymple. It was really very hard upon her, though she never complained, and I must say that she was quite as good and careful as any professional nurse could be.

A month or two ago, however, it became sadly evident that Mrs Wheeler was seriously ill. Dr Perry—who was always, I think, just the least bit afraid of her—plucked up the courage to insist that she should have a night nurse permanently on duty, and this gave Miss Dalrymple a little more freedom to come out and see her friends. One evening, shortly after the nurse had been installed, she came round to see me. I had expected her to be tired and anxious, but I was not prepared to find her quite so depressed and utterly unlike her usual cheerful self.

Naturally my first question was after Mrs Wheeler.

'She is very ill indeed,' she told me. 'Dr Perry thinks that it is most unlikely that she will recover.'

It is always difficult to know what to say on such occasions. I said, 'Oh dear!' which, I am afraid, was rather inadequate, but I tried to put as much sympathy into my voice as possible.

Miss Dalrymple said nothing for a moment or two but sat there looking very low and miserable. Finally she said, 'The trouble is, Miss Burnside, that she doesn't realize how ill she is.'

'Surely that is all to the good,' I said. 'After all, if she is going to die, it is better that she should not be troubled with any foreboding about it. It isn't as if she was a Roman Catholic,' I added, 'and in need of making a confession or anything of that kind. Not that a dear, good woman like Mrs Wheeler could have anything to confess, in any case.'

'It isn't that,' she answered, looking more miserable than ever. 'You see, Dr Perry says that she might die at any minute, and I happen to know that she has not made any will.'

I confess that I could not help feeling a little shocked—disgusted even—that Miss Dalrymple should be thinking of such things at such a time, and I thought then—as I have thought many times since! —how mistaken one can be, even about somebody one has known for a long time. Of course, I knew, like everybody in the village, that Miss Dalrymple had absolutely nothing of her own, and I knew also, because Mrs Wheeler had told me so, that her employer had intentions of making some provision for her after her death. I could quite understand Miss Dalrymple feeling disappointed at having to go out and look for another post at her age. But at the same time I could not but think that it was rather improper to be thinking of such matters, much more discussing them, while the person in question was still alive.

I must have shown something of my feelings in my expression, although I certainly did my best not to, for Miss Dalrymple immediately said, 'Please don't imagine that I'm thinking of myself, Miss Burnside.'

Naturally, I said, 'Of course not!' though I wondered very much of whom else she could possibly be thinking. But what she said next surprised me very much indeed.

'It would be a lamentable thing,' she went on, 'and, absolutely contrary to Mrs Wheeler's own wishes, if all that money of hers were to go to her son.'

Now this was the very first time that I, or anybody else so far as I was aware, had ever so much as heard that Mrs Wheeler had a son, and that only goes to show how very reticent she had always been about her own affairs, and how very loyal a companion Miss Dalrymple had been, never once to have mentioned the fact to any of her friends in the village.

'Her son, Miss Dalrymple?' I said. 'Whatever do you mean?' And then she told me all about him.

It appeared that Mrs Wheeler had a son who, as is, I am afraid, so often the case with the children of the most excellent, religious people, had turned out very badly indeed. It crossed my mind that perhaps young Charles Wheeler—that was his name, apparently —took after his father, but this was really very uncharitable of me, for, of course, I knew nothing whatever about the late Mr Wheeler except that he had made a great deal of money, and that, after all, was nothing against his character—rather the reverse. At all events, as the result of his misconduct (and although Miss Dalrymple, most properly, entered into no *details*, I gathered that it had been very grave indeed), the young man had for many years entirely cut himself off from his family. Miss Dalrymple did not so much as know where he was living, except that it was somewhere abroad, and the only communication that his mother had received from him recently was an application for money a little time before she was taken ill, which she had, of course, refused to consider in any way.

And now there was a possibility of Mrs Wheeler's money being diverted to this wicked person, to be turned by him to the most disreputable purposes! I could well understand Miss Dalrymple's agitation at such a thing, although I may as well admit that I did not *wholly* credit her assertion that she was not thinking at all of her own prospects, because, after all, we are all *human*. Speaking for myself, I felt particularly alarmed when I reflected that Mrs Wheeler's property included the right of presentation to our living and that this might well fall into the hands of an outright rascal.

I was sadly perplexed in my mind as to what advice I should give Miss Dalrymple on this difficult question, for though I am always prepared to listen to other people's troubles, and my friends have told me that I am a particularly good listener, giving advice is a responsibility which I do not care to undertake. At last it occurred to me to suggest that she should consult the vicar, who, from his position, was particularly suited to bring Mrs Wheeler to a sense of the danger which she was in, and who was himself really interested in the matter in another way. I mean, until this moment everybody regarded him as Mrs Wheeler's nearest relative, although presumably he was well aware of the existence of his ill-behaved cousin.

I could see that Miss Dalrymple did not altogether like the prospect of confiding in the vicar, but she agreed to think it over, and a little later she went home, feeling, I am sure, all the better for having had a good chat. There is, I think, nothing better than a good chat with the right sort of person to make you look on the bright side of things.

Next morning, as soon as I had breakfasted, I put on my hat and went round to the Hall to enquire. I had done this many times since Mrs Wheeler had been taken ill, of course, but on this occasion, though I am not, I trust, superstitious, I did feel a certain sense of foreboding as I did so. And sure enough, as I came round the bend in the drive, I saw that the blinds of the house had been drawn, and knew at once that our dear friend had passed away. I was about to turn round and go home again, when the front door opened and Miss Dalrymple came out. She saw me and came straight up towards me, so that, without feeling that I was in any way *intruding*, I was able to get the very first information about what had happened from her instead of having to rely upon village gossip, which is always rather undignified, in my opinion, and has the added disadvantage that one does not know what to believe!

Dear Mrs Wheeler, she told me, had taken a sudden turn for the worse at about two o'clock that morning. Dr Perry had been sent for immediately, of course, but he was out attending a maternity case, and in spite of all that Miss Dalrymple and the nurse could do, by the time that he arrived, which was not until nearly seven, all was over. The doctor had said that he could have done nothing had he been there in time, and I was glad to learn that the end had been altogether peaceful.

I dare say that I should not have been thinking of such things at such a moment, but, remembering our conversation of the evening before, I could not forbear saying, 'Then I suppose poor Mrs Wheeler was never able to make a will after all?'

Then Miss Dalrymple told me her great news! It seemed that after the first seizure Mrs Wheeler had rallied and remained quite conscious and sensible for several hours. And during that time, knowing that her last hour had come, she had been able to make her will. By that will, Miss Dalrymple told me, she had bequeathed one thousand pounds to her nephew, the vicar, and the whole of the rest of her fortune to Miss Dalrymple herself!

I could hardly believe my ears. It really seemed too good to be true, and I congratulated her most warmly, but, I hope, with the solemnity that the occasion required. Still I found it difficult to credit that the story should have had so happy an ending.

'Forgive me for asking you,' I said, 'but are you quite sure that this is really so? Have you seen the will yourself?'

'Indeed, I have,' she told me. 'We sent for the vicar, of course, as soon as we saw how gravely ill she was. The moment she recovered consciousness, she told him to write down what she wished. I saw her sign the paper, and then the vicar and I put our names underneath hers as witnesses.'

When I had got as far as this in telling the story to my nephew John, he made a most peculiar noise, something between a snort and a laugh. Of course, with his knowledge, he saw at once what was wrong; but we are not all lawyers—thank goodness!—and neither Miss Dalrymple nor I had the least idea at the time that the will was anything but perfectly legal. Nor, I am sure, had poor Mrs Wheeler, unless the knowledge was vouchsafed to her in Heaven, in which case it must have made her very unhappy, if such a thing is possible in Heaven. But it is the fact, cruel and unfair though it may seem, that the law does not allow a will to be legal unless it is witnessed by two persons, and that neither of these two persons is allowed to have any benefit from the will which they have witnessed. So that, as John put it, the only two people in the world who could not receive any of Mrs Wheeler's money under her will were the vicar and Miss Dalrymple, the only two people whom she desired to give anything to! I said then, and I think still, that it is most unreasonable and a kind of trap for innocent people like companions and country clergy who could not be expected to know anything about the law, because, after all, who could be better suited to witness an old lady's will than her nephew and the woman who had looked after her for so many years? I think they should have thought of such things when the law was made, but I suppose it is too late to alter it now.

Of course, neither Miss Dalrymple nor I knew anything of this at the time, but we were speedily undeceived. The day after the funeral she came to see me in great distress and told me that she had been to consult a lawyer as to what was to be done about Mrs Wheeler's estate, and he had told her that by witnessing the will she and the vicar had signed away all their inheritance. She told me also that the vicar had called upon her and expressed his sorrow that his ignorance had led to her losing the reward of her long years of service, not to mention his own thousand pounds, which he admitted was a serious matter for him, for the living was not a good one.

After that Miss Dalrymple left the village, and I understand she secured another post with a lady at Cheltenham, where she was not well paid, and where, I am afraid, she was anything but happy. Meanwhile we in the village awaited the dreadful moment when Mr Charles Wheeler would descend upon us to take possession of the property which had in this strange way become his after all. A week or more went by, and then we heard the great and unexpected news. I had it first from Mrs Tomlin, at the post office; and although I always suspect anything from that source, it was soon afterwards confirmed by the vicar himself. It appeared that as soon as it was established that the will was of no effect, the vicar had enquiries made for the whereabouts of the son, and these enquiries had met with a speedy and most unhoped result. Charles Wheeler was no more! He had perished, very miserably, I am sorry to say, in some foreign town, quite soon after his last letter to his mother asking for assistance. The vicar had been shown that letter at the time, and he told me that in it he had stated that he was dangerously ill. It was the vicar who had counselled Mrs Wheeler not to reply to it, thinking that the statement of his condition was only a ruse to get more money from the mother who had cast him off; and he said, very generously as I thought at the time, that he now regretted that he had not allowed his aunt to take measures which might have prolonged the unfortunate man's life a little longer. But I told him that although the sentiment did him credit, it was much better as it was, and I remember that I went so far as to say that the death of Charles Wheeler might be accounted a providential event.

So after all the vicar, as the only living relative of his aunt, came into all her possessions, and we were all so pleased at this happy turn of events that I am afraid we had very little thought to spare for poor Miss Dalrymple, who, after all, was the person whom Mrs Wheeler had mainly had in mind. And the vicar was so popular in the village—except, of course, with old Judd and people of his stamp —that there was no one who did not rejoice in his good fortune. Indeed, and this is my great difficulty at the present moment, he is still just as popular as ever, simply because nobody, myself only excepted, knows the *truth*.

Just over a week ago I spent a night in London with my brother and sister-in-law, a thing I do very rarely, except when the summer sales are in progress. They took me to the theatre that evening, I remember—it was a most amusing piece, but I do not recollect the name—and invited to join the party a Mr Woodhouse, whom I had never met before. During the interval, between the acts, he asked me where I lived and, when I told him, said, 'Then I suppose you know Mr———' (mentioning the vicar by name).

'Indeed I do,' I told him, and was about to go on to tell him something of the strange story of Mrs Wheeler's will when he interrupted me.

'I was up with him at Oxford,' he said. 'A very clever fellow, I thought him.'

'He is a very *good* man,' I answered with some emphasis, 'and I think that is more important.' One does not somehow like to hear one's vicar described as 'a very clever fellow', even if it is kindly meant.

'Oh, but he is clever too,' Mr Woodhouse persisted. 'I remember he took a first-class honours degree in Law the year I graduated.'

I was thunderstruck.

'In Law, Mr Woodhouse?' I said. 'Are you sure that you are not mistaken?'

'Quite sure,' he said. 'He was intended for the Bar, you know, but he changed his mind and went into the Church instead. Rather a waste of a good intellect, I thought.'

Luckily the curtain rose for the next act before I could ask him what he meant by his last very improper observation, and I took good care not to refer to the subject again.

All the way down in the train next day I could think of nothing but what Mr Woodhouse had told me. If the vicar had really studied the law at Oxford how was it possible that he had made such a mistake as he had done about witnessing the will? I tried to comfort myself by reflecting that he might have forgotten this particular point, but it seemed hardly possible, and indeed John has told me since that it is one of the 'first principles' of the Law of Wills—though why they should make a first principle of anything so unjust and cruel I do not in the least understand. But if he *knew* that by becoming a witness Miss Dalrymple was losing her right to Mrs Wheeler's property, however hostile to her he may have felt, why had he been content to destroy his own chances of getting a thousand pounds also? It was all most puzzling and mysterious, and I made up my mind, come what might, to speak to him at the very first opportunity. And that opportunity came last Sunday, after matins.

I still blush when I think of it—not for myself, for I feel that I only obeyed my conscience in saying what I did, but for him. His effrontery was so astonishing. I can recall—I do not think I shall ever forget—exactly what passed between us.

I met him, as I said, just as he was coming out of the vestry door after the service. He said 'Good morning' to me, and I responded as politely as I could.

Then I said, 'I met an old acquaintance of yours in London, Vicar, a Mr Woodhouse.'

'Oh, yes, Woodhouse,' he replied. 'I haven't seen him for a very long time.'

I resolved not to beat about the bush.

'He told me', I said, 'that you had studied the law at Oxford, and were awarded first-class honours for your proficiency.'

He did not show the least confusion, but merely said, 'It is pleasant to have one's little triumphs remembered.'

'Then did you not know,' I pressed him, 'that Miss Dalrymple ought not to have witnessed that will?'

'Ought not, Miss Burnside?' he asked. 'I should prefer to say that Mrs Wheeler ought not to have tried to dispose of her property in the way that she did.'

I could hardly speak for indignation.

'Then you deliberately so arranged matters that Miss Dalrymple should lose what Mrs Wheeler wished her to have?' I said.

'I did.'

'Even at the cost of losing your own legacy?'

'But you see, I have not lost it,' he answered with a smile, and then I suddenly saw the light.

'Vicar!' I said. 'You knew all the time that Charles Wheeler was dead!'

He nodded.

'I had a telegram from the British Consul informing me of his death some months ago,' he said. 'In view of my aunt's state of health I thought it wiser to keep the news from her. Do you blame me?'

I was so angry that I am afraid I lost all respect for his cloth.

'Blame you?' I said. 'I think you have behaved like a common thief!'

And then he used those awful words that I have already mentioned: 'Well, Miss Burnside, and what are you going to do about it?'

What indeed! Tomorrow it is Sunday again. I know that my absence from church would cause the most *undesirable* talk in the place, but yet I feel as if, so long as he is vicar, dear St Etheldreda's can never be the same place for me again. The Hall is up for sale and I hear dreadful rumours that it is to be bought by a *builder*. All our pleasant life in this village is at an end, so far as I am concerned. I wish somebody would answer that question for me: What am I going to do?

GLADYS MITCHELL · 1901–1983

Daisy Bell

> Daisy, Daisy, give me your answer, do!
> I've gone crazy, all for the love of you!
> It won't be a stylish marriage—
> We can't afford a carriage—
> But you'll look neat upon the seat
> Of a bicycle made for two.

In the curved arm of the bay the sea lay perfectly still. Towards the horizon was reflected back the flashing light of the sun, but under the shadow of huge cliffs the dark-green water was as quiet as a lake at evening.

Above, riding over a ridge between two small villages, went the road, a dusty highway once, a turnpike on which the coach had changed horses three times in twenty miles. That dusty road was within the memory of the villagers; in the post office there were picture postcards, not of the coaches, certainly, but of the horse-drawn station bus on the shocking gradients and hairpin bends of the highway.

The road was now slightly wider—not much, because every extra foot had to be hacked from the rocky hillside, for on one side the road fell almost sheer to the sea. A humped turf edge kept this seaward boundary (insufficiently, some said, for there had been motoring accidents, especially in the dark), and beyond the humped edge, and, treacherously, just out of sight of motorists who could see the rolling turf but not the danger, there fell away a Gadarene descent of thirteen hundred feet.

George took the road respectfully, with an eye for hairpin bends and (although he found this irksome) an occasional toot on the horn. His employer, small, spare, and upright, sat beside him, the better to admire the rolling view. Equally with the moorland scenery she admired her chauffeur's driving. She was accustomed to both phenomena, but neither palled on her. In sixteen crawling miles she had not had a word to say.

At the County Boundary, however, she turned her head slightly to the right.

'The next turning, George. It's narrow.'

His eyes on the road ahead, the chauffeur nodded, and the car turned off to the left down a sandy lane, at the bottleneck of which it drew up courteously in face of a flock of lively, athletic, headstrong moorland sheep. The shepherd saluted Mrs Bradley, passed the time of day with the chauffeur, said it was a pity all they motors shouldn't have the same danged sense, and urged his charges past the car, and kept them within some sort of bounds with the help of a shaggy dog.

At the bottom of the slope, and wedged it seemed in the hollow, was a village with a very small church. Mrs Bradley went into the churchyard to inspect the grave of an ancestress (she believed) of her own who had died in the odour of sanctity, but, if rumour did not lie, only barely so, for she had enjoyed a reputation as a witch.

Mrs Bradley, looking (with her black hair, sharp black eyes, thin hands, and beaky little mouth) herself not at all unlike a witch, spent an interesting twenty minutes or so in the churchyard, and then went into the church.

Its architectural features were almost negligible. A fourteenth-century chancel (probably built on the site of the earliest church), a badly restored nave, a good rood screen, and the only remaining bit of Early English work mutilated to allow for an organ loft, were all obvious. There seemed, in fact, very little, on a preliminary investigation, to interest even the most persistent or erudite visitor.

In the dark south wall, however, of what had been the Lady Chapel, Mrs Bradley came upon a fourteenth-century piscina whose bowl had been carved in the likeness of a hideous human head. She took out a magnifying glass and examined the carving closely. Montague Rhodes James, with his genius for evoking unquiet imaginings and terrifying, atavistic fears, might have described the expression upon its horrid countenance. All that Mrs Bradley could accomplish was a heathenish muttering indicative of the fact that, in her view, the countenance betrayed indication of at least two major Freudian complexes and a Havelock Ellis regression into infantile criminology.

'A murderer's face, ma'am,' said a voice behind her. 'Ay, as I stand, that be a murderer's face.'

She turned and saw the verger with his keys. 'Ay, they do tell, and vicar he do believe it, as carver was vouchsafed a true, just vision of Judas Iscariot the traitor, and carved he out for all to look upon.'

He smiled at her—almost with the sinister leer of the carving itself, thought Mrs Bradley, startled by the change in his mild and previously friendly expression. He passed on into the vestry, dangling his keys.

Shaking her head, Mrs Bradley dropped some money into the offertory box on the pillar nearest the porch, and took the long sloping path between the headstones of the graves to the lych-gate. Here she found George in conversation with a black-haired woman. George had always given himself (with how much truth his employer had never troubled herself to find out) the reputation of being a misogynist, and on this occasion, seated on the step of the car, he was, in his own phrase, 'laying down the law' with scornful masculine firmness. The girl had her back to the lych-gate. She was plump and bareheaded, and was wearing brown corduroy shorts, a slightly rucked-up blouse on elastic at the waist, and—visible from the back view which Mrs Bradley had of her—a very bright pink vest which showed between the rucked-up blouse and the shorts. For the rest she was brown-skinned and, seen face to face, rather pretty.

A tandem bicycle, built to accommodate two men, was resting against the high, steep, ivy-grown bank of the lane. The young woman, seeing Mrs Bradley, who had in fact strolled round to get a view of her, cut short George's jeremiads by thanking him. Then she walked across the road, set the tandem upright, pushed it sharply forward, and, in spite of the fact that the slope of the road was against her, mounted with agility and ease on to the front saddle. Then she tacked doggedly up the hill, the tandem, lacking any weight on the back seat, wagging its tail in what looked to Mrs Bradley a highly dangerous manner as it zigzagged up to the bend in the lane and wobbled unwillingly round it.

George had risen to his feet upon the approach of his employer, and now stood holding the door open.

'A courageous young woman, George?' suggested Mrs Bradley, getting into the car.

'A foolish one, madam, in my opinion,' George responded primly, 'and so I was saying to her when she was asking the way. Looking for trouble I call it to cycle one of them things down these roads. Look at the hill she's coming to, going to Lyndale this route. Meeting her husband, she says; only been married a month, and having their honeymoon now and using the tandem between them; him having to work thereabouts, and her cycling that contraption down from London, where she's living with her mother while he gets the home for her. Taken three days to do it in, and meeting him on top of Lyndale Hill this afternoon. More like a suicide pact, if you ask me what I think.'

'I not only ask you, George, but I am so much enthralled by what you think that I propose we take the same route and follow her.'

'We were due to do so in any case, madam, if I can find a place to turn the car in this lane.'

It took him six slow miles to find a suitable place. During the drive towards the sea, the big car brushing the summer hedgerows almost all the time, Mrs Bradley observed,

'I don't like to think of that young woman, George. I hope you advised her to wheel the bicycle on all dangerous parts of the road?'

'As well advise an errand boy to fit new brake-blocks, madam,' George austerely answered. 'I did advise her to that effect, but not to cut any ice. She fancies herself on that jigger. You can't advise women of that age.'

'Did you offer her any alternative route to Lyndale?'

'Yes, madam; not with success.'

At the top of the winding hill he turned to the left, and then, at the end of another five miles and a quarter of wind and the screaming seabirds, great stretches of moorland heather, bright green tracks of little peaty streams, and, south of the moor, the far-off ridges and tors, he engaged his lowest gear again and the car crept carefully down a long, steep, dangerous hill. There were warning notices on either side of the road, and the local authority, laying special emphasis on the subject of faulty brakes, had cut a parking space from the edge of the stubborn moor. The gradient of the steepest part of the hill was one in four. The car took the slant like a cat in sight of a bird.

'What do you think of our brakes, George?' Mrs Bradley inquired. George replied, in the reserved manner with which he received her more facetious questions, that the brakes were in order, or had been when the car was brought out of the garage.

'Well, then, pull up,' said his employer. 'Something has happened on the seaward side of the road. I think someone's gone over the edge.'

Her keen sight, and a certain sensitivity she had to visual impressions, had not deceived her. She followed the track of a bicycle to the edge of the cliff, crouched, lay flat, and looked over.

Below her the seagulls screamed, and, farther down, the sea flung sullenly, despite the brilliant day, against the heavy rocks, or whirlpooled, snarling, about the black island promontories, for the tide was on the turn and coming in fast. Sea-pinks, some of them brown and withered now, for their season was almost past, clung in the crevices or grew in the smallest hollows of the cliff-face. Near one root of them a paper bag had lodged. Had it been empty, the west wind, blowing freshly along the face of the cliff (which looked north to the Bristol Channel), must have removed it almost as soon as it alighted, but there it perched, not wedged, yet heavy enough to hold its place against the breeze. To the left of it, about four yards off, was a deep, dark stain, visible because it was on the only piece of white stone that could be seen.

'Odd,' said Mrs Bradley, and began to perform the feat which she would not have permitted to anyone under her control—that of climbing down to reach the dark-stained rock.

The stain was certainly blood, and was still slightly sticky to the touch. She looked farther down (having, fortunately, a mountaineer's head for heights) and thought that, some thirty feet below her, she could see a piece of cloth. It was caught on the only bush which seemed to have found root and sustenance upon the rocky cliff. It resembled, she thought, material of which a man's suit might be made.

She left it where it was and scrambled across to the bag.

'George,' she said, when she had regained the dark, overhanging lip of the rough turf edge of the cliff and had discovered her chauffeur at the top, 'I think I saw a public telephone marked on the map. Somebody ought to search the shore below these cliffs, I rather fancy.'

'It would need to be by boat, then, madam. The tide comes up to the foot,' replied the chauffeur. He began to walk back up the hill.

Mrs Bradley sat down at the roadside and waited for him to return. While she was waiting she untwisted the top of the screwed-up paper bag and examined the contents with interest.

She found a packet of safety-razor blades, a tube of toothpaste half-full, a face flannel, a wrapped cake of soap of the dimensions known euphemistically in the advertisements as 'guest-size', a very badly worn toothbrush, a set of small buttons on a card, a pipe-cleaner, half a bicycle bell, two rubber patches for mending punctures, and a piece of wormlike valve-rubber.

'Calculated to indicate that whoever left the bag there was a cyclist, George,' she observed, when her chauffeur came back from the telephone. 'Of course, nobody may have fallen over the cliff, but —what do you make of the marks?'

'Palmer tyres, gent's model—not enough clearance for a lady's —see where the pedal caught the edge of the turf?'

'Yes, George. Unfortunately one loses the track a yard from the side of the road. I should have supposed that the bicycle would have left a better account of itself if it had really been ridden over. Besides, what could have made anybody ride it over the edge? The road is wide enough, and there does not seem to be much traffic. I think perhaps I'll retrieve that piece of cloth before we go.'

'I most seriously hope you will not, madam, if you'll excuse me. I've no head for heights myself or I would get it. After all, we know just where it is. The police could get it later, with ropes and tackle for their men, if it *should* be required at an inquest.'

'Very true, George. Let us get on to the village to see whether a boat has put out. How much farther is it?'

'Another three miles and a half, madam. There's another hill after this—a smaller one.'

The car descended decorously. The hill dropped sheer and steep for about another half-mile, and then it twisted suddenly away to the right, so that an inn which was on the left-hand side at the bend appeared, for an instant, to be standing in the middle of the road.

So far as the black-haired girl on the smashed and buckled tandem was concerned, that was where it might as well have stood, Mrs Bradley reflected. The tandem had been ridden straight into a brick wall—slap into it as though the rider had been blind or as though the machine she was riding had been completely out of her control. Whatever the cause of the accident, she had hurtled irrevocably to her death, or so Mrs Bradley thought when first she knelt beside her.

'Rat-trap pedals, of all things, madam,' said George. The plump large feet in the centre-seamed cycling shoes were still caught in the bent steel traps. George tested the brakes.

'The brakes don't act,' he said. 'Perhaps a result of the accident, madam, although I shouldn't think so.' He released the girl's feet and lifted the tandem away. Mrs Bradley, first delicately and then with slightly more firmness, sought for injuries.

'George,' she said, 'the case of instruments. And then go and get some cold water from somewhere or other.'

The girl had a fractured skull. Her left leg was slightly lacerated, but it was not bruised and the bone was not broken. Her face was unmarked, except by the dirt from the roadside. It was all a little out of the ordinary, Mrs Bradley thought, seizing the thermos flask full of icy water which the resourceful George had brought from a moorland stream.

'She's alive, George, I think,' she said. 'But there have been some very odd goings-on. Are the tandem handlebars locked?'

'No, madam. They move freely.'

'Don't you think the front wheel should have been more seriously affected?'

'Why, yes, perhaps it should, madam. The young woman can't go much less than ten or eleven stone, and with the brakes out of order . . .'

'And although her feet were caught in the rat-trap pedals, her face isn't even marked. It was only a little dirty before I washed it.'

'Sounds like funny business, madam, to me.'

'And to me, too. George. Is there a hospital near? We must have an ambulance if possible. I don't think the car will do. She ought to lie flat. That skull wants trepanning and at once. Mind how you go down the hill, though. I'll stay here with her. You might leave me a fairly heavy spanner.'

Left alone with the girl, Mrs Bradley fidgeted with her case of instruments, took out gouge forceps, sighed, shook her head, and put them back again. The wound on the top of the head was extremely puzzling. A fracture of the base of the skull would have been the most likely head injury, unless the girl had crashed head-first into the wall, but, from the position in which the body had been lying, this seemed extremely unlikely. One other curious point Mrs Bradley noticed which changed her suppositions into certainty. The elastic-waisted white blouse and the shorts met neatly. It was impossible to believe that they could do so unless they had been pulled together after the girl had fallen from the saddle.

Mrs Bradley made a mental picture of the girl leaning forward over the low-slung sports-type handlebars of the machine. She must, in the feminine phrase, have 'come apart' at the back. That blouse could never have overlapped those shorts.

Interested and curious, Mrs Bradley turned up the edge of the soiled white blouse. There was nothing underneath it but the bare brown skin marked with two or three darker moles at the waist. Of the bright pink vest there was no sign; neither had the girl a knapsack or any kind of luggage into which she could have stuffed the vest supposing that she had taken it off for coolness.

'Odd,' said Mrs Bradley again, weighing the spanner thoughtfully in her hand. 'I wonder what's happened to the husband?'

At this moment there came round the bend an AA scout wheeling a bicycle. He saluted as he came nearer.

'Oh dear, madam! Nasty accident here! Poor young woman! Anything I can do?'

'Yes,' said Mrs Bradley very promptly. 'Get an ambulance. I'm afraid she's dead, but there might be a chance if you're quick. No, don't touch her. I'm a doctor. I've done all that can be done here. Hurry, please. Every moment is important.'

'No ambulance in the village, madam. Couldn't expect it, could you? I might perhaps be able to get a car. How did you get here? Was you with her when she crashed?'

'Go and get a car. A police car, if you like. Dead or alive, she'll have to be moved as soon as possible.'

'Yes, she will, won't she?' said the man. He turned his bicycle, and, mounting it, shot away round the bend.

Mrs Bradley unfolded an Ordnance Survey map of the district and studied it closely. Then she took out a reading glass and studied it again. She put out a yellow claw and traced the line of the road she was on, and followed it into the village towards which first George and then the AA scout had gone.

The road ran on uncompromisingly over the thin red contour lines of the map, past nameless bays on one side and the shoulder of the moor on a rising hill on the other. Of deviations from it there were none; not so much as the dotted line of a moorland track, not even a stream, gave any indication that there might be other ways of reaching the village besides crossing the open moorland or keeping to the line of the road. There was nothing marked on the map but the cliffs and the shore on the one hand, the open hill country on the other.

She was still absorbed when George returned with the car.

'The village has no ambulance, madam, but the bus has decanted its passengers on to the bridge and is getting here as fast as it can. It was thought in the village, madam, that the body could be laid along one of the seats.'

'I hope and trust that "body" is but a relative term. The young woman will live, George, I fancy. Somebody has had his trouble for nothing.'

'I am glad to hear that, madam. The villagers seem well-disposed, and the bus is the best they can do.'

He spoke of the villagers as though they were the aboriginal inhabitants of some country which was still in the process of being explored. Mrs Bradley gave a harsh little snort of amusement and then observed,

'Did the AA scout stop and speak to you? Or did you ask him for information?'

'No, madam, neither at all. He was mending a puncture when I passed him.'

'Was that on your journey to the village or on the return here?'

'Just now, madam. I saw no one on my journey to the village.'

'Interesting,' said Mrs Bradley, thinking of her Ordnance map. 'Punctures are a nuisance, George, are they not? If you see him again you might ask him whether *Daisy Bell* met her husband on top of the hill.'

Just then the bus arrived. Off it jumped a police sergeant and a constable, who, under Mrs Bradley's direction, lifted the girl and placed her on one of the seats, of which the bus had two, running the whole of the inside length of the vehicle.

'You take the car to the hotel, George. I'll be there as soon as I can,' said his employer. 'Now, constable, we have to hold her as still as we can. Sergeant, kindly instruct the driver to avoid the bumps in the road, and then come in here and hold my coat to screen the light from her head. Is there a hospital in the village?'

'No, ma'am. There's a home for inebriates, though. That's the nearest thing. We're going to take her there, and Constable Fogg is fetching Doctor MacBain.'

'Splendid,' said Mrs Bradley, and devoted herself thenceforward entirely to her patient.

One morning some days later, when the mist had cleared from the moors and the sun was shining on every drop of moisture, she sent for the car, and thus addressed her chauffeur:

'Well, did you give the scout my message?'

'Yes, madam, but he did not comprehend it.'

'Indeed? And did you explain?'

'No, madam, not being instructed.'

'Excellent, child. We shall drive to the fatal spot, and there we shall see—what we shall see.'

George, looking haughty because he felt befogged, held open the door of the car, and Mrs Bradley put her foot on the step.

'I'll sit in front, George,' she said.

The car began to mount slowly to the bend where the accident had come to their notice. George was pulling up, but his employer invited him to go on.

'Our goal is the top of the hill, George. That is where they were to meet, you remember. That is the proper place from which to begin our inquiry. Is it not strange and interesting to consider all the motives for murder and attempted murder that come to men's minds? To women's minds, too, of course. The greater includes the less.'

She cackled harshly. George who (although he would have found it difficult to account for his opinion) had always conceived her to be an ardent feminist, looked at the road ahead, and did not relax his expression of dignified aloofness.

Prevented, by the fact that he was driving, from poking him in the ribs (her natural reaction to an attitude such as the one he was displaying), Mrs Bradley grinned tigerishly, and the car crawled on up the worst and steepest part of the gradient.

George then broke his silence.

'In my opinion, madam, no young woman losing her brakes on such a hill could have got off so light as *she* did, nor that tandem either.'

'True, George.'

'If you will excuse the question, madam, what put the idea of an attempt on her into your mind?'

'I suppose the piscina, George.'

George concluded that she was amusing herself at his expense and accepted the reply for what it was worth, which to him was nothing, since he did not know what a piscina was (and was habitually averse to seeking such information). He drove on a little faster as the gradient eased to one in seven and then to one in ten.

'Just here, George,' said his employer. 'Run off on to the turf on the right-hand side.'

George pulled up very close to the AA telephone which he had used before. Here the main road cut away from the route they had traversed and an AA scout was on duty at the junction.

'"*Behind the barn, down on my knees*,"' observed Mrs Bradley, chanting the words in what she fondly believed to be accents of their origin, '"*I thought I heard a chicken sneeze*"—and I did, too. Come and look at this, George.'

It was the bright pink vest. There was no mistaking it, although it was stained now, messily and rustily, with blood.

'Not *her* blood, George; *his*,' remarked Mrs Bradley. 'I wonder he dared bring it back here, all the same. And I wonder where the young woman the first time fell off the tandem?' She looked again at the blood-stained vest. 'He must have cut himself badly, but, of course, he had to get enough blood to make the white stone look impressive, and he wanted the vest to smear it on with so that he need use nothing of his own. Confused thinking, George, on the whole, but murderers do think confusedly, and one can feel for them, of course.'

She sent George to fetch the AA scout, who observed,

'Was it the young woman as fell off bottom of Countsferry? Must have had a worse tumble just here by the box than Stanley seemed to think. He booked the tumble in his private log. Would you be the young woman's relatives, ma'am?'

'We represent her interests,' said Mrs Bradley, remarking afterwards to George that she thought they might consider themselves as doing so since they had saved her life.

'Well, he's left the log with me, and it do seem to show the cause of her shaking up. Must have been dazed like, and not seen the bend as it was coming, and run herself into the wall. And Stanley, they do say, must have gone over the cliff in trying to save her, for he ain't been back on duty any more. Cruel, these parts, they be.'

'Did her fall upset both her brakes, then?' Mrs Bradley inquired. She read the laconic entry in the exercise book presented for her inspection and, having earned the scout's gratitude in the customary simple manner, she returned to the car with the vest (which the scout had not seen) pushed into the large pocket of her skirt.

'Stop at the scene of the accident, George,' she said. 'She seemed,' said George admiringly later on to those who were standing him a pint in exchange for the story, 'like a bloodhound on the murderer's trail.'

'For a murderer he was, in intention, if not in fact,' continued George, taking, without his own knowledge, a recognized though debatable ecclesiastical view. 'She climbed up the bank and on to the moor as if she knew just what to look for, madam did. She showed me the very stone she reckoned he hit the young woman over the head with, and then where he sunk in the soft earth deeper than his first treads, because he was carrying the body back to the tandem to make out she crashed and fell off.'

'And didn't she crash?' his hearers wanted to know.

'Crash? What her? A young woman who, to give her her due (although I don't hold with such things), had cycled that tandem —sports model and meant for two men—all the way down there from London? No. He crashed the tandem himself after he'd done her in. That was to deceive the police or anybody else that found her. He followed her on his bike down the hill with the deed in his heart. You see, he was her husband.

'But he didn't deceive me and madam, not by a long chalk he didn't! Why, first thing I said to her, I said, "Didn't it ought to be buckled up more than that if she came down that hill without brakes?" 'Course, that was his little mistake. That, and using her vest. I hope they give him ten years!

'Well, back we went up the hill to where madam found the paper bag and its etceteras. The only blood we could see was on the only white stone.'

The barmaid at this point begged him to stop. He gave her the horrors, she said.

'So what?' one listener inquired.

'Well, the whole bag of tricks was to show that *someone*, and that someone a man and a cyclist, had gone over the cliff and was killed, like the other scout said. That was going to be our scout's alibi if the police ever got on his track, so madam thinks, but he hoped he wouldn't need to use that; it was just his stand-by, like. The other AA man had seen him go off duty. That was his danger, or so he thought, not reckoning on madam and me. He'd fixed the head of the young woman's machine while she stood talking to him at the AA telephone, so that when she mounted it threw her. That was to show (that's why he logged it, see?) as she mightn't have been herself when she took the bend. Pretty little idea.'

Three days later Mrs Bradley said to him,

'They will be able to establish motive at the trial, George. Bell—I call him that—was arrested yesterday evening. He had insured his wife, it appears, as soon as they were married, and wished to obtain possession of the money.'

'But what I would still like to know, madam,' George observed, 'is what put the thought of murder into your mind before ever we saw the accident or even the bag and the blood.'

'The bag and the blood, for some reason, sounds perfectly horrible, George.'

'But, madam, you spotted the marks he'd made on that edge with his push-bike as though you'd been *waiting* to spot them. And you fixed on him as the murderer, too, straight away.'

'Ah, that was easy, George. You see, he never mentioned that he'd seen you go by in the car, and you told me that on your journey to the village to find assistance you had not seen him either. Therefore, since he must have been somewhere along that road, I asked myself why, even if he should have left the roadside himself, his bicycle should not have been visible. Besides, he was the perfect answer to several questions which, up to that time, I had had to ask myself. One was: why did they choose to meet at the top of that hill? Another was: why did he risk bending over the injured girl to fix her feet back in those rat-trap pedals we saw and out of which, I should imagine, her feet would most certainly have been pulled if she'd had such a very bad crash?'

'Ah, yes, the AA box and the AA uniform, madam. In other words, Mr G. K. Chesterton's postman all over again.'

'Precisely, George. The obvious meeting place, in the circumstances, and the conspicuous yet easily forgotten uniform.'

'But, madam, if I may revert, what *did* turn your mind to murder?'

'The piscina, George,' Mrs Bradley solemnly reminded him. George looked at her, hesitated, then overrode the habit of years and inquired,

'What *is* a piscina, madam?'

'A drain, George. Merely a drain.

> '"Now, body, turn to air,
> Or Lucifer will bear thee quick to hell!
> O soul, be chang'd into little water drops,
> And fall into the ocean, ne'er be found!"'

MARGERY ALLINGHAM · 1904–1966

Three is a Lucky Number

At five o'clock on a September afternoon Ronald Frederick Torbay
was making preparations for his third murder. He was being very
wary, forcing himself to go slowly because he was perfectly sane and
was well aware of the dangers of carelessness.

A career of homicide got more chancy as one went on. That piece of
information had impressed him as being true as soon as he had read it
in a magazine article way back before his first marriage. Also, he
realized, success was liable to go to a man's head, so he kept a tight
hold on himself. He was certain he was infinitely more clever than
most human beings but he did not dwell on the fact and as soon as he
felt the old thrill at the sense of his power welling up inside him, he
quelled it firmly.

For an instant he paused, leaning on the rim of the wash-basin, and
regarded himself thoughtfully in the shaving glass of the bathroom in
the new villa he had hired so recently.

The face which looked at him was thin, middle-aged, and pallid.
Sparse dark hair receded from its high narrow forehead and the
well-shaped eyes were blue and prominent. Only the mouth was
really unusual. That narrow slit, quite straight, was almost lipless
and, unconsciously, he persuaded it to relax into a half smile. Even
Ronald Torbay did not like his own mouth.

A sound in the kitchen below disturbed him and he straightened
his back hastily. If Edyth had finished her ironing she would be
coming up to take her long discussed bubble-bath before he had
prepared it for her and that would never do. He waited, holding his
breath, but it was all right: she was going out of the back door. He
reached the window just in time to see her disappearing round the
side of the house into the small square yard which was so exactly like
all the other square yards in the long suburban street. He knew that
she was going to hang the newly pressed linen on the line to air and
although the manœuvre gave him the time he needed, still it irritated
him.

Of the three homely middle-aged women whom so far he had

persuaded first to marry him and then to will him their modest possessions, Edyth was proving easily the most annoying. If he had told her once not to spend so much time in the yard he had done it a dozen times in their six weeks of marriage. He hated her being out of doors alone. She was shy and reserved but now that new people had moved in next door there was the danger of some over-friendly woman starting up an acquaintance with her and that was the last thing to be tolerated at this juncture.

Each of his former wives had been shy. He had been very careful to choose the right type and felt he owed much of his success to it. Mary, the first of them, had met her fatal 'accident' almost unnoticed in the bungalow on the housing estate very like the present one he had chosen but in the north instead of the south of England. At the time it had been a growing place, the coroner had been hurried, the police sympathetic but busy and the neighbours scarcely curious except that one of them, a junior reporter on a local paper, had written a flowery paragraph about the nearness of tragedy in the midst of joy, published a wedding day snapshot and had entitled the article with typical northern understatement 'Honeymoon Mishap'.

Dorothy's brief excursion into his life and abrupt exit from it and her own, had given him a little more bother but not much. She had deceived him when she had told him she was quite alone in the world and the interfering brother who had turned up after the funeral to ask awkward questions about her small fortune might have been a nuisance if Ronald had not been very firm with him. There had been a brief court case which Ronald had won handsomely and the insurance had paid up without a murmur.

All that was four years ago. Now, with a new name, a newly invented background and a fresh area in which to operate, he felt remarkably safe.

From the moment he had first seen Edyth, sitting alone at a little table under the window in a seaside hotel dining-room, he had known that she was to be his next subject. He always thought of his wives as 'subjects'. It lent his designs upon them a certain pseudo-scientific atmosphere which he found satisfying.

Edyth had sat there looking stiff and neat and a trifle severe but there had been a secret timidity in her face, an unsatisfied, half-frightened expression in her short-sighted eyes and once, when the waiter said something pleasant to her, she had flushed nervously and had been embarrassed by it. She was also wearing a genuine diamond brooch. Ronald had observed that from right across the room. He had an eye for stones.

That evening in the lounge he had spoken to her, had weathered the initial snub, tried again and, finally, had got her to talk. After that the acquaintance had progressed just as he had expected. His methods were old-fashioned and heavily romantic and within a week she was hopelessly infatuated.

From Ronald's point of view her history was even better than he could have hoped. After teaching in a girls' boarding school for the whole of her twenties she had been summoned home to look after her recluse of a father whose long illness had monopolized her life. Now at forty-three she was alone, comparatively well off and as much at sea as a ship without a rudder.

Ronald was careful not to let her toes touch the ground. He devoted his entire attention to her and exactly five weeks from the day on which they first met, he married her at the registry office of the town where they were both strangers. The same afternoon they each made wills in the other's favour and moved into the villa which he had been able to hire cheaply because the holiday season was at an end.

It had been the pleasantest conquest he had ever made. Mary had been moody and hysterical, Dorothy grudging and suspicious but Edyth had revealed an unexpected streak of gaiety and, but for her stupidity in not realizing that a man would hardly fall romantically in love with her at first sight, was a sensible person. Any other man, Ronald reflected smugly, might have made the fatal mistake of feeling sorry for her, but he was 'above' all that, he told himself, and he began to make plans for what he described in his own mind rather grimly as 'her future'.

Two things signed her death warrant earlier than had been his original intention. One was her obstinate reticence over her monetary affairs and the other was her embarrassing interest in his job.

On the marriage certificate Ronald had described himself as a salesman and the story he was telling was that he was a junior partner in a firm of cosmetic manufacturers who were giving him a very generous leave of absence. Edyth accepted the statement without question, but almost at once she had begun to plan a visit to the office and the factory, and was always talking about the new clothes she must buy so as not to 'disgrace him'. At the same time she kept all her business papers locked in an old writing-case and steadfastly refused to discuss them however cautiously he raised the subject. Ronald had given up feeling angry with her and decided to act.

He turned from the window, carefully removed his jacket and began to run the bath. His heart was pounding, he noticed, frowning. He wished it would not. He needed to keep very calm.

The bathroom was the one room they had repainted. Ronald had done it himself soon after they had arrived and had put up the little shelf over the bath to hold a jar of bathsalts he had bought and a small electric heater of the old-fashioned two-element type, which was cheap but white like the walls and not too noticeable. He leant forward now and switched it on and stood looking at it until the two bars of glowing warmth appeared. Then he turned away and went out on to the landing, leaving it alight.

The fuse box which controlled all the electricity in the house was concealed in the bottom of the linen cupboard at the top of the stairs. Ronald opened the door carefully and using his handkerchief so that his fingerprints should leave no trace pulled up the main switch. Back in the bathroom the heater's glow died away; the bars were almost black again by the time he returned. He eyed the slender cabinet approvingly and then, still using the handkerchief, he lifted it bodily from the shelf and lowered it carefully into the water, arranging it so that it lay at an angle over the waste plug, close to the foot where it took up practically no room at all. The white flex ran up over the porcelain side of the bath, along the skirting board, under the door and into the wall socket, just outside on the landing.

When he had first installed the heater Edyth had demurred at this somewhat slipshod arrangement, but when he had explained that the local Council was stupid and fussy about fitting wall sockets in bathrooms since water was said to be a conductor she had compromised by letting him run the flex under the lino where it was not so noticeable.

At the moment the heater was perfectly visible in the bath. It certainly looked as if it had fallen into its odd position accidentally but no one in his senses could have stepped into the water without seeing it. Ronald paused, his eyes dark, his ugly mouth narrower than ever. The beautiful simplicity of the main plan, so certain, so swiftly fatal and above all, so safe as far as he himself was concerned gave him a thrill of pleasure as it always did. He turned off the bath and waited, listening. Edyth was coming back. He could hear her moving something on the concrete way outside the back door below and he leant over to where his jacket hung and took a plastic sachet from its inside breast pocket. He was re-reading the directions on the back of it when a slight sound made him turn his head and he saw, to his horror, the woman herself not five feet away. Her neat head had appeared suddenly just above the flat roof of the scullery, outside the bathroom window. She was clearing the dead leaves from the guttering and must, he guessed, be standing on the tall flight of steps which were kept just inside the back door.

It was typical of the man that he did not panic. Still holding the sachet lightly he stepped between her and the bath and spoke mildly.

'What on earth are you doing there, darling?'

Edyth started so violently at the sound of his voice that she almost fell off the steps and a flush of apprehension appeared on her thin cheeks.

'Oh, how you startled me! I thought I'd just do this little job before I came up to change. If it rains the gutter floods all over the back step.'

'Very thoughtful of you, my dear.' He spoke with that slightly acid amusement with which he had found he could best destroy her slender vein of self assurance. 'But not terribly clever when you knew I'd come up to prepare your beauty bath for you. Or was it?'

The slight intonation on the word 'beauty' was not lost on her. He saw her swallow.

'Perhaps it wasn't,' she said without looking at him. 'It's very good of you to take all this trouble, Ronald.'

'Not at all,' he said with a just amount of masculine, offhand insensitivity. 'I'm taking you out tonight and I want you to look as nice as—er—possible. Hurry up, there's a good girl. The foam doesn't last indefinitely and like all these very high-class beauty treatments the ingredients are expensive. Undress in the bedroom, put on your gown and come straight along.'

'Very well, dear.' She began to descend at once while he turned to the bath and shook the contents of the sachet into the water. The crystals, which were peach coloured and smelled strongly of roses, floated on the tide and then, as he suddenly turned the pressure of water full on, began to dissolve into thousands of irridescent bubbles. A momentary fear that their camouflage would not prove to be sufficient assailed him, and he stooped to beat the water with his hand, but he need not have worried. The cloud grew and grew into a fragrant feathery mass which not only obscured the bottom of the bath and all it contained, but mounted the porcelain sides, smothering the white flex and overflowing on to the wall panels and the bath-mat. It was perfect.

He pulled on his jacket and opened the door.

'Edyth! Hurry, dearest!' The words were on the tip of his tongue but her arrival forestalled them. She came shrinking in, her blue dressing-gown strained round her thin body, her hair thrust into an unbecoming bathing cap.

'Oh, Ronald!' she said, staring at the display aghast. 'Won't it make an awful mess? Goodness! All over the floor!'

Her hesitation infuriated him.

'That won't matter,' he said savagely. 'You get in while the virtue of the foam is still there. Hurry. Meanwhile I'll go and change, myself. I'll give you ten minutes. Get straight in and lie down. It'll take some of the sallowness out of that skin of yours.'

He went out and paused, listening. She locked the door as he had known she would. The habit of a lifetime does not suddenly change with marriage. He heard the bolt slide home and forced himself to walk slowly down the passage. He gave her sixty seconds. Thirty to take off her things and thirty to hesitate on the brink of the rosy mass.

'How is it?' he shouted from the linen cupboard doorway.

She did not answer at once and the sweat broke out on his forehead. Then he heard her.

'I don't know yet. I'm only just in. It smells lovely.'

He did not wait for the final word, his hand wrapped in his handkerchief had found the main switch again.

'One, two . . . three,' he said with horrible prosaicness and pulled it down.

From the wall socket behind him there was a single spluttering flare as the fuse went and then silence.

All round Ronald it was so quiet that he could hear the pulses in his own body, the faraway tick of a clock at the bottom of the stairs, the dreary buzzing of a fly imprisoned against the window glass and, from the garden next door, the drone of a mower as the heavy, fresh-faced man who had moved there, performed his weekly chore shaving the little green lawn. But from the bathroom there was no sound at all.

After a while he crept back along the passage and tapped at the door.

'Edyth?'

No. There was no response, no sound, nothing.

'Edyth?' he said again.

The silence was complete and, after a minute, he straightened his back and let out a deep sighing breath.

Almost at once he was keyed up again in preparing for the second phase. As he knew well, this next was the tricky period. The discovery of the body had got to be made but not too soon. He had made that mistake about Dorothy's 'accident' and had actually been asked by the local inspector why he had taken alarm so soon, but he had kept his head and the dangerous moment had flickered past. This time he had made up his mind to make it half an hour before he began to hammer loudly at the door, then to shout for a neighbour and finally to force the lock. He had planned to stroll out to buy an evening paper in the interim, shouting his intention to do so to Edyth from the front step for any passer-by to hear, but as he walked back along the landing he knew there was something else he was going to do first.

Edyth's leather writing-case in which she kept all her private papers was in the bottom of her soft-topped canvas hatbox. She had really believed he had not known of its existence, he reflected bitterly. It was locked, as he had discovered when he had at last located it, and he had not prized the catch for fear of putting her on her guard, but now there was nothing to stop him.

He went softly into the bedroom and opened the wardrobe door. The case was exactly where he had last seen it, plump and promising, and his hands closed over it gratefully. The catch was a little more difficult than he had expected but he got it open at last and the orderly contents of the leather box came into view. At first sight it was all most satisfactory, far better than he had anticipated. There were bundles of savings certificates, one or two thick envelopes whose red seals suggested the offices of lawyers and, on top, ready for the taking, one of those familiar blue books which the Post Office issues to its savings bank clients.

He opened it with shaking fingers and fluttered through the pages. Two thousand. The sum made him whistle. Two thousand eight hundred and fifty. She must have paid in a decent dividend there. Two thousand nine hundred. Then a drop as she had drawn out a hundred pounds for her trousseau. Two thousand eight hundred. He thought that was the final entry but on turning the page saw that there was yet one other recorded transaction. It was less than a week old. He remembered the book coming back through the mail and how clever she had thought she had been in smuggling the envelope out of sight. He glanced at the written words and figures idly at first but then as his heart jolted in sudden panic stared at them, his eyes prominent and glazed. She had taken almost all of it out. There it was in black and white: *September 4th Withdrawal Two thousand seven hundred and ninety-eight pounds*.

His first thought was that the money must still be there, in hundred-pound notes perhaps in one of the envelopes. He tore through them hastily, forgetting all caution in his anxiety. Papers, letters, certificates fell on the floor in confusion.

The envelope, addressed to himself, pulled him up short. It was new and freshly blotted, the name inscribed in Edyth's own unexpectedly firm hand. Ronald Torbay, Esqre.

He wrenched it open and smoothed the single sheet of bond paper within. The date, he noted in amazement, was only two days old.

Dear Ronald,

If you ever get this I am afraid it will prove a dreadful shock to you. For a long time I have been hoping that it might not be necessary to write it but now your behaviour has forced me to face some very unpleasant possibilities.

I am afraid, Ronald, that in some ways you are very old-fashioned. Had it not occurred to you that any homely middle-aged woman who has been swept into hasty marriage to a stranger must, unless she is a perfect idiot, be just a little suspicious and touchy on the subject of *baths*?

Your predecessor James Joseph Smith and his Brides are not entirely forgotten, you know.

Frankly, I did not want to suspect you. For a long time I thought I was in love with you, but when you persuaded me to make my will on our wedding day I could not help wondering, and then as soon as you started fussing about the bathroom in this house I thought I had better do something about it rather quickly. I am old-fashioned too, so I went to the police.

Have you noticed that the people who have moved into the house next door have never tried to speak to you? We thought it best that I should merely talk to the woman over the garden wall, and it is she who has shewn me the two cuttings from old provincial newspapers each about women who met with fatal accidents in bubble-baths soon after their marriages. In each case there was a press snapshot of the husband taken at the funeral. They are not very clear but as soon as I saw them I realized that it was my duty to agree to the course suggested to me by the inspector who has been looking for a man answering that description for three years, ever since the two photographs were brought to his notice by your poor second wife's brother.

What I am trying to say is this: if you should ever lose me, Ronald, out of the bathroom I mean, you will find that I have gone out over the roof and am sitting in my dressing-gown in the kitchen next door. I was a fool to marry you but not quite such a fool as you assumed. Women may be silly but they are not so stupid as they used to be. We are picking up the idea, Ronald.

Yours, Edyth

P.S. On re-reading this note I see that in my nervousness I have forgotten to mention that the new people next door are not a married couple but Detective Constable Batsford of the CID and his assistant, Policewoman Richards. The police assure me that there cannot be sufficient evidence to convict you if you are not permitted to attempt the crime again. That is why I am forcing myself to be brave and to play my part, for I am very sorry for those other poor wives of yours, Ronald. They must have found you as fascinating as I did.

With his slit mouth twisted into an abominable 'O', Ronald Torbay raised haggard eyes from the letter.

The house was still quiet and even the whine of the mower in the next door garden had ceased. In the hush he heard a sudden clatter as the back door burst open and heavy footsteps raced through the hall and up the stairs towards him.

NICHOLAS BLAKE · 1904–1972

The Assassins' Club

'No,' thought Nigel Strangeways, looking round the table, 'no one would ever guess.'

Ever since, quarter of an hour ago, they had assembled in the ante-room for sherry, Nigel had been feeling more and more nervous —a nervousness greater than the prospect of having to make an after-dinner speech seemed to warrant. It was true that, as the guest of honour, something more than the usual post-prandial convivialities would be expected of him. And of course the company present would, from its nature, be especially critical. But still, he had done this sort of thing often enough before; he knew he was pretty good at it. Why the acute state of jitters, then? After it was all over, Nigel was tempted to substitute 'foreboding' for 'jitters'; to wonder whether he oughtn't to have proclaimed these very curious feelings, like Cassandra, from the house-top—even at the risk of spoiling what looked like being a real peach of a dinner party. After all, the dinner party did get spoiled, anyway, and soon enough, too. But, taking all things into consideration, it probably wouldn't have made any difference.

It was in an attempt to dispel this cloud of uneasiness that Nigel began to play with himself the old game of identity-guessing. There was a curious uniformity amongst the faces of the majority of the twenty-odd diners. The women—there were only three of them —looked homely, humorous, dowdy-and-be-damned-to-it. The men, Nigel finally decided, resembled in the mass sanitary inspectors or very minor Civil Servants. They were most of them rather undersized, and ran to drooping moustaches, gold-rimmed spectacles, and a general air of mild ineffectualness. There were exceptions, of course. That elderly man in the middle of the table, with the face of a dyspeptic and superannuated bloodhound—it was not difficult to place him; even without the top hat or the wig with which the public normally associated him, Lord Justice Pottinger could easily be recognized—the most celebrated criminal judge of his generation. Then that leonine, mobile face on his left; it had been as much photographed as any society beauty's; and well it might, for Sir

Eldred Traver's golden tongue had—it was whispered—saved as many murderers as Justice Pottinger had hanged. There were one or two other exceptions, such as the dark-haired, poetic-looking young man sitting on Nigel's right and rolling bread-pellets.

'No,' said Nigel, aloud this time, 'no one would possibly guess.'

'Guess what?' inquired the young man.

'The bloodthirsty character of this assembly.' He took up the menu-card, at the top of which was printed in red letters

THE ASSASSINS

Dinner, December 20th.

'No,' laughed the young man, 'we don't look like murderers, I must admit—not not even murderers by proxy.'

'Good lord! are you in the trade, too?'

'Yes. Ought to have introduced myself. Name of Herbert Dale.'

Nigel looked at the young man with increased interest. Dale had published only two crime-novels, but he was already accepted as one of the *élite* of detective writers; he could not otherwise have been a member of that most exclusive of clubs, the Assassins; for, apart from a representative of the Bench, the Bar, and Scotland Yard, this club was composed solely of the princes of detective fiction.

It was at this point that Nigel observed two things—that the hand which incessantly rolled bread-pellets was shaking, and that, on the glossy surface of the menu-card Dale had just laid down, there was a moist finger-mark.

'Are you making a speech, too?' Nigel said.

'Me? Good lord, no. Why?'

'I thought you looked nervous,' said Nigel, in his direct way.

The young man laughed, a little too loudly. And, as though that was some kind of signal, one of those unrehearsed total silences fell upon the company. Even in the street outside, the noises seemed to be damped, as though an enormous soft pedal had been pressed down on everything. Nigel realized that it must have been snowing since he came in. A disagreeable sensation of eeriness crept over him. Annoyed with this sensation—a detective has no right to feel psychic, he reflected angrily, not even a private detective as celebrated as Nigel Strangeways—he forced himself to look round the brilliantly lighted room, the animated yet oddly neutral-looking faces of the diners, the *maître d'hôtel* in his white gloves—bland and un-creased as his own face, the impassive waiters. Everything was perfectly normal; and yet . . . Some motive he was never after able satisfactorily to explain forced him to let drop into the yawning silence:

'What a marvellous setting this would be for a murder.'

If Nigel had been looking in the right direction at that moment, things might have happened very differently. As it was, he didn't even notice the way Dale's wineglass suddenly tilted and spilt a few drops of sherry.

At once the whole table buzzed again with conversation. A man three places away on Nigel's right raised his head, which had been almost buried in his soup-plate, and said:

'Tchah! This is the one place where a murder would never happen. My respected colleagues are men of peace. I doubt if any of them has the guts to say boo to a goose. Oh, yes, they'd *like* to be men of action, tough guys. But, I ask you, just look at them! That's why they became detective writers. Wish fulfilment, the psychoanalysts call it— though I don't give much for that gang, either. But it's quite safe, spilling blood, as long as you only do it on paper.'

The man turned his thick lips and small, arrogant eyes towards Nigel. 'The trouble with you amateur investigators is that you're so romantic. That's why the police beat you to it every time.'

A thick-set, swarthy man opposite him exclaimed: 'You're wrong there, Mr Carruthers. We don't seem to have beaten Mr Strangeways to it in the past every time.'

'So our aggressive friend is *the* David Carruthers. Well, well,' whispered Nigel to Dale.

'Yes,' said Dale, not modifying his tone at all. 'A squalid fellow, isn't he? But he gets the public all right. We have sold our thousands, but David has sold his tens of thousands. Got a yellow streak though, I'll bet, in spite of his bluster. Pity somebody doesn't bump him off at this dinner, just to show him he's not the infallible Pope he sets up to be.'

Carruthers shot a vicious glance at Dale. 'Why not try it yourself? Get you a bit of notoriety, anyway; might even sell your books. Though,' he continued, clapping on the shoulder a nondescript little man who was sitting between him and Dale, 'I think little Crippen here would be my first bet. You'd like to have my blood, Crippen, wouldn't you?'

The little man said stiffly: 'Don't make yourself ridiculous, Carruthers. You must be drunk already. And I'd thank you to remember that my name is Cripps.'

At this point the president interposed with a convulsive change of subject, and the dinner resumed its even tenor. While they were disposing of some very tolerable trout, a waiter informed Dale that he was wanted on the telephone. The young man went out. Nigel was trying at the same time to listen to a highly involved story of the president's and decipher the very curious expression on Cripps's face, when all the lights went out too. . . .

There were a few seconds of astonished silence. Then a torrent of talk broke out—the kind of forced jocularity with which man still comforts himself in the face of sudden darkness. Nigel could hear movement all round him, the pushing-back of chairs, quick, muffled treads on the carpet—waiters, no doubt. Someone at the end of the table, rather ridiculously, struck a match; it did nothing but emphasize the pitch-blackness.

'Stevens, can't someone light the candles?' exclaimed the president irritably.

'Excuse me, sir,' came the voice of the *maître d'hôtel*, 'there are no candles. Harry, run along to the fuse-box and find out what's gone wrong.'

The door banged behind the waiter. Less than a minute later the lights all blazed on again. Blinking, like swimmers come up from a deep dive, the diners looked at each other. Nigel observed that Carruthers's face was even nearer his food than usual. Curious, to go on eating all the time——— But no, his head was right on top of the food—lying in the plate like John the Baptist's. And from between his shoulder-blades there stood out a big white handle; the handle —good God! it couldn't be; this was too macabre altogether—but it *was*—the handle of a fish-slice.

A kind of gobbling noise came out of Justice Pottinger's mouth. All eyes turned to where his shaking hand pointed, grew wide with horror, and then turned ludicrously back to him, as though he was about to direct the jury.

'God bless my soul!' was all the Judge could say.

But someone had sized up the whole situation. The thick-set man who had been sitting opposite Carruthers was already standing with his back to the door. His voice snapped:

'Stay where you are, everyone. I'm afraid there's no doubt about this. I must take charge of this case at once. Mr Strangeways, will you go and ring up Scotland Yard—police surgeon, fingerprint men, photographers—the whole bag of tricks; you know what we want.'

Nigel sprang up. His gaze, roving round the room, had registered something different, some detail missing; but his mind couldn't identify it. Well, perhaps it would come to him later. He moved towards the door. And just then the door opened brusquely, pushing the thick-set man away from it. There was a general gasp, as though everyone expected to see something walk in with blood on its hands. It was only young Dale, a little white in the face, but grinning amiably.

'What on earth————?' he began. Then he, too, saw . . .

An hour later, Nigel and the thick-set man, Superintendent Bateman, were alone in the ante-room. The princes of detective fiction were huddled together in another room, talking in shocked whispers.

'Don't like the real thing, do they, sir?' the Superintendent had commented sardonically; 'do 'em good to be up against a flesh-and-blood problem for once. I wish 'em luck with it.'

'Well,' he was saying now. 'Doesn't seem like much of a loss to the world, this Carruthers. None of 'em got a good word for him. Too much food, too much drink, too many women. But that doesn't give us a motive. Now this Cripps. Carruthers said Cripps would like to have his blood. Why was that, d'you suppose?'

'You can search me. Cripps wasn't giving anything away when we interviewed him.'

'He had enough opportunity. All he had to do when the lights went out was to step over to the buffet, take up the first knife he laid hands on—probably thought the fish-slice was a carving-knife—stab him, and sit down and twiddle his fingers.'

'Yes, he could have wrapped his handkerchief round the handle. That would account for there being no fingerprints. And there's no one to swear he moved from his seat; Dale was out of the room—and it's a bit late now to ask Carruthers, who was on his other side. But, if he *did* do it, everything happened very luckily for him.'

'Then there's young Dale himself,' said Bateman, biting the side of his thumb. 'Talked a lot of hot air about bumping Carruthers off before it happened. Might be a double bluff. You see, Mr Strangeways, there's no doubt about that waiter's evidence. The main switch was thrown over. Now, what about this? Dale arranges to be called up during dinner; answers call; then goes and turns off the main switch —in gloves, I suppose, because there's only the waiter's fingerprints on it—comes back under cover of darkness, stabs his man, and goes out again.'

'Mm,' ruminated Nigel, 'but the motive? And where are the gloves? And why, if it was premeditated, such an outlandish weapon?'

'If he's hidden the gloves, we'll find 'em soon enough. And————' the Superintendent was interrupted by the tinkle of the telephone at his elbow. A brief dialogue ensued. Then he turned to Nigel.

'Man I sent round to interview Morton—bloke who rang Dale up at dinner. Swears he was talking to Dale for three to five minutes. That seems to let Dale out, unless it was collusion.'

That moment a plain-clothes man entered, a grin of ill-concealed triumph on his face. He handed a rolled-up pair of black kid gloves to Bateman. 'Tucked away behind the pipes in the lavatories, sir.'

Bateman unrolled them. There were stains on the fingers. He glanced inside the wrists, then passed the gloves to Nigel, pointing at some initials stamped there.

'Well, well,' said Nigel. 'H. D. Let's have him in again. Looks as if that telephone call *was* collusion.'

'Yes, we've got him now.'

But when the young man entered and saw the gloves lying on the table his reactions were very different from what the Superintendent had expected. An expression of relief, instead of the spasm of guilt, passed over his face.

'Stupid of me,' he said, 'I lost my head for a few minutes, after———— But I'd better start at the beginning. Carruthers was always bragging about his nerve and the tight corners he'd been in and so on. A poisonous specimen. So Morton and I decided to play a practical joke on him. He was to 'phone me up; I was to go out and throw the main switch, then come back and pretend to strangle Carruthers from behind—just give him a thorough shaking-up—and leave a blood-curdling message on his plate to the effect that this was just a warning, and next time the Unknown would do the thing properly. We reckoned he'd be gibbering with fright when I turned up the lights again! Well, everything went all right till I came up behind him; but then—then I happened to touch that knife, and I knew somebody had been there before me, in earnest. Afraid, I lost my nerve then, especially when I found I'd got some of his blood on my gloves. So I hid them, and burnt the spoof message. Damn silly of me. The whole idea was damn silly, I can see that now.'

'Why gloves at all?' asked Nigel.

'Well, they say it's your hands and your shirt-front that are likely to show in the dark; so I put on black gloves and pinned my coat over my shirt-front. And, I say,' he added in a deprecating way, 'I don't want to teach you fellows your business, but if I had really meant to kill him, would I have worn gloves with my initials on them?'

'That is as may be,' said Bateman coldly, 'but I must warn you that you are in————'

'Just a minute,' Nigel interrupted. 'Why should Cripps have wanted Carruthers's blood?'

'Oh, you'd better ask Cripps. If he won't tell you, I don't think I ought to————'

'Don't be a fool. You're in a damned tight place, and you can't afford to be chivalrous.'

'Very well. Little Cripps may be dim, but he's a good sort. He told me once, in confidence, that Carruthers had pirated an idea of his for a plot and made a best-seller out of it. A rotten thing to do. But—dash it—no one would commit murder just because————'

'You must leave that for us to decide, Mr Dale,' said the Superintendent.

When the young man had gone out, under the close surveillance of a constable, Bateman turned wearily to Nigel.

'Well,' he said, 'it may be him; and it may be Cripps. But, with all these crime-authors about, it might be any of 'em.'

Nigel leapt up from his seat. 'Yes,' he exclaimed, 'and that's why we've not thought of anyone else. And'—his eyes lit up—'by Jove! now I've remembered it—the missing detail. Quick! Are all those waiters and chaps still there?'

'Yes; we've kept 'em in the dining-room. But what the————?'

Nigel ran into the dining-room, Bateman at his heels. He looked out of one of the windows, open at the top.

'What's down below there?' he asked the *maître d'hôtel*.

'A yard, sir; the kitchen windows look out on it.'

'And now, where was Sir Eldred Travers sitting?'

The man pointed to the place without hesitation, his imperturbable face betraying not the least surprise.

'Right; will you go and ask him to step this way for a minute. Oh, by the way,' he added, as the *maître d'hôtel* reached the door, '*where are your gloves?*'

The man's eyes flickered. 'My gloves, sir?'

'Yes; before the lights went out you were wearing white gloves; after they went up again, I remembered it just now, you were not wearing them. Are they in the yard by any chance?'

The man shot a desperate glance around him; then the bland composure of his face broke up. He collapsed, sobbing, into a chair.

'My daughter—he ruined her—she killed herself. When the lights went out, it was too much for me—the opportunity. He deserved it. I'm not sorry.'

'Yes,' said Nigel, ten minutes later, 'it was too much for him. He picked up the first weapon to hand. Afterwards, knowing everyone would be searched, he had to throw the gloves out of the window. There would be blood on them. With luck, we mightn't have looked in the yard before he could get out to remove them. And, unless one was looking, one wouldn't see them against the snow. They were white.'

'What was that about Sir Eldred Travers?' asked the Superintendent.

'Oh, I wanted to put him off his guard, and to get him away from the window. He might have tried to follow his gloves.'

'Well, that fish-slice might have been a slice of bad luck for young Dale if you hadn't been here,' said the Superintendent, venturing on a witticism. 'What are you grinning away to yourself about?'

'I was just thinking, this must be the first time a Judge has been present at a murder.'

CARTER DICKSON · 1906–1977

The House in Goblin Wood

In Pall Mall, that hot July afternoon three years before the war, an open saloon car was drawn up to the curb just opposite the Senior Conservatives' Club.

And in the car sat two conspirators.

It was the drowsy post-lunch hour among the clubs, where only the sun remained brilliant. The Rag lay somnolent; the Athenæum slept outright. But these two conspirators, a dark-haired young man in his early thirties and a fair-haired girl perhaps half a dozen years younger, never moved. They stared intently at the Gothic-like front of the Senior Conservatives'.

'Look here, Eve,' muttered the young man, and punched at the steering-wheel, 'do you think this is going to work?'

'I don't know,' the fair-haired girl confessed. 'He absolutely *loathes* picnics.'

'Anyway, we've probably missed him.'

'Why so?'

'He can't have taken as long over lunch as that!' her companion protested, looking at a wrist-watch. The young man was rather shocked. 'It's a quarter to four! Even if . . .'

'Bill! There! Look there!'

Their patience was rewarded by an inspiring sight.

Out of the portals of the Senior Conservatives' Club, in awful majesty, marched a large, stout, barrel-shaped gentleman in a white linen suit.

His corporation preceded him like the figurehead of a man-of-war. His shell-rimmed spectacles were pulled down on a broad nose, all being shaded by a Panama hat. At the top of the stone steps he surveyed the street, left and right, with a lordly sneer.

'Sir Henry!' called the girl.

'Hey?' said Sir Henry Merrivale.

'I'm Eve Drayton. Don't you remember me? You knew my father!'

'Oh, ah,' said the great man.

'We've been waiting here a terribly long time,' Eve pleaded.

'Couldn't you see us for just five minutes?—The thing to do,' she whispered to her companion, 'is to keep him in a good humour. Just keep him in a good humour!'

As a matter of fact, H. M. was in a good humour, having just triumphed over the Home Secretary in an argument. But not even his own mother could have guessed it. Majestically, with the same lordly sneer, he began in grandeur to descend the steps of the Senior Conservatives'. He did this, in fact, until his foot encountered an unnoticed object lying some three feet from the bottom.

It was a banana skin.

'Oh, dear!' said the girl.

Now it must be stated with regret that in the old days certain urchins, of what were then called the 'lower orders', had a habit of placing such objects on the steps in the hope that some eminent statesman would take a toss on his way to Whitehall. This was a venial but deplorable practice, probably accounting for what Mr Gladstone said in 1882.

In any case, it accounted for what Sir Henry Merrivale said now.

From the pavement, where H. M. landed in a seated position, arose in H. M.'s bellowing voice such a torrent of profanity, such a flood of invective and vile obscenities, as has seldom before blasted the holy calm of Pall Mall. It brought the hall porter hurrying down the steps, and Eve Drayton flying out of the car.

Heads were now appearing at the windows of the Athenæum across the street.

'Is it all right?' cried the girl, with concern in her blue eyes. 'Are you hurt?'

H. M. merely looked at her. His hat had fallen off, disclosing a large bald head; and he merely sat on the pavement and looked at her.

'Anyway, H. M., get up! Please get up!'

'Yes, sir,' begged the hall porter, 'for heaven's sake get up!'

'Get up?' bellowed H. M., in a voice audible as far as St James's Street. 'Burn it all, how *can* I get up?'

'But why not?'

'My behind's out of joint,' said H. M. simply. 'I'm hurt awful bad. I'm probably goin' to have spinal dislocation for the rest of my life.'

'But, sir, people are looking!'

H. M. explained what these people could do. He eyed Eve Drayton with a glare of indescribable malignancy over his spectacles.

'I suppose, my wench, *you're* responsible for this?'

Eve regarded him in consternation.

'You don't mean the banana skin?' she cried.

'Oh, yes, I do,' said H. M., folding his arms like a prosecuting counsel.

'But we—we only wanted to invite you to a picnic!'

H. M. closed his eyes.

'That's fine,' he said in a hollow voice. 'All the same, don't you think it'd have been a subtler kind of hint just to pour mayonnaise over my head or shove ants down the back of my neck? Oh, lord love a duck!'

'I didn't mean that! I meant . . .'

'Let me help you up, sir,' interposed the calm, reassuring voice of the dark-haired and blue-chinned young man who had been with Eve in the car.

'So you want to help too, hey? And who are *you*?'

'I'm awfully sorry!' said Eve. 'I should have introduced you! This is my fiancé. Dr William Sage.'

H.M.'s face turned purple.

'I'm glad to see,' he observed, 'you had the uncommon decency to bring along a doctor. I appreciate that, I do. And the car's there, I suppose, to assist with the examination when I take off my pants?'

The hall porter uttered a cry of horror.

Bill Sage, either from jumpiness and nerves or from sheer inability to keep a straight face, laughed loudly.

'I keep telling Eve a dozen times a day,' he said, 'that I'm not to be called "doctor". I happen to be a surgeon————'

(Here H.M. really did look alarmed.)

'—but I don't think we need operate. Nor, in my opinion,' Bill gravely addressed the hall porter, 'will it be necessary to remove Sir Henry's trousers in front of the Senior Conservatives' Club.'

'Thank you very much, sir.'

'We had an infernal nerve to come here,' the young man confessed to H.M. 'But I honestly think, Sir Henry, you'd be more comfortable in the car. What about it? Let me give you a hand up?'

Yet even ten minutes later, when H.M. sat glowering in the back of the car and two heads were craned round towards him, peace was not restored.

'All right!' said Eve. Her pretty, rather stolid face was flushed; her mouth looked miserable. 'If you won't come to the picnic, you won't. But I did believe you might do it to oblige me.'

'Well . . . now!' muttered the great man uncomfortably.

'And I did think, too, you'd be interested in the other person who was coming with us. But Vicky's—difficult. She won't come either, if you don't.'

'Oh? And who's this other guest?'

'Vicky Adams.'

H.M.'s hand, which had been lifted for an oratorical gesture, dropped to his side.

'Vicky Adams? That's not the gal who . . . ?'

'Yes!' Eve nodded. 'They say it was one of the great mysteries, twenty years ago, that the police failed to solve.'

'It was, my wench,' H.M. agreed sombrely. 'It was.'

'And now Vicky's grown up. And we thought if you of all people went along, and spoke to her nicely, she'd tell us what really happened on that night.'

H.M.'s small, sharp eyes fixed disconcertingly on Eve.

'I say, my wench. What's your interest in all this?'

'Oh, reasons.' Eve glanced quickly at Bill Sage, who was again punching moodily at the steering-wheel, and checked herself. 'Anyway, what difference does it make now? If you won't go with us . . .'

H.M. assumed a martyred air.

'I never said I *wasn't* goin' with you, did I?' he demanded. (This was inaccurate, but no matter.) 'Even after you practically made a cripple of me, I never said I *wasn't* goin'?' His manner grew flurried and hasty. 'But I got to leave now,' he added apologetically. 'I got to get back to my office.'

'We'll drive you there, H.M.'

'No, no, no,' said the practical cripple, getting out of the car with surprising celerity. 'Walkin' is good for my stomach if it's not so good for my behind. I'm a forgivin' man. You pick me up at my house tomorrow morning. G'bye.'

And he lumbered off in the direction of the Haymarket.

It needed no close observer to see that H.M. was deeply abstracted. He remained so abstracted, indeed, as to be nearly murdered by a taxi at the Admiralty Arch; and he was half-way down Whitehall before a familiar voice stopped him.

'Afternoon, Sir Henry!'

Burly, urbane, buttoned up in blue serge, with his bowler hat and his boiled blue eye, stood Chief Inspector Masters.

'Bit odd,' the Chief Inspector remarked affably, 'to see you taking a constitutional on a day like this. And how are you, sir?'

'Awful,' said H.M. instantly. 'But that's not the point. Masters, you crawlin' snake! You're the very man I wanted to see.'

Few things startled the Chief Inspector. This one did.

'You', he repeated, 'wanted to see *me*?'

'Uh-huh.'

'And what about?'

'Masters, do you remember the Victoria Adams case about twenty years ago?'

The Chief Inspector's manner suddenly changed and grew wary.

'Victoria Adams case?' he ruminated. 'No, sir, I can't say I do.'

'Son, you're lyin'! You were sergeant to old Chief Inspector Rutherford in those days, and well I remember it!'

Masters stood on his dignity.

'That's as may be, sir. But twenty years ago . . .'

'A little girl of twelve or thirteen, the child of very wealthy parents, disappeared one night out of a country cottage with all the doors and windows locked on the inside. A week later, while everybody was havin' screaming hysterics, the child reappeared again: through the locks and bolts, tucked up in her bed as usual. And to this day nobody's ever known what really happened.'

There was a silence, while Masters shut his jaws hard.

'This family, the Adamses,' persisted H. M., 'owned the cottage, down Aylesbury way, on the edge of Goblin Wood, opposite the lake. Or was it?'

'Oh, ah,' growled Masters. 'It was.'

H.M. looked at him curiously.

'They used the cottage as a base for bathin' in summer, and ice-skatin' in winter. It was black winter when the child vanished, and the place was all locked up inside against drafts. They say her old man nearly went loopy when he found her there a week later, lying asleep under the lamp. But all she'd say, when they asked her where she'd been, was, "*I don't know.*"'

Again there was a silence, while red buses thundered through the traffic press of Whitehall.

'You've got to admit, Masters, there was a flaming public rumpus. I say: did you ever read Barrie's *Mary Rose*?'

'No.'

'Well, it was a situation straight out of Barrie. Some people, y'see, said that Vicky Adams was a child of faerie who'd been spirited away by the pixies . . .'

Whereupon Masters exploded.

He removed his bowler hat and wiped his forehead. He made

remarks about pixies, in detail, which could not have been bettered by H.M. himself.

'I know, son, I know.' H.M. was soothing. Then his big voice sharpened. 'Now tell me. Was all this talk strictly true?'

'What talk?'

'Locked windows? Bolted doors? No attic-trap? No cellar? Solid walls and floor?'

'Yes, sir,' answered Masters, regaining his dignity with a powerful effort, 'I'm bound to admit it *was* true.'

'Then there wasn't any jiggery-pokery about the cottage?'

'In your eye there wasn't,' said Masters.

'How d'ye mean?'

'Listen, sir.' Masters lowered his voice. 'Before the Adamses took over that place, it was a hideout for Chuck Randall. At that time he was the swellest of the swell mob; we lagged him a couple of years later. Do you think Chuck wouldn't have rigged up some gadget for a getaway? Just so! Only . . .'

'Well? Hey?'

'We couldn't find it,' grunted Masters.

'And I'll bet that pleased old Chief Inspector Rutherford?'

'I tell you straight: he was fair up the pole. Especially as the kid herself was a pretty kid, all big eyes and dark hair. You couldn't help trusting her.'

'Yes,' said H.M. 'That's what worries me.'

'Worries you?'

'Oh, my son!' said H.M. dismally. 'Here's Vicky Adams, the spoiled daughter of dotin' parents. She's supposed to be "odd" and "fey". She's even encouraged to be. During her adolescence, the most impressionable time of her life, she gets wrapped round with the gauze of a mystery that people talk about even yet. What's that woman like now, Masters? What's that woman like now?'

'Dear Sir Henry!' murmured Miss Vicky Adams in her softest voice.

She said this just as William Sage's car, with Bill and Eve Drayton in the front seat, and Vicky and H.M. in the back seat, turned off the main road. Behind them lay the smoky-red roofs of Aylesbury, against a brightness of late afternoon. The car turned down a side road, a damp tunnel of greenery, and into another road which was little more than a lane between hedgerows.

H.M.—though cheered by three good-sized picnic hampers from Fortnum & Mason, their wickerwork lids bulging with a feast—did not seem happy. Nobody in that car was happy, with the possible exception of Miss Adams herself.

Vicky, unlike Eve, was small and dark and vivacious. Her large light-brown eyes, with very black lashes, could be arch and coy; or they could be dreamily intense. The late Sir James Barrie might have called her a sprite. Those of more sober views would have recognized a different quality: she had an inordinate sex appeal, which was as palpable as a physical touch to any male within yards. And despite her smallness, Vicky had a full voice like Eve's. All these qualities she used even in so simple a matter as giving traffic directions.

'First right,' she would say, leaning forward to put her hands on Bill Sage's shoulders. 'Then straight on until the next traffic light. Ah, clever boy!'

'Not at all, not at all!' Bill would disclaim, with red ears and rather an erratic style of driving.

'Oh, yes, you are!' And Vicky would twist the lobe of his ear, playfully, before sitting back again.

(Eve Drayton did not say anything. She did not even turn round. Yet the atmosphere, even of that quiet English picnic party, had already become a trifle hysterical.)

'Dear Sir Henry!' murmured Vicky, as they turned down into the deep lane between the hedgerows. 'I do wish you wouldn't be so materialistic! I do, really. Haven't you the tiniest bit of spirituality in your nature?'

'Me?' said H.M. in astonishment. 'I got a very lofty spiritual nature. But what I want just now, my wench, is grub.—Oi!'

Bill Sage glanced round.

'By that speedometer,' H.M. pointed, 'we've now come forty-six miles and a bit. We didn't even leave town until people of decency and sanity were having their tea. Where are we *goin'*?'

'But didn't you know?' asked Vicky, with wide-open eyes. 'We're going to the cottage where I had such a dreadful experience when I was a child.'

'Was it such a dreadful experience, Vicky dear?' inquired Eve.

Vicky's eyes seemed far away.

'I don't remember, really. I was only a child, you see. I didn't understand. I hadn't developed the power for myself then.'

'What power?' H.M. asked sharply.

'To dematerialize,' said Vicky. 'Of course.'

In that warm, sun-dusted lane, between the hawthorn hedges, the car jolted over a rut. Crockery rattled.

'Uh-huh. I see,' observed H.M. without inflection. 'And where do you go, my wench, when you dematerialize?'

'Into a strange country. Through a little door. You wouldn't understand. Oh, you *are* such Philistines!' moaned Vicky. Then, with a sudden change of mood, she leaned forward and her whole physical allurement flowed again towards Bill Sage. '*You* wouldn't like me to disappear, would you, Bill?'

(Easy! Easy!)

'Only', said Bill, with a sort of wild gallantry, 'if you promised to reappear again straightaway.'

'Oh, I should have to do that.' Vicky sat back. She was trembling. 'The power wouldn't be strong enough. But even a poor little thing like me might be able to teach you a lesson. Look there!'

And she pointed ahead.

On their left, as the lane widened, stretched the ten-acre gloom of what is fancifully known as Goblin Wood. On their right lay a small lake, on private property and therefore deserted.

The cottage—set well back into a clearing of the wood so as to face the road, screened from it by a line of beeches—was in fact a bungalow of rough-hewn stone, with a slate roof. Across the front of it ran a wooden porch. It had a seedy air, like the long, yellow-green grass of its front lawn. Bill parked the car at the side of the road, since there was no driveway.

'It's a bit lonely, ain't it?' demanded H.M. His voice boomed out against that utter stillness, under the hot sun.

'Oh, yes!' breathed Vicky. She jumped out of the car in a whirl of skirts. 'That's why *they* were able to come and take me. When I was a child.'

'They?'

'Dear Sir Henry! Do I need to explain?'

Then Vicky looked at Bill.

'I must apologize,' she said, 'for the state the house is in. I haven't been out here for months and months. There's a modern bathroom, I'm glad to say. Only paraffin lamps, of course. But then,' a dreamy smile flashed across her face, 'you won't need lamps, will you? Unless . . .'

'You mean,' said Bill, who was taking a black case out of the car, 'unless you disappear again?'

'Yes, Bill. And promise me you won't be frightened when I do.'

The young man uttered a ringing oath which was shushed by Sir

Henry Merrivale, who austerely said he disapproved of profanity. Eve Drayton was very quiet.

'But in the meantime,' Vicky said wistfully, 'let's forget it all, shall we? Let's laugh and dance and sing and pretend we're children! And surely our guest must be even more hungry by this time?'

It was in this emotional state that they sat down to their picnic.

H.M., if the truth must be told, did not fare too badly. Instead of sitting on some hummock of ground, they dragged a table and chairs to the shaded porch. All spoke in strained voices. But no word of controversy was said. It was only afterwards, when the cloth was cleared, the furniture and hampers pushed indoors, the empty bottles flung away, that danger tapped a warning.

From under the porch Vicky fished out two half-rotted deck chairs, which she set up in the long grass of the lawn. These were to be occupied by Eve and H.M., while Vicky took Bill Sage to inspect a plum tree of some remarkable quality she did not specify.

Eve sat down without comment. H.M., who was smoking a black cigar opposite her, waited some time before he spoke.

'Y' know,' he said, taking the cigar out of his mouth, 'you're behaving remarkably well.'

'Yes,' Eve laughed. 'Aren't I?'

'Are you pretty well acquainted with this Adams gal?'

'I'm her first cousin,' Eve answered simply. 'Now that her parents are dead, I'm the only relative she's got. I know *all* about her.'

From far across the lawn floated two voices saying something about wild strawberries. Eve, her fair hair and fair complexion vivid against the dark line of Goblin Wood, clenched her hands on her knees.

'You see, H.M.,' she hesitated, 'there was another reason why I invited you here. I—I don't quite know how to approach it.'

'I'm the old man,' said H.M., tapping himself impressively on the chest. 'You tell me.'

'Eve, darling!' interposed Vicky's voice, crying across the ragged lawn. 'Coo-ee! Eve!'

'Yes, dear?'

'I've just remembered,' cried Vicky, 'that I haven't shown Bill over the cottage! You don't mind if I steal him away from you for a little while?'

'No, dear! Of course not!'

It was H.M., sitting so as to face the bungalow, who saw Vicky and Bill go in. He saw Vicky's wistful smile as she closed the door after them. Eve did not even look round. The sun was declining, making fiery chinks through the thickness of Goblin Wood behind the cottage.

'I won't let her have him,' Eve suddenly cried. 'I won't! I won't! I won't!'

'Does she want him, my wench? Or, which is more to the point, does he want her?'

'He never has,' Eve said with emphasis. 'Not really. And he never will.'

H.M., motionless, puffed out cigar smoke.

'Vicky's a faker,' said Eve. 'Does that sound catty?'

'Not necessarily. I was just thinkin' the same thing myself.'

'I'm patient,' said Eve. Her blue eyes were fixed. 'I'm terribly, terribly patient. I can wait years for what I want. Bill's not making much money now, and I haven't got a bean. But Bill's got great talent under that easy-going manner of his. He *must* have the right girl to help him. If only . . .'

'If only the elfin sprite would let him alone. Hey?'

'Vicky acts like that,' said Eve, 'towards practically every man she ever meets. That's why she never married. She says it leaves her soul free to commune with other souls. This occultism————'

Then it all poured out, the family story of the Adamses. This repressed girl spoke at length, spoke as perhaps she had never spoken before. Vicky Adams, the child who wanted to attract attention, her father, Uncle Fred, and her mother, Aunt Margaret, seemed to walk in vividness as the shadows gathered.

'I was too young to know her at the time of the "disappearance", of course. But, oh, I knew her afterwards! And I thought . . .'

'Well?'

'If I could get *you* here,' said Eve, 'I thought she'd try to show off with some game. And then you'd expose her. And Bill would see what an awful faker she is. But it's hopeless! It's hopeless!'

'Looky here,' observed H.M., who was smoking his third cigar. He sat up. 'Doesn't it strike you those two are being a rummy-awful long time just in lookin' through a little bungalow?'

Eve, roused out of a dream, stared back at him. She sprang to her feet. She was not now, you could guess, thinking of any disappearance.

'Excuse me a moment,' she said curtly.

Eve hurried across to the cottage, went up on the porch, and opened the front door. H.M. heard her heels rap down the length of the small passage inside. She marched straight back again, closed the front door, and rejoined H.M.

'All the doors of the rooms are shut,' she announced in a high voice. 'I really don't think I ought to disturb them.'

'Easy, my wench!'

'I have absolutely no interest,' declared Eve, with the tears coming into her eyes, 'in what happens to either of them now. Shall we take the car and go back to town without them?'

H.M. threw away his cigar, got up, and seized her by the shoulders.

'I'm the old man,' he said, with a leer like an ogre. 'Will you listen to me?'

'No!'

'If I'm any reader of the human dial,' persisted H.M., 'that young feller's no more gone on Vicky Adams than I am. He was scared, my wench. Scared.' Doubt, indecision crossed H.M.'s face. 'I dunno what he's scared of. Burn me, I don't! But . . .'

'Hoy!' called the voice of Bill Sage.

It did not come from the direction of the cottage.

They were surrounded on three sides by Goblin Wood, now blurred with twilight. From the north side the voice bawled at them, followed by crackling in dry undergrowth. Bill, his hair and sports coat and flannels more than a little dirty, regarded them with a face of bitterness.

'Here are her blasted wild strawberries,' he announced, extending his hand. 'Three of 'em. The fruitful (excuse me) result of three-quarters of an hour's hard labour. I absolutely refuse to chase 'em in the dark.'

For a moment Eve Drayton's mouth moved without speech.

'Then you weren't . . . in the cottage all this time?'

'In the cottage?' Bill glanced at it. 'I was in that cottage,' he said, 'about five minutes. Vicky had a woman's whim. She wanted some wild strawberries out of what she called the "forest".'

'Wait a minute, son!' said H.M. very sharply. 'You didn't come out that front door. Nobody did.'

'No! I went out the back door! It opens straight on the wood.'

'Yes. And what happened then?'

'Well, I went to look for these damned . . .'

'No, no! What did *she* do?'

'Vicky? She locked and bolted the back door on the inside. I remember her grinning at me through the glass panel. She———'

Bill stopped short. His eyes widened, and then narrowed, as though at the impact of an idea. All three of them turned to look at the rough-stone cottage.

'By the way,' said Bill. He cleared his throat vigorously. 'By the way, have you seen Vicky since then?'

'No.'

'This couldn't be . . . ?'

'It could be, son,' said H.M. 'We'd all better go in there and have a look.'

They hesitated for a moment on the porch. A warm, moist fragrance breathed up from the ground after sunset. In half an hour it would be completely dark.

Bill Sage threw open the front door and shouted Vicky's name. That sound seemed to penetrate, reverberating, through every room. The intense heat and stuffiness of the cottage, where no window had been raised in months, blew out at them. But nobody answered.

'Get inside,' snapped H.M. 'And stop yowlin'.' The Old Maestro was nervous. 'I'm dead sure she didn't get out by the front door; but we'll just make certain there's no slippin' out now.'

Stumbling over the table and chairs they had used on the porch, he fastened the front door. They were in a narrow passage, once handsome with parquet floor and pine-panelled walls, leading to a door with a glass panel at the rear. H.M. lumbered forward to inspect this door, and found it locked and bolted, as Bill had said.

Goblin Wood grew darker.

Keeping well together, they searched the cottage. It was not large, having two good-sized rooms on one side of the passage, and two small rooms on the other side, so as to make space for bathroom and kitchenette. H.M., raising fogs of dust, ransacked every inch where a person could possibly hide.

And all the windows were locked on the inside. And the chimney-flues were too narrow to admit anybody.

And Vicky Adams wasn't there.

'Oh, my eye!' breathed Sir Henry Merrivale.

They had gathered, by what idiotic impulse not even H.M. could have said, just outside the open door of the bathroom. A bath-tap dripped monotonously. The last light through a frosted-glass window showed three faces hung there as though disembodied.

'Bill,' said Eve in an unsteady voice, 'this is a trick. Oh, I've longed for her to be exposed! This is a trick!'

'Then where is she?'

'H.M. can tell us! Can't you, H.M.?'

'Well . . . now,' muttered the great man.

Across H.M.'s Panama hat was a large black handprint, made there when he had pressed down the hat after investigating the chimney. He glowered under it.

'Son,' he said to Bill, 'there's just one question I want you to answer in all this hokey-pokey. When you went out pickin' wild strawberries, will you swear Vicky Adams didn't go with you?'

'As God is my Judge, she didn't,' returned Bill, with fervency and obvious truth. 'Besides, how the devil could she? Look at the lock and bolt on the back door!'

H.M. made two more violent black handprints on his hat.

He lumbered forward, his head down, two or three paces in the narrow passage. His foot half skidded on something that had been lying there unnoticed, and he picked it up. It was a large, square section of thin, waterproof oilskin, jagged at one corner.

'Have you found anything?' demanded Bill in a strained voice.

'No. Not to make any sense, that is. But just a minute!'

At the rear of the passage, on the left-hand side, was the bedroom from which Vicky Adams had vanished as a child. Though H.M. had searched this room once before, he opened the door again.

It was now almost dark in Goblin Wood.

He saw dimly a room twenty years before: a room of flounces, of lace curtains, of once-polished mahogany, its mirrors glimmering against white-papered walls. H.M. seemed especially interested in the windows.

He ran his hands carefully round the frame of each, even climbing laboriously up on a chair to examine the tops. He borrowed a box of matches from Bill; and the little spurts of light, following the rasp of the match, rasped against nerves as well. The hope died out of his face, and his companions saw it.

'H.M.,' Bill said for the dozenth time, 'where is she?'

'Son,' replied H.M. despondently, 'I don't know.'

'Let's get out of here,' Eve said abruptly. Her voice was a small scream. 'I kn-know it's all a trick! I know Vicky's a faker! But let's get out of here. For God's sake let's get out of here!'

'As a matter of fact,' Bill cleared his throat, 'I agree. Anyway, we won't hear from Vicky until tomorrow morning.'

'*Oh, yes, you will,*' whispered Vicky's voice out of the darkness.

Eve screamed.

They lighted a lamp.

But there was nobody there.

Their retreat from the cottage, it must be admitted, was not very dignified.

How they stumbled down that ragged lawn in the dark, how they piled rugs and picnic hampers into the car, how they eventually found the main road again, is best left undescribed.

Sir Henry Merrivale has since sneered at this—'a bit of a goosy feeling; nothin' much'—and it is true that he has no nerves to speak of. But he can be worried, badly worried, and that he was worried on this occasion may be deduced from what happened later.

H.M., after dropping in at Claridge's for a modest late supper of lobster and *Pêche Melba*, returned to his house in Brook Street and slept a hideous sleep. It was three o'clock in the morning, even before the summer dawn, when the ringing of the bedside telephone roused him.

What he heard sent his blood pressure soaring.

'Dear Sir Henry!' crooned a familiar and sprite-like voice.

H.M. was himself again, full of gall and bile. He switched on the bedside lamp and put on his spectacles with care, so as adequately to address the phone.

'Have I got the honour,' he said with dangerous politeness, 'of addressin' Miss Vicky Adams?'

'Oh, yes!'

'I sincerely trust,' said H.M., 'you've been havin' a good time? Are you materialized yet?'

'Oh, yes!'

'Where are you now?'

'I'm afraid'—there was coy laughter in the voice—'that must be a little secret for a day or two. I want to teach you a really *good* lesson. Blessings, dear.'

And she hung up the receiver.

H.M. did not say anything. He climbed out of bed. He stalked up and down the room, his corporation majestic under an old-fashioned nightshirt stretching to his heels. Then, since he himself had been waked up at three o'clock in the morning, the obvious course was to wake up somebody else; so he dialled the home number of Chief Inspector Masters.

'No, sir,' retorted Masters grimly, after coughing the frog out of his throat, 'I do *not* mind you ringing up. Not a bit of it!' He spoke with a certain pleasure. 'Because I've got a bit of news for you.'

H.M. eyed the phone suspiciously.

'Masters, are you trying to do me in the eye again?'

'It's what you always try to do to me, isn't it?'

'All right, all right!' growled H.M. 'What's the news?'

'Do you remember mentioning the Vicky Adams case to me yesterday?'

'Sort of. Yes.'

'Oh, ah! Well, I had a word or two round among our people. I was tipped the wink to go and see a certain solicitor. He was old Mr Fred Adams's solicitor before Mr Adams died about six or seven years ago.'

Here Masters's voice grew suave with triumph.

'I always said, Sir Henry, that Chuck Randall had planted some gadget in that cottage for a quick get-away. And I was right. The gadget was . . .'

'You were quite right, Masters. The gadget was a trick window.'

The telephone so to speak, gave a start.

'What's that?'

'A trick window.' H.M. spoke patiently. 'You press a spring. And the whole frame of the window, two leaves locked together, slides down between the walls far enough so you can climb over. Then you push it back up again.'

'*How in lum's name do you know that?*'

'Oh, my son! They used to build windows like it in country houses during the persecution of Catholic priests. It was a good enough *second* guess. Only . . . it won't work.'

Masters seemed annoyed. 'It won't work now,' Masters agreed. 'And do you know why?'

'I can guess. Tell me.'

'Because, just before Mr Adams died, he discovered how his darling daughter had flummoxed him. He never told anybody except his lawyer. He took a handful of four-inch nails, and sealed up the top of that frame so tight an orang-outang couldn't move it, and painted 'em over so they wouldn't be noticed.'

'Uh-huh. You can notice 'em now.'

'I doubt if the young lady herself ever knew. But, by George!' Masters said savagely, 'I'd like to see anybody try the same game now!'

'You would, hey? Then will it interest you to know that the same gal has just disappeared out of the same house AGAIN?'

H. M. began a long narrative of the facts, but he had to break off because the telephone was raving.

'Honest, Masters,' H. M. said seriously, 'I'm not joking. She didn't get out through the window. But she did get out. You'd better meet me'—he gave directions—'tomorrow morning. In the meantime, son, sleep well.'

It was, therefore, a worn-faced Masters who went into the Visitors' Room at the Senior Conservatives' Club just before lunch on the following day.

The Visitors' Room is a dark, sepulchral place, opening on an air-well, where the visitor is surrounded by pictures of dyspeptic-looking gentlemen with beards. It has a pervading mustiness of wood and leather. Though whisky and soda stood on the table, H. M. sat in a leather chair far away from it, ruffling his hands across his bald head.

'Now, Masters, keep your shirt on!' he warned. 'This business may be rummy. But it's not a police matter—yet.'

'I know it's not a police matter,' Masters said grimly. 'All the same, I've had a word with the Superintendent at Aylesbury.'

'Fowler?'

'You know him?'

'Sure. I know everybody. Is he goin' to keep an eye out?'

'He's going to have a look at that ruddy cottage. I've asked for any telephone calls to be put through here. In the meantime, sir————'

It was at this point, as though diabolically inspired, that the telephone rang. H. M. reached it before Masters.

'It's the old man,' he said, unconsciously assuming a stance of grandeur. 'Yes, yes! Masters is here, but he's drunk. You tell me first. What's that?'

The telephone talked thinly.

'Sure I looked in the kitchen cupboard,' bellowed H. M. 'Though I didn't honestly expect to find Vicky Adams hidin' there. What's that? Say it again! Plates? Cups that had been . . .'

An almost frightening change had come over H. M.'s expression. He stood motionless. All the posturing went out of him. He was not even listening to the voice that still talked thinly, while his eyes and his brain moved to put together facts. At length (though the voice still talked) he hung up the receiver.

H. M. blundered back to the centre table, where he drew out a chair and sat down.

'Masters,' he said very quietly, 'I've come close to makin' the silliest mistake of my life.'

Here he cleared his throat.

'I shouldn't have made it, son, I really shouldn't. But don't yell at me for cuttin' off Fowler. I can tell you now how Vicky Adams disappeared. And she said one true thing when she said she was going into a strange country.'

'How do you mean?'

'She's dead,' answered H. M.

The word fell with heavy weight into that dingy room, where the bearded faces look down.

'Y'see,' H. M. went on blankly, 'a lot of us were right when we thought Vicky Adams was a faker. She was. To attract attention to herself, she played that trick on her family with the hocused window. She's lived and traded on it ever since. That's what sent me straight in the wrong direction. I was on the alert for some *trick* Vicky Adams might play. So it never occurred to me that this elegant pair of beauties, Miss Eve Drayton and Mr William Sage, were deliberately conspirin' to murder *her*.'

Masters got slowly to his feet.

'Did you say . . . murder?'

'Oh, yes.'

Again H. M. cleared his throat.

'It was all arranged beforehand for me to be a witness. They knew Vicky Adams couldn't resist a challenge to disappear, especially as Vicky always believed she could get out by the trick window. They wanted Vicky to *say* she was goin' to disappear. They never knew anything about the trick window, Masters. But they knew their own plan very well.

'Eve Drayton even told me the motive. She hated Vicky, of course. But that wasn't the main point. She was Vicky Adams's only relative; she'd inherit an awful big scoopful of money. Eve said she could be patient. (And, burn me, how her eyes meant it when she said that!) Rather than risk any slightest suspicion of murder, she was willing to wait seven years until a disappeared person can be presumed dead.

'Our Eve, I think, was the fiery drivin' force of that conspiracy. She was only scared part of the time. Sage was scared all of the time. But it was Sage who did the real dirty work. He lured Vicky Adams into that cottage, while Eve kept me in close conversation on the lawn . . .'

H. M. paused.

Intolerably vivid in the mind of Chief Inspector Masters, who had seen it years before, rose the picture of the rough-stone bungalow against the darkening wood.

'Masters,' said H. M., 'why should a bath-tap be dripping in a house that hadn't been occupied for months?'

'Well?'

'Sage, y'see, is a surgeon. I saw him take his black case of instruments out of the car. He took Vicky Adams into that house. In the bathroom he stabbed her, he stripped her, and *he dismembered her body in the bath-tub.—Easy, son!*'

'Go on,' said Masters, without moving.

'The head, the torso, the folded arms and legs, were wrapped up in three large square pieces of thin, transparent oilskin. Each was sewed up with coarse thread so the blood wouldn't drip. Last night I found one of the oilskin pieces he'd ruined when his needle slipped at the corner. Then he walked out of the house, with the back door still standin' unlocked, to get his wild-strawberry alibi.'

'Sage went out of there,' shouted Masters, 'leaving the body in the house?'

'Oh, yes,' agreed H. M.

'But where did he leave it?'

H. M. ignored this.

'In the meantime, son, what about Eve Drayton? At the end of the arranged three-quarters of an hour, she indicated there was hanky-panky between her fiancé and Vicky Adams. She flew into the house. But what did she do?'

'She walked to the back of the passage. I heard her. *There she simply locked and bolted the back door*. And then she marched out to join me with tears in her eyes. And these two beauties were ready for investigation.'

'Investigation?' said Masters. '*With that body still in the house?*'

'Oh, yes.'

Masters lifted both fists.

'It must have given young Sage a shock,' said H. M., 'when I found that piece of waterproof oilskin he'd washed but dropped. Anyway, these two had only two more bits of hokey-pokey. The "vanished" gal had to speak—to show she was still alive. If you'd been there, son, you'd have noticed that Eve Drayton's got a voice just like Vicky Adams's. If somebody speaks in a dark room, carefully imitatin' a coy tone she never uses herself, the illusion's goin' to be pretty good. The same goes for a telephone.

'It was finished, Masters. All that had to be done was remove the body from the house, and get it far away from there . . .'

'But that's just what I'm asking you, sir! Where was the body all this time? And who in blazes *did* remove the body from the house?'

'All of us did,' answered H. M.

'What's that?'

'Masters,' said H. M., 'aren't you forgettin' the picnic hampers?'

And now, the Chief Inspector saw, H. M. was as white as a ghost. His next words took Masters like a blow between the eyes.

'Three good-sized wickerwork hampers, with lids. After our big meal on the porch, those hampers were shoved inside the house, where Sage could get at 'em. He had to leave most of the used crockery behind, in the kitchen cupboard. But three wickerwork hampers from a picnic, and three butcher's parcels to go inside 'em. I carried one down to the car myself. It felt a bit funny . . .'

H. M. stretched out his hand, not steadily, towards the whisky.

'Y'know,' he said, 'I'll always wonder whether I was carrying the—head.'

MICHAEL INNES · 1906–

The Furies

'The death of Miss Pinhorn,' said Appleby, 'was decidedly bizarre. But it was some time before we realized that it was sinister, too. Indeed, if it hadn't been for my aunt we might never have thought of it. She takes a great interest, you know, in criminal investigation.'

'I remember Miss Pinhorn slightly.' The vicar set down his tankard. 'My daughter called on her once when collecting for European relief. She owned a cottage here, I think, and so it appeared reasonable to treat her as a resident. But she opened her purse—in the actual rather than the metaphorical sense—and gave the poor girl sixpence.'

The doctor chuckled. 'Then you may take it she was stretching a point, and that your daughter's eloquence had moved her in uncommon degree. She was quite astonishingly mean. I was abroad when she died, and I don't know anything about her end. But I should guess that the chronic malnutrition of the pathological miser had a hand in it. Is that right?'

Appleby shook his head. 'Certainly she was terribly mean—and about her food among other things. She would have lived, if she could, on free samples of breakfast cereals. But she died, nevertheless, of something odder than starvation. In a sense she died of drink.'

'Dear, dear!' The vicar's features composed themselves momentarily upon strictly professional lines. 'It is a deplorable fact that elderly unmarried women———'

'And it was the drink that worried my aunt. She simply would not believe Miss Pinhorn capable of paying out good money for the pleasure of drinking two pints of beer as it is today. It worried me, too. There did seem to be something rather incredible about that beer. But I see I must tell the story.'

'Capital,' said the doctor. 'And we'll try a second pint ourselves.'

'Amelia Pinhorn was a woman of considerable fortune and marked eccentricity. But while she enjoyed the benefits of her fortune all the time, her eccentricity was intermittent. For most of the year she lived in London the normal life of a leisured person of her sort: two servants, a fixed circle of acquaintances, concert-going, church-going —that sort of thing. Then for a couple of months each summer she came down here—her parents had been Sheercliffe folk—and led a solitary and miserly existence in a small cottage not half a mile from where we are sitting now. She had no contacts with anybody—not even the milkman. I don't exaggerate. Everything was sent down from town before she arrived. She lived on tins. It was said that she believed the Sheercliffe shopkeepers to be peculiarly malignant, and eager to poison her. In all this there is, perhaps, nothing very out of the way. Here was an old woman who had formed the habit of concentrating a tendency towards mild insanity within a two months' spell at the sea, when she lived alone and was a nuisance to nobody. It was a public-spirited and rather heroic disposition of things. I used to see her taking her daily walk along the cliff—a handsome grey-haired woman, not carelessly or strangely dressed, but talking to herself in some withdrawn state that was decidedly alarming. And then one day she was drowned.'

'Drowned?' The doctor looked surprised. 'It sounds a bit of an anti-climax. Unless you mean that somebody drowned her in those two pints of beer?'

Appleby shook his head. 'The beer was an agent, not a medium. Miss Pinhorn simply tumbled into the sea and was drowned. Or at least it is supposed that she was drowned. For we never, you see, recovered the body. The poor lady went over the cliff just short of the lighthouse. You must know about the current that sweeps in there and then goes out to sea again past the Furies. Two or three times in a century the thing happens. If a body goes through there at a certain depth it gets sucked right down and trapped in nobody knows what monstrous system of submarine caverns lying beneath those three placid-looking pinnacles. And poor Miss Pinhorn passed that way. Which meant that all the king's dolphins and all the king's divers couldn't between them have dredged her up for a coroner's jury to sit upon. And this was awkward when the rumours began to go round. It might have been particularly awkward for Jane Pinhorn. Old women over their teacups would have credited the poor girl with the most masterly crime of the age.'

The vicar looked disturbed. 'This is not *really* a crime story, I hope?'

'It certainly is—but whether masterly or not, you must judge. The initial facts were perfectly simple, and fell within the observation of a number of people who were about here at the time. Miss Pinhorn emerged from her cottage, locked the door behind her, and set out on what appeared to be one of her normal solitary rambles. She came in the direction of this pub, and as she neared it she was seen to be hurrying—like a seasoned toper, somebody said, who is afraid of being beaten to it by closing time. But she wasn't known to drink, and she had certainly never been in this very comfortable private bar before. Well, in she came, talking to herself as usual and looking quite alarmingly wild. She called for two pints of beer in quick succession, floored them, planked down half a crown, and bolted out again. By this time she was singing and throwing her arms about.

'If the few people here had possessed any gumption they'd have followed the old girl and seen that she did herself no mischief. But she was known to be a bit dotty, and they hung back. Besides, she appeared to be making for home again. It was only when she had gone some way that she appeared to lose direction and wheel round towards the brow of the cliff. By that time she was in a thorough-going state of mania, and she went straight to her death. Perhaps, you may say, she had a repressed tendency to suicide—we found out after-wards that her father had made away with himself—and the need for that took charge when her inhibitions were destroyed by the poison. For this is a story of poisoning—as you, doctor, have no doubt realized.

'I've said that my aunt was the first person to suspect foul play. That needs qualifying, maybe. For the notion of poisoning seems to have arisen almost at once at what you might call a folk-level. Everybody was whispering it, and on no very ponderable evidence. You may remember how it was believed that poor Miss Pinhorn was *afraid* of being poisoned. That may or may not have been true. I should be inclined to call it an aetiological myth—one invented for the purpose of accounting for an observed fact: namely, that Miss Pinhorn would buy neither food nor drink locally. What my aunt certainly spotted was the significance of the beer. It indicated, she said, a sudden pathological thirst. Together with the very rapid onset of a violent mania or delirium, it should give us a very good guide to the sort of poison at work.

'When I say "us" I mean, of course, the local police and myself. It's a queer thing that I seldom quit Scotland Yard to spend a week in Sheercliffe with my eminently respectable kinswoman without her involving me in something of a busman's holiday. But I felt bound to peer about. For a very little thought suggested to me that my aunt—in this instance at least—was talking sense. Had the body been recoverable I'd never have bothered my head. It was the fact that we had in that quarter an absolutely unknown x, so to speak, that got me really interested.

'Well, the first question clearly concerned the possibility of Miss Pinhorn's having poisoned herself, whether inadvertently or of set purpose. Her cottage was not a difficult place to search thoroughly—I shall come to that in a moment—and the hunt yielded what seemed at first a significant result. There was a tremendous store of patent medicines—something quite out of the way even with a maiden lady—all put up in very small packs. But each was more utterly harmless than the last. They were, in fact, almost without exception, free samples which had been stored away for a long time. I doubt if one can get very much in that way nowadays.

'A related inquiry to this was that into the dead woman's recent medical history. There was something of a hold-up over this, because in such matters she had been of a decidedly secretive habit. We did learn from her maids in town, however, that a few months previously she had been having trouble with her eyes, and that for some unknown reason she had to be hurried off to a nursing home. I ought to have seen a bit of light when I heard that.' Appleby paused. 'I can see, Doctor, that it at once conveys something to you.'

The doctor shook his head. 'Perhaps so. But I can't say that I see much sense———'

'Exactly.' Appleby applied himself briefly to the pewter mug before him. 'And what you might call the irony of this queer yarn lies just there. But now I must tell you about the chocolates.

'You see, it really comes down to a sort of sealed-room mystery. Miss Pinhorn is poisoned—and yet *nothing* has gone into her cottage for days. Or so we thought until I happened, during the search, to take a second look at this half-pound box of chocolates. It was lying in the sitting-room, with the top layer gone. It wasn't anything about the chocolates themselves that struck me. It was the lid. You know that slightly padded sort of lid that confectioners go in for? It was of that kind. And just visible on it was the impress of three or four parallel wavy lines. That box had been through the post, lightly wrapped, and here was a faint trace of the postmark.'

'Most astonishing!' The vicar was enthusiastic. 'My dear Appleby, a fine feat of detection, indeed.'

'I don't know that I'd call it that. But at least it sent me to the waste-paper basket. And there, sure enough, with a London post-mark and Miss Pinhorn's address, was the scrap of wrapping I expected. And there was something more—a slip of notepaper with the words: "To Aunt Amelia on her birthday, with love from Jane."

'So I hunted out the postman. Apart from a few letters, he had delivered nothing at Miss Pinhorn's for weeks—until the very morning of the day on which she died. On that day he had delivered a small oblong parcel.

'I looked like being hot on a trail. That evening, while the remaining chocolates were being analysed with what was to prove an entirely negative result, I went up to town and sought out Jane Pinhorn. And I didn't care for what I found. Jane was as nice a girl as you could wish to meet, and she had liked her eccentric aunt. This birthday box of chocolates had been an annual occasion with her. She was a highly intelligent girl, too.

'Miss Pinhorn's symptoms, so far as we knew about them, were consistent with the ingestion of some poison of the atropine group. The sudden thirst, and the delirium resulting from inco-ordinate stimulation of the higher centres of the cerebrum, were consistent with this. Deadly nightshade, as you may know, is not in fact all that deadly. But one could no doubt cram a chocolate with quite enough to cause a great deal of mischief, and Jane Pinhorn had possessed the opportunity to do this. Moreover she had a motive. Along with a male cousin—a ne'er-do-well in Canada—she was the dead woman's only relative and co-heir. I saw suspicion inevitably attaching itself to this girl. It was overwhelmingly unlikely, indeed, that any case against her could be proved. But that was a matter of the sheerest chance. Miss Pinhorn's body had gone for ever—a thing the girl could not possibly have reckoned on. As a crime of intelligence and calculation the thing would not do. The sealed-room aspect of Miss Pinhorn's way of living while at Sheercliffe, and the penetrating of the defences thus created by this single gift which was so easily traceable to the sender: it just didn't make sense—unless indeed Jane Pinhorn had a repressed suicidal strain herself.

'I came back to Sheercliffe that night seriously troubled, and as soon as I arrived I went straight out to the dead woman's cottage. It was locked and sealed, but I had been given a key. The rest of that night—and I remember it as very long—I spent prowling from one room to another hunting for I didn't know what. Essentially I was casting about inside my own head for some logic in the thing that had escaped me. I don't think I had any notion of hitting upon a further material clue. And then, quite suddenly, I found that I had come to a halt in the little hall and was staring at an envelope lying beside the telephone directory on a small table. It was a plain manilla envelope, stamped ready for post, and creased down the middle. For a second I didn't see the significance of that crease. What had touched off some spring in my mind was the address—a single-spaced typescript affair of the most commonplace sort. *International Vitamin Warehouses Limited*, if mildly absurd, was nothing out of the way and wouldn't have troubled me. The snag lay in what followed. I know my East London fairly well. And the street in which this pretentious organiz- ation claimed an abode contains nothing but mean private houses and a few shabby little shops. And so the truth came to me . . . The truth, to begin with, about that crease. This envelope had come to Miss Pinhorn folded inside another one.

'I slit the thing open there and then. "*Send no money. Simply fill up the back of this form. . . .*" It had been a diabolically clever scheme. And it had, of course, been a completely fatuous one as well.'

Appleby paused. The vicar was looking largely puzzled. But the doctor drew a long breath. 'The nephew in Canada!'

'Precisely. He knew about the sealed-room effect. He knew about Jane's annual birthday gift. And he knew about his aunt's idiosyn- crasy to belladonna. Some months before, its use by her oculist in a normal clinical dose had made her so seriously unwell as to take her into a nursing-home. He believed that he could get on the gum of a reply-paid envelope a quantity which in her special case would be fatal. Miss Pinhorn, you remember, could never resist a free sample of anything. So she would fill in the form, lick the envelope—and perish! There are Elizabethan plays, you know, rather like that; people die in them quite horribly after kissing a poisoned portrait. The envelope, if posted, would go to what was in fact a shady accommodation address in London, and our precious nephew would pick it up when he came over to England. He would also pick up the half of his aunt's fortune—or the whole of it if the unfortunate Jane was hanged on the strength of her chocolates.

'In point of fact, however many wicked nephews you may have in Canada, you need never have any qualms about licking an envelope doped with belladonna. Or rather, qualms are all that you *will* have. This amateur in poison had sadly confused a lethal with a toxic dose. With this particular drug, as it happens, the margin between the two is unusually wide. Having her special susceptibility to it, poor old Miss Pinhorn did go horribly delirious, just as she had on a previous occasion. But that she chose to hurry on to this pub near the cliff, and thus put herself in the way of tumbling into the sea when the attack was at its worst, was pure chance.'

Appleby paused and stood up. 'It wasn't, as it happened, the last stroke of chance in the Pinhorn case. You may wonder what happened to the nephew.'

The vicar nodded vigorously. 'Yes, indeed. He was certainly a murderer.'

'He had aimed at being that, and he showed a certain efficiency. From a small town in Canada he had timed his stroke so nicely that the bogus circular reached his aunt just when he intended: on her birthday, and when Jane Pinhorn's customary chocolates would be arriving too.

'But he hadn't the stuff that an effective killer is made of. No sooner had he set his plot in motion, it seems, than he cracked up badly and went on a drinking-bout. Staggering home one morning in the small hours, and making his way through some public park, he fell into a very small pond and was drowned in six inches of water. At just about the same hour, that tremendous current must have been drawing Amelia Pinhorn's body to unknown depths beneath the Furies.'

CHRISTIANNA BRAND · 1907–1988

The Hornets' Nest

'We've got hornets nesting again in that old elm,' said Mr Caxton,
gulping down his last oyster, wiping thick fingers on his table napkin.
'Interesting things, hornets.' He interrupted himself, producing a
large white handkerchief and violently blowing his nose. 'Damn
these colds of mine!'

'I saw you were treating them,' said Inspector Cockrill; referring,
however, to the hornets. 'There's a tin of that WASP-WAS stuff on
your hall table.'

Cyrus Caxton ignored him. 'Interesting things, I was saying. I've
been reading up about them.' Baleful and truculent, he looked round
at the guests assembled for his wedding feast. 'At certain times of the
year,' he quoted, 'there are numerous males, the drones, which have
very large eyes and whose only activity is to eat—' he glared round at
them again, with special reference to the gentlemen present '—and
to participate in the mass flight after the virgin queen.' He cast upon
his bride a speculative eye. 'You are well named Elizabeth, my
dear,' he said. 'Elizabeth, the Virgin Queen.' And added with ugly
significance, 'I hope.'

'But only one of the hornets succeeds in the mating,' said Inspector
Cockrill into the ensuing outraged silence. 'And he dies in the process.' He sat back and looked Cyrus Caxton in the face, deliberately;
and twiddled his thumbs.

Cyrus Caxton was a horrid old man. He had been horrid to his first
wife and now was quite evidently going to be horrid to his second
—she had been the late Mrs Caxton's nurse, quite young still and
very pretty in a blue-eyed, broken-hearted sort of way. And he was
horrid to his own stout son, Theo, who was only too thankful to live
away from papa, playing in an amateurish way with stocks and shares,
up in London; and horrid to his stepson, Bill, who, brought into the
family by the now departed wife, had immediately been pushed off to
relatives in the United States to be out of Mr Caxton's way. And he
was horrid to poor young Dr Ross who, having devotedly attended

the wife in her last illness, now as devotedly attended Mr Caxton's own soaring blood pressure and resultant apoplectic fits; and horrid to his few friends and many poor relations, all of whom he kept on tenterhooks with promises of remembrances in his will when one of the choking fits should have carried him off. He would no doubt have been horrid to Inspector Cockrill; but—Mr Caxton being incapable of keeping peaceably to a law designed for other people as well as for himself—Cockie got in first and was horrid to *him*. It must have been Elizabeth, he reflected, who had promoted his invitation to the wedding.

The little nurse had stayed on to help with things after the poor wife died; had gradually drifted into indispensability and so into accepting the pudgy hand of the widower. Not without some heart-searching however; Inspector Cockrill himself had, in his off-duty moments, lent a shoulder in those days of Mr Caxton's uninhibited courtship; and she had had a little weep there, and told him of the one great love lost to her, and how she no longer looked for that kind of happiness in marriage; but was sick of work, sick of loneliness, sick of insecurity . . . 'But a trained nurse like you can get wonderful jobs,' Inspector Cockrill had protested. 'Travel all over the place, see the world.' She *had* seen the world, she said, and it was too big, it scared her; she wanted to stay put, she wanted a home: and a home meant a man. 'There are other men?' he had suggested; and she had burst out that there were indeed other men, too many men, all men—it was dreadful, it was frightening, to be the sort of woman that, for some unknown reason, all men looked at, all men gooped at, all men —wanted. 'With him, at least I'll be safe; no one will dare to—to drool over me like that when he's around.' Inspector Cockrill had somewhat hurriedly disengaged his shoulder. He was a younger man in those days of Mr Caxton's second marriage and subsequent departure from this life; and taking no chances.

And so the affair had gone forward. The engagement and imminent wedding had been announced and in the same breath the house-hold staff—faithful apparently in death as in life, to the late Mrs Caxton—had made their own announcement: they had Seen it Coming and were now sweeping out in a body, preferring, thank you very much, not to continue in service under That Nurse. The bride, unchaperoned, had perforce modestly retired to a London hotel and from thence left most of the wedding arrangements to Son Theo and Stepson Bill—Theo running up and down from London, Bill temporarily accommodated for the occasion beneath the family roof.

Despite the difficulties of its achievement, Mr Caxton was far from satisfied with the wedding breakfast. 'I never did like oysters, Elizabeth, as you must very well know. Why couldn't we have had smoked salmon? And I don't like cold meat, I don't like it in any form. Not in *any* form,' he insisted, looking once again at his virgin queen with an ugly leer. Inspector Cockrill surprised upon the faces of all the males present, drones and workers alike, a look of malevolence which really quite shocked him.

She protested, trembling. 'But, Cyrus, it's been so difficult with no servants. We got what was easiest.'

'Very well, then. Having got it, let us have it.' He gestured to the empty oyster shells, 'With all these women around—am I to sit in front of a dirty plate for ever?'

The female relations upon this broad hint rose from their places like a flock of sitting pheasants and began scurrying to and fro, clearing used crockery, passing plates of chicken and ham. 'Don't over-do it, my dears,' said Mr Caxton, sardonically watching their endeavours. 'You're all out of the will now, you know.'

It brought them up short: the crudeness, the brutality of it —standing staring back at him, the plates in their shaking hands. Half of them, probably, cared not two pins for five, or five-and-twenty pounds in Cyrus Caxton's will, but they turned, nevertheless, upon the new heiress questioning—reproachful?—eyes. 'Oh, but Cyrus, that's not true,' she cried; above his jeering protests insisted: 'Cyrus has destroyed his old will, yes; but he's made a new one and—well, I mean, no one has been forgotten, I'm sure, who was mentioned before.'

The lunch progressed. Intent, perhaps, to show their disin- terestedness, the dispossessed scuttled back and forth with the cold meats, potato mayonnaise, sliced cucumber—poured delicious barley water (for Mr Caxton was a rabid teetotaller) into cut glass tumblers, worthy of better things. The bridegroom munched his way through even the despised cold viands in a manner that boded ill, thought Inspector Cockrill, for the wretched Elizabeth, suddenly coming alive to the horror of what she had taken upon herself. She sat silent and shrinking and made hardly any move to assist with the serving. Son Theo carved and sliced, Stepson Bill handed plates, even young Dr Ross wandered round with the salad bowl; but the bride sat still and silent and those three, thought Cockie, could hardly drag their eyes from the small white face and the dawning terror there. The meat plates were removed, the peaches lifted one by one from their tall bottles and placed, well soused with syrup, on their flowery plates. Stepson Bill dispensed the silver dessert spoons and forks, fanned out ready on the sideboard. The guests sat civilly, spoons poised, ready to begin.

Cyrus Caxton waited for no one. He gave a last loud trumpeting blow to his nose, stuffed away his handkerchief, picked up the spoon beside his plate and somewhat ostentatiously looked to see if it was clean: plunged spoon and fork into the peach, spinning dizzily before him in its syrup, and, scooping off a large chunk, slithered it into his mouth: stiffened—stared about him with a wild surmise—gave one gurgling roar of mingled rage and pain, turned first white, then purple, then an even more terrifying dingy, dark red; and pitched forward across the table with his face in his plate. Elizabeth cried out: 'He's swallowed the peach stone!'

Dr Ross was across the room in three strides, grasped the man by the hair and chin and laid him back in his chair. The face looked none the more lovely for being covered in syrup and he wiped it clean with one swipe of a table-napkin; and stood for what seemed a long moment, hands on the arms of the chair, gazing down, intent and abstracted, at the spluttering mouth and rolling eyes. Like a terrier, Elizabeth was to say later to Inspector Cockrill, alert and suspicious, snuffing the scent. Then with another of his swift movements, he was hauling Mr Caxton out of his chair, lowering him to the floor; calling out, 'Elizabeth!—my bag. On a chair in the hall.' But she seemed struck motionless by the sudden horror of it all and only stammered out, imploring, 'Theo?' Stout Theo, nearest the door, bestirred himself to dash out into the hall, appearing a moment later with the bag. Stepson Bill, kneeling with the doctor beside the heaving body, took it from him, opened it out. Elizabeth, shuddering, said again: 'He must have swallowed the stone.'

The doctor ignored her. He had caught up the fallen table-napkin and was using it to grasp, with his left hand, the man's half-swallowed tongue and pull it forward to free the air-passages; at the same time with his right groping blindly towards the medical bag. 'A finger-stall—it's just on top, somewhere. . . .' Bill found it immediately and handed it to him; he shuffled it on and thrust the middle finger of his right hand down the gagging throat. 'Nothing there,' he said, straightening up, standing looking down, absently wiping his fingers on the table-napkin, rolling off the finger-stall—all again with that odd effect of sniffing the air; galvanizing into action once more, however, to fall on his knees beside the body. With the heel of his left hand he began a quick, sharp pumping at the sternum, with his right he gestured towards the medical bag. 'The hypodermic. Adrenalin ampoules in the left pocket.' Bill fumbled, unaccustomed, and he lifted his head for a moment and said, sharply: 'For heaven's sake—Elizabeth?' She jumped, startled. 'Yes? Yes?' she said, staccato; and seemed to come suddenly to her senses. 'Yes, of course. I'll do it.' She dropped to her knees beside the bag, found the ampoules, filled the syringe. 'Keep it ready,' he said. 'Somebody cut away the sleeve.' He took both hands to the massage of the heart. 'While I do this—can someone give him the kiss of life?'

It was a long time since anyone, his affianced not excluded, had willingly given Mr Caxton a kiss of any kind and it could not now be said that volunteers came eagerly forward. The doctor said again, 'Elizabeth?' but this time on a note of doubt. She looked down, faltering at the gaping mouth, dreadfully dribbling. 'Must I?'

'You're a nurse,' said Dr Ross. 'And he's dying.'

'Yes. Yes, of course I must.' She brought out a small handkerchief, scrubbed at her own mouth as though somehow irrationally to cleanse it before a task so horrible; moved to crouch where she would not interfere with the massage of the heart. 'Now?'

Mercifully, Cyrus Caxton himself provided the answer—suddenly and unmistakably giving up the ghost. He heaved up into a last great, lunging spasm, screamed briefly and rolled up his eyes. She sat back on her heels, the handkerchief balled against her mouth, gaping. Dr Ross abandoned the heart massage, thrust her aside, himself began a mouth-to-mouth breathing. But even he soon admitted defeat. 'It's no use,' he said, straightening up, his hands to his aching back. 'He's gone.'

Gone: and not one, perhaps, in all that big ugly ornate room but felt a sort of lightening of relief, a sort of little lifting of the heart because with the going of Cyrus Caxton so much of ugliness, crudity, cruelty also had gone. Not one, at any rate, even pretended to grief. Only the widowed bride, still kneeling by the heavy body, lifted her head and looked across with a terrible question into the doctor's eyes; and leapt to her feet and darted out into the hall. She came back and stood in the doorway. 'The tin of cyanide,' she said. 'It's gone.'

Dr Ross picked up the dropped table-napkin and quietly, unobtrusively yet very deliberately, laid it over the half eaten peach.

Inspector Cockrill's underlings dealt with the friends and relations, despatching them to their deep chagrin about their respective businesses, relieved of any further glorious chance of notoriety. The tin had been discovered without much difficulty, hidden in a vase of pampas grass which stood in the centre of the hall table: its lid off and a small quantity of the paste missing, scooped out, apparently, with something so smooth as to show no peculiarities of marking, at any rate to the naked eye. It had been on the table since some time on the day before the wedding. Cockie himself had seen it there, just before the lunch.

He thought it all over, deeply and quietly—for it had been a plot deeply and quietly laid. 'I'll see those four for myself,' he said to his sergeant. 'Mrs Caxton, of course, the son and the stepson and the doctor.' These were the principals and one might as well tease them a little and see what emerged; but for the rest of course—he knew[1]: the how and the when and the why, and therefore the who. Some details to be sorted out, naturally; but for the rest—he knew; a few words recollected, a dozen, no more—and with a little reflection, how clear it all became! Curious, thought Cockie, how two brief sentences, hardly attended to, might so twist themselves about and about as to wind themselves at last into a rope. Into a noose.

He established himself in what had been Cyrus Caxton's study and sent for Elizabeth. 'Well, Mrs Caxton?'

White teeth dug into a trembling lower lip to bite back hysteria. 'Oh, Inspector, at least don't call me by that horrible name!'

'It is your name now; and we're engaged upon a murder investigation. There's no time for nonsense.'

'You don't really believe———'

'You know it,' said Cockie. 'You were the first to know it.'

'Dr Ross was the first,' she said. 'You saw him yourself, Inspector, leaning over Cyrus as he was lying back in that chair; sort of—snuffing. Like a terrier on the scent. He could smell the cyanide on his breath, I'm sure he could; like bitter almonds they say it is.'

It had not needed an analyst to detect the white traces of poison on the peach and in the heavy syrup. 'Who brought the food for the luncheon, Mrs Caxton?'

'Well, we all . . . We talked it over, Theo and Bill and I. It was so difficult, you see, with no servants; and me being in London. I ordered most of the stuff to be sent down from Harrod's and Theo brought down—well, one or two things from Fortnum and Mason's . . .' Her voice trailed away rather unhappily.

---

[1] And so should the reader.

'Which one or two things? The peaches, you mean?'

'Well, yes, the peaches. He brought them down himself, yesterday. He was up and down from London all the time, helping Bill. But,' she cried, imploringly, 'why should Theo possibly have done this terrible thing? His own father! For that matter, why should anyone?'

'Ah, as to that!' said Cockie. Had not Cyrus Caxton spoken his own epitaph? *At certain times there are numerous males, the drones, which have very large eyes and whose only activity is to eat and to participate in the mass flight after the virgin queen.* He had seen them himself, stuffing down Mr Caxton's oysters and cold chicken and ham, their eyes, dilated with devotion, fixed with an astonishing unanimity upon Mr Caxton's bride. '*Only one of them mates, however,*' he repeated to himself, '*and he dies in the process.*' That also had been seen to be true. 'Elizabeth,' he said, forgetting for a moment that this was a murder investigation and there was to be no nonsense, 'from the hornet's-eye angle, I'm afraid you are indeed a virgin queen.'

And Theo, the young drone, stout and lethargic, playing with his stocks and shares in his cosy London flat . . . Inspector Cockrill had known him since his boyhood. 'You needn't think, Cockie, that I wanted my father's money. I'm all right: I got my share of my mother's money when she died.'

'Oh, did you?' said Cockrill. 'And her other son, Bill?'

'She left it to my father, to pass on if he thought it was right.'

'Wasn't that a bit unfair? He wasn't Bill's own father; and it was her money.'

'I think she'd probably sort of written him off. I mean, it's easy enough to hop across from America nowadays, isn't it? But he never came to see her. Though I believe the servants let him know, when she was dying; and they did correspond. In secret; my father would never have allowed it, of course.'

'Of course!' said Cockie. He dismissed the matter of money. 'How well, Theo, did you know your father's new wife?'

'Not at all well. I saw her when I came to visit my mother during her illness, and again at the funeral after she died. But of course . . .' But of course, his tone admitted, a man didn't have to know Elizabeth well, to . . . There was that something . . .

'You never contemplated marrying her yourself?'

But Theo, lazy and self-indulgent, was not for the married state. 'All the same, Inspector, it did make me pretty sick to think of it. I mean, my own father . . .'

Would Theo, dog in the manger, almost physically revolted by the thought of his adored in the gross arms of his own father—would Theo kill for that? 'These bottled peaches, Theo. You served them out, I know; but who actually opened them? I mean, had they been unsealed in advance?'

'No, because they'd have lost the bouquet of the Kirsch. Right up to the last minute, they were sealed.'

'Can you prove that?'

'Elizabeth can bear me out. We nipped in here on the way to the wedding—I drove her down from London—for me to go to the loo in case I should start hopping in church. And she took a quick dekko just to see that everything looked all right. She'll tell you the bottles were still sealed up then; you can ask her.'

'How quick a dekko? Tell me about this visit.'

'Oh, good heavens, Inspector!—the whole thing took three minutes, we were late and you know what the old man was. We rushed in, I dashed into the cloakroom, when I came out she was standing at the dining-room door, looking in, and she said, "It all looks wonderful," and what a good jòb Bill and I had done. Then *she* went into the cloakroom and we both got into the car and went off again.'

'Was the tin of cyanide on the hall table then?'

'Yes, because she said thank goodness Bill seemed to have got it for her and saved her more trouble with Father.'

'No one else was in the house at this time?'

'No, Bill had gone on to the church with my father.'

'OK. Well, send this Bill to me, will you, Theo? And tell him to bring his passport with him.'

He was ten years older than his stepbrother; well into his thirties: blond-headed, incisive, tough, an ugly customer probably on a dirty night; but rather an engaging sort of chap for all that. Cockie turned over the pages of the passport. 'You haven't been in this country since you were a boy?'

'No, they shipped me out as a kid, my new papa didn't want me and my mother doesn't seem to have put up too much of a fight for me. So I wasn't all that crazy to come rushing home on visits.'

'Not even when she died?'

'At that time I was—prevented,' he said briefly.

'By what, if I may ask?'

'By four stone walls,' said Stepson Bill, ruefully. 'Which in my case, Inspector, did a prison make. In other words, I was doing time, sir. I got into a fight with a guy and did six months for him. I only got out a few weeks ago.'

'A fight about what?'

'About my wife, if you have to know,' he said, sullenly, 'I was bumming around, I admit it, and I guess he got her on the rebound. Well, bum or not, I took and chucked her out and that was the end of her. And I took and pulled him in, and that was the end of *him*—in the role of seducer, anyway.'

'You divorced your wife?'

'Yeh, I divorced her.' He looked at Inspector Cockrill and the hard, bright eyes had suddenly a look almost of despair. 'I think now I made some pretty bad mistakes,' he said.

'At any rate, having got out, you learned that your stepfather was marrying the nurse; that your mother's money was in jeopardy, perhaps? So you came across hot foot, to look the lady over?'

And having looked her over . . . Another drone, drawn, willy-nilly—the more so for having been for long months starved of the company of women, for having been deprived of the wife whom he still loved—into the mass flight after the virgin queen. 'It was you, I believe, who brought the poison into the house?'

'Yes, I did. The old man was furious with Elizabeth because she hadn't ordered it. How could she, poor girl, when she wasn't here half the time? So I went down and fetched it, just to save her more trouble, and put it on the hall table so he'd think she'd got it.'

'But she was in London: how could she?'

'Oh, heck, he couldn't care: if it wasn't there, she was responsible.'

'And after all this alleged fuss and urgency, it never got used?'

'Didn't I tell you—it was only to make more trouble for Elizabeth. He was a man that just loved to find fault.'

'I see. Well, we agree it was you who introduced the cyanide. Was it not also you who handed a plate of cold meat to your stepfather?'

'Was it I who———? For heaven's sakes, Inspector! Those old ladies were running around like a lot of decapitated hens, snatching plates out of our hands, dumping them down in front of just anyone who'd accept them.'

'You might, however, have said specifically to one of them, "This plate is especially for Mr Caxton."'

'I might at that,' said Bill, cheerfully. 'Why don't you ask around and find her: she'll tell you.' He shrugged. 'Anyway, what does it matter? The poison wasn't on the meat, was it? It had been put on the peach.'

'If it had,' said Cockie, 'it had been put there by someone very clever.' He dwelt on it. 'How could it have been placed there so that the whole dose—to all intents and purposes—was on the one mouthful that he happened to take? The first mouthful?'

And he sent Stepson Bill away and summoned Dr Ross. 'Well, doctor—so we have it. *Only one mates; and he dies in the process.*'

'You're referring to the thing about the hornets?' said Dr Ross rather stiffly.

'That's right: to the thing about the hornets. But nobody could call *you* a drone, doctor. So busy with that little bag of yours that you had it with you out in the hall, all ready to hand.'

'At intervals of about one week,' said Dr Ross, 'policemen like yourself exhort us not to leave our medical bags in unattended cars.' He fixed Inspector Cockrill with a dark and very angry eye. 'Are you suggesting that it was I who murdered my own patient?'

'Will you declare yourself outside the mass flight, Dr Ross? You must have seen a good deal of our little queen in the sickroom of the late Mrs Caxton.'

'I happen to have a little queen of my own, Inspector. Not to mention several little drones, not yet ready for flighting.'

'I know,' said Cockie. 'It must have been hell for you.' He said it very kindly. He added: 'I accuse you of nothing.'

Disarmed, he capitulated, immediately, wretchedly. 'I've never so much as touched her hand, Inspector. But it's true—there's something about her . . . And to think of that filthy old brute . . .'

'Well, he's gone,' said Cockie. 'Murdered under your nose—and mine. And talking of noses————'

'I smelt it on his breath. Oh, gosh, the faintest whiff—but there was something. I thought it must be just the Kirsch—the Kirsch on the peaches.'

'Such a curious meal!' said Inspector Cockrill, brooding over it. 'He was the bridegroom: you'd think somebody would be falling over themselves to please him. But no: he didn't like oysters, but he has to have oysters, he hated cold meat but all there is, is cold meat, he was violently teetotal but he's given peaches with liqueur on 'em.' He sat with his chin on his hand, his bright eyes gazing away into nothingness. 'There has been a plan here, doctor: no simple matter of a lick of poison scraped out of a fortuitous tin, smeared on to a fortuitous peach-in-liqueur; but a very elaborate, deep-laid, long-thought-out, absolutely sure-fire plan. But who planned it, who carried it out and with what ultimate motive . . .' He broke off. He said at last, slowly:

'Of course whatever's in the will, as the law goes now she will still be a rich widow; more agreeable to her, presumably, than being a rich wife.'

'You don't honestly think that Elizabeth————?'

'Elizabeth had nothing to do with the preparation of the food; she hasn't been in the house for the past three days, except for that brief interlude when she and Theo came in on their way to the church. Each of them was alone for a period of a minute or two—Elizabeth probably for less. Not nearly enough time to have chanced prising open the tin, scooping out the stuff, doctoring the peaches (which anyway were still in sealed bottles) or the cold meat or oysters. On the other hand—Elizabeth is a trained nurse . . .' He mused over it. 'He had a bad cold. Could she have persuaded him to take some drug or other? On the way back from the church, for example.'

'He was a man who wouldn't touch medicines. He got these colds, the place was stiff with pills and potions I'd prescribed for him, but he'd never even try them. Besides,' he insisted, as Bill had before him, 'the stuff was on the peach.' And it was that fat slob Theo who had been responsible for the peach. Not that he wanted to suggest, he added rather hurriedly, that Theo would have murdered his own father. But . . . 'You needn't think I haven't seen him gooping at her.'

'You needn't think I haven't seen you all gooping at her.'

'I've made up my mind,' said the doctor, quietly and humbly, 'if I can get out of this business with my family still safe and sound, never, so long as I can help it, to see Elizabeth again.'

'You are a worker,' said Cockie. 'Not a true drone. It will be easier for you. Bill is a drone; he admits it—only *he* calls it a bum.'

And so was fat Theo a drone. Bill, Theo, the doctor . . .

But the doctor had a family of his own, whom he had had no intention, ever, of deserting for Elizabeth the Virgin Queen. And for that matter, so had Bill a wife of his own, whom, even now, even knowing Elizabeth, he cared for. And Theo was sufficient unto himself and would go no further than a little yearning, a little mooning, an occasional sentimental somersaulting of the fatty heart. *Only one of them mates* . . . Of the four, mass flighting after the queen, only one in fact had been a potential mate; and sure enough had died.

Of the three remaining—which might be capable of murder, only to prevent that mating?

Investigation, interrogation—the messages to Harrod's, to Fortnum's, to the chemist's shop in the village; the telephone calls to Mr

Caxton's lawyers, to Stepson Bill's few contacts in America, to the departed domestic staff . . . The afternoon passed and the light summer evening came; and he stood with the four of them, out on the terrace of the big, ugly, anything-but-desirable residence which must now be Elizabeth's own. 'Elizabeth—Mrs Caxton—and you three gentlemen . . . In this business there is only one conceivable motive. Money doesn't come into it. The new will had been signed, Mr Caxton's death now or later made no difference to its contents. None of you appears to have been in any urgent financial need. So there's only one motive, and therefore only one question: who would commit murder to prevent Cyrus Caxton from ever holding Elizabeth in his arms?'

Stout Theo?—who might yet have keen enough feelings, whose sick revulsion might be the more poignant because his own father had been involved. Or Stepson Bill?—who for this same unendurable thought of the belovèd in the arms of another, could half-kill a man and cast off for ever the woman he still loved. Or the doctor?—who, of them all, had most closely known Elizabeth; who, as Cyrus Caxton's medical adviser, knew only too intimately the gross body and crude appetites of the conquering male . . .

Theo, Bill, Dr Ross. Out of these three . . . Softly, softly catchee monkey, said Inspector Cockrill to himself. Aloud he said: 'This murder was a planned murder; nothing would have been left to chance. So why, I go on asking myself, should his first mouthful of peach have been the fatal one? And I answer myself: "Think about that spoon!"'

'You mean the spoon Theo was using to dish out the peaches?' said Elizabeth quickly. 'But no, because Theo didn't hand the plate to his father. He couldn't know which peach he'd get.'

'Unless he directed a special plate to his father?' suggested Bill, casting a quizzical glance at Inspector Cockrill. He reassured a suddenly quaking Theo. 'OK pal, take it easy. We've already worked through that one.'

'In any event, it wouldn't account for the first mouthful being the poisoned one. And Elizabeth,' said Inspector Cockrill severely, 'please don't go trying to put me off! That was a red-herring—to draw my attention away from the other spoon: the spoon handed directly to your husband by Master Bill here.'

She began to cry, drearily, helplessly, biting on the little white screwed-up ball of her handkerchief. 'Inspector, Cyrus is dead, all this won't bring him back. Couldn't you——? Couldn't we——?'

And she burst out that if it was all because of her, it was so dreadful for people to be in all this trouble . . .

'But your husband has been murdered: what do you expect me to do, let it go at that, just because his murderer had a sentimental crush on you?' He came back to the spoon. 'If that spoon had been smeared with poison————'

She stopped crying at once, raised her head triumphantly. 'It couldn't have been. Cyrus looked at it to see that it was polished clean; he always did after the servants left, he said that I . . .' The lower lip began to wobble again. 'I know he's dead; but he wasn't very kind,' she said.

Not Theo then: who could not have known that the poisoned peach would reach his father. Not Bill, who could not have poisoned the peach at all. 'And so,' said Dr Ross, 'you come to me?'

It was very quiet out there on the terrace; the sun had gone down now and soon the stars would be out, almost invisible in the pale evening sky. They stood, still and quiet also, and for a little while all were silent. Elizabeth said slowly: 'Inspector—Dr Ross has a wife of his own; and children.'

'He still might not care for the vision of you in the arms of "that filthy old brute" as he has called him.'

'That went for us all,' said the doctor.

'But it was you that went for Mr Caxton, doctor—wasn't it? Or *to* him, if you prefer. Went to him and put down his throat a finger protected by a rubber finger-stall.'

A finger-stall—thrust down the throat of a man having an everyday choking fit. A finger-stall dabbled in advance in a tin of poison.

'You don't believe this?' said Dr Ross, staring aghast. 'You can't believe it? Murder my own patient!' Elizabeth caught his arm, crying out, 'Of course he doesn't mean it!' but he ignored her. 'And murder him in such a way! And anyway, how could I have known he would have a choking fit?'

'He was always having choking fits,' said Cockie.

'But Dr Ross couldn't have *got* the poison,' said Elizabeth. 'It wasn't he who fetched the bag from the hall.' She broke off. 'Oh, Theo, I didn't intend————'

'I got the bag,' said Theo. 'But that doesn't mean anything.'

'It could mean it was you who dabbled the finger-stall in the poison.'

Theo's round face lost colour. 'Me, Inspector? How could I have?

How could I know anything about it? *I* don't know what they use finger-stalls for and what they don't.'

'Anyway, he wouldn't have had time,' said Elizabeth. 'Not to think it all out, undo the poison tin, find the finger-stall in the bag. Finger-stalls are kept in a side pocket, not floating about at the top of a medical bag.'

But in fact that was just where it had been: floating about at the top of the medical bag. Bill, crouching beside the doctor over the heaving body, had located it immediately and handed it to him. 'I had used it on a patient just before I came to the church,' said Dr Ross patiently. 'You can check if you like. I threw it into boiling water, dried it and chucked it back into the bag. I was in a hurry to come to the wedding.'

In a hurry—to come to Elizabeth's wedding. 'So the finger-stall was in the fore-front of your mind then, doctor?—when you brought in your medical bag and put it down on the chair and your eye fell on that tin of poison. Everyone is milling about, just back from the ceremony, not thinking of anyone except the bride and bridegroom. You take a little scoop of the poison, using the finger-stall—just in case occasion arises. And occasion does arise. What a bit of luck!'

'Inspector Cockrill,' said Elizabeth steadily, 'this is all nonsense. Dr Ross smelt the stuff on Cyrus's breath, long before he put the finger-stall down his throat. You saw him yourself, like I said, sort of—snuffing . . .'

'Sort of snuffing at nothing,' said Cockie. 'There was nothing to snuff at, was there, doctor?—not yet. But it placed the poison, you see, in advance of the true poisoning with the finger-stall. The man chokes, the doctor leans over him, pretends to be suspicious. *Then* the finger-stall down the throat; and this time there *is* something to snuff at. And when the finger-stall is later examined, the fact of its having been down the man's throat will account for traces of cyanide on it. Now all that remains is to pin-point the earlier source of the poison. Well, that's easy: he wipes off the finger-stall on the napkin; and then, so innocently!—places the napkin over the peach.' His bright eyes, bird-like, looked triumphantly round upon them.

They all stood rigid, staring at the doctor: horrified, questioning. Elizabeth cried out: 'Oh, it isn't true!' but on a note of doubt.

'I don't think so, no,' said Cockie. 'This isn't a crime where anything was left to chance. And this is based on the chance that the old man might have a choking fit.'

She went over to the doctor, put her two little hands on his arm, laid her forehead for a moment against his shoulder in a gesture devoid of coquetry. 'Oh, thank God! He frightened me.'

'He didn't frighten me,' said Dr Ross stoutly; but he looked all the same exceedingly pale. To Cockrill he said: 'He got these choking fits, yes: but—once or twice in a year. You couldn't risk all that on the chance of his having one.'

'So that brings us back to you, Theo,' said Inspector Cockrill blandly. 'Who gave him peaches in Kirsch and *made* him have one.'

Theo looked as likely as his father had ever done, to have a choking fit. '*I* made him have one?'

'My dear Theo! A man is a rabid teetotaller. You provide him with a peach in a thick syrup of Kirsch—observing that he has a heavy cold and won't smell the liqueur in advance. He takes a great gulp of it and realizes that he's been tricked into taking alcohol. You knew your father: he would go off into one of his spluttering rages and if he didn't choke on the peach, he'd choke on his own spluttering. And it isn't true, is it? that you didn't know about choking fits, and how the air-passages may be freed with a finger, covered with a finger-stall. You must have seen your father in these attacks at least once or twice; he'd been having them for years.'

He began to splutter himself. 'I couldn't have done it. Gone out into the hall, you mean, to get the bag, and put the stuff on the finger-stall then? Elizabeth showed that earlier; I wouldn't have had time.'

'We were all preoccupied, getting your father out of his chair and lowered on to the floor. The seconds pass quickly.'

But she couldn't bear it for Theo, either. 'Don't listen to him, Theo, don't be frightened! This is no more true than the other theory. He's—he's sort of teasing us; needling us, trying to make us say something. If Theo did it, Inspector, what about Dr Ross? Why should he have sniffed at Cyrus's breath, when he was lying back in the chair. There would have been nothing to smell, yet. You say he was pretending; but if it was Theo who put the poison on the finger-stall—why should the doctor have pretended? Unless . . .' She broke off, clapped her hand to her mouth; took it away immediately, began to fiddle unconcernedly with the handkerchief. Inspector Cockrill said: 'Yes, Elizabeth? Unless———?'

'Nothing,' said Elizabeth. 'I just mean that the doctor wouldn't have put on an act if it had been Theo who'd done it.'

Unless . . . He thought about it and his eyes were brilliant as stars. 'Unless, Elizabeth, you were going to say—unless they were in it together.' And he looked round at the three of them and smiled with the smile of a tiger. 'Unless they were all three in it together.'

Three men—united: united in loving the same woman, united in not wishing actually to possess her; united in determination, however, that a fourth man should not.

The first casual exchange of thought, of feeling, of their common disgust and dread; the first casual discussion of some sort of action, some sort of rescue, the vague threats, hardening into determination, into hard fact, into realistic plotting. But—murder! Even backed up by the rest—which one of them would positively commit murder? And, none accepting—divide the deed, then, amongst them: as in an execution, where a dozen men fire the bullets, no one man kills.

Bill's task to acquire the poison, see that it remains available in the hall. Theo's task to ensure, as far as possible, that a chance arises to use the poisoned finger-stall. The doctor, of course, actually to employ it. But lest that seem too heavy a share of the guilt for any one partner to carry, let Theo be the one to go out into the hall and poison the finger-stall; let Bill take the bag from him, hand the poisoned thing to the doctor. Executioners: does he who administers the poison, kill more than he who procures it?—does he who presents the victim to the murderer, kill the less because he does not do the actual slaying? All for one and one for all! And all for the purity of Elizabeth, the Virgin Queen.

Elizabeth stood with him, weeping, in the hall, while a sergeant herded the three men into the huge, hideous drawing-room and kept them there till the police car should come. 'I don't believe it: I utterly don't believe it, Inspector. Those three? A plot———'

He had said it long ago: from the very beginning. 'A very deep-laid, elaborate, absolutely sure-fire plan.'

'Between the doctor and Theo then, if you must. But Bill—why drag Bill into it?'

'Ah, Bill,' he said. 'But without Bill . . .? You have been very loyal; but I think we must now come into the open about Bill?'

And he was back with her, so many weeks ago now, when Cyrus Caxton's proposed new marriage had first become an open secret. 'With your job, Elizabeth, you could travel, you could see the world.' 'I *have* seen the world,' she had answered. 'All right,' she admitted now, in a small voice. 'Yes. I did go to America, with a private patient. I did get married there. Cyrus knew that I'd been married and divorced. I didn't tell other people because he didn't like anyone knowing that I was—well, he called it second-hand.'

Married; and divorced. Married to one who 'bumming around' had heard through the devoted family servants that his mother's illness would be her last. 'Inspector, we were desperate. He wouldn't work, he gambled like a maniac, my nursing wouldn't keep the two of us. And yet I couldn't leave him. I told you that I had had a lost love; well, that was true in its own way. My love he was—and yet not lost really after all: my love he is still and to my ruin ever shall be. I suppose some women are like that.'

'And some men,' said Cockie; thinking of that suddenly desolate look with which he had said, 'I think now that I made some pretty big mistakes.'

'I've been so ashamed, Inspector,' she said, weeping again. 'Not only of what we were doing; but of all the lies, all the acting.'

'Yet you went through with it.'

'You don't know Bill,' she said. 'But yes—it's true. He wrote to his mother secretly, through the servants. He said a girl would get in touch with her, a wonderful nurse, who would soon be coming over to England. He told her to say nothing to the old man but to try to get this girl engaged to look after her; of course the girl was me, Inspector. The idea at first was simply to look after his interests, to try to get his mother's money ensured to him, before she died. But then he got this other idea. The old man would soon be a widower; and he thought of him as a *very* old man, old and, he knew, in bad health. He hadn't seen his stepfather for years; to an adolescent, all adults seem far more aged than they are. He imagined an old crock far more in need of a nurse than of a wife. So—the first thing was a divorce. He beat up a man whom he accused of having an affair with me; he over-did that a bit and landed himself in prison; but even that he didn't mind, it helped in speeding up the divorce because of the reason for the assault.'

'Without a divorce, you couldn't have inherited, of course. The marriage with the old man had to be water-tight.'

'Inspector,' she said, in anguish, 'don't believe for one moment that this began as a murder plot. It started from small beginnings, as I've said; and then in that gambler's mind of his, it just grew and grew. Here was this golden chance. He knew that I had this—this power over men; something that I just have, I can't help it, you've seen for yourself how, without any effort on my part, it works. With such an asset—how could he bear not to exploit it? A sick old man, recently widowed, a pretty little nurse already installed: how could it fail?'

'And he was prepared to wait?'

'He saw the thing in terms of a year or two, no longer. Meanwhile he would remain in England, we could see one another—after all, he was a member of the family. And I would provide him with money, I suppose; and he would gamble.'

'But before this happy condition of things, you must nurse the dying mother; and then get to work succeeding in her place with the widower.'

She turned away her head. 'I know you think it sounds terrible; put that way, it seems terrible to me too—and it always has done. But—well, of course I had only Bill's picture of the situation, the picture of an ailing old man who would want a—a nurse rather than a wife . . . And when I found out differently—well, once again, you don't know Bill. What Bill says, you have to do. And I did nurse her: she was dying, I couldn't make any difference to that, but I did nurse her and care for her—almost her last words were of gratitude to me. When she died, I could hardly bear it. I rang up Bill in America and told him I couldn't go through with it. But . . . Well, he just said——'

'He said you *must* go through with it: and came over here himself, to make sure that you did?'

'To make sure of that—and of something else,' she said, faintly.

'Yes,' he said, thinking it over. 'Of something else too. Because he's still in love with you, Elizabeth, in his own way. And he might drive you to the altar with a horrible old man; but he would never let you get as far as the old man's bed.'

And in that determination, he had found unexpected allies. 'I suppose, Inspector, he may have meant to do it himself—God knows, he never to me breathed a word of such a thing. As I say, back in the States, he was visualizing this old-man-and-nurse relationship. But anyway, he's a gambler, here was this chance and nothing must stand in the way of it. Then he came over here and saw me again: and saw me with his stepfather . . . And then, perhaps, finding how the other two felt about it, I suppose he roped them in. Another gambler's chance: so typical of Bill. Only this one will come off for a change, because in this way the law can't do anything to them?'

'How do you mean?—can't do anything?'

'Well, but—who has committed any crime? Bill has bought a tin of stuff for killing wasps: there's nothing wrong in that? Theo has bought a bottle of peaches—nothing wrong in that either? The doctor—well, I suppose he did put the finger-stall down Cyrus's throat. But *he* didn't poison it. None of them has actually done one wrong action. They can't even be put in prison?'

'Only for a very short time,' acknowledged Cockie.

'For a short time?' she said, startled.

'Till they're taken out and hanged,' said Inspector Cockrill.

'You don't truly mean that? All three of them could be—executed?'

'All three,' said Cockie. 'For being concerned in a murder: that's the law. The flight of the queen, Elizabeth—*at certain times of the year the drones sit around eating*—well, we saw them do that—*and gazing with huge eyes upon the virgin queen*—well, we saw them do that too. And then, *the mass flight after the queen*: and that also we've seen. But here something goes wrong with the comparison; because only one succeeds in the mating; and therefore—only one dies.'

'You mean that these three————?'

'I mean that these three are not going to die. It would be too inartistic an ending to the metaphor.'

'What can save them?' said Elizabeth, beginning to tremble.

'Words can save them: and will save them.'

'Words?'

'A dozen words; carelessly spoken, hardly listened to, attended to not at all. Except by me when later I remembered them. Your husband saying, "Why couldn't I have had smoked salmon?" and you replying, "We got what was easiest."' A plain-clothes man who had all this time sat quietly on a chair by the front door, got up, as quietly, and came forward; and Inspector Cockrill shot out a hand and circled, with steely hard fingers, her narrow wrist. 'Why should oysters have been easier than smoked salmon, Elizabeth?' he said.

A very elaborate, long-thought-out, deep-laid, absolutely sure-fire plan . . .

The ugly collusion between husband and wife, to implant in the household of the dying mother, a new bride for the rich widower soon to be. On the husband's part, probably nothing more—nothing worse intended than an impatient waiting from then on, for the end of a life whose expectations had been somewhat underestimated. On hers—ah! she had been on the spot to recognize in advance the long years she might yet have to serve with a man who at the least sign of rebellion would pare down her inheritance to the limit the law allowed. Had she really confessed to Cyrus Caxton an earlier marriage? Not likely! 'You are well named Elizabeth—the virgin queen,' he had said; and added, 'I hope!' Of them all, the one who had had most cause to dread Mr Caxton's marriage bed, had been Elizabeth herself.

The plot then, laid: but in one mind alone. Use the ex-husband, expendable now, as red-herring number one; ensnare with enchantments long proved irresistible, such other poor fools as might serve to confuse the issue. With gentle persistence, no injury pin-pointable, alienate servants too long faithful and now in the way. And, the scene set, sit, sweet and smiling, little hands fluttering, soft eyes mistily blue—and in the back of one's scheming mind, think and think and plan and plan . . .

'You can't know,' she said, spitting it out at him, as they drove away from the house, the three men left sick and bewildered, utterly confounded, watching her go: sitting between himself and his sergeant in the smooth black police car, ceaselessly, restlessly struggling against their grip on her wrists. 'You don't know. It's all a trick, trying to lead me up the garden path.'

'No,' said Cockrill. 'Not any more. We've been up enough garden paths: with you leading *me*.' His arm gave slackly against the tug and pull of her hand, but his fingers never left their firm hold. 'How well you did it!—poking the clues under my nose, snatching each of them back when you saw it wasn't going to work—and all with such a touching air of protecting your poor dear admirers, fallen into this terrible trap, for love of you. But I matched you,' he said with quiet satisfaction, 'trick for trick.'

'You can't know,' she repeated again.

'I knew from the first moment,' he said. 'From the first moment I remembered his asking why he couldn't have had smoked salmon. *You* ordered the meal: accuse who you will—whatever you had said about the meal, that would have been decided. So why give him oysters; which would only make him angry? If one thought about it—taking all the other factors into consideration—the answer had to be there.'

'But the tin! You saw it yourself when we came into the dining-room. I never left the dining-room—how could I have hidden it in the vase?'

'You hid it when you went out to "look"; it wouldn't take half a second and you had your little hankie in your hand, didn't you?—all ready to muffle your fingerprints.' And with his free hand he smote his knee. 'By gum!—you'd thought this thing out, hadn't you?—right down to the last little shred of a handkerchief.'

She struggled, sitting there between them, ceaselessly wrenching to ease their grip on her wrists. 'Let me go, you brutes! You're hurting me.'

'Cyrus Caxton didn't have too comfortable a time, a-dying.'

'That old hog!' she said, viciously. 'Who cares how such an animal dies?'

'As long as he dies.'

'You'll never prove that I killed him, Inspector. How, for example,' she said, triumphantly, subsiding a little in her restless jerking to give her whole mind to it, 'how could I have taken the poison from the tin?'

'You could have taken it while you were in the house with Theo, on the way to the church. Theo went off to the downstairs cloak-room————'

'For half a minute. How long does a man take, nipping into the loo? To get the stuff out of the tin, do all the rest of it————'

'Ah, but I don't say you did "do all the rest of it"—not then. "All the rest of it" had been prepared in advance. We'll find—if we look long enough; and we will—some chemist in London where you bought a second tin of cyanide. The tin here was a blind; there was time enough even during Theo's half-minute, to take a quick scoop out of it (no doubt you'd arranged to have it left on the hall table)—just as a blind. That lot, I suppose, you disposed of in the cloak-room when you went there, after Theo.'

'You know it all, don't you?' she said, sarcastically; but she was growing weary, helpless, she had ceased to struggle, sitting limply between them now, slumped against the seatback.

A very deep-laid, elaborate, absolutely sure-fire plot: and all to be conceived in the mind of one little woman—a woman consumed, destroyed, by the dangerous knowledge of her own invincibility in the hearts of men. But the cleverness, thought Cockie; the patience! The long preparation, the building-up, piece by piece, of the 'book' itself, the stage-props, the make-up, the scenery: as a producer will work long months ahead on a projected production. Then—the stage set at last, the puppet actors chosen: curtain up! The 'exposition' —'Bill, for goodness sake collect the things from the chemist for me, the old man will slay me if I don't get his wretched wasp stuff. Just leave it on the hall table, let him think I got it . . .' And, 'Theo, I've ordered the stuff from Harrod's, but I never thought about a dessert.

You couldn't hop across to Fortnum's and get some of those peaches-in-Kirsch?—I've seen them there and they look so delicious. Teetotal?—oh, lord, so he is! But still, why should everyone else suffer?—perhaps this will make up to them for having no champagne. And he's got his usual fearful cold, maybe he won't even notice.' In the excitement and confusion, who would remember accurately, who would carry in their heads, all the commands and counter-commands, all the myriad unimportant small decisions, and who had made them? Who, for that matter, of her three cavaliers, would shelter behind her skirts to cry out, 'It was Elizabeth who told me to.' So Bill introduces the poison into the house, and Theo the peach which is to be found guilty of conveying the poison; and if the doctor does not bring in his medical bag, then busy little Elizabeth, ex-nurse, will be there to remind him of police exhortations. The stage set; the cast assembled; the puppet actors (Inspector Cockrill himself included to do the observing)—moved this way and that at the twitch of a thread, held in a small hand already dyed red with the victim's blood.

For even as he swallowed his last oyster, munched his way resentfully through his cold meat, began on his peach—already Cyrus Caxton had been a dying man: had not the doctor smelt the cyanide upon his breath? 'Why couldn't you have got smoked salmon?' he had asked angrily: and, after all, smoked salmon could have been sent down from Harrod's as easily as oysters. But 'We got what was easiest,' she had replied; and even then, Inspector Cockrill had asked himself—why? Why should oysters, which require cut lemon, a little red pepper and perhaps some brown bread and butter, have been easier than smoked salmon which requires just the same?

Answer: because you cannot conceal a capsule of poison as easily in a plate of smoked salmon, as you can in a dozen oysters.

A man who likes oysters will retain them in his mouth, will chumble them a little, gently, savouring their peculiar delight for him. A man who does not care for oysters—and Mr Caxton was not one to make concessions—will swallow them down whole and be done with it.

Cyrus Caxton had had a heavy cold, he was always having colds and the house was full of specifics against the colds, though he would not touch any of them. Among the specifics would certainly be found bottles of small capsules of slow-dissolving gelatine, filled with various compounds of drugs. A capsule emptied out might be filled with just so much of the preparation of cyanide as would kill a man. An oyster, slit open with a sharp knife, might form just such a pocket as would accommodate the capsule and close over it again.

No time of course, as she had truly said, to have achieved it all in the brief moment available when she and Theo had visited the house. But an oyster bar would be found in London, if Cockie searched long enough—where a little, blue-eyed woman had yesterday treated herself to a dozen oysters: and left behind her, if anyone had troubled to count them, only eleven shells. A small plastic bag, damp with liquor from the oyster, would no doubt have also been got rid of in the downstairs cloakroom. For the rest—it wouldn't have taken a moment to duck into the dining-room (Theo having been sent off like a small boy to the loo 'in case he started hopping in church') and replace one oyster with another, on Cyrus Caxton's plate.

Ten minutes later Elizabeth, the Virgin Queen, had given her hand to a man who within that hour and by that same hand, to her certain knowledge would no longer be alive; and had promised before God to love, cherish, and keep him till death did them part.

Well, if there was an after-life, reflected Inspector Cockrill coming away from the Old Bailey a couple of months later, at least they would be soon re-united.

Meanwhile, he must remember to look up hornets; and see whether the queens, also, have a sting.

The Murderer

Howard Carey had always been what he thought of as fastidious, and his wife Ellen once called downright prudish, in sexual matters, and at first he did not understand what the woman was saying to him.

He glanced at his watch, under the vague impression that she had said something about the time. Then she repeated the suggestion in words that were unmistakable. He recoiled slightly, shook his head and walked on, but she moved on with him using obscenities, murmuring things that appalled him. He turned on her, ready to threaten her with the police, and saw under the street lamp that this was not a woman but a young girl. She wore a white mackintosh, had hair that under the light seemed a remarkable shade of reddish gold, and her features were delicate and pale. She could not be more than sixteen, was perhaps less. He would have liked to say to her that she should be at home, that she might contract a disease, half a dozen other things. In fact he only quickened his step and hurried away from her. 'Too old for it, are you?' she shouted after him.

The encounter worried and upset him. This was suburban London, not the centre of town where he knew that such things went on. They were no more than a couple of minutes from the Underground station, and less than ten minutes' walk from his home. He had read in the local paper about prostitution and mugging, and about drivers who crawled along beside the kerb trying to pick up women, but had never truly believed in such things. How could any woman bring herself to say such things as the girl had suggested to him? He arrived home in a state of shock.

The house was called Mon Repos. It was one in a short road of exactly similar houses, all of which had names, names which included Eagle's Nest, Chez Nous, Everest and Happy Landings. The houses had been built between the wars. They were red brick semi-detached, with bow windows in the front covered by lace or net curtains. Variety was provided by the doors, which were in different colours, as well as by the house names. A few bold spirits had replaced the wooden doors by glass ones with a design engraved on them. The Dempseys next door at Happy Landings had a glass door which showed mermaids rising from the waves. Howard and Ellen had discussed it at length. Ellen liked the design, but Howard thought that it was vulgar.

Once indoors he felt a little better. It was reassuring to see the three-piece suite, with both chairs and sofa facing the television set, the nest of tables that were pulled out when friends came in for coffee, the prints of local scenes on the walls, the photograph of Rod and Jean. Rod had been living in Canada for two years now, and was doing very well in his job as some kind of engineer. There was more space, he said, more opportunity, you had a better life altogether. Perhaps he was right, perhaps they would go out and pay the visit they had often talked about.

He looked at his watch. Ellen might be home soon, or she might be another hour or two. She had worked for several years as secretary in a firm of solicitors and her chief, Mr McIntyre, asked her to work late a couple of evenings a week. Howard himself, knowing this, had done some little jobs at the insurance firm where he was deputy sub-controller of the small Complaints Section. It had always been a source of gratification to Howard that they both worked in such sound occupations. He would not have liked it if Ellen had been employed in something rather doubtful, like an art gallery.

He went upstairs to wash his hands—that was how he thought of it, for he did not like to name his bodily necessities—and looked in the bathroom glass. It showed a lean face with thinning grey hair, lines on either side of the narrow nose, deep-set grey-blue eyes, a thin mouth. The expression was anxious, as though he were expecting something unpleasant to happen.

'Too old for it, are you?' He was fifty-three, Ellen six years younger. They had married young, because Rod was on the way. The birth had been difficult. After it Ellen had not seemed to welcome his attentions for a while, and then—well, it had not been easy to make ends meet on his salary, and if he were frank he would have to say that it had always been in his mind that an unintended successor to Rod would be a disaster. And then they had both been immensely occupied with Rod, with finding the money to send him to a good private day school and to University, so that it had seemed nothing else much mattered. Of course things had been easier financially after Ellen took a typing course and got a job.

He became aware that he was still staring into the glass. In it he seemed to see a different world from the one in which Ellen and he played bridge sometimes with neighbours and went occasionally to local whist drives or socials, in which he mowed the small lawn at the back once a week from spring to autumn, wound the grandfather clock in the hall every Sunday night, and never used any word with a sexual connotation or a swear word of any kind. In that other world people spoke as the young girl with reddish gold hair had spoken to him, used every possible word and committed every possible action, first making themselves insensible by drugs or drink to the very idea of right or wrong. In the other world they would sneer at everything that was right, reasonable, and respectable. He had a sudden vision of the girl standing in their living-room with others of her kind and doing dirty things everywhere, not just breaking things up but making an actual trail of filth all around . . .

He closed his eyes and the vision became more vivid, opened them again and it had disappeared, leaving his own face looking anxiously into the glass. He went down to the kitchen and got himself biscuits and cheese. Ellen cooked in the evenings, but when she worked late he ate a hot lunch and had something light for supper. They never took food into the living-room for fear of leaving crumbs, and he ate at the kitchen table while he read the evening paper. The front-page story was about a pop star who was leaving England because taxes were too high. He was shown smiling, about to board a plane, with a girl on either arm. In the story below the picture he said that they were two of his harem. Inside the paper there was a full-page story about a schoolgirl who had killed herself because several others had been bullying her, forcing the girl to steal from her parents under threat of being tortured.

Howard went into the living-room and turned on the TV. He enjoyed sports programmes, a family drama, or anything historical, but tonight there seemed to be nothing but what were called thrillers, with people being hit on the head or shot. He watched one of them to pass the time, but did not care for it. At nine o'clock it occurred to him that Ellen was later than usual. Perhaps Mr McIntyre had taken her to supper, which had happened occasionally when there was a lot of work to be done.

The bell rang just after ten o'clock. A policeman stood there, with sergeant's stripes on his arm.

'Mr Carey? May I come in?'

'What is it?' His thoughts moved at once, for some reason, to the girl in the white mackintosh.

'Your wife is Mrs Ellen Carey? I am afraid I have some bad news. Best to sit down.'

Howard sat in one of the armchairs, looking up at the sergeant, who had a dark blue chin in need of a shave.

'Do you know a Mr John McIntyre?'

'I have never met him, but yes, he is my wife's employer.'

'Your wife was a passenger in Mr McIntyre's car tonight when it was involved in an accident.'

'Ellen's been hurt? She's in hospital?'

'I said the news was bad, sir. The car came out of a side road and was hit broadside on by a lorry. We haven't got all the details of just how it happened. The lorry driver is in hospital with concussion.'

'And Ellen?'

'I'm sorry, sir. Both car passengers were killed outright.'

Everybody was tremendously kind. Sergeant Stubbs (that was his name) had talked to Bill and Carol Dempsey at Happy Landings next door, and Howard spent the night there, and the next couple of days as well. Ellen's elder sister Norah, whom Howard had never much liked, came up from the country and stayed nearly a week. At the office the manager, Mr Langport, had called him and had a long chat, which ended with the suggestion that Howard should take some time off.

'Go away somewhere, stay with relatives.'

'I have no close relatives except my son in Canada. Otherwise only cousins.'

'What about staying with one of them?'

Howard shook his head. 'We haven't been in touch for years.'

'Your wife's relatives then?'

'No, I don't think that would do.' The thought of staying with Norah was not to be contemplated. 'I think the best thing is to go on working.'

'Very well. But if you change your mind and decide you'd like a few days off, just say the word.'

Yes, kindness everywhere. And nobody kinder than Rod, who flew over for the inquest. Jean stayed behind because she was expecting. Rod had filled out since he left England, and now seemed twice the size of his father. He stood in front of the gas fire in the living-room and asked: 'What are you going to do, dad?'

'Do? I don't know what you mean.'

'What I mean is——' Rod gave it up and began again. 'Why not come back with me? Jean would love to see you, and there's plenty of room.'

No doubt that was so. He had seen photographs of Rod's home, which was said to be a ranch-style house whatever that was, and it certainly looked much bigger than Mon Repos. He stayed silent while Rod elaborated the theme.

'Even the old skinflint where you work has said you ought to get away. If you come back with me you can look round and see how you like it. Then if you did, you could put this little place on the market————'

'You mean stay there, go to live in Canada? Give up my position in the firm?'

'Oh come on, dad, you know you're just a dogsbody. I mean, that's why mum went to work, isn't it?' He went on hurriedly. 'I know, it was to pay for my education and all that. Maybe the firm has a branch out there and could transfer you. Or if they didn't, no need to worry, you could stay with us as long as you liked while you found a job.'

Howard said stiffly, 'Thank you, Rod. I appreciate the offer, but I couldn't possibly leave this house.'

'Mon Repos? This stuffy little place? But dad, don't you see things will be different for you now mum's gone? At least move out into a flat, something easier to manage————'

'That's enough, Rod. I'm sure you mean well, but I shouldn't think of moving from here. It may be a stuffy little place, but it is where you were brought up.'

That was the end of the discussion. After a week Rod flew back, and to his surprise Howard found that he was not sorry to see his son go. He wanted, more than anything, time to reflect and to be alone.

At the inquest what happened had been explained. The car had come out of a side turning on a curve and the driver's view of the road, which would have been poor anyway, had been obscured by a parked car. The lorry driver had probably been travelling faster than he should have been, but he could not have seen the car until it was too late to brake.

There was only one puzzling thing. The office was in the City, and the accident had taken place some miles away, in St John's Wood. The point did not concern the coroner and was not mentioned at the inquest, but it worried Howard because he could not understand it. Ellen had said that if Mr McIntyre took her out to eat, it was always somewhere near the office.

There seemed to be a conspiracy to prevent him from being alone. The Dempseys asked him in to supper once or twice a week and regularly for Sunday lunch, other neighbours dropped in for a chat, the vicar came round and so did a member of the committee that ran the church socials, to ask if he could lend a hand with the next outing. His chief Hebden, the sub-controller, with whom he had never been particularly friendly, surprised Howard by asking him to dinner. He accepted on the spur of the moment, but the evening was not a success. Hebden and he had little in common, and Mrs Hebden kept referring to what she called his tragic loss, and said that she thought lorries should not be allowed on the same roads as cars. Howard left, determined not to accept another invitation.

He had to show determination in getting free of the Dempseys. Carol had taken to coming round almost every evening, bringing hot soup or a piece of jam tart. When she offered to sort through Ellen's clothes and give them to some good cause she favoured, he said that he would do it himself.

'But Howard, that's foolish.' The Dempseys were a little older than the Careys, but Carol dressed and acted younger than her years. She was a dumpy little woman who always wore bright clothes, which he disliked. 'I mean, you're just making things more painful for yourself.'

The clothes, Howard decided, were not the only things he disliked about Carol. She had a slightly lop-sided nose that he found distasteful. 'It's very kind of you, but I can do them.'

'At least let me help. Two do these things so much more easily than one. I shouldn't pry into anything.'

He found suddenly that his whole body was shaking. 'What do you mean? What would there be to pry into, as you call it?'

'Nothing, Howard. I didn't mean————'

'Why do you want to stick your nose into our affairs?' As he spoke the nose, with its small but decisive turn near the end, looked enormously enlarged and seemed to quiver with a life of its own.

'If that's your attitude I won't mention it again.'

'And I don't want this stuff.'

Howard went to give back the bowl of fruit jelly she had brought in, but it slipped from his hands and fell to the floor, breaking the bowl. Carol said nothing, but walked out of the kitchen. Later he bought a replacement bowl and put it outside their back door. After that there were no more invitations to dinner, and no little dishes were brought in.

Nevertheless, Carol had been right in saying that he must do something about Ellen's things. He threw into the dustbin the pots of cosmetics, scent, and other things on her dressing table—she must have spent a lot of money on such stuff—but her dresses hung in the cupboard, her other clothes were in a chest of drawers. He packed a suitcase full of them, and took it down to the local Oxfam shop in the little Morris car they had had for years. That's that, he thought as he returned, and it's been done without any help from that sly-nosed bitch next door.

He was surprised to find himself thinking so coarsely.

On the next evening he found the letters.

There was one drawer in the chest that Ellen had always kept locked. It was her personal drawer, she said, and when he asked what she meant by that, she laughed and said that curiosity killed the cat. The key had been in her bag at the time of the accident, and was returned to him after the inquest. When he turned it in the lock he expected to find little more than Ellen's jewellery, which she had told him she kept there.

The jewellery was there, the few inexpensive bits he had been able to afford and other things too, a diamond ring, a pair of pearl earrings, what looked like a ruby necklace. He had never seen them before. Had they belonged to Ellen's mother? The box containing the ring looked modern. There were other things that occasioned him no surprise, a photograph taken on their wedding day and pictures of Rod at school.

And there were the letters.

There were more than twenty of them, in their envelopes, addressed to Mrs Howard Carey. He remembered one of them arriving. Ellen had said it was from an old school friend, and he had said that she wrote a good firm hand. He had said nothing further, and he would never have thought of looking at her correspondence. But these letters were from no old school friend. They began 'Dearest Ellen' or 'Darling', and were signed 'Mac'. They told the story of a love affair. The first letter had been written several years ago, the last was less than three months old.

Howard Carey was a methodical man. He sat down on the bed with the letters and read them in chronological order, so that he had the whole story. Mac of course was Mr McIntyre, and it seemed that they had become lovers soon after she went to work for him. He was married, but his wife was hopelessly neurotic, in and out of mental institutions. The letters had been written when McIntyre had taken his wife away on holiday during short periods of recovery, and so had not seen Ellen for two or three weeks. The wife's illness made any thought of marriage impossible, but those evenings when she had been 'working late' had been spent in his St John's Wood apartment. There were references to 'the agony of parting' and 'sending you back to that crusty dry old stick who thinks of you only as his housekeeper'. And there were other remarks about Howard. 'I cannot bear to think of you in his arms, but then from what you say he never holds you in them . . . You say that if you left him it would break his heart, but what makes you think he has one? He has never cared for you, does not know what love means.' Then there were passages about 'burning for you' and 'longing for you', as well as explicit words and phrases about making love, words that reminded him of what had been said by the young girl in the street.

He took two of the pills prescribed for him by the doctor, but could not sleep. What had Ellen been like? He switched on the light and looked long and earnestly at the photograph beside the bed, trying to discover in the features of the woman he had known the slut who had entered McIntyre's bed. She was in her forties. Did women have the desires mentioned in the letters at such an age? When he turned off the light again, sexual images rioted through his mind, he saw Ellen happily shrieking obscenities. Then he must have slept, because she appeared with extraordinary vividness before him, laughing and saying: 'Of course I do it, I do it with anybody—*except you.*' He woke crying out, and did not sleep again.

It was from this evening onwards that Howard Carey felt he really understood the meaning of the world around him, and knew the purpose of his life. He did his work in the Complaints Department with reasonable efficiency, although Hebden told Mr Langport that Carey hardly seemed to be there half the time and in his opinion should be compelled to take some leave. The manager called Carey in for a chat, but saw nothing wrong. When he asked how things were going Carey said very well, he was much clearer in his mind now. It was a slightly odd answer, but hardly justified sending a man on leave.

So Howard went on working, arriving and leaving punctually. He shopped at the local supermarket, mostly foods that could be heated quickly. He washed up after eating, and then used the vacuum cleaner, so that Mon Repos was scrupulously clean. After eating, washing up, and cleaning the house, he went for a long walk in the winter night. If while out walking he saw neighbours, like the Dempseys, he ignored them. His walk usually ended at one or other local pub, where he drank half a pint of beer and looked keenly at the women who came in unaccompanied. One evening a man told him that if he was looking for a bit of stuff, he'd find plenty at the Rising Sun. After that his walks ended there, but he did not find what he was looking for. He was accosted outside the pub a couple of times, but brusquely rejected the invitations made to him. Every night, after his return, he read the letters. He now knew several parts of them by heart.

He saw the knife on a night when the pavements and road gleamed with rain, a slanting rain that he trudged through with hat pulled down over his eyes. The knife was in the window of a seedy little shop, among shears, scissors, and nail clippers. It had a long thin blade narrowing to a point, so that it resembled a miniature sword, and it seemed to Howard that it glittered like a jewel among all the rubbish beside it. Beneath it was a label: *Stiletto type blade, many uses*.

The shop was closed when he came home in the evening, but he bought the knife at the weekend.

'Very nice little job, sir,' the man behind the counter said appreciatively. 'Beautiful cutting edge. Clicks back into the handle too. On a spring.' He demonstrated.

Howard held it with the point on his palm, moved it fractionally downwards. A bead of blood showed.

'You have to be careful of that point, sir. I'll get you something.'

'It doesn't matter.' Howard dabbed with a handkerchief. 'I'll take it.'

When he returned from this expedition the Dempseys were at their gate. He was passing them with a nod when Carol spoke.

'Horrible weather. Don't know when the winter's going to end. And you have to be out in it such a lot, don't you? We've seen you coming home once or twice.'

They had been spying on him! He did not reply, simply glared. But she went on.

'Why not come in tomorrow for Sunday lunch? So long since we've seen you.'

He muttered that he was too busy, had no time, and slammed his gate, leaving them staring after him.

After that he took the car out at nights and became one of the kerb crawlers. He had seen their technique in his walks. They moved along, hardly ever at more than five miles an hour, stopping when they saw one or two girls together, sometimes flashing their lights. There would be a brief discussion. Then the girls might move away or one—occasionally both—would get into the car, which speeded up as it drove away.

Now he did this himself. Girls came up and spoke to him, offering various 'services' as they called it, none of which he accepted. After a few days he became known, and some of the rejected girls were annoyed. One abused him at the car window.

'What do yer bleedin' want, then? Know what you are, just a dirty old man wants to hear girls talk about it and that's all. You keep out of my way or I'll tell my feller. He'll do you over, I can tell you that.'

After that he moved to another area a few streets away, one which he had avoided because it contained so many blacks, and he was a little afraid of them. Sure enough, one night a black girl opened the car door and sat down beside him. A black man came to the window grinning, and said, 'You want little Joanna?'

'No. I didn't ask her to get in, I don't want her.'

'That ain't what he said, is it Joanna? You hurt my little girl's feelings, I don't like that, you better give her a fiver, show you don't mean it.'

'I'll call the police.'

The man came round to Howard's door, opened it, stuck his head inside and said, 'You won't call pussy.'

The knife was in his pocket, but he dared not draw it. He gave the girl the money and drove away, pursued by raucous laughter.

In the end he found her by chance, in a street remote from the areas of prostitution. He was driving down it when he saw ahead of him the white mackintosh and the reddish gold hair. He pulled up beside her and opened the passenger door.

'Get in.'

She looked doubtfully at him, then said, 'No, thank you.'

Of course she was nervous, it was off her beat. He leant over, pulled her arm, jerked her into the car and closed the door in one motion, drove off.

'What the hell are you doing?' she said.

He spoke rapidly. 'Look, we met before and I said no then but I didn't mean it, everybody wants it, my wife did, she loved it. She liked to be held in his arms naked and why not?' His right hand was in his pocket, he had the knife out and open.

'I don't know what you're talking about. Just let me out.'

'This is what everybody wants,' he said. He leaned over and put in the knife. 'Ellen,' he said. 'Hold me, Ellen.'

She did not cry out, so he withdrew the knife and plunged it in again. Now she leaned over and, with a sigh, came to rest in his arms. He pulled up, and put an arm round her. They were under a street lamp and only now, as the blood from her white mackintosh stained his hand and the light showed her features clearly, a rather coarse face with a twisted nose strangely like Carol Dempsey's, did he realize that he had picked up the wrong girl.

MICHAEL GILBERT · 1912–

The Killing of Michael Finnegan

'They burned him to death,' said Elfe. He said it without any attempt to soften the meaning of what he was saying. 'He was almost certainly alive when they dumped him in the car and set fire to it.'

Deputy Assistant Commissioner Elfe had a long, sad face and grey hair. In the twenty years that he had been head of the Special Branch he had seen more brutality, more treachery, more fanaticism, more hatred than had any of his predecessors in war or in peace. Twice he had tried to retire, and twice had been persuaded to stay.

'He couldn't have put up much of a fight,' said Mr Calder, 'only having one arm and one and a half legs.'

They were talking about Michael Finnegan, whose charred carcass had been found in a burnt-out stolen car in one of the lonelier parts of Hampstead Heath. Finnegan had been a lieutenant in the Marines until he had blown off his right arm and parts of his right leg whilst defusing a new type of anti-personnel mine. During his long convalescence his wife Sheilagh had held the home together, supplementing Michael's disability pension by working as a secretary. Then Finnegan had taught himself to write left-handed, and had gained a reputation, and a reasonable amount of cash for his articles; first only in service journals, but later in the national press, where he had constituted himself a commentator on men and affairs.

'It's odd,' as Mr Behrens once observed, 'you'd think that he'd be a militant chauvinist. Actually he seems to be a moderate and a pacifist. It was Finnegan who started arguing that we ought to withdraw our troops from Ireland. That was long before the IRA made it one of the main planks in their platform.'

'You can never tell how a serious injury will affect a man,' said Mr Calder. This was, of course, before he had become professionally involved with Michael Finnegan.

'For the last year you've been acting as his runner, haven't you?' said Elfe. 'You must have got to know him well.'

'Him and his wife,' said Mr Calder. 'They were a great couple.' He thought about the unremarkable house at Banstead with its tiny flower garden in front and its rather larger kitchen garden at the back, both of which Michael Finnegan tended one-armed, hobbling down between whiles for a pint at the local. A respected man with many friends, and acquaintances, none of whom knew that he was playing a lonely, patient, dangerous game. His articles in the papers, his casual contacts, letters to old friends in Ireland, conversations with new friends in the pub, all had been slanted towards a predetermined end.

The fact was that the shape of the IRA's activities in England was changing, a change which had been forced on them by the systematic penetration of their English groups. Now, when an act of terrorism was planned, the operators came from Ireland to carry it out, departing as soon as it was done. They travelled a roundabout route, via Morocco or Tunis, entering England from France or Belgium and returning by the same way. Explosives, detonators, and other material for the job came separately, and in advance. Their one essential requirement was an operational base where materials could be stored and the operators could lodge for the few days needed for the job.

It was to hold out his house as such a safe base that every move in Michael Finnegan's life had been planned.

'We agreed,' said Mr Calder, 'that as far as possible, Michael should have no direct contacts of any sort with the security forces. What the Department did was to lease a house which had a good view, from its front windows, of Michael's back gate. They installed one of their pensioners in it, old Mrs Lovelock————'

'Minnie Lovelock?' said Elfe. 'She used to type for me forty years ago. I was terrified of her, even then.'

'All she had to do was to keep Michael's kitchen window sill under observation at certain hours. There was a simple code of signals. A flower pot meant the arrival of explosives or arms. One or more milk bottles signalled the arrival of that number of operators. And the house gave us one further advantage. Minnie put it about that she had sublet a room on the first floor to a commercial gentleman who kept his samples there, and occasionally put up there for the night. For the last year the commercial gent was me. I was able to slip out, after dark, up the garden path and in at the back door. I tried to go at least once a month. My ostensible job was to collect any information Michael might have for us. In fact, I believe my visits kept him sane. We used to talk for hours. He liked to hear the gossip, all about the inter-departmental feuds, and funny stories about the Minister.'

'And about the head of the Special Branch?'

'Oh, certainly. He particularly enjoyed the story of how two of your men tried to arrest each other.'

Elfe grunted and said, 'Go on.'

'And there was one further advantage. Michael had a key of this room. In a serious emergency he could deposit a message—after dark, of course—or even use it as an escape hatch for Sheilagh and himself.'

'Did his wife know what he was up to?'

'She had to be told something, if only to explain my visits. Our cover story was that Michael was gathering information about subversion in the docks. This was plausible, as he'd done an Intelligence job in the Marines. She may have suspected that it was more than that. She never interfered. She's a grand girl.'

Elfe said, 'Yes.' And after a pause, 'Yes. That's really what I wanted to tell you. I've had a word with your chief. He agrees with me. This is a job we can't use you in.'

'Oh,' said Mr Calder coldly. 'Why not?'

'Because you'd feel yourself personally involved. You'd be unable to be sufficiently dispassionate about it. You knew Finnegan and his wife far too well.'

Mr Calder thought about that. If Fortescue had backed the prohibition it would be little use kicking. He said, 'I suppose we *are* doing something about it.'

'Of course. Superintendent Outram and Sergeant Fallows are handling it. They're both members of the AT squad, and very capable operators.'

'I know Tom Outram,' said Mr Calder. 'He's a sound man. I'll promise not to get under his feet. But I'm already marginally involved. If he wants to question Sheilagh he'll have to do it at my cottage. I moved her straight down there as soon as I heard the news. Gave her a strong sleeping pill and put her to bed.'

'They wondered where she'd disappeared to. I'll tell them she's living with you.'

'If you put it quite like that,' said Mr Calder, 'it might be misunderstood. She's being chaperoned, by Rasselas.'

'I think,' said Superintendent Outram, 'that we'd better see Mrs Finnegan alone. That is, if you don't mind.'

He and Sergeant Fallows had driven out to Mr Calder's cottage, which was built on a shoulder of the North Downs above Lamperdown in Kent.

'I don't mind,' said Mr Calder. 'But you'll have to look out for Rasselas.'

'Your dog?'

'Yes. Mrs Finnegan's still in a state of shock, and Rasselas is very worried about it. The postman said something sharp to her—not meaning any harm at all—and he went for him. Luckily I was there and I was able to stop him.'

'Couldn't we see her without Rasselas?'

'I wouldn't care to try and shift him.'

Outram thought about it. Then he said, 'Then I think you'd better sit in with us.'

'I think that might be wise,' said Mr Calder gravely.

Sheilagh Finnegan had black hair and a white face out of which looked eyes of startling Irish blue. Her mouth was thin and tight and angry. It was clear that she was under stress. When Outram and Fallows came in she took one look at them and jerked as though an electric shock had gone through her.

Rasselas, who was stretched out on the floor beside her, raised his head and regarded the two men thoughtfully.

'Just like he was measuring us for a coffin,' said Fallows afterwards.

Mr Calder sat on the sofa, and put one hand on the dog's head.

It took Outram fifteen minutes of patient, low-keyed questioning to discover that Mrs Finnegan could tell him very little. Her husband, she said, had suggested that she needed a break, and had arranged for her to spend a week in a small private hotel at Folkestone. She wasn't sorry to agree because she hadn't had a real holiday in the last three or four years.

Outram nodded sympathetically. Had the holiday been fixed suddenly? Out of the blue, like? Sheilagh gave more attention to this than she had to some of the earlier questions. She said, 'We'd often talked about it before. Michael knew I had friends at Folkestone.'

'But on this occasion it was your husband who suggested it? How long before you left?'

'Two or three days.'

'Then it *was* fairly sudden.'

'Fairly sudden, yes.'

'Did he give any particular reason? Had he had an unexpected message? Something like that.'

'He didn't say anything about a message. I wouldn't have known about it, anyway. I was out at work all day.'

Outram said, 'Yes, of course.'

There was nothing much more she could tell them. A quarter of an hour later the two men drove off. As their car turned down the hill they passed Mr Behrens, who was walking up from Lamperdown. Mr Behrens waved to the superintendent.

'Looks a genial old cove,' said Sergeant Fallows.

'That's what he looks like,' agreed Outram.

When Mr Behrens reached the cottage he found Mr Calder and Sheilagh making coffee in the kitchen. They added a third cup to the tray and carried it back to the sitting-room where Rasselas was apparently asleep. By contrast with what had gone before it was a relaxed and peaceful scene.

Mr Calder tried the coffee, found it still too hot, put the cup carefully back on its saucer, and said, 'Why were you holding out on the superintendent?'

'How did you know I was holding out?'

'Rasselas and I both knew it.'

Hearing his name the great dog opened one brown eye, as though to confirm what Mr Calder had said, and then shut it again.

'If I tell you about it,' said Sheilagh, 'you'll understand why I was holding out.'

'Then tell us at once,' said Mr Behrens.

'Of course I knew something was in the wind. I didn't know exactly what Michael was up to. He was careful not to tell me any details. But whatever it was he was doing, I realized it was coming to a head. That was why he sent me away. He said it shouldn't be more than two or three days. He'd get word to me as soon as he could. That was on the Friday. I had a miserable weekend, you can imagine. Monday came, and Tuesday, and still no word. By Wednesday I couldn't take it any longer. What I did was wrong, I know, but I couldn't help myself.'

'You went back,' said Mr Calder. He said it sympathetically.

'That's just what I did. I planned it carefully. I wasn't going to barge in and upset all Michael's plans. I just wanted to see he was all right and go away again. He'd given me a key of that room in Mrs Lovelock's house. I got there after dark. There's a clear view from the window straight into our kitchen. The light was on and the curtains weren't drawn.'

As she talked she was living the scene. Mr Behrens pictured her, crouched in the dark, like an eager theatre-goer in the gallery staring down onto the lighted stage.

She said, 'I could see Michael. He was boiling a kettle on the stove and moving about, setting out cups and plates. There were two other

people in the room. I could see the legs of a man who was sitting at the
kitchen table. Once, when he leant forward, I got a glimpse of him.
All I could tell you was that he was young and had black hair. The
other was a girl. I saw her quite plainly. She was dark, too. Medium
height and rather thin. The sort of girl who could dress as a man and
get away with it. I got the impression, somehow, that they'd just
arrived, and Michael was bustling about making them at home. The
girl still had her outdoor coat on. Maybe that's what gave me the idea.
Just then I saw another man coming. He was walking along the road
which runs behind our kitchen garden, and when he stopped, he was
right under the window where I was sitting. When he opened the
gate I could see that he was taking a lot of trouble not to make any
noise. He shut the gate very gently, and stood there for a moment,
looking at the lighted kitchen window. Then he tiptoed up the garden
path and stood, to one side of the kitchen window, looking in. That's
when I saw his face clearly for the first time.'

Sheilagh was speaking more slowly now. Mr Calder was leaning
forward with his hands on his knees. Rasselas was no longer pretending to be asleep. Mr Behrens could feel the tension without understanding it.

'Then he seemed to make up his mind. He went across to the
kitchen door, opened it, without knocking, and went in quickly, as
though he was planning to surprise the people inside. Next moment,
someone had dragged the curtains across. From the moment I first
saw that man I knew that he meant harm to Michael. But once the
curtains were shut I couldn't see what was happening.'

'You couldn't see,' said Mr Calder. 'But could you hear?'

'Nothing. On account of Mrs Lovelock's television set in the room
just above me. She's deaf and keeps it on full strength. All I could do
was sit and wait. It must have been nearly an hour later when I saw
the back door open. All the lights in the house had been turned out
and it was difficult to see but Michael was between the two men. They
seemed to be supporting him. The girl was walking behind. They
came out and turned up the road. Then I noticed there was a car
parked about twenty yards further up. They all got into it. And I went
on sitting there. I couldn't think what to do.'

There was a moment of silence. Neither of the men wanted to
break it. Sheilagh said, 'I do realize now that I should have done something. I should have run down, screamed, made a fuss. Anything
to stop them taking Michael away like that. But I didn't know what
was happening. Going with them might all have been part of his plan.'

'It was an impossible situation,' said Mr Calder.

'When you thought about it afterwards,' said Mr Behrens, 'am I right about this? You got the impression that things had been going smoothly until that other man arrived, and that he was the one who upset things.'

'He was the one who gave Michael away,' said Sheilagh. 'I'm sure of it.' There was a different note in her voice now. Something hard and very cold.

'I agree with Calder,' said Mr Behrens. 'You couldn't have done anything else at the time. But as soon as you knew that things had gone wrong for Michael why didn't you tell the police everything that you've just told us? Time was vital. You could give a good description of two of the people involved. Surely there wasn't a moment to lose.'

Sheilagh said, 'I didn't go to the police because I recognized the man, the one who arrived on foot. I'd seen his photograph. Michael had pointed it out to me in the paper. I only saw him clearly as he stood outside the lighted window, but I was fairly certain I was right.' She paused, then added, 'Now I'm quite certain.'

Both men looked at her.

She said, 'It was Sergeant Fallows.'

The silence that followed was broken unexpectedly. Rasselas gave a growl at the back of his throat, got up, stalked to the door, pushed it open with his nose, and went out. They heard him settling down again outside.

'That's where he goes when he's on guard,' said Mr Calder.

There was another silence.

'I know what you're thinking,' said Sheilagh. 'You both think I'm crazy, but I'm not. It *was* Fallows.'

'Not an easy face to forget,' agreed Mr Calder, 'and it would explain something that had been puzzling me. We'd taken such tight precautions over Michael that I didn't see how they could suddenly have known that he was a plant. He might eventually have done something, or said something, which gave him away. They might have got suspicious. But not certain. Not straight away. It could only have happened like that if he was betrayed, and the only person who could have betrayed him was someone working in the Squad.'

Mr Behrens's mind had been moving on a different line. He said, 'When they got into the car, and turned the lights on, you'd have been able to see the number plate at the back, I take it.'

'That's right. I saw it, and wrote it down. I've put it here. LKK 910P.'

'Good girl. Now think back. When you were talking about the last man to arrive you called him "the one who came on foot". What made you say that?'

Sheilagh said, 'I'm not sure. I suppose because he came from the opposite direction to where the car was parked. So I assumed————'

'I'm not disputing it. In fact, I'm sure you were right. Fallows wouldn't have driven up in a police car. He wouldn't even have risked taking his own car. He'd have gone by bus or train to the nearest point and walked the rest of the way.'

Mr Calder said, 'Then the car belonged to the Irish couple. Of course, they might have stolen it, like the one they left on the Heath.'

'They might. But why risk it? It would only draw attention to them, which was the last thing they wanted. My guess is that they hired it. Just for the time they were planning to be here.'

'If you're right,' said Mr Calder, 'there's a lot to do and not much time to do it. You'd better trace that car. And remember, we've been officially warned off, so you can't use the police computer.'

'LKK's a Kent number. I've got a friend in County Hall who'll help.'

'I'll look into the Fallows end of it. It'll mean leaving you alone here for a bit, Sheilagh, but if anyone should turn up and cause trouble Rasselas will attend to him.'

'In case there might be two of them,' said Mr Behrens, 'you'd better take this. It's loaded. That's the safety-catch. You push it down when you want to fire.'

The girl examined the gun with interest. She said, 'I've never used one, but I suppose, if I got quite close to the man, pointed it at his stomach, and pulled the trigger————'

'The results should be decisive,' said Mr Behrens.

Fallows was whistling softly to himself as he walked along the carpeted corridor to the door of his flat. It was on the top floor of a new block on the Regent's Park side of Albany Street and seemed an expensive pad for a detective sergeant. He opened the door, walked down the short hall into the living-room, switched on the light and stopped.

A middle-aged man, with greying hair and steel-rimmed glasses was standing by the fireplace regarding him benevolently. Fallows recognized him, but had no time to be surprised. As he stepped forward something soft but heavy hit him on the back of the neck.

When he came round, about five minutes later, he was seated in a heavy chair. His arms had been attached to the arms of the chair and his legs to its legs by yards of elastic bandage, wound round and round. Mr Behrens was examining the contents of an attaché case which he had brought with him. Mr Calder was watching him. Both men were in their shirt sleeves and were wearing surgical gloves.

'I think our patient is coming round,' said Mr Calder.

'What the bloody hell are you playing at?' said Fallows.

Mr Behrens said, 'First, I'm going to give you these pills. They're ordinary sleeping pills. I think four should be sufficient. We don't want him actually to go to sleep. Just to feel drowsy.'

'Bloody hell you will.'

'If you want me to wedge your mouth open, hold your nose and hit you on the throat each time until you swallow, I'm quite prepared to do it, but it'd be undignified and rather painful.'

Fallows glared at him, but there was an implacable look behind the steel spectacles which silenced him. He swallowed the pills.

Mr Behrens looked at his watch, and said, 'We'll give them five minutes to start working. What we're trying'—he turned courteously back to Fallows—'is an experiment which has often been suggested but never, I think, actually performed. We're going to give you successive doses of scopalamine dextrin to inhale, whilst we ask you some questions. In the ordinary way I have no doubt you would be strong enough to resist the scopalamine until you became unconscious. There are men who have sufficient resources of will power to do that. That's why we first weaken your resistance with a strong sedative. Provided we strike exactly the right balance, the results should be satisfactory. About ready now, I think.'

He took a capsule from a box on the table and broke it under Fallows's nose.

'The snag about this method,' he continued, in the same level tones of a professor addressing a class of students, 'is that the interreaction of the sedative and the stimulant would be so sharp that it might, if persisted with, affect the subject's heart. You'll appreciate therefore —head up, Sergeant—that by prolonging our dialogue you may be risking your own life. Now then. Let's start with your visit to Banstead———'

This produced a single, sharp obscenity.

Fifty minutes later Mr Behrens switched off his tape recorder. He said, 'I think he's gone. I did warn him that it might happen if he fought too hard.'

'And my God, did he fight,' said Mr Calder. He was sweating.

'We'd better set the scene. I think he'd look more convincing if we put him on his bed.'

He was unwinding the elastic bandages and was glad to see that, in spite of Fallows's struggles, they had left no mark. The nearly empty bottle of sleeping pills, a half empty bottle of whisky and a tumbler were arranged on the bedside table. Mr Behrens closed Fallows's flaccid hand round the tumbler, and then knocked it onto the floor.

'Leave the bedside light on,' said Mr Calder. 'No one commits suicide in the dark.'

'I've done a transcript of the tape for you,' said Sheilagh. 'I've cut out some of the swearing, but otherwise it's all there. There's no doubt, now, that he betrayed Michael, is there?'

'None at all,' said Mr Behrens. 'That was something he seemed almost proud of. The trouble was that when we edged up to one of the things we really wanted to know, an automatic defence mechanism seemed to take over and when we fed him a little more scopalamine to break through it, he started to ramble.'

'All the same,' said Mr Calder, 'we know a good deal. We know what they're planning to do, and roughly when. But not how.'

Mr Behrens was studying the neatly typed paper. He said, 'J.J. That's clear enough. Jumping Judas. It's their name for Mr Justice Jellicoe. That's their target all right. They've been gunning for him ever since he sent down the Manchester bombers. I've traced their car. It was hired in Dover last Friday, for ten days. The man they hired it from told them he had another customer who wanted it on the Monday afternoon. They said that suited them because they were planning to let him have it back by one o'clock that day. Which means that whatever they're going to do is timed to be done sometime on Monday morning, and they aim to be boarding a cross-Channel ferry by the time it happens.'

'They might have been lying to the man,' said Sheilagh.

'Yes. They might have been. But bear in mind that if they brought the car back on Saturday afternoon or Sunday the hire firm would be shut for the weekend and they'd have to leave the car standing about in the street, which would call attention to it. No. I think they've got a timetable, and they're sticking to it.'

'Which gives us three days to find out what it is,' said Mr Calder. 'If the pay-off is on Monday there are two main possibilities. Jellicoe spends his weekends at his country house at Witham, in Essex. He's pretty safe there. He's got a permanent police guard and three boxer dogs who are devoted to him. He comes up to court on Monday by car, with a police driver. All right. That's one chance. They could arrange some sort of ambush. Detonate one of their favourite long-distance mines. Not easy, though, because there are three different routes the car can take. This isn't the Ulster border. They can't go round laying minefields all over Essex.'

'The alternative,' said Mr Behrens, 'is to try something in or around the Law Courts. We'll have to split this. You take the Witham end. Have a word with the bodyguard. They may not know that we've been warned off, so they'll probably co-operate. I'll tackle the London end.'

'Isn't there something I could do?' said Sheilagh.

'Yes,' said Mr Calder. 'There is. Play that tape over again and again. Twenty times. Until you know it by heart. There was something, inside Fallows's muddled brain, trying to get out. It may be a couple of words. Even a single word. If you can interpret it, it could be the key to the whole thing.'

So Friday was spent by Mr Calder at Witham, making friends with a police sergeant and a police constable; by Sheilagh Finnegan listening to the drug-induced ramblings of the man who had been responsible for her husband's death; and by Mr Behrens investigating the possibility of blowing up a judge in court.

As a first step he introduced himself to Major Baines. The major, after service in the Royal Marines, had been given the job of looking after security at the Law Courts. He had known Michael Finnegan, and was more than willing to help.

He said, 'It's a rambling great building. I think the chap who designed it had a Ruritanian palace in mind. Narrow windows, heavy doors, battlements and turrets, and iron gratings. The judges have a private entrance, which is inside the car park. Everyone else, barristers, solicitors, visitors, all have to use the front door in the Strand, or the back door in Carey Street. They're both guarded, of course. Teams of security officers, good men. Mostly ex-policemen.'

'I was watching them for a time, first thing this morning,' said Mr Behrens. 'Most people had to open their bags and cases, but there were people carrying sort of blue and red washing bags. They let them through uninspected.'

'They'd be barristers, or barristers' clerks, and they'd let them through because they knew their faces. But I can assure you of one thing. When Mr Justice Jellicoe is on the premises everyone opens everything.'

'Which court will he be using?'

Major Baines consulted the printed list. 'On Monday he's in Court Number Two. That's one of the courts at the back. I'll show you.'

He led the way down the vast entrance hall. Mr Behrens saw what he meant when he described it as a palace. Marble columns, spiral staircases, interior balconies, and an elaborately tessellated floor.

'Up these stairs,' said Baines. 'That's Number Two Court. And there's the back door, straight ahead of you. It leads out into Carey Street.'

'So that anyone making for Court Number Two would be likely to come this way?'

'Not if they were coming from the Strand.'

'True,' said Mr Behrens. 'I think I'll hang around for a bit and watch the form.'

He went back to the main hall and found himself a seat, which commanded the front entrance.

It was now ten o'clock and the flow of people coming in was continuous. They were channelled between desks placed lengthways, and three security guards were operating. They did their job thoroughly. Occasionally, when they recognized a face, a man was waved through. Otherwise everyone opened anything they were carrying and placed it on top of the desk. Suitcases, briefcases, even women's handbags were carefully examined. The red and blue bags which, Mr Behrens decided, must contain law books were sometimes looked into, sometimes not. They would all be looked into on Monday morning.

'It seemed pretty water-tight to me,' said Mr Behrens to Sheilagh and Mr Calder, as they compared notes after supper. 'Enough explosive to be effective would be bulky and an elaborate timing device would add to the weight and bulk. They might take a chance and put the whole thing in the bottom of one of those book bags and hope it wouldn't be looked at, but they don't seem to me to be people who take chances of that sort.'

'Could the stuff have been brought in during the weekend and left somewhere in the court?'

'I put it to Baines. He said no. The building is shut on Friday evening and given a thorough going-over on Saturday.'

'Sheilagh and I have worked one thing out,' said Mr Behrens. 'There's a reference, towards the end, to "fields". In the transcript it's been reproduced as "in the fields", and the assumption was that the attempt was going to be made in the country, when Jellicoe was driving up to London. But if you listen very carefully it isn't "in the fields". It's "in fields" with the emphasis on the first word, and there's a sort of crackle in the tape before it which makes it difficult to be sure, but I think what he's saying is "Lincoln's Inn Fields".'

They listened once more to the tape.

Mr Calder said, 'I think you're right.'

'And it does explain one point,' said Mr Behrens. 'When I explored the area this morning it struck me how difficult it was to park a car. But Lincoln's Inn Fields could be ideal—there are parking spaces all down the south and east sides, and the south-east corner is less than two hundred yards from the rear entrance to the courts.'

'Likely enough,' said Mr Calder, 'but it still doesn't explain how they're going to get the stuff in. Did you get anything else out of the tape, Sheilagh?'

'I made a list of the words and expressions he used most often. Some were just swearing, apart from that his mind seemed to be running on time. He said "midday" and "twelve o'clock" a dozen times at least. And he talks about a "midday special". That seemed to be some sort of joke. He doesn't actually use the word "explosion", but he talks once or twice about a report, or reports.'

'Report?' said Mr Calder thoughtfully. 'That sounds more like a shot from a gun than a bomb.'

'It's usually in the plural. Reports.'

'Several guns.'

'Rather elaborate, surely. Hidden rifles, trained on the Bench, and timed to go off at midday?'

'And it still doesn't explain how he gets the stuff past the guards,' said Mr Behrens.

He took the problem down the hill with him to his house in Lamperdown village and carried it up to bed. He knew, from experience, that he would get little sleep until he had solved it. The irritating thing was that the answer was there. He was sure of it. He had only to remember what he had seen and connect it up with the words on the tape, and the solution would appear, as inevitably as the jackpot came out of the slot when you got three lemons in a row.

Visualize the people, pouring through the entrance into the building, carrying briefcases, book bags, handbags. One man had had a camera slung over his shoulder. The guard had called his attention to a notice prohibiting the taking of photographs in court. This little episode had held up the queue for a moment. The young man behind, a barrister's clerk Mr Behrens guessed, had been in a hurry, and had pushed past the camera-owner. He had not been searched, because he hadn't been carrying a case. But he had been carrying *something*. When Mr Behrens reached this point he did, in fact, doze off, so that the solution must have reached him in his sleep.

Next morning, after breakfast, he telephoned his solicitor, catching him before he set out for the golf course. He said, 'When you go into court, and have to tell the judge what another judge said in another case————'

'Quote a precedent, you mean.'

'That's right. Well, do you take the book with you, or is it already in court?'

'Both. There's a complete set of Reports in court. Several sets, in fact. They're for the judges. And you bring your own with you.'

'That might mean lugging in a lot of books.'

'A trolleyful sometimes.'

'Suppose you had, say, five or six sets of Reports to carry. How would you manage?'

'I'd get my clerk to carry them.'

'All right,' said Mr Behrens patiently; 'how would he manage?'

'If it was just half a dozen books, he's got a sort of strap affair, with a handle.'

'That's what I thought I remembered seeing,' said Mr Behrens. 'Thank you very much.'

'I suppose you've got some reason for asking all these questions?'

'An excellent reason.'

His solicitor, who knew Mr Behrens, said no more.

'We'll get there early,' said Mr Calder, 'and park as close as we can to the south-east corner. There's plenty of cover in the garden and we can watch both lines of cars. As soon as one of us spots LKK 910P he tips off the others using one of these pocket radios. Quite easy, Sheilagh. Just press the button and talk. Then let it go, and listen.'

'That doesn't sound too difficult,' said Sheilagh, 'what then?'

'Then Henry gets busy.'

'Who's Henry?'

'An old friend of mine who'll be coming with us. His job is to unlock the boot of their car as soon as they're clear of it. By my reckoning he'll have ten minutes for the job, which will be nine and a half minutes more than he needs.'

The man and girl walked up Searle Street, not hurrying, but not wasting time, crossed Carey Street, climbed the five shallow steps and pushed through the swing doors and into the court building.

Mr Behrens had got there before them. He was standing on the far side of the barrier. A little queue had already formed and he had plenty of time to observe them.

They had dressed for the occasion with ritual care. The man in a dark suit, cream shirt, and dark red tie. The girl in the uniform of a female barrister, black dress, black shoes and stockings, with a single touch of colour, the collar points of a yellow shirt showing at the throat.

As he watched them edge forward to the barrier Mr Behrens felt a prickle of superstitious dread. They might have been nervous, but they showed no sign of it. They looked serious and composed, like the young crusaders who, for the more thorough purging of the holy places, mutilated the living bodies of their pagan prisoners; like the novices who watched impassively at the *auto-da-fé* where men and women were burned to the greater glory of God.

Now they were at the barrier. The girl was carrying a book bag and a satchel. She opened them both. The search was thorough and took time. The man showed very slight signs of impatience.

Mr Behrens thought: they've rehearsed this very carefully.

When it came to the man's turn he placed the six books, held together in a white strap, on the counter and opened the briefcase. The guard searched the briefcase, and nodded. The man picked up the books and the case and walked down the short length of corridor to where the girl was standing. He ignored her, turned the corner and made for Court Number Two. Although it was not yet ten o'clock there were already a number of people in the courtroom. Two elderly barristers were standing by the front bench discussing something. Behind them a girl was arranging a pile of books and papers. The young man placed his six books, still strapped together, on the far end of the back bench, and went out as quietly as he had come in. No one took any notice of him.

A minute later Mr Behrens appeared, picked up the books, and left. No one took any notice of him either.

When the young man came out he had joined the girl and they moved off together. Having come in by the back entrance it was evidently their intention to leave by the front. They had gone about ten paces when a man stopped them. He said, 'Excuse me, but have you got your cards?'

'Cards?' said the young man. He seemed unconcerned.

'We're issuing personal identity cards to all barristers using the court. Your clerk should have told you. If you'd come with me I'll give you yours.'

The girl looked at the man, who nodded slightly, and they set off after their guide. He led the way down a long, empty passage towards the western annexe to the courts.

The young man closed up behind him. He put his hand into a side pocket, pulled out a leather cosh, moved a step closer, and hit the man on the head. Their guide went forward onto his knees and rolled over onto his face.

The young man and the girl had swung round and were moving back the way they had come.

'Walk, don't run,' said the young man.

They turned a corner, and went down a spiral staircase which led to the main hall and the front entrance.

When they were outside, and circling the court building, the girl said, 'That man. Did you notice?'

'Notice what?'

'When you hit him. He was expecting it.'

'What do you mean?'

'He started to fall forward just before you hit him. It must have taken most of the force out of the blow.'

Without checking his pace the young man said, 'Do you think he was a plant? Holding us up so they could get to the car ahead of us?'

'I thought it might be.'

The young man put one hand on the shoulder-holster inside his coat, and said, 'If that's right, you'll see some fireworks.'

There was no one waiting by the car. The nearest person to it was a small man, with a face like a friendly monkey, who was sitting on a bench inside the garden reading the *Daily Mirror*.

No one tried to stop them as they drove out of Lincoln's Inn Fields and turned south towards the Embankment. 'Twenty past ten,' said the young man, 'good timing.' They were five miles short of Dover, on the bare escarpment above Bridge, before he spoke again. He said, 'Twelve o'clock. Any time now.'

Either his watch was fast or the timing mechanism was slow. It was fully five minutes later when their car went up in a searing sheet of white flame.

MICHAEL UNDERWOOD · 1916–

Murder at St Oswald's

'I think he should be sentenced to be boiled in oil,' said Wace, who was aged eleven.

His friend, Webster, nodded enthusiastically. 'Yes, then be thrown into a pit full of poisonous spiders and scorpions.'

Nigel Kilby frowned impatiently. He was the recognized leader of their form and the acknowledged foreman of their self-constituted jury, for it so happened that middleschool (the name of their form) had exactly twelve pupils.

'That's silly,' he said scathingly. 'Where'd you get enough oil?'

'And where would you find poisonous spiders and scorpions?' inquired Marsden, the form's best all-rounder.

'I'd steal them from a zoo,' Webster said robustly.

'And I'd get oil from a garage,' added Wace, 'and heat it in a cauldron.'

Nigel Kilby was still frowning. 'We've got to think of some terribly clever way of killing him,' he said. 'Something that can never be detected.'

'I was reading in a magazine about a tribe in some jungle who kill their enemies with poison darts. They use blow-pipes and the poison is so deadly that the person dies immediately.' This contribution came from Perry mi who was the smallest and, at ten, the youngest boy in the form.

Kilby nodded. 'Poison is definitely the best way.'

'We could push him over the cliff on a walk,' Marsden said. 'We'd say it was an accident, that he went too close to the edge and it crumbled.'

'That'd be all right if we could be certain it'd kill him,' Kilby conceded. 'But supposing he was only injured. Supposing he managed to hang on to something . . .'

A silence fell as each of them contemplated the full horror of such a plan going awry. The existing tyranny would be nothing compared with what would inevitably follow.

There was no doubt that Mr Cheeseman was the most unpopular

master at St Oswald's, and the boys of middleschool, of which he was the form-master, were further convinced that he must be the most hated master in any of the preparatory schools strung out along the Sussex coast in that year of 1929. Whenever they compared notes with boys from neighbouring schools, it served to confirm their morbid conviction that 'Cheesepot' was Attila the Hun, Ghengis Khan, and Fouquier-Tinville rolled into one. They accepted from Kilby that you couldn't find a nastier trio in history.

Mr Cheeseman—Cheesepot behind his back—was a tall, lean man with a heavy moustache and a deep voice which could sound more threatening than any roll of thunder. He had drifted into teaching after coming out of the army in 1919 and had been at St Oswald's for six years. Like many of his sort at the time, he had no academic qualifications, merely a basic knowledge of the subjects he taught, and an ability to maintain discipline and lend a crude hand at games. Even allowing for the boys' natural exaggeration, a dispassionate adult eye could not have failed to notice that he took a distinct relish in tormenting his pupils. He was not only a bully, he was also unfair. For example, just recently he had kept Webster behind and made him late for prayers and had then told the head-master there was no reason why Webster should not have been there on time. When Webster had made a muted protest, Mr Cheeseman had given a nasty sort of laugh and said, 'Life *is* unfair, boy. The sooner you realize it, the better.'

'I bet Mrs Cheeseman'll be glad when he dies,' Wace said, breaking the silence that had fallen.

The Cheesemans lived in a cottage on the edge of the school grounds and Mrs Cheeseman helped matron with the boys' clothes. She was a small, pale, soft-spoken woman, who appeared to be as much dominated by her husband as were the boys of his form. She aroused their sense of chivalry and they had little doubt that she would welcome her husband's demise as much as they would.

'I bet he pulls her hair,' Webster added.

'How are we going to poison him, Kilby?' Marsden asked, getting the discussion back on course again.

'What we need,' Kilby said slowly to his now attentive audience, 'is a poison that'll take a bit of time to work. I mean, we can mix it with his porridge at breakfast, but we don't want him to drop dead until later, so that no one will guess when he took it.'

'Like when he's in the shed mending the mower,' Marsden remarked.

One of Mr Cheeseman's responsibilities was looking after the school's large motor mower. He appeared to have a far greater affinity for its oily workings than he did for his pupils and he was forever tinkering with its engine.

'But where'll you get the poison, Kilby?' Wace asked.

'I'll have to look in my book. It'll probably mean making our own poison. There are all sorts of poisonous things in the school wood.'

'It'd have to be tasteless,' Marsden observed.

'That's not difficult,' Kilby said confidently. 'And, anyway, the porridge is so revolting, no one could tell whether it'd been poisoned or not.'

Perry mi gave a sudden, frightened start and bent studiously over his desk. One or two boys turned their heads and then quickly followed suit, for standing in the doorway with a disagreeable gleam in his eye was Mr Cheeseman. How long he had been there and what, if anything, he had overheard they were not to know, but a chilly fear gripped each of them.

They sat in two rows of six and it was Mr Cheeseman himself who had sardonically likened them unto a jury. They now gazed at him with expressions of anxious innocence as he mounted the small dais and faced them across the top of his desk.

The silence which followed became quickly oppressive, so that Wace felt compelled to break it.

'Good morning, sir,' he said.

Mr Cheeseman now focused his attention on Wace. His moustache twitched.

'Is it, Wace?'

Wace was nonplussed and gave a nervous giggle.

'What's the joke, Wace? Come on, share it, don't keep it to yourself,' the deep voice boomed.

'Joke, sir? There isn't any joke, sir.'

'But you giggled, Wace. There must be a joke. Or are you so feather-brained that you giggle at nothing?'

'I didn't know I did giggle, sir,' Wace said in a tone of alarm, endeavouring to extricate himself from a rapidly deteriorating situation.

'I didn't hear him giggle, sir,' Webster said loyally.

'Webster and Wace, our twin buffoons,' Mr Cheeseman observed, glancing at the faces turned towards him. Then in his most sepulchral tone he added, 'But buffoonery can be a dangerous sport, so take warning!'

He picked up the top exercise book from the pile he had brought into the classroom with him. It was their French composition of the previous afternoon which he had corrected.

'Brook?'

'Here, sir.'

'Evans?'

'Here, sir.'

'Perry mi?'

'Here, sir.'

As each boy answered to his name, his exercise book was skimmed at him like a quoit. Anyone failing to catch was made to stand with the book balanced on his head.

'Everyone got their books?' Mr Cheeseman asked in a doom-laden tone.

'No, sir, you haven't given me mine,' Wace said nervously.

'Nor I have, Wace. I've kept yours back for special presentation. Just step up here, will you?'

Wace rose and made his way slowly round the end of the desks, an expression of apprehension on his face. He paused when he reached the edge of the dais.

'Stand here, Wace,' Mr Cheeseman said, pointing at the floor beside his desk, 'and face the rest of the class.'

Mr Cheeseman rose and stepped across to stand behind him. In one hand he held the exercise book; his other hand seized the hair in the nape of Wace's neck.

'What gender is *maison*, Wace?'

'Er . . . feminine, sir.'

'Then why did you put *le maison*?' he barked, giving the hair a vicious tweak.

'Ouch!'

'And what is the plural of *hibou*?'

'I can't think sir, you're hurting, sir.'

There was another tweak followed by a further cry of pain.

'Come on, Wace, the plural of *hibou*?'

'*H-I-B-O-U-S.*'

This time there was a shriek as Mr Cheeseman jerked his head back.

'*H-I-B-O-U-X*, you ignorant boy! There are more mistakes in your composition, than there are pips in a pot of raspberry jam. You're lazy, Wace, and you don't pay attention.'

'I do, sir.'

'Don't argue with me,' Mr Cheeseman thundered, slowly rotating the hand which held the hair.

By now Wace was scarlet and tears were tumbling down his cheeks.

'Crying doesn't cut any ice with me, Wace. You'll stay in this afternoon and copy out the first ten pages of your French Grammar. Later I shall come and hear you and there'd better not be any mistakes. Now get back to your desk!' As he spoke he slapped him across the top of his head with the exercise book and then flung it after him.

A grim silence ensued in which only Wace's strangulated sobs could be heard. Webster tried to comfort his friend by picking up the book for him and helping him look for his pen which had rolled off the desk.

The rest of the lesson was passed in a more oppressive atmosphere than ever and it was not until the school bell had been rung to signal the end of the period and Mr Cheeseman had swept out that anyone dared speak.

'Don't worry, Wace,' Kilby said, 'it won't be for much longer.'

'Couldn't we put a spell on him?' Perry mi asked.

'What sort of spell?' Marsden inquired with interest.

'A spell to make him fall down and break both his legs.'

'How do you do that?'

'I'm not really sure. But if we formed a sort of circle and held hands and closed our eyes and muttered an incantation, it might work.'

'What's an incantation?' Webster asked.

'It's words for casting spells,' Kilby broke in. 'But I doubt if we could make it work. I still think poison's the best way. I tell you what, I'm excused games this afternoon because of my new spectacles, so I'll go into the wood and collect poisonous things. I'll look in my book first and see what would make the deadliest poison.'

'I'll come with you,' Perry mi said. 'Matron's excused me games because of my cold.'

Kilby nodded his approval. 'We'll go off immediately after lunch while everyone's changing.'

At this, even Wace managed to look more cheerful. Life without Cheesepot came as close to paradise as his imagination could bring him.

Nigel Kilby was the last to enter the classroom when they reassembled just before half-past four. He was carrying a brown cardboard box which he quickly slipped into his desk.

'What did you get?' Marsden asked.

Kilby removed the lid of the box and they all craned forward to have a look. What they saw was some mysterious pale berries, a root resembling a parsnip and a number of different leaves.

'Are they all poisonous?' Webster asked eagerly.

Kilby nodded gravely and one or two boys pulled back from the deadly contents. Yarrow even held his breath in case any fumes were being given off.

'But you can't sprinkle that lot on his porridge,' Marsden remarked.

'Of course not. The poison's got to be made. The leaves have to be boiled and then the grated root and the crushed berries must be added. It's what's left at the end that's the poison.' Kilby cast a quick glance towards the door before going on. 'I've got a tin and I'll boil the leaves on the gas-ring outside Matron's room when she's down at staff dinner tonight. But someone'll have to keep watch at the end of the corridor in case she comes back early.'

'I'll do that,' Marsden volunteered.

'It'll be better if Perry does it. He's smaller and can hide under the table.'

'What'll the poison look like?' Wace asked.

Nigel Kilby blinked behind his spectacles. The truth was that he had no idea, but no leader could possibly make such an admission.

'It'll be a sort of nondescript powder,' he said. 'We'll put it on his porridge at breakfast tomorrow. You know the way he goes and talks to Mr Saunders after serving us, I'll do it then.'

'Suppose he doesn't have any porridge tomorrow?' Webster asked.

'Then we'll have to wait until the next day. But he always has porridge.'

'He didn't one day last week. I remember noticing.'

'That was because he'd been out drinking the night before. He's only like that on Mondays.' Kilby glanced round at his eleven fellow jurors. 'Don't forget we're in this together. We must take an oath of silence and swear never to tell a single soul whatever happens. If we stick together, nobody'll ever find out.'

'Not even the top Scotland Yard detective,' Wace added in a burst of confidence.

'So, are we all agreed, Cheesepot must die?' Kilby said, looking from face to face.

Everyone nodded, though some a trifle apprehensively.

Shortly afterwards the object of their death sentence strode into the classroom. But for once he seemed preoccupied. It was supposed to be an English lesson, but all he did was to give them an essay subject and then, while they wrote, stare with a glowering expression out of the window. He didn't even shout or attempt to cuff Wace when he dropped his pen.

It was almost as if he realized he hadn't much longer for this life.

Nigel Kilby was already awake when the school bell rang at half-past seven the next morning. He jumped out of bed, put on his spectacles and ran over to the radiator on top of which he had left his lethal mixture to mature. He noted with satisfaction that it had turned into a greyish paste. He held it to his nose and sniffed, and decided that it smelt of shoe polish, but not too strongly.

Twenty minutes later the first bell rang for breakfast. In the dining-hall where they sat by forms, middleschool was at one end of the room. This meant that the boys on one side had their backs against a wall and those sitting on the opposite side had theirs turned to the rest of the room, which provided Kilby with as much cover as he could hope to have when the crucial moment arrived.

Before leaving the dormitory, he had transferred the mixture to a paper bag which he put in his trouser pocket.

'How much are you going to give him?' Wace had asked.

'I reckon it's so deadly, it won't need much.'

'How are you going to sprinkle it on?' Perry mi had inquired earnestly. 'It looks all sticky.'

'I'll just put in a few bits. If Cheesepot comes back too soon, you'll have to kick me under the table, Marsden.'

'Aren't you frightened of getting some on your own plate, Kilby?' someone else had asked.

He shook his head. 'I shall be extra careful and wash my hands as soon as breakfast is over.'

The novelty of this struck silence into his audience and a couple of minutes later the second bell rang and they trooped downstairs to the dining-hall.

Mr Cheeseman came in late, just as the headmaster was starting to say grace. He gave the boys a curt nod and began ladling out the porridge. He was never very communicative at breakfast, but this morning there seemed something subtly different about him. Nothing which could be called an improvement, but nevertheless different. His eyes looked as they did when he had a hangover, but there wasn't the usual smell that went with that condition. He had a grimly brooding air.

Kilby wondered whether others had noticed the difference as he watched Mr Cheeseman through his own quite different eyes. The eyes of an executioner.

When each boy had been served, Mr Cheeseman filled his own bowl and then, as they had hoped, stalked away to the table presided over by Mr Saunders.

Kilby had given the strictest instructions that, when this moment was reached, everyone must eat normally and not gaze up the table in his direction, as this could give the whole thing away. Despite the warning, he observed Wace leaning forward and staring at him as though about to witness a conjuring trick. He gave him a furious glare at the same time as Webster kicked him on the ankle. Wace blushed and quickly picked up his spoon.

Removing the crumpled paper bag from his pocket, Kilby slid to the very end of the bench so that his movements would be masked from everyone save those of his own form on the opposite side of the table. Quickly he shook out four pellets of the grey paste on to the waiting plate, where they promptly sank from sight beneath the surface of equally grey porridge.

He was halfway through his own porridge before Mr Cheeseman returned to the table and sat down. With twelve pairs of eyes trying not to stare at him, he began to eat. At one moment, he made a face and appeared to remove something from the tip of his tongue, but otherwise he ate without comment. Porridge was followed by kippers and the meal ended with a slice of bread and margarine, covered by a film of marmalade.

There was a grating noise as the headmaster pushed back his chair and said, 'I'll say grace for those who've finished.'

This was followed by a noisy exodus, leaving only the dreamers and slow-eaters to continue chewing their wholesome cud.

Mr Cheeseman had left with the majority without having spoken a single word during the meal. Kilby was puzzled and Perry mi voiced the theory that their form-master had already had a vision of the angel of death.

'How long will it take to work?' Webster asked as he and Kilby went out of the dining-hall together.

Kilby shrugged non-committally. 'Difficult to say.'

'I hope it means we miss French.'

As events turned out, they missed history as well.

History should have been the first lesson of the day and at twenty to nine, five minutes before it was due to start, middleschool were at their desks.

'I wonder if he'll come out in spots first,' Wace whispered to Webster.

'I don't want to see him actually die in here,' Webster said with a slight shiver.

Noise from other classrooms along the corridor began to die away, indicating the arrival of teachers for the start of the day's work. But there was no sign of Mr Cheeseman. A quarter to nine came and went. Then ten to nine and five to nine. But still no Cheesepot.

'It must have worked already,' Marsden said in a hoarse whisper, and Kilby swallowed nervously. 'I mean, he's never been as late as this before. What are we going to do?'

'If he hasn't come by the time the school clock strikes nine, I'll go and have a look around,' Kilby said.

It seemed no time at all before nine o'clock struck, hurling them into a state of high tension such as they had never experienced.

Kilby rose from his desk. 'Everyone stay here. If anyone comes, say I've gone to look for Cheesepot.'

He slipped out of the classroom, half-closing the door behind him. It was doubtful whether middleschool had ever sat in silence for so long. Even Webster and Wace barely exchanged a whispered word.

It was a quarter of an hour before Kilby returned and they could see at once from his expression that something had happened. His face was white and he kept on blinking behind his spectacles. With great deliberation, he moistened his lips.

'He's dead all right,' he announced in a quavering voice. 'He's lying on the floor of the mower shed.'

The news was greeted in stunned silence, apart from a few quick gasps. Deliverance had come, but their reaction was not as they had anticipated. There was no urge to cheer or bang their desk tops, just a feeling of fearful unease.

Perry mi was the first to break the silence.

'Did you feel his pulse?' he asked.

Kilby shook his head. 'I didn't go into the shed. I looked through the keyhole and could see him lying there in a sort of heap.'

'How do you know it was Cheesepot?' Marsden asked.

'I could tell by his jacket. The black and white check one he was wearing at breakfast. He must have been bending over the mower when he collapsed.'

'He might have still been breathing,' Perry mi remarked in a worried tone.

'No, he was dead all right. I'd have noticed if he was breathing. His chest would have been going up and down.'

'What are we going to do?' Wace asked, a note of panic in his voice.

The question was answered for them by the sudden appearance in the doorway of Mr Repping, the headmaster.

'What are you all doing?' he asked sharply. 'Where's Mr Cheeseman?'

'We don't know, sir,' Kilby replied. 'He hasn't turned up.'

'Hasn't turned up! But he was at breakfast.'

'Yes, sir,' agreed a chorus of voices.

'Well, get on with some work while I go and find out what's happened. Now, no talking, do you understand?'

'May I make a suggestion, sir?' Kilby said.

'Well, what is it, Kilby?'

'Mr Cheeseman often goes to the mower shed between breakfast and first period, sir.'

'I'm aware of that, Kilby.'

'Sorry, sir, I just thought it might be a good idea to look there. He might have had an accident and be trapped.'

Mr Repping frowned. 'That sounds most far-fetched. You're letting your imagination run away with you, Kilby. Now, get on with your work while I go and attend to the matter.'

It was half an hour before the headmaster returned. Half an hour during which the minutes ticked away with agonizing slowness and very little work was done. When he did reappear in the classroom, they stared at him in fascinated horror while waiting to hear how he would break the news.

'Well, I'm afraid the mystery remains unsolved for the time being,' he said briskly. 'I've tried to phone Mr Cheeseman's home, but can't get any answer, so both he and Mrs Cheeseman must be out. I believe Mr Price is free next period so I'll ask him to come and take you. What is your next period by the way?'

'French, sir,' Marsden said when no one else spoke.

'Very well, stay in your classroom and I'll go and speak to Mr Price.'

'Excuse me, sir.'

'Yes, what is it, Kilby?'

'Didn't you look in the mower shed, sir?'

'As a matter of fact, I did, Kilby. I told you that you were letting your imagination run away with you, lad. There wasn't a single sign of Mr Cheeseman having been in there this morning.'

Fifty minutes of French with the benign Mr Price would normally have been something of a treat, but middleschool agreed afterwards that they had never known the clock to move so slowly. It seemed as if the mid-morning break would never come. And when at last it did, Nigel Kilby found himself facing a barrage of questions which would have undermined the confidence of anyone less self-assured. As it was, however, he stuck to his story and remained outwardly unshaken. Cheesepot had definitely been lying on the floor beside the mower, his black and white check jacket being unmistakable. If he was no longer there when Mr Repping inspected the shed, it meant only one thing. His body had been removed.

'But who'd have done it, Kilby?'

'And why, Kilby?'

To these and similar questions, Nigel Kilby did not pretend to have answers, but his trump card which he played over and over again was to remind his audience that Cheesepot had indisputably disappeared.

'Body-snatching is not unknown,' he added in a tone which hinted at personal experience of the practice.

And so the day dragged by with Mr Cheeseman's twelve jurors fermenting in an agony of feverish speculation.

When bedtime came, still without any news of their form-master, the prospect of sleep could not have seemed more distant.

It was Perry mi who suggested that, like a wild animal aware of its approaching end, Cheesepot had gone off to die in a cave. But Kilby crushed this theory by pointing out that it didn't begin to fit the facts.

'I wish now we'd never sentenced him to death,' Wace whispered to Webster in the next bed.

'So do I,' Webster said. 'I'm scared.'

At breakfast the next morning, the head boy was deputed to sit at the end of their table and serve the porridge. He and Marsden then spent the whole time discussing England's cricket prospects in the coming season.

When breakfast was over, various masters were to be observed exchanging conspiratorial whispers, but of Mr Cheeseman there was neither sign nor mention.

By twenty minutes to nine, middleschool were sitting at their desks wondering what to expect. Their first lesson was Latin and it seemed possible that the headmaster himself might take it.

Kilby had reminded them all of the need to stand firm and not break ranks because they had all been in it together. Anyone who sneaked could expect a fate little better than Cheesepot's.

'What have you done with the rest of the poison?' Perry mi asked.

'I flushed it down the lav last night,' Kilby replied.

The sound of approaching footsteps in the corridor brought them to silence and a moment later the headmaster entered, followed by a stranger. He was dressed in a tweed suit and had an outdoor appearance. To Kilby, he looked much more like a farmer than a teacher. Though teacher he must presumably be.

Mr Repping mounted the dais and clutched both sides of the high desk in front of him. The stranger stood at his side letting his gaze roam impassively over the two rows of faces. He had blue eyes which gave the impression of missing nothing. He certainly didn't look to be a tyrant in the same mould as Cheesepot; equally, he didn't give the appearance of being a soft touch.

This line of thought was passing through a number of heads as the boys sought to assess him. Thus the jolt they received when the headmaster spoke was like a severe electric shock.

'Boys, this is Detective Inspector Cartwright. He has some questions he wants to ask you about Mr Cheeseman's disappearance and I expect you to be completely truthful in your answers.' He turned to the officer. 'I shall be in my study if you want me, inspector.' Glancing back at the two rows of anxious upturned faces, he added, 'Inspector Cartwright has said that he would like to speak to you alone. That's why I'm leaving the classroom. But he'll certainly report to me if anyone misbehaves.'

Inspector Cartwright watched Mr Repping's departure and waited for the door to be closed. Then he looked at the boys and gave them a broad wink.

'You look just like a jury sitting there,' he said in an amused tone. Kilby gulped and several other boys blushed, all of which he observed. 'As the headmaster told you, I want to ask you some questions about Mr Cheeseman. When did you last see him?'

'At breakfast yesterday, sir,' Kilby said when no one else answered.

'That would have been at eight o'clock. Right? And he never turned up for your first lesson at eight forty-five, is that right?'

'Yes, sir,' Kilby said, while others nodded.

'Did anyone go and look for him?' Inspector Cartwright became aware that no one was looking at him any longer, all eyes having become suddenly cast down. 'Didn't anyone go looking for him? Surely it would have been quite a natural thing to do?'

'I did, sir,' Kilby said at the end of an oppressive silence.

'What's your name?'

'Kilby, sir.'

'Where did you go and look, Kilby?'

'The shed where the mower's kept, sir.'

'Ah! That would explain why you urged Mr Repping to look there, eh? And what did you discover?'

Kilby swallowed hard and then met Inspector Cartwright's gaze full on. 'I saw his body, sir, when I looked through the keyhole. He was lying in a heap beside the mower. I knew it was him, sir, because I recognized his jacket.'

'It must have given you quite a shock, eh?'

'Yes, sir.'

'But it didn't come as a total surprise?'

'Sir?'

'Seeing him dead on the shed floor?'

Even Kilby felt defenceless in the face of this *deus ex machina*.

'No, sir,' he said in a faint whisper.

'Not a very popular master, I gather?'

'No, sir.'

'Did anyone like him?' He glanced from boy to boy as he spoke.

'He was the most unpopular master in the whole of England, sir,' Perry mi broke in.

Inspector Cartwright received this news with pursed lips and a thoughtful nod.

'It must be a relief to you to know he won't be teaching you any more.' He paused. 'Well, I think that's about all . . . unless anyone has a question to ask me.'

Everyone looked towards Kilby who appeared to be fighting some inner battle.

'Have you found the body yet, sir?' he blurted out at last.

Inspector Cartwright looked solemn. 'Yes, it was down a crevice at the top of the cliffs. We'd never have discovered it if we hadn't been told.'

'But who put it there, sir?'

'Whose body are we talking about?' Inspector Cartwright inquired in a tone of mock puzzlement.

'Mr Cheeseman's, sir,' half a dozen voices called out.

'Oh! Oh, his body's at the police station.'

'Then whose body was it on the cliff, sir?' Kilby asked in a bewildered voice.

'Mrs Cheeseman's.'

'Is she dead, too?'

'Hers is the only body I know about.'

'But I thought you said, sir, that Mr Cheeseman . . .'

'Is at the police station, charged with the murder of his wife. We picked him up outside Dover last night. He and his lady-friend were about to cross the Channel, but he was recognized when he went into a chemist's shop. It seems he'd had horrible griping pains in his stomach all day. But for that, he'd almost certainly have got away.' Inspector Cartwright's eye had a strange glint as he went on, 'As it is, he has told us everything, including how he placed an old bolster dressed in his jacket and trousers in the mower shed, which he removed as soon as he'd seen Kilby look through the keyhole. He reckoned that if he and his lady-friend could disappear abroad and his wife's body was never found, the mystery would never be solved. The assumption would be that his wife had murdered *him* and then vanished. But those tummy pains were his undoing. And all because he underestimated your ability to make the porridge nastier than I'm sure it is.' Inspector Cartwright stepped off the dais as if to go, then paused. 'I'd like to offer you boys just two bits of advice. The first is not to take the law into your own hands and the second is, if you do, make sure your intended victim doesn't overhear your plans.'

He reached the door and paused again. 'But as things have turned out, you seem to have gained the best of both worlds. Got rid of a bully of a master and helped the police catch a murderer.'

P. D. JAMES · 1920–

Great Aunt Allie's Flypapers

'You see, my dear Adam,' explained the Canon gently as he walked with Chief Superintendent Dalgliesh under the vicarage elms, 'useful as the legacy would be to us, I wouldn't feel happy in accepting it if Great Aunt Allie came by her money in the first place by wrongful means.'

What the Canon meant was that he and his wife wouldn't be happy to inherit Great Aunt Allie's £50,000 if, sixty-seven years earlier, she had poisoned her elderly husband with arsenic in order to get it. As Great Aunt Allie had been accused and acquitted of just that charge in a 1902 trial which, for her Hampshire neighbours, had rivalled the Coronation as a public spectacle, the Canon's scruples were not altogether irrelevant. Admittedly, thought Dalgliesh, most people faced with the prospect of £50,000 would be happy to subscribe to the commonly held convention that once an English Court has pronounced its verdict the final truth of the matter has been established once and for all. There may possibly be a higher judicature in the next world, but hardly in this. And so Hubert Boxdale might normally be happy to believe. But, faced with the prospect of an unexpected fortune, his scrupulous conscience was troubled. The gentle but obstinate voice went on:

'Apart from the moral principle of accepting tainted money, it wouldn't bring us happiness. I often think of that poor woman, driven restlessly around Europe in her search for peace, of that lonely life and unhappy death.'

Dalgliesh recalled that Great Aunt Allie had moved in a predictable progress with her retinue of servants, current lover, and general hangers-on from one luxury Riviera hotel to the next, with stays in Paris or Rome as the mood suited her. He was not sure that this orderly programme of comfort and entertainment could be described as being restlessly driven around Europe, or that the old lady had been primarily in search of peace. She had died, he recalled, by falling overboard from a millionaire's yacht during a rather wild party given by him to celebrate her eighty-eighth birthday. It was perhaps

not an edifying death by the Canon's standards but he doubted
whether she had, in fact, been unhappy at the time. Great Aunt Allie
(it was impossible to think of her by any other name), if she had been
capable of coherent thought, would probably have pronounced it a
very good way to go. But this was hardly a point of view he could put
to his companion.

Canon Hubert Boxdale was Superintendent Adam Dalgliesh's
godfather. Dalgliesh's father had been his Oxford contemporary and
life-long friend. He had been an admirable godfather, affectionate,
uncensorious, genuinely concerned. In Dalgliesh's childhood he had
been mindful of birthdays and imaginative about a small boy's
preoccupations and desires. Dalgliesh was very fond of him and
privately thought him one of the few really good men he had known.
It was only surprising that the Canon had managed to live to
seventy-one in a carnivorous world in which gentleness, humility,
and unworldliness are hardly conducive to survival let alone success.
But his goodness had in some sense protected him. Faced with such
manifest innocence, even those who exploited him, and they were
not a few, extended some of the protection and compassion they
might show to the slightly subnormal.

'Poor old darling,' his daily woman would say, pocketing pay for six
hours when she had worked five and helping herself to a couple of
eggs from his refrigerator. 'He's really not fit to be let out alone.' It
had surprised the then young and slightly priggish Detective Constable Dalgliesh to realize that the Canon knew perfectly well about
the hours and the eggs but thought that Mrs Copthorne with five
children and an indolent husband needed both more than he did. He
also knew that if he started paying for five hours she would promptly
work only four and extract another two eggs and that this small and
only dishonesty was somehow necessary to her self-esteem. He was
good. But he was not a fool.

He and his wife were, of course, poor. But they were not unhappy;
indeed it was a word impossible to associate with the Canon. The
death of his two sons in the 1939 war had saddened but not destroyed
him. But he had anxieties. His wife was suffering from disseminated
sclerosis and was finding it increasingly hard to manage. There were
comforts and appliances which she would need. He was now, be-
latedly, about to retire and his pension would be small. A legacy of
£50,000 would enable them both to live in comfort for the rest of their
lives and would also, Dalgliesh had no doubt, give them the pleasure
of doing more for their various lame dogs. Really, he thought, the

Canon was an almost embarrassingly deserving candidate for a modest fortune. Why couldn't the dear silly old noodle take the cash and stop worrying? He said cunningly:

'She was found not guilty, you know, by an English jury. And it all happened nearly seventy years ago. Couldn't you bring yourself to accept their verdict?'

But the Canon's scrupulous mind was impervious to such sly innuendoes. Dalgliesh told himself that he should have remembered what, as a small boy, he had discovered about Uncle Hubert's conscience; that it operated as a warning bell and that, unlike most people, he never pretended that it hadn't sounded or that he hadn't heard it or that, having heard it, something must be wrong with the mechanism.

'Oh, I did, while she was alive. We never met, you know. I didn't wish to force myself on her. After all, she was a wealthy woman. My grandfather made a new will on his marriage and left her all he possessed. Our ways of life were very different. But I usually wrote briefly at Christmas and she sent a card in reply. I wanted to keep some contact in case, one day, she might want someone to turn to and would remember that I am a priest.'

And why should she want that, thought Dalgliesh. To clear her conscience? Was that what the dear old boy had in mind? So he must have had doubts from the beginning. But of course he had! Dalgliesh knew something of the story and the general feeling of the family and friends was that Great Aunt Allie had been extremely lucky to escape the gallows. His own father's view, expressed with reticence, reluctance, and compassion had not in essentials differed from that given by a local reporter at the time.

'How on earth did she expect to get away with it? Damn lucky to escape topping if you ask me.'

'The news of the legacy came as a complete surprise?' asked Dalgliesh.

'Indeed yes. I only saw her once at that first and only Christmas six weeks after her marriage when my grandfather died. We always talk of her as Great Aunt Allie but in fact, as you know, she married my grandfather. But it seemed impossible to think of her as a step-grandmother. There was the usual family gathering at Colebrook Croft at the time and I was there with my parents and my twin sisters. I was barely four and the twins were just eight months old. I can remember nothing of my grandfather or of his wife. After the murder—if one has to use that dreadful word—my mother returned home with us children leaving my father to cope with the police, the solicitors, and the newsmen. It was a terrible time for him. I don't think I was even told that grandfather was dead until about a year later. My old nurse, who had been given Christmas as a holiday to visit her own family, told me that soon after my return home I asked her if grandfather was now young and beautiful for always. She, poor woman, took it as a sign of infant prognostication and piety. Poor Nellie was sadly superstitious and sentimental, I'm afraid. But I knew nothing of grandfather's death at the time and certainly can recall nothing of that Christmas visit or of my new step-grandmother. Mercifully, I was little more than a baby when the murder was done.'

'She was a music hall artiste, wasn't she?' asked Dalgliesh.

'Yes, and a very talented one. My grandfather met her when she was working with a partner in a hall in Cannes. He had gone to the south of France with a manservant for his health. I understand that she extracted a gold watch from his chain and, when he claimed it, told him that he was English, had recently suffered from a stomach ailment, had two sons and a daughter, and was about to have a wonderful surprise. It was all correct except that his only daughter had died in childbirth leaving him a granddaughter, Marguerite Goddard.'

'And all easily guessable from his voice and appearance,' said Dalgliesh. 'I suppose the surprise was the marriage?'

'It was certainly a surprise, and a most unpleasant one for the family. It is easy to deplore the snobbishness and the conventions of another age and, indeed, there was much in Edwardian England to deplore. But it was not a propitious marriage. I think of the difference in background, education, and way of life, the lack of common interest. And there was this great disparity of age. My grandfather had married a girl just three months younger than his own grand-daughter. I cannot wonder that the family were concerned; that they felt that the union could not, in the end, contribute to the contentment or happiness of either party.'

'And that was putting it charitably,' thought Dalgliesh. The marriage certainly hadn't contributed to their happiness. From the point of view of the family it had been a disaster. He recalled hearing of an incident when the local vicar and his wife, a couple who had actually dined at Colebrook Croft on the night of the murder, first called on the bride. Apparently old Augustus Boxdale had introduced her by saying:

'Meet the prettiest little variety artiste in the business. Took a gold watch and notecase off me without any trouble. Would have had the elastic out of my pants if I hadn't watched out. Anyway she stole my heart, didn't you, sweetheart?' All this accompanied by a hearty slap on the rump and a squeal of delight from the lady who had promptly demonstrated her skill by extracting the Reverend Arthur Venables's bunch of keys from his left ear.

Dalgliesh thought it tactful not to remind the Canon of this story.

'What do you wish me to do, sir?' he enquired.

'It's asking a great deal, I know, when you're so busy. But if I had your assurance that you believed in Aunt Allie's innocence I should feel happy about accepting the bequest. I wondered if it would be possible for you to see the records of the trial. Perhaps it would give you a clue. You're so clever at this sort of thing.'

He spoke without flattery but with an innocent wonder at the strange avocations of men. Dalgliesh was, indeed, very clever at this sort of thing. A dozen or so men at present occupying security wings in HM prisons could testify to Chief Superintendent Dalgliesh's cleverness; as, indeed, could a handful of others walking free whose defending Counsel had been, in their own way, as clever as Chief Superintendent Dalgliesh. But to re-examine a case over sixty years old seemed to require clairvoyance rather than cleverness. The trial judge and both learned Counsel had been dead for over fifty years. Two world wars had taken their toll. Four reigns had passed. It was highly probable that, of those who had slept under the roof of Colebrook Croft on that fateful Boxing Day night of 1901, only the Canon still survived. But the old man was troubled and had sought his help and Dalgliesh, with a day or two's leave due to him, had the time to give it.

'I'll do what I can,' he promised.

The transcript of a trial which had taken place sixty-seven years ago took time and trouble to obtain, even for a Chief Superintendent of the Metropolitan Police. It provided little potential comfort for the Canon. Mr Justice Bellow had summed up with that avuncular simplicity with which he was wont to address juries, regarding them apparently as a panel of well-intentioned but cretinous children. And the facts could have been comprehended by any intelligent child. Part of the summing up set them out with admirable lucidity:

'And so, gentlemen of the jury, we come to the night of December 26th. Mr Augustus Boxdale, who had perhaps indulged a little unwisely on Christmas Day, had retired to bed in his dressing-room after luncheon suffering from a recurrence of the slight indigestive trouble which had afflicted him for most of his life. You have heard that he had taken luncheon with the members of his family and ate nothing which they too did not eat. You may feel you can acquit luncheon of anything worse than overrichness.

'Dinner was served at eight p.m. promptly, as was the custom at Colebrook Croft. There were present at that meal, Mrs Augustus Boxdale the deceased's bride; his elder son Captain Maurice Boxdale with his wife; his younger son the Reverend Henry Boxdale with his wife; his granddaughter Miss Marguerite Goddard; and two neighbours, the Reverend and Mrs Arthur Venables.

'You have heard how the accused took only the first course at dinner which was ragoût of beef and then, at about eight-twenty, left the dining-room to sit with her husband. Shortly after nine o'clock she rang for the parlour-maid, Mary Huddy, and ordered a basin of gruel to be brought up to Mr Boxdale. You have heard that the deceased was fond of gruel, and, indeed, as prepared by Mrs Muncie the cook, it sounds a most nourishing and comforting dish for an elderly gentleman of weak digestion.

'You have heard Mrs Muncie describe how she prepared the gruel according to Mrs Beaton's admirable recipe and in the presence of Mary Huddy in case, as she said, "the master should take a fancy to it when I'm not at hand and you have to make it". After the gruel had been prepared, Mrs Muncie tasted it with a spoon and Mary Huddy carried it upstairs to the main bedroom, together with a jug of water to thin the gruel if it were too strong. As she reached the door, Mrs Boxdale came out, her hands full of stockings and underclothes. She has told you that she was on her way to the bathroom to wash them through. She asked the girl to put the basin of gruel on the washstand by the window and Mary Huddy did so in her presence. Miss Huddy has told you that, at the time, she noticed the bowl of flypapers soaking in water and she knew that this solution was one used by Mrs Boxdale as a cosmetic wash. Indeed, all the women who spent that evening in the house, with the exception of Mrs Venables, have told you that they knew it was Mrs Boxdale's practice to prepare this solution of flypapers.

'Mary Huddy and the accused left the bedroom together and you have heard the evidence of Mrs Muncie that Miss Huddy returned to the kitchen after an absence of only a few minutes. Shortly after nine o'clock the ladies left the dining-room and entered the drawing-room to take coffee. At nine-fifteen p.m. Miss Goddard excused herself to the company and said that she would go to see if her grandfather needed anything. The time is established precisely because the clock struck the quarter-hour as she left and Mrs Venables commented on the sweetness of its chime. You have also heard Mrs Venables's evidence and the evidence of Mrs Maurice Boxdale and Mrs Henry Boxdale that none of the ladies left the drawing-room during the evening; and Mr Venables has testified that the three gentlemen remained together until Miss Goddard appeared about three-quarters of an hour later to inform them that her grandfather had become very ill and to request that the doctor be sent for immediately.

'Miss Goddard has told you that, when she entered her grandfather's room, he was just finishing his gruel and was grumbling about its taste. She got the impression that this was merely a protest at being deprived of his dinner rather than that he genuinely considered that there was something wrong with the gruel. At any rate, he finished most of it and appeared to enjoy it despite his grumbles.

'You have heard Miss Goddard describe how, after her grandfather had had as much as he wanted of the gruel, she took the bowl next door and left it on the washstand. She then returned to her grandfather's bedroom and Mr Boxdale, his wife, and his granddaughter played three-handed whist for about three-quarters of an hour.

'At ten o'clock Mr Augustus Boxdale complained of feeling very ill. He suffered from griping pains in the stomach, from sickness, and from looseness of the bowel. As soon as the symptoms began Miss Goddard went downstairs to let her uncles know that her grandfather was worse and to ask that Doctor Eversley should be sent for urgently. Doctor Eversley has given you his evidence. He arrived at Colebrook Croft at ten-thirty p.m. when he found his patient very distressed and weak. He treated the symptoms and gave what relief he could, but Mr Augustus Boxdale died shortly before midnight.

'Gentlemen of the jury, you have heard Marguerite Goddard describe how, as her grandfather's paroxysms increased in intensity, she remembered the gruel and wondered whether it could have disagreed with him in some way. She mentioned this possibility to her elder uncle, Captain Maurice Boxdale. Captain Boxdale has told you how he at once handed the bowl, with its residue of gruel, to Doctor Eversley with the request that the Doctor should lock it in a cupboard in the library, seal the lock, and himself keep the key. You have heard how the contents of the bowl were later analysed and with what result.'

An extraordinary precaution for the gallant captain to have taken, thought Dalgliesh, and a most perspicacious young woman. Was it by chance or by design that the bowl hadn't been taken down to be washed up as soon as the old man had finished with it? Why was it, he wondered, that Marguerite Goddard hadn't rung for the parlour-maid and requested her to remove it? Miss Goddard appeared the only other suspect. He wished he knew more about her.

But, except for the main protagonists, the characters in the drama did not emerge very clearly from the trial report. Why, indeed, should they? The British accusatorial system of trial is designed to answer one question: is the accused guilty, beyond reasonable doubt, of the crime charged? Exploration of the nuances of personality, speculation, and gossip have no place in the witness-box. The two Boxdale brothers came out as very dull fellows indeed. They and their estimable, respectable, sloping-bosomed wives had sat at dinner in full view of each other from eight until after nine o'clock (a substantial meal that dinner) and had said so in the witness-box more or less in identical words. The ladies' bosoms might have been heaving with far from estimable emotions of dislike, envy, embarrassment, or resentment of the interloper. If so, they didn't tell the court.

But the two brothers and their wives were clearly innocent, even if a detective of that time could have conceived of the guilt of gentlefolk so well respected, so eminently respectable. Even their impeccable alibis had a nice touch of social and sexual distinction. The Reverend Arthur Venables had vouched for the gentlemen, his good wife for the ladies. Besides, what motive had they? They could no longer gain financially by the old man's death. If anything, it was in their interests to keep him alive in the hope that disillusion with his marriage, or a return to sanity, might occur to cause him to change his will. So far Dalgliesh had learned nothing that could cause him to give the Canon the assurance for which he hoped.

It was then that he remembered Aubrey Glatt. Glatt was a wealthy amateur criminologist who had made a study of all the notable Victorian and Edwardian poison cases. He was not interested in anything earlier or later, being as obsessively wedded to his period as any serious historian, which, indeed, he had some claim to call himself. He lived in a Georgian house in Winchester—his affection for the Victorian and Edwardian age did not extend to its architecture —and was only three miles from Colebrook Croft. A visit to the London Library disclosed that he hadn't written a book on the case, but it was improbable that he had totally neglected a crime so close at hand and so in period. Dalgliesh had occasionally helped him with technical details of police procedure. Glatt, in response to a telephone call, was happy to return the favour with the offer of afternoon tea and information.

Tea was served in his elegant drawing-room by a parlour-maid in goffered cap with streamers. Dalgliesh wondered what wage Glatt paid her to persuade her to wear it. She looked as if she could have played a role in any of his favourite Victorian dramas, and Dalgliesh had an uncomfortable thought that arsenic might be dispensed with the cucumber sandwiches.

Glatt nibbled away and was expansive.

'It's interesting that you should have taken this sudden and, if I may say so, somewhat inexplicable interest in the Boxdale murder. I got out my notebook on the case only yesterday. Colebrook Croft is being demolished to make way for a new housing estate and I thought I would visit it for the last time. The family, of course, haven't lived there since the 1914–18 war. Architecturally it's completely undistinguished but one grieves to see it go. We might drive over after tea if you are agreeable.

'I never wrote my book on the case, you know. I planned a work entitled "The Colebrook Croft Mystery", or "Who Killed Augustus Boxdale?" But the answer was all too obvious.'

'No real mystery?' suggested Dalgliesh.

'Who else could it have been but Allegra Boxdale? She was born Allegra Porter, you know. Do you think her mother could have been thinking of Byron? I imagine not. There's a picture of her on page two of the notebook, by the way, taken by a photographer in Cannes on her wedding day. I call it beauty and the beast.'

The photograph had scarcely faded and Great Aunt Allie smiled clearly at Dalgliesh across nearly seventy years. Her broad face, with its wide mouth and rather snub nose, was framed by two wings of dark hair swept high and topped in the fashion of the day by an immense flowered hat. The features were too coarse for real beauty, but the eyes were magnificent, deep-set and well-spaced, and the chin round and determined. Beside this vital young Amazon, poor Augustus Boxdale, smiling fatuously at the camera and clutching his bride as if for support, was but a frail and undersized beast. Their pose was unfortunate. She looked as if she were about to fling him over her shoulder.

Glatt shrugged. 'The face of a murderess? I've known less likely ones. Her counsel suggested, of course, that the old man had poisoned his own gruel during the short time she left it on the washstand to cool while she visited the bathroom. But why should he? All the evidence suggests that he was in a state of post-nuptial euphoria, poor senile old booby. Our Augustus was in no hurry to leave this world, particularly by such an agonizing means. Besides, I doubt whether he even knew the gruel was there. He was in bed next door in his dressing-room, remember.'

Dalgliesh asked:

'What about Marguerite Goddard? There's no evidence about the exact time when she entered the bedroom.'

'I thought you'd get on to that. She could have arrived while her step-grandmother was in the bathroom, poisoned the gruel, hidden herself either in the main bedroom or elsewhere until it had been taken in to Augustus, then joined her grandfather and his bride as if she had just come upstairs. It's possible, I admit. But is it likely? She was less inconvenienced than any of the family by her grandfather's second marriage. Her mother was Augustus Boxdale's eldest child and married, very young, a wealthy patent-medicine manufacturer. She died in childbirth and the husband only survived her by a year. Marguerite Goddard was an heiress. She was also most advantageously engaged to Captain the Honourable John Brize-Lacey. It was quite a catch for a Boxdale—or a Goddard. Marguerite Goddard, young, beautiful, secure in her possession of the Goddard fortune, not to mention the Goddard emeralds and the eldest son of a Lord, was hardly a serious suspect. In my view, defence counsel, that was Roland Gort Lloyd remember, was wise to leave her strictly alone.'

'It was a memorable defence, I believe.'

'Magnificent. There's no doubt Allegra Boxdale owed her life to Gort Lloyd. I know that concluding speech by heart.

'"Gentlemen of the jury, I beseech you, in the sacred name of Justice, to consider what you are at. It is your responsibility, and yours alone, to decide the fate of this young woman. She stands before you now, young, vibrant, glowing with health, the years stretching before her with their promise and their hopes. It is in your power to cut off all this as you might top a nettle with one swish of your cane. To condemn her to the slow torture of those last waiting weeks; to that last dreadful walk; to heap calumny on her name; to desecrate those few happy weeks of marriage with the man who loved her so greatly; to cast her into the final darkness of an ignominious grave."

'Pause for dramatic effect. Then the crescendo in that magnificent voice. "And on what evidence, gentlemen? I ask you." Another pause. Then the thunder. "On what evidence?"'

'A powerful defence,' said Dalgliesh. 'But I wonder how it would go down with a modern judge and jury.'

'Well, it went down very effectively with that 1902 jury. Of course the abolition of capital punishment has rather cramped the more histrionic style. I'm not sure that the reference to topping nettles was in the best of taste. But the jury got the message. They decided that, on the whole, they preferred not to have the responsibility of sending the accused to the gallows. They were out six hours reaching their verdict and it was greeted with some applause. If any of those worthy citizens had been asked to wager five pounds of their own good money on her innocence, I suspect that it would have been a different matter. Allegra Boxdale had helped him, of course. The Criminal Evidence Act, passed three years earlier, enabled him to put her in the witness-box. She wasn't an actress of a kind for nothing. Somehow she managed to persuade the jury that she had genuinely loved the old man.'

'Perhaps she had,' suggested Dalgliesh. 'I don't suppose there had been much kindness in her life. And he was kind.'

'No doubt. No doubt. But love!' Glatt was impatient. 'My dear Dalgliesh! He was a singularly ugly old man of sixty-nine. She was an attractive girl of twenty-one!'

Dalgliesh doubted whether love, that iconoclastic passion, was susceptible to this kind of simple arithmetic but he didn't argue. Glatt went on:

'And the prosecution couldn't suggest any other romantic attachment. The police got in touch with her previous partner, of course. He was discovered to be a bald, uxorious little man sharp as a weasel, with a buxom wife and five children. He had moved down the coast after the partnership broke up and was now working with a new girl. He said, regretfully, that she was coming along nicely, thank you, gentlemen, but would never be a patch on Allie and that, if Allie got her neck out of the noose and ever wanted a job, she knew where to come. It was obvious even to the most suspicious policeman that his interest was purely professional. As he said: "What was a grain or two of arsenic between friends?"'

'The Boxdales had no luck after the trial. Captain Maurice Boxdale was killed in 1916, leaving no children, and the Reverend Henry lost his wife and their twin daughters in the 1918 influenza epidemic. He survived until 1932. The boy Hubert may still be alive, but I doubt it. That family were a sickly lot.

'My greatest achievement, incidentally, was in tracing Marguerite Goddard. I hadn't realized that she was still alive. She never married Brize-Lacey or, indeed, anyone else. He distinguished himself in the 1914–18 war, came successfully through, and eventually married an eminently suitable young woman, the sister of a brother officer. He inherited the title in 1925 and died in 1953. But Marguerite Goddard may be alive now for all I know. She may even be living in the same modest Bournemouth hotel where I found her. Not that my efforts in tracing her were rewarded. She absolutely refused to see me. That's the note that she sent out to me by the way.'

It was meticulously pasted into the notebook in its chronological order and carefully annotated. Aubrey Glatt was a natural researcher; Dalgliesh couldn't help wondering whether this passion for accuracy might not have been more rewardingly spent than in the careful documentation of murder.

The note was written in an elegant upright hand, the strokes black and very thin but unwavering.

'Miss Goddard presents her compliments to Mr Aubrey Glatt. She did not murder her grandfather and has neither the time nor inclination to gratify his curiosity by discussing the person who did.'

Aubrey Glatt said: 'After that extremely disobliging note, I felt there was really no point in going on with the book.'

Glatt's passion for Edwardian England extended to more than its murders and they drove to Colebook Croft through the green Hampshire lanes, perched high in an elegant 1910 Daimler. Aubrey wore a thin tweed coat and deerstalker hat and looked, Dalgliesh thought, rather like a Sherlock Holmes with himself as attendant Watson.

'We are only just in time, my dear Dalgliesh,' he said when they arrived. 'The engines of destruction are assembled. That ball on a chain looks like the eyeball of God, ready to strike. Let us make our number with the attendant artisans. You, as a guardian of the law, will have no wish to trespass.'

The work of demolition had not yet begun, but the inside of the house had been stripped and plundered, and the great rooms echoed to their footsteps like gaunt and deserted barracks after the final retreat. They moved from room to room, Glatt mourning the forgotten glories of an age he had been born thirty years too late to enjoy, Dalgliesh with his mind on more immediate and practical concerns.

The design of the house was simple and formalized. The first floor, on which were most of the main bedrooms, had a long corridor running the whole length of the façade. The master bedroom was at the southern end with two large windows giving a distant view of Winchester Cathedral tower. A communicating door led to a small dressing-room.

The main corridor had a row of four identical large windows. The brass curtain-rods and wooden rings had been removed (they were collectors' items now) but the ornate carved pelmets were still in place. Here must have hung pairs of heavy curtains giving cover to anyone who wished to slip out of view. And Dalgliesh noted with interest that one of the windows was exactly opposite the door of the main bedroom. By the time they had left Colebrook Croft and Glatt had dropped him at Winchester Station, Dalgliesh was beginning to formulate a theory.

His next move was to trace Marguerite Goddard, if she were still alive. It took him nearly a week of weary searching, a frustrating trail along the south coast from hotel to hotel. Almost everywhere, his enquiries were met with defensive hostility. It was the usual story of a very old lady who had become more demanding, arrogant, and eccentric as her health and fortune waned; an unwelcome embarrassment to manager and fellow guests alike. The hotels were all modest, a few almost sordid. What, he wondered, had become of the Goddard fortune?

From the last landlady he learned that Miss Goddard had become ill, really very sick indeed, and had been removed six months previously to the local district general hospital. And it was there that he found her.

The Ward Sister was surprisingly young, a petite, dark-haired girl with a tired face and challenging eyes.

'Miss Goddard is very ill. We've put her in one of the side wards. Are you a relative? If so, you're the first one who has bothered to call and you're lucky to be in time. When she is delirious she seems to expect a Captain Brize-Lacey to call. You're not he by any chance?'

'Captain Brize-Lacey will not be calling. No, I'm not a relative. She doesn't even know me. But I would like to visit her if she's well enough and is willing to see me. Could you please give her this note?'

He couldn't force himself on a defenceless and dying woman. She still had the right to say no. He was afraid she would refuse him. And if she did, he might never learn the truth. He thought for a second and then wrote four words on the back page of his diary, signed them, tore out the page, folded it and handed it to the Sister.

She was back very shortly.

'She'll see you. She's weak, of course, and very old, but she's perfectly lucid now. Only please don't tire her.'

'I'll try not to stay too long.'

The girl laughed:

'Don't worry. She'll throw you out soon enough if she gets bored. The chaplain and the Red Cross librarian have a terrible time with her. Third door on the left. There's a stool to sit on under the bed. We ring a bell at the end of visiting time.'

She bustled off, leaving him to find his own way. The corridor was very quiet. At the far end he could glimpse through the open door of the main ward the regimented rows of beds, each with its pale blue coverlet; the bright glow of flowers on the over-bed tables and the laden visitors making their way in pairs to each bedside. There was a faint buzz of welcome, a hum of conversation. But no one was visiting the side wards. Here in the silence of the aseptic corridor Dalgliesh could smell death.

The woman propped high against the pillows in the third room on the left no longer looked human. She lay rigidly, her long arms disposed like sticks on the coverlet. This was a skeleton, clothed with a thin membrane of flesh, beneath whose yellow transparency the tendons and veins were plainly visible as if in an anatomist's model. She was nearly bald, and the high-domed skull under its spare down of hair was as brittle and vulnerable as a child's. Only the eyes still held life, burning in their deep sockets with an animal vitality. But when she spoke, her voice was distinctive and unwavering, evoking, as her appearance never could, the memory of imperious youth.

She took up his note and read aloud four words:

'"It was the child." You are right, of course. The four-year-old Hubert Boxdale killed his grandfather. You signed this note Adam Dalgliesh. There was no Dalgliesh connected with the case.'

'I am a detective of the Metropolitan Police. But I'm not here in any official capacity. I have known about this case for a number of years from a dear friend. I have a natural curiosity to learn the truth. And I have formed a theory.'

'And now, like that poseur Aubrey Glatt, you want to write a book?'

'No. I shall tell no one. You have my promise.'

Her voice was ironic.

'Thank you. I am a dying woman, Mr Dalgliesh. I tell you that not to invite your sympathy, which it would be an impertinence for you to offer and which I neither want nor require, but to explain why it no longer matters to me what you say or do. But I too have a natural curiosity. Your note, cleverly, was intended to provoke it. I should like to know how you discovered the truth.'

Dalgliesh drew the visitors' stool from under the bed and sat down beside her. She did not look at him. The skeleton hands still holding his note did not move.

'Everyone in Colebrook Croft who could have killed Augustus Boxdale was accounted for, except the one person whom nobody considered, the small boy. He was an intelligent, articulate, and lonely child. He was almost certainly left to his own devices. His nurse did not accompany the family to Colebrook Croft, and the servants who were there had the extra work of Christmas and the care of the delicate twin girls. The boy probably spent much time with his grandfather and the new bride. She too was lonely and disregarded. He could have trotted around with her as she went about her various activities. He could have watched her making her arsenical face wash and when he asked, as a child will, what it was for, could have been told "to make me young and beautiful". He loved his grandfather, but he must have known that the old man was neither young nor beautiful. Suppose he woke up on that Boxing Day night, overfed and excited after the Christmas festivities. Suppose he went to Allegra Boxdale's room in search of comfort and companionship, and saw the basin of gruel and the arsenical mixture together on the washstand. Suppose he decided that here was something he could do for his grandfather.'

The voice from the bed said quietly:

'And suppose someone stood unnoticed in the doorway and watched him.'

'So you were behind the window curtains on the landing looking through the open door?'

'Of course. He knelt on the chair, two chubby hands clasping the bowl of poison, pouring it with infinite care into his grandfather's gruel. I watched while he replaced the linen cloth over the basin, got down from his chair, replaced it with careful art against the wall and trotted out into the corridor and back to the nursery. About three seconds later Allegra came out of the bathroom, and I watched while she carried the gruel in to my grandfather. A second later I went into the main bedroom. The bowl of poison had been a little heavy for Hubert's small hands to manage, and I saw that a small pool had been spilt on the polished top of the washstand. I mopped it up with my handkerchief. Then I poured some of the water from the jug into the poison bowl to bring up the level. It only took a couple of seconds, and I was ready to join Allegra and my grandfather in the bedroom and sit with him while he ate his gruel. I watched him die without pity and without remorse. I think I hated them both equally. The grandfather who had adored, petted, and indulged me all through my childhood had deteriorated into this disgusting old lecher, unable to keep his hands off his woman even when I was in the room. He had rejected me and his family, jeopardized my engagement, made our name a laughing-stock in the country—and for a woman my grandmother wouldn't have employed as a kitchen-maid. I wanted them both dead. And they were both going to die. But it would be by other hands than mine. I could deceive myself that it wasn't my doing.'

Dalgliesh asked: 'When did she find out?'

'She knew that evening. When my grandfather's agony began, she went outside for the jug of water. She wanted a cool cloth for his head. It was then that she noticed that the level of water in the jug had fallen and that a small pool of liquid on the washstand had been mopped up. I should have realized that she would have seen that pool. She had been trained to register every detail; it was almost subconscious with her. She thought at the time that Mary Huddy had spilt some of the water when she set down the tray and the gruel. But who but I could have mopped it up? And why?'

'And when did she face you with the truth?'

'Not until after the trial. Allegra had magnificent courage. She knew what was at stake. But she also knew what she stood to gain. She gambled with her life for a fortune.'

And then Dalgliesh understood what had happened to the Goddard inheritance.

'So she made you pay?'

'Of course. Every penny. The Goddard fortune, the Goddard emeralds. She lived in luxury for sixty-seven years on my money. She ate and dressed on my money. When she moved with her lovers from hotel to hotel, it was on my money. She paid them with my money. And if she has left anything, which I doubt, it is my money. My grandfather left very little. He had been senile and had let money run through his fingers like sand.'

'And your engagement?'

'It was broken, you could say by mutual consent. A marriage, Mr Dalgliesh, is like any other legal contract. It is most successful when both parties are convinced they have a bargain. Captain Brize-Lacey was sufficiently discouraged by the scandal of a murder in the family. He was a proud and highly conventional man. But that alone might have been accepted with the Goddard fortune and the Goddard emeralds to deodorize the bad smell. But the marriage couldn't have succeeded if he had discovered that he had married socially beneath him, into a family with a major scandal and no compensating fortune.'

Dalgliesh said: 'Once you had begun to pay you had no choice but to go on. I see that. But why did you pay? She could hardly have told her story. It would have meant involving the child.'

'Oh no! That wasn't her plan at all. She never meant to involve the child. She was a sentimental woman and she was fond of Hubert. No, she intended to accuse me of murder outright. Then, if I decided to tell the truth, how would it help me? How could I admit that I had watched Hubert, actually watched a child barely four years old preparing an agonizing death for his grandfather without speaking a word to stop him? I could hardly claim that I hadn't understood the implication of what I had seen. After all, I wiped up the spilled liquid, I topped up the bowl. She had nothing to lose, remember, neither life nor reputation. They couldn't try her twice. That's why she waited until after the trial. It made her secure for ever. But what of me? In the circles in which I moved reputation was everything. She needed only to breathe the story in the ears of a few servants and I was finished. The truth can be remarkably tenacious. But it wasn't only reputation. I paid in the shadow of the gallows.'

Dalgliesh asked, 'But could she ever prove it?'

Suddenly she looked at him and gave an eerie screech of laughter. It tore at her throat until he thought the taut tendons would snap.

'Of course she could! You fool! Don't you understand? She took my handkerchief, the one I used to mop up the arsenic mixture. That was her profession, remember. Some time during that evening, perhaps when we were all crowding around the bed, two soft plump fingers insinuated themselves between the satin of my evening dress and my flesh and extracted that stained and damning piece of linen.'

She stretched out feebly towards the bedside locker. Dalgliesh saw what she wanted and pulled open the drawer. There on the top was a small square of very fine linen with a border of hand-stitched lace. He took it up. In the corner was her monogram delicately embroidered. And half of the handkerchief was still stiff and stained with brown.

She said: 'She left instructions with her solicitors that this was to be returned to me after her death. She always knew where I was. She made it her business to know. You see, it could be said that she had a life interest in me. But now she's dead. And I shall soon follow. You may have the handkerchief, Mr Dalgliesh. It can be of no further use to either of us now.'

Dalgliesh put it in his pocket without speaking. As soon as possible, he would see that it was burnt. But there was something else he had to say. 'Is there anything you would wish me to do? Is there anyone you want told, or to tell? Would you care to see a priest?'

Again there was that uncanny screech of laughter, but it was softer now:

'There's nothing I can say to a priest. I only regret what I did because it wasn't successful. That is hardly the proper frame of mind for a good confession. But I bear her no ill will. No envy, malice, or uncharitableness. She won; I lost. One should be a good loser. But I don't want any priest telling me about penance. I've paid, Mr Dalgliesh. For sixty-seven years I've paid. And in this world, young man, the rich only pay once.'

She lay back as if suddenly exhausted. There was silence for a moment. Then she said with sudden vigour:

'I believe your visit has done me good. I would be obliged if you would make it convenient to return each afternoon for the next three days. I shan't trouble you after that.'

Dalgliesh extended his leave with some difficulty and stayed at a local inn. He saw her each afternoon. They never spoke again of the murder. And when he came punctually at 2 p.m. on the fourth day it was to be told that Miss Goddard had died peacefully in the night with apparently no trouble to anyone. She was, as she had said, a good loser.

A week later Dalgliesh reported to the Canon.

'I was able to see a man who has made a detailed study of the case. He had already done most of the work for me. I have read the transcript of the trial and visited Colebrook Croft. And I have seen one other person, closely connected with the case but who is now dead. I know you will want me to respect confidences and to say no more than I need.'

It sounded pompous and minatory but he couldn't help that. The Canon murmured his quiet assurance. Thank God he wasn't a man to question. Where he trusted, he trusted absolutely. If Dalgliesh gave his word there would be no more questioning. But he was anxious. Suspense hung around them. Dalgliesh went on quickly:

'As a result I can give you my word that the verdict was a just verdict and that not one penny of your grandfather's fortune is coming to you through anyone's wrongdoing.'

He turned his face away and gazed out of the vicarage window at the sweet green coolness of the summer's day, so that he did not have to watch the Canon's happiness and relief. There was a silence. The old man was probably giving thanks in his own way. Then he was aware that his godfather was speaking. Something was being said about gratitude, about the time he had given up to the investigation.

'Please don't misunderstand me, Adam. But when the formalities have been completed, I should like to donate something to a charity named by you, one close to your heart.'

Dalgliesh smiled. His contributions to charity were impersonal; a quarterly obligation discharged by banker's order. The Canon obviously regarded charities as so many old clothes; all were friends, but some fitted better and were more affectionately regarded than others.

But inspiration came:

'It's good of you to think of it, sir. I rather liked what I learned about Great Aunt Allie. It would be pleasant to give something in her name. Isn't there a society for the assistance of retired and indigent variety artists, conjurers and so on?'

The Canon, predictably, knew that there was and could name it.

Dalgliesh said: 'Then I think, Canon, that Great Aunt Allie would agree that a donation in her name would be entirely appropriate.'

EDMUND CRISPIN · 1921–1978 and GEOFFREY
BUSH ·

Baker Dies

Wakefield was attending a series of philosophy lectures at London
University, and for the past ten minutes his fellow-guests at Haldane's had been mutely enduring a précis of the lecturer's main
contentions.

'What it amounts to, then,' said Wakefield, towards what they
hoped was the close of what they hoped was his peroration, 'is that
philosophy deals not so much with the answers to questions about
man and the universe as with the problem of *what questions may
properly be asked.* Improper questions'—here a little man named
Fielding, whom no one knew very well, choked suddenly over his
port and had to be led out—'improper questions can only confuse the
issue. And it's this aspect of philosophy which in my opinion defines
its superiority to other studies, such as—such as'—Wakefield's eye
lighted on Gervase Fen, who was stolidly cracking walnuts opposite
—'such as, well, criminology, for instance.'

Fen roused himself.

'Improper questions,' he said reflectively. 'I remember a case
which illustrates very clearly how———'

'Defines,' Wakefield reiterated at a higher pitch, 'its superiority
to———'

But at this point Haldane, perceiving that much more of Wakefield
on epistemology would certainly bring the party to a premature end,
contrived adroitly to upset his port into Wakefield's lap, and in the
mêlée which ensued it proved possible to detach the conversational
initiative from Wakefield and confer it on Fen.

'*Who killed Baker?*' With this rather abrupt query Fen established
a foothold while Wakefield was still scrubbing ineffectually at his
damp trousers with a handkerchief. 'The situation which resulted in
Baker's death wasn't in itself specially complicated or obscure, and in
consequence the case was solved readily enough.'

'Yes, it would be, of course,' said Wakefield sourly, 'if you were
solving it.'

'Oh, but I wasn't.' Fen shook his head decisively, and Wakefield, shifting about uncomfortably in the effort to remove wet barathea from contact with his skin, glowered at him. 'The case was solved by a very able detective-inspector of the county CID, by name Casby, and it was from him that I heard of it quite recently, while we were investigating the death of that Swiss schoolmaster at Cotten Abbas. As nearly as I can, I'll tell it to you the way he told me. And I ought to warn you in advance that it's a case in which the mode of telling is important—as important, probably, as the thing told. . . .

'At the time of his death Baker was about forty-five, a self-important little man with very black, heavily brilliantined hair, an incipient paunch, dandified clothes, and a twisted bruiser's nose which was the consequence not of pugnacity but of a fall from a bicycle in youth. He was not, one gathers, at all a pleasing personality, and he had crowned his dislikeable qualities by marrying, and subsequently bullying, a wife very much younger and more attractive than himself. For a reason which the sequel will make obvious, there's not much evidence as to the form this bullying took, but it was real enough—no question about that—and three years of it drove the wretched woman, more for consolation than for passion, into the arms of the chauffeur-handyman, a gloomy, sallow young man named Arnold Snow. Since Snow had never read D. H. Lawrence, his chief emotion in the face of Mary Baker's advances was simple surprise, and, to do him justice, he seems, never to have made the smallest attempt to capitalize his position in any of the obvious ways. But, of course, the neighbours talked; there are precedents enough for such a relationship's ending in disaster.'

Haldane nodded. 'Rattenbury,' he suggested, 'and Stoner.'

'That sort of thing, yes. It wasn't a very sensible course for Mary Baker to adopt, the more so as she was a devout Catholic with a real horror of divorce. But she was one of those warm, good-natured, muddle-headed women—not, in temperament, unlike Mrs Rattenbury—to whom a man's affection is overwhelmingly necessary, as much for emotional as for physical reasons; and three years of Baker had starved that side of her so effectively that when she did break out she broke out with a vengeance. I've seen a photograph of her and can tell you that she was rather a big woman (though not fat), as dark as her husband or her lover, with a large mouth and eyes, and a Rubensish figure. Why she married Baker in the first place I really can't make out. He was well-to-do—or, anyway, seemed so—but Mary was the sort of woman to whom money quite genuinely means nothing; and, oddly enough, Snow seems to have been as indifferent to it as she.

'Baker was a manufacturer. His factory just outside Twelford made detailed and expensive model toys—ships, aeroplanes, cars, and so forth. The demand for such things is strictly limited—people who know the value of money very properly hesitate before spending fifteen guineas on a toy which their issue are liable to sit on, or drop into a pond, an hour later—and when Philip Eckerson built a factory in Ruislip for producing the same sort of thing, only slightly more cheaply, Baker's profits dropped with some abruptness to rather less than half what they'd been before. So for five years there was a price-war—a price-war beneficial to the country's nurseries, but ruinous to Baker and Eckerson alike. When eventually they met, to arrange a merger, or try to, both of them were dangerously close to bankruptcy.

'It was on March 10th of this year that they met—not on neutral territory, but in Baker's house at Twelford, where Eckerson was to stay the night. Eckerson was an albino, which is uncommon, but apart from that the only remarkable thing about him was obstinacy, and since he confined this trait to business, the impression he made on Mary Baker during his visit to her house was in every respect colourless. She was aware, in a vague, general way, that he was her husband's business rival, but she bore him not the least malice on that account; and as to Snow, the mysteries of finance were beyond him, and from first to last he never understood how close to the rocks his employer's affairs had drifted. In any case, neither he nor Mary Baker had much attention to spare for Eckerson, because an hour or two before Eckerson arrived Baker summoned the pair of them to his study, informed them that he knew of their liaison, and stated that he would take steps immediately to obtain a divorce.

'It's doubtful, I think, if he really intended to do anything of the kind. He didn't sack Snow, he didn't order his wife out of the house, and apparently he had no intention of leaving the house himself—all of which would amount, in law, to condoning the adultery and nullifying the suit. No, he was playing cat-and-mouse, that was all; he knew his wife's horror of divorce, and wished quite simply to make her miserable for as long as the pretence of proceedings could be kept up; but neither Mary nor Snow had the wit to see that he was duping them for his own pleasure, and they assumed in consequence that he meant every word he said. Mary became hysterical—in which condition she confided her obsession about divorce to Snow. And Snow, a remarkably naïve and impressionable young man, took it all *au grand sérieux*. He had not, up to now, displayed any notable animus against Baker, but Mary's terror and wretchedness fanned hidden fires, and from then on he was implacable. They were a rather pitiful pair, these two young people cornered by an essentially rather trivial issue, but their very ignorance made them dangerous, and if Baker had had more sense he'd never have played such an imbecile trick on them. Psychologically, he was certainly in a morbid condition, for apparently he was prepared to let the adultery go on, provided he could indulge his sadistic instincts in this weird and preposterous fashion. What the end of it all would have been, if death hadn't intervened, one doesn't, of course, know.

'Well, in due course Eckerson arrived, and Mary entertained him as well as her condition would allow, and he sat up with Baker till the small hours talking business. The two men antagonized one another from the start; and the more they talked, the more remote did the prospect of a merger become, until in the latter stages all hope of it vanished, and they went to their beds on the very worst of terms, with nothing better to look forward to than an extension of their present cut-throat competition and eventual ruin. You'd imagine that self-interest would be strong enough, in a case like that, to compel them to some sort of agreement, but it wasn't—and, of course, the truth of the matter is that each was hoping that, if competition continued, the other would crack first, leaving a clear field. So they parted on the landing with mutual, and barely concealed, ill-will; and the house slept.

'The body was discovered shortly after nine next morning, and the discoverer was Mrs Blaine, the cook. Unlike Snow, who lived in, Mrs Blaine had a bed-sitting-room in the town, and it was as she was making her way round to the back door of Baker's house, to embark on the day's duties, that she glanced in at the drawing-room window and saw the gruesome object which lay in shadow on the hearthrug. Incidentally, you mustn't waste any of your energy suspecting Mrs Blaine of the murder; I can assure you she had nothing to do with it, and I can assure you, too, that her evidence, for what little it was worth, was the truth, the whole truth, and nothing but the truth. . . .

'Mrs Blaine looked in at the window, then, and her first thought, to use her own words, "was that 'e'd fainted". But the blood on the corpse's hair disabused her of this notion without much delay, and she hurried indoors to rouse the household. . . . Well, in due course Casby arrived, and in due course assembled such evidence as there was. The body lay prone on a rug soaked with dark, venous blood, and the savage cut which had severed the internal jugular vein had obviously come from behind, and been wholly unexpected. Nearby and innocent of fingerprints, lay the sharp kitchen knife which had done the job. Apart from these things, there was no clue.

'No clue, that is, of a positive sort. But there *had* been an amateurish attempt to make the death look like a consequence of burglary—or rather, to be more accurate, of housebreaking. The pane of a window had been broken, with the assistance of flypaper to prevent the fragments from scattering, and a number of valuables were missing. But the breakfast period is not a time favoured by thieves, there were no footprints or marks of any kind on the damp lawn and flower bed beneath the broken window (which was not, by the way, the window through which Mrs Blaine had looked, but another, at right angles to it, on a different side of the house), and finally—and in Casby's opinion most conclusive of all—one of the objects missing was a tiny but very valuable bird-study by the Chinese emperor Hui Tsung, which Baker, no connoisseur or collector of such things, had inherited from a great-uncle. The ordinary thief, Casby argued, would scarcely give a Chinese miniature a second glance, let alone remove it; and the one or two burglars who specialized in loot of that nature would be unlikely to break into the house of a man not known to be a collector. No, the burglary was bogus; and unless you postulated an implausibly sophisticated double-bluff, then the murder had been done by one of the three people sleeping in the house. As to motive—well, you know all about that already; and one way and another it didn't take Casby more than twenty-four hours to make his arrest.'

Somewhat grudgingly, Fen relinquished the walnuts and applied himself to stuffed dates instead. His mouth full, he looked at the company expectantly; and with equal expectancy the company looked back at him. It was Wakefield who broke the silence.

'But that can't be *all*,' he protested.

'Certainly it's all,' said Fen. 'I've told you the story as Casby told it to me, and I now repeat the question he asked me at the end of it—and which I was able to answer, by the way: *who killed Baker?*'

Wakefield stared mistrustfully. 'You've left something out.'

'Nothing, I assure you. If anything, I've been rather more generous with clues than Casby was. But if you still have no idea who killed Baker, I'll give you another hint: he died at 9 a.m. Does that help?'

They thought about this. Apparently it did not help in the least.

'All right,' Wakefield said sulkily at last, 'we'll buy it. Who did kill Baker?'

'The public executioner killed him,' said Fen blandly, 'after he had been tried and convicted for the murder of Eckerson.'

For a moment Wakefield sat like one stupefied; then he emitted a howl of rage. 'Unfair!' he shouted, banging on the table. 'Trickery!'

'Not at all.' Fen was unperturbed. 'It's a trick story, admittedly, but you were given ample warning of that. It arose out of a discussion about the propriety of asking certain questions; and there was only one question—*who killed Baker?*—which I asked. What's more, I emphasized at the outset that the mode of telling was as important as the thing told.

'But quite apart from all that, you had your clue. Mrs Blaine, looking in through a window at a figure lying in shadow, concluded that violence had been done for the reason that she saw blood on the hair. Now that blood, as I mentioned, was dark, venous blood; and I mentioned also that Baker had black, heavily brilliantined hair. Is it conceivable that dark blood would be *visible* on such hair—visible, that is, when the body was in shadow and the observer outside the window of the room in which it lay? Of course not. Therefore the body was not Baker's. But it couldn't have been Mary Baker's, or Snow's, since they, too, were black-haired—and that leaves only Eckerson. Eckerson was an albino, which means that his hair was white; and splotches of blood would show up on white hair all right—even though it was in shadow, and Mrs Blaine some distance away. Who, then, would want to kill Eckerson? Baker obviously, and Baker alone—I emphasized that both Snow and Mary were quite indifferent to the visitor. And who, after the arrest, would be likely to kill (notice, please, that I never at any time said "murder") Baker? There's only one possible answer, I think, to that. . . .

'And what happened to the wife?' Haldane asked. 'Did she marry Snow?'

'No. He melted,' said Fen complacently, 'away. She married someone else, though, and, according to Casby, is very happy now. Baker's and Eckerson's businesses both collapsed, after their deaths, under the weight of debt they'd accumulated, and, having been one-man affairs, exist no longer.'

There was a pause; then:

'The nature of existence,' said Wakefield suddenly, 'has troubled philosophers in all ages. What are the sensory and mental processes which cause us to assert that this table, for instance, is *real*? The answer given by subjective idealism————'

'Will have to wait,' said Haldane firmly, 'till we meet again.' He stood up. 'And now shall we join the ladies?'

A Dangerous Thing

There are places in London into which it is not given to everyone to
enter. Yet of one of these, a holy of holies, Mrs Craggs, daily cleaner,
was an habituée. This was the Reading Room at the British Museum
Library, to which entry is restricted to approved scholars only. But it
was as well that Mrs Craggs's duties took her in there too. Definitely
as well.

Of course, she saw little of the Reading Room while it was properly
in use, when the Readers were there deep in volumes from that huge
collection to which by law every single book, magazine, fascicle, or
pamphlet published in Great Britain must be sent. But she liked the
stately, quiet atmosphere of the huge round chamber under its
shallow glass dome as she polished its great floor early in the
mornings before the hour of opening. She liked the encircling shelves
of leather-smelling tomes, the British Union Catalogue of Periodicals, the Bibliothèque Nationale Catalogue des Imprimes, the
Cumulative Book Index, the Annual Register, the Calendars of State
Papers, Halsbury's 'Statutes of England', 'Notes and Queries', and the
long run of 'The Gentleman's Magazine'. And she very much liked
what she saw of the learned people who began to come in at 9.30 a.m.

They might not be, she would often think, any great shakes as
specimens of physical beauty, running as they did for the most part to
shoulders stooped and rounded by long hours bent over volumes laid
out on desks and to posteriors more adapted to the seated attitude
than to the soldierly march or the elegance of the dance. But, by and
large, the love of their work, the love of scholarship for the sake of
scholarship, shone in their eyes, gleamed clearly through spectacle
lenses often—neglectfully smeared. And Mrs Craggs, though she
was the first to acknowledge that she was not much of a reader herself,
loved them for that.

Not that she loved every single one she chanced to see after her
chief duty of polishing that enormous circular floor with its radiating
spokes of Readers' desks was over and she was occupied in seeing to
parts of the huge learning machine not open to the public, even to

that privileged section in possession of Readers' Admission Tickets. There were a few individuals she had picked out as being, for all their industry at their desks, not proper scholars, not people dedicated to the pursuit of knowledge for its own sake. Most of these 'whizzers', as Mrs Craggs called them in her own mind, were comparatively young, though they were not all necessarily so. And she would have had difficulty, had she been asked, in saying just what it was about them that marked them out for her.

Perhaps it was the way they always hurried. They hurried to be first in the short queues waiting to hand in book application slips at the small circular area that forms the hub of the Room's great wheel. They hurried, first thing in the morning, to occupy some particular one of the 390 blue-leather covered desks which they considered to be nearest the particular reference works on the Room's perimeter that they might need. They hurried, when Closing Time came, to be first in the queues to hand back books for safe keeping during the night. 'Whizzers' was Mrs Craggs's name for them, and in her eyes they spoilt the slow, quiet, studious atmosphere of the place much as a garish half-squashed Coke can spoils the beauty of some ancient close-mown lawn on to which it has been carelessly thrown.

Once she overheard one of her gentlemen, one of the ones who was certainly not a whizzer, quoting a couple of lines of poetry to himself as he toddled away to get some lunch at midday.

> A little learning is a dang'rous thing;
> Drink deep, or taste not the Pierian spring.

She had often wondered what the heck a Pierian spring was, but she had had no difficulty in at once agreeing with the bit about 'a little learning'. It was a dangerous thing, she knew that in her bones. And it was the whizzers who had it, and would be dangerous some day to someone somewhere.

Before long there came a time when she had startling proof of this. It was on a day that began no differently from any other. Except for one funny thing.

Mrs Craggs had been standing at the entrance to the Reading Room in the lofty inner hall of the vast Museum itself talking to a friend of hers, one of the warders who check people going in to make sure they are in possession of a Reader's Ticket. It was a slack time, shortly after the first small rush of Readers when the Museum opens, and Mr Meiklejohn, a Scot who had lost none of his Scottishness for long residence in London, had been glad of a few moments' chat.

They had just got on to the subject of 'whizzers', though Mrs Craggs was keeping her pet name for them to herself, and Mr Meiklejohn, who was a pretty formidable scholar himself, if the faces of Readers, past, present, long-term and temporary, is a subject for scholarship, was agreeing that there were 'bodies you can pick out who are never your regular Reader the way a Reader ought tae be' when a very, very elderly man came slowly, slowly up to the entrance.

He looked, thought Mrs Craggs, about as old as anybody could be. He had a little stooped frail body that shuffled forwards under an enormous old overcoat, despite the summer heat, like a tortoise in its shell. His head, on which a few white hairs were spread this way and that, poked out on the end of a scrawny thin length of neck round which an old grey woollen muffler was wrapped. And he surveyed the world cautiously through a pair of tiny glinting pince-nez spectacles.

Mr Meiklejohn stepped forward and asked with grave Scottish courtesy if he could see his Reader's Ticket.

'Reader's Ticket?' said the old gentleman, as if such an object were something he had once heard of, dimly. 'Reader's Ticket? Well, yes, I suppose I have a Reader's Ticket. Must have been given one when I first used the Library, in '99, I think that must have been. Ninety-nine or '98, can't quite remember.'

Mr Meiklejohn shot Mrs Craggs a quick glance of amazement. Could the old boy really be meaning that he had first come to the Reading Room in the year 1899, or even 1898, eighty years ago? Was it possible?

And Mrs Craggs, looking at that peering scaly tortoise head on its long thin desiccated scarf-wound neck, thought that, well, it might be. It might really be. It would make the old boy probably a hundred years old, a bit less if he had begun to come to the Reading Room as a bright lad of eighteen or nineteen, but anyhow within a few months of his century. And he looked old enough to be a centenarian, every bit.

'Have you got your Ticket on you now, sir?' Mr Meiklejohn asked, pitching his voice a wee bit loudly in case the old gentleman was hard of hearing.

'On me? Now? I might have. I suppose I might have. Somewhere. But why on earth do you want to know?'

Mr Meiklejohn strove not to allow too astonished a look to appear on his features.

'We have to examine Readers' Tickets now, sir,' he said. 'It's a Regulation. Has been for—For a good many years, sir.'

'Oh. Oh, I see. Unauthorized fellers trying to make their way inside, eh?'

'Something like that, sir. And there had been thefts, sir, I'm sorry to say.'

'Thefts? Thefts, eh? What is the world coming to when a scholar and gentleman will steal from his own Library?'

'Aye, it's a terrible thing, sir. A terrible thing. But I'm afraid it means I'll have to see your Ticket, sir.'

'Oh, of course. Of course.'

The old gentleman brought one rather trembly grey woollen gloved hand to join the other and with extreme slowness plucked off the right-hand glove. He then seemed in some doubt about what to do with it.

'Might I hold that for you, sir?' asked Mr Meiklejohn.

'Oh. Oh, yes. Yes. Good of you.'

Mr Meiklejohn secured the grey glove—the tips of its fingers had been carefully darned once, many years ago—and the old gentleman plunged his free hand into the recesses of his overcoat.

A sudden rattling noise, like a quick burst of fire from a Kalashnikov automatic rifle, came from just behind them. Mrs Craggs and Mr Meiklejohn looked round. It was a Reader, a Reader wanting to enter and coughing to draw attention to his need. And, in that one quick, half-second glance, Mrs Craggs put him down at once as a whizzer, a whizzer plainly in a fury because he was being held up from plunging into the Reading Room and his waiting books.

'One moment, if you please, Mr Tipton-Martin,' said Mr Meiklejohn, authority on Readers' faces.

Mr Tipton-Martin, who was about twenty-four or twenty-five with a pale, slightly fat face and pale, well-brushed hair, wearing not the neglected clothes that most Readers seemed to possess but a well-pressed light blue safari suit with a shirt in broad blue and white stripes to match, gave Mr Meiklejohn a glance of suppressed rage. But there was nothing he could do about getting through the narrow entrance to the Reading Room before the old gentleman.

For perhaps as much as a minute or more the latter fished waveringly inside his overcoat. But then his hand emerged gripping a time-polished leather wallet. With trembling fingers, rather hampered by the grey glove still on his other hand, he attempted to pull out from it a small card that once might have been white but was now grey with age.

'Should I give you a hand, sir?' asked Mr Meiklejohn.

Behind the old gentleman young Mr Tipton-Martin produced a snort of quick disgust.

'That's very good of you,' said the old gentleman, handing over the wallet.

Mr Meiklejohn deftly extracted the card and gave it a glance.

'Mr Walter Grappelin,' he read. 'Thank you, sir.'

He was about to slip the card back into the old gentleman's wallet when he suddenly stopped and gave it another scrutiny.

'I'm verra sorry, sir,' he said, 'but this Ticket's out of date. It doesna' appear to have been renewed since————'

He stopped, and then continued in a voice from which he strove to eliminate the incredulity.

'. . . since 1943, sir.'

'Yes,' said old Mr Grappelin. 'Yes, that would be right. I suppose it must have been a year or so after that that I last had occasion to use the Library. Just about the time of the end of the Second World War, the one with that chap Hitler, you know. I retired from my Editorship about then, and the Bodleian at Oxford has been sufficient for my needs up till now. But I found yesterday that I really ought to look up that novel of George Sand that was suppressed, you know, and the Bodleian hasn't a copy. So I thought I'd better come up here.'

'Quite so, sir,' said Mr Meiklejohn reassuringly. 'But I'm afraid you really will have to get your Ticket renewed. The office is just by the main entrance doors down there, sir. Round to your right.'

'Ah. Good. Thank you. Thank you.'

And the old man shuffled away, moving not much faster than the tortoise he so much resembled.

'Your Ticket, Mr Tipton-Martin then,' Mr Meiklejohn said briskly.

'Oh, Er-Er-Ticket? Oh, yes, my Ticket.'

Young safari-suited Mr Tipton-Martin seemed not at all his usual whizzing self. Mrs Craggs wondered why.

And, for once, her curiosity was satisfied. Instead of shooting into the Reading Room and zipping round to secure himself some particularly advantageous desk, Mr Tipton-Martin stayed where he was and actually began to gossip with Mr Meiklejohn. To gossip. There was, thought Mrs Craggs, no other word for it.

'Do you know who that was?' he asked the warder.

'Gentleman name of Grappelin, sir.'

'Yes. But he's no ordinary gentleman. He's Professor Walter Grappelin. You know, the Editor of the Oxford Dictionary of Nineteenth-Century French, one of the great works of scholarship of our time. I thought he was dead years ago. The Dictionary came out in 1945, and he was quite old then. He retired as soon as he'd seen it through the press. He must be damned near a hundred now.'

'A verra remarkable man, sir,' said Mr Meiklejohn, in suitably awed tones. 'Verra remarkable indeed.'

Mr Tipton-Martin laughed. It was an unexpected sound. Mrs Craggs reckoned that whizzers didn't often laugh. But then this seemed to be a day of unexpected events.

'You may say old Walter Grappelin's remarkable,' Mr Tipton-Martin said. 'But he wasn't half as remarkable as his young brother!'

'Indeed not, sir? Then young Mr Grappelin must have been verra, verra remarkable.'

'He was. He was. He was the poet, you know.'

Mr Meiklejohn shook his head.

'I'm not verra much o' what you'd call a poetry man mesel', sir,' he said.

'No? I should have thought that everyone had heard of Maurice Grappelin. After all, next to Rupert Brooke he was probably our finest poet of the '14–'18 War.'

'Indeed, sir? Weel now, that's verra interesting.'

'That's as may be,' said Mr Tipton-Martin a little sharply. 'But the poetry's by no means the most interesting thing about Maurice Grappelin. Not many people remember this, or even know it. But he wasn't only a poet. He was a remarkable scholar as well. A philologist, of course, in the family tradition, following his elder brother's footsteps. But if you ask me he'd have far outshone him if he'd lived. If his discoveries in the field of—But, never mind, you'd hardly understand.'

'The poor gentleman died early then, sir?' Mr Meiklejohn asked with undeterred sympathy.

'Died early?' Mr Tipton-Martin snapped. 'Why, he was killed, man. Killed in 1914. Didn't you even know that?'

'I'm afraid not, sir,' Mr Meiklejohn said.

He sounded thoroughly ashamed of his ignorance, and Mrs Craggs, who in the ordinary way would not have ventured to address a Reader, quite suddenly jumped into the conversation in his defence.

'An' 'ow come you know such a lot about his philolwhatsit an' all that?' she asked, politeness abandoned.

Mr Tipton-Martin looked utterly affronted. As perhaps he had reason to be, suddenly spoken to by a person in a flowered apron with a rather squashed-looking red hat on her head.

'As a matter of fact,' he said, chilliness in every word, 'I work in the same discipline myself and I was also privileged, as an undergraduate, to re-catalogue the library at Castle Mandeville, a task which had been abandoned by none other than the young Maurice Grappelin at the outbreak of the 1914–1918 War. So naturally I know something of the man, perhaps rather more than any other scholar in the field.'

And with that he turned on his heel and flounced into the Reading Room, omitting to show Mr Meiklejohn his Reader's Ticket.

But Mr Meiklejohn was unperturbed. He shook his head wonderingly.

'Losh,' he said, 'it's always amazing to me just how much a real scholar knows.'

Mrs Craggs sniffed.

'Real scholar,' she said.

'Och, come now, Mrs Craggs. The wee man's been spoken of as one of the rising people. There was a gentleman the other day who told me that when next month a certain learned journal comes out it's to have an article in it by the young man that's likely to astonish everybody in the field and make his name for him once and for all. Not that anyone else will ken what it's all about, mind. But in his wee world he's fair bent to be a king-pin.'

'That's as may be,' Mrs Craggs said, not at all impressed by this example of a whizzer whizzing. 'But all the same, 'e only knew all about that Maurice Grappelin 'cos 'e 'appened to 'ave 'ad a job in the selfsame place where the feller worked afore 'e went off an' got shot fer 'is country. I don't see what's so ruddy amazing about that.'

The next thing that happened on this day which was to turn out to be extraordinary in every way was that Mrs Milhorne lost her handbag. Mrs Millhorne, long Mrs Craggs's friend, different in so many ways though they were, liked to work in the same place if she could and she had been a cleaner in the Reading Room almost as long as Mrs Craggs. But her view of the Readers was not at all the same as her friend's. She regarded them all, scholars and whizzers alike, as creatures of an extraordinary, superior order, as not so much human beings with human beings' imperfections and weaknesses as walking Brains, beyond and above ordinary ways as the stars are above the humdrum earth.

So naturally when she realized she had left her handbag tucked into one of the knee-hole shelves at desk Number F8 when she had dusted it that morning—dusting was her forte, just as good hard floor polishing was Mrs Craggs's—she felt entirely incapable of simply going quietly into the Reading Room and retrieving it.

'I'd disturb them,' she said to Mrs Craggs, much as she might have been saying 'I'd assassinate them'. 'I couldn't do it. I couldn't. Me nerves would go all to pieces. I just could not set foot in That Room.'

'Then you'll 'ave ter manage without yer old bag.'

'But I must have it. I must. It's got me pills in it. I need them pills. One every four hours I got to take. The Doctor said so.'

'Then go in and fetch it.'

'I couldn't. I can't. But I must have it. I must.'

Mrs Craggs sighed. She had known from the start what would happen in the end.

'All right,' she said. 'I'll go.'

And into the Reading Room with its ranks of bowed studious heads she went, walking quietly as she could but unable, of course, to do anything about her shoes, which squeaked abominably and always had.

But only one person took any notice, and that was a whizzer, one of the female variety, a lady dressed in a severe grey suit with a pointed nose and heavy purple-rimmed spectacles. She hissed at Mrs Craggs like an affronted goose. But otherwise nothing stopped her making her way between the radiating spokes of face-to-face desks with their high separating partitions until she got to Number F8.

She recognized at once its occupant. It was the old, old man, Professor Grappelin. He must have succeeded in renewing his Reader's Ticket without any trouble, she thought, and here he was now sitting patiently at his desk waiting for that book he wanted to come from where it must lie in the deep underground bookstore among the row on rows of close-packed volumes.

Or rather, Mrs Craggs thought, he ain't so much waiting as 'aving a nice bit of a zizz till 'is book comes. He had, she saw, been reading a magazine, one of them magazines that the learned gents of the Reading Room were always reading. She could see its title. 'The Journal of Philological Studies.' Whatever 'philological' meant. And she could see the date on it, too. Today's date. The old boy still keeping up with all the latest, even if he was damn nearly a hundred years old.

She decided that she could probably rescue Mrs Milhorne's handbag from the knee-hole shelf without disturbing the old boy. And she would have succeeded in doing so, too. Only, just as she stooped to reach in beside the old chap's unmoving little frail body, a crumpled piece of paper that someone had dropped on the floor just under the desk caught her eye. Tidying-up was a discipline to Mrs Craggs. If there was dirt or mess about she could no more stop herself dealing with it than she could have stopped herself breathing. So she reached down and picked up the piece of paper—it was a sheet of plain paper, very stiff and just lightly squeezed together—and thrust it into the pocket in front of her flowered apron with the intention of popping it into a waste-paper basket as soon as she had got out of the quietly calm atmosphere of the Reading Room.

But, in reaching just a little further than she had meant to so as to get hold of that piece of rubbish, the edge of her shoulder had lightly brushed against the sleeping professor's jutting-out elbow. And when it did so the old, old man, his body weighing hardly more than that of any lucky little girl's giant doll, toppled over out of his chair to lie, just in the position he had been in, curled up on the floor.

Mrs Craggs gasped. And then she gave a little short sharp involuntary scream.

Because, as the old man had fallen, his long grey muffler had come away and, looking down, Mrs Craggs's eyes had been drawn as if by two tugging black threads to the handle of a small shining silver paperknife that was protruding from the back of that frail old tortoise neck.

Mrs Craggs had recovered herself in a moment and had gone straight along to the central round desk to report the murder, all the more disturbed because of a nagging feeling at the back of her mind that somewhere before she had seen the murder weapon, that little silver paperknife. Its handle was funny. In the shape of a stubby, short-armed cross. She had seen that before somewhere, couldn't mistake it.

Just as she was about to report she noticed a yard or two further round the counter young Mr Tipton-Martin, standing waiting to hand back books he had finished with. So, remembering that he had known who old Professor Grappelin was, she went round, took him by the elbow and marched him back, despite his initial protests, to help her tell her story.

It was a good thing she had done so, because, once a police constable had been summoned from the courtyard outside the

Museum, Mr Tipton-Martin was able to advance matters in a decidedly swift way. Or so it seemed.

'Constable,' he said, when things had begun to be sorted out a little and they were waiting for the full might of Scotland Yard to arrive, 'there's something I think you ought to know.'

'Oh, yes, sir?'

'I hesitate to tell you, because it may seem like launching an accusation against a person who may be perfectly innocent. But on the other hand he is still here, and————'

'Who is this, sir?' the constable asked, with some urgency.

Mr Tipton-Martin pulled at the corners of the collar of his smart blue-and-white striped shirt.

'It's Francis Lecroix,' he said. 'I don't suppose you'll have ever heard of him, officer, but he's quite well known in his field, in a way. He's a philologist. Or he was. Well, he almost certainly still thinks of himself as one.'

'I'm sorry, sir,' said the constable. 'But I don't quite see what you're getting at.'

'No? No, I'm sorry. Well, you see, it's quite simply really. Lecroix years ago was one of Professor Grappelin's assistants on his great work, the Oxford Dictionary of Nineteenth-Century French. But he quarrelled with him. It was a professional disagreement over the definition of a certain group of words. And he resigned. And then, I'm afraid, he never got another job in the academic world. People thought he wasn't sound, you know. But he still persisted with his notion that Professor Grappelin had committed a serious crime in compiling that section of the Dictionary. He became obsessed with the idea. He even wrote a little book to explain his theories, and he had it privately printed and sent copies to every philologist of note. It's very well known in its way, a sort of joke. Because, you see, the chap is mad, of course. Mad as a hatter. But he happens to be here in the Reading Room now, and it was today that Professor Grappelin suddenly surfaced here when everybody thought he must be dead long ago.'

'I see, sir,' said the constable. 'And just where is this other gentleman now, this Mr-er-Lecroix, was it?'

'He's there, officer. Just there.'

And Mr Tipton-Martin extended a long arm and pointed right over to a far corner, just near Desk P9.

Mrs Craggs, who like everybody else had followed that long pointing arm, felt a sudden thump of dismay somewhere in the region of her heart. Because she recognized the man Mr Tipton-Martin had named. He was the old scholar she had once heard muttering to himself that 'a little learning is a dang'rous thing'. And, worse, the moment she saw him she knew where it was that she had seen that silver paperknife with the stubby cross handle. She had seen it more than once. On whatever desk it had been that Francis Lecroix was occupying. He always had it with him. He was always reading those old books that had uncut pages and he used the knife constantly to open them up.

Of course the constable had gone straight over and asked old Francis Lecroix—he must be seventy-five if he's a day, Mrs Craggs thought—to step over this way if he would. And there he had been by the Central Desk when from Scotland Yard to take charge of the inquiry there had arrived, with an impressive escort of detective-sergeants and fingerprint men and photographers and a scene-of-crime officer, the great towering form of Superintendent Mouse.

Mrs Craggs recognized him from his photo in the papers, that slab-sided six-foot-six-inches body, that solid wall of a face. But what she had never seen in the papers was what Superintendent Mouse pulled from the top pocket of his tent-like grey suit when Mr Tipton-Martin repeated his account of old Professor Grappelin, the Oxford Dictionary of Nineteenth-Century French and Mr Lecroix —a pair of heavy horn-rim spectacles. He put them on the bridge of his massive squabby nose and peered through them at little, safari-suited Mr Tipton-Martin.

'Hm,' he said. 'The ODNCF, eh? Masterly piece of work, of course. I do a little reading on those lines myself from time to time, and I couldn't do without it.'

Mr Tipton-Martin positively preened himself.

'Then perhaps you'll know that little book "The Great Oxford Dictionary of Nineteenth-Century French Scandal", Lecroix's polemic?' he said.

'Hm. Ha. Yes. Yes, interesting piece of work. In its way.'

'But the work of—' Mr Tipton-Martin dropped his voice since old Francis Lecroix was, after all, standing there blinking from one to the other—'a total lunatic.'

'Oh, yes, yes. Undoubtedly. Lunatic, yes, lunatic.'

Superintendent Mouse removed his heavy horn-rims and tucked them decisively into his top pocket.

'Well, thank you, Mr-er-Tupton-Marlowe,' he said. 'And now I think, Mr Lecroix, if you'll accompany me to Scotland Yard we can have this business cleared up before very much longer.'

'Oh, no, you don't,' said Mrs Craggs.

She was surprised, really, to hear her own voice, right out loud like that in the tremendous hush that had fallen on the wide-domed Reading Room after the first excitement had died down. But she had spoken. The words had been forced out of her from somewhere.

And she was glad that they had.

But everyone was looking at her now. Superintendent Mouse's ham-like left hand was groping again for his horn-rims. She had to justify what she had said.

'Look,' she began, 'you can't take him away like that. Well, there ain't no need to.'

Superintendent Mouse dropped his horn-rims, which he had got half way out of his top pocket, back in. Plainly, this was not a matter where the more intellectual side of life could be called into play.

'You're the lady that found the body,' he pronounced. 'Cleaning woman, isn't it? Mrs Bloggs, I believe.'

'If you believe that, you'll believe anything that likes ter come into your 'ead,' Mrs Craggs retorted. 'No, my name's Craggs, an' always has been ever since we was united more years ago than I cares to remember. An' if you believe a gentleman like old Mr Lecroix 'ere, what's what I calls a real scholar, could've done what was done to that pore old professor, then you're worse nor what I thought.'

Superintendent Mouse drew himself up to his full six foot six. The breadth of his body was enormous.

'That's quite enough of that,' he said. 'When I want a charwoman to tell me who's a scholar and who isn't I'll sell every book in my library. I dare say Mr Lecroix here looks like a scholar to you, clothes he hasn't changed for the best part of six months and spectacles with their left lens cracked, but that doesn't make him any different from any other person or persons. And he's got a little bit of explaining to do back at the Yard.'

He turned his massive bulk to face the aged author of 'The Great Oxford Dictionary of Nineteenth-Century French Scandal', who did indeed look a dusty and neglected figure.

'Now, just you come along with me,' he said.

But Mrs Craggs thrust herself, flowered apron, squashed red hat, between the Superintendent and his prey.

'He ain't going,' she said. How she brought herself to say it she never knew. 'He ain't going, or not until you've listened to reason for 'alf a minute.'

'My good woman.'

'Don't you "good woman" me. An' just you listen. Mr Lecroix is a scholar. Ain't I seen 'im in 'ere day after day? Nose down in those old books of 'is? Cutting away at every single page as 'as been stuck together ever since the book was printed and nobody else cared what was inside?'

But Superintendent Mouse's massive face had suddenly lit up with an inner fire.

'Cutting away at uncut pages?' he said. 'And what was he using to do that? Come along now, speak up.'

It was then that Mrs Craggs thought that all she had done was to make matters worse for her nice old gentleman. But it was his knife that was still sticking deep into the frail neck of old Professor Grappelin, and she knew it was. And not telling the truth wasn't going to make matters one bit better for anyone.

So she told the truth. And Superintendent Mouse put on his heavy horn-rims and went over and gave the shiny silver handle of the paperknife a short personal examination.

Then he returned to the Central Desk where the group of them were still standing.

'Yes,' he said. 'Well, come along now, Mr Lecroix.'

Mrs Craggs felt terrible. She knew that old Mr Lecroix, the man who could toddle out of the Reading Room muttering 'a little learning is a dang'rous thing', for all that he might have a bit of a bee in his bonnet about some complicated bit of studying in that huge big dictionary they were all on about, could not have plunged his paperknife into the old professor's neck and then covered up its jutting silver handle with the grey muffler. He could not have done that. It wasn't right for a man like him.

But how had his knife, his very own knife in the form of a cross, that she herself had seen him with so often, how could that knife have got to have been used for the horrible purpose that it had, if he was not the person who had used it?

And then she knew.

It came to her in a flash. No, old Mr Lecroix, the real scholar, had not used that knife. It had been used by none other than Mr Tipton-Martin, whizzer. She realized that not only did she know this, but she knew why Mr Tipton-Martin had done what he had done. No wonder he had gabbled and gabbled on like that after the sudden appearance of the old, old professor when everyone had thought he was long ago dead. Professor Walter Grappelin, whose brother had been Maurice Grappelin, the poet who had been tragically killed in 1914. The poet and the philol-whatsit. A philol-whatsit like Mr Tipton-Martin himself, Mr Tipton-Martin who had once worked in a library somewhere where Maurice Grappelin had been working until he had dropped everything to go and fight in the war. Had left behind—she knew this to be true, as if she had seen the evidence with her own eyes—some discovery or other in philol-whatsit that young Tipton-Martin years later had found. Had found and had pinched, safe in the knowledge that no one would know that Maurice Grappelin had done the work before him. Only, what was more likely than that Walter Grappelin would recognize his brilliant young brother's work when, just next month, it came out in the Journal of Philol-thingamebob Studies? The very magazine the old, old man had been reading this month's copy of just before he had fallen asleep at his desk over there.

And young whizzer Tipton-Martin had realized his danger, and then had realized that the perfect scapegoat for the murder that would get him out of his trouble and let him whizz on up to being king-pin of philol-whatsit was there in the Reading Room, asking to be made use of. Even down to providing him with a weapon that would point back to its owner like a ruddy illuminated street-sign.

But how was she to prove all this? How was she to convince Superintendent Mouse when plainly he had lapped up every word that his fellow so-called scholar, young Safari Suit, had ladled out to him?

Old Mr Lecroix had said hardly a word up till now. He had agreed that he was who he was, but beyond that he had kept silent, looking from face to face as each development occurred. But now he spoke.

'Grappelin was wilfully mistaken over the vocabulary of the *midinettes,*' he said. 'Wilfully, you know. You've only to read my book to see why. But I wouldn't have wished him any harm.'

'There,' said Mrs Craggs. 'There. You see. Mild as Dutch cheese. 'Ow can you say he'd of done a thing like that.'

'Mrs Bloggs,' said Superintendent Mouse, 'I should be reluctant to have you charged with obstruction, but, believe me, I shall if you persist in this.'

His huge left hand reached up to his horn-rims as if he would like just to peruse the relevant section of the Act before instituting proceedings.

It's now or never, thought Mrs Craggs. Whatever shall I do?

And then—Then, as if the spirit of Athene, goddess of wisdom, had descended on her from the great domed roof above, the answer came to her. She had had it. She had had it all along.

So now she produced it. It came out of her pocket, out of the pocket of her flowered apron. A piece of crumpled paper. A stiff lightly crumpled sheet of paper.

'Look,' she said. 'Just you look at this, an' you'll see.'

So charged were her words that Superintendent Mouse, man-œuvring his huge bulk round in the direction of the Readers' Entrance and extending a ham fist in the direction of old Mr Lecroix's elbow, stopped and swung himself back round again.

'Look at what?' he demanded.

'Look at this piece o' paper what I picked up just under old Professor Grappelin's desk,' Mrs Craggs said. 'Get your old 'orn-rims out, mate, and 'ave a gander at this. Look, a piece of paper, stiff paper what's been wrapped round something. Ain't it? Ain't it?'

Superintendent Mouse, who, to do him justice, had ignored the word 'mate' and had got out his horn-rims and settled them across the bridge of his great squabby nose, peered and agreed.

'Yes. Stiff paper and wrapped round an object.'

'An' you know why, don't you?' said Mrs Craggs. 'Fingerprints. That's why. Well, if someone was keen to keep 'is fingerprints off of that there paperknife, it can only 'ave been 'cos it wasn't the chap who owned the knife what used it. Everyone knew it was old Mr Lecroix's knife, so there wouldn't 'ave been no point in 'im keeping 'is paw marks off it, would there? An', look, you can see the print o' that there cross handle on the paper, can't yer? Can't yer?'

Mr Tipton-Martin began to sidle very gently in the direction of the Readers' Entrance. But Superintendent Mouse, moving his great bulk with surprising speed, put it between him and the wide open spaces beyond. Then he looked at Mrs Craggs.

'It's Mrs—Mrs Craggs, isn't it?' he said. 'Well, just give your full name and address to one of my officers, Mrs Craggs. I have a feeling we'll be needing you to give evidence sooner or later, and a witness who really knows what she's talking about is always a pleasure to have on hand.'

And from old Mr Lecroix there came a murmured rider to that statement.

'Yes,' he said, almost as if he was speaking to himself, 'drink deep or taste not the Pierian spring.'

RUTH RENDELL · 1930–

Thornapple

The plant, which was growing up against the wall between the gooseberry bushes, stood about two feet high and had pointed, jaggedly toothed, oval leaves of a rich dark green. It bore, at the same time, a flower and a fruit. The trumpet-shaped flower had a fine, delicate texture and was of the purest white, while the green fruit, which rather resembled a chestnut though it was of a darker colour, had spines growing all over it that had a rather threatening or warning look.

According to *Indigenous British Flora*, which James held in his hand, the thornapple or Jimson's Weed or *datura stramonium* also had an unpleasant smell, but he did not find it so. What the book did not say was that *datura* was highly poisonous. James already knew that, for although this was the plant's first appearance in the Fyfields' garden, he had seen it in other parts of the village during the previous summer. And then he had only had to look at it for some adult to come rushing up and warn him of its dangers, as if he were likely at his age to eat a spiky object that looked more like a sea urchin than a seed head. Adults had not only warned him and the other children, but had fallen upon the unfortunate *datura* and tugged it out of the ground with exclamations of triumph as of a dangerous job well done.

James had discovered three specimens in the garden. The thornapple had a way of springing up in unexpected places and the book described it as 'a casual in cultivated ground'. His father would not behave in the way of those village people but he would certainly have it out as soon as he spotted it. James found this understandable. But it meant that if he was going to prepare an infusion or brew of *datura* he had better get on with it. He went back thoughtfully into the house, taking no notice of his sister Rosamund who was sitting at the kitchen table reading a foreign tourists' guide to London, and returned the book to his own room.

James's room was full of interesting things. A real glory-hole, his mother called it. He was a collector and an experimenter, was James, with an enquiring, analytical mind and more than his fair share of curiosity. He had a fish tank, its air pump bubbling away, a glass box containing hawk moth caterpillars, and mice in a cage. On the walls were crustacean charts and life cycle of the frog charts and a map of the heavens. There were several hundred books, shells and dried grasses, a snakeskin and a pair of antlers (both naturally shed), and on the top shelf of the bookcase his bottles of poison. James replaced the wild flower book and, climbing on to a stool, studied these bottles with some satisfaction.

He had prepared their contents himself by boiling leaves, flowers, and berries and straining off the resulting liquor. This had mostly turned out to be a dark greenish brown or else a purplish red, which rather disappointed James who had hoped for bright green or saffron yellow, these colours being more readily associated with the sinister or the evil. The bottles were labelled *conium maculatum* and *hyoscyamus niger* rather than with their common English names, for James's mother, when she came in to dust the glory-hole, would know what hemlock and henbane were. Only the one containing his prize solution, that deadly nightshade, was left unlabelled. There would be no concealing, even from those ignorant of Latin, the significance of *atropa belladonna*.

Not that James had the least intention of putting these poisons of his to use. Nothing could have been further from his mind. Indeed, they stood up there on the high shelf precisely to be out of harm's way and, even so, whenever a small child visited the house, he took care to keep his bedroom door locked. He had made the poisons from the pure, scientific motive of *seeing if it could be done*. With caution and in a similar spirit of detachment, he had gone so far as to taste, first a few drops and then half a teaspoonful of the henbane. The result had been to make him very sick and give him painful stomach cramps which necessitated sending for the doctor who diagnosed gastritis. But James had been satisfied. It worked.

In preparing his poisons, he had had to maintain a close secrecy. That is, he made sure his mother was out of the house and Rosamund too. Rosamund would not have been interested, for one plant was much the same as another to her, she shrieked when she saw the hawk moth caterpillars and her pre-eminent wish was to go and live in London. But she was not above tale-bearing. And although neither of his parents would have been cross or have punished him or peremptorily have destroyed his preparations, for they were reasonable, level-headed people, they would certainly have prevailed upon him to throw the bottles away and have lectured him and appealed to his better nature and his common sense. So if he was going to add to his collection with a potion of *datura*, it might be wise to select Wednesday afternoon when his mother was at the meeting of the Women's Institute, and then commandeer the kitchen, the oven, a saucepan, and a sieve.

His mind made up, James returned to the garden with a brown paper bag into which he dropped five specimens of thornapple fruits, all he could find, and for good measure two flowers and some leaves as well. He was sealing up the top of the bag with a strip of Scotch tape when Rosamund came up the path.

'I suppose you've forgotten we've got to take those raspberries to Aunt Julie?'

James had. But since the only thing he wanted to do at that moment was boil up the contents of the bag, and that he could not do till Wednesday, he gave Rosamund his absent-minded professor look, shrugged his shoulders and said it was impossible for *him* to forget anything *she* was capable of remembering.

'I'm going to put this upstairs,' he said. 'I'll catch you up.'

The Fyfield family had lived for many years—centuries, some said—in the village of Great Sindon in Suffolk, occupying this cottage or that one, taking over small farmhouses, yeomen all, until in the early nineteen hundreds some of them had climbed up into the middle class. James's father, son of a schoolmaster, himself taught at the University of Essex at Wivenhoe, some twenty miles distant. James was already tipped for Oxford. But they were very much of the village too, were the Fyfields of Ewes Hall Farm, with ancestors lying in the churchyard and ancestors remembered on the war memorial on the village green.

The only other Fyfield at present living in Great Sindon was Aunt Julie who wasn't really an aunt but a connection by marriage, her husband having been a second cousin twice removed or something of that sort. James couldn't recall that he had ever been particularly nice to her or specially polite (as Rosamund was) but for all that Aunt Julie seemed to prefer him over pretty well everyone else. With the exception, perhaps, of Mirabel. And because she preferred him she expected him to pay her visits. Once a week these visits would have taken place if Aunt Julie had had her way, but James was not prepared to fall in with that and his parents had not encouraged it.

'I shouldn't like anyone to think James was after her money,' his mother had said.

'Everyone knows that's to go to Mirabel,' said his father.

'All the more reason. I should hate to have it said James was after Mirabel's rightful inheritance.'

Rosamund was unashamedly after it or part of it, though that seemed to have occurred to no one. She had told James so. A few thousand from Aunt Julie would help enormously in her ambition to buy herself a flat in London, for which she had been saving up since she was seven. But flats were going up in price all the time (she faithfully read the estate agents' pages in the *Observer*), her £28.50 would go nowhere, and without a windfall her situation looked hopeless. She was very single-minded, was Rosamund, and she had a lot of determination. James supposed she had picked the raspberries herself and that her 'we've got to take them' had its origins in her own wishes and was in no way a directive from their mother. But he didn't much mind going. There was a mulberry tree in Aunt Julie's garden and he would be glad of a chance to examine it. He was thinking of keeping silkworms.

It was a warm sultry day in high summer, a day of languid air and half-veiled sun, of bumble bees heavily laden and roses blown but still scented. The woods hung on the hillsides like blue smoky shadows, and the fields where they were beginning to cut the wheat were the same colour as Rosamund's hair. Very long and straight was the village street of Great Sindon, as is often the case in Suffolk. Aunt Julie lived at the very end of it in a plain, solidly built, grey brick, double-fronted house with a shallow slate roof and two tall chimneys. It would never, in the middle of the nineteenth century when it had been built, have been designated a 'gentleman's house', for there were only four bedrooms and a single kitchen, while the ceilings were low and the stairs steep, but nowadays any gentleman might have been happy to live in it and village opinion held that it was worth a very large sum of money. Sindon Lodge stood in about two acres of land which included an apple orchard, a lily pond, and a large lawn on which the mulberry tree was.

James and his sister walked along in almost total silence. They had little in common and it was hot, the air full of tiny insects that came off the harvest fields. James knew that he had only been invited to join her because if she had gone alone Aunt Julie would have wanted to know where he was and would have sulked and probably not been at all welcoming. He wondered if she knew that the basket in which she had put the raspberries, having first lined it with a white paper table napkin, was in fact of the kind that is intended for wine, being made with a loop of cane at one end to hold the neck of the bottle. She had changed, he noticed, from her jeans into her new cotton skirt, the Laura Ashley print, and had brushed her wheat-coloured hair and tied a black velvet ribbon round it. Much good it would do her, thought James, but he decided not to tell her the true function of the basket unless she did anything particular to irritate him.

But as they were passing the church Rosamund suddenly turned to face him and asked him if he knew Aunt Julie now had a lady living with her to look after her. A companion, this person was called, said Rosamund. James hadn't known—he had probably been absorbed in his own thoughts when it was discussed—and he was somewhat chagrined.

'So what?'

'So nothing. Only I expect she'll open the door to us. You didn't know, did you? It isn't true you know things I don't. I often know things you don't, I *often* do.'

James did not deign to reply.

'She said that if ever she got so she *had* to have someone living with her, she'd get Mirabel to come. And Mirabel wanted to, she actually liked the idea of living in the country. But Aunt Julie didn't ask her, she got this lady instead, and I heard Mummy say Aunt Julie doesn't want Mirabel in the house any more. I don't know why. Mummy said maybe Mirabel won't get Aunt Julie's money now.'

James whistled a few bars from the overture to the *Barber of Seville*. 'I know why.'

'Bet you don't.'

'OK, so I don't.'

'Why, then?'

'You're not old enough to understand. And, incidentally, you may not know it but that thing you've got the raspberries in is a wine basket.'

The front door of Sindon Lodge was opened to them by a fat woman in a cotton dress with a wrap-around overall on top of it. She seemed to know who they were and said she was Mrs Crowley but they could call her Auntie Elsie if they liked. James and Rosamund were in silent agreement that they did not like. They went down the long passage where it was rather cold even on the hottest day.

Aunt Julie was in the room with the french windows, sitting in a chair looking into the garden, the grey cat Palmerston on her lap. Her hair was exactly the same colour as Palmerston's fur and nearly as fluffy. She was a little wizened woman, very old, who always dressed in jumpers and trousers which, James thought privately, made her look a bit like a monkey. Arthritis twisted and half-crippled her, slowly growing worse, which was probably why she had engaged Mrs Crowley.

Having asked Rosamund why she had put the raspberries in a wine basket—she must be sure to take it straight back to Mummy—Aunt Julie turned her attention to James, demanding of him what he had been collecting lately, how were the hawk moth caterpillars and what sort of a school report had he had at the end of the summer term? A further ten minutes of this made James, though not unusually tender-hearted towards his sister, actually feel sorry for Rosamund, so he brought himself to tell Aunt Julie that she had passed her piano exam with distinction and, if he might be excused, he would like to go out and look at the mulberry tree.

The garden had a neglected look and in the orchard tiny apples, fallen during the 'June drop', lay rotting in the long grass. There were no fish in the pond and had not been for years. The mulberry tree was loaded with sticky-looking squashy red fruit, but James supposed that silkworms fed only on the leaves. Would he be allowed to help himself to mulberry leaves? Deciding that he had a lot to learn about the rearing of silkworms, he walked slowly round the tree, re-membering now that it was Mirabel who had first identified the tree for him and had said how wonderful she thought it would be to make one's own silk.

It seemed to him rather dreadful that just because Mirabel had had a baby she might be deprived of all this. For 'all this', the house, the gardens, the vaguely huge sum of money which Uncle Walter had made out of building houses and had left to his widow, was surely essential to poor Mirabel who made very little as a free-lance designer and must have counted on it.

Had he been alone, he might have raised the subject with Aunt Julie who would take almost anything from him even though she called him an *enfant terrible*. She sometimes said he could twist her round his little finger, which augured well for getting the mulberry leaves. But he wasn't going to talk about Mirabel in front of Rosamund. Instead, he mentioned it tentatively to his mother immediately Rosamund, protesting, had been sent to bed.

'Well, darling, Mirabel did go and have a baby without being married. And when Aunt Julie was young that was a terrible thing to do. We can't imagine, things have changed so much. But Aunt Julie has very strict ideas and she must think of Mirabel as a bad woman.'

'I see,' said James, who didn't quite. 'And when she dies Mirabel won't be in her will, is that right?'

'I don't think we ought to talk about things like that.'

'Certainly we shouldn't,' said James's father.

'No, but I want to know. You're always saying people shouldn't keep things secret from children. Has Aunt Julie made a new will, cutting Mirabel out?'

'She hasn't made a will at all, that's the trouble. According to the law, a great niece doesn't automatically inherit if a person dies intestate—er, that is, dies . . .'

'I know what intestate means,' said James.

'So I suppose Mirabel thought she could get her to make a will. It doesn't sound very nice put like that but, really, why shouldn't poor Mirabel have it? If she doesn't, I don't believe there's anyone else near enough and it will just go to the state.'

'Shall we change the subject now?' said James's father.

'Yes, all right,' said James. 'Will you be going to the Women's Institute the same as usual on Wednesday?'

'Of course I will, darling. Why on earth do you ask?'

'I just wondered,' said James.

James's father was on holiday while the university was down and on the following day he went out into the fruit garden with a basket and his weeder and uprooted the thornapple plant that was growing between the gooseberry bushes. James, sitting in his bedroom, reading *The Natural History of Selborne*, watched him from the window. His father put the thornapple on the compost heap and went hunting for its fellows, all of which he found in the space of five minutes. James sighed but took this destruction philosophically. He had enough in the brown paper bag for his needs.

As it happened, he had the house to himself for the making of his newest brew. His father announced at lunch that he would be taking the car into Bury St Edmunds that afternoon and both children could come with him if they wanted to. Rosamund did. Bury, though not London, was at any rate a sizeable town with plenty of what she liked, shops and restaurants and cinemas and crowds. Once alone, James chose an enamel saucepan of the kind which looked as if all traces of *datura* could easily be removed from it afterwards, put into it about a pint of water and set this to boil. Meanwhile, he cut up the green spiny fruits to reveal the black seeds they contained. When the water boiled he dropped in the fruit pieces and the seeds and leaves and flowers and kept it all simmering for half an hour, occasionally stirring the mixture with a skewer. Very much as he had expected, the bright green colour hadn't been maintained, but the solid matter and the liquid had all turned a dark khaki brown. James didn't dare use a sieve to strain it in case he couldn't get it clean again, so he pressed all the liquor out with his hands until nothing remained but some soggy pulp.

This he got rid of down the waste disposal unit. He poured the liquid, reduced now to not much more than half a pint, into the medicine bottle he had ready for it, screwed on the cap and labelled it: *datura stramonium*. The pan he scoured thoroughly but a few days later, when he saw that his mother had used it for boiling the peas they were about to eat with their fish for supper, he half-expected the whole family to have griping pains and even tetanic convulsions. But nothing happened and no one suffered any ill effects.

By the time the new school term started James had produced a substance he hoped might be muscarine from boiling up the fly agaric fungus and some rather doubtful cyanide from apricot kernels. There were now ten bottles of poison on the top shelf of his bookcase. But no one was in the least danger from them, and even when the Fyfield household was increased by two members there was no need for James to keep his bedroom door locked, for Mirabel's little boy was only six months old and naturally as yet unable to walk.

Mirabel's arrival had been entirely impulsive. A ridiculous way to behave, James's father said. The lease of her flat in Kensington was running out and instead of taking steps to find herself somewhere else to live, she had waited until the lease was within a week of expiry and had turned up in Great Sindon to throw herself on the mercy of Aunt Julie. She came by taxi from Ipswich station, lugging a suitcase and carrying the infant Oliver.

Mrs Crowley had opened the door to her and Mirabel had never got as far as seeing Aunt Julie. A message was brought back to say she was not welcome at Sindon Lodge as her aunt thought she had made clear enough by telephone and letter. Mirabel, who had believed that Aunt Julie would soften at the sight of her, had a choice between going back to London, finding a hotel in Ipswich or taking refuge with the Fyfields. She told the taxi to take her to Ewes Hall Farm.

'How could I turn her away?' James heard his mother say. Mirabel was upstairs putting Oliver to bed. 'There she was on the doorstep with that great heavy case and the baby screaming his head off, poor mite. And she's such a little scrap of a thing.'

James's father had been gloomy ever since he got home. 'Mirabel is exactly the sort of person who would come for the weekend and stay ten years.'

'No one would stay here for ten years if they could live in London,' said Rosamund.

In the event, Mirabel didn't stay ten years, though she was still there after ten weeks. And on almost every day of those ten weeks she tried in vain to get her foot in the door of Sindon Lodge. Whoever happened to be in the living-room of Ewes Hall Farm in the evening—and in the depths of winter that was usually everyone —was daily regaled with Mirabel's grievances against life and with denunciations of the people who had injured her, notably Oliver's father and Aunt Julie. James's mother sometimes said that it was sad for Oliver having to grow up without a father, but since Mirabel never mentioned him without saying how selfish he was, the most imma- ture, heartless, mean, lazy, and cruel man in London, James thought Oliver would be better off without him. As for Aunt Julie, she must be senile, Mirabel said, she must have lost her wits.

'Can you imagine anyone taking such an attitude, Elizabeth, in this day and age? She literally will not have me in the house because I've got Oliver and I wasn't married to Francis. Thank God I wasn't, that's all I can say. But wouldn't you think that sort of thing went out with the dark ages?'

'She'll come round in time,' said James's mother.

'Yes, but how much time? I mean, she hasn't got that much, has she? And here am I taking shameful advantage of your hospitality. You don't know how guilty it makes me, only I literally have nowhere else to go. And I simply cannot afford to take another flat like the last, frankly, I couldn't raise the cash. I haven't been getting the contracts like I used to before Oliver was born and of course I've never had a penny from that unspeakable, selfish, pig of a man.'

James's mother and father would become very bored with all this but they could hardly walk out of the room. James and Rosamund could, though after a time Mirabel took to following James up to the glory-hole where she would sit on his bed and continue her long, detailed, repetitive complaints just as if he were her own contemporary.

It was a little disconcerting at first, though he got used to it. Mirabel was about thirty but to him and his sister she seemed the same age as their parents, middle-aged, old, much as anyone did who was over, say, twenty-two. And till he got accustomed to her manner he hardly knew what to make of the way she gazed intensely into his eyes or suddenly clutched him by the arm. She described herself (frequently) as passionate, nervous, and highly strung.

She was a small woman and James was already taller than she. She had a small, rather pinched face with large prominent dark eyes and she wore her long hair hanging loose like Rosamund's. The Fyfields were big-boned, fair-headed people with ruddy skins but Mirabel was dark and very thin and her wrists and hands and ankles and feet were very slender and narrow. There was, of course, no blood relationship, Mirabel being Aunt Julie's own sister's granddaughter.

Mirabel was not her baptismal name. She had been christened Brenda Margaret but it had to be admitted that the name she had chosen for herself suited her better, suited her feyness, her intense smiles and brooding sadnesses, and the clinging clothes she wore, the muslins and the trailing shawls. She always wore a cloak or a cape to go into the village and James's mother said she couldn't remember Mirabel ever having possessed a coat.

James had always had rather a sneaking liking for her, he hadn't known why. But now that he was older and saw her daily, he understood something he had not known before. He liked Mirabel, he couldn't help himself, because she seemed to like him so much and because she flattered him. It was funny, he could listen to her flattery and distinguish it for what it was, but this knowledge did not detract a particle from the pleasure he felt in hearing it.

'You're absolutely brilliant for your age, aren't you, James?' Mirabel would say. 'I suppose you'll be a professor one day. You'll probably win the Nobel prize.'

She asked him to teach her things: how to apply Pythagoras' Theorem, how to convert Fahrenheit temperatures into Celsius, ounces into grammes, how to change the plug on her hair dryer.

'I'd like to think Oliver might have half your brains, James, and then I'd be quite content. Francis is clever, mind you, though he's so immature and lazy with it. I literally think *you're* more mature than he is.'

Aunt Julie must have known for a long time that Mirabel was staying with the Fyfields, for nothing of that kind could be concealed in a village of the size of Great Sindon, but it was December before she mentioned the matter to James. They were sitting in front of the fire in the front sitting-room at Sindon Lodge, eating crumpets toasted by Mrs Crowley and drinking Earl Grey tea, while Palmerston stretched out on the hearthrug. Outside a thin rain was driving against the window panes.

'I hope Elizabeth knows what she's doing, that's all. If you're not careful you'll all be stuck with that girl for life.'

James said nothing.

'Of course you don't understand the ins and outs of it at your age, but in my opinion your parents should have thought twice before they let her come into their home and bring her illegitimate child with her.' Aunt Julie looked at him darkly and perhaps spitefully. 'That could have a very bad effect on Rosamund, you know. Rosamund will think immoral behaviour is quite all right when she sees people like Mirabel getting rewarded for it.'

'She's not exactly *rewarded*,' said James, starting on the tea cakes and the greengage jam. 'We don't give her anything but her food and she has to sleep in the same room as Oliver.' This seemed to him by far the worst aspect of Mirabel's situation.

Aunt Julie made no reply. After a while she said, looking into the fire, 'How d'you think you'd feel if you knew people only came to see you for the sake of getting your money? That's all Madam Mirabel wants. She doesn't care for me, she couldn't care less. She comes here sweet talking to Mrs Crowley because she thinks once she's in here I'll take her back and make a will leaving everything I've got to her and that illegitimate child of hers. How d'you think you'd like it? Maybe you'll come to it yourself one day, your grandchildren sucking up to you for what they can get.'

'You don't *know* people come for that,' said James awkwardly, thinking of Rosamund.

Aunt Julie made a sound of disgust. 'Aaah!' She struck out with her arthritic hand as if pushing something away. 'I'm not green, am I? I'm not daft. I'd despise myself, I can tell you, if I pretended it wasn't as plain as the nose on my face what you all come for.'

The fire crackled and Palmerston twitched in his sleep.

'Well, I don't,' said James.

'Don't you now, Mr Pure-and-holy?'

James grinned. 'There's a way you could find out. You could make a will and leave your money to other people and tell me I wasn't getting any—and then see if I'd still come.'

'I could, could I? You're so sharp, James Fyfield, you'll cut yourself badly one of these fine days.'

Her prophecy had a curious fulfilment that same evening. James, groping about on the top shelf of his bookcase, knocked over the bottle of muscarine and cut his hand on the broken glass. It wasn't much of a cut but the stuff that had been inside the bottle got onto it and gave him a very comfortable and anxious hour. Nothing happened, his arm didn't swell up or go black or anything of that sort, but it made him think seriously about the other nine bottles remaining. Wasn't it rather silly to keep them? That particular interest of his, no longer compelling, he was beginning to see as childish. Besides, with Oliver in the house, Oliver who was crawling now and would soon walk, to keep the poisons might be more than dangerous, it might be positively criminal.

His mind made up, he took the bottles down without further vacillation and one by one poured their contents away down his bedroom washbasin. Some of them smelt dreadful. The henbane smelt like the inside of his mouse cage when he hadn't cleaned it out for a day.

He poured them all away with one exception. He couldn't quite bring himself to part with the *datura*. It had always been his pride, better even than the nightshade. Sometimes he had sat there at his desk, doing his homework, and glanced up at the *datura* bottle and wondered what people would think if they had known he had the means in his bedroom to dispose of (probably) half the village. He looked at it now, recalling how he had picked the green spiny thornapples in the nick of time before his father had uprooted all the beautiful and sinister plants—he looked at it and replaced it on the top shelf. Then he sat down at the desk and did his Latin unseen.

Mirabel was still with them at Christmas. On Christmas Eve she carried up to Sindon Lodge the pale blue jumper, wrapped in holly-patterned paper, the two-pound box of chocolates, and the poinsettia in a golden pot she had bought for Aunt Julie. And she took Rosamund with her. Rosamund wore her new scarlet coat with the white fur which was a Christmas present in advance, and the scarf with Buckingham Palace and the Tower of London printed on it which was another, and Mirabel wore her dark blue cloak and her angora hat and very high-heeled grey suede boots that skidded dangerously about on the ice. Oliver was left behind in the care of James's mother.

But if Mirabel had thought that the presence of Rosamund would provide her with an entrée to the house she was mistaken. Mrs Crowley, with a sorrowful expression, brought back the message that Aunt Julie could see no one. She had one of her gastric attacks, she was feeling very unwell, and she never accepted presents when she had nothing to give in return. Mirabel read a great deal, perhaps more than had been intended, into this valedictory shot.

'She means she'll never have anything to give me,' she said, sitting on James's bed. 'She means she's made up her mind not to leave me anything.'

It was a bit—James sought for the word and found it—a bit *degrading* to keep hanging on like this for the sake of money you hadn't earned and had no real right to. But he knew better than to say something so unkind and moralistic. He suggested tentatively that Mirabel might feel happier if she went back to her designing of textiles and forgot about Aunt Julie and her will. She turned on him in anger.

'What do you know about it? You're only a child. You don't know what I've suffered with that selfish brute of a man. I was left all alone to have my baby, I might have been literally destitute for all he cared, left to bring Oliver up on my own and without a roof over my head. How can I work? What am I supposed to do with Oliver? Oh, it's so unfair. Why shouldn't I get her money? It's not as if I was depriving anyone else, it's not as if she'd left it to someone and I was trying to get her to change anything. If I don't get it, it'll just go to the government.'

Mirabel was actually crying by now. She wiped her eyes and sniffed. 'I'm sorry, James, I shouldn't take it out on you. I think I'm just getting to the end of my tether.'

James's father had used those very words earlier in the day. He was getting to the end of his tether as far as Mirabel was concerned. Once get Christmas over and then, if James's mother wouldn't tell her she had outstayed her welcome, he would. Let her make things up with that chap of hers, Oliver's father, or get rooms somewhere or move in with one of those arty London friends. She wasn't even a relation, he didn't even like her, and she had now been with them for nearly three months.

'I know I can't go on staying here,' said Mirabel to James when hints had been dropped, 'but where am I to go?' She cast her eyes heavenwards or at least as far as the top shelf of the bookcase where they came to rest on the bottle of greenish-brown liquid labelled: *datura stramonium*.

'What on earth's that?' said Mirabel. 'What's in that bottle? *Datura* whatever-it-is, I can't pronounce it. It isn't cough mixture, is it? It's such a horrible colour.'

Six months before, faced with that question, James would have prevaricated or told a lie. But now he felt differently about those experiments of his, and he also had an obscure feeling that if he told

Mirabel the truth and she told his mother, he would be forced to do something his own will refused to compel him to and throw the bottle away.

'Poison,' he said laconically.

'*Poison?*'

'I made it out of something called Jimson's Weed or thornapple. It's quite concentrated. I think a dose of it might be lethal.'

'Were you going to kill mice with it or something?'

James would not have dreamt of killing a mouse or, indeed, any animal. It exasperated him that Mirabel who ought to have known him quite well, who had lived in the same house with him and talked to him every day, should have cared so little about him and been so uninterested in his true nature as not to be aware of this.

'I wasn't going to kill anything with it. It was just an experiment.'

Mirabel gave a hollow ringing laugh. 'Would it kill me? Maybe I'll come up here while you're at school and take that bottle and—and put an end to myself. It would be a merciful release, wouldn't it? Who'd care? Not a soul. Not Francis, not Aunt Julie. They'd be glad. There's not a soul in the world who'd miss me.'

'Well, Oliver would,' said James.

'Yes, my darling little boy would, my Oliver would care. People don't realize I only want Aunt Julie's money for Oliver. It's not for me. I just want it to give Oliver a chance in life.' Mirabel looked at James, her eyes narrowing. 'Sometimes I think you're the only person on earth Aunt Julie cares for. I bet if you said to her to let bygones be bygones and have me back, she'd do it. I bet she would. She'd even make a will if you suggested it. I suppose it's because you're clever. She admires intellectuals.'

'If I suggested she make a will in Oliver's favour, I reckon she just might,' said James. 'He's her great-great-nephew, isn't he? That's quite a good idea, she might do that.'

He couldn't understand why Mirabel had suddenly become so angry, and with a shout of 'Oh, you're impossible, you're as bad as the rest of them!' had banged out of his room. Had she thought he was being sarcastic? It was obvious she wanted him to work on Aunt Julie for her and he wondered if she had flattered him simply towards this end. Perhaps. But however that might be, he could see a kind of justice in her claim. She had been a good niece, or great-niece, to Aunt Julie, a frequent visitor to Sindon Lodge before the episode of Francis, a faithful sender of birthday and Christmas cards, or so his mother said, and attentive when Aunt Julie had been ill. On the practical or selfish side, getting Mirabel accepted at Sindon Lodge would take her away from Ewes Hall Farm where her presence frayed his father's temper, wore his mother out, made Rosamund sulk, and was beginning to bore even him. So perhaps he would mention it to Aunt Julie on his next visit. And he began to plan a sort of strategy, how he would suggest a meeting with Oliver, for all old people seemed to like babies, and follow it up with persuasive stuff about Oliver needing a home and money and things to make up for not having had a father. But, in fact, he had to do nothing. For Mrs Crowley had been offered a better job in a more lively place and had suddenly departed, leaving Aunt Julie stiff with arthritis and in the middle of a gastric attack.

She crawled to the door to let James in, a grotesque figure in red corduroy trousers and green jumper, her witch's face framed in a woolly fuzz of grey hair, and behind her, picking his way delicately, Palmerston with tail erect.

'You can tell that girl she can come up here tonight if she likes. She'd better bring her illegitimate child with her, I don't suppose your mother wants him.'

Aunt Julie's bark was worse than her bite. Perhaps, indeed, she had no real bite. When James next went to Sindon Lodge some three weeks later Mirabel was settled in as if she had lived there all her life, Oliver was on the hearthrug where he had usurped Palmerston's place and Aunt Julie was wearing Mirabel's Christmas present.

She hardly spoke to James while her great-niece was in the room. She lay back in her armchair with her eyes closed and though the young woman's clothes she wore gave to her appearance a kind of bizarre mockery of youth, you could see now that she was very old. Recent upheavals had aged her. Her face looked as if it were made of screwed-up brown paper. But when Mirabel went away—was compelled to leave them by Oliver's insistent demands for his tea—Aunt Julie seemed to revive. She opened her eyes and said to James in her sharpest and most offhand tone: 'This is the last time you'll come here, I daresay.'

'Why do you say that?'

'I've made my will, that's why, and you're not in it.'

She cocked a distorted thumb in the direction of the door. 'I've left the house and the furniture and all I've got to *her*. And a bit to someone else we both know.'

'Who?' said James.

'Never you mind. It's not you and it's none of your business.' A curious look came into Aunt Julie's eyes. 'What I've done is leave my money to two people I can't stand and who don't like me. You think that's silly, don't you? They've both sucked up to me and danced attendance on me and told a lot of lies about caring for me. Well, I'm tired, I'm sick of it. They can have what they want and I'll never again have to see that look on their faces.'

'What look?'

'A kind of greedy pleading. The kind of look no one ought to have unless she's starving. You don't know what I'm talking about, do you? You're as clever as they come but you don't know what life is, not yet you don't. How could you?'

The old woman closed her eyes and there was silence in which the topmost log crumpled and sank into the heart of the fire with a rush of sparks, and Palmerston strode out from where he had taken refuge from Oliver, rubbed himself against James's legs and settled down in the red glow to wash himself. Suddenly Aunt Julie spoke.

'I didn't want you corrupted, can you understand that? I didn't want to *spoil* the only one who means more than a row of pins to me. But I don't know . . . If I wasn't too old to stand the fuss there'd be I'd go back on what I've done and leave the house to you. Or your mother, she's a nice woman.'

'She's got a house.'

'Houses can be sold, you silly boy. You don't suppose Madam Mirabel will *live* here, do you?' Mirabel must have heard that, James thought, as the door opened and the tea trolley appeared, but there was no warning Aunt Julie or catching her eye. 'I could make another will yet, I could bring myself to it. They say it's a woman's privilege to change her mind.'

Mirabel looked cross and there was very little chance of conversation after that as Oliver, when he was being fed or bathed or played with, dominated everything. He was a big child with reddish hair, not in the least like Mirabel but resembling, presumably, the mean and heartless Francis. He was now ten months old and walking, 'into everything', as James's mother put it, and it was obvious that he tired Aunt Julie whose expression became quite distressed when screams followed Mirabel's refusal to give him chocolate cake. Oliver's face and hands were wiped clean and he was put on the floor where he tried to eat pieces of coal out of the scuttle and, when prevented, set about tormenting the cat. James got up to go and Aunt Julie clutched his hand as he passed her, whispering with a meaning look that virtue was its own reward.

It was not long before he discovered who the 'someone else we both know' was. Aunt Julie wrote a letter to James's parents in which she told them she was leaving a sum of money to Rosamund in her will. Elizabeth Fyfield said she thought there was something very unpleasant about this letter and that it seemed to imply Rosamund had gone to Sindon Lodge with 'great expectations' in mind. She was upset by it but Rosamund was jubilant. Aunt Julie had not said what the sum was but Rosamund was sure it must be thousands and thousands of pounds—half a million was the highest figure she mentioned—and with her birthday money (she was eleven on 1 March) she bought herself a book of photographs of London architecture, mostly of streets in Mayfair, Belgravia, and Knightsbridge, so that she could decide which one to have her flat in.

'I think we made a great mistake in telling her,' said James's father.

For Rosamund had taken to paying weekly visits to Sindon Lodge. She seldom went without some small gift for Aunt Julie, a bunch of snowdrops, a lop-sided pot she had made at school, a packet of peppermints.

'Wills can be changed, you know,' said James.

'That's not why I go. Don't you dare say that! I go because I love her. You're just jealous of me and you haven't been for weeks and weeks.'

It was true. He saw that Rosamund had indeed been corrupted and he, put to the test, had failed it. Yet it was not entirely disillusionment or pique which kept him from Sindon Lodge but rather a feeling that it must be wrong to manipulate people in this way. He had sometimes heard his father use the expression 'playing God' and now he understood what it meant. Aunt Julie had played God with him and with Rosamund and with Mirabel too. Probably she was still doing it, hinting at will-changing each time Mirabel displeased her. So he would go there to defy this manipulating, not to be a puppet moved by her strings, he would go on the following day on his way home from school.

But although he went as he had promised himself he would, to show her his visits were disinterested and that he could stick to his word, he never saw her alive again. The doctor's car was outside when he turned in at the gate. Mirabel let him in after he had rung the bell three times, a harassed, pale Mirabel with Oliver fretful in her arms. Aunt Julie had had one of her gastric attacks, a terrible attack which had gone on all night. Mirabel had not known what to do and Aunt Julie had refused to let her call an ambulance, she wouldn't go into hospital. The doctor had come first thing and had come back later and was with her now.

She had had to scrub out the room and actually *burn* the sheets, Mirabel said darkly. The mess had been frightful, worse than James could possibly imagine, but she couldn't have let the doctor see her like that. Mirabel said she hoped the worst was over but she didn't look very hopeful, she looked unhappy. James went no further inside than the hall. He said to tell Aunt Julie he had been, please not to forget to tell her, and Mirabel said she wouldn't forget. He walked away slowly. Spring was in the air and the neat, symmetrical front garden of Sindon Lodge was full of daffodils, their bent heads bouncing in the breeze. At the gate he met Palmerston coming in with the corpse of a fieldmouse dangling from his mouth. Without dropping his booty, Palmerston rubbed himself against James's legs and James stroked him, feeling rather depressed.

Two days later Aunt Julie had another attack and it killed her. Or the stroke which she had afterwards killed her, the doctor said. The cause of death on the certificate was 'food poisoning and cerebral haemorrhage', according to Mrs Hodges who had been Aunt Julie's cleaner and who met James's mother in the village. Apparently on death certificates the doctor has to put down the main cause and the contributory cause, which was another piece of information for James to add to his increasing store.

James's parents went to the funeral and of course Mirabel went too. James did not want to go and it never crossed his mind that he would be allowed to on a school day, but Rosamund cried when they stopped her. She wanted to have her red and white coat dyed black and to carry a small bouquet of violets. The provisions of the will were made known during the following days, though there was no dramatic will-reading after the funeral as there is in books.

Sindon Lodge was to go to Mirabel and so was all Aunt Julie's money with the exception of Rosamund's 'bit', and bit, relatively speaking, it turned out to be. Five hundred pounds. Rosamund cried (and said she was crying because she missed Aunt Julie) and then she sulked, but when the will was proved and she actually got the money, when she was shown the cheque and it was paid into her Post Office Savings account, she cheered up and became quite sensible. She even confided to James, without tears or flounces, that it would have been a terrible responsibility to have half a million and she would always have been worried that people were only being nice to her for the sake of the money.

James got Palmerston. It was set out in the will, the cat described and mentioned by name, and bequeathed 'if the animal should survive me, to James Alexander Fyfield, of Ewes Hall Farm, Great Sindon, he being the only person I know I can trust . . .'

'What an awful thing to say,' said Mirabel. 'Imagine, literally to have a thing like that written down. I'm sure James is welcome to it. I should certainly have had it destroyed, you can't have a cat about the place with a baby.'

Palmerston had lived so long at Sindon Lodge that he was always going back there, though he kept instinctively out of Mirabel's way. For Mirabel, contrary to what Aunt Julie had predicted, did not sell the house. Nor did she make any of those changes the village had speculated about when it knew she was not going to sell. Sindon Lodge was not painted white with a blue front door or recarpeted or its kitchen fitted out with the latest gadgets. Mirabel did nothing ostentatious, made no splash and bought herself nothing but a small and modest car. For a while it seemed as if she were lying low, keeping herself to herself, mourning in fact, and James's mother said perhaps they had all misjudged her and she had really loved Aunt Julie after all.

Things began to change with the appearance on the scene of Gilbert Coleridge. Where Mirabel had met him no one seemed to know, but one day his big yellow Volvo estate car was seen outside Sindon Lodge, on the next Mirabel was seen in the passenger seat of that car, and within hours it was all over the village that she had a man friend.

'He sounds a nice, suitable sort of person,' said James's mother, whose bush telegraph system was always sound. 'Two or three years older than she and never had a wife—well, you never know these days, do you?—and already a partner in his firm. It would be just the thing for Oliver. He needs a man about the house.'

'Let's hope she has the sense to marry this one,' said James's father.

But on the whole, apart from this, the Fyfield family had lost interest in Mirabel. It had been galling for them that Mirabel, having got what she wanted with their help, first the entrée to Sindon Lodge and then the possession of it, had lost interest in *them*. She was not to be met with in the village because she scarcely walked anywhere if she could help it, and although Rosamund called several times, Mirabel was either not at home or else far too busy to ask anyone in. James overheard his mother saying that it was almost as if Mirabel felt she had said too much while she stayed with them, had shown too openly her desires, and now these were gratified, wanted as little as possible to do with those who had listened to her confidences. But it suited the Fyfields equally, for the arrival of Mirabel was always followed by trouble and by demands.

The summer was hotter and dryer than the previous one had been, and the soft fruit harvest was exceptionally good. But this year there was no Aunt Julie to cast a cynical eye over baskets of raspberries. And Jimson's Weed, *datura*, the thornapple, did not show itself in the Fyfields' garden or, apparently, in any part of Great Sindon. A 'casual', as the wild plant book described it, it had gone in its mysterious way to ground or else wandered to some distant place away over the meadows.

Had it appeared, it would have exercised no fascination over James. He had his thirteenth birthday in June and he felt immeasurably, not just a year, older than he had done the previous summer. For one thing, he was about six inches taller, he had 'shot up' as his mother said, and sometimes the sight in a mirror of this new towering being could almost alarm him. He looked back with incredulous wonder on the child he had been, the child who had boiled noxious fruits and leaves in a pot, who had kept white mice in a cage and caterpillars in a box. He had entered his teens and was a child no more.

Perhaps it was his height that led directly to the drama—'the absolutely worst day of my life', Rosamund called it—or it might have been Mrs Hodge's operation or even the fact, that, for once in a way, the Women's Institute met on a Tuesday rather than a Wednesday. It might have been any of those factors, though most of all it happened because Mirabel was inevitably and unchangingly Mirabel.

The inhabitants of Ewes Hall Farm knew very little about her life since they hardly ever saw her. It came as a surprise to Elizabeth Fyfield to learn how much time Mrs Hodges had been spending sitting in with Oliver or minding him in her own home. It was Mrs Hodges's daughter who told her, at the same time as she told her that her mother would be three weeks in hospital having her hysterectomy and another goodness knows how many convalescing. Mirabel would have to look elsewhere for a baby-sitter.

She looked, as they might have known she would, to the Fyfields.

Presenting herself on their doorstep with Oliver on one arm and a heavy shopping basket on the other, she greeted James's mother with a winsome, nervous smile. It might have been last year all over again, except that Oliver was a little boy now and no longer a baby. James, home for the long summer holidays, heard her sigh with despair and break into a long apology for having 'neglected' them for so long. The fact was she was engaged to be married. Did Elizabeth know that?

'I hope you'll be very happy, Mirabel.'

'Gilbert will make a marvellous father,' said Mirabel. 'When I compare him with that stupid, immature oaf, that Francis, it just makes me—oh, well, that's all water under the bridge now. Anyway, Elizabeth dear, what I came to ask you was, do you think James or Rosamund would do some baby-sitting for me? I'd pay them the going rate, I'd pay them what I pay Mrs Hodges. Only it's so awful for me never being able to go out with my fiancé, and actually tomorrow I'm supposed to be meeting his parents for the first time. Well, I can't take a baby of Oliver's age to a dinner party, can I?'

'Rosamund's out of the question,' said James's mother, and she didn't say it very warmly. 'She's only eleven. I couldn't possibly let her have sole charge of Oliver.'

'But James would be all right, wouldn't he? James has got so *tall*, he looks almost a grown man. And James is terribly mature, anyway.'

His mother didn't answer that. She gave one of those sighs of hers that would have effectively prevented James asking further favours. It had no effect on Mirabel.

'Just this once. After tomorrow I'll stay at home like a good little mum and in a month Mrs Hodges will be back. Just from seven till—well, eleven would be the absolute latest.'

'I'll sit with Oliver,' said James's mother.

Mirabel's guarantee came to nothing, however, for far from staying home with Oliver, she turned up at Ewes Hall Farm three days later, this time to leave him with them while she went shopping with Gilbert's mother. She was gone for four hours. Oliver made himself sick from eating toffees he found in Rosamund's room and he had uprooted six houseplants and stripped off their leaves before James caught him at it.

Next time, James's mother said she would put her foot down. She had already promised to sit with Oliver on the coming Saturday night. That she would do and that must be the end of it. And this resolve was strengthened by Mirabel's failure to return home until half-past one on the Sunday morning. She would have told Mirabel so in no uncertain terms, Elizabeth Fyfield told her family at breakfast, but Gilbert Coleridge had been there and she had not wanted to embarrass Mirabel in front of him.

On the Tuesday, the day to which the Women's Institute meeting had been put forward, the fine weather broke with a storm which gave place by the afternoon to steady rain. James was spending the day turning out the glory-hole. He had been told to do it often enough and he had meant to do it, but who would be indoors in a stuffy bedroom when the sun is shining and the temperature in the eighties? That Tuesday was a very suitable sort of day for disposing of books one had outgrown, tanks and cages and jars that were no longer inhabited, for throwing away collections that had become just boxfuls of rubbish, for making a clean sweep on the path to adulthood.

Taking down the books from the top shelf, he came upon an object whose existence he had almost forgotten—the bottle labelled *datura stramonium*. That was something he need not hesitate to throw away. He looked at it curiously, at the clear greenish-brown fluid it contained and which seemed in the past months to have settled and clarified. Why had he made it and what for? In another age, he thought he might have been an alchemist or a warlock, and he shook his head ruefully at the juvenile James who was no more.

So many of these books held no interest for him any longer. They were kids' stuff. He began stacking them in a 'wanted' and an 'unwanted' pile on the floor. Palmerston sat on the window-sill and watched him, unblinking golden eyes in a big round grey face. It was a good thing, James thought, that he had ceased keeping mice before Palmerston arrived. Perhaps the mouse cage could be sold. There was someone in his class at school who kept hamsters and had been talking of getting an extra cage. It wouldn't do any harm to give him a ring.

James went down to the living-room and picked up the receiver to dial Timothy Gordon's number; the phone was dead. There was no dialling tone but a silence broken by occasional faint clicks and crepitations. He would have to go up the lane to the call box and phone the engineers, but not now, later. It was pouring with rain.

As he was crossing the hall and was almost at the foot of the stairs the doorbell rang. His mother had said something about the laundry coming. James opened the door absent-mindedly, prepared to nod to the man and take in the laundry box, and saw instead Mirabel.

Her car was parked on the drive and staring out of its front window was Oliver, chewing something, his fingers plastering the glass with stickiness. Mirabel was dressed up to the nines, as Aunt Julie might have said, and dressed very unsuitably for the weather in a trailing, cream-coloured pleated affair with beads round her neck and two or three chiffon scarves and pale pink stockings and cream shoes that were all straps no thicker than bits of string.

'Oh, James, you are going to be an angel, aren't you, and have Oliver for me just for the afternoon? You won't be on your own, Rosamund's in, I saw her looking out of her bedroom window. I did try to ring you but your phone's out of order.'

Mirabel said this in an accusing tone as if James had purposely broken the phone himself. She was rather breathless and seemed in a hurry.

'Why can't you take him with you?' said James.

'Because, if you must know, Gilbert is going to buy me something rather special and important and I can't take a baby along.'

Rosamund, under the impression that excitement was afoot, appeared at the bend in the staircase.

'It's only Mirabel,' said James.

But Mirabel took the opportunity, while his attention was distracted, of rushing to the car—her finery getting much spotted with rain in the process—and seizing the sticky Oliver.

'You'd like to stay with James and Rosamund, wouldn't you, sweetheart?'

'Do we have to?' said Rosamund, coming downstairs and bestowing on Oliver a look of such unmistakable distaste that even Mirabel flinched. Flinched but didn't give up. Indeed, she thrust Oliver at James, keeping his sticky mouth well clear of her dress, and James had no choice but to grab hold of him. Oliver immediately started to whine and hold out his arms to his mother.

'No, darling, you'll see Mummy later. Now listen, James. Mrs Hodges's daughter is going to come for him at five-thirty. That's when she finishes work. She's going to take him back to her place and I'll pick him up when I get home. And now I must fly, I'm meeting Gilbert at three.'

'Well!' exploded Rosamund as the car disappeared down the drive. 'Isn't she the end? Fancy getting lumbered with *him*. I was going to do my holiday art project.'

'I was going to turn my room out, but it's no good moaning. We've got him and that's that.'

Oliver, once the front door was closed, had begun to whimper.

'If it wasn't raining we could go in the garden. We could take him out for a walk.'

'It *is* raining,' said James. 'And what would we take him in? Mum's basket on wheels? The wheelbarrow? In case you hadn't noticed, dear

Mirabel didn't think to bring his push chair. Come on, let's take him in the kitchen. The best thing to do with him is to feed him. He shuts up when he's eating.'

In the larder James found a packet of Penguin biscuits, the chocolate-covered kind, and gave one to Oliver. Oliver sat on the floor and ate it, throwing down little bits of red and gold wrapping paper. Then he opened the saucepan cupboard and began taking out all the pots and pans and the colander and the sieves, getting chocolate all over the white Melamine finish on the door. Rosamund wiped the door and then she wiped him which made him grizzle and hit out at her with his fists. When the saucepans were spread about the floor, Oliver opened all the drawers one after the other and took out cutlery and cheese graters and potato peelers and dishcloths and dusters.

James watched him gloomily. 'I read somewhere that a child of two, even a child with a very high IQ, can't ever concentrate on one thing for more than nineteen minutes at a time.'

'And Oliver isn't two yet and I don't think his IQ's all that amazing.'

'Exactly,' said James.

'Ink,' said Oliver. He kicked the knives and forks out of his way and came to James, hitting out with a wooden spoon. 'Ink.'

'Imagine him with ink,' said Rosamund.

'He's probably not saying ink. It's something else he means only we don't know what.'

'Ink, ink, ink!'

'If we lived in London we could take him for a ride on a bus. We could take him to the zoo.'

'If we lived in London,' said James, 'we wouldn't be looking after him. I tell you what, I reckon he'd like television. Mirabel hasn't got television.'

He picked Oliver up and carried him into the living-room. The furniture in there was dark brown leather and would not mark so it seemed sensible to give him another Penguin. James switched the television on. At this time of day there wasn't much on of interest to anyone, let alone someone of Oliver's age, only a serial about people working at an airport. Oliver, however, seemed entranced by the colours and the movement, so James shoved him into the back of an armchair and with a considerable feeling of relief, left him.

There was a good deal of clearing up to be done in the kitchen. Oliver had got brown stains on two tablecloths and James had to wash the knives and forks. Rosamund (typically he thought) had vanished.

Back to her art project, presumably, making some sort of collage with dried flowers. He put all the saucepans back and tidied up the drawers so that they looked much as they had done before Oliver's onslaught. Then he thought he had better go back and see how Oliver was getting on.

The living-room was empty. James could soon see why. The serial had come to an end and the bright moving figures and voices and music had been replaced by an old man with glasses talking about molecular physics. Oliver wasn't anywhere downstairs. James hadn't really imagined he could climb stairs, but of course he could. He was a big strong boy who had been walking for months and months now.

He went up, calling Oliver's name. It was only a quarter past three and his mother wouldn't be back from the village hall until four-thirty at the earliest. The rain was coming down harder now, making the house rather dark. James realized for the first time that he had left his bedroom door open. He had left it open—because Palmerston was inside—when he went downstairs to phone Timothy Gordon about the mouse cage, and then Mirabel had come. It all seemed hours ago but it was only about forty minutes.

Oliver was in James's bedroom. He was sitting on the floor with the empty *datura* bottle clutched in his hands, and from the side of his mouth trickled a dribble of brown fluid.

James had read in books about people being rooted to the spot and that was exactly what happened at that moment. He seemed anchored where he stood. He stared at Oliver. In his inside there seemed to swell up and throb a large hard lump. It was his own heart beating so heavily that it hurt.

He forced himself to move. He took the bottle away from Oliver and automatically, he didn't know why, rinsed it out at the washbasin. Oliver looked at him in silence. James went down the passage and banged on Rosamund's door.

'Could you come, please? Oliver's drunk a bottle of poison. About half a pint.'

'What?'

She came out. She looked at him, her mouth open. He explained to her swiftly, shortly, in two sentences.

'What are we going to do?'

'Phone for an ambulance.'

She stood in the bedroom doorway, watching Oliver. He had put his fists in his eyes, he was rubbing his eyes and making fretful little sounds.

'D'you think we ought to try and make him sick?'

'No. I'll go and phone. It's my fault. I must have been out of my tree making the stuff, let alone keeping it. If he dies . . . Oh, God, Roz, we can't phone! The phone's out of order. I was trying to phone Tim Gordon but it was dead and I was going to go down to the call-box and report it.'

'You can go to the call-box now.'

'That means you'll have to stay with him.'

Rosamund's lip quivered. She looked at the little boy who was lying on the floor now, his eyes wide open, his thumb in his mouth. 'I don't want to. Suppose he dies?'

'You go,' said James. 'I'll stay with him. Go to the call-box and dial nine-nine-nine for an ambulance and then go into the village hall and fetch mum. OK?'

'OK,' said Rosamund, and she went, the tears running down her face.

James picked Oliver up and laid him gently on the bed. There were beads of perspiration on the child's face but that might have been simply because he was hot. Mirabel had wrapped him very warmly for the time of year in a woolly cardigan as well as a jumper and a tee-shirt. He had been thirsty, of course. That was what 'ink' had meant. 'Ink' for 'drink'. Was there the slightest chance that during the year since he had made it the *datura* had lost its toxicity? He did not honestly think so. He could remember reading somewhere that the poison was resistant to drying and to heat, so probably it was also resistant to time.

Oliver's eyes were closed now and some of the bright red colour which had been in his face while he was watching television had faded. His fat cheeks looked waxen. At any rate, he didn't seem to be in pain, though the sweat stood in tiny glistening pinpoints on his forehead. James asked himself again why he had been such a fool as to keep the stuff. An hour before he had been on the point of throwing it away and yet he had not. It was useless to have regrets, to 'job backwards', as his father put it.

But James was looking to the future, not to the past. Suddenly he knew that if Oliver died he would have murdered him as surely, or almost as surely, as if he had fired at him with his father's shotgun. And his whole life, his entire future, would be wrecked. For he would never forgive himself, never recover, never be anything but a broken person. He would have to hide away, live in a distant part of the country, go to a different school, and when he left that school get some obscure job and drag out a frightened, haunted existence. Gone would be his dreams of Oxford, of work in some research establishment, of happiness and fulfilment and success. He was not over-dramatizing, he knew it would be so. And Mirabel . . . ? If his life would be in ruins, what of hers?

He heard the front door open and his mother come running up the stairs. He was sitting on the bed, watching Oliver, and he turned round slowly.

'Oh, James . . . !'

And James said like a mature man, like a man three times his age, 'There's nothing you can say to me I haven't already said to myself.'

She touched his shoulder. 'I know that,' she said. 'I know you.' Her face was white, the lips too, and with anger as much as fear. 'How dare she bring him here and leave him with two *children*?'

James hadn't the spirit to feel offended. 'Is he—is he *dying*?'

'He's asleep,' said his mother and she put her hand on Oliver's head. It was quite cool, the sweat had dried. 'At least I suppose he is. He could be in a coma, for all I know.'

'It will be the end of me if he dies.'

'James, oh, James . . .' She did something she had not done for a long time. She put her arms round him and held him close to her, though he was half a head taller than she.

'There's the ambulance,' said James. 'I can hear the bell.'

Two men came up the stairs for Oliver. One of them wrapped him in a blanket and carried him downstairs in his arms. Rosamund was sitting in the hall with Palmerston on her lap and she was crying silently into his fur. It seemed hard to leave her but someone had to wait in for Mrs Hodges's daughter. James and his mother got into the ambulance with Oliver and went with him to the hospital.

They had to sit in a waiting room while the doctors did things to Oliver—pumped his stomach, presumably. Then a young black doctor and an old white doctor came and asked James a whole string of questions. What exactly was the stuff Oliver had drunk? When was it made? How much of it had been in the bottle? And a host of others. They were not very pleasant to him and he wanted to prevaricate. It would be so easy to say he hadn't known what the stuff really was, that he had boiled the thornapples up to make a green dye, or something like that. But when it came to it he couldn't. He had to tell the bald truth, he had to say he had made poison, knowing it might kill.

After they had gone away there was a long wait in which nothing happened. Mrs Hodges's daughter would have come by now and

James's father would be home from where he was teaching at a summer seminar. It got to five-thirty, to six, when a nurse brought them a cup of tea, and then there was another long wait. James thought that no matter what happened to him in years to come, nothing could actually be worse than those hours in the waiting room had been. Just before seven the young doctor came back. He seemed to think James's mother was Oliver's mother and when he realized she was not he just shrugged and said as if they couldn't be all that anxious, as if it wouldn't be a matter of great importance to them:

'He'll be OK. No need for you to hang about any longer.'

James's mother jumped to her feet with a little cry. 'He's all right? He's really all right?'

'Perfectly, as far as we can tell. The stomach contents are being analysed. We'll keep him in for tonight, though, just to be on the safe side.'

The Fyfield family all sat up to wait for Mirabel. They were going to wait up, no matter what time she came, even if she didn't come till two in the morning. A note, put into the letter-box of Sindon Lodge, warned her what had happened and told her to phone the hospital.

James was bracing himself for a scene. On the way back from the hospital his mother had told him he must be prepared for Mirabel to say some very unpleasant things to him. Women who would foist their children on to anyone and often seemed indifferent to them were usually most likely to become hysterical when those children were in danger. It was guilt, she supposed. But James thought that if Mirabel raved she had a right to, for although Oliver had not died and would not, he might easily have done. He was only alive because they had been very quick about getting that deadly stuff out of him. Mirabel wouldn't be able to phone Ewes Hall Farm, for the phone was still out of order. They all had coffee at about ten and James's father, who had gone all over his room to make sure there were no more killing bottles and had given James a stern but just lecture on responsibility, poured himself a large whisky.

The yellow Volvo came up the drive at twenty to twelve. James sat tight and kept calm the way he had resolved to do while his father went to answer the door. He waited to hear a shriek or a sob. Rosamund had put her fingers in her ears.

The front door closed and there were footsteps. Mirabel walked in, smiling. She had a big diamond on the third finger of her left hand. James's mother got up and went to her, holding out her hands, looking into Mirabel's face.

'You found our note? Of course you must have. Mirabel, I hardly know what to say to you . . .'

Before Mirabel could say anything James's father came in with the man she was going to marry, a big teddy bear of a man with a handlebar moustache. James found himself shaking hands. It was all very different from what he had expected. And Mirabel was all smiles, vague and happy, showing off her engagement ring on her thin little hand.

'What did they say when you phoned the hospital?'

'I didn't.'

'You didn't phone? But surely you . . . ?'

'I knew he was all right, Elizabeth. I didn't want to make a fool of myself telling them he'd drunk half a pint of coloured water, did I?'

James stared at her. And suddenly her gaiety fell from her as she realized what she had said. Her hand went up to cover her mouth and a dark flush mottled her face. She stepped back and took Gilbert Coleridge's arm.

'I'm afraid you underrate my son's abilities as a toxicologist,' said James's father, and Mirabel took her hand down and made a serious face and said that of course they must get back so that she could phone at once.

James knew then. He understood. The room seemed to move round him in a slow circle and to rock up and down. He knew what Mirabel had done, and although it would not be the end of him or ruin things for him or spoil his future, it would be with him all his life. And in Mirabel's eyes he saw that she knew he knew.

But they were moving back towards the hall now in a flurry of excuses and thank yous and good nights, and the room had settled back into its normal shape and equilibrium. James said to Mirabel, and his voice had a break in it for the first time: 'Good night. I'm sorry I was so stupid.'

She would understand what he meant.

ROBERT BARNARD · 1936–

The Oxford Way of Death

St Pothinus's Hall is not one of the most distinguished colleges of the University of Oxford. Its academic record is frankly deplorable—a fact in which many of the dons take a twisted kind of pride. Nor is it one of the younger and livelier colleges. I myself, at forty-seven, am the second youngest of the Fellows. The vast majority are well into their sixties or older. I once saw one of them reading over a list of the members of the Russian or Chinese politburo, with their ages, and chuckling so much he blew snuff all around the Senior Common Room. But compared to more normal institutions we are very old indeed. It has happened twice in the last year that a student would begin to read his weekly essay to a normally comatose old gentleman, only to find on concluding his piece that he had been reading for some time to a corpse. One of the young gentlemen to whom this happened let out a howl of horror and ran amok into Burton's Quad, screaming and tearing his hair. The other retrieved his books from the floor around him, placed his essay back in its folder, and went and had a quiet word with Jenkyns the porter. His conduct was much approved.

On the evening this all starts, I sat at High Table and looked around at my fellow Fellows (that is the sort of joke they like), and thought what a pathetic lot they all were. Wrinkled, bald, shrivelled, having trouble with dentures, respiration, and prostate glands. With some old people you can say, in effect: 'Well, at least they've had a good life———' or an interesting or exciting one. But the lives of these dons made A. E. Housman's, by comparison, an existence jam-packed with incident. The Senior Common Room was still chuckling about a brief and unsuccessful fling our Mr Peddie (Divinity) had had with a lady don at St Anne's. And that was back in 1934.

So anyway, there we all sat. Macnaughton, the Master, Peddie of the brief fling, Hugo Carmody (History), Pritchard-Jones (Medicine), Wittling (Classics) and the rest who play little part in this story, and who shall be left nameless. And myself, Peter Borthwick (English). Oh yes—and Auberon Smythe, the one who is younger

than I. Auberon was elected in 1970, and at the interview he looked
sober, discreet, well-washed. He came, we knew, from a minor
public school, as we all did. When he arrived to take up residence six
months later he had hair a foot long, wore kaftans, was into drugs,
revolution, and the gay scene, and used language that hadn't been
heard at High Table since the eighteenth century. We were properly
conned. Twelve years or so had tamed him, as it had most of his
generation, but he was still spoken of as our Big Mistake.

As we were spooning the last of the cabinet pudding into our
mouths (St Pothinus's is not renowned for its kitchen either), the
Master launched himself, as was inevitable, into the subject of
the next meeting of the Senior Common Room, to take place the
following week. These little excitements in our lives cast long
shadows before them.

'A busy time is ahead of us, I fear,' he began, in that disagreeable
chainsaw voice of his which nevertheless had a certain authority, and
ensured silence when he raised it above its normal whine. 'And a long
meeting too. For a start there is the question of Admissions for next
year.'

All the old gentlemen around him sighed. If they had their way
there would be no Admissions. No more undergraduates. They had a
vague sense that two hundred years ago this would have been
possible, and that they lived in a degenerate age.

'No problem, surely, about Admissions,' said Peddie, as the port
began to go round. 'They all come up and take the scholarship exams,
and then we give the places to the sons of Old Boys as usual.'

'You forget,' neighed the Master, 'that the Old Boys are not
producing many sons. Not *enough*.'

'No. Hardly a philoprogenitive lot,' said Wittling, with his
horrid laugh like twenty French horns doing the prelude to *Der
Rosenkavalier*.

'We could always give the places to the best applicants,' I said
cautiously, for new ideas are not welcome at Potty's.

'I know what that means!' yelped Peddie, wagging an accusing
finger. 'You want brains! *Brains!* Ha!'

'Besides,' said Pritchard-Jones seriously, 'it would mean reading
their scholarship papers.'

'What are you talking about, EH?' bellowed Hugo Carmody from
the foot of the table.

'Admissions,' I shouted back.

'Well, really!' said Hugo Carmody with a knowing wink. He is quite infuriating. He was a friend of Waugh and Acton and people back in the 'twenties, but if he was a dog then, he certainly has had his day by now. He uses his deafness as a weapon, and when we shout at him he invariably seems to turn what we say in his mind into something indecent, making us feel like smutty schoolboys. To shut him up the Master proposed a toast.

'Our benefactor, the poet-priest Heatherington,' he neighed.

More priest than poet, more gentleman than priest, more bon-viveur and hanger of poachers and discontented peasantry than gentleman. We drank the health of Edmund Heatherington (1711–1779), whose entry in the *Oxford Companion to English Literature* runs to one and a half lines. It was due to the happy accident of his having died immediately after writing the one will (of some thirty) which disinherited both his son and his daughter simultaneously that the college was rolling in money. We repeated his name in hushed tones, and sipped, reverently.

'Then,' said the Master, 'there is the question of Elections.'

'What are you talking about—EH?' yelled Carmody again.

'About ele . . . about appointing new Fellows,' I shouted back.

'Really!' sniggered Carmody. 'Whatever next?'

We all sighed.

'There are of course two places to fill, due to the untimely deaths of poor Purvis and Matheson,' resumed the Master. St Pothinus's is the only place in the world where death at 76 and 81 could be described as untimely. 'It has been suggested to me by the Vice-Chancellor that this time we should make an all-out effort—'

There was a sigh. He had lost his audience already. That phrase had put them all off.

'—to appoint somebody younger. To ensure the future of the college, as he put it.'

He looked around sardonically. Everyone looked bewildered.

'What frightful balderdash,' said Peddie, looking from face to face, seemingly quite confident that not only he, but all of us, would be blessed with eternal life on earth.

'We could make another Big Mistake,' muttered Pritchard-Jones, in the sort of mutter designed to call cattle home on the hills of North Wales.

'Oh God,' said Auberon Smythe, 'when will I graduate to being just a Little Mistake?'

'I told the Vice-Chancellor,' said the Master, satisfied with our reactions, 'I fear with a touch of asperity, that the cult of the young cut no ice with us, and would not be allowed to destroy the traditional ethos of St Pothinus's. No, indeed! Nevertheless, there are these elections. We have to have a new Fellow in French. You know my opinion of studying *mod*ern languages at a uni*v*ersity, but there it is: the Fellowship is vacant. And then, perhaps more difficult, there is the Fellowship in Ancient Persian . . .'

The Fellowship in Ancient Persian had been held by Harold Purvis, whose death had sent his one pupil screaming into Burton Quad. Since his death his pupil had been as lacking in tuition as he undoubtedly was in *savoir faire*, since there was only one such Fellowship in the University. Not surprisingly. Many were the years when Purvis managed to attract not one single undergraduate pupil.

'I don't see the difficulty,' suddenly chirped up Wittling. There was an edge to his voice that I knew and did not like. It meant mischief. Wanton, senile malice.

'Oh?' whinnied the Master. 'You have a candidate?'

'*I* don't have a candidate. I know there will *be* a candidate. There is only *one* person in Britain qualified for the position, and that person will certainly apply, positions in that field being by no means plenteous.'

'No, indeed: we are nearly, very nearly unique,' breathed the Master, with immense satisfaction. 'I hope this is not a *young* person, Wittling?'

'Thirty-two, I believe, Master.'

'Oh dear. *Very* young indeed. It seems the decision will be taken out of our hands. You say there is virtually no alternative?'

'No, Master,' said Wittling, with what was obviously some secret satisfaction. 'And I'm told that Sandowa Bulewa is brilliant, absolutely brilliant.'

There was a moment's silence.

'What was that name?' bellowed Carmody (who could hear when he wanted to) from the end of the table. 'Don't tell me it's some damned foreigner, for God's sake.'

'No, no. Born in Britain. Quite the homemade article.'

'But the name,' insisted the Master. 'It's not——'

'Not English, no. Tanganyikan, I believe, or whatever they call the place these days. Mother was Kenyan, I'm told.'

'Then he's not . . . you're not telling us——'

'Black. Black as your hat. Yes, Master.'

'Gracious heavens!' said the Master. 'Whatever next?'

'It's a retreat to barbarism,' said Peddie.

'Something must be done,' neighed the Master, at his most imperative. 'I feel the modern world has suddenly rapped most brutally at our door.'

'Personally,' said Auberon Smythe, 'I rather fancy the idea.'

It was all too clear what form the idea took for Smythe. Exclusively sexual. He was imagining a splendid black lover. But I felt I had to back him up.

'If we refused to appoint the man,' I said, 'we would certainly be in contravention of the Race Relations Act.'

'Heavens above,' said Pritchard-Jones. 'What's that?'

I explained at some length, ending up: 'If we have no adequate grounds for refusing him the Fellowship, he could certainly appeal to the Tribunal.'

'Admirably expounded,' cut in Wittling as I concluded, and now his voice had a suggestion of real mirth which absolutely made the blood run cold. 'But I must correct you, pedantically no doubt, on one little detail. You have been referring to Sandowa Bulewa throughout as "he". However the correct personal pronoun would be the third person *feminine*: "she", dear boy, "she".' And he chortled that awful laugh that sounded like whooping, Straussian French horns.

'But that's splendid. She's not elig . . .' The Master's voice faded away. This third shock left him looking as if he had heard the opening of Beethoven's Fifth played by massed Midlands brass bands and amplified a thousandfold. He looked at Wittling with outraged reproach.

For the powers that be at St Pothinus's had been caught in a trap of their own devising. Some years before, when all the Oxford colleges were changing their statutes, recruiting female dons, even admitting women students, we had, under strong pressure from the university authorities, declared all our senior appointments open to female applicants. We (or rather *they*) had done this on the clear understanding that nothing whatever was to come of it. I distinctly remembered Wittling at the meeting chuckling his horrible chuckle and saying: 'We declare them eligible, and we just don't appoint any. He-he-he!' It had seemed to most of them an awfully jolly wheeze at the time. I had no doubt that the Master was remembering this now.

'Wittling,' he said. 'This is at least in part your doing. I shall rely on you to find some way of getting us out of it.'

'Out of it?' crowed Wittling. 'Why should I want to get us out of it? Jolly good idea. Pretty young black thing. Brighten the place up.

Spruce us up a bit too. I believe she's a very lively little thing —modern, and all that. What's the phrase?—"with it". He-he-he.'

'Then what on earth is she studying Ancient Persian for?' demanded Pritchard-Jones.

'I'm told she has a Protestant Mission background from her parents. Went up to Cambridge to study theology. Got into New Testament Greek. Went on from there. Lost her religion, but proved a—he-he-he—whizzkid in ancient languages. Studied Persian at the Sorbonne.'

'Heavens above!' bellowed Carmody. 'It doesn't seem possible. What are gels coming to?'

'I have it! I have it!' shrieked the Master, a rare and terrifying smile wreathing his aged face. 'The Fellowship can be changed. Its terms can be altered. We can turn it into a Fellowship in Geography. Or Spanish. Or Comparative Something-or-other. That,' he concluded triumphantly, 'is possible under the terms of Edmund Heatherington's will. The endower of the Fellowship.'

'Quite,' said Wittling. 'It is possible. *Providing the Fellows are unanimous in desiring the change.*'

'Well?' Magisterially.

'They will not be unanimous. I myself do not desire the change. I must uphold the importance of the dead languages.' He sniggered. 'I have no doubt that Mr . . . er, *Dr*' (sneer) 'Smythe, being a *modern* young man, will not wish the nature of the Fellowship to be changed in order to exclude a member of the female sex.'

Now Auberon Smythe is one of the few homosexuals who seem genuinely to dislike women. But he too felt himself caught in one of Wittling's fork-like traps.

'No. No, of course not,' he muttered.

'And you, Borthwick,' continued Wittling, turning to me, 'a liberal young fellow like you would naturally like to see the College open to women.'

'Of course,' I said, with a touch of priggishness that comes, I think, from my Scottish ancestry. 'I would certainly be against changing the terms of the Fellowship if that were the motive.'

'Three dissenting!' said Wittling, in tones of triumph. 'Not a chance of a unanimous vote, Master. Not a chance!'

It was death to the Master's hopes. All his powers of command seemed to have left him. He summoned Jenkyns the porter, who led him from table, back to his Residence. As he staggered off, I saw him removing his dentures, something he only does in public when he is very upset. The rest of us broke up raggedly, and the evening concluded in less of an alcoholic fugg than usual.

I am not quite sure why Wittling did all this. I'm convinced that when he suggested altering the statutes to admit women he had no such far-sighted project as this in mind. Nor, of course, did he have any particular love of women as such. I'm sure no tingling of lust warmed his aged loins, or had, since about the time of *Chu Chin Chow*. I think it was just mischief. That's the trouble when you get older. Either you think you're immortal, and this gives you a godlike carelessness of consequences, or else you know you'll soon be dead, and won't have to put up with the results of your mischief. If the latter was Wittling's calculation, he was all too soon to be proved right.

In the week that followed I absented myself from College as much as possible, for squabbling geriatrics are hardly congenial companions. My only insight into how things were going I obtained one evening when, after a late tutorial, I went over to the buttery bar to have a beer before going home for dinner. The door stood open, and I heard the booming voice of Hugo Carmody.

'Well, I don't know if the Master has any plans, but I'm damned sure *some*thing's got to be done.' I lingered in the twilight outside the door. 'If only we could *get* something on them.'

'Absolutely,' I heard, in the sharp voice of Peddie.

'Smythe would be easy, what? Threaten to go to the police about his boyfriends.'

'That wouldn't do. It's not illegal any more.'

'What? Not illegal? Good heavens! I must stop slipping Higgins five-pound notes.'

Higgins was Carmody's scout. He was reaching retirement age, so he wouldn't greatly miss his five-pound notes. There was silence for a moment.

'Then there's Borthwick. Not much to be got on him. A somewhat *dim* personality, what?'

'His wife is sleeping with the milkman, you know,' came the thin, malicious voice of Peddie. They chuckled about this like crazy.

'But all the Fellows' wives sleep with one or other of the roundsmen. I always said that marriage doesn't *do*. And really it's hardly a *lever*.'

They subsided into silence, and I made a bustling entrance. I had a quick beer, and resolved to be home more in the mornings.

Nothing much happened that I knew of until the night before the Senior Common Room meeting. My wife was at an Oxfam gathering, she said, and I was forced to eat in Hall. Dinner was uneventful but unpleasant. No one was talking to Wittling, so he was forced to talk to me and Smythe. Given the choice I preferred Pritchard-Jones, who was at least inoffensive, or even Hugo Carmody, because I was always hoping to get out of him details of a trip he made to Paris with Waugh in 1924. But Wittling it was, and we were forced to put up with his crackling malice, his sly self-satisfaction, his trumpeted chortlings. After dinner we adjourned as usual to the Senior Common Room. I poured myself a second glass of port, and Wittling did the same. Smythe took a hard slug of whisky, and the master took coffee and brandy. Wittling stood by the mantelpiece, and though the rest of us wanted to cluster round the fire, we none of us wanted to be too near him.

'St Pothinus!' said the Master, who had placed himself in the centre of the room. We all toasted the patron saint of the College (dead at ninety, in a dungeon), and then the Master fixed Wittling with an eye, bleary, but designed to threaten and command.

'Well, Wittling, we're all hoping to hear you've changed your mind.'

'Changed my mind, Master?' Innocently.

'About altering the terms of the Fellowship.'

Oh, *that*———' (dismissively, as if the matter had passed completely out of his head). 'No, Master, I fear that my opinions on that subject are very much as they were last week.'

'I see, I see-e-e. So, to satisfy a foolish whim, to enjoy a bit of wilful trouble-making, you are prepared to jeopardize the best traditions of St Pothinus.'

'What did Winston Churchill say about the traditions of the Navy? Rum, sodomy, and the lash? I suppose you could say that St Pothinus's were port, sodomy, and the third-class honours degree. Personally, I believe traditions should be evaluated empirically. The obsolete ones discarded, what?'

'What you are proposing,' snapped Peddie, 'is a craven concession to the spirit of modernity.'

'Concession?' chortled Wittling. 'Not at all. I propose welcoming it in! A breath of fresh air from the contemporary scene. A propos of which, I have a *picture*—' he skipped, chuckling and snuffling, over to his briefcase in a corner by the door—'a snapshot, I think you call it, of the young lady herself, some years ago, taken when she was performing in the Cambridge Footlights Review . . . Ah, here it is.'

He produced from his case an old, slightly brown copy of the *Sun* newspaper, and we clustered round to view a picture of a distinctly handsome black girl, in leopardskin briefs, apparently topless, clutching a microphone in the centre of a stage, swaying her hips and crooning into it.

'My word!' said Carmody, 'I suppose that was taken after she lost her faith.'

None of the rest of us could think of anything more adequate to say.

'There,' said Wittling triumphantly, looking around at us and thrusting the photograph at the Master who was wandering over from the fireplace. 'Now you can see that Miss Bulewa will certainly provide something different in the College, what? Can't see anyone paying to see us topless, eh? Except perhaps Dr Smythe in some dubious Soho locale.' He pottered back towards the fire. 'No, this *is* going to be a bit of a change, isn't it? I hope she fits in. Do you feel she will? Don't you sometimes feel you've got into a bit of a rut here, all of you? That life is lacking in zest? Needs a bit of spice. Suddenly our lives are going to acquire a whole new flavour.'

He picked up his glass of port, and drank triumphantly. Suddenly an expression of horror, or rage, crossed his face, which set in a terrible grimace. His hand dropped the glass and went to his throat, a strangled cry escaped him, and he crashed forward on to the hearthrug.

'Dear me,' said the Master. 'Mr Wittling appears to be unwell.'

I was down on the hearthrug beside him, pulling open his dinner jacket, feeling his pulse. No one else moved. I didn't need long.

'He's dead,' I said.

'How unfortunate,' said the Master, taking a fortifying sip of his brandy. 'Struck down in his prime. In the midst of life . . . The ways of Providence are strange.'

'Providence, my foot!' I said brutally. 'You saw how he died. He's been poisoned.'

'Mr Borthwick! Mis-ter Borthwick! What an extraordinary suggestion! Most improper. You've been reading too many books by —what's that *thriller* writer?—Mr Wilkie Collins.'

'Can't you smell it? Almonds. It must have been in the port.'

'Gad! Founder's Port,' said Hugo Carmody.

'I can't smell a thing,' said Peddie. 'Look—I'm drinking port. It's perfectly all right.' And he downed his drink.

'I'm drinking port too,' I said. 'It must have been put in his *glass*. He'd already drunk half of it. It must have been put in his glass while we were all looking at his damned newspaper.'

'Come, come, Mr Borthwick, let us not lose grip of our logic,' said the Master in his unpleasant, silken whine. 'If we were all looking at his newspaper, none of us could have put anything in his glass.'

'One of us must have held back,' I said, crinkling my forehead with effort. 'One of us wasn't there.' I had a vision of the paper being thrust at the Master as he came from the direction of the fireplace. I looked at him, and he stared unwaveringly back.

'We were all gaping at it, far as I remember,' said Pritchard-Jones. 'Handsome filly.'

'Quite,' said the Master. 'We were all over that side of the room. Now let us forget this frivolous suggestion, and————'

'No doctor on earth is going to sign a death certificate, Master,' I said. 'There'll have to be an autopsy.'

'I'm sure Dr Pritchard-Jones will have no hesitation in signing the necessary formalities,' said the Master smoothly.

'Pritchard-Jones? He hasn't practised medicine since before penicillin was invented.'

'I believe you are eligible to sign the necessary forms?' inquired the Master in his high whinny, turning to Pritchard-Jones.

''Course I am. Most uncalled-for remark. Offensive.'

'I believe there *was* some history of heart trouble, wasn't there?'

'Think there was. Know he went to his doctor last week. I can square it with Smithers. Man's practically senile. Needn't be any question of a post-mortem.'

'There we are, then. That's all quite clear. There need be no question.'

'Master, even if you have a certificate,' I explained patiently, 'no undertaker is going to bury that corpse without getting a police clearance first.'

'Why on earth not?'

'Well—look!' I turned over the corpse. The face of Mr Wittling, blue, and twisted into a hideous grimace of torment that seemed to drag his wrinkled skin tight over his aged skull, gazed horrifyingly up at us.

'Well, he was nobody's idea of a dreamboat at the best of times,' said Auberon Smythe.

'I've no doubt Lockitt will not make any trouble,' said the Master. 'We'll get *old* Lockitt. Not the boy, he's a fusser. Old Lockitt is quite as old as any of us, and nearly blind. He's very understanding. He won't want to lose us—we've been one of their most regular customers, over the years.'

'You are covering up! You are accessories after a murder!'

'Covering up? Really, Mr Borthwick. You'll be suggesting next that I committed murder myself.'

He looked at me, and I, weakly, looked down at the floor.

'Well, how do I know that you didn't? How do I know that you're not all in it? Pritchard-Jones, what poison is it that smells like almonds?'

'Don't know, m'boy. Have to look it up in m'books.'

'It must have been brought here.' I looked desperately round the room. 'Look! Here it is.' I picked up from one of the side tables a tiny glass phial. 'This is how it was brought.'

'No doubt it contained some medicament that poor Wittling was taking for his heart,' said the Master.

'He did not have heart trouble,' I said. 'We'd have heard about it endlessly if he had. Smythe: you can see what's happening, can't you? Can I rely on you to support me?'

'Fight your own battles,' said Auberon Smythe, making for the door. 'I've no love for the police, believe me. As far as I'm concerned, I went straight to my rooms after Hall. Haven't been near the SCR all evening. 'Bye, duckies.'

'What did he say?' roared Carmody, but we ignored him.

'Right,' I said. 'If I have to fight my own battles, so be it.' I marched over to the telephone, recently installed in the SCR as a concession to the times. 'If you won't listen to me, perhaps you'll listen to the police.'

'The police?' neighed the Master. 'Really, Mr Borthwick, if we can't settle a little matter like this without calling in outside authorities, what has become of academic freedom?'

I didn't deign to answer, and was just beginning to dial when the Master spoke again, with that authoritative undertone to his whine that always got his point across.

'Mr Borthwick, you really must be careful, you know. I don't *think* you have quite thought this thing through.'

'What do you mean?' I demanded.

'Well, let us say, for argument's sake, that we are all "in it", as you put it a moment ago. It will be very easy, will it not, for us, all of us, to inform the police of a most unfortunate altercation, really quite violent, that took place last week between you and poor Wittling————'

'Altercation? There was no altercation. I hardly spoke to the man if I could help it.'

'Precisely. Your hostility was well known to us. And in an enclosed community such as our own, it is well known how little things can fester, and become great ones. There was that altercation, as I say. On the subject of—what was it?—Milton's debt to Virgil. Yes, I think that was it. We all heard it, of course. Now, would the police believe your story, of a collusion between a large number of elderly and impeccably respectable academic gentlemen to murder one of their colleagues? Or would they not rather accept our unanimous view that you—your mind unhinged, perhaps, by the notorious infidelities of your wife—had a brainstorm and decided to do away with a colleague with whom you were publicly on the worst of terms?'

'That's ridiculous.'

'Or say our splendid British police discovered that this was the work of one man. Say Mr Peddie. Say Mr Carmody. Say, even, myself. Leaving the rest of the SCR intact. You have been so taken up, I fear, with the terms of the Fellowship in Ancient Persian that you have forgotten the terms of your own Fellowship . . .'

'My own————'

'As some of us here remember, when the Jeremy Collier Fellowship in English was established, English was still a comparatively new university subject. Many of us hoped it would go away. So, in their wisdom, the governing Fellows made this Fellowship renewable every five years.'

'But that's just a formali————'

'*It has been hitherto.* Quite. We have been generous, as is our habit. However, the Fellowship comes up for renewal, does it not, *next year.* I think you may find that the SCR will not take kindly to the idea of renewing the Fellowship of one who has been responsible for arraigning one of their colleagues on a capital charge.'

'Damned bad form,' said Carmody.

'Quite,' said Peddie.

'Quite,' said all of them, sounding like a flock of ducks in St James's Park.

'You wouldn't dare,' I said, but my voice sounded hollow.

'I think you would find that to get a job at your time of life is far from easy. A cold academic wind is blowing, is it not, Borthwick? Positions are being abolished, rather than created, I believe. I'm told that even in the Colonies the universities are no longer the refuge for Oxonians that they once were. And though you are a great *reader*, Borthwick, you are hardly a prolific *writer*, are you? Isn't that what they want these days? Acres of little papers on this and that? It doesn't bear thinking about, does it, Borthwick? One of the great army of three million unemployed.'

I took my hand slowly from the telephone. He had me over a bubbling cauldron of boiling oil. When threatened where it hurts most, our jobs and our pockets, we liberal intellectuals do not hesitate. Or rather, we hesitate, because that is in our natures, but in the end . . .

I took a symbolic step away from the telephone.

'Splendid!' neighed the Master, rubbing his hands. 'I felt quite sure you'd see you'd been mistaken. Sad that the death of a respected and valued colleague should have been disfigured in this way. Now I fear I must to the Residence, to set in motion the necessary formalities.' He looked around the room carefully. He took up the little phial from the table, and hurled it into the fire. Then he took the copy of the *Sun* and placed it carefully in his briefcase.

'I shall ring Lockitt's, talk to the old man. I'll tell him to bring along a certificate for you to sign, Pritchard-Jones. Perhaps you would stay here too, Peddie, to see if there's anything else? The rest of us can go, I think. Borthwick, we'll quite understand if you are too upset to attend tomorrow's meeting: you have taken the death of your friend very hard, we can all see that. I shall propose to change the terms of the Heatherington Fellowship to one in Chinese. I think Wittling would have approved, with his concern for the older languages. And it will show that we in Potty's can, in our small way, adapt ourselves to the new patterns of the modern world.'

And that's how it turned out. We appointed two new Fellows. One was a Chinese scholar of great age and Buddha-like inscrutability, the other an elderly Winchester schoolmaster who was having disciplinary problems. They fitted in very well. Life in college goes on pretty much as before. For a time I did not care to go to High Table. I dined constantly at home, driving my wife to a frenzy of irritation. Even when I started to eat in Hall again, I avoided the port. But Time takes the edge off most things. Now I take my glass of Founder's Port with the rest, with scarcely a thought.

It's amazing what we liberal intellectuals can take in our strides, when we set our minds to it.

REGINALD HILL · 1936–

Bring Back the Cat!

It was a cold, clear morning, shortly after ten, when Joe Sixsmith arrived at the house in Brock Wood Lane. He checked the number, then set out on the long walk up the drive. It was an imposing double-fronted villa whose bay windows proclaimed middle-class wealth like an alderman's belly.

An upstairs curtain twitched but it might have been a draught.

He rang the doorbell.

After a pause, the door was opened by a woman of about forty, good-looking, well dressed in a county kind of way, with an accent to match.

'Y . . . e . . . s?'

It came out long as a sentence. A death sentence.

'Sixsmith.'

'Sorry?'

He handed her his card.

'You rang my office,' he said.

She studied the card till he retrieved it. He only had one card and he wanted it to last.

'Ah, *that* Sixsmith. I was expecting . . .'

He knew what she was expecting. Paul Newman, or Humphrey Bogart at least. What she wasn't expecting was a balding West Indian in a balding corduroy jacket.

'Yes,' she said again. It was another sentence, suspended this time. She was making up her mind. Suddenly she closed the door.

At least once she'd made up her mind she didn't fuck around with conscience-cleansing excuses, he thought.

'You see, it works.'

He looked around. He was alone.

'You try it from your side.'

The voice came from between his feet. He looked down. A small flap in the door at ground level was being swung on its hinge.

He stooped and said, 'Mrs Ellison?'

'Push it, Mr Sixsmith,' she said impatiently.

He studied her meaning for a moment, then pushed it.

'Again.'

He pushed it again.

'There, you see. It works both ways. Quite adequate for both ingress and egress, don't you agree?'

He said, 'Mrs Ellison, it certainly works. But I don't think I'm going to be able to make it. Also I don't know if . . .'

The door opened. Mrs Ellison looked down at him.

'Come in, Mr Sixsmith,' she said.

He went in. It was a long broad hallway smelling of lavender polish and hung with prints of *The Cries of Old London*. A girl of sixteen or seventeen was standing by a small table on which she was arranging a vase of flowers. She was rather plump and wore a tight sweater, short skirt and leg-warmers. She tore savagely at the flower-stems as if they had offended her.

A flight of stairs ran up from the hall to a landing, then turned back on itself. Sitting on the landing was a boy only slightly younger than the girl. His hair had blue highlights. He stared morosely at a spot between his feet.

'This is my daughter, Tittie. That is my son, Auberon,' said Mrs Ellison.

The boy didn't move but the girl said, 'Is he the new au pair?'

'Don't be ridiculous,' said Mrs Ellison. 'This way.' Sixsmith followed her into a large, airy lounge. An upholstered bench ran round the window-bay. A coffee-table stood in the bay. Opposite the window was a mock Adam fireplace. In the grate before it stood a large well-cushioned cat-basket. A chintz-covered suite of three armchairs and a huge sofa rested on the pale blue fitted carpet. At one end of the sofa with his legs up sat a man in his forties, shirt-sleeved, unshaven, and reading a *Daily Mail*. He looked up, caught Sixsmith's eye, winked and said, 'Hello, Sherlock.'

The woman ignored him and led Sixsmith to the window-seat. He sat in the bay and she perched herself at the angle of window and wall.

'Mr Sixsmith,' she said, 'I would like you to investigate a disappearance. The disappearance of my cat.'

This was what Sixsmith had begun to fear. He rubbed his fingers across the worn ribs of his corduroy jacket and wondered how to react. He didn't have the kind of mind which made decisions or even deductions very quickly and he recognized this as a disadvantage in his chosen profession. But he liked to think that in the end he got it right.

'Well?' urged the woman.

He sighed and said, 'I'm sorry, Mrs Ellison. We've all got to draw lines. I draw mine at chasing stray cats.'

He began to rise. There was a snort of what sounded like suppressed laughter from the sofa. This hurt him. He thought he'd sounded rather dignified, even if what he'd meant was he saw no way of tracking down a stray cat, so didn't reckon there was much chance of squeezing his fee out of Mrs Ellison.

'Sit down, Mr Sixsmith,' she ordered peremptorily.

He paused in a semi-squat, neither rising nor sitting. It wasn't the woman's tone that froze him. He'd long since developed tone-deafness to the accents of the bourgeoisie. The petrification derived from what he could see waiting for him through the open doorway into the hall. The girl, Tittie, stood there. She was regarding him sullenly and at the same time rolling up her tight sweater till it circled like a life-belt beneath her armpits. She wore no bra and lived up to her name.

Sixsmith sat down. The girl put out her tongue and turned away. Her brother appeared behind her and closed the door.

'What is hard to understand,' resumed the woman, certain it was her simple command that had done the trick, 'is why he should stray. Everything he wants or needs is here. He never goes further than the herbaceous border at the back or the shrubbery at the front. His little door stays open day and night. And as you saw for yourself, there's no chance of it sticking.'

From the hallway came the sound of a hand cracking hard across flesh and a female voice saying furiously, 'Piss off!'

'So what's your conclusion, Mr Sixsmith?' said Mrs Ellison, ignoring the interruption.

'Pardon?'

'You're a private detective. What conclusion do you draw from the facts I've just given you?'

He said, 'Oh yes. Look, Mrs Ellison, I don't have much experience of cats, I admit, but what seems likely to me is that either your cat strayed out on the road and got knocked down. Or maybe someone stole it. For one of those research places. I'm sorry.'

'Research places?'

'That's right. You know, medical research. Vivisection. There's a lot of pet-thieving goes on, I believe. Sorry.'

The woman rose now, her face twisted in grief.

'Vivisection? You mean . . . cut up? Oh no! I'd know . . . I'd feel it . . . how disgusting!'

There were tears in her eyes. She went to the far end of the room, where a couple of decanters and some crystal glasses stood on an authentic reproduction Jacobean cocktail cabinet, poured herself a drink and went out of the room.

The man on the sofa said, 'She weren't so bothered when she took him to be doctored.'

'Doctored?' said Sixsmith.

'Castrated. They smell like cats, else. That's two of us she's had done now.'

'You're Mr Ellison, are you, sir?'

Sixsmith spoke hesitantly. The man's appearance, manner, and broad northern accent jarred with this Hertfordshire stockbroker belt setting.

'That's me, son,' said the man. 'Surprised? Not as surprised as she were, I bet, when she clapped eyes on thee!'

Mrs Ellison returned. From the tintinnabulation of her glass she'd clearly gone in search of ice rather than solitude.

'Forgive me, Mr Sixsmith,' she said. 'There is something of the Celt in me, emotionally speaking. I get upset very easily.'

It struck Sixsmith that she had not as yet acknowledged her husband's presence.

He said, 'You miss your cat so much, Mrs Ellison, I presume you've taken steps already to get him back?'

'True. I've advertised widely. I've contacted the RSPCA. I've even informed the police. They were not sympathetic.'

Ellison said, 'She contacted the cops in Bedfordshire, Cambridgeshire, and Essex. We live in Herts, and she expects the cops in Bedfordshire, Cambridgeshire, and Essex to be sympathetic!'

He shook the pages of his paper in angry disbelief.

His wife ignored him and said, 'I've also conducted a search of my own, Mr Sixsmith, though with limited resources and no assistance, it has not been easy.'

Sixsmith screwed up his face and tried to look professional.

'Did you search on a systematic basis, Mrs Ellison?' he asked.

'Yes. I've kept a record. Would you like to see it?'

'Please.'

She left the room again and Ellison emerged from his paper once more.

'You know how she's spent most of her spare time, which means most of her time, this past week?' he demanded. 'I'll tell you. She gets into her car and she sets off driving round the countryside.

From time to time she gets out and she starts calling. *Darkie! Darkie!'*

'Sorry?' said Sixsmith.

'Darkie. That's the cat's name.'

Sixsmith scratched his nose, sighed, and said, 'Go on. She calls his name . . .'

'But that's not all. Oh no. Before she drives on, she removes some part of her clothing and lays it in a ditch or drapes it over a hedge. I bet half the police in Hertfordshire are out looking for the mad rapist of Baldock!'

'How do you know this, Mr Ellison? Do you accompany your wife?'

'No fear! No, my daughter went with her once. She told me.'

Mrs Ellison came back once more carrying a large desk diary and an Ordnance Survey map.

'I've got it all charted and recorded here,' she said.

'Thank you. Mrs Ellison, why do you leave items of clothing scattered round the countryside?'

She said, 'How do you know about that?'

Sixsmith sighed again and said, 'I'm a detective, Mrs Ellison.'

'I see. Well, it's smell, Mr Sixsmith. The framework of a cat's living space is smell. They lay a boundary of odour outside which they are in foreign territory. Darkie, wherever he is, is clearly lost. By leaving my garments where he might possibly find them, I am providing an oasis of familiarity in a desert of frightening strangeness.'

'Have you had any results yet?'

'How can I know? I leave the clothes for comfort, not as bait.'

Sixsmith said, 'I mean, have you caught a glimpse of . . . er . . . Darkie yet? Have you had any replies to your ads? Have the police or the RSPCA been able to help?'

'No. Nothing. The RSPCA keep me posted about any strays they get. The police, I fear, have done nothing. I've had several replies to my advertisements but they have so far either been frivolous or extortionate. Twice I have been offered cats which allegedly fitted the description. They were nothing like Darkie! The tricksters who tried to pass them off became quite aggressive when I told them what I thought. But it was clearly an attempt at fraud. Look, he is so distinctive, isn't he?' She handed him a colour photograph. It showed a cat rearing out of a wellington boot. It had a red ribbon round its neck. But it still managed to look dignified. And it was certainly distinctive, jet black except for a white patch on its head which involved most of its left eye and ear.

'Very nice,' said Sixsmith. It was time to talk business, he decided. When you were being hired by a wife who treated her husband as non-existent, it made sense to find who controlled the purse strings. He had a sliding scale, based on how much he felt the customer could carry and how much he needed the work. So far it hadn't slid off the bottom. This one was different.

He said, 'Mrs Ellison, before we go any further, let's put things on a firm professional basis. My terms are sixty pounds a day plus expenses, with two days' pay in advance. How's that grab you?'

She looked at him with the cold eyes of her class which admits silliness about anything except money. But before she could speak, Ellison said, 'Sixty quid a day? Jesus fucking Christ!'

That did the trick.

'That's perfectly agreeable, Mr Sixsmith. I'll give you a cheque before you leave,' said the woman.

'I'm a cash man, as far as possible,' said Sixsmith. 'And before I start would be better.'

He thought he'd gone too far, but after a moment she left the room once more.

'My God, you're cool for a darkie,' said Ellison. '*Darkie!* Hey, there's a thing!'

'Yes, sir, there's a thing,' agreed Sixsmith. 'Tell me, Mr Ellison, do you and your wife *never* speak, or is this just a lull in the storm?'

'Don't get cheeky, son,' said Ellison with no real resentment. 'And don't think just because she can dig up a hundred quid from her china pig that she's the banker round here. This is *my* house and it's *my* money that makes this family tick, God help us.'

'I believe you, man,' said Sixsmith. 'What do you do, Mr Ellison?'

'Apart from lying around here reading the paper, you mean? Precious little. I'd better tell you about myself, if only because I don't reckon you've been at this game long enough to nose around, asking questions about me, without causing embarrassment. I had my own business up in Bradford till ten years ago. Then I got took over. I didn't complain, I made a packet and part of the deal was an executive directorship on the board of the boss company, which meant a move down here, which pleased her ladyship no end. Last year, they managed to shuffle me out altogether. Golden handshake again, so I'm comfortably set up for life only I've not yet made up my mind what life is. That answer your question, son?'

'Great,' said Sixsmith, wondering among other things why Ellison should assume that pursuing his wife's cat should involve asking questions about his own background and character.

The door opened and the boy, Auberon, came in.

'Is Mum doing lunch?' he demanded. 'Tittie says she's not doing it again.'

'Why don't you have a go?' retorted his father.

'Jesus! This household's falling apart, you know that? Have we advertised or anything?'

'Only about the cat,' said Ellison. 'Now, shove off and make a few sandwiches, you don't need O-levels for that!'

Surlily the boy left, slamming the door behind him.

'You got kids, Sixsmith?' asked Ellison.

'Not to keep,' said Sixsmith.

'Bloody wise,' grunted the man.

'You having domestic trouble? I mean, with domestics?'

'Both,' said Ellison. 'We're what you call between help. Or do I mean beyond help? Time was when women could control a kitchen and their daughters were pleased to give a hand. We've grown beyond that, it seems. You don't cook, do you, Sixsmith?'

'That'd cost you another sixty, man,' said Sixsmith.

The door opened and Mrs Ellison returned carrying an envelope.

'When are we getting someone new to help in the kitchen?' demanded Ellison instantly.

This sudden rupture of their angry silence did not disturb the woman in the least.

'What's the matter? Finding your appetite again, are you?' she replied with icy scorn.

The answer meant a great deal more than it said, judged Sixsmith.

Mrs Ellison handed him the envelope.

'I think you'll find that in order,' she said.

He put it in his pocket.

'Not counting it?' said Ellison.

'Never got beyond ten,' said Sixsmith. 'Mrs Ellison, now I'm officially on the case, can I have a word in private?'

The woman looked at the man. He grinned ferociously and stretched himself out on the sofa.

'Follow me,' said Mrs Ellison.

She led him into the hallway. Through an open door he glimpsed the boy sawing at a loaf of bread in a high-tech kitchen. The girl had vanished but the distant thud of a stereo suggested she was upstairs. Mrs Ellison opened a door which gave him a glimpse of a small booklined room with a television set and a couple of deep armchairs.

'No,' she said, changing her mind. 'In here.'

They went back down the hall and into a dining-room.

Perhaps she believes we really do all have huge uncontrollable dicks and wants to keep a table between us, thought Sixsmith.

He was almost disappointed when she pulled out a couple of chairs and invited him to sit alongside her.

'Yes, Mr Sixsmith?' she prompted.

'Let's get down to cases, Mrs Ellison,' he said with what he hoped sounded like brisk professionalism. 'What do you really think happened to your cat?'

'I beg your pardon?'

'Lady, just because you're paying me to act clever don't mean you've got to act dumb,' he said in exasperation. 'Look. Your cat goes missing. Most probably it's strayed. That's what you work on, advertising and searching and such. But there's something else bothering you, and when you get no results, you call in a private eye. Me. Now, you're not paying me sixty a day and expenses just to find a stray cat, are you, Mrs Ellison?'

'It would be cheap if you could find him,' she answered. 'But no, you're right, of course. But I'm not sure how to put what I half suspect. It sounds so absurd . . .'

For a second she looked vulnerable enough for Sixsmith to glimpse her with a couple of decades peeled off. Twice the girl her pudgy daughter was, he guessed. He thought of those boobs and shuddered.

'You reckon someone's either stolen your cat, or maybe killed it, am I right?'

She nodded as if this were a less binding form of agreement.

'Right. Who's your money on, Mrs Ellison?' he said.

Immediately she was herself again, formidable and contained.

'My money is on you, Mr Sixsmith. Quite a lot of it,' she said. 'I suggest you start earning it.'

'All right,' he said, reaching into his inner pocket for a notebook and ballpoint. 'Let's get the facts. Mrs Ellison, when did you last see your pussy?'

For a woman plunged in such grief at a pet's disappearance, Mrs Ellison proved to be rather vague about her last sighting.

It had been a Friday almost three weeks earlier. Then she had been away for the weekend and when she returned on the Monday, Darkie had disappeared.

'Where was he when you saw him?' asked Sixsmith.

'Going out,' she replied promptly.

'Through the cat-flap, you mean.'

'Yes.'

'What time was that?'

'Late,' she said after a hesitation.

'Late. Before you went away for the weekend?'

'That I should have thought was a sixty-pence rather than a sixty-pound question,' she said acidly.

'Yes, right. Sorry. Was the whole family away with you, Mrs Ellison?'

'No,' she said shortly. 'I went by myself.'

'Uh-huh,' he said. 'Who took care of Darkie while you were away normally? Your husband? The children? The au pair?'

'I don't know,' she said.

That really surprised him.

'Don't know?'

'No, what I mean is, not being here, I can't be sure . . .'

'That's a sixty-pence answer, Mrs Ellison,' he grinned.

'Don't be impertinent!' she snapped. 'All I meant was that normally when I'm away, I leave strict instructions in writing for his feed and changes of water.'

'I see. And you leave these instructions with . . . ?'

'With the au pair normally,' she said.

'And did you do this on this occasion?'

'No, I didn't,' she said.

'Why not?'

'It wasn't possible. The au pair was not available.'

'You mean she'd left?'

'Yes. She'd left.'

Sixsmith digested this. Three weeks of looking after themselves! How had the Ellisons survived?

'So presumably the family looked after the cat that weekend,' he said. 'I'll need to talk to them, Mrs Ellison.'

'Of course,' she said.

'Presumably you've already questioned them.'

'To very little effect,' she said savagely.

'How little?'

'The children cannot distinctly recall seeing Darkie any time during the weekend.'

'And your husband?'

'I'll leave you to question my husband, Mr Sixsmith.'

So there it is, thought Sixsmith. Suspect Number One is Ellison. Two and Three, presumably the kids. And is there a Four?

He said, 'Neighbours. I may need to talk to them as well. To check on sightings. Will you mind?'

'*I* shan't mind,' she said significantly. 'You can confine yourself to the Bullivants next door. As you will have observed, Mr Sixsmith, to the rear and the left, this house abutts on to Brock Wood. Our sole immediate neighbours therefore are the Bullivants to the right. She is a rather silly but on the whole harmless woman. He . . . well, I'll let you judge for yourself.'

'They would know Darkie?'

'Oh yes,' she said significantly. 'They would know Darkie. Bullivant and I have had many conversations about Darkie. That stupid man on more than one occasion has accused the poor dear of scratching up his seed-beds and even of damaging his cold frames. He has uttered threats, Mr Sixsmith, and doubtless will utter them again when you see him.'

Sixsmith scratched his bald spot with his ballpoint.

'You've spoken to him already, I suppose?' he said.

'Indeed,' she replied.

Jesus! He's going to love me! thought Sixsmith, beginning to wonder if he'd undercharged.

'Just one more thing,' he said. 'Brock Wood. Do you get many people in there?'

'Too many,' she retorted. 'There's a great deal of activity in there, day and night. Children mainly; courting couples—it can be quite disgusting! And shooting too. We frequently hear gunshot. Pigeons, I presume. Crows. Anything that moves. They're like Frenchmen round here. Frenchmen!'

Sixsmith wasn't clear if she meant the shooters or the lovers. He didn't ask, but said, 'Did Darkie ever get into the wood?'

'Never,' she said firmly. 'We have a heavy duty security fence between our grounds and the wood. Apart from our own private gate which is kept invariably locked when not in use, there is no way through, not even for a cat.'

Sixsmith doubted this, but again he held his peace.

'I'd like to talk to the children now, if I may,' he said.

'Auberon is in the kitchen. Tittie is upstairs, I think. I'll tell her you want to see her.'

'In a couple of minutes,' he said. 'I'll parley with the boy first.'

In the kitchen, Auberon was devouring a sandwich like a pair of badly laid bricks. The table on which he'd prepared it was a bomb site. Sixsmith sat down opposite and looked in vain for a place to put his elbows.

'Good, is it?' asked Sixsmith.

The sandwich was lowered momentarily and the chutney-ringed lips said, ''S all right.'

'Can't be much fun, making your own eats, though,' continued Sixsmith.

This question was treated as rhetorical.

'Your mum's upset about her cat,' said Sixsmith. 'What about you, Auberon? Are you upset?'

The boy swallowed.

'Not much,' he said. 'Always under your feet. Got locked in my room once and pissed in my wardrobe.'

'What did you do?'

'Put my boot up its arse, what do you think?'

Sixsmith pushed his chair back and studied the boy's feet. They were large. In fact, the boy was pretty large all over. The immature face and blue-tinted hair distracted attention from the fact that there was a man's body beneath them. Probably also a man's desire. Sixsmith recalled the slap he'd heard just after the girl had flashed her tits at him. He guessed the boy had tried to kop a feel. Christ, when you were that age and not getting it, you'd give one of your ears for a grope and both for a real bounce! Incest taboos didn't come into it.

Which was not to the point. What was to the point was that a good kick from one of those highly expensive bovver boots could break a cat's neck.

He said, 'Tell me about that weekend.'

'What weekend?'

The boy spoke aggressively but his eyes were on the defensive.

'You know,' said Sixsmith confidently.

'Nothing to tell,' said the boy, taking refuge in his sandwich.

Sixsmith let him chew, noting he had to help mastication with a slurp of milk straight from a bottle. Dry mouth, he told himself, feeling like a real detective.

'Start at the beginning. Friday. What did you do after your mother left?'

'Went back to bed,' said the boy sullenly.

Sixsmith was surprised.

'Hey, man, I know you're a growing boy and need your rest, but wouldn't that be just a little before your normal bedtime?'

'It was midnight. Mebbe later. Don't you know anything?'

The question was meant as a piece of rhetorical scorn, but Sixsmith could see the boy downgrading it to simple interrogative and being surprised by the answer.

'Look, what's all this about? The cat? I never saw the fucking cat, OK? I didn't even know it was missing till Mum came home on the Monday and started making a fuss. She was more concerned about the fucking cat than who was going to do the cooking! Christ, it really makes you realize where you come in the pecking order when your own mother's happy to let you starve so she can go out looking for a bloody cat!'

There were all kinds of things in here, Sixsmith felt. Facts, atmospheres, implications. But he didn't have the kind of mind to make instant computations. His synapses were pre-micro-chip stock. You had to wait around for results.

The kitchen door opened.

'Bloody hellfire! What a mess!'

It was Ellison, who regarded the kitchen table with angry amazement.

'I was going to clean it up,' said the boy unconvincingly.

'You were going to make me a sandwich.'

'All right. What do you want?'

The tone was surly still, but Sixsmith detected a genuine desire to please his father.

'I should like beef dripping on a slice of fresh baked bread, but I don't suppose we run to that, so make it cheese and onion on wholemeal, and don't stint the onion. What about you, Sixsmith? At sixty quid a day, do you give yourself a lunch-break?'

'I'll just tighten my belt a while,' said Sixsmith. 'I've got an appointment with your daughter.'

He went out into the hallway. Ellison followed him.

'Third on the left when you reach the landing,' he said. 'If your bloodhound nose misses the scent, just follow your droopy ears.'

The gibe set Sixsmith's clockwork mental calculator clicking a couple of notches.

'First thing you said to me was *Hello Sherlock*, Mr Ellison,' he said. 'So?'

'So how'd you know I was a detective?'

'Mebbe my wife told me,' said Ellison.

'I don't think so,' said Sixsmith. 'I mean, communication hasn't exactly been flowing like the crystal stream between you two. Also, she was surprised when she spotted I was no WASP. You weren't. Just amused.'

Ellison didn't answer straightaway, then said speculatively, 'Could be you're not so daft after all.'

'Meaning?'

Ellison said, 'My wife got you out of the Yellow Pages, Mr Sixsmith. Nice ad you've got there. I heard her make the call. I like to know what my family's getting for their money, so I made a couple of calls myself. What did I find? That until two months ago the head of *Sixsmith Investigation Inc.* was a lathe operator at Robco Engineering who took his redundancy money, got himself an office on a six months' lease, and set up as a private eye. This your first case?'

'Second,' said Sixsmith. 'I did a tailing job. Divorce case.'

'How'd that work out?'

'Not so hot. I got pulled in on sus, loitering outside the Four Seasons Restaurant. Well, I couldn't afford to go in there, could I, man?'

Ellison hooted with laughter. The Four Seasons was the area's top restaurant, famous for its food, infamous for its prices.

So, I've reassured him, thought Sixsmith as he went up the stairs. But why should this man, who likes to be sure his family gets the best value for money, need to be reassured that his wife had got herself the most inexperienced and inefficient gumshoe in town?

The landing ran left and right. The noise of the music came from the left. Sixsmith turned right.

There were four doors. One opened on a palatial bathroom, another on the master bedroom, the third on a room which had once been a nursery and was now a store room for all the sad relics of childhood. The fourth revealed another bedroom, probably normally reserved for guests but currently, from the evidence of discarded clothing, being used by Ellison.

The other end of the landing also had four doors. There was another bathroom, a bedroom which was clearly Auberon's, then the girl's room. The door was ajar. Through it he could glimpse the bottom half of a bed with the girl's legs sprawled across it. The boom of the hi-fi and the thickness of the carpet gave him ample cover and he moved swiftly by to the fourth door. This led into another bedroom, but this one had the bed stripped and was devoid of ornament and all other evidence of present use.

'What do you think you're doing here?'

So much for cover! The girl had come up behind him.

'Hi,' he said. 'I was just looking for you.'

'You deaf or something? I'm in here.'

She led him into her pulsating room and said something. He grimaced and cupped his ear with his hand. She rolled her eyes in irritation and switched the hi-fi down.

'Mum says I've to talk to you,' she said.

He sat down in an old basket chair and said, 'You always do what Mum tells you?'

'Look, just get on with it, Sixsmith or whatever your name is.'

'That's my name, honey,' he agreed.

'It'll be your slave name, won't it?' she flashed. 'And don't call me honey.'

'What'll I call you then? Missie Ellison. *Ms* Ellison? Or why don't you call me Joe, so you won't have to soil your tongue with no slave name, and I'll call you Tittie. That's a nice old-fashioned name, now. Short for Titania, is it? Or Letitia?'

'It could be long for Tit,' she answered, studying him slyly to see his reaction.

'Man, from what I've seen, it just wouldn't be long enough,' he replied with a grin.

'You liked that, did you?' she said. 'Gave you a thrill?'

'Listen, girl,' he said seriously. 'I think you've been reading too many books about them poor repressed negroes in Alabam' and such places, who get off on a white woman's ankles, and get burned alive if they're caught looking. You want to give instant thrills, you stick to that brother of yours!'

'Him? God, he's disgusting. He's just obsessed. He once offered me five quid to jerk him off. Five quid! Can you imagine?'

Whether he was being invited to express indignation at the proposal or merely the price wasn't clear. Sixsmith's affections tended to blossom as leisurely as his deductions, but he was beginning to doubt if he could love this family. At the same time he suddenly found himself feeling genuinely concerned at the fate of poor old Darkie.

He cast around for his best line of questioning and into his head popped something that Auberon had said. 'I went *back* to bed.'

He said, 'That weekend, that Friday night, what time did you get to bed?'

She looked at him doubtfully and he chanced his arm and said, 'The first time, I mean.'

'Just after midnight,' she said, as if reassured that he was merely confirming what he already knew.

'And how long was it before . . . ?' he tailed off, crossing his fingers.

'Half an hour. Twenty minutes maybe. It didn't take long!' she said with indignant scorn.

'No,' agreed Sixsmith. 'That evening, what kind of evening had it been? For you I mean?'

Surprisingly he seemed to have hit a good line.

'Oh, it was all right, you know. A bit draggy, really. I mean, you'd have thought we could have gone somewhere a bit lively, a night club maybe, but Mummy likes queening it at the Four Seasons. Me, I'm trying to diet, and they cover everything in cream, so all I got out of it was a bit of salad. But it pleased them, and then there was going to be the party . . . oh Christ, it was so awful! I've never been so humiliated . . .'

To Sixsmith's dismay the podgy face screwed up in grief. Tits he could deal with; tears were beyond him.

'It must have been awful,' he said. 'Really awful.'

'It was, oh, it was!' she agreed tearfully.

But what was? And what had it all to do with the bloody cat?

'To get things quite clear,' he said. 'You were all at the Four Seasons? All four of you?'

'Five,' she said viciously.

Five? For a crazy second he thought she meant they'd taken the cat! Then the old machinery clicked.

'I meant the four of you in the family. Plus, of course . . . what's her second name, by the way?'

'Netzer. Astrid Netzer.'

'Yes. Plus Astrid. You got back here before midnight . . .'

'About half eleven. Daddy said, was I going to open my presents at midnight? and I said, no, I'd leave them till the morning, and Daddy said he'd open a bottle of champagne anyway, and Mummy said she had a bit of a headache so she thought she'd go on up. Off she went. Daddy got the champagne, opened it and filled our glasses. Midnight struck, they all toasted me and wished me happy birthday . . .'

At last! It had been the kid's birthday, seventeenth probably, on the Saturday. Friday night had been family celebration night with the posh dinner out. But the big occasion as far as the girl was concerned was to be her own party on Saturday night.

He began to guess the rest, but pressed for confirmation.

'Who went upstairs first, you or your brother?'

'We went at the same time. He drank his champers straight down and wanted some more. He was a bit tiddly, he gets like that very easily, and Daddy said he'd be better drinking coffee and he got on his high horse and said in that case he was off to bed. I said I'd go up too. I didn't want to risk waking up with a headache and spoiling things. God, it makes me sick just thinking about it. I went to bed not to spoil things. Perhaps if I'd sat up a bit longer . . .'

'You went to bed, leaving your father and Astrid downstairs?'

'Yes. He said he'd finish the bottle and she said she'd clear up. I got undressed and into bed. And then, it hardly seemed any time at all before I heard the yelling.'

'The yelling?'

'Yes. Mummy. God, what a noise! I thought we must be under attack. By the time I got downstairs, she'd quietened down a bit, but that was worse. When she goes all icy and under control, that's far worse than yelling.'

'But you gathered what had happened.'

'Oh yes. Well, it was clear enough. Daddy was busy buttoning up, but that bitch didn't even bother. Mummy had got tired of waiting for Daddy to come to bed and gone downstairs. She looked in the snug . . .'

'The snug. That's the little television room?'

'That's right. The lounge, you see, is right underneath their bedroom, so they'd gone into the snug. And there they were, hard at it . . .'

The girl was once more close to tears. Perhaps, thought Sixsmith, he'd misjudged her. Even spoilt brats had feelings.

'There, there,' he said awkwardly. 'It'll be all right.'

She took a deep breath.

'How can it be all right?' she demanded. 'There was a terrible row and Mummy packed her case, and said she wouldn't be back while that creature was in the house and walked out, and the next day . . . the next day . . .'

Her sobs were almost choking her.

'Yes, honey?' urged Sixsmith.

'The next day I had to cancel my fucking party!'

So what have I got so far? Sixsmith asked himself as he walked up the driveway of the house next to the Ellisons.

A neurotic woman, a frustrated man, a pair of spoilt, self-centred kids, and a randy au pair.

And Darkie.

The woman loves Darkie as much as she loves anything, but in her rage at finding Ellison on the job, she sweeps out without a thought for him. Understandable in the circumstances. But where does that leave the cat?

In a houseful of enemies, that's where. Enemies in many ways. Well, three ways anyway. He mentally catalogued.

(1) *Enemies by neglect*.

A cat, used to the best of everything from its mistress, suddenly finds its source of warmth, comfort, and gourmet meals is cut off. Not enough to kill it, though, but maybe enough to make it take a powder.

(2) *Enemies by accident and irritation*.

In the emotional atmosphere of the house that weekend, who'd pay any heed to the cat? And if it was too imperative in its demands for attention, well, he already had the boy's admission that he wasn't above taking a swing at it with his boot.

(3) *Enemies by malice aforethought*.

Mrs Ellison must have been the object of considerable antagonism after she left, and what better way of taking revenge than striking at the thing she loved? Ellison, tired of playing second fiddle to a cat and in that excess of righteous fury known only to those caught in the wrong, could have done the deed. Or Astrid, told to pack her bags and still smarting from the stream of nasty things Mrs Ellison doubtless called her, may have looked for some particularly bloody parting shot. Even Tittie may have blamed her mother as much as her father for the cancellation of her party. Auberon alone seemed to have no motive for deliberate slaughter, but who knows what goes on in the mind of a mixed-up adolescent?

Well satisfied that with such a fine analysis, a solution could not lag far behind, Sixsmith rang the bell of the Bullivant residence.

Ten minutes later his analysis had been modified to include two more prime suspects, one of which came very close to an open confession on the part of the other. The talkative one was Bullivant himself, a small dark prickly man, like a blackthorn bush in motion. Sixsmith, unsure of his reception, had mentioned the cat with some diffidence. Immediately he was swept round the side of the house into the rear garden to be shown the variety of anti-personnel devices which Bullivant had erected in his war against Darkie and all other four-legged intruders. These devices ranged from the merely deterrent such as pepper, netting, and a tight-mesh wire fence, to the captivating, such as pitfalls and mink-traps.

The final weapon in Bullivant's armoury was unequivocally lethal.

'It's all right. He won't harm you without my say-so,' said Bullivant confidently. 'Will you, Kaiser?'

Sixsmith looked uneasily at his second new suspect, a huge black Dobermann who returned his gaze assessingly.

'You let this thing run loose?' he inquired.

'He has the run of the garden at night, yes. No pests here, I tell you. Saves on his food bill too.'

He laughed as he spoke and patted the dog's head approvingly.

'You mean, he catches . . . things, and eats them?'

'That's it.'

'Including cats?'

'Especially cats!'

Sixsmith looked at the animal with a distaste which was clearly mutual and said, 'What about traces? I mean, if he's eaten something, would you know?'

'Oh, a bit of blood on the grass maybe. Sometimes I hear a bit of squealing in the night,' said Bullivant cheerfully.

'Two weekends ago, did you spot any blood, or hear any squealing?'

'Two weekends ago?' Bullivant's tight little face screwed up like a Brussels sprout in the effort of memory.

'You're wondering about that monster of Ellison's, aren't you? No I don't recollect any blood or squealing. But there was something, I remember. Early Saturday morning, or was it Sunday? He woke me up. Doesn't bark much, but I'm a light sleeper. I had a look out. Nothing in the garden, but he seemed to have caught a noise in the woods. Over there.'

He pointed diagonally across his own garden. Sixsmith followed the line of the finger through the dividing fence and across the neighbouring garden, and found himself looking at Ellison standing in his shrubbery, watching them. Their eyes met, then Ellison turned away and walked back towards his house.

'Do you often get disturbances in the woods?'

'All the time,' said Bullivant. 'Kids in the day, God knows what at night. Lot of people are scared to go walking in the woods these days. But not me, not when I've got Kaiser! Which reminds me. It's time for his constitutional now. Come, Kaiser. You can see yourself out, can't you?'

'Sure,' said Sixsmith, watching as Bullivant set off down his garden with the dog at his heels. There was a solid, heavily padlocked metal gate in the wire fence leading into the woods. Bullivant unlocked it and sent the dog out ahead of him.

Turning back, he called, 'Tell Ellison, yes, Kaiser could have had that moggy, it's true. But where's your proof, eh? Where's your proof!'

And with a bark of laughter, he followed the silent dog into the wood.

As he returned to the Ellisons, Sixsmith said to himself, 'Joe boy, you were wrong. Sixty a day is no fair payment for trading with the natives of Brock Wood Lane! They're cannibals, man, real cannibals!'

Ellison met him at the front door. He looked very angry.

'Who the hell gave you the right to start bothering my neighbours!'

Bullivant would have been surprised by this protectiveness, Sixsmith guessed. He also guessed Ellison was more concerned that the squalid details of his private life were being bandied about than with his neighbour's privacy.

He was saved the trouble of defending himself by Mrs Ellison's appearance.

'I will remind you that this man is in my employ. Mine is the only authority he needs to question anyone!'

'You think so? This is still my house!'

'Still *half* your house. Even our grossly biased divorce laws allow the woman that right.'

Ellison glowered at her, then to Sixsmith's surprise became relatively conciliatory.

'All right, all right. No need to talk like that, not in public. Look, don't you think this has gone far enough? The bloody cat has obviously just taken off. Mebbe it got knocked down, like this fellow said when he first arrived. Well, all right, it's sad and I'm sorry. But either it'll come back or else you can get yourself another. You can get yourself a whole bloody cattery for what you're likely to end up paying Sherlock here!'

Sixsmith couldn't fault the man's logic. He wished he'd made it clear the advance was non-returnable. He made a mental note to get such things written down in future. If there was a future. With only three months of his lease left to run, he was a long way from making a living. Not that there wasn't the work, but half a dozen prospective clients in this liberal, integrated country had shied off when they realized what they'd caught by the toe.

Happily Mrs Ellison was not in the mood for right reason.

She ignored her husband and said, 'Come with me, Mr Sixsmith, and report.'

Meekly he followed her into the house.

They went into the lounge once more.

'Well?' she said.

'It's early days,' he said.

'At sixty pounds an early day, I'm entitled to an hourly update if I so require,' she retorted.

She had a point.

He took a deep breath and said, 'All I've worked out is probably what you could have told me when I first arrived, Mrs Ellison. Which is that, the way things were that weekend, anyone in this house might have harmed Darkie. Or at least encouraged him to leave.'

'Anyone?' she said, giving nothing away.

'Mr Ellison. The kids. Even the au pair. Maybe particularly the au pair.'

He threw this in out of charity. If there was no positive solution, and this seemed the probable outcome, then it would hurt least to have the most distant suspect in terms of space and relationship elected the most likely.

'You know about that?' she said, very chill, very formal.

'I had to know. It was relevant,' he said.

'I suppose so. And you think that that *woman* might have been responsible?'

She made *woman* sound like it had four letters.

'Could be. You probably tore a strip off her, right? She may have resented that so much that . . . well, it depends what sort of girl she was.'

'Wanton,' she said crisply. 'I can find out her home address through the agency.'

He shook his head in disbelief.

'Lady, you don't really want me to go to Germany, do you?' he said.

She thought a moment, then said, 'No, I suppose not. But if that creature did do something to Darkie, then he must be still around somewhere, mustn't he?'

It was a fair deduction. Astrid was hardly going to pass through Customs with a dead cat in her holdall.

Sixsmith nodded.

'Then at least earn your money by finding him so that we can give him a proper burial!'

She left the room swiftly and Sixsmith thought he heard a scuffle of footsteps on the stairs. He wondered if he should have offered his alternative theory, which was that Kaiser had disposed of Darkie. Kaiser, too, was outside the family. On the other hand, she had to live next door to the monster. Both monsters.

He went into the hallway and ran lightly up the stairs. Tittie's room was closed, but the door to her brother's was ajar.

He pushed it open and went in. The boy was lying on the bed.

'Don't you knock before coming through doors?' he demanded.

'Don't you knock before listening at them?' replied Sixsmith.

He sat on the edge of the bed and said, 'When do the bins get picked up round here?'

'What?'

'The dustbins, man. Those big round containers you dump the rubbish in.'

'I don't know. Thursday, I think. Or Friday. That's right, Friday. They come early and make such a fucking din, they wake me up.'

'That's terrible,' said Sixsmith.

So a dustbin disposal was unlikely. You might dump your dead cat there if the bins were going to be picked up very soon, but not when it was almost a week away.

'Do you think Astrid could have killed the cat?' he asked suddenly.

The boy sat up, alarmed.

'I don't know. Why ask me?'

'Because you know the girl. I don't. Listen, son, I know all about what went on that weekend. I'm sorry, believe me. But it happens. An attractive young chick can turn anyone on, so don't blame your dad too much.'

'I don't,' said the boy in a muffled voice, slumping back on the pillows.

'No? Well, OK.'

A thought occurred to Sixsmith. Ellison senior had proved susceptible, true; but the real centre of unsatisfied male desire in this household lay on the bed before him.

'You ever fancy her yourself, Auberon?'

The boy did not reply, but he didn't need to. His face was flushed like a dawn sky.

Sixsmith said, 'And did you ever try your hand?'

'Shut up! Shut up! Just go away and leave me!'

'OK, OK!' said Sixsmith, standing up. 'Sorry I spoke, man. Look, I'm going. Don't let it worry you, though. We all get the cold finger some time, believe me.'

His words of consolation were clearly falling more like hailstones than the soothing rain.

He left.

Tittie's door opened as he went by.

'You still prowling around up here?' she said.

'I've been talking to your brother,' he said. 'About Astrid.'

'What about her?' she demanded.

'Just about the play he made for her.'

'Play? You call it play to wander naked into her room? Child's play, maybe. That's what he is, a child. Imagine thinking just because she let Daddy do it, she'd be happy to accommodate poor little Auberon too!'

She laughed stridently, humourlessly.

Sixsmith said, 'Where do I get the key to the garden gate?'

'Why?'

'I'd like to go into the woods at the bottom of the garden,' said Sixsmith. 'To see if I can spot any fairies.'

'Oh. It's hanging up in the kitchen. But you'll have to ask Daddy.'

'You ask Daddy,' he said. 'Daddy and I ain't exactly speaking.'

She followed him into the kitchen and offered no help as he examined a selection of keys on a row of hooks.

'You don't sound like a West Indian,' she said suddenly. 'Only sometimes.'

'I've been here a long time,' he said. 'More than twice as long as you, which is to say, all my life. This the one?'

She ignored the question and said, 'You're going bald. I didn't know that kind of hair went bald.'

'It don't,' he said. 'We shave it off and sell it to bed manufacturers to stuff mattresses with. What about this one?'

But she wasn't going to answer. She simply stood there with sudden tears in her eyes. She looked about twelve.

Don't start feeling sorry for them, Sixsmith told himself. That's the way you end in chains.

He took the three most likely keys and went into the garden.

The gate was even bigger and solider than Bullivant's. It fitted snugly into an iron mesh fence whose ugly angularity was hidden from the house by a boundary of shrubs and further disguised by clematis, and ivy, and various other climbing species.

The first key fitted and Sixsmith passed through the gate. He saw at once that the woods were far too extensive for one man to have much hope of finding the small patch of disturbed ground under which a cat might be buried, but this didn't bother him. All he really wanted was a quiet stroll and a bit of space for thinking in.

He had paused just through the gateway and he became aware that Ellison's metal fence was not the outermost boundary of his garden. Before the fence, a mixed hedge of beech, hawthorn, blackthorn and bramble must have ringed the property. The fence had been built about three feet inside the hedge and since then the unchecked growth of the vegetation had formed a narrow tunnel between the metal and the vegetable barriers.

It was a noise somewhere along this tunnel that attracted Sixsmith's attention, a snuffling, scraping noise. He thought of investigating, then heard another noise which at the same time solved the problem and made him glad he'd stayed put.

'Kaiser! Kaiser! Where are you, damn you!'

It was Bullivant's voice and a moment later the man himself appeared.

'Oh, it's you,' he said ungraciously. 'You haven't seen that blasted dog, have you?'

'I think it's up there,' said Sixsmith, pointing.

Bullivant stooped down and began to make his way along the tunnel. Sixsmith hesitated, then the clockwork of his mind clicked with unwonted speed, and he turned and followed.

They found Kaiser about twenty yards in, scrabbling away with his front paws at a patch of ground thickly covered in dead leaves. But where the dog had shifted the leaves, it was clear the revealed earth had been recently disturbed.

'Kaiser, what the hell are you playing at? *Still*, boy. *Still!*'

The dog growled in its throat, but obeyed.

'Must be a bone. Or maybe a rabbit burrow,' said Bullivant.

Sixsmith shook his head sadly.

'Neither,' he said. 'I reckon it's a cat.'

'A cat?'

For a moment Bullivant was puzzled, then suddenly he laughed.

'Oh, you mean *that* cat?' What's this, then? Dirty work at the crossroads? Someone in there dislike it as much as me, did they?'

'Why don't you shut up?' said Sixsmith. 'If you stop here, I'll go and get a spade.'

'Why bother?' said the man. 'Kaiser'll have it up in no time.'

'Look, man,' said Sixsmith. 'You get a grip on that fucking beast of yours, right? It couldn't catch the cat alive, I see no reason why it should get to maul him dead. Also it's going to be painful enough for Mrs Ellison as things are without finding Fido here chewing at the remains.'

Bullivant was clearly not happy at Sixsmith's assumption of command, but he contented himself with saying, 'Could be the poor moggy's been mauled around already!' and gripped Kaiser's collar.

It was Sixsmith's hope that he could get back to the house and find a spade without being spotted, but he was out of luck.

Ellison was in the garden once more approaching the open gate. Behind him was Tittie.

'What the hell are you up to, Sixsmith? You've no right to go pushing your way round this house as though you own it!'

'Sorry,' said Sixsmith. 'But I think I've found the cat. I'll need a spade.'

'Oh Christ. Where?'

'In that sort of tunnel between the fence and the hedge. Mr Bullivant's there with his dog.'

Ellison looked towards Tittie, his face pale with an emotion which could have been anything from shock, through pity, to guilt. The girl didn't look much better.

And now to make things worse, Mrs Ellison, seeing them from the kitchen window, came running down the garden, followed by Auberon.

'You've found something, haven't you?' she cried.

'No,' said Ellison savagely. 'You stay here! Auberon, look after your mother.'

He turned and headed for the gate with Tittie close behind.

Auberon put a hand on his mother's arm, but she shook it off.

'Wait!' she cried. 'Wait!'

And she too was gone.

'Where will I find a spade?' Sixsmith said to the boy, who looked as though he was feeling sea-sick.

'In there,' he choked, pointing towards a garden shed.

Then he too went running after the others.

The shed was locked. None of the keys Sixsmith had with him opened it, so he went back to the kitchen in search of the right one.

He could hear the front doorbell ringing, but he had no time for that.

He tried his new selection, found one that fitted and opened the shed.

From the comprehensive supply of tools, he selected a spade and hurried back through the door, almost crashing into the bosom of a uniformed policeman.

'Hello,' said the officer.

Sixsmith paused and studied the man.

He was a young constable. In his hand he carried a plastic carrier bag.

'You the owner?' asked the constable doubtfully, adding, 'Sir?' just to be on the safe side.

'No,' said Sixsmith. 'I just work here.'

'Ah,' said the youth, relieved. 'Gardener, eh? Look, is there anyone around? I've been ringing the bell.'

'What's it about?' asked Sixsmith.

The constable looked inclined to tell him it was none of his business, but then changed his mind. The reason why became quickly apparent. He wanted information.

'The lady, Mrs Ellison, is she all right?' he asked, with an intonation which made it clear it was mental health he was interested in.

'A bit highly strung,' said Sixsmith. 'Why?'

'It's these,' said the constable, opening the bag.

It was full of bits of female clothing.

'They've been found all over. There was a laundry mark on some of them, that's how we've got on to Mrs Ellison. Then someone remembered she'd been causing a stink lately about a lost cat, you know, going on like it had been kidnapped or murdered.'

Suddenly Sixsmith saw a chance to be out of the way when this miserable business came to its sad and grisly climax.

'Here,' he said thrusting the spade into the young man's hand. 'They're all out there. Through the gate, turn left straight away. There's a sort of a tunnel. The whole family's there.'

'Eh? What're they doing? And what's this for?' demanded the constable, examining the spade dubiously.

'They've gone to dig up a body,' said Sixsmith. 'That's called a spade. It's for digging. You could do yourself a bit of good, maybe.' He didn't wait for a response but headed for the house. He reckoned his expenses covered at least one stiff drink and he went into the lounge, poured himself a large whisky and slumped into one of the deep armchairs to enjoy a moment of peace before the Ellisons returned and the recriminations began.

As he took a long pull at his drink, he heard a noise from the hallway. A sort of click. The letter-box perhaps, but it lacked the metallic sharpness of a letter-box. It was more like the . . .

There was another click, this one in his mind. He sat up and stared at the open door.

It caused him small surprise but the beginning of infinite horror when a small black cat, with a white patch over its left eye and ear, came round the corner, miaowed a greeting, then jumped on to his lap and began purring in clear anticipation of being made much of.

Now his mind was clicking and whirring like a clockmaker's repair room.

'Oh Jesus!' he said aghast. 'Oh Jesus, Jesus, Jesus!'

The cat purred on.

The telephone rang on Joe Sixsmith's leather-topped desk.

He picked it up.

'Sixsmith,' he said crisply.

'Hello. Is that the Mr Sixsmith who solved the Astrid Netzer case?'

'The very same.'

'Good, that's fine. Look, Mr Sixsmith, I'd like to hire you to do a job . . .'

'Hold it,' said Sixsmith, riffling through his desk diary. 'I can't talk now, I'm on my way out. Anyway, I like to see my clients before I take a job. Wednesday morning, eight-thirty, I can fit you in. That suit?'

'Not till Wednesday? I hoped . . .'

'Sorry. When you get the best, you get the busiest. Shall I put you in?'

'Yes, I suppose so.'

The details noted, Sixsmith replaced the receiver, connected his answering machine and stretched luxuriously.

The past three months had been good to him. The case had still to come to trial and the police were still uncertain who was to be charged with what, but that didn't matter to the media. There'd been a crime of passion. A dead au pair always made for good headlines, but this time they'd been handed a new folk-hero on a plate, a man for all political seasons.

What better symbol of the times could there be than a balding, redundant, West Indian lathe-operator who'd made good?

Joe Sixsmith glanced at his watch. It was time to go. He was lunching with a client and had a reputation for punctuality to keep up.

As he stood up, there was a protesting noise from the bottom drawer of his desk. He pulled it open and a small black cat with a white patch over its left eye and ear yawned up at him.

Mrs Ellison was resting her shattered nerves in a Swiss sanatorium and Sixsmith had agreed to look after the cat. He charged no fee but had made one condition, a simple matter of nomenclature.

'Sorry, Whitey,' he said. 'They don't allow no live animals where I'm going, but I'll bring you back a slice of rare beef, shall I?'

The cat purred its agreement. It had a loud rasping purr when it was happy. It sometimes reminded Joe Sixsmith of his old lathe.

He smiled at the memory, checked to see that his well-filled wallet was bulging in his inside pocket like a shoulder-holster, and went out to walk down the mean streets that led to the Four Seasons Restaurant.

How's Your Mother?

'It's all right, Mother. Just the postman,' Humphrey Partridge called up the stairs, recognizing the uniformed bulk behind the frosted glass of the front door.

'Parcel for you, Mr Partridge.' As he handed it over, Reg Carter the postman leant one arm against the door-frame in his chatting position. 'From some nurseries, it says on the label.'

'Yes———'

'Bulbs, by the feel of it.'

'Yes.' Humphrey Partridge's hand remained on the door, as if about to close it, but the postman didn't seem to notice the hint.

'Right time of year for planting bulbs, isn't it. November.'

'Yes.'

Again Reg was impervious to the curtness of the monosyllable. 'How's your mother?' he asked chattily.

Partridge softened. 'Not so bad. You know, considering.'

'Never seem to bring any letters for her, do I?'

'No. Well, when you get to that age, most of your friends have gone.'

'Suppose so. How old is she now?'

'Eighty-six last July.'

'That's a good age. Doesn't get about much.'

'No, hardly at all. Now if you'll excuse me, I do have to leave to catch my train.'

Humphrey Partridge just restrained himself from slamming the door on the postman. Then he put his scarf round his neck, crossed the ends across his chest and held them in position with his chin while he slipped on his raincoat with the fleecy lining buttoned in. He picked up his brief-case and called up the stairs, 'Bye bye, Mother. Off to work now. Be home usual time.'

In the village post office Mrs Denton watched the closing door with disapproval and shrugged her shawl righteously around her. 'Don't like that Jones woman. Coming in for *The Times* every morning. Very lah-di-dah. Seems shifty to me. Wouldn't be surprised if there was something going on there.'

'Maybe.' Her husband didn't look up from his morbid perusal of the *Daily Mirror*. 'Nasty business, this, about the woman and the RAF bloke.'

'The Red Scarf Case,' Mrs Denton italicized avidly.

'Hmm. They say when the body was found————' He broke off as Humphrey Partridge came in for his *Telegraph*. 'Morning. How's the old lady?'

'Oh, not too bad, thank you. Considering . . .'

Mrs Denton gathered her arms under her bosom. 'Oh, Mr Partridge, the vicar was in yesterday, asked me if I'd ask you. There's a jumble sale in the Institute tomorrow and he was looking for some able-bodied helpers just to shift a few————'

'Ah, I'm sorry, Mrs Denton, I don't like to leave my mother at weekends. She's alone enough with me being at work all week.'

'It wouldn't be for long. It's just————'

'I'm sorry. Now I must dash or I'll miss my train.'

They let the silence stand for a moment after the shop-door shut. Then Mr Denton spoke, without raising his eyes from his paper. 'Lives for his mother, that one.'

'Worse things to live for.'

'Oh yes. Still doesn't seem natural in a grown man.'

'Shouldn't think it'd last long. Old girl must be on the way out. Been bedridden ever since they moved here. And how long ago's that? Three years?'

'Three. Four.'

'Don't know what he'll do when she goes.'

'Move maybe. George in the grocer's said something about him talking of emigrating to Canada if only he hadn't got the old girl to worry about.'

'I expect he'll come into some money when she goes.' When Mrs Denton expected something, it soon became fact in the village.

Humphrey Partridge straightened the ledgers on his desk, confident that the sales figures were all entered and his day's work was done. He stole a look at his watch. Five-twenty-five. Nearly time to put his coat on and————

The phone rang. Damn. Why on earth did people ring up at such inconvenient times? 'Partridge,' he snapped into the receiver.

'Hello, it's Sylvia in Mr Brownlow's office. He wondered if you could just pop along for a quick word.'

'What, now? I was about to leave. Oh, very well, Miss Simpson. If it's urgent.'

Mr Brownlow looked up over his half-glasses as Partridge entered. 'Humphrey, take a pew.'

Partridge sat on the edge of the indicated chair, poised for speedy departure.

'Minor crisis blown up,' said Brownlow languidly. 'Know I was meant to be going to Antwerp next week, for the conference?'

'Yes.'

'Just had a telex from Parsons in Rome. Poor sod's gone down with some virus and is stuck in an Eyetie hospital, heaven help him. Means I'll have to go out to Rome tomorrow and pick up the pieces of the contract. So there's no chance of my making Antwerp on Monday.'

'Oh dear.'

'Yes, it's a bugger. But we've got to have someone out there. It's an important conference. Someone should be there waving the flag for Brownlow and Potter.'

'Surely Mr Potter will go.'

'No, he's too tied up here.'

'Evans?'

'On leave next week. Had it booked for yonks. No, Partridge, you're the only person who's free to go.'

'But I'm very busy this time of year.'

'Only routine. One of the juniors can keep it ticking over.'

'But surely it should be someone whose standing in the company———'

'Your standing's fine. Be good experience. About time you took some more executive responsibility. Bound to be a bit of a reshuffle when Potter retires and you're pretty senior on length of service . . . Take that as read then, shall we? I'll get Sylvia to transfer the tickets and hotel and———'

'No, Mr Brownlow. You see, it's rather difficult.'

'What's the problem?'

'It's my mother. She's very old and I look after her, you know.'

'Oh come on, it's only three days, Partridge.'

'But she's very unwell at the moment.'

'She always seems to be very unwell.'

'Yes, but this time I think it's . . . I mean I'd never forgive myself if . . .'

'But this is important for the company. And Antwerp's not the end of the earth. I mean, if something happened, you could leap on to a plane and be back in a few hours.'

'I'm sorry. It's impossible. My mother . . .'

Mr Brownlow sat back in his high swivel chair and toyed with a paper-knife. 'You realize this would mean I'd have to send someone junior to you . . .'

'Yes.'

'And it's the sort of thing that might stick in people's minds if there were a question of promotion or . . .'

'Yes.'

'Yes. Well, that's it.' Those who knew Mr Brownlow well would have realized that he was extremely annoyed. 'I'd better not detain you any longer or I'll make you late for your train.'

Partridge looked gratefully at his watch as he rose. 'No, if I really rush, I'll just make it.'

'Oh terrific,' said Mr Brownlow, but his sarcasm was wasted on Partridge's departing back.

'Mother, I'm home. Six-thirty-five on the dot. Had to run for the train, but I just made it. I'll come on up.'

Humphrey Partridge bounded up the stairs, went past his own bedroom and stood in the doorway of the second bedroom. There was a smile of triumph on his lips as he looked at the empty bed.

Partridge put two slices of bread into his toaster. He had had the toaster a long time and it still worked perfectly. Better than one of those modern pop-up ones. Silly, gimmicky things.

He looked out of the kitchen window with satisfaction. He felt a bit stiff, but it had been worth it. The earth of the borders had all been neatly turned over. And all the bulbs planted. He smiled.

The doorbell rang. As he went to answer it, he looked at his watch. Hmm, have to get his skates on or he'd miss the train. Always more difficult to summon up the energy on Monday mornings.

It was Reg Carter the postman. 'Sorry, couldn't get these through the letter-box.' But there was no apology in his tone; no doubt he saw this as another opportunity for one of his interminable chats.

Partridge could recognize that the oversize package was more brochures and details about Canada. He would enjoy reading those on the train. He restrained the impulse to snatch them out of the postman's hand.

'Oh, and there was this letter too.'

'Thank you.'

Still the postman didn't hand them over. 'Nothing for the old lady today neither.'

'No, as I said last week, she doesn't expect many letters.'

'No. She all right, is she?'

'Fine, thank you.' The postman still seemed inclined to linger, so Partridge continued, 'I'm sorry. I'm in rather a hurry. I have to leave for work in a moment.'

The next thing Reg Carter knew, the package and letter were no longer in his hands and the door was shut in his face.

Inside Humphrey Partridge put the unopened brochures into his brief-case and slid his finger along the top of the other envelope. As he looked at its contents, he froze, then sat down at the foot of the stairs, weak with shock. Out loud he cried, 'This is it. Oh, Mother, this is it!'

Then he looked at his watch, gathered up his brief-case, scarf, and coat and hurried out of the house.

'There's more about the Red Scarf Case in the *Sun*,' said Mr Denton with gloomy relish.

'It all comes out at the trial. Always does,' his wife observed sagely.

'Says here he took her out on to the golf links to look at the moon. Look at the moon—huh!'

'I wouldn't be taken in by something like that, Maurice. Serves her right in a way. Mind you, he must have been a psychoparth. Sergeant Wallace says nine cases out of ten———'

Partridge entered breezily. '*Telegraph*, please. Oh, and a local paper, please.'

'Local paper?' Mrs Denton, starved of variety, pounced on this departure from the norm.

'Yes, I just want a list of local estate agents.'

'Thinking of buying somewhere else?'

'Maybe not buying,' said Partridge, coyly enigmatic.

He didn't volunteer any more, so Mr Denton took up the conversation with his habitual originality. 'Getting colder, isn't it?'

Partridge agreed that it was.

Mrs Denton added her contribution. 'It'll get a lot colder yet.'

'I'm sure it will,' Partridge agreed. And then he couldn't resist saying, 'Though with a bit of luck I won't be here to feel it.'

'You are thinking of moving then?'

'Maybe. Maybe.' And Humphrey Partridge left the shop with his newspapers, unwontedly frisky.

'I think,' pronounced Mrs Denton, focusing her malevolence, 'there's something going on there.'

'You wanted to see me, Partridge?'

'Yes, Mr Brownlow.'

'Well, make it snappy. I've just flown back from Rome. As it turns out I could have made the Antwerp conference. Still, it's giving young Dyett a chance to win his spurs. What was it you wanted, Partridge?' Mr Brownlow stifled a yawn.

'I've come to give in my notice.'

'You mean you want to leave?'

'Yes.'

'This is rather unexpected.'

'Yes, Mr Brownlow.'

'I see.' Mr Brownlow swivelled his chair in irritation. 'Have you had an offer from another company?'

'No.'

'No, I hardly thought . . .'

'I'm going abroad. With my mother.'

'Of course. May one ask where?'

'Canada.'

'Ah. Reputed to be a land of opportunity. Are you starting a new career out there?'

'I don't know. I may not work.'

'Oh, come into money, have we?' But he received no answer to the question. 'OK, if you'd rather not say, that's your business. I won't inquire further. Well, I hope you know what you're doing. I'll need a month's notice in writing.'

'Is it possible for me to go sooner?'

'A month's notice is customary.' Mr Brownlow's temper suddenly gave. 'No, sod it, I don't want people here unwillingly. Just go. Go today!'

'Thank you.'

'Of course, we do usually give a farewell party to departing staff, but in your case . . .'

'It won't be necessary.'

'Too bloody right it won't be necessary.' Mr Brownlow's eyes blazed. 'Get out!'

Partridge got home just before lunch in high spirits. Shamelessly using Brownlow and Potter's telephones for private calls, he had rung an estate agent to put his house on the market and made positive enquiries of the Canadian High Commission about emigration. He burst through the front door and called out his customary, 'Hello, Mother. I'm home.'

The words died on his lips as he saw Reg Carter emerging from his kitchen. 'Good God, what are you doing here? This is private property.'

'I was doing my rounds with the second post.'

'How did you get in?'

'I had to break a window.'

'You had no right. That's breaking and entering. I'll call the police.'

'It's all right. I've already called them. I've explained it all to Sergeant Wallace.'

Partridge's face was the colour of putty. 'Explained what?' he croaked.

'About the fire.' Then again, patiently, because Partridge didn't seem to be taking it in. 'The fire. There was a fire. In your kitchen. I saw the smoke as I came past. You'd left the toaster on this morning. It had got the tea towel and the curtains were just beginning to go. So I broke in.'

Partridge now looked human again. 'I understand. I'm sorry I was so suspicious. It's just . . . Thank you.'

'Don't mention it,' said Reg Carter with insouciance he'd learned from some television hero. 'It was just I thought, what with your mother upstairs, I couldn't afford to wait and call the fire brigade. What with her not being able to move and all.'

'That was very thoughtful. Thank you.' Unconsciously Partridge was edging round the hall, as if trying to usher the postman out. But Reg Carter stayed firmly in the kitchen doorway. Partridge reached vaguely towards his wallet. 'I feel I should reward you in some way . . .'

'No, I don't want no reward. I just did it to save the old lady.'

Partridge gave a little smile and nervous nod of gratitude.

'I mean, it would be awful for her to be trapped. Someone helpless like that.'

'Yes.'

Up until this point the postman's tone had been tentative, but, as he continued, he became more forceful. 'After I'd put the fire out, I thought I ought to see if she was all right. She might have smelt burning or heard me breaking in and been scared out of her wits . . . So I called up the stairs to her. She didn't answer.'

The colour was once again dying rapidly from Partridge's face. 'No, she's very deaf. She wouldn't hear you.'

'No. So I went upstairs,' Reg Carter continued inexorably. 'All the doors were closed. I opened one. I reckon it must be your room. Then I opened another. There was a bed there. But there was no one in it.'

'No.'

'There was no one in the bathroom. Or anywhere. The house was empty.'

'Yes.'

The postman looked for a moment at his quarry, then said, 'I thought that was rather strange, Mr Partridge. I mean, you told us all your mother was bedridden and lived here.'

'She does—I mean she did.' The colour was back in his cheeks in angry blushes.

'Did?'

'Yes, she died,' said Partridge quickly.

'Died? When? You said this morning when I asked after her that———'

'She died a couple of days ago. I'm sorry, I've been in such a state. The shock, you know. You can't believe that it's happened and———'

'When was the funeral?'

A new light of confusion came into Partridge's eyes as he stumbled to answer. 'Yesterday. Very recently. It's only just happened. I'm sorry, I'm not thinking straight. I don't know whether I'm coming or going.'

'No.' Reg Carter's voice was studiously devoid of intonation. 'I'd better be on my way. Got a couple more letters to deliver, then back to the post office.'

Humphrey Partridge mumbled more thanks as he ushered the postman out of the front door. When he heard the click of the front gate, he sank trembling on to the bottom stair and cried out loud, 'Why, why can't they leave us alone?'

Sergeant Wallace was a fat man with a thin, tidy mind. He liked everything in its place and he liked to put it there himself. The one thing that frightened him was the idea of anyone else being brought in to what he regarded as his area of authority, in other words, anything that happened in the village. So it was natural for him, when the rumours about Humphrey Partridge reached unmanageable proportions, to go and see the man himself rather than reporting to his superiors.

It was about a week after the fire. Needless to say, Reg Carter had talked to Mr and Mrs Denton and they had talked to practically everyone who came into the post office. The talk was now so wild that something had to be done.

Humphrey Partridge opened his front door with customary lack of welcome, but Sergeant Wallace forced his large bulk inside, saying he'd come to talk about the fire.

Tea chests in the sitting-room told their own story. 'Packing your books I see, Mr Partridge.'

'Yes. Most of my effects will be going to Canada by sea.' Partridge assumed, rightly, that the entire village knew of his impending departure.

'When is it exactly you're off?'

'About a month. I'm not exactly sure.'

Sergeant Wallace settled his uninvited mass into an armchair. 'Nice place, Canada, I hear. My nephew's over there.'

'Ah.'

'You'll be buying a place to live . . . ?'

'Yes.'

'On your own.'

'Yes.'

'Your mother's no longer with you?'

'No. She . . . she died.'

'Yes. Quite recently, I hear.' Sergeant Wallace stretched out, as if warming himself in front of the empty grate. 'It was to some extent about your mother that I called.'

Partridge didn't react, so the Sergeant continued. 'As you know, this is a small place and most people take an interest in other people's affairs . . .'

'Can't mind their own bloody business, most of them.'

'Maybe so. Now I don't listen to gossip, but I do have to keep my ear to the ground—that's what the job's about. And I'm afraid I've been hearing some strange things about you recently, Mr Partridge.'

Sergeant Wallace luxuriated in another pause. 'People are saying things about your mother's death. I realize, being so recent, you'd probably rather not talk about it.'

'Fat chance I have of that. Already I'm getting anonymous letters and phone calls about it.'

'And you haven't reported them?'

'Look, I'll be away soon. And none of it will matter.'

'Hmm.' The Sergeant decided the moment had come to take the bull by the horns. 'As you'll probably know from these letters and telephone calls then, people are saying you killed your mother for her money.'

'That is libellous nonsense!'

'Maybe. I hope so. If you can just answer a couple of questions for me, then I'll know so. Tell me first, when did your mother die?'

'Ten days ago. The 11th.'

'Are you sure? It was on the 11th that you had the fire and Reg Carter found the house empty.'

'I'm sorry. A couple of days before that. It's been such a shock, I . . .'

'Of course.' Sergeant Wallace nodded soothingly. 'And so the funeral must have been on the tenth?'

'Some time round then, yes.'

'Strange that none of the local undertakers had a call from you.'

'I used a firm from town, one I have connections with.'

'I see.' Sergeant Wallace looked rosier than ever as he warmed to his task. 'And no doubt it was a doctor from town who issued the death certificate?'

'Yes.'

'Do you happen to have a copy of that certificate?' the Sergeant asked sweetly.

Humphrey Partridge looked weakly at his tormentor and murmured, 'You know I don't.'

'If there isn't a death certificate,' mused Sergeant Wallace agonizingly slowly, 'then that suggests there might be something unusual about your mother's death.'

'Damn you! Damn you all!' Partridge was almost sobbing with passion. 'Why can't you leave me alone? Why are you always prying?'

The Sergeant recovered from his surprise. 'Mr Partridge, if a crime's been committed————'

'No crime's been committed!' Partridge shouted in desperate exasperation. 'I haven't got a mother. I never saw my mother. She walked out on me when I was six months old and I was brought up in care.'

'Then who was living upstairs?' asked Sergeant Wallace logically.

'Nobody. I live on my own, I always have lived on my own. Don't you see, I hate people.' The confession was costing Partridge a lot, but he was too wound up to stop its outpouring. 'People are always trying to find out about you, to probe, to know you. They want to invade your house, take you out for drinks, invade your privacy. I can't stand it. I just want to be on my own!'

Sergeant Wallace tried to interject, but Partridge steamrollered on. 'But you can't be alone. People won't let you. You have to have a reason. So I invented my mother. I couldn't do things, I couldn't see people, because I had to get back to my mother. She was ill. And my life worked very well like that. I even began to believe in her, to talk to her. She never asked questions, she didn't want to know anything about me, she just loved me and was kind and beautiful. And I loved her. I wouldn't kill her—I wouldn't lay a finger on her—it's you, all of you who've killed her!' He was now weeping uncontrollably. 'Damn you, damn you.'

Sergeant Wallace took a moment or two to organize this new information in his mind. 'So what you're telling me is, there never was any mother. You made her up. You couldn't have killed her, because she never lived.'

'Yes,' said Partridge petulantly. 'Can't you get that through your thick skull?'

'Hmm. And how do you explain that you suddenly have enough money to emigrate and buy property in Canada?'

'My premium bond came up. I got the letter on the morning of the fire. That's why I forgot to turn the toaster off. I was so excited.'

'I see.' Sergeant Wallace lifted himself ponderously out of his chair and moved across to the window. 'Been digging in the garden, I see.'

'Yes, I put some bulbs in.'

'Bulbs, and you're about to move.' The Sergeant looked at his quarry. 'That's very public-spirited of you, Mr Partridge.'

The post office was delighted with the news of Partridge's arrest. Mrs Denton was firmly of the opinion that she had thought there was something funny going on and recognized Partridge's homicidal tendencies. Reg Carter bathed in the limelight of having set the investigation in motion and Sergeant Wallace, though he regretted the intrusion of the CID into his patch, felt a certain satisfaction for his vital groundwork.

The Dentons were certain Reg would be called as a witness at the trial and thought there was a strong possibility that they might be called as character witnesses. Mrs Denton bitterly regretted the demise of the death penalty, feeling that prison was too good for people who strangled old ladies in their beds. Every passing shopper brought news of the developments in the case, how the police had dug up the garden, how they had taken up the floor-boards, how they had been heard tapping the walls of Partridge's house. Mrs Denton recommended that they should sift through the ashes of the boiler.

So great was the community interest in the murder that the cries of disbelief and disappointment were huge when the news came through that the charges against Partridge had been dropped. The people of the village felt that they had been robbed of a pleasure which, by any scale of values, was rightfully theirs.

But as the details seeped out, it was understood that Partridge's wild tale to Sergeant Wallace was true. There had been no one else living in the house. He had had a large premium bond win. And the last record of Partridge's real mother dated from four years previously when she had been found guilty of soliciting in Liverpool and sentenced to two months in prison.

The village's brief starring role in the national press was over and its people, disgruntled and cheated, returned to more domestic scandals. Humphrey Partridge came back to his house, but no one saw him much as he hurried to catch up on the delay to his emigration plans which his wrongful arrest had caused him.

It was two days before his departure, in the early evening, when he had the visitor. It was December, dark and cold. Everyone in the village was indoors.

He did not recognize the woman standing on the doorstep. She was dressed in a short black and white fun-fur coat, which might have been fashionable five years before. Her hair was fierce ginger, a strident contrast to scarlet lipstick, and black lashes hovered over her eyes like bats' wings. The stringiness of her neck and the irregular bumps of veins under her black stockings denied the evidence of her youthful dress.

'Hello, Humphrey,' she said.

'Who are you?' He held the door, as usual, ready to close it.

The woman laughed, a short, unpleasant sound. 'No, I don't

expect you to recognize me. You were a bit small when we last met.'

'You're not . . . ?'

'Yes, of course I am. Aren't you going to give your mother a kiss?'

She thrust forward her painted face and Partridge recoiled back into the hall. The woman took the opportunity to follow him in and shut the front door behind her.

'Nice little place you've got for yourself, Humphrey.' She advanced and Partridge backed away from her into the sitting-room. She took in the bareness and the packing cases. 'Oh yes, of course, leaving these shores, aren't you? I read in the paper. Canada, was it? Nice people, Canadians. At least, their sailors are.' Another burst of raucous laughter.

''Cause of course you've got the money now, haven't you, Humphrey? I read about that too. Funny, I never met anyone before what'd won a premium bond. Plenty who did all right on the horses, but not premium bonds.'

'What do you want?' Partridge croaked.

'Just come to see my little boy, haven't I? Just thinking, now you're set up so nice and cosy, maybe you ought to help your Mum in her old age.'

'I don't owe you anything. You never did anything for me. You walked out on me.'

'Ah, that was ages ago. And he was a nice boy, Clinton. I had to have a fling. I meant to come back to you after a week or two. But then the council moved in and Clinton got moved away and————'

'What do you want?'

'I told you. I want to be looked after in my old age. I read in the paper about how devoted you were to your old mother.' Again the laugh.

'But you aren't my mother.' Partridge was speaking with great care and restraint.

'Oh yes, I am, Humphrey.'

'You're not.'

'Yes. Ooh, I've had a thought—why don't you take your old mother to Canada with you?'

'You are not my mother!' Partridge's hands were on the woman's shoulders, shaking out the emphasis of his words.

'I'm your mother, Humphrey.'

His hands rose to her neck to silence the taunting words. They tightened and shuddered as he spoke. 'My mother is beautiful and kind. She is nothing like you. She always loved me. She still loves me!'

The spasm passed. He released his grip. The woman's body slipped down. As her head rolled back, her false teeth fell out with a clatter on to the floor.

Sergeant Wallace appeared to be very busy with a ledger when Humphrey Partridge went into the police station next morning. He was embarrassed by what had happened. It didn't fit inside the neat borders of his mind and it made him look inefficient. But eventually he could pretend to be busy no longer. 'Good morning, Mr Partridge. What can I do for you?'

'I leave for Canada tomorrow.'

'Oh. Well, may I wish you every good fortune in your new life there.'

'Thank you.' A meagre smile was on Partridge's lips. 'Sergeant, about my mother . . .'

Sergeant Wallace closed his ledger with some force. 'Listen Mr Partridge, you have already had a full apology and————'

'No, no, it's nothing to do with that. I just wanted to tell you . . .'

'Yes?'

'. . . that I *did* kill my mother.'

'Oh yes, and then I suppose you buried her in the garden, eh?'

'Yes, I did.'

'Fine.' Sergeant Wallace reopened his ledger and looked down at the page busily.

'I'm confessing to murder,' Partridge insisted.

The Sergeant looked up with an exasperated sigh. 'Listen, Mr Partridge, I'm very sorry about what happened and you're entitled to your little joke, but I do have other things to do, so, if you wouldn't mind . . .'

'You mean I can just go?'

'Please.'

'To Canada?'

'To where you bloody well like.'

'Right then, I'll go. And . . . er . . . leave the old folks at home.'

Sergeant Wallace didn't look up from his ledger as Partridge left the police station.

Outside, Humphrey Partridge took a deep breath of air, smiled and said out loud, 'Right, mother, Canada it is.'

ACKNOWLEDGEMENTS

The editor and publishers are grateful for permission to include the following copyright material in this anthology:

MARGERY ALLINGHAM, 'Three is a Lucky Number' reprinted from *The Allingham Case Book* (Chatto, 1969), © P & M Youngman Carter 1969, by permission of Curtis Brown, London and John S. Robling Ltd.

H. C. BAILEY, 'The Dead Leaves' reprinted from *Clue For Mr Fortune* (Gollancz, 1936), copyright 1936 by H. C. Bailey, by permission of Tessa Sayle Agency.

E. C. BENTLEY, 'The Genuine Tabard' reprinted from *Trent Intervenes* (Nelson, 1938).

ANTHONY BERKELEY, 'The Avenging Chance', © The Society of Authors 1974. Reprinted by permission of The Society of Authors.

ROBERT BERNARD, 'The Oxford Way of Death' reprinted from *Death of a Salesman* (Collins Crime Club, 1989), by permission of Collins Publishers.

NICHOLAS BLAKE, 'The Assassins' Club' first published in *Ellery Queen Magazine* and reprinted by permission of the Peters Fraser & Dunlop Group Ltd.

CHRISTIANNA BRAND, 'The Hornet's Nest' reprinted from *What Dread Hand* (M. Joseph, 1968) by permission of A. M. Heath on behalf of the author's estate.

SIMON BRETT, 'How's Your Mother?' from *A Box of Tricks*, published in the United States in *Tickled to Death*, © 1985 Simon Brett. Reprinted by permission of Victor Gollancz Ltd., and Charles Scribner's Sons, an imprint of Macmillan Publishing Company.

JOHN DICKSON CARR, 'The House in Goblin Wood' reprinted from *The Queen's Awards 2* (Gollancz) by permission of David Higham Associates Ltd.

AGATHA CHRISTIE, 'The Witness for the Prosecution' reprinted from *The Hound of Death*, copyright 1933 Agatha Christie Mallowan, by permission of Aitken & Stone Ltd., Harold Ober Associates Inc., and the Putnam Publishing Group.

G. D. H. and M. COLE, 'Superintendent Wilson's Holiday' reprinted from *Superintendent Wilson's Holiday* (Collins, 1928) by permission of David Higham Associates Ltd.

EDMUND CRISPIN and GEOFFREY BUSH, 'Baker Dies' ('Who Killed Baker?') reprinted from *Fen Country* by permission of A. P. Watt Ltd. on behalf of Jean Bell and Geoffrey Bush, and Walker and Company.

FREEMAN WILLS CROFTS, 'The Mystery of the Sleeping-Car Express' reprinted from *The Mystery of the Sleeping-Car Express* (Hodder, 1956) by permission of A. P. Watt Ltd. on behalf of the Authors' Contingency Fund.

R. AUSTIN FREEMAN, 'The Mysterious Visitor' reprinted from *The Puzzle Lock* (Hodder, 1925) by permission of A. P. Watt Ltd. on behalf of Winifred Briant.

MICHAEL GILBERT, 'The Killing of Michael Finnegan' reprinted from *Mr Calder and Mr Behrens* (Hodder, 1982) copyright © Michael Gilbert 1981, by permission of Curtis Brown Group Ltd., London.

CYRIL HARE, 'Miss Burnside's Dilemma' reprinted from *Best Detective Stories of Cyril Hare* (Faber, 1959) by permission of A. P. Watt Ltd. on behalf of the Revd. C. P. Gordon Clark.

REGINALD HILL, 'Bring Back the Cat' reprinted from *There Are No Ghosts in the Soviet Union* by permission of Collins Publishers and of Foul Play Press, a division of The Countryman Press, Inc.

MICHAEL INNES, 'The Furies' reprinted from the *Evening Standard Detective Book* (2nd series, 1951). Used with permission.

P. D. JAMES, 'Great Aunt Allie's Flypapers' reprinted from *Verdict on Thirteen: A Detective Club Anthology* (Faber, 1979), © 1969 P. D. James, by permission of Elaine Greene Ltd.

H. R. F. KEATING, 'A Dangerous Thing' reprinted from *The Mystery Guild Anthology* (1980) by permission of the author.

RONALD KNOX, 'Solved by Inspection' reprinted from *My Best Detective Story* (Faber, 1931) by permission of A. P. Watt Ltd. on behalf of the Earl of Oxford and Asquith.

NGAIO MARSH, 'Death on the Air' reprinted from *Ellery Queen's Mystery Magazine*, Jan. 1948, copyright 1947 by the American Mercury, Inc., copyright renewed 1975 by Ngaio Marsh, by permission of Harold Ober Associates Inc., and Aitken & Stone Ltd.

GLADYS MITCHELL, 'Daisy Bell' reprinted from *Detective Stories of Today* (Faber, 1940) by permission of the Curtis Brown Group Ltd. on behalf of the Gladys Mitchell Estate.

ARTHUR MORRISON, 'The Case of Laker, Absconded' reprinted from *Chronicles of Martin Hewitt*, by permission of Ward Lock.

RUTH RENDELL, 'Thornapple' reprinted from *The Fever Tree* by permission of Century Hutchinson Ltd.

JOHN RHODE, 'The Purple Line' reprinted from the *Evening Standard Detective Book* (1st series, 1950). Used by permission.

DOROTHY L. SAYERS, 'Hangman's Holiday' reprinted from *Murder at Pentecost* (Gollancz, 1933) by permission of David Higham Associates Ltd.

JULIAN SYMONS, 'The Murderer' reprinted from *The Tigers of Subtopia* (Macmillan, 1982) copyright © Julian Symons 1982, by permission of Curtis Brown Group Ltd., London.

MICHAEL UNDERWOOD, 'Murder at St Oswald's' reprinted from *Verdict on Thirteen: A Detective Club Anthology* (Faber, 1979) by permission of the author.

ROY VICKERS, 'The Hen-Pecked Murderer' reprinted from *The Department of Dead Ends* (Faber, 1949), copyright Roy Vickers, by permission of Curtis Brown Ltd, London.

BIOGRAPHICAL NOTES

MARGERY ALLINGHAM (1904–66). Born in London. Author of twenty-four crime novels, many featuring the quintessential 'silly ass' detective, Albert Campion, and sixty-two stories. Goes in for humorous understatement and a cheerful, if occasionally showy, manner.

HENRY CHRISTOPHER BAILEY (1878–1961). Born in London; classical scholar at Corpus Christi College, Oxford, drama critic, war correspondent, and leader-writer for the *Daily Telegraph*. Author of many novels. Best known for his 'Reggie Fortune' stories, which appeared in twelve volumes between 1920 and 1940.

ROBERT BARNARD (b. 1936). Born in Essex. Professor of English Literature at the University of Tromsø. Ebullient and highly regarded crime novelist and author of an appreciation of Agatha Christie, *A Talent to Deceive* (1980).

EDMUND CLERIHEW BENTLEY (1875–1956). Born in London. After Oxford, joined the editorial staff of the *Daily News* and later became the chief leader-writer on the *Daily Telegraph*. Gave his name to a particular kind of four-line verse (the clerihew), and achieved fame with *Trent's Last Case* published in 1913.

ANTHONY BERKELEY (1893–1971). One of the pseudonyms of Anthony Berkeley Cox, who, under the name of Francis Iles, gained a new respectability for the crime novel (*Malice Aforethought*, 1931). Creator of the debonair detective Roger Sheringham, who first appeared in *The Layton Court Mystery* (1925). Light-hearted and influential detective novelist.

NICHOLAS BLAKE (1904–72). The Poet Laureate C. Day Lewis wrote twenty crime novels under the name of Nicholas Blake, starting with *A Question of Proof* (1935). Famous for having brought a literary flavour to detective fiction.

CHRISTIANNA BRAND (1907–88). Born Mary Christianna Lewis. Author of thirteen detective novels, including the intriguing *Green for Danger* (1944), set in a wartime hospital, and thirty-nine stories.

SIMON BRETT (b. 1945). Author of many television and radio scripts, and accomplished detective novelist (starting in 1975 with *Cast, in Order of Disappearance*). Often agreeably satirical about the world of the theatre.

GEOFFREY BUSH (b. 1920). Born in London; composer and author. Collaborated with Bruce Montgomery on the story 'Baker Dies'.

GILBERT KEITH CHESTERTON (1874–1936). Distinguished man of letters and creator of the priest-detective Father Brown. *The Innocence of Father Brown* (1911) was the first of the series featuring this character. Most of the fifty 'Father Brown' cases are cast in the form of the moral parable, but there are one or two genuine detective plots to be found among them.

AGATHA CHRISTIE (1890–1976). Outstanding author of sixty-six crime novels and 149 stories, mostly collected in fourteen volumes. Unsurpassed as far as technical ingenuity is concerned, and one of the most popular detective writers of all time.

G. D. H. and M. COLE (1890–1959; 1893–1980). The Coles's detective Superintendent Wilson first appeared in *The Brooklyn Murders* of 1923 (by G. D. H. Cole alone). The husband-and-wife team went on to write a good many novels and a handful of stories featuring this character, while at the same time gaining a considerable reputation within the Labour movement. Their detective fiction is, at its best, very deft and entertaining.

EDMUND CRISPIN (1921–78). The pseudonym of Robert Bruce Montgomery, whose principal occupation was as a composer (chiefly of film music). Author of nine novels and forty-three stories. Creator of the don-detective Gervase Fen, and altogether a stylish and astute practitioner of the genre.

FREEMAN WILLS CROFTS (1879–1957). A railway engineer, born in Dublin and educated in Belfast, Freeman Wills Crofts created the first and most resolute of the painstaking professionals, Inspector French, who specializes in breaking one apparently unbreakable alibi after another. Crofts is famous for instilling interest into the 'railway timetable' brand of detecting.

CARTER DICKSON (1906–77). Equally well known under his real name of John Dickson Carr, Carter Dickson is the creator of the stout detective Sir Henry Merrivale, and one of the most inspired, and inspiriting, of detective writers. Born in Pennsylvania, but spent most of his life in England (working for MI5 during the Second World War). Brings a prestidigitator's skills to bear on the detective plot, especially in relation to the 'locked room' mystery with which he is chiefly associated.

ARTHUR CONAN DOYLE (1859–1930). With the first appearance of Sherlock Holmes in *A Study in Scarlet* (1887), the detective genre found both a form and an impetus, and has never looked back since. Doyle himself regretted what he considered the undue popularity of Holmes, and could have done with more acclaim for his work in other fields—but his name remains inextricably linked with the first and most distinctive detective figure of all.

R. AUSTIN FREEMAN (1862–1943). Born in London, and—like Conan Doyle—took up the study of medicine. First novel published under his own name was *The Red Thumb Mark* of 1907, which introduced readers to the indefatigably 'scientific' Dr Thorndyke. Many Thorndyke stories followed, with the hero carrying his 'portable laboratory'—a square case covered in green Willesden canvas and containing scientific instruments—to the scene of every crime.

MICHAEL GILBERT (b. 1912). Wit and aplomb are two of the characteristics of Michael Gilbert, whose career includes wartime service in North Africa and Italy, and a long association with a firm of solicitors. Has created a number of series characters including Inspector Hazelrigg and Sergeant Petrella, and the formidable duo of Mr Calder and Mr Behrens. A versatile and unpredictable author.

CYRIL HARE (1900–58). Pseudonym of the barrister Alfred Gordon Clark, who wrote nine engaging novels and thirty-eight stories. Wryness of tone, a talent for plotting and legal expertise all contributed to Cyril Hare's achievement.

REGINALD HILL (b. 1936). Best known for his 'Dalziel and Pascoe' novels (starting in 1970 with *A Clubbable Woman*). Has shown himself to be a master of a good range of tones, from the bleak to the exuberant. Often very funny and outrageous.

MICHAEL INNES (b. 1906). Pseudonym of retired Oxford don J. I. M. Stewart (who writes non-detective fiction under his real name). Author of many urbane detective novels featuring policeman John Appleby, starting with *Death at the President's Lodging* in 1936.

P. D. JAMES (b. 1920). Author of eleven detective novels and some uncollected stories, P. D. James has worked as an administrator of the North-West Regional Hospital Board and in an advisory capacity at the Home Office. Though her books are immensely absorbing and adroitly planned, she has always refused to treat murder as a game, and does not shirk its more distressing aspects. Her stories are perhaps lighter in effect, though no less impressive.

H. R. F. KEATING (b. 1926). Author of highly regarded novels about Inspector Ghote of the Bombay CID, and has also created the resourceful charlady Emma Craggs, who appears in one novel (*Death of a Fat God*, 1963) and a number of stories. Also well known as a critic and historian of the genre.

FR. RONALD KNOX (1888–1957). A Monsignor of the Roman Catholic Church who turned to detective writing in 1925 (*The Viaduct Murder*) and continued to work in the genre over the next twelve years. Humorously devised a list of rules for detective writers (in his introduction to *The Best*

Detective Stories of 1928) which made a starting-point for the Detection Club founded in the following year.

NGAIO MARSH (1899–1982). Born in New Zealand. Famous for having created the aristocratic policeman Roderick Alleyn, who appeared in many exuberant novels after the first one, *A Man Lay Dead* (1934). Like Margery Allingham's, her books have an element of drawing-room comedy and high jinks.

GLADYS MITCHELL (1901–83). Born in Oxfordshire, and a schoolteacher for all of her working life, Gladys Mitchell is one of the most diverting and idiosyncratic of British crime writers. She began in 1929 with *Speedy Death*, which marked the first appearance of the redoubtable Mrs Bradley (later Dame Beatrice). Sixty-five novels and a number of stories followed.

ARTHUR MORRISON (1863–1945). Born in Kent. Worked in journalism and in the Civil Service. Author of stories concerning nineteenth-century London slum life, such as *Tales of Mean Streets* (1894), and also of *Painters of Japan* (1911). His 'Martin Hewitt' stories—in three volumes, starting with *Chronicles of Martin Hewitt* in 1894—made him the first detective writer of substance to follow Conan Doyle.

RUTH RENDELL (b. 1930). Writes both orthodox detective novels, starring Inspector Wexford of the Kingsmarkham (Sussex) CID, and psychological thrillers of a breathtaking ingenuity. Has received considerable acclaim for her audacity and inventiveness.

JOHN RHODE (1884–1964). Pseudonym of Major Cecil John Charles Street, who also wrote under the name of Miles Burton. Prolific and straightforward author of crime-and-detection stories. Best known for his 'Dr Priestley' novels, starting with *The Paddington Mystery* of 1925.

CLARENCE ROOK (d. 1915). Best known for his *Hooligan Nights* (1899), which purports to be a factual account of goings-on in the London under-world—'certain scenes from the life of a young criminal', as the author describes it in his Introduction. In this book, Clarence Rook refers to himself as an American living in London, and little more than this seems to be known about him.

DOROTHY L. SAYERS (1893–1957). One of the most prominent and entertaining of all detective writers, and creator of the egregious Lord Peter Wimsey, who appeared in eleven novels (starting with *Whose Body?* in 1923) and twenty-one stories. Gave up detective fiction after 1937, and went on to become a Christian apologist and translator of Dante's *Divine Comedy*.

JULIAN SYMONS (b. 1912). Distinguished biographer, social and literary historian, crime writer and critic of the genre (his *Bloody Murder* of 1972 has been called 'the classic study of crime fiction'). Author of many absorbing detective novels and some astringent stories.

MICHAEL UNDERWOOD (b. 1916). Pseudonym of John Michael Evelyn, a barrister who puts his legal background to good use in his detective novels. Probably his most famous creation is the young London solicitor Rosa Epton, who has featured in a number of murder cases (beginning with *The Unprofessional Spy*, 1964).

ROY VICKERS (1899–1965). One-time journalist and crime reporter, and editor of the *Novel Magazine*. Best known for his series of remarkably ingenious stories concerning *The Department of Dead Ends* (1949).